THE ISLE OF THE BLEST

The Isle of the Blest

A novel

by

EUGENE CHRISTY

Adelaide Books
New York / Lisbon
2021

THE ISLE OF THE BLEST
A novel
By Eugene Christy

Published by Adelaide Books, New York / Lisbon
adelaidebooks.org

Editor-in-Chief
Stevan V. Nikolic

For any information, please address Adelaide Books
at info@adelaidebooks.org

or write to:

Adelaide Books
244 Fifth Ave. Suite D27
New York, NY, 10001

ISBN: 978-1-956635-00-3

Printed in the United States of America

For Aisling

Contents

Volume V

THE FINAL VOLUME
OF
THE TWENTIETH CENTURY QUINTET

The race is not to the swift, nor the battle to the strong . . .

but time and chance happeneth to them all.

Ecclesiastes 9:11

Chapter 1

Stout-Hearted Men of the County Mayo

I landed in Ireland about a fortnight after Internment began in August of 1971.

Pre-dawn raids, imprisonment without trial, the news was a worldwide sensation. Turgid reports of torture at the hands of British soldiers followed the wave of angry reaction that ripped through the North; there were burning barricades, pitched gun-battles, incidents of devastating violence.

My name is Nick Petrovich. I was a young man on board an Aer Lingus 707, flying into this maelstrom.

My father was a coal miner from Pershing, PA, down near the West Virginia line. My mother was a stitcher in the sweatshops of Milltown, MA. I mention this because I was the first from my family ever to go to college. Where I learned to think, to question and to rebel. That, and the war in Vietnam, and my all-consuming love for a farmer's daughter from the West of Ireland, Sheila Blake, a gorgeous, dark-haired, maddening flirt, were all clashing together, in a cauldron of emotion, alienating me from my native home, turning me overnight into a 24-year-old, self-exiled American, fleeing the Nixon regime.

I had good reason to feel this way. Back home in Milltown, I had a decent administrative position in a Johnson-era poverty program. I was using that college education. I was providing for my wife of three years, Sheila, and our little daughter Aisling, already, incredibly, a year-and-three months.

All that was ended by a little visit to my boss from the FBI. Photos of me organizing anti-war rallies on the Milltown Common, spread out on his desk.

Nixon's Amerika.

From my seat in a 707, I drank in a window-view of the world from 35,000 feet above the steel-ribbed Atlantic.

I was alive with such anticipation that I could not concentrate on the book in my lap.

Would my life be forever changed in a six-hour flight?

As we began the descent and emerged into sunshine under a canopy of cloud-banks, I saw below me a gently-approaching bucolic patchwork of neat parcels and crookedy rural roads, white houses and winding hills.

It did not look like a land torn by conflict. Shining in the sunlight, it was a peaceful, pastoral vision, a green pastel postcard.

The Isle of the Blest, I called it, knowing, in my own mind, the words of the music of the books and the poems and the illuminated manuscripts of her saints and scholars and writers and rebels.

My love for Sheila had given rise to an insatiable thirst, in my grad school days, for the Irish storytelling of Joyce and Yeats and O'Casey; James Stephens and Brendan Behan and JP Donleavy; all in a wishful dream of deepening my love for her, Sheila, the one who was my soul and my life. Because this was the place my dark-haired Sheila loved. This was where she wished to dwell, with me and our beloved daughter. Where she had spent her own idyllic, country girlhood.

Two weeks before I had sent them on ahead, to the place Sheila called home. And wherever Sheila was, was my home, too.

My brother-in-law, Patrick Blake, picked me up at Shannon Airport to take me the 80 miles or so home to Mayo in his battered cobalt-blue Austin mini.

It was just as well I was traveling light—a rucksack with hardcover books, *Moby Dick, The Brothers Karamazov* (in the compact Modern Library edition from the 1930s with the maniacal Freudian paper cover) and Tolstoy's *War and Peace*—three books on my list after Whitman. On my back, my father's old WWII Navy pea-coat, which, at the last minute, I had snatched off the hook in the back hall, when leaving my mother's door, thinking Ireland might be a chilly place. I had to take off the pea-coat to fit in the mini.

There we were, two strangers meeting for the first time. Had I been a sketch-book artist, I would have drawn my blue-eyed brother-in-law with a wind-blown head of hair, not nearly as neat as a thatched roof (hair the color of a stand of hay bleached in sunlight) with the sort of complexion called 'ruddy' in books by Thomas Hardy; strictly an outdoors man, dressed in a tartan-print flannel shirt, and farmer's boots. I hardly know how he would have drawn me—a refugee from America? (did such a thing exist?)—a disenfranchised scholar, wearing John Lennon gold-rimmed glasses, and a floor-mop of hair borrowed from an Albert Einstein cartoon, with the dark moustache to match?

Though completely foreign to one another, you might have thought we had known each other all our lives, as, cosseted shoulder to shoulder, pell-mell, in a mini being driven like an hysterical European bullet-train, we plunged immediately into political discussions of the most precise, arcane and detailed kind. I was amazed to think that, as far as I knew, my new relation had as yet to attend any political science courses at University, being about my brother Jack's age, which was 19.

"Why don't you lot just get out of Vietnam?" said Patrick Blake to me. "You've no business being there any more than I would."

I didn't know what to say. It felt as if I were being personally blamed, a new sensation for someone like me who had never been outside the United States. "Patrick, look, I've just been fired from my job for protesting the War—."

"Oh, you'll have to tell me that story."

"So I hardly think that there's popular support in America for continuing the war. The problem is—."

"Nixon."

"And Kissinger."

"And the shape of the table."

"But tell me about the North. Is it as bad as we've seen on television back home?"

"Oh, aye. Desperate. But, you see, it goes back directly to 1921 and the Treaty talks and that imperialist bastard Churchill and the partition."

"What did Churchill have to do with it?"

"Only everything." Spoken as if I had a lot to learn about Ireland, which I did. "Churchill had a seat at the table as Minister of War for the Brits, and he was the one who threatened Michael Collins with genocidal annihilation if he refused to sign."

"I didn't know that."

"You'll have to speak with my da. He came up a young man in them days. He'll fill you in."

As we passed through Galway City we stopped in Eyre Square for lunch in Garvey's Inn. I had my first splash of Guinness and I thought it was the most disgusting thing I'd ever tasted. As we left town, heading for Castlebar, in Mayo, it seemed we had poured the stout into the gas-tank, rather than ourselves. We were traveling faster, and not in a straight line.

"Patrick, if I asked you to slow down, would you?"

"Not at all."

"I'd like to see Sheila and the baby again before I die."

"No fear. Dead or alive, we're getting there."

The village of Kilcross was situated at what the locals called 'the hook of the road.'

It was located more or less on a shoulder of Lough Conn, a lake nine miles long. And it was under the brow of a mountain called Nephin: spelled Nephin, but pronounced 'Nay-fin.' (Spelling and punctuation, my specialties—but didn't I say I had a lot to learn? This Ireland thing was going to be a big adjustment for the likes of me, with my master's degree, and a head full of notions, as Sheila would have said.)

In one direction, more or less northeast, it was four miles to Crossmolina, (Crossmoliney) twelve miles to Ballina (no ball in it, as in 'baseball,' and the two a's pronounced differently, the first, soft, as in 'bad,' the second as in the dentist telling you to 'say ah!') Going the other way, south, it was twenty miles to Castlebar. Pronounced just the way it looks (except, of course, with my Boston accent, I couldn't put in the 'r' at the end of the word!)

The point is, this village, Kilcross, was as remote as any place I had ever seen or imagined.

The mountain, Nephin, loomed over the roof-line of Delaney's pub, post-office and petrol station, which was across the hook of the road from the small stone church called St Patrick's; the church, enclosed, like every field for miles around, by stone walls, in this case, with a wrought-iron gate entering upon a footpath leading up to the front door.

Everywhere you went in the village, which had a population of about 178 souls, and may have had as many as 17 or so houses strung out along the main road, wherever you went, the mountain seemed always to be shadowing you over your shoulder.

There were three pubs in the place, Delaney's, Garrett's and Reynolds'. Frank Delaney was the local T.D., a member of the Dáil in Dublin.

That was the extent of it. One petrol pump, a church and three pubs.

This was where my Sheila had spent her childhood and youth. This was where she had grown up, played, gone to the National School, fed chickens and milked cows. And it seemed, to me, the furthest outpost of Europe that you could find before you ran into Iceland.

The mountain called Nephin was the only thing you could see from a distance for miles around. In daylight it knelt down in the bog like a round-shouldered sheep. At night it formed a blot upon the darkness. The mountain gave me the feeling that it was ever-present, and in this way, it evoked eternity itself. You could walk out any door in Kilcross, and there it was, confronting you, waiting for you. It was, like fate, implacable.

And the nights in Kilcross were the darkest I had ever seen, with never a star to shine because the clouds never went away, and then the morning came and the clouds, the lake and the mountain, all were veiled by fog and mist, like a land composed purely of imagination.

Sheila's place was not actually on the main road of the village at all. After you passed the last row-houses, you turned blind right into an opening in the hedgerows, which you couldn't see unless you already knew it was there, and headed down a dirt road, which the Blakes called 'the boreen,' the Irish word for a small, secondary, unpaved road. The boreen led all the way to the lake, bordered with hedgerows on both sides.

The Blakes' house was the first one on the right. The dark, shadowy hedge parted and you came upon it suddenly. It was a cinder-block, four-room farmhouse with a slate roof. The front of the house was pebbledash, the sides and back plain and smooth, cement-colored from the rain. A tiny front garden resided at the edge of the boreen, enclosed by a low wall, with corner posts. A gate in the middle opened on the footpath up to the front door. The front walk was only a dozen or so footsteps long, with a flat lawn on either side. Chimneys stuck up above the rooflines at the gable-ends of the house. It looked like a little Dutch house on a canal. The front door was painted blue and had no window; the door, windowsills and mantles over the fireplaces were the only wood in the place besides the furniture. To a stranger like me from America, where all the houses were wood-frame, it looked oddly bare.

On the right side of the house, there was a neatly piled stack of turf sticking out under a dingy blue plastic tarp beneath a shanty-stick tin roof. It looked like a post-office wall with each individual sod of turf in its own slot. The turf told you this dwelling was anchored on the solid island of *Éire*. Electricity had come to Kilcross in 1960, but there was no running water. The family had a well out back behind the henhouse.

Inside, the floors were uncarpeted cement. The house was heated with a fireplace in each room, but in August, usually, the fire was going only for cooking and making tea on the crane in the fireplace of the big room.

The door on the right in the middle of the central hallway let you into the big room. Opposite that door, two bedrooms, front and back, were on the left of the hallway. Sheila and the baby and I had the back bedroom on that side. Her mother and father had the small oblong bedroom beyond the big room on the right side of the house.

The big room ran the depth of the house and served as breakfast, lunch and living room all in one. A big table could be pushed up against the wall by the door or pulled out into the middle of the room. Beyond the door was the tall cupboard storing cups and saucers, which Jane Blake called 'the press.' Sheila's mother cooked on the open turf fire, but she also had a small 60cm gas-cooker and oven fueled by a 5-gallon butane tank in the wash-room, down the back, at the end of the central hall, where her big four-legged washtub lived. The family jacks, behind that, was a sort of a semi-detached outhouse with a commode and a single-stall shower you could stand up in. You drew the plastic curtain closed around you and pumped the handle and an Irish mist came out of the perforated ring suspended over your head.

It might have looked primitive to my city-boy eyes, and like roughing it to my library-ensconced posterior, but as soon as I entered this house for the first time, I felt the love that inhabited the rooms, the warmth that came off the turf fire in the big room.

And imagine the culture-shock I felt, who had long ago, at my own mother's elbow, watched Hattie McDaniel in *Gone With the Wind* on TV, to hear my Sheila calling her mother *'Mammy,'* in strict accordance with the local usage!

To begin at the beginning, I had to enter the house, for the first time, through the front door, head down the hall, carrying my duffel-bag behind me, being directed by brother-in-law Pat, to turn in the first door on the right, and then—confront the consequences.

There they stood, my father-in-law, Patrick Blake the elder, his daughter Ann and his son Martin, in front of the fire. Before I could say anything, Sheila's mother emerged from her bedroom door.

My first thought was, *my God, Sheila's the spitting image of her mother!*

Jane Blake came out of her bedroom in a long high-necked granny dress and a cardigan and took her place alongside the others in front of the fire, looked down demurely, after smiling in my direction, and crossed her arms in front of herself, modestly closing the cardigan and holding her elbows in her hands.

When she had turned to shut the bedroom door behind her I had glimpsed a long pony-tail all the way down her back, the same dark color of silky hair as Sheila's, only dulled by the years with wisps of greyish strands. With her ankle-length dress, and the lace collar up to her neck, she could have been Sheila's twin sister in a hippie commune back home.

And remarkably, instantly, I could see that Patrick, Martin and Ann, the children, all three, along with their older sisters Mary and Bridie back in Massachusetts, took after their father's side—although Patrick Blake the elder was a head taller than any of them, a good six-foot, at least.

Himself now stepped forward to extend his hand to me on behalf of the family, and I could see that he had the same thatch of hair as his son Patrick, only a bit more straw-colored.

"Welcome to Ireland, young man," he said, "I hope you'll find soon enough you have friends here you never knew you had."

He stepped back with a quick nod, abruptly bird-like, and seemed highly bemused and unable to know what to make of me.

I smiled and stupidly said nothing and looked around for Sheila to rescue me, but where was she?

Over there in the corner by the back window, holding Aisling in her arms.

Tactfully, Jane Blake suggested, "You must be tired after your trip."

Again, as I was awkwardly speechless, Mammy spoke up. "Sheila, take him down to the room and let the poor boy relax a while before we're all upon him. We'll call you both when it's time for dinner."

We had barely closed the bedroom door before Sheila threw one arm around my neck.

"Stop!" she gasped, "you'll bruise my lips, what will my mother think?"

"She'll think I missed you."

"Don't crush the child."

"Put her down and I'll crush you instead."

"You are a randy fellow, but you'll just have to mind your manners and wait, won't you?"

I picked up little Aisling and hugged her close. "Did you miss me?"

"No," she said, frowning.

"She's jealous now she'll have to share me," said Sheila.

The tiny bedroom we were in was the size of a monk's cell, long and narrow, with a cot big enough for one resident pushed up against the wall, only inches from the fireplace, and a small sleeping pallet on the floor under the rear window for 'the child.' I stretched out on the cot and balanced Aisling on my chest. "Your legs are getting long, little girl."

Sheila made room to sit down with us and said, "Well, how was your trip?"

"I thought your brother was going to kill us both driving up here from Shannon."

"And the flight? No turbulence? Soft landing?"

"Sheila, I didn't know what to say to your father."

"Not to worry. He's easy."

"But what will they all think of me?"

"That you're a typical Yank, out of his road."

And that I was.

But after lying back, I started to yawn uncontrollably. "Why am I so tired?"

"Oh, aye, that. Jet-lag."

And after napping, my appetite, alertness, and affability restored, I enjoyed dinner, (put on specially for me; I had no concept, as yet, of 'tea') and picked up the conversation with my new family right where Pat and I had left it in the Austin mini.

And then it was time to retire to the back bedroom again.

They say that absence makes the heart grow fonder but in my case it might better be said that it stiffens one's resolution. Sheila and I had been separated by an ocean for approximately two weeks, yet we fell upon one another like a deprived pris-on-inmate and his conjugal visitor.

And so in the end I had my soft landing.

I was invited the next night to an evening of doing-the-rounds in Delaney's, evidently a custom of the country. Whenever anyone in Kilcross had a 'visitor' in the house, that is, some novel creature from a foreign land, they were expected to bring them up to Delaney's for a pint, upon which occasion all the village could satisfy their curiosity as to the dimensions, peccadilloes, and seducements of the stranger. Was he or she round and chubbable, like a pillow, or spiky like a hedgehog? Could they take a joke, and most importantly, could they give as good as they got? In my case, since Sheila's arrival with the babby a fortnight previously, it was understood that I was married into the family, and so they were to be stuck with me. Still, who was he, that he wooed away one of our own?

I myself was most delighted to be introduced to Toss Ribbons, the teacher at the National School in Kilcross, as he represented an individual molded, like myself, by higher education, and therefore I was not alone in this western outpost.

"How in the world did you ever get a name like Toss Ribbons?"

"Unfortunately, my mother named me Thomas, and, early on, one of the twisted local wits tagged me with the nickname, and it stuck like egg yolk on a china plate."

Evidently, Toss did not consider there to be anything unusual about the surname, 'Ribbons,' but I thought it wiser not to pursue the matter, and reserved it for later. It took a mighty effort, too, to stifle myself.

Frank Delaney the T.D. and his missus were gathered at the round table, along with Naughton and Langan, a pair of cronies who hovered about Patrick Blake the elder, also known as Long Pat, to distinguish him from his son Patrick; wherever Long Pat went, especially should he stick his nose inside Delaney's, which was rarely more than once or twice or three or four or five times a week, and always on Sunday after Mass (and never in Garret's or Reynolds,' God forbid) there would you find Langan and Naughton close behind. There was Sheila, of course, and her brother Pat, and with Pat, news to me, a girlfriend, by the name of Pippa, an interloper, like me, only in her case, from, of all places, Ye Olde England; Pippa was quite determined to seek out the authentic 'life on the land' here in the wilds of Mayo. She was a friendly sort, a modestly attractive young woman who wore sensible shoes, and leggings, and trimmed her hair with a bowl on her head, and I was happy for my brother-in-law Pat, surprised too, as he had neglected to mention Pippa at any point in the eighty miles between Shannon and Kilcross.

I wondered what other hidden depths that I knew not of lay behind those teasingly blue eyes of Young Pat's.

After Ned Fogerty, the local boatman, came up to our round table, enquiring as to whether I would be wanting to go fishing out in Lough Conn, and was rebuffed, he made no further advances, having concluded I must be 'not one of them Yanks' who come equipped with credit cards, a truly unique event in his experience; did I not know that the brooks here-abouts were rife all summer with avid trout-fisherman from Germany? Indeed.

I decided that my best bet for making my entrée among the locals a qualified success, at optimum, was to play the polit-ical card, and so I let it filter into the roundtable conversation that I had been on familiar terms with the Noraid people back in Boston and had even attended speechmaking by Bernadette Devlin herself on the Boston Common.

Then all I had to do was to sit back and listen, as I had set the match to the haystack.

In the end, it was Toss Ribbons who was urging me to get involved with the upcoming re-enactment of Humbert's march to Castlebar across the Windy Gap in 1798, a project upon which he and his group of cohorts were busily engaged, in the planning phase, and which was set to be staged on the anniversary of the historic events themselves, coming up shortly on 8 September.

I learned a very valuable lesson that evening in Delaney's, which I kept to myself, but observed ever afterwards in Ireland, and it stood me in good stead: say little, ask no pokey questions, just listen. And that way you will learn a great deal that you didn't know enough to ask.

After a week or so of settling in, of re-connecting with Sheila under the covers of our narrow trundle-bed, with a gentle, low fire going in the grate, which solicitously, Sheila insisted upon, even though it was August; after a week of being a proud Papa with my little Aisling, and of being treated as an honored guest in a wayside inn; a certain restlessness encroached upon the shores of my consciousness, a bit like the little wavelets that lapped up on the gravel aprons of Lough Conn. Sheila and I took a walk down the boreen to the edge of the water, with the child suspended by the arms between us; happily, Aisling went tapping every other step on the ground playfully, the mile or so it took to get there.

It almost seemed as if time were suspended, things moved so slowly. Although the house was a hub of activity all the day long, there was no such thing as a nine-to-five day at the office. My mother-in-law Jane was always the first up before six in the morning, raking the ashes in the main fireplace to uncover yesterday's still-warm coals and throw on a sod or two of fresh turf to get the fire going and make tea. Soft butter smeared on bread was the breakfast swallowed by young Pat on his way out the door to milk the cows.

The cowshed was a concrete affair on a pedestal of cement perched catty-corner across the boreen from the house and surrounded by scrub trees. Looking in the door, you could see three milking-stalls. The cows were surprisingly agile at hopping up onto the steep apron to go in the door. After milking, they were taken down to the lower field. Long Pat was also up and about early to assist his son in whatever needed to be done.

It was all a mystery to me. Jane fed her chickens and hens, there was one roast chicken a week to eat, on Sundays mutton perhaps, and the rest of the week, boiled potatoes, with their jackets on, heaped in a bowl for lunch. The one or two hired hands who worked alongside young Pat would troop in the door and sit down at the big table, pushed lengthwise up against the wall so that both sides could be seated. Mammy would carry in the big steaming pot from the cooker down back using pot-holders. Young Pat, Martin and the lads would plunge hands onto the big bowl of boiling-hot spuds, hold one up and, with a flick of the wrist, peel down the skin on the hot potato with a knife, while they twirled them on their fingertips, as quick as they could, attempting to keep their fingers from being burnt; it was like the devil dancing on hot coals; then smash them with a fork on their plate, douse them in HP sauce and butter, throw salt on, and dig in, steam rising. Inside of five minutes they were out the door again. Free lunch being provided was evidently a part of their wages for the lads, but the economy of subsistence farming eluded me just as much as the economy of the Detroit automobile industry would have. I was clearly out of my bailiwick on the Blakes' farm in Kilcross.

I did think that I detected undercurrents going on, however. It seemed to me that young Pat was inclined to be in a hurry to take things over from his da. It came out that he had left school at 16 in order to get a head start. That he was schooling himself in methods of scientific farming with the help of the

Department of Agriculture; the agents they sent out into the field were to identify young men such as himself with forward-looking progressive outlooks and a background and commitment in farming. Young Pat had taken out a bank loan to buy a tractor and start his own business serving all the farmers in Kilcross by collecting their milk cans in the morning for transport to the creamery in Killala Bay. He had started a flock of sheep up on the sides of Nephin.

These were things his father had not done. They represented the changing of the guard, as it were.

Young Pat stood to inherit the two fields that belonged to the family, the upper and the lower; the first was behind the house and was steep and hilly and served as the potato-patch. A dirt footpath, worn away by the ages, which was used by the villagers as a shortcut, ran below it and this footpath crossed from the boreen all the way to the main road, below the hook in the road and behind the church. The second field was much flatter, as it was situated on the left of the boreen partway to the lake and beyond the two other farmhouses that shared the fields at this end of Kilcross.

Between these two fields and his dozen or so head of dairy cattle and his flock of sheep, Young Pat had forged his dreams of one day building his own home, so much grander and larger, and starting his own family, in the upper field, with its rocky outcrop: from which serene views of Lough Conn, in one direction, and Nephin, in the other, inspired him.

The map of the West of Ireland lodged inside my head was altogether of another sort. It consisted not of farms and fields but of literary landmarks. I was aware that here in Kilcross I was situated about halfway between Drumcliff Churchyard in Sligo and Nora Barnacle's Connemara in Galway.

Now that I was here I had not yet quite left behind the person I had become through four years at Boston College, topped with two more in grad school in South County, Rhode Island: the aspiring writer who had hitchhiked to Roanoke to pick the brains of James Dickey and Larry McMurty; the poet who had been published by Ray Deeds in New York and delivered Saturday afternoon readings at Dr Deeds, Ray's pub in Manhattan, on 2nd Avenue and 72nd St. In fact, I, too, was full of grandiose plans for a future in Ireland, every bit as much as my brother-in-law. His example inspired me and I was challenged to compete with him. Certainly, we came from polar worlds, but I was going to industriously set about sending out my resume and find a teaching position through which I could utilize my master's degree. I was going to husband the thousand bucks I had saved up for Sheila, Aisling and me, till I could get an income stream going that would provide support for my family. My future was going to be in Ireland. I was now officially a political exile from the United States, and when I sat over a pint at Delaney's with Toss Ribbons, it became clearer than ever that this was the case. Because of Sheila I had been presented with opportunities I could not have imagined as recently as five years previously.

Then 'The Muse' placed her hand on my shoulder, silently and unexpectedly, from behind, just as she had that night at the Stardust Lounge, so many years ago.

I asked Sheila if there was anything about the place with which I could write.

Her sister Ann came forward with just the thing.

Still in school, Ann had always liked to draw, and she was home from London for the summer. Over there, she waited on tables while attending night school once a week to study art. She took the occasion of my arrival in the house to acquire an ally who could buttress her dreams of becoming an artist, preferably in London.

Ann was young and tender-hearted and although she looked very much like her older sisters Mary and Bridie back in Boston, taking after her da's side, as they did, her personality was nothing like theirs. Indeed, it almost seemed to me that Ann was more like me than any of her own family. She did not see herself going for motherhood or being the wife of a farmer in Kilcross. She did not see herself as belonging in Kilcross, actually, any more than I did. She welcomed me as giving her the chance to indulge in long conversations about the world of Picasso, Andy Warhol, and the Rolling Stones. I thought it was remarkable to find such an aesthetic soul had grown up in this family and in this house. Running away to London was Ann's gambit for independence.

It was my sister-in-law Ann who gave me the blue copy-book from the National School, and the biro, with which to fill in its blank pages.

Jane said I could go down to the front bedroom, if I liked, the room belonging to Patrick and Martin, and shut the door, for a little peace and quiet.

It occurred to me that The Muse had her handmaidens in Kilcross. And they were conspiring with her to place me upon my path.

To my utter astonishment, what came pouring out of me was the past, and it came without hesitation or hindrance. From the vantage point of the present, and with the perspective of three thousand miles of separation, my eyes turned back toward America.

An idea seized hold of me. I think it came from pop music, the concept album. What the Beatles did with *Pepper. Tommy,* by The Who. The Kinks, *Village Green,* definitely. When I got to *Village Green,* I knew that was it. A unified storyline. But what was the storyline to be, the theme? Then it hit me like a block of wood in the face. And the impetus hearkened back two thousand years, more: to the explosion of tragedy in the convoluted maze between father and son, minotaur and man; to the burning birth of religion, the love between mother and son on the harrowing hill of Gethsemane.

That was it. Mother and father tangled together to make the son. Twisted together, like strands of DNA. Chapter One, the Father. Chapter Two, the Mother. And Three, the Son. The holy, or unholy, trinity. *Unholy* was stillborn in the idea, but obscurely, still there, refusing to bow down, raising rebellion, staked on conflict.

Yet none of it was so unexpected as the first lines I wrote, which, to my bafflement, were in praise of my father, my real father, not some mythical, or heavenly, figure, but a real man, of mud, dust and blood.

Where daylight drowns the dregs of night,
coal-miners rise in the wire cage,
eyes downcast, wincing at the light:
the graveyard shift, lurching onstage.

Rage locked in a skull of bones,
a face like the dust-blackened leaf,
a heart like the withered pine-cone,
sisters rocking in chairs of grief.

With pick and shovel, under the ground,
my father labored. No sweet, bright
chorus embraced the splintered sound—
but his headlamp split the night.

It soon became apparent that I was taking dictation from the cool, country air, unstained with smoke. From the window of the front bedroom I could see through a gap in the hedgerows all the way down the hill to the water, where, on an island in the middle of Lough Conn, there stood Ferranti's estate. He was the Milanese industrialist who had bought the island in the lake to be his summer residence. At this distance, the big house peeking through the broccoli-bunch trees on the island seemed to be floating in mid-air. White clouds scudding overhead on a sunlit afternoon were racing like sailboats. Sometimes they turned flat-bottomed and grey so that they were like the undersides of rowboats. Everything was in motion, the spinning reel of a movie in my mind, and the words I was setting on the page were passing across the screen faster than I could write them down. Printed lines unrolling on the clouds. Thoughts rising from the lake, clothed in the morning mist.

Vague, formless, obscure, the idea coalesced.

Out of the fog of daybreak, out of the mysterious breath rising from the lake, the big house on the island emerged.

So now the stakes were set, the race was in motion. Who would finish first, the favorite, with the big money on his back, or the longshot, running on his heart?

When it was time for tea, Sheila would nudge open my door and invite me across to the big room.

In the evenings Long Pat would not let me sit in a chair by the window. "You'll catch your death," he said. "Come on over here by me, in front of the fire." We would arrange two chairs facing one another while he took down his pipe from the mantel and I would be reading my *Moby Dick.*

There was a radio in the big room but no television, and the radio would be silenced after the evening news from RTE at six. I found out from Sheila's brother Martin, known to all as 'Matt,' that he intended to go in for a television repairman programme after secondary school. Meanwhile, the boy stuck close on the heels of his older brother Pat, working the farm in tandem with his idol, both of them directed in no uncertain terms by their da, Long Pat, who was, these days, resigning himself, by fits and starts, to his new role as 'elder statesman' of the family.

Artistic Ann would be lying on the floor with her charcoal pencils and a big sketch-pad drawing birds and dogs. Long Pat would be explaining to me the difference between the political parties Fianna Fail and Fine Gael. He himself was a DeValera man, he avowed, and always would be. I had no real idea how serious a matter this was until I happened to mention that Seán Ó Faoláin had been my teacher at Boston College and that I had read some of his short stories about the IRA in the 1920s, especially his tales of the Civil War. This opened the spigots for my father-in-law and I got the impression that Long Pat himself had been involved, on the Dev, or anti-Treaty, side of the bitterness. And bitterness it was, if I could tell from him. I followed my rule, asked nothing, and tried to listen. He was not specific about anything, and I got the sense that he was sparing all of us in the room from hearing what he actually knew or had witnessed as he said, sighing, "It was a terrible, terrible time," puffing on his pipe. I wondered exactly how old Long Pat was. Could he be actually 70 years old? He would have to have been in order to be old enough to be involved in the War of Independence or the Civil War. And it was obvious that he was considerably older than my mother-in-law Jane. I didn't want to ask, but it gave poignancy to the time I remembered when we'd had to drag Sheila to St Elizabeth's in Brighton when she'd been seized with visions of her da dying.

One day Young Pat suggested that I go on an excursion with him. He took me across the main road from the mouth of the boreen to another side-road I had never noticed which led in the opposite direction, towards the mountain instead of the lake. We went on foot, late in the day. In Kilcross, that might be nine or ten at night in August, as I was finding out that this was the land of the midnight sun I'd heard tell of, but never had connected to Ireland.

I often wondered why Sheila, in all the time I'd known her, five years or more now, had never told me about this, and so many other things. I supposed it was something she took for granted and, in spite of being intimate with me, and knowing my voracious curiosity, thought it not worth mentioning. Or could it be that when she was away in America, Ireland was a memory too private, precious and personal to share even with me? As I was finding my yearning for a lost America spooling itself out on the blank pages of an Irish schoolgirl's blue copybook?

I found it difficult to keep up with young Pat, his stride was so vigorous, especially when we diverted from the damp dirt road to scramble through the boggy bottom leading to our destination. He had taken me off the boreen in order to square up the view for me. Where he nimbly and sure-footedly hopped form tuft to tuft in the bogland, I sank up to my ankles getting my shoes and myself miserably wet. I envied him his skills. From this one excursion I could tell how admirably he was suited to his native ground and how hopelessly out of it I was.

Finally he stopped and let me catch up. He gestured expansively uphill on the side of the mountain.

There I saw what could not be seen from the main road. An entire village of abandoned stone dwellings with caved-in roofs. Window-openings in walls looked out, eyes without pupils; empty doorways yawned, empty except for the ghosts of haunted lives.

"This is the old village of Kilcross, the famine village," said Pat. "Everyone who ever lived here perished here and nobody ever wanted to go back to it. I thought you might like to see it. When the village was rebuilt again, after the famine, they put the road through further down the mountainside and closer to the lake, so that they wouldn't have to come back here again."

We were silent for a long while, and then I said, "We should say a prayer for them."

"Go ahead, if you like," said Pat. "I'm sure they wouldn't object, though it mightn't do them much good now."

He turned and began to walk back again, and I followed. The irony was that the stones of the walls of the famine village called back to my mind a picture of my own fieldstone house, back in the Spicket Falls of my childhood.

Thus was born the third chapter. The mother, the father, the children all lived in the stone house. *This storied house.* I had the title of my book.

And so the next time I sat in the window in my brother-in-law's front bedroom which he shared with his brother Matt, and now, with me, in that small cinder-block farmhouse with the slate roof, I found poems about the fieldstone house in Spicket Falls introducing themselves into my blank pages, with an insistent, if subterranean, force.

And it became crystallized in my mind that we are all one, that all of us are brothers and sisters, that we all are descended from the inhabitants of the famine village, that we are connected, in one way or another.

So the book grew, from page to page, beyond the father, the mother and the son, to fill in yet more blank pages with an ever-larger, growing family, encompassing the past, leading to the present, foretelling the future, holding in its cupped hands the whole world.

This was cemented within me by the luscious kiss that Mrs. Delaney planted on my lips one night.

We were up in the pub carousing, and Sheila excused herself as being tired and would see me when I got home. Pat and his girlfriend Pippa also had a drive ahead of them to get her back to her place. I suppose I had taken too much of the Guinness as I wasn't noticing that Mr. Delaney and Naughton and Langan and my father-in-law were all, one by one, taking their leave.

In fact, it was me and Mrs. Delaney who were left there by ourselves, and the pub now empty. Whereupon Mrs. Delaney invited me to continue the party in her kitchen, which was on the other side of the wall from the pub.

So we retired there and Mrs. Delaney persuaded me to regale her with tales of the student life back in Boston. What were the parties like, and didn't I have more than several girl-friends stashed away where Sheila wouldn't find them, a handsome young curly-mop like myself? And didn't I look dashing in my Navy pea-coat? It was enough to make a lady swoon.

I tried to explain to Mrs. Delaney that I liked to spend my time in libraries, but she was too busy filling my glass to listen to anything I had to say, when suddenly, she threw her am around my neck, pulled me close in a headlock, and showered me with a big fat wet one right on the kisser.

"Missus Delaney!" I protested, pushing my chair back. "What would Mister Delaney say?"

"Isn't it convenient he isn't here?"

As fast as I could in my stumbling state, I ran all the way home. Thank God Sheila was asleep when I got there. All I could hear was Mrs. Delaney laughing like a braying donkey behind me, all the way to the boreen.

Beside this licentious woman, my mother-in-law Jane was the picture of piety. I was sure a gentler soul I had never encountered. Before she was married, she had been Jane Loftus. She remembered very well the day back in the 1930s when her sister Theresa and her sister Ann and her brother Anthony left for America. "We had the American wake in our house that day," said Jane. I asked her did it not bother her that she had never seen them again from that day to this?

"Oh, no, not at all," said Jane, "for I knew that they were happy there, from the letters over the years, and they were always sending money and presents home to us, and they were so thoughtful that way towards my children, before they even had a chance to meet them, and wasn't it handy when my own children grew up, that they had someone over there in Boston that could help them get started, it was God's blessing that it all worked out the way that it did, and besides, in those days, you know, there wasn't any air travel, was there? and how could they be taking time off from work two months at a time to travel across the ocean in a boat and back again, and then, there was the war in Europe, of course, and that put a stop to things, and by that time, well."

I used to elbow Sheila in the ribs in the morning and say to her, "Get up, you lazy thing, and go help your mother with the tea."

She would yawn and sigh and turn over to face me, saying, "Oh, she can very well do for herself, she's used of it, and anyways, wouldn't you rather I stay here in the bed with you, with the sun rising and all?"

"Did they hold the American wake for you in the house when you were leaving?" said I, propped up on one elbow.

"They did not. That's an old-fashioned custom belonging to Mammy's day and before. Jesus, what are you doing, Nicky, writing a book? Come here," she said, pulling me by what she considered my thinking apparatus, "and remind me why you're mad about me."

The next time I informed Jane that I was going down the lake to take some exercise for myself, she said, "I'll walk you to the gate."

This was another of the lovely customs of the country that endeared my relations to me. As I went away down the boreen, I looked back over my shoulder and happened to see my mother-in-law looking after me and crossing herself in the doorway with the Sign of the Cross.

I said to myself, that woman is a saint if ever there was one. Imagine raising six kids in this god-forsaken place with nothing but toil and tears to show for it.

It must have been that very day when I saw the two farmer's daughters standing in the field of hay.

I was proceeding to the lake with *Moby Dick* (with its beautiful woodcuts by Rockwell Kent, in the hardcover Modern Library edition) walking slowly and reading (like one of the priests at Boston College with his breviary in his hand) when I glanced up and spied them.

Jack Ryan had the house on the left closest to the lake. He was one broad field away from the Blake's lower field. Behind his house, the land sloped upwards in a round mound, just after the flatness of the Blake's cow-pasture. Mr. Ryan's cash crop was hay, and this was the time of the year for taking the hay in. The mounded field was dotted with haystacks. A single horse facing away from me stood placidly while Ryan used his pitchfork to toss the hay up on the back of the hayrick. Getting it all in before bad weather might spoil it was the reason the man had his daughters out there to help him—he had no sons. But the scene I saw was straight from a nineteenth century painting in a museum, something like 'The Toilers,' by Heysen.

There were things I'd seen in Kilcross that belonged to olden times. The donkey cart on the main road that Sheila called the 'ass'n'cart,' whose only concession to modernity was the rubber tires on the back. The famine village. The stone church at the hook of the road. The multitudinous stone walls criss-crossing everywhere. This hayrick pulled by the single horse.

Jack Ryan's two daughters peeked out from behind the rickety contraption. They had heard about the stranger living in the house up the boreen. Overcome by curiosity, determined to clap eyes on me as long as they could keep me in view, bashful as lambs, and bold as shameless strumpets, they stared at me, as if they were gazing through telescopes at an astronomical oddity.

They were a pair of young, gangly, long-legged yearlings, in dresses knocking about their knees.

Oh, God, I'm going straight to hell for what I'm thinking right now.

I turned my face resolutely to the wind and marched on doggedly to the lake, certain I'd be struck by lightning bolts at the step after next, if not sooner.

Day after day I spent my afternoons dwelling in the window of the front bedroom. My scribbling in the blue copybook was going so well I was sure that another hand was guiding mine. The most surprising thing was that I was writing poem after poem in rhymed stanzaic forms, and they were coming easily, without strain, and the end-rhymes were flowing within the logic of sense, not forced into being so as to fit patterns, but emerging out of the needs demanded by the context.

Most definitely I could not be doing this purposely. If I tried to do it, how would I? But I was not trying, it was just flowing.

Having read my share of my contemporaries, that is, my competitors; having been promised by Ray Deeds in New York that soon one of my pieces was to be appearing in *Esquire* magazine; having found my first book, published by Dr Deeds, on the shelf at Grolier's in Harvard Square; having introduced myself to Jack Powers, Boston's leading entrepreneur of poets, in the basement of Goodspeed's on Beacon Hill; all before I left home; here I was, in a window of a farmhouse in Mayo, going against the grain of the established, stamp-of-approval poetics of the day.

What was going on? It was exciting. Having contacts in Boston and New York, hoping one day soon to add Dublin to that lineup, I couldn't wait to see what the reaction of other writers to these poems would be. Would they reject them as old-fashioned in an obsolete style? Perversely, I plowed on. I would confront them, I would knock them down like candle-pins at the Recreation Lanes.

As time went on I was developing three chapters based on the concept that the strands of DNA from my father's and mother's side would join together in the fieldstone house. Chapter one, the miner; chapter two, the tailor; chapter three, the scion of these two lines. This would be my next book of poems.

Was it not the primal family? Was it not the lineage of all humankind I was plunging into?

Behind these mounting poems, day by day numbering twenty, thirty, forty, stood the family surrounding me in this isolated farmhouse. Behind them stood another family three thousand miles away. Behind them stood families strewn like islands of an archipelago across oceans of water, and then continents of land. Behind them stood ancestors fading like blue mountains in the distance of recorded time.

In my siege mentality, I felt I had stumbled across the age-old experience of the bard. There existed an irreversible, inevitable moment, in timeless time, when Dylan Thomas turns away from the microphone in the BBC studio in London and retreats to his writing shed overlooking the water in Wales.

Behind my back, my shoulders hunched over the page, Sheila was opening the door a crack to call me to tea. Behind her stood The Muse from the Stardust Lounge. They had blended together to form one driving feminine hand that was guiding me across the blank pages of the blue-lined copybook from the National School.

Here in the West of Ireland, finally, I was living the life. As the days wore on I began to feel pangs of guilt that I had not yet made my pilgrimage to Yeats' grave, to thank him.

In the evenings I would sit across from Long Pat reading my *Moby Dick* by firelight. It was the most gorgeous prose ever penned in English, I proposed to my father-in-law, who removed the pipe from between his teeth to assert, "I suppose I wouldn't know about that, but—if you say so." I shared those rock-ribbed illustrations of Rockwell Kent with sister Ann, on the floor with her sketch-pad, as I came upon them, turning the page. She was now copying illustrated dress-adverts from the Mayo News. One night I laughed out loud at a certain paragraph, and Long Pat said, "Must be a very comical book." I looked up at him and replied with one twinkling word: "Queequeg."

How do you sum up Queequeg? How do you express the worlds Queequeg contains? How do you translate a nineteenth-century, seafaring, South Seas nomad to a twentieth-century survivor of the Irish Civil War, in so many words? What conversation can bridge that gap? What theory can verbalize the connections? *You have to read the book to understand.* No mere summary jammed into the spoken word of a single sentence can express the essence of all the worlds contained by the great works of the great minds. It's as if another world, parallel to ours, ran alongside the petty realities of our daily lives, a world that en-compassed the secret, beating heart of this one.

As my writing approached culmination, I began to feel guilty also about my lackadaisical, loafing ways. Here I was living off the generosity of people who, it seemed to me, had little enough to spare. The most I had yet done around the house was to once in a while go out to fetch sods for the fire, thrusting them into the old smudged white laundry sack with the drawstring, to carry the bulging bulk back on my shoulder into the big room for Mammy. I said to Sheila, "You know, I think I'm gonna have to get off my duff and do something." I volunteered one afternoon, to Long Pat, that I might try my hand at some useful chore. He reached behind the door of the big room and pulled out his knobby blackthorn stick. "Take this and go down to the lower field and bring up the cows for the evening milking. And if they don't mind you, just give 'em a clip o' this in the butt o' the thurl."

"In the what?"

"In the hind-quarters, lad."

The lower pasture was enclosed by stout hedgerows, but the opening to the boreen was covered by a swinging gate with three metal, paint-chipped bars crossed by a diagonal. I managed to figure out that I would not get the cows, about a dozen or so head, out the gate unless I pushed it all the way back. That turned out to be about the only thing I did right. The cows were all gathered in one corner of the squared-off field. I approached them tentatively from behind. It suddenly occurred to me that these were enormous beasts. I yelled encouragment to them. "Okay, girls, let's go home!"

That accomplished exactly nothing, so I took my father-in-law's instructions to heart and gave one of them a clip in the rear with the knobby stick.

This cow then reared up on her hind-legs, squealed in protest, and set out at a dead run across the field to cower in the next corner of squared-off hedgerow, upon which all the other cows, in a panic, followed, to huddle alongside her.

I repeated the approved procedure, and the same thing happened again.

I was getting frustrated but I reasoned that if I headed them off at the open gateway this time, I could direct them out to the boreen. Of course, I didn't think beforehand that if I executed this maneuver, I might get trampled, but it quickly became all too clear. I dodged out of the way, and was left with a gaggle of spooked cows huddling in a corner.

I swore oaths at Long Pat and realized he'd been having me on, as the local saying went. Finally, sweating profusely and trying to wave away swarms of flies, I managed to get them out the gate to the road. There was no time to go back and shut the gate again. They were already trotting away. I was desperately thankful only that they weren't headed in the direction of the lake. Already I could see that one of them had wandered into the front garden of the Cochran's house, the one on the left. The woman of that place came out and helped me get Long Pat's cow out of her lawn. She was too kind to laugh directly in my face, but I felt so ridiculous that by the time I got them up to the Blake's cowshed, I was in a red-faced fury. I went into the house, and there was Long Pat sitting in his chair in front of the fire, puffing on his pipe, saying blandly, "Ah, that was a good deal more comical than Queequeg."

I could only think of how this story would go the rounds up at Delaney's to universal hilarity at my expense.

Then Young Pat came to me, and said kindly, "Come on with me, and we'll go up the mountain and pay a visit to the flock." He added, with a grin, "Not to worry, no tricks."

So we headed up the famine village road but diverted in another direction past it and ventured higher up. Nephin was a different animal up close. I was surprised to find that no matter how high you went, soggy bogland seemed to prevail, though I shouldn't have been wondering, as most days there was a fine mist blowing half of the day, interrupted by either showers or a downpour, sometimes on the order of what Sheila called 'teeming torrents,' so that the land never had time to dry out.

On odd days we'd get fine weather and sun. The mountain glowered often, wreathed in morning fog along her bottom skirts, or clouded at the brow with vividly purple afternoon thunderclouds. There were no trees on Nephin, so there was no relief to her inscrutable face. She was a mountain of many moods, and sometimes you could see the sunlight chasing cloud-shadows across her forehead, so that she resembled nothing less than a tempestuous lover plotting her next revenge.

But on this day the rain was holding off and again I had to appreciate young Pat's mountain-goat deftness at dodging every muddle and keeping his feet dry.

"I have to come up here at least once a week, more for the dog than the sheep. I trained her myself, you know, but she's young and this is her first year I've let her up here on her own."

How does one train a sheepdog? Where does one get the knowledge? Is it something born and bred in a farmer, a matter of inherited bloodlines? I marveled at my, relatively, taciturn brother-in-law. As far as I knew, there were no schools, no textbooks, for training a sheep-dog. Either you had it or you didn't.

"I started the flock, sort of, to have another line of cash-crop for the business. When shearing time comes, you can sell the wool. And you can pasture sheep up here on the mountain-side, so there's little to no expense involved. It's not as if you have to buy up another field, borrowing from the bank. It's all free up here. Nobody owns it. All you need do is keep your sheep-dog fed and he looks after the flock for you. I'm thinking next of perhaps getting into mushrooms. We've the climate for that. They thrive on darkness."

I could see that Young Pat was brimming over with ideas, planning all the while that house he was going to build on the hillock of the upper field, with views of the lake and the mountain, front and back.

Afterwards, Pat lay back on the mountain and folded his hands behind his head and looked up at the wayward sky.

"Well, that's it. We're done for the day. Nothing left to do and we can relax and enjoy ourselves watching the clouds go by. Nick, it's the life of the farmer for me. I wouldn't trade it for anything."

My time in Mayo was coming to a close, though I didn't know it. I should have. Because I was coming to the end of my poem-writing. I had turned a lump of coal in my mind this way and that and examined it from every facet, trying to extract poetic ore, and still I did not know whether my lump was diamond or dust. But I knew I had crushed the life out of it, that there was no blood left in the stone. Finally, I decided I had to go up to Drumcliff Churchyard to visit the great man and see what his ghost had to say, before I lost the chance altogether.

"I remember when I was a child, one time, when Yeats himself came to our classroom," said Jane Blake.

"Really? One of his most famous poems is 'Among School Children.'"

"I wouldn't know about that, but I do remember we were told we had to be on our best behavior."

"Would you like to come with me, then? We could go together."

"And who would mind the babby and feed the chickens? I'm better off staying here, but thank you for the thought."

I could get no-one else to go with me, either. Sheila also had to mind the babby and feed the chickens. Ann had her drawing to attend to and Matt had school. Long Pat said cemeteries gave him the chills. Young Pat was tied up delivering daily milk-runs to the creamery in Killala Bay daily. So I had to go alone.

I waited for the bus to Ballina up at Delaney's. It usually passed through twice a day. I was intending to make it a day-trip so as to save money rather than paying for accommodations overnight. It was my first day away from the house since I'd arrived. Sheila had already been up to Ballina to open a bank account for us and deposited my monopoly-money, my thousand bucks per annum, but I was overly aware of trying to make it last. I really had no idea of the cost of living in this country, but so far I hadn't needed to make my own way; even at Delaney's, nobody let me buy a pint. I was getting too used to living for free. Perhaps the great man would tell me from the far side of the grave that it was time to face facts and get a move on.

It wasn't far from Ballina to Sligo Town. The bus I transferred to took less than an hour. As soon as I crossed into Sligo, though, I thought I detected a change in the demeanor of the place. Between the two counties, Sligo was that much tidier and less desolate-looking. This feeling became the more pronounced as you entered the town of Sligo. There was a low bridge across a narrow neck of the River Garavogue exactly where it meets Sligo Bay. Drumcliff Churchyard itself was only 15 minutes further north by another bus.

It looked exactly like pictures I'd seen in the biography of Yeats by Richard Ellman. You could almost reach out and touch Ben Bulben, it was so prominent, dominating the view. Right across the road was a round tower. The stone walls bordering the graveyard were capped and so much neater than the ragged stone walls of Mayo. The medieval church where Yeats' grand-father had been the rector was pristine. I found Yeats' headstone and knelt before it to read the famous inscription. The day was fine, no thunder sounded, the earth did not shake. I prayed that, through the ground I knelt on, I would absorb some residue of the spirit of poetry that resided in the man and the place.

When I was going home on the bus, it struck me that I now called 'home' a farmhouse in the village of Kilcross. Was this a temporary illusion, a trick of the mind, or something deeper, more profound? I did not feel transformed, I had no roots, I was floating, but I felt buoyed on the low-lapping waters of Lough Conn, the minor-key *lupp-lupp* of the wavelets slapping the gravel strand.

That evening, sitting with my book opposite Long Pat, I had the merry thought of spooking him, so I leaned over into his face and said, "Do you know what it says on that headstone, Pat? 'Cast a cold eye on life, on death, Horseman, pass by.'"

"God save us," said my father-in-law.

The bowl of spuds suffered daily destruction in the big room when the farmhands sat down to eat. I was sometimes there, reading by the fire, feeling I hadn't earned a place at the table with the first shift, who had worked for their lunch. They thought, and I thought, I was reading, but sometimes I was listening in.

"Did you hose down the milking parlor properly, then, Pádraig?" Young Pat would say, almost every day.

And 14-year-old Pádraig Gilboy, who was a bit of a bother, would say, "Don't I every day?"

I had no idea of people's names in the local Irish, which some people in Kilcross spoke, while others didn't bother. I thought the boy's name was 'Pawrig,' that's the way it sounded to me.

Pat would have been gone all the morning after collecting the milk cans of the vicinity for the long run up to Killala, which was twenty miles from Kilcross, and the longer he was away the more anxious he was to get back to the house, feeling that everything had to be done by himself, to be done properly. "I won't need you then," he said to Pádraig, "till you're after the milking tonight and washing down the girls and the machinery."

"Have you nothing for me this afternoon?" said Pádraig, smashing potatoes smeared with HP sauce into his gob.

"Not unless you want to flush the loo today?"

"I do that tomorrow."

"I thought you might say so. Well—I have the vet coming in for the sheep today. I'll be up on Nephin. So, you're off for the afternoon."

"And when am I to be driving the tractor again?"

At this Pat's brother Matt and his friend Liam McGowan would dip their heads down over their plates, knowing the storm was coming if Pádraig provoked Pat any further.

"When you're able, Pádraig" said Pat with finality.

"You promised," said Pádraig.

"I promised when I could fit you in, but work comes first."

Long Pat would also be there, as the table would fit five with one chair on the end. He had resigned himself to the role of Pat's second, and no longer performed any of the heavy lifting, but he had long ago earned his place at the table. A nod from his father in Pat's direction was customarily enough to indicate 'that's enough now, till later.'

Then the lot of them were out the door again for another long, lazy afternoon of the dairy farmer, the time of day between early-to-rise and late-to-bed that caused the young man to turn his thoughts to young women in their summer dresses.

And my saintly mother-in-law Jane would carry in the remainder of the big two-handled pot of steaming spuds from the cooker out back and it was my turn to sit at the table with Sheila and Aisling and Ann and Jane herself and smash spuds and douse them in softened butter and HP sauce and plenty of salt.

It was some time later when Pat came to me to say, "I have had no time off at all, in a while now. Would you ever fancy taking a trip somewhere with me, oh, for four or five days or so."

"Where to? In the Austin mini?"

"Oh, aye. I was thinking we might head north, that maybe you might like to see the Giant's Causeway."

"What's that?"

"Oh, it's something all the tourists flock to, one of the sights."

"Is that what I am?—a tourist."

"I've never seen it myself, and I live here."

"I don't know if I'd go just for that."

"Well, would you go just for me? Mind you, we'll stop a while in Derry, maybe Belfast, too."

"Now you're talking. Sign me up."

So we went, leaving the business of the farm to Long Pat and his other son, Martin, to do the daily milk-runs, but we didn't get any further the first night than Ballina.

Pat parked the car outside a brightly-lit emporium in the dark.

"What's this?" said I.

"A dance on a Saturday night."

"Pat—I'm a married man!"

"That you are. To my sister."

"Well, why would I be wanting to go to a dance then, without her?"

"Well, would you go just for me? I'm not asking you to go in there and commit adultery, only stand there next to me and give out with that American accent and we'll be surrounded in no time, you'll be a bird-magnet."

We went inside and shortly thereafter I was right back in the State Ballroom on Massachusetts Avenue on the night I first met Sheila, with the very same band in the very same country-and-western red jackets on the stage blasting the Texas-twang-guitars through the speakers.

"Jesus," said Pat, "would you look at the talent in this place? There's lashin's of 'em."

"Don't you have a girlfriend?"

"Would you look at the state of yer one?"

"Her name is Pippa, I believe?"

"Aye, but I'm not married to her, now, am I?"

In unison, our four eyes, or I should say, six, if you count my specs, swiveled to follow the progress of three lovely pairs of legs in high heels with skirts on up to here.

"I'm going to hell for this. I'll wait for you at the bar."

I nursed a Guinness or maybe two for the rest of the evening while Pat succeeded in proving he had no need for my services as a bird-magnet and I managed to survive the night with my virtue intact.

In the morning he nudged my shoulder aside where I had been drooling all night on the top edge of the driver's seat and I rubbed my eyes open to a view of a stone bridge on the River Moy outside the town, with a row-boat drawn up on the bank.

"Sleep well, did you? What is this? Disgusting."

"Where were you all night while I was trying to sleep?"

"Paddling downstream, and thank God it wasn't upstream."

He started the motor and we were off, except that swarms of flies were clinging to the windscreen, which I tried to flap off and squish off with my Charlestown, Massachusetts scally-cap on the end of my arm stuck out the window.

"If there's anything I hate," I said, "it's flies on the windscreen."

Pat looked narrowly at me. "And if it's anything I hate, it's dead flies on the windscreen."

After a time, driving away, smiling to himself, he remarked, casually, "Did you ever make love in the bottom of a row-boat?"

"Is that where you were? Thank God Guinness makes me sleepy. I was sure you'd gone into the house across the road."

"Well, we started there, but that was only round one, as it turned out. Round two we went for a swim. Then we decided on a paddle. In the boat, I mean. Then we started playing kissy-face. Then we continued on to playing hide the biscuit. And it was lovely. Something so soothing about it. I recommend it highly. It's like rocking away to a lullaby."

We crossed the border into Fermanagh at Belcoo. There was an imperceptible river of the same name, a bridge about twenty-five feet long, and a Customs Post on the left. Two customs men in dark uniforms came up to the windows on either side of the mini. Everything was flat for miles around, not a hill to be seen. The tiny customs post was after the bridge. There was no British Army in sight. I had forgotten to bring my passport, but Pat had said to play the dumb Yank. They asked politely, "Where are you going?" and "What is your business in Northern Ireland?" Pat said, "We're going to the Giant's Causeway," and "We're just here for the tourism, this is my brother-in-law from the States." I looked up at the Customs man and said, in as broad American as I could, smiling with my teeth, "Howdy. How are ya?" The other one asked Pat to open the boot so he got out and did, but the Customs fellow could have just looked through the windows of the mini. All we had in the back was my shaving kit and loose clothes thrown around, no bags or suitcases. Pat said, "We'll only be a couple of days at the most." They passed us on. The only papers they asked for were Pat's driver's license, so I didn't need my passport after all.

Everything was quiet and peaceful, no queue of cars or lorries, just us, the place seemed deserted. But about a mile further on in the town we passed a British Army installation: forbidding-looking cement blockade-walls topped with high fencing surmounted with barbed wire; a Saracen parked in the street, the vehicle caged inside chicken-wire rising about twice its height; three soldiers poised behind very large cement blocks with automatic weapons at the ready, pointing at the road. We passed them too fast to really see their faces, but they seemed to take only cursory notice of a cobalt-blue Austin mini going by.

Now we had left the N16 in Ireland and were cruising along the A4 in the UK, and the only difference detectable was that the speed limit signs looked different.

"What's the deal with the passports, Pat?"

"I'm Irish, Nick. This is Ireland we're in. The border is only a nuisance on paper. It's all one country. And in any case, you wouldn't need a passport to cross the Irish Sea and enter Wales or England itself if you're Irish. It's all open borders. Why? Did you bring your passport? Because you needn't have."

"I forgot it."

"That's why I didn't remind you. I knew you didn't need it."

"You didn't know I'd forgotten it, are you daft?"

"I didn't need to know. Are we talkin' the same language here?"

In another hour we were in Derry, slowly turning the corner in front of the gable wall I'd seen in all the newsprint photos, the one that read,

YOU ARE NOW ENTERING FREE DERRY

We found a pub in the Bogside that looked likely enough, and inside, it was Sunday afternoon, and all the lads were standing themselves at the bar with their friends after Sunday Mass, just as they did in Kilcross, except that here there were no women or kids. They were watching Billie Jean King on the telly in the US Open in New York and all agreed that they'd like to filet a fish with Billie Jean one of these days. We bought a round and they bought a round and the talk turned to politics and the British Army and Internment and the consensus was that the Special Powers Act was the best thing that had ever happened to the Provos, so we drank another round to 'Up the Rebels' and went on our way.

Pat thought we had better not be sleeping in the car this night, though, so we stopped in a B&B a good distance outside Derry on the A37, and then went on in the morning to Coleraine, where we enquired the road to the Giant's Causeway, and with directions, headed north to the coastal, scenic route that took us to Portrush.

This turned out to be a lovely, quaint, remote seaside resort town, I thought, in the unlikeliest place in the world, looking straight out on the forbidding Arctic Ocean, but, no, there was an Amusement Arcade, oceanfront hotels, it was as lively as Revere Beach in a bygone era of my long-lost childhood. I wondered what brought all the vacationers to this decidedly British getaway spot. What were they getting away from? The headlines and the nightly news? Or did people here have lives like the rest of the world did? Did children play sandcastles and parents worry they'd better not stay in the cold water too long?

If I thought Portrush was a local version of a middle-class Shangri-la, the Giant's Causeway was an international destination. The province of Ulster was turning out to be a revelation. Given the stereotypes hammered into codified concrete by the media presentation of 'The Troubles' back home, with which I'd come pre-programed on this sojourn to Ireland, I was not prepared for the gangs of families on tour who had come, like my brother-in-law, to take this chance-of-a-lifetime opportunity to gaze upon, and walk upon, and take snapshots of themselves upon, these flat-topped cube-sticks of caramel-colored rocks, jutting up from the earth at the edge of the ocean like an army of toy soldiers marching shoulder-to-shoulder into the sea. Young Patrick Blake was joyfully in his element on this grey afternoon, delighted to be realizing the ambition to see this storied place, and I was glad I'd come along, because I knew how hard he worked and what awaited him when he got back to Mayo.

When we were leaving, Pat decided that the best plan by far was to stick to the scenic coastal roads and linger awhile, avoiding the larger motorways that were meant only to get you speedily from Derry to Belfast to Dublin, and so we crawled around at a leisurely pace, meandering over the northeast shoulder of Antrim till we came to a place called Ballycastle where we were told that if we made our way along the narrow and precipitous local road called Torr Road we would come to Torr Head and the most spectacular view of Scotland to be had on a fine day like this.

We tried it, and we were not disappointed. As we closed in on the place, we found a wee car-park fitting only four or five cars, and from there we had to walk.

We crossed a grassy glen, an upturned bowl in the earth, which Pat thought would have been a marvelous pasture for his sheep. High up above us a rocky outcropping scarred with stone walls and other protrusions looked forbiddingly steep. There was only one path up from the glen, a time-worn balding track out of the long grass which followed a ridge-line up, up, up, to structures that resembled ancient forts.

But at the top you could tell from the dull brown cement walls and slit-window, blockhouse-type rooms that this was not an ancient fort but a derelict lookout station, probably British Army, vintage WWII. When you got to the edge of the apparently medieval stone walls that overlooked the sea, straight down hundreds of feet below, there, eastward, only ten miles away, was the Mull of Kintyre in Scotland.

You could almost reach out your hand and touch it.

The lookout station must have been added on to some earlier structures in order to watch for German U-boats approaching Scotland or the west of England through the narrowness of the North Channel separating Ireland from Britain.

A haunted place if there ever was one. I thought immediately of the abandoned Civil War turrets of Jamestown Island in Narragansett Bay, back home, where I had written the poem about David and Susan sitting on the wall, holding onto each other.

Here there were no young lovers, nothing but a long, lingering twilight over the Irish Sea.

When we had exhausted our capacity to gaze any longer, and were leaving in the Austin mini to head for Belfast, I grabbed my notebook from under the wrinkled shirts in the boot, and wrote these lines:

I wish that we could part the veil, and see the other side,
So we could meet the coming night, at the end of the sky . . .
I would then return again, to a certain world I know,
Evening in the glens of Antrim, falling gently on your eye . . .

When we crossed the border again, we had a boot full of rebel records to listen to on Pat's portable record player back home in Mayo. We'd picked them up in a shop in the Falls Road in Belfast, and this time, no Customs men in 'Northern Ireland' garb wanted to look into the boot of the Austin mini, since we were now leaving the Six Counties. They were concerned only with what people were bringing in, not what they night be taking out. And the gardai on the 26-counties customs post didn't care about a load of records, either, so we got away clean with our contraband, and were as pleased as a couple of poteen smugglers.

I was delighted when we got back home again to add another poem to the pile, and one which portended chapters yet to come beyond where I'd left off, thinking everything completed, which fired my ambitions for an auspicious near-future for my writing.

But I was thrilled to discover that at last there was something useful I could do around the house and the land, as Jane Blake announced that she'd only been waiting our return to start getting the house ready for The Stations in October.

This meant that I could utilize my old trade of house-painter, and I blessed the name of Russell Sage for having originally initiated me into the brotherhood.

So I happily wielded my bucket and brush, painting the house trim a buttery golden yellow and the pebbledash exterior walls a nice corncrake-blue, and digging into my lunch of spuds with both an appetite and a clear conscience.

Next I sent off letters to Robbie MacDuff and Ray Deeds with the exciting news of my recent digs in the poetry pit and how I had covered myself in glittering coal-dust.

But I did not, in the end, manage to avoid offending Irish piety.

It fell out this way.

I was not known in the family to go anywhere without a book in my hand, even if it was only in moving to another room. Up at Delaney's, villagers who had encountered me on the dirt footpath which led the shortcut behind the main road and the stone church testified that they had seen me wandering with a book. Now ever since my arrival in Kilcross back in August my attendance at Sunday mass had been required, or so I was advised by Sheila, and I was respectful of the custom of the country, and actually, not displeased to return to my better self of old Boston College days, when I had the example of the Jesuits before my eyes on a daily basis. I did tempt fate, however, by enquiring of Sheila how it was that I had never seen her anxious to get out of bed of a Sunday morning and rush off to Mass when we were living in Narragansett, RI, only a stone's throw from St Mary's-of-the-Sea? To which Sheila told me, "Oh, shut your gob, would you?"

Now I bore my trials with fortitude, but I was so bored by the Sunday sermons of the pastor of St Patrick's in Kilcross, Father John Latchford, that finally I determined I was going to bring a book to Mass in order stay awake.

So, I appeared in the big room one Sunday ready to walk out to church with the family with a book in my hand. I had moved on from *Moby Dick* to *The Brothers Karamazov*.

Long Pat pulled Sheila aside when he saw this. Sheila took me down to our bedroom in the back and told me, "Daddy says you cannot take a book to mass with you, you'll disgrace us in front of the whole village." So I put down that book and picked up the Sunday Missal which my mother had bought for me for my Confirmation, which was one of the four books I'd brought to Ireland—I don't know why, but I did. I said, "Surely he can't object to me following along with the Mass in the daily missal, can he?"

However, he did, and I had to bring my Missal back to the bedroom and stow it away again.

That was the Sunday I bumped into Toss Ribbons on the steps of Delaney's before Mass. People in Kilcross lingered about on Sunday mornings till the last possible second, smoking fags and chatting, waiting for the signal for Mass to begin, upon which they would step on their butts and rush in so as not to be late. The signal was the moment when they would spy Father Latchford come running round the corner of the church with his skirts flying and his stick waving, the blackthorn stick, with which to beat the buttocks of the young lads of his flock who were lounging about sitting on the stone wall by the gate: upon which the boys would scatter like a flock of pigeons and fly in the church door.

Said I to Toss Ribbons, trilling my R's, "The stench of Ir-r-rish piety is r-r-r-ising in me nos-tr-r-r-ils."

"Oh, aye," said Toss.

"I'm starting to feel neglected," said Sheila.

"I've been busy painting for the Stations."

"You've spent more time with my brother lately than you have with me."

"We couldn't fit you in the mini."

"And I'm jealous of whoever you're writing all those love letters to."

"They're poems. And they're all to you."

"I'm more married to the child than I am to you."

"Well. Let me see. What if. You know you haven't shown me around Nephin as yet? I've been here all this time, and one walk down to the lake is all I get? And that with Aisling swinging by the hand between us?"

So we devised a plan to have Mammy watch the child for us while we took a whole day to ourselves to go strolling up the mountainside.

And since we were lucky enough to get the weather to cooperate with us, we had sunshine to light the way. We had every earnest intention of actually climbing the mountain, thinking what a wonderful view of the whole countryside for miles around there must be if we could make it all the way to the top.

So we packed a picnic lunch of marmalade sandwiches covered by white cloth in a basket with a handle and set out down the side road and up the hill past the old famine village. We quickly ran out of road and I needn't have worried about wetting our shoes in the bog as the steepness soon set in and after a bit we were laboring mightily to keep going. After what seemed like hours we were only halfway up or less and we were exhausted. All about us was heather and bald rock outcroppings. Looking down it seemed that the main road and the village were miniatures encased in a globe of sunshine and any infrequent passing vehicles were the size of fleas. I looked at Sheila and she at me, and we said simultaneously, "I'm knackered."

So we broke open the sandwiches wrapped in a rather opaque white wax-paper, not at all like Cut-Rites, back home, and despite the fatigue factor, managed enough strength to chew.

"Whatever made us think we could make it to the top?" said Sheila.

"We'd need a week" I leaned backwards and tilted my head. "I can't even see the top."

Sheila tried it, with the same result.

"It's two-thousand-four-hundred-and-sixty feet tall," I said.

"Who told you that?"

"Toss Ribbons."

"Jesus, I've lived here all my life and I didn't know that."

"The man knows everything. He has the Irish, too, you know. You need it to teach school. And something called the H.Dip. Which I don't have. It's like the Teaching Certificate back home that you get if you go through the School of Education at BC to become a high school teacher. Which I never did. So, it looks like finding a job teaching here is not going to be as easy as I thought, even with my Master's Degree. But, hey, the hell with it. It's too nice of a day to go wasting it."

At this point we had finished our sandwiches and were already leaning back on the lumpy ground gazing at the sky skimming overhead in cerulean splendor and not a cloud to be seen.

I looked at her and she at me. "Are you thinking what I'm thinking?"

"You wouldn't dare."

"Nobody can see us up this high. They'd need binoculars."

"We'd be like the beasts in the fields."

"Ah, but think of the story you'll be able to tell your grandchildren, Sheila."

"You are a rogue."

In this passionate fancy of ours, Nephin turned out to be our co-conspirator, as the spot where we'd stopped for lunch was no more than a few feet from a kind of natural couch formation in the rock, where two arms, like those of a love-seat, beckoned to us; and so Sheila put her back to the brace of villages below, both the inhabited one and the ghost village of the ancestors, and her backside as well, to the main road, and the boreen, and the lake, and the three pubs and the seventeen houses and the stone church at the hook of the road, and sat on my lap, and I stretched my back snugly up against the mountain and with a slow, rocking motion, we made love on the mountainside. Soon we were floating as if we were in the bottom of a rowboat on the River Moy. And I gazed out over her shoulder at the tiny world below until my eyes blissfully closed.

I began to think, imaginatively, that I might almost manage on the farm, and in spite of my bookishness and fourth-cousin relationship to reality (those shining qualities of my personality that caused Sheila to re-assure her mother, affectionately, "he's full of himself, he is,") I began to think, irrationally, that I might turn myself into a farmhand after all. What good are those advanced college degrees of mine anyway? Not much.

But I was destined to have my eyes opened, or closed, as the case may be, by the first chance I took to accompany Pat on the morning delivery of milk-cans up to the Creamery in Killala Bay.

We hadn't gotten as far as the outskirts of Crossmoliney when the skies opened.

I was standing on the trailer hitch behind Pat, who sat the driver's seat on the tractor. I had one hand on his shoulder, like a passenger on the back of a motorcycle, and one hand on the top rail of the trailer behind me, bouncing with all the jangling, rattling milk-cans.

My first thought was, so this is what Sheila means by 'teeming torrents.'

"How're ye keeping back there?"

"Drowned as a rat in the Charles River, with all the dirty water in Boston."

"Mind you don't slip off."

It was twenty miles from the boreen to the Creamery, if it was a step, and for sixteen of those, the heavens poured down on my head. I had my father's Navy pea-coat on and it became so soaked through I had to wonder what good it was on board an ocean-going vessel. My Charlestown scally-cap was about as useful for a head-covering as a wet dish-rag.

Well, I wanted to find out what was involved in delivering those milk-cans six days a week to the Creamery, and I guess I found out.

I began to think that mother nature had come along for the ride, joining us for the purpose of curing me of my farmboy fantasies.

The tractor. The tractor was Young Patrick Blake's prize possession. A British-Leyland Invincible, painted royal blue, with a pretty chrome-plated smokestack, gleaming silver, beaded with raindrops. It was the key to all his projections of success as a dairy farmer in a village in the West with 178 people, most of whom were up against it as subsistence farmers, mired in the past, immured in their poverty, from generations long gone. The Blakes' house was not the only one in Kilcross with missing children who had grown up only to emigrate to the States, to England, to Glasgow, to Hamburg, to Adelaide, Australia. The children of the place were like a crop grown for export.

Pádraig Gilboy was one of these. And he resented it. On a good day he was sullen and cross. You could see the envy in his watery eyes, with the dirty blond hair hanging down in them, every time he looked at Pat Blake. You would think Pádraig took Pat for his personal oppressor when all Pat had done was to give him a job when nobody else would.

I didn't like Pádraig much. He was always pushing. And he had needled Pat into letting him drive the tractor.

It suited Pat to let him when it came time to hunt for a few dry days in late September to get the turf up from the bog. Everyone in the village was dependent on it for heat for the winter. Pat used his tractor to help Mrs. Cochran and Jack Ryan, his neighbors in the boreen, as well as some of the elderly and infirm in the village, and a widow or two, by bringing their stack up to their houses for them. But he needed time better spent on his cattle and sheep, so here was the time and place to let Pádraig get a bit of experience handling the British-Leyland. And maybe then the pestilent boy might shut his gob for once and all.

Kilcross was fortunately placed by not only Lough Conn and the mountain called Nephin, but also by the blanket bog in the lowland just below the village on the Castlehill road. This bog was called the Conlatristan Fen. Ever since the end of the war between England and Germany, it had been under ownership and worked by Bord na Mona, the national Turf Board. They built the bog roads into it, which were laid out in a rectangular grid pattern like the streets of New York City. In Conlatristan, these were narrow causeways perched on top of embankments. Nowadays people did not cut their own turf by hand, it was done for them by the Turf Board with machinery, but each family in the village had their own assigned plot of turf. The families were still responsible to stack the turf beside the bog road in spring so that it could get a chance to dry out all summer, hopefully, and then in the fall, they had to fetch it up to their houses.

Young Matt Blake was out helping his brother Pat on the farm, so Pat asked me to go along with Liam MacGowan and Pádraig Gilboy, and the three of us spent about a week before we finally got round to bringing up the Blakes' own stack, on Friday.

That's when it happened.

The bog had the look of a townland of brown cottages, as it was so flat, with turf-stacks that stood six to eight feet tall at intervals everywhere along the causeway roads. It was large and level, big enough to fit three villages the size of Kilcross.

Up close, down in it, it was a different world. Not the somber brown waste that could be seen from the Castlehill road, but a panorama of hues, pinkish-purple to clover-green to tints of yellow. Tall wisps of cattails and the tufted heads of sedge, rushes and reeds and nameless bushes grew in the wet bottom-land. Bog-cotton, silky and spidery on wisps of stalks. Patches of purple heather proliferating with bunches of tiny flowers. Spiny, thorny whin-bushes crawling over sections of turf-weed, still green in their shade. Buttons of butter-yellow buttercups over bright green stretches of clover, islands of an archipelago.

We weren't the only ones there, several parties were just as busy as we were, some with a horse and wagon, some with the ass'n'cart, even the children were not too young to lend a hand. The bog roads were too narrow to allow two vehicles to pass so occasionally you had to wait.

Liam and I were sitting back on top of a sheet of plywood in the trailer during down-time when our turn came. Padraig was napping in the tractor-seat with his head in the crook of his elbow. Farm life was full of stop and go, sitting and waiting, and boredom. I yelled at him. "We're up, Pádraig, let's go!"

It was the end of a long day, the end of a full week of frustration. We'd already brought two-thirds of the stack up to the house, and it was now seven o'clock, and noontime since we'd had anything to eat. My hands were reddened and rough, torn by the tough, knotty, machine-cut sods of turf, sliced by the razor-edges of the dried turf-weed that grew out of the sods, making them look like loaves of hard bread crusted with hair. Death by a million paper-cuts. And then there were the midges. Clouds of them rising every time you touched the turf-stack, clawing at the corners of your eyes and mouth, lodging in your ears, gathering in a complicated, whizzing halo around your head. A sane man could go mad from the midges, sniping at your nostrils, under your collar, up your sleeves.

Now we had to hurry as it was beginning to mist over. I looked up at Nephin to check her worried brow. All we needed at this point was a cloudburst. We had only the last third of the Blakes' stack to load, and we'd be done.

Padraig pulled up alongside the stack, just beyond it, and left the tractor running.

The accelerating mist did nothing to discourage the midges.

The three of us, getting into and out of each other's way, kept throwing sod after sod into the open back of the trailer.

Now it seemed to be drizzling.

"Pile it high, pile it high," I said, hoping we'd not underestimated the remainder and had enough room. The last thing any of us wanted at this point was to have to make yet another trip.

I waved my arm uselessly at the cloud of midges and wondered why I'd bothered to say anything. Pádraig wouldn't listen to Pat, at the best of times, why would he heed me now, when we were sweating, tired, and plagued?

When we were actually finished, we kept on, hunting and pecking the odd, stray sod here and there, and throwing that one up, too.

Held in by the high sides of the trailer-slats, our pyramid of turf looked oddly like Nephin herself.

On the embankment, there was the satisfying sight of a clearly-outlined, damp, rectangular patch, where, that morning, wet sods were rotting at the bottom of the Blake's turf-stack.

It was a thing to stand back and admire.

"Oh, no," said Padraig.

Liam said, "God above."

Then it struck me.

We'd forgotten to take the empty trailer up to the right-angle intersection to turn it around and head it nose out on the bog road before we pulled up to the stack—before we loaded it with a mountain of turf.

As we'd been doing all week.

"Shit!" I said.

"Why didn't you say something, Yank!" Pádraig cried, tugging wildly at his disheveled blond hair.

"Me? You were driving, Pádraig!"

"A lot of good you are. Jesus Christ—what are we gonna do?"

"Pádraig, you'll just have to back it out to the main road!"

"Are you mad? It's a quarter-mile if it's an inch! It's nearly half-a-mile, if I measured. I'd never make it. You try backin' this thing up with a load of turf behind it, see how far you'll get. You must be daft."

"Well, what are you gonna do? Nevermind. I'm going up the house and get Pat."

"No, no, no! Wait. I can do it. All we have to do is make two turns. I'll go down to the intersection, turn left, get her straight, and one more turn at the next intersection, and we're out! I can do it. Don't get Pat, I don't want him to hear of this, give me a chance, would you, to just fix it. Anyway, I need you both here to help."

"What can *we* do, Pádraig?"

"You can steady the back of the trailer for me!"

But he was already in the driver's seat of the British-Leyland.

I threw my cap down on the road, I was so angry, and then I kicked it uselessly down the causeway, as, with a groan of machinery, Padraig set the thing in motion.

"Hold on to the slats, one on each side, and push if she slides!" yelled Pádraig, as he nosed the tractor left at the intersection.

He had to judge it nicely and veer out without sending the big right-rear wheel over the edge of the embankment. Or the left one, for that matter.

I was holding my breath until it appeared, by some miracle, he made the first left turn.

Now if he could only straighten it out.

"Slowly, slowly!" I cried, as Liam and I were both pushing the back end of the trailer rightwards with every ounce we could muster. The heavy load made it shifty and wobbly, and the whole shebang was perched precariously on the two wheels in the mid-driff of the under-carriage.

At that moment, when I knew we'd made the straightaway again without a disaster, I remembered my cap, as it was now coming down steadily.

But this was not the time to go back and get souvenirs.

"Listen, you two!" called Pádraig. "Climb up on top and both of you get your weight over on the right side of the turf-pile, up against the slats, and give me some balance for the next turn. I could feel her wobbling. We must have too much weight on one side!"

By this time I, too, was so worried about Pat's reactions that I couldn't think of reasons to object and so Liam and I both clambered up there.

I looked at Liam and he was terrified. "Say your prayers, Liam. And whatever you do, be ready to jump."

Slowly, slowly, at the next intersection, Padraig leaned into the turn, urging, coaxing the thing with his body.

The Invincible coughed and chugged as he nearly choked her out.

Then it leapt forward with a jerk.

It groaned, it wheezed. Puff-balls of smoke came from the stack. Liam and I were pushing as hard as we could up against the slats, but the stack we were sitting on top of, we had piled it so high that we had little purchase with our tail-bones.

I couldn't see it, but I felt it.

It wasn't the trailer-wheels that slipped, but the tall left-rear tractor wheel, with its gigantic treads.

The mountain of turf shifted abruptly, towards the front of the trailer-slats, and we yawed to the left.

"Jump!"

Liam and I landed on the roadway.

People were running towards us from two intersections away.

I couldn't see Pádraig.

The massive weight of the slipping trailer was dragging the British-Leyland down the embankment.

A long way off, someone was exiting the bog and heading at a run uphill towards the village.

As we got up, Padraig was coming toward us with woe-begone anguish all over his face. "He'll have my skin, Pat will."

The bog was gasping and chortling as it sucked down both ends of the rig, trailer and tractor, too.

Up at the village I saw Pat, followed by Matt, rounding the corner at the hook in the road by the church, Pat atop a saddled horse of Jack Ryan's, with a length of looped rope in one hand, flailing at the horse to urge him on, the three of them, horse, man and boy, moving as fast as they could, followed by the whole village, who, by this time, had heard, and, wanting to see for themselves was it true, what they were saying up at Delaney's Pub, petrol station and Post Office, about 'The Bog That Ate the Tractor?'

By the time Young Patrick Blake had thrown his lasso, the only thing showing above the bog was the Invincible's pretty chrome-plated smokestack, gleaming silver, beaded with rain-drops.

The 26th of September was a Sunday. It was the best day in the week for the farming folk of Kilcross to hold a commemoration such as the one Toss Ribbons had been planning for weeks, and which had suffered delay due to weather. Now at last we were going to carry out the long-planned Re-enactment of Humbert's March across the Windy Gap to victory over the British Army in the Battle of Castlebar in 1798.

In view of the news pouring from the North during the month after Internment (now nearing on a month-and-a-half) not a soul in Kilcross intended to be absent from this demonstration of the faithfulness and loyalty of the people of Connacht to their Republican traditions, passed down by word of mouth from generation to generation, ever since the Rising of '98.

In fact, it was through this very village of Kilcross that the stirring events of those days were made possible at all. Back in 1798, it was Father Andrew Conroy himself, of the stone church at the hook in the road (at that time only recently rescued from the grip of the local Protestant Ascendancy and the Church of Ireland) who gave General Humbert and his French troops the advice that led to their success—to take the old road through the mountains—and indeed, it was the good Father Conroy himself led them through the Windy Gap to Castlebar.

That road was still there, though unpaved and little-used, and it diverted from the present-day main road at the edge of the village near the hook in the road just after the last two houses adjacent to Delaney's and just before the blanket bog.

And so it was that my dear friend Toss Ribbons, the schoolteacher and village historian, was standing on the steps of Delaney's, with Father John Latchford at his side, making the dedication speech for the Re-enactment, before every man, woman and child of Kilcross.

"As you know, friends and neighbors, or as you may not know, as the case may be, it was right here, where we are standing now, that the original Irish Republic, long before Pearse and Connolly, long before 1916, originated, and came down to us in the history books under the name, as it was sometimes called, or misnomered, as the case may be, the Republic of Connacht, and it was our own Men of the West who marched alongside the one-thousand French troops of General Humbert, our own Father Conroy, of St Patrick's in Kilcross, and our own George Blake, who led us to victory in Castlebar, and who, subsequently, were sent to the gallows at the hands of the forces of the Crown. So I've asked Father Latchford to lead us in prayer, as we remember the martyrs of 1798, who gave their lives that we, their descendants, may enjoy the freedom of the Irish Republic that we know and love today, and I ask you, too, now, to bow your heads. Father Latchford?"

And the pastor of St Patrick's lead them in prayer, in Irish, as well as in English, and I stood there, wondering, uncomprehending, at the mention of the name of George Blake.

And then the whole village moved off as one herd, with a Celtic Cross and the Irish Tricolor flying at the head of the column, off onto the old road, downhill at first, then rapidly turning upland towards the Windy Gap itself, and I maneuvered my way, with Aisling in my arms, and Sheila at my side, and Pat and Pippa, and Matt Blake, and Ann Blake, not far behind, to the side of Toss Ribbons, to interrogate him.

"Who's this George Blake you were speaking of, that Sheila never mentioned to me?"

"Well, he came from near here, a place called Garracloon, on the other side of Lough Conn, and he was the grandson of the original George Blake who acquired the estate when it passed to him from his father-in-law, Marcus Lynch, upon his death in 1765. All this is documented in the records of the Church of Ireland's Parish of Addergoole, which I've researched, and of course, they're available to the general public."

"Sheila! Why did you never tell me about this George Blake connection?"

"Oh—I'm not as clever as Toss, now."

"Pat—is it true that the family is descended from one of the martyrs of '98?"

"Are none of the family secrets safe anymore?" said Young Pat.

Sheila and Pat were both grinning, and I couldn't tell if they were having me on, as the saying goes, or not, so I turned back to Toss for some facts.

"We know, for a fact, that George Blake was hanged, along with Father Conroy, after the Battle of Ballinamuck, in Longford, where the British caught the French with their guard down, or maybe was it their trousers?"

That was good for a laugh as we trudged along uphill, Pat adding, "Knowing the French lads, as well as the Longford colleens, it must've been their knee-britches."

Pippa and Sheila took this in good humor, but they really had no choice, if they wanted to march with us, but to partake in ribaldry, as they well knew. Fortunately the pious Father

Latchford was elsewhere, no doubt explaining the trinity with the example of a three-legged stool.

"And I'll tell you another thing," said Toss Ribbons, "that I found out from the civil parish of Addergoole. There was a certain grandson of Blake the martyr, who, sometime in the mid-19th century, about 1850 or so, sold off 200 acres of the Garracloon estate, and the sellers were George Martyn, a son-in-law, who came into it on inheritance, and one Abraham Stoker, who was married to Charlotte Matilda Blake Thornley Stoker, and they were the parents of the Bram Stoker who wrote Dracula."

"And you without a literary bone in your body," I said to Sheila.

"You're lit'ry enough for the both of us, I'm sure."

"But what I'm really intrigued about," said Toss, "and I'm so encouraged in this by the turnout today, is that we are literally sitting on a tourism goldmine, here in Kilcross, if I can ever get it organized to the point where it would need to be—I mean, what are we known for?–not to be putting down the Yanks, Nick, but they're here, yourself excepted, every summer, for one of two things—the fishing, or the golf. Isn't that right, girls? And yet, is it completely forgotten in Kilcross, and it's not that long ago, mind you, that we gave no less than 14 souls of the parish to the tragic disaster of the Titanic? Why, there's folks still with us in Kilcross who were within living memory of it, though they might have been children at the time."

"Sheila," I said, "we know just such a person, don't we? Remember Marshall Andrews, in Rhode Island? Remember when we went to his lecture? He was one of the children on board that night, Toss, when the ship went down, and he survived only because he was put into a lifeboat with his mother. He was eleven years old at the time."

"Well, he was luckier than many of ours were," said Toss, "as the village of Kilcross lost 11 of the 14 who set foot on board—and that, my friends, means that our little village gave more lives to the Titanic than any other spot on the face of the earth—not to mention, all of Ireland."

"And what are you going to do with that information, Toss?" said Sheila.

"Well, I'm going to form a committee, certain sure, to look into it and develop some plans to exploit the thing, on behalf of the village, with Bord Failte Eireann. I'm sure they'll have the resources to put us on the right track, and no matter how many years it takes—."

"Too bad you won't be around to see it, Nick," said Sheila.

"Why?" said Toss. "You're not leaving us, are you?"

"Toss—I need to feel city pavements under my feet again."

"He's off to Dublin, to look for work," said Sheila.

"What about the pottery in Bofeenan?" said Pippa, who knew of my aesthetic inclinations.

"I'm useless with my hands, Pippa. Ask Pat."

"Oh, he could kill flies on my windscreen, all right. Thank Christ the wipers were working."

"Well," said Toss Ribbons, "we'll have to raise a glass in your memory this night in Castlebar. Fortunately, I know a watering hole or two in that town. I reckon we'll have a thirst worked up by the time we get there."

And so the lasting image of Mayo that I carried away with me, in the book-riddled rucksack of my heart, was one of marching to Castlebar, alongside people I had come to care for, like some extended village of my own,; marching at the crest of the Windy Gap, with drums beating, pipes playing and pennants flying, and the dancing red message on the torn white banner, rippling in the wind, bobbing along between two tall poles, which read,

DOWN WITH / / INTERNMENT / / / / / / BRING OUR BOYS HOME / /

Chapter 2

Half-Eleven at the Metropole

At last I could feel the solidity of city streets under my feet again. No more boggy bottom for this boy. At last I could feel the enchantment of being drawn in by Dublin, a city prominent on the literary map of the world, a place, to me, sanctified by literature, enshrined in immortal words by Sean O'Casey, Brendan Behan, James Joyce, and yes, Yeats, Synge, Lady Gregory and the Abbey Theatre.

What other cities on the world stage had I known or explored? Boston, New York? Somehow they did not compare. Somehow they did not throb in my temples the way Dublin did, from a distance, back in the day when I labored at the library in Kingston, Rhode Island, and Dublin was but an ephemera encountered on the page, a pipe-dream, in the opium-haze of spells cast by Oscar Wilde, James Stephens, J.P. Donleavy. All these I had devoured, and they devoured me, and now I found myself, on my first day in the actual, real city, standing outside the Amiens Street Station, waiting for the lights to change; gazing across the wide car-crossed, bicycle-thronged acre of tarmac at the North Star Hotel, as a wind came whistling up from the quays; and I was wondering where I was going to stay that night; a wide white crosswalk in front of me, and who knew what else, in this magical place.

The stoplight did change, and I stepped into the street. A man on a bicycle rolled up, squeezing his handbrakes, letting down one foot. Along behind the first ranks of cars, Fiats, Vauxhalls, Volvos and Citroens, a hodge-podge of Europe on wheels, came the No. 23 bus for Fairview, wheezing to a stop: a tall, gawkly tin-man of a double-decker, wrapped in the Navy blue and cream-colored cardigan of the CIE, whatever that was; a bus presenting, for all the world, the wire-rimmed demeanor of a doddering old-age pensioner: the chrome-slatted grill shiny like a runny nose, the cranked-open windscreen peeking like bi-focals. Dublin!

I came to the foot of Talbot Street with no idea which way to go. I had hitch-hiked across the country and had an uneventful time of it, except for the rainstorm that made me hide under a tree outside Roscommon town, and perhaps the farmer who drove me into Mullingar, who might have been offended when I kept saying, thanks, no, I didn't smoke. I was now encountering Dublin in this unlikely spot where my latest ride had decided to drop me. Pennants were fluttering deep in the distance at the far end of Talbot Street, a long, narrow tube. I decided to head that way, as there must be something up there. In a city, I trusted my instincts, to find my way, in a manner which eluded me completely, down the country.

I passed the padlocked grills of shuttered shops at this lower end of Talbot Street. Wristwatches behind wire, Japanese radios, surplus clothing, hardware, appliances, a sign shaped like a key: Locksmith. Tribal figures walked past me, as if in a dream: teenaged girls wearing garish ear-rings, dressed in blue-denim mini-skirts, or jeans with the cuffs rolled up, in the style which, back in the States, dated to the 1950s; these pleasingly undersea creatures were wearing red-and-white button-down blouses over round-necked, colored jumpers, and tiny gold-crucifixes on 5-and-10p gold chains; on their delicate feet they wore soft shoes like slippers, with pennies in the in-step straps. Invariably, they were hanging on the arms of young fellows with shaved round heads wearing ankle-length Edwardian overcoats with velvet collars: the skinheads and their dolly-birds. Or, to my astonishment, along would come two girls linking arms like lovers, even holding hands. And as I gazed on in culture-shock, such pairs were by no means scarce. What did it signify? Sadly, as the saying goes, I hadn't a clue.

A dingy black-iron elevated line carried the railway from Amiens Street station over this end of Talbot Street, casting a derelict glamor on a cinema in its shadow. A long queue of young people waited on the footpath, leaning on the grills of the shops. On the white marquee, in red letters, beside the elevated: *Bruce Lee Meets the Kings of Kung-Fu.*

I came to Lower Gardiner Street, and found it was a wide, welcoming street studded with signs advertising Bed & Breakfast. Waiting for the lights, I could see to my left Busaras, the main bus station, and behind it, the bus rank in Eden Quay. Up ahead, straight up Talbot Street, where pennants fluttered, I guessed that might be O'Connell Street. To the right, Lower Gardiner Street started climbing a tall hill. This looked a likely place to me, and I assumed a Bed & Breakfast meant something like two for the price of one. First things first. I had come up to the city to look for work. But I had to be situated in order to do that. I did my hitch-hiking on the weekend, thinking it more likely to catch through-rides more easily from long-distance travelers. Here was Saturday night in Dublin coming up, my first night in the city of my dreams, and there would be no-job hunting till Monday. So I headed across the street for *The Lake Isle B&B.* After all, I had to make my thousand bucks stretch out through the whole school-year, so fancy hotels were out of the question, not that I'd seen any as yet, or knew where they were.

Like all the other former townhouses in Lower Gardiner Street, The Lake Isle had steep steps mounting to a front door. This street reminded me of something like Marlborough Street in Boston, except that grey limestone stood in for the brownstone back home. Twisting the doorknob, I found it locked.

I peeked through the tall narrow pane in one half of the double door. There was a light on, but no one there. This was like a motel in the States where you pulled up and walked through open doors into a lobby, and found nobody there, the front desk deserted.

But how did you get in? I could see a staircase, faded flowery wallpaper, an abbreviated, tall counter. Then I saw the bell-handle in the door. I turned it, and the rotary-bell rang out as shrill as a bicycle bell.

A middle-aged woman came down the steps inside, tiny, in an apron frilled from her shoulders to her knees. She opened the inner door, and came down one more step. "I was in the loo!" she shouted through the glass. "What do you want?"

"The sign says 'Vacancy.'"

Opening the outer door, she stuck her head out. "I'm Mrs Warren. Who are you?"

"Just looking for a room for the night."

"You're not a regular guest here. There are some people, when they come up from the country, who will only stop in the Lake Isle."

"Do you have a vacancy or not?" I'm afraid I was rudely American with the old biddy.

Mrs Warren looked me up and down. "Where are your suitcases?"

I jiggled the blue Aer Lingus bag in my hand. "This is all I have."

"Who referred you?"

"Nobody referred me."

"You must have a reference."

"I don't know anyone in Dublin."

"Who do you know down the country?"

It was on the tip of my tongue. "Frank Delaney, the TD in Kilcross."

"Don't know him. Never stayed here, he didn't. Respectable people carry suitcases."

I turned to go.

"Wait a minute." She opened the door wide. "Come into the light, then, where I can get a good look at you."

I stepped inside the tiny front landing, and then the inner door. Mrs Warren went behind the tall counter till only the top of her head showed. There was a pot of plastic flowers, a plaster statuette of the Holy Virgin, and a chrome desk bell. Mrs Warren made her mind up and spun the register at me, holding out a biro. "Sign here."

"How much is a room?"

"How long are you staying?"

"Well, two nights, anyway."

"One pound, in advance."

I pulled out my wallet, handed her a pound-note, and signed.

"That's a pound per night, laddie."

"Do you want the money for tomorrow, too?"

"Ah, never mind. Pay as you go, pay as you go." Mrs Warren sighed. "Breakfast is at seven. Don't bother coming down if you leave it till past nine." She held out a key. "Top floor, on the right." I took the key and she twirled the register. "License, please."

"I don't have a license. I don't have a car."

"How on earth did you get here without a car?

"By thumb. Can I ask you one question? How did you know I came up from the country?"

"Don't I know a Culchie when I see one standing on my doorstep?"

"I'm not a Culchie. I'm a Yank."

"Ah, that's what they all say."

I threw my bag on the counter and zipped it open. I showed her my passport. "See?"

"Proves nothing. They're giving them things out to anybody at all these days." Nevertheless, she took back her biro and jotted down the passport number. "Police regulations."

I zipped up the bag. "I think I'll go up to my room now, if I may, Mrs Warren?"

"Suit yourself." As I went up the stair, she called after me. "I lock the door at midnight. If you come after that, don't bother ringing."

I looked down and watched her disappear into a small door in the rear wall behind the staircase. First night in Dublin and I have to be in by midnight!

My room was bare and narrow. A cot with a grey wool blanket occupied most of it. The cot was hospital iron. When I closed the door, there was a single shelf fixed angle-wise behind it where two walls joined. A lone window overlooked the head of the bed. Looking out, I could see the stoplights at the inter-section three stories below. I put my toothbrush and razor on the sink in the corner, under the mirror, next to the window, and my Modern Library edition of *The Brothers Karamazov* on the woolen bed. I went out again, locking the door to secure my valuables, such as they were. After all, on Monday, I would have to be clean-shaven to go job-seeking—or even tonight, to go out on the town.

On the third-floor landing was a white door: the WC.

A claw-foot tub, a sink tobacco-stained with rust, a cracked mirror, and a commode with no seat. I ran the water, rinsed my hands, and splashed my face. No towel. Well, handsome, that's that. Be home by twelve, and stay out of mischief. At least there's indoor plumbing.

Downstairs, on my way out, I gave a ring to the desk-bell. Mrs Warren came out of the little door, wiping her hands on her apron.

"Would it be possible to get a key for the front door?"

"Why didn't you ask me before?" From behind the counter, she pulled out a long skeleton key. "There you are."

Like any American tourist, the first place I headed for was the world-famous O'Connell Street, reputed to be the widest boulevard in Europe. I came out of Earl Street and there was the GPO, staring right at me out of old photographs of the Easter Rising in 1916. It was said that the bullet-holes made by British Army machine-gun fire could still be seen in the outer walls, and I wanted to see if that could possibly be true, but I had to be careful crossing the street as the traffic was like Times Square in New York, as was, to my surprise, the commercial glare of lights. I wanted my O'Connell Street virginal and preserved in amber, not made tawdry with neon.

It was true what they said about the pock-marked pillars.

But the couples crowding the footpaths, mobs waiting at the crosswalks, all the crush of Saturday night, car-horns, noisy diesel buses, people walking fast to get to their destinations, were heedless of history, wrapped up as they were, and had to be, in their own lives, problems, daily concerns, petty quarrels and quiet joys. It was only an interloper like me, inveterately out-of-place wherever I went, to whom life seemed novel, strange, simultaneous and beckoning, only an incorrigible reader like me to whom every surface was in need of interpretation, to uncover meanings hidden underneath.

Now I plunged leftwards into that mass of bobbing heads in search of my first sighting of the legendary River Liffey.

I found O'Connell Bridge not pristine but hired out to the penny-grasping multitudes looking for a chipper parked by bridge-side where they could queue up for fish and chips. And there were no less than four of them, one at each corner of the bridge, in each traffic direction, little white houses perched on the flatbed back of pick-ups, with peaked roofs and white flaps opened on the footpath-side to dispense delicious open-air fried potatoes wrapped in newspaper, bubbled on the spot in fryola-tors, tended by a pair of sweating white-clad cooks in white paper hats, who doled out the chips and rang them up.

I made a mental note of the tempting aromas wafting through the twilight, vowing to return at the first opportunity when there were no long queues; while, facing the other way, upriver, leaning over the balustrades, I observed the long, lingering northern-lat-itude twilight that came sweeping down the Liffey from the west, brushing over the spidery arch of the Ha'penny Bridge, to light on the foreheads of the west-facing buildings on the far side of O'Connell Street, splashing them with vibrant copper coins that made the top storeys glow like fevered brows.

Every place has it enchantments, if only you are there, with fresh eyes, at the precise, exact moments when they occur, and only if your eyes are open, and your mind made up to memorize them, because you know they're likely never to recur again, or that, if and when they do, you will have changed, and will no longer possess the fresh eyes to see them.

On the other side of the bridge, after crossing when the lights changed, I was standing on the footpath, looking up at the sign for D'Olier Street, wondering how to pronounce it, when a passerby tapped my elbow. "Are you lost?"

I laughed. "Do I look lost? I guess I must be, then."

"Perhaps I can help?"

Harry Smith, the bus-conductor, having been swaying on the rear deck all day, and now back on solid ground, was fond of walking home after work, swinging his ticket-dispenser by the leather strap,. "I've to get back my land-legs, and a pint or two along the way won't hurt—make me human again by the time I get home and have to face up to the missus and the little bleeders. Would you care to join me?"

Harry took me straight on to College Green, narrating the sights as we went: the Bank of Ireland (where I had my dwindling-by-the-day thousand bucks in an account that Sheila opened for us back in Ballina) was first: that which, once, was Grattan's Parliament; Trinity College on the left, Nassau Street, straight on, and, ah, Grafton Street. "Here's where we'll find my local, which is Sinnott's, in King Street, none better."

Harry Smith, the dedicated member of the Irish Transport and General Workers' Union, proceeded to regale me with stories his father, the wagon-driver, told him, all about Jim Larkin and the times of the General Strike in 1913; and I told him of what I knew about the Bread and Roses Strike of 1912, in Milltown, the place where I came from, and of my father, Andy Petrovich, another staunch union man, who was a member of John L. Lewis's United Mine Workers in the 'Thirties; and we talked well past Harry's tea-time, and he wouldn't let me pay for a pint, and we adjourned then to John Rice's, next door, for another pint or two and more stories which Harry told often—"whenever I can locate someone who hasn't heard them already—"all about "the German woman with the radio transmitter who made all those trips to Ulster during the war, and Dev refused to have her arrested, right in our street she lived, wasn't that neutral of him?" Or the day his wife had their seventh child, and Harry had the bus-driver drop him in Jervis Street, "and when I got to the hospital, wasn't she gone home the day before! But you know, Nick, with all them little codgers and their feckless sisters to provide for, I needed the overtime, didn't I?"

We parted in Owen Roe's, by the Portobello Bridge, Harry Smith and I, by that time, the finest of friends, and I waved to him from the street, with a thumb's up, and a seriously man-gled "Up the General Transport Workers' Union, now! Brilliant! Have a great week!"

Harry pursued me before leaving. "Aragh, remember. Liberty Hall. Look us up."

Then I made my way home the same way I'd come, back to Mrs Warren's again in Lower Gardiner Street, having learned my way in Dublin, thanks to Harry Smith, as far as the South Circular Road and back.

Starting Monday, rising early, I would step out to buy the Dublin Herald and the Irish Press at a shop in Talbot Street, and then walk back to The Lake Isle with an appetite. Over rashers and eggs in Mrs Warren's little dining room at the back of the stair, I'd peruse the Help Wanted adverts. You had to say 'adverts.' If you referred to the 'ad' you'd seen in the paper, they didn't know what you were talking about. "Oh, the advert, you mean. Yes, that's filled. Sorry." I felt about as dreary as the autumn weather. Dublin was uniformly grey. My interval in Mayo, when inspiration was flying in the window and pushing my biro across the blue-lined copybook page, seemed a lifetime ago. Was it really only July when I had my own office back home in Milltown and I was the one turning supplicants away? Job-hunting was clearly not uplifting to my spirits. But there was no help for it. How would one get copies of a resume made in the wilds of Mayo? You would have to go 4 miles, or 8 miles, or 12 miles to a town, wait all day for a bus to appear at Delaney's, or stick out your thumb, and wait, for the odd, infrequent car. Dublin was really no different than Boston, it had the same amenities, the same services. But at least it had them.

Yet by the same reasoning it was just as discouraging job-hunting in Dublin as it would be in Boston. Longing for a good, strong coffee, I'd sip at the lukewarm tea that was served, down my breakfast, and go out again to locate a bus in O'Connell Street, or Eden Quay, and go for an interview. You didn't call people, or phone them, you 'rang them up,' from a red phone-box in the street. Then a long bus ride to see someone in Fingal or Rialto, or way out the Naas Road to the Industrial Estate.

> Forecourt Attendant. Must be reliable
> and trustworthy. Reference required.
> Experience not necessary. Apply at
> the premises, Lannigan's BP, Sandymount
> Green.

I was learning Dublin the hard way. No suite of rooms in the Intercontinental Hotel with room service and a telephone.

Dublin was full of small garages tucked into back lanes, stitching rooms in lofts, shoe-repairs in shops, bars, lounges, pubs. Everyone in close to the city centre, (*not* 'downtown') was in service: book-selling, dry-cleaning, job-printing, food, hotels. Other than small shops, everyone worked for the Dublin Corporation, or the Irish Government, the banks, the assurance companies, the travel bureaus, the buses and the railways, Trinity College, the newspapers, or Guinness' Brewery. I tried the job-printers, as I'd learned offset printing at Liberty Mutual in Boston, but without luck. Here such positions were skilled professional trades, highly-sought-after, and by the time I got there, someone who had a motor or knew their way around or had gotten a lift from a friend had beat me to it.

Janitor. Clean work. Jervis Street
Hospital, 2nd shift. Apply at the
Office, rear entrance.

I had to save time and save bus fares. It was a long way out to the Dublin Airport just to put in an application: I once worked a couple of summers at Logan, in Boston, loading aircraft for Flying Tiger Lines, my wife is Irish, we're trying to get settled. I would get odd looks. You came *here* looking for work? To Ireland, I mean? Oughtn't it to be the other way round? Look!—here's a fellow who's emigrated in reverse! "We'll call you." Call me where? I hadn't any fixed abode. I had to give out Mrs Warren's number and hope the old lady would take a message. In my blue Aer Lingus bag, I had a notebook, and now it was filling with phone numbers and addresses instead of poem-writing. A notebook and my hardcover copy of Dostoevsky, which I would dip into on the long bus rides. I spent too much time on the buses: all the bigger factories were out past the

South Circular Road or the North Circular Road, Jacob's Biscuits, Carroll's Cigarettes, the big ESB generating plant, the oil refinery out in Ringsend, Digital Equipment out at the Industrial Estate. There were no Americans working at this American company. Wasn't that the idea? Give them a big tax break so they'll come here and provide jobs for us, the Irish?

I sometimes despaired, as it seemed I'd wasted my time completely, spending six years studying literature at two universities. Even with two degrees, I still didn't have the qualifications needed for an entry-level teaching position in an Irish school. Still, I had to make a stab at it. Perhaps in Dublin, it might be different, as it was completely hopeless in Mayo, where they had to send one of Delaney's kids running down to the boreen on foot to let you know someone had rung you up—and then you had to go up to Delaney's to ring them back.

So the very first Monday morning the very first thing I did was to drop in on the Ministry of Education in Tara Street.

The receptionist was most polite.

"Yes, we're hoping to get re-settled, the wife and I. She's from Mayo, you see."

"Ah, Mayo, God help us." She would disappear down a corridor of closed office doors. And then bring back the nation-wide list of teacher vacancies.

"You already sent me this, in the mail, down to Mayo."

"Well—perhaps this one's updated."

I sat losing my appetite in Caffola's in O'Connell Street. I poked at the puddle on my plate, Frankfurter Grill, only one bite gone from the curled, notched, half-burnt meat wilting in red sauce, which smothered baked beans. One week in Dublin. I sat with my *Karamazov* propped in front of me, held open by the sugar bowl and the napkin dispenser. I had flown to Ireland with such elation, and now, although I set out each morning enthusiastic and venturesome, believing that today I'd hear, *yes, you're hired,* instead of *sorry, it's been filled,* or, *leave off your application, we'll be in touch;* at the end of each long day on the buses, deflation would set in. I had come to Ireland with no plans but to read the three books I had stowed in my airlines bag within the coming year. I had polished off the Melville in Mayo, now I was on to Dostoevsky, and then I had next on the list Tolstoy's *War and Peace.* Three classics which I had deliberately put off reading during the entire two years of graduate school while I was correcting freshman essays, plunging into radical teaching methods, and plotting to end the Vietnam fiasco; put off to some later, ideal time when I was free. But now, instead of free, I was trapped on a treadmill.

I went into Caffola's because the place had a vaguely Italian name. What I found was a version of Horn and Hardart's in New York. I came in here because breakfast was the only meal in the day I could get out of Mrs Warren. If I wanted a second meal, I'd have to pay for it. That thousand dollars in that account at the Bank of Ireland?—it was dribbling away day after day. I came in here because it was cheap, and what I found was an empty napkin dispenser, flies crawling across the mirrors on the square pillars, grease floating on the surface of the Coca-Cola, men in long grey overcoats gathered at the rear trying to catch some warmth from the steam tables.

Next week it would be October. This time last year, I was in New York, and Ray Deeds was greeting me warmly from behind the bar, showing me his hand-printed flyer: *A Reading, by Nick Petrovich, Saturday afternoon at Dr D's, 2 pm.* I picked up my book and bag and walked out of Caffola's.

Traffic blared in O'Connell Street. People queueing at the bus-ranks, dashing under the awnings of Clery's Department Store. The marquee of The Embassy, bleak-white, announcing in lipstick-red: Elaine May, Walter Matthau, in *A New Leaf.* I paused for the lights at North Earl Street, and my heart went sore: a young fellow and his girl, holding hands, just stepping off the kerb.

In Mayo I was greeted. In Mayo I was treated to the Ireland of the Welcomes. Here I was just another bloke with empty pockets.

I missed Sheila. I missed waking in the morning beside her in the trundle-bed down in the back bedroom. I missed being there to watch my mother-in-law rake the ashes to start the fire for the tea. Time wears away the scent of a touch, the love in a look. You strain to call it up. It's there, just out of reach. After one week, I struggled to see before me the innocent face of my little daughter Aisling. Out of sight, out of mind. How could this be? At the end of a long week in the turbulent city, a cruel loneliness creeps up behind you.

Days later I happened to find myself in Lower Dorset Street, and I decided to look up Eccles Street, where Leopold Bloom lowered himself over the railings in Joyce's novel. The railings were there, but the door to No. 7 was not.

All that was left of the three-story redbrick Georgian row-house was the shell of the ground floor and a pile of rubble in the vacant lot behind the ruin of the windowless front wall.

Where Bloom's front door once stood there was a sheet of corrugated tin pinned to the doorjambs with rusty nails, topped by a fanlight bereft of glass.

Someone had stolen the door.

Sacrilege.

The love that once was shared between Molly and Leopold in that house was erased forever now.

It mattered not to me that they never really existed, that they never really lived here. To me they were more real than I was.

Thursday evening, I rang down to Mayo from a phonebox in the street outside the Talbot Lounge. They sent a young one down the boreen to fetch Sheila up to Delaney's. I stood outside the phonebox waiting for what seemed hours but must've been thirty minutes at least, worried all the time that someone would be occupying it just when Sheila rang back the number I'd given. Finally the phone jangled, my nerves jumped, and I thrust myself through the door. Needlessly, I told Sheila yet again that I'd bring her and Aisling up just as soon as I got a job and a proper place for them to stay. Yeah, I'm fine. No, I'm in a B&B. But I miss you. How's the kid?

"She wants to know where her Daddy is. She keeps looking round corners to find where we've hidden you."

When I went back to my table in the Talbot Lounge, all I could think of was a long stretch of sea-wall out the bus-window somewhere out by Howth Head in the darkness.

The interior of the Talbot Lounge was dim and rather tawdry, with a discolored lino floor and faded prussian-green wallpaper. The light was low and there were cheap prints of turn-of-the-century trams and wagons loaded with barrels of Dublin porter on the walls.

I first went in there because I was looking for an alternative to a dump like Caffola's, and passing by in Talbot Street, the door intrigued me.

The door had a porthole of bubbled glass, like the eye of the Cyclops. The windows were high in the wall and you could not see inside. It looked private, strictly locals, not for tourists.

That's what I wanted, a small slice of Dublin to call my own, a neighborhood bar where nobody would bother me. And I found the shepherd's pie on offer quite palatable, and I could sit and have my supper and read my book.

So I began going every evening, after job-hunting. It was much preferable to returning to my empty room at the Lake Isle to sit and stare at walls. Since it was usually mostly deserted, they didn't mind if I sat there and nursed a Guinness all night.

The one redeeming feature of the Talbot was the snug tucked into the back wall opposite the door. The trim was gleaming oak and the glass panels were frosted with art nouveau ferns, white on white.

As I was returning several nights in a row, I soon noted that the same two ladies occupied the snug every night. From my table, I could not see all of them, just enough to speculate. One was rather blonde, the other dark-haired. A pair of girlfriends, well-preserved at about 35 years of age or so. Still young and trim enough to wear skirts above the knee and peep-toed heels with pull-over straps. I thought they must be office-workers in the city centre on the way home, but taking their time. I never saw them eat anything, only drink. No wonder they were so trim. Sometimes when they shifted and re-crossed their legs I would look up from my book, but I didn't want to stare. Usually, I would get so absorbed in the tangled drama of the mad Karamazovs that I wouldn't notice that the two girlfriends had gone, and the snug was empty.

Friday night came and I felt restless. I still had no job offer, only a second week full of rejection. I couldn't concentrate on yet another night of Dmitri and Ivan. I was fed up with sameness repeating itself, and I wanted badly a little diversion. So after finishing my dinner, I picked up my glass and book and walked over to the snug, and stood there in the doorway.

"Well, aren't you going to going to invite me to sit down?"

"Oh, look, Kay, it's the mysterious stranger," said the blonde.

"Rosemary, it's a Yank," said the dark-haired one.

Swiftly, they made room—in between them.

I seated myself on the warmed bench between them, and Rosemary, the blonde, said, "Kay was sure you were from the Romanian Navy."

"We were wondering were you going to speak in some barnacle tongue we wouldn't understand," said Kay, "and here you're a Yank, plain and simple."

"Why would you think I'm a sailor?"

"Well, I didn't, and I told Kay the Romanian Navy has never been known to visit Dublin."

"But I said, he is so one, and has left the wife home wilting on the vine while he's off to a girl in every port."

"How do you know I'm married?"

"Isn't that a naval jacket you're wearing," said Rosemary.

"And isn't that a wedding ring on your finger?" said Kay.

"And where is she, then? Why are you eating alone every night?"

"Yes, we want to know."

"She's down in Mayo."

"Oh, Kay—Mayo, God help us."

"Shocking it is, Rosemary."

"Nevermind," said Rosemary, "didn't we leave our husbands at home, all week, till we could find out what was what with the mysterious stranger."

"Do you like to go dancing?" said Kay eagerly.

"You're safe with us, we're already taken."

"And you are as well, so good for us, too."

And so in short order I found myself walking up Talbot Street headed for the Metropole with Rosemary on one arm and Kay on the other.

Rosemary was, up close, a strawberry blonde, with peacock-blue eyes and freckles and a turned-up bounce to her hairstyle as she strode, and Kay had an eggshell-white complexion with dark Spanish eyes; she was a silky brunette whose dark hair hung over dark eyes in seductress-sexy curls. I kept looking back and forth between them. "And why don't you go dancing with your husbands?" I asked.

"They're a pair of bleedin' doorknobs, that's why."

"Can't handle us."

"Usually, we go to the Metropole on a Friday night and dance with each other, just to go dancing, you know? So this is our lucky night—we get to dance with you."

"You'll have to share us, however. No playing favorites."

Upstairs, at the Metropole, the ball of mirrors suspended from the ceiling sent ovals of mauve and pink and blue lights spinning round and round the ballroom floor. I took a turn first with one and then the other and soon we were dizzy, with laughing faces, passing in and out of swirling lights and diving shadows. Round tables where exhausted couples rested between numbers surrounded the dance-floor. Around the balcony, more couples sat leaning on the balustrades with drinks in their hands to watch the dancers below. Brian Mathews, radio host of the BBC's Top of the Pops Programme, was the headliner, and the MC for the evening. Tommy Sheiling's Orchestra played the numbers he introduced. After each preamble, Mathews retreated to a small card-table at the side of the stage where he sipped a drink. The orchestra played the top-forty tunes he called out from sheet-music balanced on music-stands mono-grammed baby-blue with the initials, *TS.* A chubby and petite female vocalist who sounded to me like Brenda Lee belted out *Candida,* and a cry went up from the audience, but she followed with *Knock Three Times,* and they were screaming, only to collapse in hysterics when she started on *Build Me Up, Buttercup,* but when she came to *Never-Ending Love Song,* and she was joined by a male partner, so that they sounded exactly like Delaney & Bonnie on the original record, the fans rushed the floor like a flock of pigeons let out of a cage.

At a quarter past eleven, we tumbled down the stairs and just managed to make it in time to the bus rank in Aston Quay so that the girls could catch the No. 23 to Fairview, and when they jumped aboard the rear platform, they hung off the chrome-plated pole, waving and laughing, jumping up and down, crying "Half-eleven—last bus to heaven!" and, to the tune of the Beatles, "We love you, Ni-i-icky, oh, yes we do!"

And then the bus accelerated, and they disappeared up the stair to the top deck, and I stood there waving, long past the time when they could see me.

I felt so wildly, ridiculously happy that I didn't want to go home right away. To prolong the evening, I walked over to the nearest chipper in O'Connell Bridge, and joined the long queue.

Foot tapping, smiling at the passersby, a rock'n'roll song dancing in my heart, I then strolled leisurely back to my room at the Lake Isle, planning to use Mrs Warren's skeleton key to let myself in, so as not to disturb the poor old thing, and those fried potatoes, wet with white vinegar, wrapped in newspaper, balanced in one hand, burning the tongue, tossed around my mouth to cool off as I walked: they tasted wicked good.

"Fancy a fag, mate?"

It was Saturday night in McDaid's, in Harry Street, just off Grafton Street, and I was jammed in elbow to elbow at the end of the short bar. On my left a man was offering an open box of Benson & Hedges with one cigarette pulled half-out. "Thanks—I don't smoke."

"Why not? You look fully grown to me."

"Never got into the habit, I guess."

"Ah, well, you're right. Bad habit. Worse luck for me. Peter Murphy's my name, import-export's my game. What about yourself?"

It was hard to hear in this noisy, tiny, packed bar, but I thought I detected an accent of some kind I hadn't heard before. "I don't have a game."

"Ah, but you do have an accent. Let me guess. You're from west of here. I'd say far west. Hollywood. You're the illegitimate son of Anthony Quinn and he's set up a trust fund to get rid of you and you're out to spend it as fast as you legally can."

"I wish. No trust fund, no Hollywood."

"What the hell are you doing here in this rutting tourist trap, then?"

"McDaid's is Brendan Behan's local."

"Brendan, eh? Personal friend of yours?"

"Hardly. He's dead."

"Oh. So that means you're not expecting him tonight. Oh, good, you thought that witty. I'm not doing so badly, eh? Now, look, I've told you my name and it's dead unfriendly of you not to tell me yours."

"Nick Petrovich."

As I shook hands with Peter Murphy, he said, "Very good. We're mates now, ain't we?"

We could hardly be mates, being perfect strangers, but in my time in Ireland thus far, especially down the country, I'd become accustomed to the idea that you might walk into a bar full of strangers and walk out with a raft of new friends.

Peter Murphy then said, or I should say, shouted, "You were telling me about your friend Brendan. What's his game?"

"He was a writer. And a playwright. *Borstal Boy*, I suppose, is his best-known work but he also wrote a hit play on Broadway, *The Quare Fellow.*"

"I dunno about that. Not my game. Do you actually read these things, then, books, as they're called?"

"Oh, yes. Newspapers, too." My attempt at wit was falling short. "Flyers, handouts, matchboxes. Anything that stays still long enough."

"Listen—if you're not meeting your friend Brendan here tonight—what if I told you I knew of a place where we could actually hear one another? Would you be interested?"

I wasn't sure. If he didn't know who Brendan Behan was, we didn't have much in common. He detected my doubts.

"Listen—we're mates, ain't we? If you can't trust me, Nick, who can you? You stick with me and you won't get wet in the rain."

I wasn't persuaded.

"Look—have you got that beer as yet? I don't know about you, but I'm getting thirsty."

I did have to admit that I hadn't come into McDaid's solely for the atmosphere.

"Now, I'm not going to tell you I'm buying, but—what if I told you that I've a pair of birds waiting to meet me tonight, and I can't handle both of them—and I'd even let you have your choice."

"I'm married, Peter."

"Perfect. Why, it's the thought of a married man that gets their knickers soaked."

That did it. I had to laugh, and admit that he was trying hard—and didn't look as if giving up anytime soon, and—I could always politely dis-attach myself later—so I let myself be persuaded.

Out on the footpath, I got my first good look at him. Shined black shoes, grey slacks, a maroon suit-jacket, white shirt, and a burgundy necktie: under the white collar, over the gold collar-pin, near the knot in the necktie, gold-mono-grammed initials: PM. A spiffy black umbrella used like a cane, or for self-defense. A narrow-brimmed grey-plaid fedora, with a sporting feather in the hatband. The thin face with the self-amused grin was not made for television, but neither would it make women run away, and his pinch-able, flushed pink cheeks added to the gamin-appeal, calling out to the maternal instincts.

"Now, look, Nick," said Peter Murphy as we set off down the pedestrian mall of Grafton Street towards College Green. "I'm going to give you a piece of advice, so listen carefully. If you want to know someone's name, never come out and say, 'What's your name?' bald as brass like that. No, no. Instead, you stick out your hand and say, 'I'm Nick, et cetera, et cetera, and, lo and behold, the reaction you have just provoked is that they'll shake your hand and give you their name, without you having to ask. Works every time."

"I'll keep it in mind."

"It's good advice. Now, just exactly what are you doing in Dublin?"

"Looking for work."

"Not half. So am I. We'll look together. After all, we're mates, ain't we?"

"I thought you said you were in the import-export trade."

"Well, that's an on-again, off-again thing. Sometimes I'll take a position just to tide me over, like."

"You're English, not one of the Irish Murphys, I take it."

"Oh, but I am. That is, the auld fella is, all right. As Irish as they come. Quite the hand at turning sods into pound-notes. Emigrated to England and made a fortune. Employs all the navvies in Liverpool, Irish, English, Scots and Welsh. PM Builders, Ltd." Murphy thumbed his tie. "See? Filthy rich, mon père, really. Can't stick the bastard. So—I've run away from home."

Wynn's Hotel in Abbey Street was where Murphy was taking me. Double-glass doors, venerable descendants of the reign of Queen Victoria. Wynn's was a bespectacled philistine, on the watch for riff-raff. But the porter, who wore a long grey greatcoat with red epaulets, and was as stout as a barrel, opened the door respectfully for Peter Murphy. "Good evening, sir."

I stepped into the vestibule. My pea-coat, wind-blown curly-mop of dark hair, dungarees, the attire I had worn daily down on the farm, or on campus, for that matter, my usual Jerry Garcia garb, were remarked by the porter.

Inside, a broad staircase, richly-red-carpeted, came sweeping down out of gas-lamp-glow upper reaches. The registration desk in the main lobby of Wynn's Hotel was discreetly out of view of the entrance. Obviously, any person to whom Wynn's gave a key could be trusted to let themselves directly upstairs.

I admit I was impressed. Compared to the B&B where I was staying in Lower Gardiner Street, this was the upper crust.

In the lobby, ancient, elderly, and merely old guests, were arranged in commodious chairs, lamps at the elbow on round tables. Only their eyes moved. *Oh my God—they've been here longer than the furniture.* A chandelier shed a confidential light across the furry, wine-red carpeting, mahogany moldings, potted palms. The desk clerk looked a young spartan in black-rimmed glasses, observing me with folded hands. I crept by on padded feet.

The bar in Wynn's was an ell-shaped sitting room, like being at home, in your own front parlor. The lounge regulars, middle-aged businessmen sipping dry sherrys, young lovers trying to forget, married couples trying to remember.

At the door to the lounge, Murphy stopped me with a hand. "Watch this."

He marched up to the bar and hailed the barman loudly. "Double-scotch, straight-up, if you will, and whatever my American friend here fancies."

Ladies heads swiveled. I wished I were a turtle and could sink into my collar.

The same eyes looked Murphy up and down and dismissed him as a vulgar drummer who'd misplaced his case of samples.

Murphy dropped his voice low over his shoulder. "You want to watch your billfold in a kip like this." He sipped his Scotch. I waited for my pint to settle. "Well, how do you like my digs? You're welcome to stop here, with me, you know."

I took my pint. "Thanks. I'm in a B&B in Lower Gardiner Street." I didn't want to say which one.

Thumbing the knot in his tie, Murphy looked round the bar. "I have my business contacts in here to the lounge for luncheon. Exclusive, you know? I've a deal or two on for imported goods."

"I thought you were looking for a job?" He was beginning to repeat himself, I was getting bored. Why did he bring me here? He must have some angle.

Murphy countered with, "The type of position I'm in line for is not presently vacant."

"Right. Prince Charles is kinda stuck."

"Look—I've tried leeching off the auld bastard, and it's no go. I'm not exactly one of his forms to be filled out in triplicate."

I took a stool. Just to make conversation, which was flagging, I said, "So how does it feel to be back home, Peter?"

"Christ, I can feel my ancestors rotting under the floorboards. Stinking little island. Give me England."

"So why don't you go back there?""

"Just waiting for my ship to come in."

"So—what is this import-export business you're in, exactly?"

"Well—import-export, you might say. I imports the goods and I exports the money." Murphy enjoyed his joke. "Would you believe—olive oil?"

"No."

Murphy hung his umbrella on the curved oak lip of the bar and lowered his voice confidentially. "Guns for the IRA?"

"Excuse me?"

"Sounds glamorous, though. And what harm, when it isn't true, and you're not going to be taken seriously anyway?" Murphy looked to the left and right. "It is quite illegal, what I do, if you must know."

"Drugs, right?"

"Oh, God, no. I'm not looking for rent-free in the Joy courtesy of the Branch."

"What, then?"

"French letters. Condoms, mate. Prophylactics. You know, contraceptives."

I laughed out loud.

"You may laugh, Nick, but it's really quite serious. In a country as randy as this, it amounts to a national crisis. Why, you might say I'm performing a vital service. And what happens to me if one of these honest Irish virgins has a fit of the guilts and goes to confession on Saturday? It's a short trip from

Wynn's Hotel to accommodations courtesy of the Ban-the-Birth-Control Republic. Stop laughing. You'll embarrass me in front of my public."

"So that's it! You imports the rubbers, and you exports the money!"

"Look, mate, I'm not into Wellies."

"No, no. 'Rubbers' is just American slang for the same thing."

"Well, cheers. Learn something new every night in Wynn's, eh, mate? What did I do with my fags? Listen, Nick, could you loan me a fiver, just temporary-like. You'll get it back, every shilling, not to worry. We're mates, ain't we?"

I said good-bye, and good riddance, to Peter Murphy, but not without risking five quid, which I was certain sure, as they say in Mayo, I'd never see again.

And then on Monday morning it was back to the salt-mines, riding the buses.

First thing, Tara Street again. The receptionist was straight out with phone calls incoming, so I perused the Help-Wanted 'adverts' while I waited, till she finally looked up. "Any luck so far?" says she, "I haven't anything new in since last week. A pity you started so late—the academic year began first of September. But—it's only Monday."

Well, I started so late because I was bloody-well busy creating deathless verse at the behest of The Muse, I felt like saying, but what was the use?

More and more I was coming to see my time in Mayo as an interlude, all too brief, before the business of resuming life as usual for the unemployed. A mist was drifting through the air, and I was drifting, aimlessly, up O'Connell Street, clerks and shop-girls brushing me by. In Boston, it would have been Jordan Marsh, Filene's and R.H. White's: here it was Roche's, Clery's, and Guiney's. Same difference. Monday morning's workaday world.

On the pillars of the GPO, a flyer from Saturday's rally, which I'd missed, still stuck, wilting in the mist: *No Surrender*. I'd been reading the Dublin papers on the buses, as well as the Employment sections. The headlines were black this morning. The Irish Press was saying, *The newly-organized Northern Resistance Movement (NRM) is to meet in conference today in Omagh to coordinate the activities of Defence Committees and to organize mass demonstrations in protest of Internment, according to Frank McManus, MP for Fermanagh-South Tyrone . . .* Events were passing me by while I was stalled in B&B land, neither a tourist nor a dues-paying citizen.

The women in the stalls in Moore Street advised me to give the office of Paddy Power a try. I thought not. I was not quite ready to go out on day-laborer assignments quite yet. *No Surrender.*

Back in O'Connell Street, I chanced across Macmillan's Bookshop. By the volumes in the window, I knew they were the same publisher as in New York. And I well-remembered my old dog-eared paperback copy of Yeat's *Selected Poems,* with the bright red cover, by them. Next to the plate-glass windows, a street-door led upstairs. What did I have to lose?

The receptionist at Macmillan's had her own office, serving doubly as a waiting room. Large windows at the front looked out across O'Connell Street to The Royal Dublin. Fiona was very nice. I mentioned as how I'd given readings in New York and was on the roster of the Dr Deeds' Poets Series and had seen my first volume in the shops in Boston and Cambridge at Goodspeed's and Grolier's and that I was very excited about my current project, which I'd begun in Mayo and which looked so promising. I even remembered Peter Murphy's advice on how to find out her name—and it worked. Meanwhile, behind her desk, in the inscrutable oak-panelled wall, the mysterious studded door led inwards to the guardians of literature: the editors.

Fiona leaned back in her leather-upholstered swivel-chair, dropping the telephone receiver gently into its cradle with two fingers. "Our general practice is that we ask to see typed manuscript—especially from someone who hasn't submitted before. But—have you thought of having it published in America? We handle American books to be re-printed in the British Isles. Which means, they're published over there first. And the taste of the British audience for American books—unless they're established classics—Faulkner, Steinbeck, Hemingway—."

I was hearing this sort of thing everywhere I went. 'Where have you worked in Dublin before? Have you any references? Yes—we understand that you're trying to get re-settled here with your family, but—.'

What I didn't want to get into was having been dismissed in my last job. The FBI. The photos, and all that. Not exactly a recommendation.

So I lied, or omitted the truth. What else could I do?

I threw myself into the effort of racing around the city by double-decker, Monday afternoon, all day Tuesday, all day Wednesday. Dishwasher, grille-cook, forecourt attendant, unskilled laborer, janitor, news reporter, travel office clerk, factory assembler. Nothing was too low or high for me. I timed myself. How many interviews today? Got to do more than that tomorrow.

I had too much time on those buses to brood. I was doing everything the wrong way around. If I wanted a career in poetry,

I'd have to teach in higher academia. If I wanted to get into a Phd program, I should've kissed ass on my professors while I had the chance to get those letters of recommendation. But, no, I couldn't. That wasn't me. The longer I stayed in grad school, the angrier I got over Vietnam and the hypocrisy of the whole establishment. Why would I want to join them and become just like them? Never trust anyone over thirty. If I wanted to have just a nice little life in the suburbs of Milltown, I would never have tried to bring the war home to the Common. But then, I would have been a hypocrite, just like them. I couldn't do it. I wouldn't be looking for a job now . . . If I wanted to be an American poet, I should've stayed in America. There's precious little market for poetry over there—but then, to run away and try to get published from here, when all your uprushing river of words is coming from there . . . I needed my head examined.

It rained the rest of the week. One morning near Busaras the fog was as thick as bottled Bovril. A white wrapper, starred with a green shamrock, *Jacob's Biscuits,* flew up from the kerb on a gust of wind like a licking tongue. It fled between wheels, darting, dodging, swept aside by whizzing traffic till it came to rest beneath a grey van, stripped, bonnet open, wires ripped, wheels gone, on its axles in the gutter. The swish of tires on the wet pavements was synonymous with the mutter of the constant rain.

Friday the rain stopped suddenly at seven in the morning, but the sky remained a soggy shade of washed-out carbon-paper.

Maurice Woolf, Ltd. No. 38, Usher's
Island Quay. Dispatch Controller. Apply
on premises.

It began to rain again, big spots on the *Wanted* section in my hand. I stepped aboard the bus in Aston Quay. The driver dropped me at the corner of Bridgefoot Street, which was almost all the way out to Kingsbridge. I had no idea what I was looking for. I stopped a passerby who told me the driver had left me off short and it was the next quay up, that this was Usher's Quay.

It was all very confusing. I walked west on the south side of the Liffey and opposite, on the north side, it did not look a very savory neighborhood: anonymous shops, all shuttered, closed, boarded up, out-of-business, a long red-brick block crowned with an ancient grey-blue cornice with the advert spelled out:
Battersby & Co., Auctioneers, Estate Agents, Est. 1815
On my side of the river the view mounted steeply uphill to the monolithic brown peaks of Guinness' Brewery in Thomas Street. I kept walking west till I came to a street sign in Irish, *Sraid Watling,* at the next bridge over the Liffey. I had seen nothing at all that looked like a place called *Maurice Woolf Ltd,* but there was a small sweet-shop called O'Rourke's on the corner of Watling Street, opposite a pub facing the bridge on the other corner. They told me to go back.

Never a number on anything. I wandered back towards Bridgefoot Street, but there was nothing but a thick, medieval inscrutability, blanks walls stranded out of time, grey stone darkening with rain. Nobody ever got a job on a Friday anyway.

The only possible thing was a stub of slightly inclined tarmac apron. Just a pair of tall garage-doors, closed. I had already passed it twice. If you didn't know it was there, you would drive right by in a bus or a car and never see it. Could this be it? There was no number 38 or anything, but I had passed a lone No. 15 earlier. I stood there looking up at a ramshackle corrugated tin roof thrown up over a laneway between the butt of a stone wall and the next building over, which was blank with a windowless wall. But now I spied a tiny nameplate on a half-door in one of the tall garage-doors. Going up close I read

> Maurice Woolf, Ltd.
> Foam Cushions.
> Mattresses and Bunk-Beds

A cast-iron latch handle, which I lifted, opened the half-door. Dark inside. The smell was wet concrete, petrol fumes, engine oil, damp canvas. Blocking my view was a one-ton lorry, parked in a high-raftered bay. Yards away, past the side of the lorry, up behind it, into the narrow tunnel of the covered lane, flourescent tubes made nighttime out of morning; whitely-illuminated benches were packed with foam-filled-mattresses waiting to be edge-stitched.

It seemed as if nobody was about at all. But to my left, jerry-rigged plywood walls partitioned off a cubicle-sized office. Obviously, this had been built up against the wall of the abandoned building next door.

This is not a building at all. It's a covered-over lane-way. God only knows how many centuries it's been here, or whether this was some narrow street where people lived hundreds of years ago.

A skinny man in a stained white knee-length smock came from around the back of the lorry.

Sallow, mushroom-colored cheeks, rutted with black, unshaven stubble, eyes ringed with fatigue. He looked at me questioningly. "May I help you with something?"

"You filled that job already, did you?"

"What job?"

"The one in the Dublin Herald. Dispatch Controller.

"There's an advert in the paper, is there? Let me see that."

I handed the folded newspaper with the circled part to him.

"Isn't that just like them? Never tell me a thing. Head office. Pearse Street. I'm just the manager here, that's all. Bleedin' fiasco is what it is." Handing me back the paper, he ran his hands backs over his head till a cowlick popped astray behind one ear—a round ear, like a tea-pot handle. He had another one on the other side, too. "Look—do you fancy work? I'm in desperate need of a good man. To straighten up this mess. It's a disaster. I've been on to them for a fortnight on the phone to get me a man, and the only result is that I'm a fortnight behind in me own work." Employees were climbing through the half-door behind me, squeezing between me, the lorry and the makeshift office, and the manager was distracted for a moment. "Where was I? Oh, yeah. It's heavy work. Lifting bunk-beds onto that lorry there. About eight stone apiece. Well, you're big enough. My name's Sugarman, Noel Sugarman. And you?"

"Nick Petrovich."

Young fellows passing looked curiously at me over their shoulders.

"Would you pardon me, just one second?" Sugarman caught up with a man in an overcoat passing up under the flourescent tubes, and I stepped aside into the doorway of the little office.

Papers, pink, blue, yellow and white, bills of lading, receipts, order forms, price lists, brochures and one-page flyers, dockets, tickets, tags and labels, held down with scissors, staplers and staple-guns serving as paper-weights, were strewn across the long plywood bench under the office windows. They were fastened down with pins, thumb-tacks and paper-clips, threaded over and under a long, snaking cord plugged into a black telephone, speared on spindles, tossed into trays, buried under telephone directories, street directories, road-maps, catalogs, three-ring folders.

I tested the plywood floor with my weight: it bent and bounced back. The cubicle-door was jammed open with a prism-shaped black-plastic name-plate from the desk: *Noel Sugarman, Mgr.*

It was then I noticed a pair of over-sized hobnail boots stood planted—thick ankles in stove-pipe black trousers—in the doorway. A corduroy jacket over a dirty grey sweatshirt, shoulders a yard wide, sleeves too short for the long arms: a bullet-headed, baby-faced giant grinning at me, blocking the doorway. Behind this bloated boy, three skinheads craned their necks, two of them short and blondish, the third lanky and black-haired, with a gold earring in his left ear. Another young one strolled past: a denim jacket that came short in the small of his back, silver studs on the shoulder seams, spiked hair.

One of the blond boys said, "After the job, are you?"

The black-haired one with the earring looked at me, suspiciously arrogant.

"G'luck," said the shorter blond, gesturing at the corduroy-jacketed giant. "Pay him no mind—'tis only Wee Willie."

Sugarman clapped his hands. "Start-up, boys, start-up."

They gave way with a sort of surly reluctance, schoolboys at the sound of the bell. But not before the shorter blond advised me with a wink, "The Dispatcher before you lasted three weeks in it."

Sugarman climbed into the plywood booth with me. "See what I mean? It's a disaster, I tell you."

Behind Sugarman, at a studious, un-ruffled pace came a short, stoutish man, also dressed in a long-white smock, a man with round spectacles perched on a balding pink forehead whose few remaining strands tickled pink ears with silken grey. He must have been the gentleman I saw earlier in the overcoat.

"This is Mr Higginbotham," said Sugarman. "In full charge of Assembly. I was just telling him about you, my boy, and as you can see, he's come down straightaway. We'd just like to ask you—what did you say your name was?"

"Nick Petrovich."

"Not an Irish name, certainly," said Higginbotham.

With his head to one side, this man regarded me with an unblinking, owlish detachment. He placed his glasses sliding down on his nose, the better to observe me. Where Sugarman's smock was discolored and stained with motor-oil, Higginbotham wore his immaculately white. Even the threads, bits of foam-rubber, and snippets of tubular plastic edging-strips stuck all over him like static-clinging wool, were clean. He could have been a chemistry professor emerging from his lab, smiling at the foolishness of the premise of his experiment. "Have you ever done this kind of work before, young man?"

"Well, yes. Not recently—but I'd look on the chance as an opportunity to learn more?"

"And what part of the world might you be from?"

"I'm from Boston."

"I thought as much. He's a Yank, Noel."

"But the reason I'm here is I'm married to a girl from Mayo."

"Ah, Mayo, God help us," said Higginbotham, while Sugarman, arms folded, looked me up and down with a wondrous regard. Higginbotham adjusted his glasses on his nose. "I'm thinking now—have you ever worked in a factory? Somehow, you don't sound the sort."

"My latest job was in an insurance company in Boston," I lied. "I was routing the delivery of computer tapes—through the whole building. Six stories." I was thinking as fast as I could, remembering someone I'd seen doing that job, pushing his cart, at Liberty Mutual, when I was in the form-printing division: does that sound impressive, something like, Dispatcher? "I worked for a couple of years before that in Malden Mills, a textile company, in the Dryer Department—we handled foam-rubber, too like you're doing here." I was becoming more glib as I went. "And I loaded aircraft—for Flying Tigers Lines, out at Logan Airport, in Boston, drove a forklift, warehouse, inside, outside, the whole bit, lifting 80-lb boxes of ITT-cable into the belly of a Lockheed Electra, prop-jet, you know?" I was trying to talk my way into it. "Listen, Mr Higginbotham, I think I can do this job. Just show me what you want done, I'll do it."

"Well, Noel. Suit yourself. Not my department. Now I've got to get back there and put an eye on those hooligans before they rob us blind."

That left me with Sugarman. I was almost there.

"Look, may I call you Nick? It's easier, wouldn't you say?"

"Sure, go ahead."

"There's one small matter, Nick. Have you the card from the Labor Exchange? Your work-permit, so to speak?"

"I don't know that I would need any—seeing as my wife is a citizen here?"

"Is she? Still carries her Irish passport, does she? Good. Good. Good."

"After all, we're married—and have a child, too."

"Do you? A boy, is it?"

"A girl, going on two-and-a-half, named Aisling."

"Oh, a lovely Irish name. Fancy that, now."

"All I'm asking is a start, Mr Sugarman. You won't regret it, sir."

"Indeed, indeed." Sugarman folded his arms again as he leaned up against the door-jamb. "I've three children myself, all boys. Eleven, nine and seven. Quite odd, actually." He chuckled at his little joke. "Well, I'd say that does it, Nick. I think we've got our man. You'll start at eight sharp, Monday morning. It's seventeen pound, ten shillings a week, the standard married man's wages, and you'll have your stamps, of course, and, oh, it's three months provisional status, company rule, but then, thereafter you're made permanent, all routine, nothing to concern yourself with—well, shall we take care of all that messing about Monday morning, my boy? Look at this desk. It's a disaster among disasters. It'll be a pleasure having the likes of you about to help take up the slack. Your sort don't often come my way, I don't mind telling you."

I was so elated I could hardly sit still on the bus back to the city centre. You would think I had just bought the whole town. I hadn't a care in the world. I was an overnight success. I forgot to read my book. I was planning to visit the Garden of Remembrance, Trinity College, Stephen's Green, the National Gallery, the Book of Kells, all in the one day.

I did manage to screw my head back on long enough to check the adverts in the Herald for someplace more suitable to stay than a B&B.

I was thrilled to think that soon I'd be calling Sheila down in Mayo from a phonebox in the street to give her the great news.

But I decided it would take me till at least tomorrow to calm down enough to handle that.

Meanwhile, I spotted an advert for a single bedsitter in the Palmerston Road. Apply at McTeague's, Ranelagh Road.

I went to the Bank of Ireland in O'Connell Street and took out money. I stepped aboard a No. 44 bus and got off at Charleston Road in Ranelagh. McTeague's was the tobacconist on the corner.

I went in and asked the young girl behind the counter for the man renting the bedsitter. "There's no Mr McTeague," said a woman's voice from the dark back of the shop. "I'm his missus, and thanks be to God he worked at it while he was with us and left me better off than he found me, God rest his soul. Breda! Come down and mind the shop for your sister!"

As we set off down the Charleston Road, Mrs McTeague found me in an ebullient mood and willing, no eager, to listen. "Are you a student? I'd welcome a bit of that tourist trade to trouble me. We all have our dreams, don't we? Are you surprised, at my age? Here we are now at Belgrave Square. Isn't it lovely? And this is Palmerston Road. We turn here. We'll be there in a minute. You're a fast walker, wait for me now. Well, here it is. 'Tisn't much, but there's an electric kettle in it, and the electric fire if you're not used of the damp as yet. You can hang your clothes on this bar and put your socks in here. That's the shilling meter there, behind the door. Do you know how to work it?"

Between the single bed and the wall, there wasn't much room to stand side by side with Mrs McTeague.

"I'll let you have it for four pounds a week. That's decent for this neighborhood. I could get more, but I suspect you won't be staying long anyway. Good. That's set, then. Are you coming or going? Right—I'll have fresh linen on before you come back, then."

I couldn't stand the excitement one minute longer so I found a phonebox back in Ranelagh Road. "Hello, I want to call Kilcross, Co. Mayo."

"What exchange, please?"

"Ballina. The number I want is Kilcross 4."

"Hello. Hello, hello. Ballina? Can you connect me to Kilcross 4? Please place ten bob in the coin slot. It's ringing. Kilcross 4? I have a call from Dublin."

"Who's that?" It was Mrs Delaney in the village post office. I didn't recognize her voice, but of course, she remembered me—or maybe, my lips.

"I'm sending young Declan down straightaway, Nick. Hurry on, now, and fetch up Sheila from the Blakes.' No, I won't tell her. I'll let you. How're you keeping, Nick? It's grand to hear your voice again. I'll ring off, now—or this'll cost you a fortune. Oh, aye, I have the number written down. Good-bye!"

For five minutes, ten, twenty, twenty-five minutes, I paced the footpath, round and round, guarding my phonebox, imploring anyone who wanted to use it to please go find another. A solid half-hour went by—and the phone rang—and I leapt at it, as if I'd choke the life out of the receiver. "Hello, hello, is it you? Yes, it's me! The news is—I've got a job, to start Monday morning! Now, I need about a week or so—but as soon as I've found a suitable place, I'll be ringing you back to take the train up from Castlebar with the babby. Give her a kiss for me, will you? Do you miss me! Yes, I love you, too, but I can't talk now, or it'll cost you a fortune there with Mrs Delaney. No, I've left the B&B, I'm in a single-bedsitter in Palmerston Road, it's nice, but there's no room enough for only me hardly. I need time to find something better—and meanwhile start a new job. I love you, Sheila, please take care of yourself and we'll be together again soon, darling!"

Now a bad penny will turn up again.

In my excitement somehow I missed the Garden of Remembrance and the Book of Kells and landed instead at The Lake Isle B&B, and it took me the best part of the afternoon in Lower Gardiner Street to square things with Mrs Warren, who, as equivocal as she was to see me coming, the first time I met her, was now unequivocally distraught to see me going, and wished to inform me at great length that I was now considered to be one of her regulars and that the next time I was in Dublin I was to see her and no-one else and she'd keep my room for me up on the third floor till then, so be it, dear boy.

I thought that now I really must have a decent meal for myself, for the first time in a month, and that, after all my travails, I certainly deserved it, and hang the cost.

But I didn't know anyplace, really, for that fine repast I was dreaming of, and yet another Shepherd's Pie at the Talbot Lounge was simply not making it.

But where could I go that I knew of that reliably?—the only place I could think of, that I'd been in, that I was familiar with, was, of course, Wynn's Hotel, in Abbey Street.

Not in a million years did I think I would bump into somebody who owed me money, having kissed that particular fiver good-bye, believing it most likely without any doubt went on a ticket for the ferry to Liverpool from Dun Laoghaire harbor, just so a certain mate of mine could safely be out of range of ever having to pay it back.

But as soon as I stepped into the lobby at Wynn's, I heard a hale-fellow-well-met shout from the lounge. "Nick! Well, of all the bloody luck! Haven't I been looking all over for you—!"

"Desperate, no doubt, to pay back a fiver?"

"I am, I am. Nick, you've got to come in and sit down and meet someone. Nick, this is Liz, Liz this is me mate, auld Nick I was telling you about."

"Yes, you're quite famous, how do you do? Do sit down. We're all mates here, aren't we?"

Liz was a quite nice-looking, well-preserved forty-or-so, tweed-ish sort, with frosted hair, who crossed her legs modestly, pinned her skirt to her kneecap decorously, and spoke with a superior Dublin accent, nothing like the rough and ready déclassé North Side dialect of the young lads I'd met that morning at Maurice Woolf's, where I'd finally, finally, secured that object of my dreams, a job. Nor did she sound anything like Mrs Warren, or Mrs McTeague, for that matter, a pair of Dublin landladies who gave the very definition of the term to the Oxford dictionary. I was quite honestly curious to ask the Lady Liz all about herself, and namely, to the point, whatever in the world was she doing with a bloke like Murphy, as well-appointed, pedicured and pedigreed a person as she was; but just at that moment we were accosted by the desk clerk, accompanied by a large-shouldered, beefy-headed traffic-squad-member of the Garda Síochána.

"This is him, officer. Mr Peter Murphy. An Englishman."

Murphy raised his voice so that everyone in the lounge that Friday evening could hear how wronged he was by this pettifogging worm of a desk-clerk. "I'll have you know I haven't been in my room for the *Last Eleven Days!*"

"Yes, that's right, officer, the maid says he hasn't slept in his bed for the last eleven nights. But, Mr Murphy, sir—*You Never Checked Out!*"

"A certain discretion in your tone would be appreciated," Murphy hissed at the desk clerk.

"You owe me eleven days' board."

"I know your sort—snivelling, runny-nosed, penny-gripping snout!"

"You are no gentleman, sir."

"Officer, I'd like this insolent bugger locked up for his impertinence."

"Why, you crawling, slithering Liverpool louse, you!"

"You'll come along quietly, now," the big garda said to Murphy with a wave of his white traffic baton.

"On what charge?" Murphy demanded.

"This is getting ridiculous," said Liz, fuming, as she opened her handbag. "Murphy, give the man what you owe him and quit this carry-on!"

"I won't, till I have an apology." Heads turned at the bar as Murphy collected the wad of bills Liz held out to him.

"For pity's sake, man," said the clerk to the policeman, "This is a polite establishment—do something!"

"All right," said the officer, disgusted with both of them, "you apologize, and he'll give you the wherefore, and I can get back to work. Come on, now."

The desk clerk's neck turned red as he choked out the one word, "Sorry."

"Ah, ah, ah. Sorry, *Mr. Murphy*—if you please."

The clerk snatched his money and strode out of the bar.

"Better watch the blaggard count it, officer. Three days is what I owe, and I want no accusations."

The garda smiled. "Murphy is your name, is it? Not a hard name to remember." He touched the white baton to the tip of his visor, in Liz' direction. "Good evening, dearie."

"God," said Peter Murphy, "get us a drink, Lizzie. I'm broke again."

Liz withdrew a sort of business-sized card from her hand-bag, a card printed florally with the day and time of her weekly 'at-homes,' and pressed it into my palm, along with a five-pound note in lovely Irish money, so delicately printed that when you held it up to the light, the transparent bill revealed watermarks you didn't know were there.

"You see, now, I'm not a welsher, am I?" said Murphy.

"Come and see me sometime in Fitzwilliam Square," said Liz to me. "I'd like to show you my house."

That Friday night was the first night I spent in the single-bed-sitter in Palmerston Road. I had gotten undressed and climbed into bed and was reading my book, propped on my chest, so neglected these past days because I couldn't clear my mind of— what? Anxiety? What was I worried about? I have a job now! Everything's going to be all right!

So I settled back to turn the page, so to speak—when the lights went out.

Welcome to your new life.

I fished around the pockets of my dungarees on the floor, but came up only with an octagonal-shaped ten-bob piece, no shillings. I still wasn't used to the money, and had to think twice, but I was out of luck and couldn't feed the meter. I shut the book and threw it on the floor. I lay back on Mrs McTeague's fresh-smelling pillow, thinking, with a ghastly light thrown through the one window by a streetlamp.

The next thing I knew it was bright daylight coming through that window.

I had no idea of the time. I felt so refreshed and unburdened that I thought I must have overslept by hours and hours. *This will never do, I'm going to have to get a wristwatch or something, I have to be on time for work Monday morning.*

I splashed cold water in my face from the sink in the room, but now that I wasn't in Mrs Warren's B&B any longer, where could I get washed up and shaved?

I went down the end of the hall outside and fortunately the bathroom was unoccupied. Someone coming out of their room gave me the time—almost noon! There was an old-fashioned tub, beige shower curtains suspended from a chrome ring in the air, towels on a shelf, even a medicine cabinet.

I used the toilet, took a shower, shaved, got dressed, got out of that depressing, tiny room, leaving my blue airlines bag and my shaving kit on the bed, grabbed my Dostoyevsky, and once outdoors, felt like a stamping thoroughbred, full of racing energy.

I'd had that great dinner of steak and potatoes the night before at Wynn's Hotel, and now I set out to do something I'd been putting off and putting off: *to live.* Yes, and to live in Dublin, which was a dream of mine. Wasn't it Mrs McTeague who said, just yesterday: *we all have our dreams—are you surprised?*

I suppose that when you are all tensed up and worried for a time you feel such a sense of relief, of release, when it's over, that it's like–being let out of the starting gate.

And it was all going to start today.

Because that job at Maurice Woolf Ltd. means that I'm going to be able to stay in Dublin. Permanently!

After grabbing a pot-pie lunch in a Madigan's in Ranelagh and swilling down a Guinness, which I now knew to be definitely an acquired taste, I set out for the city centre to find that necessary wristwatch, probably, I hoped, in Clery's or Roche's.

But first I had to stop in my same-old phonebox in Ranelagh Road and call down to Mayo again, so that I could bubble over again with Sheila, and give her my list of things to bring up to me in Dublin, especially clothes, and my copy of *War and Peace*, the book which was third on my list.

I swore eternal love and listed some of the things that we were going to do to each other when re-united, and I think she could catch the contagion of my excitement through the 150 miles of telephone wire.

Then it was the next No. 44 bus heading for the city centre I had to wait for.

The result was that it was somewhere between two and three in the afternoon, that Saturday, when I finally got to O'Connell Street, and what I saw there stopped me cold.

Countless numbers, a human multitude, covered the wide, open space between the pillars of the GPO and Clery's, across the street.

Uncountable thousands were jammed into the one city block between Abbey Street and Earl Street.

All traffic had been closed off, even my No. 44 bus had to be disembarked in the loop of Westmoreland and D'Olier Streets.

As I approached across the bridge, I could see distant figures sprawled, hanging, clinging, standing, sitting, on top of parked cars, on the base of Daniel O'Connell's statue, on the roofs of bus-shelters, dangling from lamp-posts. Every head was turned in the same direction, towards the tiny figures on the flatbed trailer in front of the GPO, heads and shoulders bobbing as they attempted to get a glimpse over the crowd in front of them—a sea of swinging buoys, a meadow of waving cornflowers.

I had been avoiding this scene, up till now.

Riding the buses, trying to focus on Help-Wanted, I could not avoid the headlines from the North.

I'd had no television or radio, but I only needed my own eyes to see what was going on, every single Saturday in O'Connell Street.

Now that I had that job, I need not turn my face away any longer, for fear of distracting myself from first things first.

So now I did approach the shores of the human ocean in O'Connell Street and tried to insinuate myself forward into the crowd, weaving my way as politely as I could, to get as close to the front as possible.

Loud-hailers hung from cornices and street-lamps, strung together with wires that quivered with every exhortation from the flatbed, and swayed with every shout from the audience.

A parade of speakers, testifying one by one, approached the lone mike-stand on the bare platform.

As I filtered my way forward, the tin murmur of the loud-hailers took on the distinctly hard-edged note of anger, the emphatic, ringing tone of indignation.

A woman introduced as Maire Drumm was speaking now.

"When the soldiers came, there was no polite knock at the door, but the butt of a British rifle." Her face was grim and hardened. Her voice was calm, measured, even. "When the door was broken down, there was no asking a mother's permission, but only the butt of an SLR in the back of your son's head."

I could feel the surge of a response coursing through the mass of people like an electric current as Maire Drumm went on.

"And when they finished wrecking your house, they were leaving with your husband, your brother, your neighbor, with no word of where they were taking him to, but only the echo of the British jackboot fading on the stair."

Her words were ripped by the wind from the loud-hailers, and they lashed the upturned faces of the crowd.

"They took my husband, and they took my son. They took a man who was seventy-seven years old. They took another man who was blind. They even arrested a dog—though no official statement has yet been released as to what crime the dog was committing at the time of his capture."

A man in the crowd called out. "Maybe he was pissing up against a Land Rover!"

Laughter rumbled in the belly of the crowd.

"No, he must have been carrying messages round his neck!" cried another.

Some else shouted, "Did he put the bite on a Brit? I hope he tore the bastard's leg off!"

As I melted further into the mass of the assemblage, I could feel myself becoming smaller, more absorbed, more molecular, like a drop of water in the river of humanity, sped along on the swift-bubbling current.

When the audience settled down, Maire Drumm spoke again.

"I am not the best one to tell you about what is going on behind the wire. Who can ever know the full extent or the complete results of the terrorizing of defenceless civilians, which we know is taking place? It may be years before we can even estimate it. But I can tell you from my own experience of the systematic terrorizing of the prisoners' families. Can anyone here imagine what it is like to phone round to government offices trying to locate where someone is being held, and to be shunted back and forth, from the Army to the RUC, and back again? Or to be told flat-out that under Special Powers, no reason need be given to you for the arrest of your loved one? Or to finally have your day in court when they will actually come up with charges, only to have the judge dismiss the charges, and the Army re-arrest the prisoner as he attempts to leave the courtroom? On what charges, sir? No charges, madam. Special Powers. Internment. But I have come here today with a message for you from the women of Belfast. I come to you today to say to the powers that be that we'll stand united with our husbands and brothers and sons. I come to you, as a mother, to say—No Surrender!"

I was now very near to the front, up close to a rank of army-jacketed men in black berets with dark glasses and folded arms, a bodyguard standing at ease in front of the flat-bed trailer. The crowd around me and behind me erupted into applause and cheering, vows of support, oaths of retaliation, as a man in a fur hat came forward to take Maire Drumm's elbow. I looked up to see a middle-aged housewife in a tweed jacket, with a corsage in her lapel: the Vice-President of the Belfast Sinn Fein. This was Maire Drumm.

She looked to me no different than a mother from Savin Hill in Dorchester whose son was brought home to her from Vietnam in a box accompanied by two US Marines.

Music burst on the air with militant trumpets blaring from the loud-hailers as I saw Maire Drumm's head disappear over the edge of the draped green-white-and-orange bunting on the rail of the trailer. Young ladies in green sashes were filtering through the packed crowd, collecting. I placed a nice fresh Irish five-pound note in the canister. I looked up to see a long-white banner, pinned to the pillars of the GPO, fluttering on every breeze, proclaiming in bold-faced green lettering:

JOIN THE REPUBLICAN MOVEMENT

Chapter 3

Pillars of the GPO

While Ranelagh still slept, I left Palmerston Road to meet Monday morning at the corner of Charleston Road. There was a bus shelter on Ranelagh Road itself only a few steps from Mrs McTeague's tobacconist's. The only residents awake were the pigeons and me. My new watch, with the leather band, so it wouldn't pinch the hairs on my wrist, worked well: you operated the alarm by pulling out the winding-wheel one notch. It was a Timex with a black face. I found it in a street-stall in Moore Street. Cost me almost four pounds, but that was better than the seven quid fifteen bob in Roche's Department Store. Anyway, I needed it. It was only half-six in the morning, but on my first day I had no way of knowing how long it would take to get to work by bus, only that I would have to go from here to the city centre and then transfer to a second bus.

It was foggy in Ranelagh Road, with only the occasional car racing through, with yellow fog-lights burning; or a bakery van, hurrying on. There was no queue at the bus-rank. Finally when I saw a sleek new No. 44 coming, I held out an open palm, as I'd seen the Dubliners do. I thought maybe if you didn't, even though you were standing at the bus-stop, they wouldn't stop for you: to each country their own practices.

The conductor blocked the aisle of the lower deck with his feet spread to keep his balance as the bus moved off. "City Centre?" he demanded. "6p."

At least I knew where to jump off, in D'Olier Street. Then I crossed over to Aston Quay to wait for a westbound bus. But I was impatient to get going on my first day, so I began to walk.

Pigeons wandered in the road, pecking at the pavement. Above the Liffey, seagulls whined under a mirthless overcast. A lorry loaded with empty chicken-crates rumbled past, heading back to the farm, white feathers eddying in its wake. Aston Quay. Rhymes with 'key,' I reminded myself, newcomer that I was. Wellington Quay. The towers of Christchurch Cathedral on the hill south of the river seemed to drift by backwards as I walked. Towers squat and browbeaten by centuries of clouds weighing on them. Merchant's Quay. Every time a bus passed me I was between stops. I was walking past an enormous housing estate, five stories, staggered around a central courtyard, the side facing me and the river solid rows of balconies. Usher's Quay seemed endless, but then, crossing Bridgefoot Street, I thought I'd gotten to Usher's Island Quay rather quickly, considering I was taking my time. Morning rush hour traffic heading for the city centre was rapidly increasing on the north side of the river. The doors of the numberless 38 looked locked. I checked the time, and it was only seven. Good. I made it an hour early. Only took a half hour from Ranelagh to here, even walking. I filed away my mental note.

There was nothing to do but to go visit the sweetshop on the corner. Fortunately, O'Rourke's was open. But I couldn't stay there because people kept rushing in to buy a packet of ten fags or 2 loose ones or a box of matches for 2p. It was too tiny, I was in the way. So I went back to my apron of tarmac, crossed to the quay wall, and hung over the stone to watch the Liffey proceeding to the sea while the gulls circled.

I was as nervous as my first day of college.

Finally, it was half-seven, and a green-back, canvas-covered lorry pulled off the quay road, reversing, tailgate-first, onto the apron outside the tall doors of Maurice Woolf, Ltd., forcing cars trying to pass to have to wait. The lorry-driver jumped down and turned his back to examine the rear tire.

Minding the traffic, now whizzing by, gathering speed for Kingsbridge and Kildare, I crossed over and sidled up between the stone wall and the lorry on the driver's side.

"Who's that! Jumpin' Jesus, you nearly scairt me to death!"

It was Wee Willie, the giant, bent now to the half-door, his corduroy coat cocking up over his backside, baring the crack of his arse, and a genuine fright blushing on the bare face turned to look back over his shoulder.

"Sorry," I said. "I didn't mean to creep up on you."

"Well, you did. And me mum says a driver has to be mighty careful these days with all the hijackers and all that lot about." The big man turned back to his work on the pad-locked half-door. "Poor mum. She hasn't a clue, has she? She's never out of the house, is she? But she reads the papers, she does. I don't mind. As long as I gets me porridge on these cold mornings."

From inside the half-door, he stuck his head back out. "She's always nagging me about the job, you know? Willie, says she, it's no job for the likes of you, lad. But they like me here. They've even let me drive the lorry. Oh, I don't take it down the country, sure, I don't. It's only the city lorry. But Needlenose has even let me to open up Monday mornings. And I can take the lorry home nights, too, any time I like. You wouldn't want to leave it in here in the bay weekends, now would you? You wouldn't find it again, come Monday morning. Well—are you comin' in?"

"Thanks." I stepped in over the high door-ledge. Inside, pitch dark.

"You can help me un-latch the doors, if you like.

We walked the big garage doors back to the stone walls on either side of the apron and Wee Willie reversed his rig into the lorry bay before we then shut the big doors again, slipping in the dead-bolts to lock them.

Then Willie came back round the lorry to me in the dark. "This is the best time of the day," he sighed, feeling his way along the darkened windows of the manager's booth. "With nobody about, I go round switching on all the lights, and then I go into Needlenose's office to fix his tea for him on his old electric plate. He likes his tea first thing, he does." The big man reached inside the office wall and flipped the light-switch. "There. Now we can see. You won't tell him I called him Needlenose, will you? All the lads do, but only behind his back."

Lakes of light splashing across the tunnel of the factory, up one wall of the narrow laneway and back down the other to the office again, as Willie hit the switches. "Come in, come in," he said. He sat in the manager's swivel-chair and threw his big hob-nail boots up on the makeshift plywood desk. There were holes in the soles, the toes flapped, and the rain had the black uppers stained with whitish aureoles. "Fancy me as the gaffer," said he, striking a pose. "Wait'll you see him. 'It's a disaster.' That's his favorite saying. Needlenose, we call him. A pin'll drop, and it's a disaster. We'll be short a foot of twine, and it's a disaster. Every minute, a bleedin' disaster. Of course, if he heard us callin' him Needlenose, we'd be for it. Many's the lad he's sacked for less. No Needlenose for him. Mister Sugarman, if you please. They all do it, though, behind his back. Fancy a cup of tea, then?"

"I won't get you in trouble?"

"But for me, he'd never clean it," said Wee Willie, getting busy over the kettle and spooning in the loose tea.

Folding my arms, I leaned back on my ass, half-on the edge of the desk.

"What do they make here, Willie?"

"Oh—beds, you know? Mattresses and the like. Pillows, cushions, all sorts of things. What job are you takin,' anyway?"

"Dispatch Controller, Needlenose said."

"You'll be my gaffer then."

"Well—you'll have to show me the ropes."

"I will, I will."

"Good. Thank you."

"Are we to be friends, then?"

"I don't see why not?"

"You don't?" Two empty teacups filling his hands, Willie leaned his head over. "Do you think I'm daft?"

"Do you think I know how to drive that big lorry there?" said I. "I don't. But it's nothing to you. A man that can handle a lorry like that isn't daft, is he?"

"Ah—wait'll mum hears." Willie turned back to the kettle's whistle. "Don't take long, do it?"

A heavy rapping shook the double-doors, all the way down the tunnel, echoing up to us in Noel Sugarman's office.

"Ah—there they are." Willie handed me his cup and bundled himself out the door. The impatient rapping sounded the end to his quiet time.

I blew on my tea and put his down on the desk. Then the dark-looking skinhead with the black eyebrows I'd noticed on Friday passed the office without looking up.

"Who's that, Willie," I asked him when he came back in.

"That's Malachi. He's mad, is Malachi. Mad Malachi Morgan. He's the divil that gets them all started."

"Started?"

"You know what I mean. I have me work to do, but there's them that loves mischief."

"What's wrong with him this morning?"

"Only the same as always. Off his form, that's all. He doesn't fancy it here a bit. Thinks he's too clever for the likes of us. You don't know him—but mind yourself. He's up, he's down, he's all around. Great with you now, and then it's daggers drawn. Some days he can't leave off slaggin' me, till it's a mercy to get the lorry loaded and be off. I used get the same at school, and didn't I leave some of them wishin' they'd kept their gobs shut?"

The rapping came again, more measured this time, and Willie went for the door. He wore a sense of his role the way the porter at Wynn's Hotel wore his epaulets. This time it was the young fellow with the spiked hair-do, and he nodded to me through the glass as he went up.

"That was Tony Daugherty," Willie said. "He's all right. Quite the bloke. There's worse than him. The Larkin brothers. You'll see. Did you know, I'm older than the lot of them? Thirty-two I am. I'm the oldest one in it, only old Susan, and Higginbotham, of course—I'm older even than old Needlenose himself. Did you enjoy your tea?"

"I did, Willie, thanks."

"I must be off now and say hello to the lads. Will you come?"

"No, I think I'd better wait here. My first day and everything."

"Cheerio, then." Willie paused a moment in the doorway. "I'm glad we're to be friends. But I don't know your name."

"You can call me Nick, Willie."

"Very good, Mister Nick. Funny name, that."

My first day, I was on time, but Mr. Sugarman was not.

"Monday morning," he said. "First disaster of the week. Well—could be worse. At least you're here on time."

As he struggled out of his raincoat, the sleeves caught on his pointed elbows. I reached over to help him.

"Thanks very much." He was slithering into the grease-stained smock that was thrown over the top of the hat-stand in the corner, one sleeve off, one sleeve on. "Wait here, now. I'll be back in a jiff."

I watched as he raced up the floor. There was something frenetic about his movements, nervous energy spent in ten directions at once. Higginbotham was in the midst of meticulously straightening his own coat and cap and umbrella on his personal hat-stand. Sugarman heaped him with a torrent of questions while Higginbotham continued his methodical methods unperturbed. Though I couldn't hear them, I caught the bemused smile creep over Higginbotham's lips: he's telling him my name—Sugarman forgot it. Calmly, the older man buttoned up his Monday-morning freshly-white-laundered smock. While Sugarman dashed back to me, Higginbotham merely lifted his chin—and the people in Assembly, recognizing this as their signal to 'Start-Up,' shifted places and drifted to their machines.

"Right, Nick—come on out with you. I'm only showing this to you the one time. Oh, bleeding hell."

Sugarman jogged back to Assembly and returned with a half-dozen plastic-sheathed, bunkbed-sized mattresses balanced precariously on his shoulder so that he listed as he ran. "That's Assembly Department over there, and our area down here is the Dispatch Department—in the back?—that I call the Disaster Area."

Between the lorry bay and the Assembly floor, there was an open area the width of the laneway. This was where the peaked roof of the lorry bay ended and horizontal rafters began. Over these, all the way back to the Disaster Area, a tubular corrugated-tin covering, similar to a quonset hut roof, closed out the sky. Here the metal bunk-bed frames that Wee Willie collected from Pearse Street were stacked on end against the left wall. The bare macadam was flanked on the right with shelving and a giant triangle-legged steel frame holding a roll of six-foot-long, 25-lb-weight brown wrapping paper, slung on a steel bar across the top.

Sugarman flung down the mattresses on the Dispatch floor. Their plastic coverings were only two colors, pink and blue. They were stamped with colorful cartoon-like teddy-bears, sail-boats, fire-engines, little girls in pinafores, cherub-cheeked blue-eyed boys in sailor suits. Sugarman grabbed the paper from the roll and spun it out across the floor, reaching to a shelf for a utility-knife. A ball of thick, prickly twine was suspended in a housing that hung from the rafters on a chain. When Sugarman yanked the twine, the ball spun inside the housing, and yards of the stuff came spiralling down in a heap.

With the knife clenched in his teeth, Sugarman measured out twine. He snapped it off with a stab of the blade at waist-level. The twine was tough, and took cutting. "All last week I had no-one for this job but that useless Bermingham who drives the lorry. He was so slow and tedious. And how could he be driving when he had to be packing? I'm back-logged with orders due delivery since Tuesday a week—a bona-fide disaster if ever I saw one."

Now the nervous, bird-like spring in his bow-legged body flew into form as Sugarman, wrestling with the brown paper and the shifting, six-ply mound of mattresses, tied his bundle, swiftly, surely and precisely. "I've timed this, you know. Thirty seconds. Bundles of six, four, eight. A dozen is a bit much. Ever tie any knots?"

"Sure," I lied.

"Best to tie just one knot—a slip-knot—just one knot, till you wrap up at the end and tie off. Just pass it over and under, the whole package comes out tight as a drum, because the tension of every loop is tugging on the tension of every other. Counter-balanced, you see? Ingenious, actually, when you think of it—bleeding hell, I should've been an engineer. Now you try it."

I took five minutes to produce a bundle, shabby and loose, with none of the famous tension.

Sugarman re-tied it for me and pointed. "Those stacks there, behind Clare's machine? I want you to start with the order for Clery's in Galway City."

All morning I struggled. Sugarman, in his swivel-chair, inside the manager's booth, with his knees up against the plywood desk, with the telephone receiver plastered to his head, shuffling papers, messing his greasy black hair with worrying fingers, looked out occasionally and frowned, but he never said a word to me. He was locked in mortal combat with his own nemeses. Just before lunch-time, he surrendered.

"The first shipment is to be out the door in the lorry by ten every morning. The second run is to be gone no later than two, to allow Willie to get to the city stores by five." Sugarman ran his hands over his head. "Sorry, man, it's not your fault, is it? It seems they're fed up with excuses in P-Street. When we don't make our deadline there, they can't make their shipments out to the country towns. Not to worry, Nick They all start like this. I'd be surprised if you hadn't the knack by the end of the week. Tomorrow, I'll show you how to do the bunks."

Sugarman patted my shoulder. "Have your lunch, lad."

He returned to his office, brooding and preoccupied.

"Tea up!" It was Wee Willie Bermingham, calling me, waving me over.

Mr. Higginbotham was coming down the aisle between the edge-stitching benches, and he nodded. "Looks like they're expecting you, eh?" he said kindly. "Mr. Sugarman and myself take our lunch in the office, and you're welcome to join us. But you'll have to get introduced to them sometime."

I could see Sugarman pulling a banana out of a brown paper bag. "Everyone eats in?"

"You have half an hour."

The rank and file employees of Maurice Woolf, Ltd. had their own electric kettle perched on a board over the fuse-box on the wall. As I approached, Susan Drummond was passing out the tea. She was a middle-aged housewife from the Oliver Bond Council Flats, round the back of Woolf's in Island Street. A mother with six children and no husband at home, and when she came to work, she mothered them on the job, too. Malachi Morgan and Tony Daugherty came from the Oliver Bond, and Clare Nelligan, as well. But Pascal Larkin and his brother Eddie came from the Mt. Pleasant Flats, over behind Benburb Street, on the north side of the Liffey. Wee Willie Bermingham and his mother lived in Phibsboro, in the North Side, and Con Lenihan was a country man from the midlands.

Con was lying full-length across some wooden bins filled with foam scraps, his head on his arm and his eyes closed. Tony was sitting on a throne of cushions with his back against the wall, eating a sandwich while he leafed through a copy of Melody Maker. Clare sat on one of the edger tables, her legs crossed at the ankles, swinging them absent-mindedly while she chewed her lunch. Malachi, the dark-haired one with the earring, paced.

"Look lads, it's the new Dispatcher."

"What's this, the welcoming committee?"

"Yeah, welcome to the lower classes. What do you think, lads?"

"Looks green to me," said Tony, without looking up from his Melody Maker.

"Shall we learn him, then?"

Clare laughed. "Malachi'll school ye."

"That he will," said Con, drowsily. "He'll wash you behind the ears."

"Go back to sleep, plough-boy. Do you think he could pot one, cross-corner, Tony?"

"Time will tell, time will tell."

Susan Drummond said, "Pay them no heed, young fella. Their bark is worse than their bite. Have you any cup?"

"I haven't," I said, slipping into the lingo, which I was doing more and more. I suppose it came from my time in Mayo, where I was surrounded with the local way of expressing things, but I also practiced my skills as a mimic, just for the hell of it, and because I thought I had a talent for it. In any case, I'd been picking it up by imitating my wife Sheila for about five years now, hadn't I?

"You'll have to bring your own cup if you want some of our tea," said Susan.

"Lesson number one," said Malachi. "And five bob a week into the jar, for provisions. That is, if you're going to have your tea with us, and not them. The last Dispatcher before you was stand-offish like that. Wouldn't consider associating with the riff-raff."

Wee Willie interjected. "You can use my cup for today, Nick."

"So that's your name," said Malachi.

"My mother gave me that name, yes."

"Did she? We heard you was a foreigner."

"I am."

"Have you noticed the rise in foreigners landing in Dublin lately, lads, looking for work? When they got word the snakes had left Ireland, they came to apply for the job."

Pascal Larkin sniggered, and Malachi walked around me with a sneering swagger. Pascal said, "Maybe he thinks this is one of Forte's cafes."

"Give over, youz," Wee Willie blurted, " and don't you start on him, Malachi."

"It's all right, Willie. Malachi's just saying hello."

"That's right," said he. "Just getting acquainted, like. You're in good company here, mister. Higgie, he's a native, but Sugarman's a bleedin' hiney. You're safer by far with the likes of us. That is, if we let ye. But tell us—what's a bloke like you doing in a kip like this anyway?"

"I was down in Mayo collecting turf in the bog. This is a step up."

"A step up, says he. Didja hear that, Connie? A step up from the bog, says he. What have I been telling you?"

"Shut up, you dirty jackeen, I'm trying to rest."

"That's Connie," said Malachi. "You can take the peasant from the soil you know, but you can never take the soil from the peasant. This over here is Tony—when he isn't looking at the papers, he's rolling them and smoking them. That over there is Clare. Show us your knickers, Clare."

"Go frig yourself, Malachi."

"I leave that low behavior to the likes of you, love. Them two, over there, that's the Larkins, Pascal and Eddie, specimens of the type produced by St Columcille's Grammar School. Tell us your letters, Pascal."

"I can't read," said Pascal, staring impassively at his dirty fingernails.

"And there you have it," said Malachi. "The Den of the Woolf."

"And you're Malachi."

"And I'm Malachi."

I held out my hand. "Where I come from, it's customary to shake hands with a new friend."

Malachi looked at the proferred hand. "Let's get one thing straight. I run this kip. No matter what Sugarman thinks—or what he tells you."

I said, "See the Dispatch floor down there? Looks to me like it's halfway between the office and here. That's where I'll be."

I still offered my hand, but Malachi hesitated. I said, "Fair enough?"

"Fair enough, Malachi," said Tony.

"What are you afraid of, Malachi?" said Pascal, sitting up in his bin.

"Shut up, you fookin' eedjit." He took my hand to shake, and added "I'll have an eye out for you."

Susan Drummond handed me some lukewarm tea in Willie's cracked mug. Pascal Larkin jumped up, saying "Time for a fag." He pulled a packet of ten Majors from the tight breast-pocket of his thin pullover, and offered one to me.

I didn't want to refuse, even if I didn't smoke. They didn't know that. And I figured I'd had enough practice inhaling pot back home to pull it off.

"Bend your head," said Pascal. "We can't let Higginbotham catch us at this."

"Youz are going to set this factory afire one day," said Susan Drummond.

"Shut up, Mammy," said Pascal. "Don't I hear it at home enough?"

"Not near enough, not near. You could do with more work and less carry-on yourself, Pascal."

"Tell him he's too young to smoke, mister, why don't you?" said Clare.

"How old are you?" I asked Pascal, who was definitely stunting his growth with cigarettes.

"Old enough, old enough."

"He's twelve," said Malachi.

"I'm not. I'm fourteen."

"He's twelve years old," said Susan, "and his brother over there is nine."

"But Sugarman thinks I'm fourteen, and don't none of youz go grass on me." Pascal looked at me. "Best place for a fag is in the jacks, mister. Malachi—show him your libary."

They took me down the back, which faced out onto Island Street. In the back it was dark and lightless, the fluorescents didn't reach back there, and it was piled with the shadows of big bulky blocks of foam rubber pads stacked alongside ramshackle shelving, with a walkway to the rear door in between: Sugarman's Disaster Area, obviously. Malachi pulled open a door in the wall. "The jacks."

An odor of stale urine washed out. Inside, there was room for a man to stand and aim, or a woman to sit with her knees jammed up against the closed door.

Malachi reached up to a ledge over the top of the WC box and pulled down a dog-eared copy of the London Daily Mirror. "Look at that," he said, turning to a photo-page of a leggy model reclining in a haystack, with the caption 'Sighful Eyefull.' "Tuppence a day if you want a wank."

"Here comes Higgy," called Pascal Larkin. "Douse them butts."

Five o'clock on my first day couldn't came fast enough. I cursed my new writstwatch because now I kept looking at it. I was tired and dying to quit but I kept it up while the others filed past me for the half-door. Malachi nudged Tony. "He's a worker, not a fookin' lurker."

Finally, they were gone. Willie Bermingham had returned from his two o'clock run by half-four and parked the lorry inside the locked doors, safe enough on a weeknight, it was thought. Higginbotham waved goodnight to me with his brelly as he passed. I pulled on my cap and went to the office door. "Need me for anything else, Mr Sugarman?"

He was scribbling under a desklamp that held down a wad of receipts. He looked up. "Eh? No, lad."

"See you in the morning."

He turned back to his figures, rubbing his temple as if he had a headache.

Outside, Pascal Larkin and his brother were sitting on the ground together, backs up against the wall of the lane.

"Aren't you two going home?"

Nine-year-old Eddie Larkin looked up and said, "What for?"

That evening, in Ranelagh Road, Mrs McTeague said, "And you're leaving me without so much as any notice? I wouldn't mind, but you could give me a week."

"I'd gladly stay. But it's so small."

"Nevermind. How am I going to let it on a Monday now, tell me that."

As sweetly as I could, I said, "Oh, Mrs McTeague, can you blame me?"

"I never believed you were the single-bedsitter type. Well— if you've a fancy to make it up to me—?"

"Ask me. Anything."

"I've a friend with a double-bedsitter in Harold's Cross. Not far from here, it is, in fact. She's having a terrible time of it finding a lodger to suit herself. I could recommend you."

"Would you? You're a darling."

"You'd be doing me the favor. Shut the old thing up for once."

"God bless you, missus."

"Go on wid-ja."

Aughrim Lane was a sheltered back-street, a block behind the dingy centre of Harold's Cross. A lone, stunted evergreen gave the lane its dubiously countrified look. I didn't know what to make of Harold's Cross. A tiny green, shabby-looking, and a greyhound race-track seemed the only attractions. It was definitely a cut or two or three below Ranelagh. No. 27, she said. Mrs. McCroomb, she said. In a gap between single-story red-brick row-houses, I could see vacant fields, overgrown, leading down to the Grand Canal and over to the Mount Jerome Cemetery.

As I stood there gazing, out of the corner of my eye I could see the corner of a curtain moving in the house next door.

A moment later, a door opening, at the back, and a woman, as formidable as a stone wall, came waddling down the brick walk. "Yoo-hoo! Is it you Mrs. McTeague sent? Come along, young man. I prefer a young man. Less trouble than an old man. Are you spliced? That's good. I prefer a young man kept out of mischief. Nose to the grindstone. You're not on the dole, I presume. Employed? That's good. This now—" Mrs. McCroomb slapped the porch-rail of a wooden house—"was once the master's hunting lodge, smoking rooms, and valet's quarters. He used retire here himself to get out of the way of the women in the house. Clever he was, that man. This place has history."

She led me down a musty hall dank with the odor of history, and soaked wood. "Two double-bedsitters, one either side.

Both presently unoccupied. Due to the difficulty of finding suitable tenants, mind you. You can have this one."

She flung open an unlocked door. This room, too, had history. It looked like a tent and it smelled like a campsite. A kitchenette, a fireplace and grate, and a naked chimney. Tall grass tickling the glass from outside the windows. "Two windows, two beds, two chairs, one cooker, one sink, one light, loo down the hall," said Mrs. McCroomb. "Double-bedsitter! When will you and the missus move in?"

"Well, I don't know, Mrs. McCroomb—there's the kid, too —and—." I was trying to look doubtful, leading up to saying 'no, it's not for us'—when she came out with—.

"No kids."

"What?"

"Don't allow them."

"You don't allow them!"

"Can't have them. They make noise. Husband's an invalid—."

"She's two years old, Mrs. McCroomb. She sleeps all night."

"You and your wife's all right, but no children."

"She's a little girl. Polite and well-behaved."

"That's none of my concern."

I did not like the tone this woman was taking with me. "But she has to stay with us, Mrs. McCroomb."

"Oh-ho, so now you think of these things, young man—it's one thing having them, but where are you going to put them, eh?"

"I'll take it, missus." My ire was up. "How much is it?"

Mrs. McCroomb fumed stoutly with her hand on the doorknob.

"Must I go up to Harold's Cross and ring the authorities, Mrs. McCroomb?"

"Ring the–! Who do you think you're dealing with!"

What I was really worried about, suddenly, was the idea that I might find some kind of 'no-children' rule to be rampant in this city. After all, so far, I'd stayed in a B&B, and a room for a single guy. I hadn't looked for accommodations for a family. With my new job to worry about, I didn't want extra, unforeseen hassles. What if I couldn't get Sheila and 'The Child' up to Dublin for another–God knows—a month? I was taking a stand now—after all she had two unoccupied bedsitters—and no wonder. I held out my open wallet. "Do you want the money, or not?"

"Five quid a week!" she spat out. "In advance."

I put a single five-pound note on the sink.

"Better count that. You don't want to be cheated."

"I'm ringing the police! I'll have you evicted, and you haven't moved in yet!"

I sat down in one of the two chairs. "I'm not budging. I'm paid up."

"I'll hang that McTeague! Sent me a bleedin' squatter, she did!"

Sunday finally came, and the sky was a grey towel hung out over Dublin to dry.

I'd survived my first week at Maurice Woolf, Ltd. without setting any bunk-bed mattresses on fire or hanging myself with twine, but towards the end I was badly in need of something to look forward to, so, why not, I called down to Mayo and told Sheila I missed them so much I just had to have her and Aisling come up to Dublin and re-unite our little family.

As this was our plan all along, and it was only waiting on me to find the job, I was hoping Sheila was as excited about the prospect as I was. But I had my misgivings. Wouldn't Sheila find Mrs McCroomb's servant-quarters as distasteful as I did myself?

So my mood rather matched the grey sky that arrived on Sunday, when I went out to Kingsbridge to the railway station that served all the country to the west of Dublin.

People still called it Kingsbridge Station, as they did the neighborhood, Kingsbridge. That was from long habit, but in 1966, the year of the 50th anniversary of the Easter Rising, the year the IRA blew up Nelson's Pillar in O'Connell Street, the authorities thought it finally much more appropriate to remove the old British royal family connotations of Kingsbridge Station, and so it was renamed Heuston Station, after Sean Heuston, one of the martyrs of 1916, a railwayman from Limerick who'd been executed by firing squad in Kilmainham Gaol after holding out in the Mendicity Institute against the overwhelming odds of the advancing British Army for a full two-and-a-half days, with only 26 men, after they were ordered to hold it, at most, for 3 to 4 hours.

All this could be read on the plaque outside the old British-built railway station (as I say, I will read anything that will stand still long enough.) Like the GPO, like the Four Courts, like Kilmainham, Heuston Station looked exactly as it did in 1916. No doubt Maurice Woolf, Ltd., jerry-built as it was into a medieval laneway, was a lot more recent than this was.

Inside, the shutters of the newspaper kiosk were drawn and padlocked. I paced up and down past empty benches; the lavatory doors, 'Fir' and 'Ban,' which I must have read fifty times; a line of ancient wooden hand-propelled luggage carts on iron-rimmed wheels. A waiting train was parked at a platform across the rails. It had two engines, one at the front of the train, one at the back. This train was always facing two ways. This train could shuttle across the country, from Dublin to Cork, or Limerick, or Galway City, and without turning around, come back again. This train. I could hear the electric engine idling, warming up, and blue sparks spitting from the contacts of the diamond-folding trolley-carriage raised up to the power-lines overhead, above the westward-facing engine.

On the western horizon, late in the afternoon, a black point moved. It crawled. Slowly it grew to the size of a water-drop on the tip of a sickle, the curving arc of the rail line. They're here! Gradually, the train itself materialized, at first, a lengthening apparition, with a sound like a teletype in another room. The rhythm of the tack-tack-tack grew steadier till it was a line of prose. From the concrete beneath my feet came a growing brittle vibration. The voice of the train from Castlebar growled. It slid into the station a howl of grinding steel.

At the far end of the platform, I could see Sheila coming down the steps of the coach, struggling with a large blue folding case and two more suitcases, Aisling clinging to her back with her arms thrown around her mother's neck.

I hurried towards her against the flow of the disembarking passengers, weekenders, and foreign visitors. "Boy, are you two a sight for sore eyes. Here, let me help you, Sheila."

She let me drag the folding case from her hand. "What a trip."

"I'm so glad to see you."

"Oh, aye, lovely to be here. I'll never ride the CIE again. Not even a clean toilet. Next time I'll thumb the lift."

"Hi, Aisling! How's my baby?" I put down the case. "Boy, did I miss you! Come here and let me hold you."

"Don't, Nick."

"What's the matter, honey?"

"Stopped in every station from Roscommon to Longford to Athlone to God knows where—and her, looking out the window for you. Are we there yet? I could've crossed the whole of the USA in the time it took us to get here—five hours."

On the No. 18 bus to Harold's Cross, after we changed from the 91B to the city centre, Aisling fell asleep on her mother's shoulder. "Wouldn't you know it," said Sheila. After I tried and tried to get her to take a nap on the train. It's the excitement, Nick, she's worn out."

After a bit, while I kept mum, seeing how haggard they both were, Sheila said, "What's this place, Harold's Cross, like?"

The dread question. It suddenly struck me like a cave-in that I had been up to Dublin for some weeks, but Sheila had never been there in her life, even though she grew up in Ireland. She had been in Boston long before she'd ever thought of coming here. In fact, but for me, she wouldn't be coming here at all, if her own words were to be believed, as she had no interest in it whatsoever, and before ever setting one little toe in it, had been told all her life that it was nothing but the stamping grounds of the Dublin jackeen, a form of life lower than earthworms.

I sighed and said, "Harold's Cross is just like the country. You wouldn't know it's in the city at all. I think you'll like it, Sheila."

She did not. When we stepped off the bus across from the tall wooden gates of the greyhound track, closed, it being Sunday, a day of worship for the pious, God-fearing Dublin jackeen, I could feel her face fall; I didn't need to look.

A grim silence ensued as I pulled the folding case on wheels and the two jam-packed suitcases down Aughrim Lane, with Sheila following behind.

When we opened the door to Mrs. McCroomb's double-bedsitter, she finally spoke.

"Nicky—this is horrid."

"I didn't think you'd like it."

"This will never do."

"It's not exactly 104 Queensberry Street, is it?"

"Where does one sit down? I'd be afraid to."

"I had to get a furnished flat, didn't I?" I said, lamely.

"It looks infested. It smells dilapidated. I'd be afraid to sleep in it in case I'd wake up and find myself crawling with vermin." Sheila went to the sink under the window. "Look at this."

Admittedly, ugly rust had corroded the sink's wan, at-one-time white, enamel, in a straight line from the faucet to the drain. Holding the sleeping child awkwardly, Sheila bent her knees to open the oven door in the cooker. "Am I supposed to cook in this? How am I ever to clean it?"

I sat down glumly. "It's a start."

"We're not stopping here, I'll tell you that!" Sheila paced back and forth, jiggling the sleeping child on her shoulder nervously.

"Come on, Sheila."

"I'd be afraid to put the baby down to sleep for fear I'd wake up and find her gnawed by rats."

"Don't be ridiculous."

"Who's ridiculous? We're in my country now and I'll talk whatever way I want."

"Will you stop?"

"I won't. There—now you've done it—you've waked the child."

"Give her to me."

"Leave her alone."

"Just give her to me, Sheila. Let her go. I don't want to argue. I don't want to fight."

"You're a fine father that wants his child now that I've dragged her clear across Ireland to you! Where were you these last weeks, when she wanted you?"

Aisling was beginning to crumble her face into scowling red tears, and to wail, and I put her down, fearful that she was going to commit Mrs. McCroomb's child-violation No. 1—making noise. "I'll tell you where I've been. Walking the streets to find a job so we could get back together, that's where I've been."

"We were happy down in Mayo—weren't we?" Sheila's face began to dissolve into tears.

I threw my hands up. "Sheila! There was no way I could've stayed down on the farm, free-loading on your family."

Aisling kicked me a wallop in the right shin. "Don't you be cross with my mam!"

I went hopping around the room. "Ow, ow, ow."

Mrs. McCroomb came running in, without knocking. "What're these ructions I hear going on?"

Aisling had planted her foot, crossed her arms, and stuck her chin out at me. "I'm not great with you any longer, Daddy. So there."

Between tears, as she picked up the child, Sheila pointed out to Mrs. McCroomb, one mother to another, "She's an awful case of the terrible twos."

On the Monday, at work, it began to sink in to me how Mr. Sugarman's view of things could well be contagious: a disaster a day, a day, a disaster. Nor did the dim clouds wear away by the time I got home to the disaster of Harold's Cross. But in Aughrim Lane, as I went up under the overhanging evergreen, to the inevitable curtain-corner lifting in Mrs. McCroombs's window, I was surprised to find the pleasant smell of cooking coming through the dank hall from our flat.

"What's this?" I said, as I went in.

"I thought you might be hungry after all day on the job," said Sheila, "so I kept it warm for you in the oven."

I didn't know what to say and stood there like the proverbial amadaun.

"Come sit down before it's gone cold."

I pulled out a chair and looked at the plate. "What is it?"

"Liver and fries. Your favorite."

Now she was joking and I knew she was great with me again. "What happened to spaghetti and meatballs?"

"Where am I going to find parmesan cheese in Dublin, love?"

"I don't know. Where did you find this?"

"A butcher-shop in Harold's Cross. The liver looked so red and juicy." Sheila sat down and took up her knife and fork. "Are you not hungry, Nick?"

"Where's Aisling?"

"Playing out the back. I fed her. I just wanted us to have a nice supper, our first night in Dublin."

"So does that mean she's great with me, too?"

"That's up to herself entirely. I know. Last night. Ganged up on you, didn't we? I was rotten, I know, but it was all the fault of the CIE and their banjaxed trains. Wait'll I tell you my news, now. But, oh—how was your day, love?"

"Sheila—don't ask."

"That bad? Oh, I'm sorry."

"Mm. This is actually good. Thank you."

"Well, Aisling and me have had a busy day. And our troubles will soon be over. We'll be in our new flat by Thursday."

"Sheila—what have you done?"

"It was that biddy, that land-lady, Nick, what's her name?"

"Mrs. McCroomb."

"Aye. As soon as you left this morning, she started in. I told that man of yours, says she, like that, I wanted no children in it. That's all I had to hear. But she couldn't stop there, you know. I don't think you two are married at all, at all, says she—spying the gold band gone from my finger. How could I tell her that I lost it down the sink, that time I went to wash it? Remember, in our house in Duncan Park? I'm not going to divulge my personal business to the likes of her. I declare, I made up my mind then and there. I don't know how I'll put up with her for even two days more."

"Poor baby. Come here."

Sheila came round the table and was sitting in my lap with her arms round my neck when Mrs McCroomb walked in. "Here, now, have you two a license for that sort of behavior?" The landlady had a frightened Aisling by the hand. "I found this little wanderer unattended in the back garden," she sniffed.

"Back garden," said Sheila. "That weed-patch would choke a goat where I come from."

"I know Culchies haven't any manners, but you could ask me in."

"You are in, missus," I said. "You let yourself in. And you can let yourself out the same way."

"Poor neglected thing," Mrs. McCroomb cooed as she let go of Aisling. "Have they fed you today, lovey?" Sheila snatched up the child, and the fat lady waddled further into the room. "I wouldn't say no to a cup of tea, now."

"You've had all you're getting from me," Sheila said, "and in advance."

"'Twasn't you paid me–'twas himself. Where were you gone all the day long, by the way?"

"I don't believe it's any of your concern," said Sheila.

"You can have our notice, missus," I added. "We'll be out of here by Thursday, isn't that right, Sheila?"

"Nevertheless, your week in advance is non-refundable. We have laws in Dublin, young man, laws for the likes of you. It's a civilized place, not the Wild West."

"A civilized place, is it?" I said. "Where landlords won't let a flat to a father with kids? Where a married man's wages is a standard seventeen quid a week? Where the law blinks at the practice of child labor? Yes, Mrs McCroomb, don't look shocked. Child

labor—here in Dublin—in the year of our lord, nineteen-hun-
dred-and-seventy-one."

Dublin was changing all the days of that week in the factory.
My outburst of Monday evening told me that I was still the
self-righteous campus radical I had been, dating back to Nixon's
Cambodian invasion, and before. Yes, I thought—that must
be when it all crystallized, and became, more or less, permanent. Now it seemed a creeping familiarity was coming over the
streets as the bus-wheels droned on through my daily commute.
A sameness spread over the shopwindows, bicycles, pedestrians,
stop-lights, bill-boards, statues. No longer was Dublin the
ancient and noble dame of varied visages, who tempted the
traveller, and the mental voyager, with her seductive charms.
Routine had stripped away her glamour, and the workaday life
settled over me with the drag of drabness. This is what it all
comes down to: to spend the days of your natural life in the
artificial night in the windowless laneway. After six years in the
ivory tower, now I was confronting the world as it is, as it was
back home in Milltown, as it was in Mayo, as it is now, in the
real Dublin. And the world didn't suit me.

Dublin changed. Her features grew wizened, whittled, mean.
She took on the aspect of an old hag, the sow who ate her own
farrow. Woolf. *Un*limited. My disillusionment was devastatingly
swift and total.

I told Sheila, "I want you to do something for me. Help me
find a better job. Help me keep those letters going out, watch
for my replies in the mailbox, make sure I don't slack off. Buy
the papers for me, so I can follow the want-ads. This thing at
Maurice Woolf's gotta be just a temporary stepping stone, just
to get us started again. If only I could catch on somewhere as a

teacher or something, and get to use my education, we could be so much better off, honey."

But I had little time now for wishes, regrets or disaffection. I was up to my neck in labels, addresses, routes, schedules, forms, tight packaging, counter-balanced tensions, loading the lorry, first off, last in.

My refuge, as always, was in books. I didn't miss television, especially the wasteland of TV in America: I hadn't watched it for the six years I'd spent in campus libraries and classrooms. I didn't miss the radio, even the radio we had in Mayo. And we had neither radio nor TV now, nor would we, on my present wages. But Dublin was full of bookshops and libraries. I had finished my Dostoevsky and I was now ready to plunge into Tolstoy. If I wasn't people-watching on the buses, I had that novel by my side, *War and Peace.* In the evenings, well, Sheila knew me, and she had Aisling. And I had my book.

"It's a sorry way to get out of the rain in an Irish town," Malachi Morgan commented one morning, as he stepped into the lorry-bay of Woolf's, dripping from head to foot. "To stop into your local British factory for shelter, I mean. Or didn't you know—Maurice Woolf, he's one of you lot, a fookin' foreigner. Look at this place. That's what you get from your fookin' absentee landlord—and a fookin' kike Englishman he is, too, to top it off. Don't look at me like that. I'm not making any profits out of this Hole of Calcutta."

Ignorance was innocence, to me, when Ireland was a mere name on a map, when the picture I had of it was drawn by Lady Augusta Gregory. Now I was learning the meaning of discontent. The discontent of the uneducated lower classes. And, remarkably, lack of opportunity did not stunt their minds. If anything, I was finding out that the average Irish person who went no further than secondary school, if that, people like my brother-in-law Patrick Blake, or, yes, people like that self-made proletarian, Malachi Morgan, were up on their history, had a grasp of what's what, politically-speaking, in a way I had never encountered back in the States. What was it? Was it centuries of oppression from foreign conquerors who instilled a native indignation that was passed down by word of mouth from hand to hand inside families for the last eight centuries since Strongbow invaded? Was it the naked oppression of feeling oneself lower-class in a society striped by class divisions, in a way that could be ignored or forgotten in egalitarian America—unless you happened to be black? My God. Yes. That's what Malachi Morgan is. In the eyes of the British investing class, he's the Irish nigger.

I hate this. That's what they taught us in school: to hate. Well. I hate pretty good. I hate very well. One of the things I do best. And I'm their product. Oh, I tried to get out. I tried to go to college to get out of spending my life in the Dryer Room on the fifth floor of the Malden Mills in the heat of August. And look where I got to. I was one of those kids coming up with just a little bit of talent at passing exams or something. I ate up everything they fed me and spit it right back at them. They couldn't give me enough. I wanted more. I took it all, and when I went out into the world to put this precious knowledge of theirs to use, this knowledge proved to be too dangerous—so they had to cut my wings—ground me—shove my nose in the shite—show me where I really belonged: in a covered lane on the Liffey quays. Where I found England to be still occupying Ireland. Still bleeding Irish pauper children of their lifeblood for a few miserable shillin's.

Thursday evening, the wife and I took our meager belongings in our two suitcases, a blue airlines bag, and the big blue case that folded in the middle to hold dresses on hangers, and took Aisling, and walked from Harold's Cross to Rathmines. From under the dropping spruce, I turned and called "Good-bye, Mrs. McCroomb! Go fumble in a greasy till—and add the sixpence to the five-pound note—." The corner of the curtain dropped again. "Romantic Ireland's dead and gone, Mrs. McCroomb! It's buried with O'Leary in Maurice Woolf's."

Anyone who saw us might have thought we were refugees fleeing the fire-bombing of Dresden as we trudged through the sidestreets of Harold's Cross carrying everything in the world we possessed.

I said to Sheila, "You're not gonna carry the kid, too? Put her down. She can walk."

'Nick—."

"You're my wife, not a beast of burden."

Although it bordered on Harold's Cross, on Dublin's South Side, and just south of the Grand Canal, Rathmines had the character of another world. Within a handful of connecting streets, the city, like a butterfly, emerged from the cocoon of a seedy, dilapidated district into the spreading wings of a bustling middle-class suburb. An almost visible line divided poverty from prosperity. On one side lay sloth and defeatism, and the domain of the dole, on the other, neat black railings and flower-boxes in the windows. Rathmines Town Hall was a Victorian edifice with a redbrick clock-tower with Roman numerals telling the time to the four corners of the compass: it reminded me of nothing less than Memorial Hall at Harvard, where I took my GREs. The magnificent church that dominated Lower

Rathmines Road was called Mary Immaculate, Refuge of Sinners, and it was a spectacular melding of eighteenth and nineteenth-century architectural idioms, with a portico of stout classical Roman temple columns facing Rathmines Road, which were, in turn, dwarfed by the truly impressive green-bronzed tulip-dome, which could be seen above the buildings all the way to Ranelagh, and which was said to have been originally intended for an orthodox church in Russia before the 1917 Revolution.

This imperial dome now hovered over Rathmines the way the mountain called Nephin shadowed Kilcross, 150 miles west, in County Mayo. The dome, peeking over the shoulder of the sidestreets, together with the Town Hall bell-tower tolling the hour, made Rathmines into a self-enclosed enclave within Dublin, a village inside the urban shell. Beside the church, enclosed in black railings, were the extensive grounds of a convent and its broad green lawn. And Rathmines had its own Post Office, a sizable one, at that, which made it self-reliant and detached from the city centre; rather, you might say, independent of it. There were not one, but two, American-style supermarkets in this urban village, H. Williams, in Rathmines Road Lower, on the same side as the Town Hall, and then further up, at the fork in the road where Upper Rathmines Road diverged from Rathgar Road, a Five-Star Supermarket, complete with a modest-sized car-park. All told, Rathmines looked to be a haven of domestic tranquillity.

But not least of the features to recommend it, to me, was the Rathmines Library, situated next door to the gem of Mary Immaculate, on the same side of Rathmines Road as the church. This library, with its nine-foot tall double-oaken doors and tall Georgian windows looking out at the street, looked to be of 1920s vintage, and it was not a branch library, but a main library, meant for Rathmines alone—and therefore, for me alone.

I marvelled at Sheila. "How did you find this place?"

"You mean a Culchie like me, still knockin' the pig-shite off me boots?"

At the corner of Church Avenue and Upper Rathmines Road, beyond Rathmines Centre and the Five-Star, on the same side as the Madigan's at Rathgar Road, and opposite a shop called Campbell's, which sold cigarettes and newspapers and loose tea and other neighborhood staples, Sheila stopped and said, "Here we are."

Part-way down Church Avenue, the side-street, the roadway divided to encircle a Protestant chapel ensconced inside black railings on its own island in the road.

Sheila said, "There's the black church, and here's our new place—No. 56 Upper Rathmines Road."

We stood in front of the left-hand side of a block of two-story Georgian townhouses which had long ago been sub-divided into flats for rent. Each painted door had a Georgian-style fanlight and white trimmings, a tiny, paved-over front garden, and tall steps leading to the front door.

"First floor," said Sheila, "window on the street. Isn't it lovely?"

We went inside, the street-door being unlocked, and our flat was the first door on the right. Only one other flat was on the first floor, behind ours. The loo was behind that, down the end of the hall. Both flats were on the right, the other side being the exterior wall of the townhouse. On that wall hung the telephone for the building; the stairs were down the back, next to the loo, and they went up to the 2nd floor, and down to the basement flats below us.

"It's a double-bedsitter?"

"For this money, it's a bargain."

"How much?"

"Six pound, ten bob a week."

"Sheila—that's over a third of my wages."

Inside our flat, behind the door, when you opened it, was the electric meter. Then along that wall came a white-painted trellis enclosing a single bed. Beside the wall shared with the hallway was the other bed, also inside a white trellis. I sat down in one of the two black vinyl armchairs. Wall-to-wall carpeting, red-and-black, like the chairs. No ceiling light, but two lamps on the walls over the beds. Another white trellis separated the kitchenette, with its ceiling light, table and four chairs, cooker and sink, from the sitting room. The carpeting stopped at the kitchenette area, where a plain beige linoleum was in place. The only window in the place had a commodious window-seat, and it was in the bed-sitting area—but in daylight, it was big enough to sit in to read. I liked it. There was running water indoors. No fireplace, but in lieu of hauling turf in from outside, there was a portable electric-fire, which, of course, ran on electricity from the meter. I ran my hand over the laminated table-top, imitation wood-grain. The bedspreads matched the carpeting, and there was a chrome-plated electric kettle standing on the cooker. Obviously, the landlord—or management company—had taken a care.

"Well," said Sheila, "what do you think? Isn't it grand?"

"Sheila—it's the size of one room in Queensberry Street in Boston."

"Yes, but I had to have two roommates there, to make the rent. Aisling can have her own bed here. And there's a huge back-garden for her to play in, behind high walls, too, so, no worry from the traffic. Well?"

"I can live in a tent—is it what you want?"

For answer, Aisling grabbed me by the hand to pull me out of my chair. "Come and see the back-garden, Daddy."

I went, of course, but I was trying to imagine how we were going to live on, what was it, eleven quid a week?–which is what we would have left over, after the rent was paid. It's a bloody good thing I still have money I made back home in an account at the Bank of Ireland. But when that's gone, what then?

Now that a few things were settled—my job, our family back together, our new accommodations in Rathmines—I turned my mind to what was really going on.

And to me, that was Internment.

So many other things had intervened. Meeting Sheila's parents and brothers and sister at home in Mayo. For the first time in my life. Unexpected gusts of poetry blowing through my body and bones. When they became a gale that blew me away, that was really unexpected. Obligatory nods to literary shrines: that was me in another life, left over from South County, Rhode Island; when, wide-eyed, we used to do things like taking a day-trip to the Gilded Age mansions of Newport, or communing with the ocean in the wind and rain of a winter nor'easter assaulting Point Judith lighthouse, or exploring antique shops on sandy backwoods roads.

But the baggage I carried from Milltown to Shannon Airport back in August included also all my unresolved conflicts about America, Nixon, the anti-war movement, the FBI calling on my supervisors at work to get me fired because I was a protester of the government that was paying my salary.

All I was trying to do was to support my family, like any man was supposed to, and, on my own time, exercise my rights as a citizen, my God-given, constitutional rights.

I had a lot of anger left over. And although it never occurred to me that I had fled America in order to join the revolution in Ireland—yet I knew very well before I ever set foot on an Aer Lingus 707 that there was a lot going on over there.

But what did it have to do with me?

On Saturday, the long work-week over, I turned to Sheila and said, "I think I'll go down to O'Connell Street for the rally this afternoon."

"Why? What's going on?"

It was a natural question. Having arrived at Shannon two weeks ahead of me, back in August, Sheila and Aisling arrived virtually on the day Internment happened, or the day or two after. The whole country was in an uproar.

"Every weekend since I've been up in Dublin, Sheila, they've been mounting these enormous rallies outside the GPO in support of the North. People from Belfast and Derry testifying on a flatbed lorry parked at the pillars. You wouldn't believe the size of the crush—thousands. I'd invite you along, but it's not a thing for Aisling to be seeing. I think she might be frightened by it."

"No, no, you go. We're fine right where we are. We can play out the back or maybe go window-shopping in Rathmines, or sight-seeing, or something. Not to worry, we'll find something."

We understood each other. Sheila was just as angry as I was about Internment, the British Army, the attacks in the North on the Catholic enclaves by the Loyalist gangs. She was outraged, of course: she was Irish. She'd heard all the same talk going the rounds down in Mayo that I had. There was not a body down the country that did not whole-heartedly stand by their brethren in the North, especially in Mayo, a bastion of the rebel heartland since time immemorial. Sheila had come along on the march across the Windy Gap, Aisling, too.

But back then, Sheila was down home, amongst her own, she knew everybody. Dublin was different, and if the likes of Mrs.

McCroomb was any example, there was no love lost; nor indeed, could Sheila put any trust in the denizens of her brand-new (to her) capital city. And there were no secrets between us. She knew exactly how I felt. In that, I was no different than her own brother, Patrick Blake, and how many times had she listened to us discussing the whole thing? Her da, her mother, sister Ann, brother Matt, we all felt the same way as Toss Ribbons and the rest of them.

So off I went.

This time, the speaker at the mike-stand was Ruairí Ó Brádaigh the national President of Sinn Fein.

"And Pádraigh Pearse said, in 1915, at the graveside of O'Donovan Rossa, that time when he was to speak at the homecoming of one of our own Wild Geese, that Ireland Unfree Shall Never Be At Peace!"

Ruairí Ó Brádaigh was a schoolmaster from Roscommon. On the flatbed, he presented a round-faced, be-spectacled harmlessness, in his plain cloth raincoat, with its notions of humble respectability.

"How prophetic he turned out to be, down to our own day," Ó Brádaigh went on. "Unfinished business is what we have at hand today, my friends."

If you met him in the street, you would never have suspected that this man was once the Chief of Staff of the IRA—that he'd spent time in English prisons—that he'd led raids across the Border in the 1950s—that he'd escaped himself from Internment, in the early '60s, at the Curragh Military Camp in Kildare.

"When Pádraigh Pearse spoke in 1915, he spoke of those graves of the Fenian dead which would not let the Irishmen and Irishwomen of his day rest with a business unfinished. Today, we have, not only those graves of the dead of generations past to remind us of our duty, but the graves of our own day, of our own Patrick Corry, of our own Sam Devenny, of Danny O'Hagan and Jim Saunders, of Patrick Rooney, Desmond Beattie and Seamus Cusack, Cathal Hughes and Billy Reid—and we have those graves of the living dead, Long Kesh, and the prison-ship Maidstone—those graveyards of Internment—to remind us of our duty. But the past can never rescue the future. It is for us in the present to seize the day and secure the future. And that is why I come before you today, comrades and friends, to ask your support, to ask your aid, to ask for your money, in Ireland's time of need, to ask you to join the Republican Movement—because I promise you that we are the generation and this is the time— this time, there will be no unfinished business—this time, we shall not fail!"

The speech-making was over and the rally was breaking up, but the President's brother, Seán Ó Brádaigh, a Vice-President of Sinn Fein, and its Information Officer, had taken over the microphone to exhort the hangers-on, and those liable to drift away when the show was over.

"For many weeks now, we have been meeting here, in growing numbers, since August the Ninth, Internment Day, in swelling numbers, and the numbers joining the Irish Republican Movement have been increasing daily. We appeal to you again today, as this rally draws to a close, to march up to the table you see here, where a Sinn Fein worker will be happy to take your name."

Seán Ó Brádaigh was a handsome, angle-faced man, thin-lipped and dark, with dark, thinning hair, a lean, tense contrast to his prosperous-looking brother. He pointed at the crowd drifting away, seeming to name with his finger one of the waverers, "Stand up, march up, join up. We need your help. There is plenty of work for all to do—man, woman and child— we need your help."

The crowd was splitting, crossing, breaking apart, separating. The open-air Mass for this Saturday, in defiance of the Penal Laws of the invader, was over. The doors of the church were opening and it was time to head across the road to the pub. Ó Brádaigh looked around the platform behind him. The heads of the Movement were climbing down from the lorry.

I watched, as a worker leaned over the bunting on the rail in front and began to unpin the green-white-and-orange banner: *Sinn Féin*

Far away, on the distant margins of the mob of thousands, I could see isolated pairs of uniformed Dublin gardai, keeping a respectful distance.

It seemed to me that non-interference must be their policy, their orders. Or, like so many others, did they, too, sympathize?

How could they not, if they were Irish police, and not, indeed, paid by the English crown?

Ó Brádaigh spoke into the mike one last time, and his voice came out of the loud-hailers suspended all over O'Connell Street. "Every man must do what he can. Please make a contribution to the workers you see filtering among you with the containers marked Northern Aid."

People in the crowd around me were stopping those with the white-wrapped canisters that resembled over-sized beer cans and pressing money on them before they hurried off to their bus-stops. A young woman, one of the collectors, turned with a can in her hand, and bumped into to me. She said nothing, but looked up at me and held out her cardboard container.

"Money," I said, "is for those with nothing else to give."

"Or for those who don't want to give at all," she said. She passed on.

Was it a rebuke? A commentary? An observation on me? What did she mean?

Again, at the microphone, Seán Ó Brádaigh was not yet ready to give up. "The Irish Republican Movement needs every able-bodied man in the land—every stout-hearted woman—there is no corner of this island for you to turn away to! Join us today! This time we shall not fail–this time, our problem shall not become our children's problem."

I thought of my father in the coal mine. My mother in the factory. Nixon on the throne—because the majority were silent. If—if—my daughter's future was to be in Ireland—as her mother, obviously, was wishing it to be—what kind of Ireland was that going to be? Divided? At war? *An Ireland unfree that would never be at peace?*

I stood there waiting until the pavement around me was emptied.

I stood alone with my own thoughts.

So many were turning away.

But some were not.

I looked around at the littered ground. A crowd this size left their prints behind. Who had the job of cleaning up this mess?

It seemed a desecration.

I made up my mind and headed for the tag end of the queue at the sign-up table, and immediately I felt better.

It was an impulse. Besides, I hated indecision—and this impulse cut the knot inside me, decisively.

But also it was seeing Sheila Blake again, across the dance floor, for the first time in my life, and realizing that I knew what it was that I wanted. It was another moment, just like that. History may not repeat itself, but it rhymes.

Everything I had in life, everything worthwhile, came from that moment, because I listened to myself, and obeyed the impulse.

I fell in with my hands in my pockets. A young man's voice, in something like a husky confidential, just-between-us-tone, said, "Joining the IRA, are you?"

I turned to see a young fellow about Patrick Blake's age mischievously, inanely grinning at me.

I turned away again, frowning to myself. I took the biro that was being held out to me. A girl in a green military skirt and green beret watched me as I bent my head to sign on the next line open on a sheet full of names and addresses. The girl read my address upside down. "Have you a telephone?"

"I do," I said. "But I .don't know the number, I've only just moved in."

The girl turned to a man in a 3-piece suit beside her. She said something close to his ear. He was a thin, ascetic-looking man who wore black-rimmed glasses. He leaned over the table to me. "Come to the Macmillan Bookshop in O'Connell Street, Monday at nine. Ask for John Martyn."

"I can't. I'll be at work."

"Can you come on your lunch hour?"

"I'll try."

"So. Remember. John Martyn."

I began to leave. There seemed to be nothing else to do. Others were behind me in the queue. I didn't want to lose this contact, once established, but they were looking to others, and I hadn't thought of them asking for a phone number.

The young bloke who'd been behind me in the queue was bantering with the girl in the military skirt. "Any vacancies for Commandants? What's the wages like?"

He was a ginger-haired lad with a thin, wispy bit of a goatee on his chin, and he was signing his name left-handed. He seemed to know he was acting like an ass and he thought it funny.

I passed it off as youth, as a case of nerves—teenage self-consciousness.

After all, I was a grown man of 24, and this fellow was 18, if that.

He could have been one of my students in one of my classes.

With that, it was time to leave, find my No. 46A bus, and go home to my loved ones in Upper Rathmines Road.

A good day's work, for a Saturday, I thought.

On Monday, I said to Sugarman, "What about my insurance cards?"

"Bleeding hell—I'd forgotten entirely. Here. Here. Take these and fill them out. The Labor Exchange is in Thomas Street."

"I know how to get there."

"Well, they're closed after five—you'll have to go on your lunch-hour."

Which was only a lunch-half-hour. But I was planning on explaining to Sugarman that the queues were long, and I'd had to wait.

In O'Connell Street, it amused me to think of the last time I'd been in Macmillan's, when I'd taken the door on the right, up the stair to the first floor, to Fiona in her swivel-chair. This time I took the glass door on the left, the entrance to the ground-floor bookshop. "Is John Martyn here, please?"

The salesgirl said, "Let me see if he hasn't gone to lunch."

She went down the inside of the glass bookcase to disappear behind a revolving rack of paperback pocket-books: the Cardinal, the Bluejay and the Swan were the imprints. John Martyn came down the counter. He was the man with the suit and glasses from the sign-up table on Saturday. He stopped at the cash register. "Have you the telephone number now?"

"I memorized it yesterday. 373-568."

John Martyn's priestly fingers slipped a small white card along the glass counter-top as if it were a communion wafer. He held a pencil poised above the white edge. "You're American, aren't you?"

"Yes."

"Well–we appreciate your interest." He wrote on the white card. "That's 373-568? You'll be contacted."

Chapter 4

Cumann Billy Reid

The telephone hanging in the hall by the front door at the new flat in Rathmines Road rang on Monday evening.

The young woman down the hall, in the flat behind ours, raced out to answer it. Then she knocked on our door. I could see by her face she was disappointed that the call wasn't for her, but I thanked her, thinking, something else new to get used to.

The message was brief, and I was equally brief as I picked up Aisling when I went back in. "I'm going out Wednesday evening."

Sheila was doing the dishes at the sink. The dishes, like the electric kettle, came with the double-bedsitter. 'A self-contained flat,' in the parlance of Jeremy Flynn. I hadn't met him, but Sheila had told me it was Jeremy Flynn who was the estate agent who'd shown her round Rathmines. His office was across the road, up a few doors from Campbell's. 'A lot of single girls up from the country, working in government offices, the hospitals and the like, or else going to school,' said Jeremy, in Sheila's re-telling, and 'they appreciated the convenience, though it was the bit extra.' What mattered to her was that Jeremy Flynn had no objection to children, or one child, anyway. She thought it decent of him—I thought, well, he doesn't own it, or live in it. He's only trying to make a commission.

As I approached with the child in my arms, her arms around my neck, happy to be picked up, Sheila said, "Where are you going?"

"To a meeting."

"A meeting?" When I hesitated, she said, "A meeting like the rally on Saturday?"

"A meeting of the Sinn Féin Cumann Billy Reid."

Now Sheila turned, to dry her hands, and face me. "Why are you doing this, Nick?"

Leaning back against the trellis, I sighed. "Do I have to explain to you, honey? Who knows me better, in the whole world?"

"You could have told me."

"I didn't want to worry you."

A child picks up every emotional twinge between her parents, and I could feel Aisling shifting, so I put her down. She immediately went to her mother to hold onto her skirt.

"I thought you were just going to a rally—not joining up." I could see the storm-clouds gathering in Sheila's face, but I didn't expect tears. "I thought it was to please me that you came to Ireland."

"Of course it was. And now we're here. This is it. The flat you picked out. Aren't you happy?"

"It's just that I wonder sometimes if you think of Aisling and me as much as you think of other people."

Electric torch in hand, Paddy Clarke himself escorted the Cumann Billy Reid up to their brand-new meeting room on his top floor, apologizing for the lack of light. "Mind the twist in the stair, lads," he called back under his arm from the landing at the top.

Paddy was only too glad to accommodate them. His uncle, Old Joe Clarke, now in his eighties, but still an active Sinn Féiner, was known all over Dublin as a grandfather to the Movement, a sort of a figurehead, beloved to the members. A veteran of the Easter Rising, Old Joe Clarke had been shot in the head, but survived in English prisons, and upon his release, back in Ireland, was then interned once more during the Civil War. Paddy Clarke, his nephew, owned the pub in Aungier Street with his own name over the doors and windows, and he and his family lived on the first floor, above the pub, but they never used the attic, two rooms squeezed under the mansard roof. Inside the first room, he flicked on the wall-switch. "At least this light works."

Behind him on the stair, Alita Hughes peered into the shadows of the second room. She was the member of Cumman na Ban in the green military skirt who'd taken my name at the rally.

In the lighted room, Alita wandered over to the front of the house and looked out the dormer windows, scouting out Aungier Street, three stories below. At the end of October, with the clocks changing, it was already dark by 5 pm. Now at 8 o'clock, the shadows were thick around the stout pillars and under the arched gateway of the Carmelite Priory across the street. Cars went by with the park-lights on. It was raining slightly, people walking, everything regular.

Alita Hughes was the first officer of Cumman Billy Reid, and she liked to use the title Chairman: she fancied neither Chairwoman, which she thought sounded like a ladies' charity-circle, nor Chairperson, which was new-fangled and foreign. She didn't mind being thought a traditionalist, nor, for that matter, what anyone thought of her at all. What mattered at the moment to Alita was the street below.

Paddy Clarke's pub was two blocks down from the corner of Kevin Street. No. 4A Kevin Street was the Headquarters office of Sinn Féin. The headquarters of the Irish Special Branch were just a hop and a skip the other way down Aungier Street, in Dublin Castle. Paddy Clarke's pub was dead in the middle between the two. Though the Party, Sinn Féin, was legal, open, above-board and so on, you still sometimes saw the black Ford Cortina, the model typically used by the Branch, parked across the road a few doors down from 4a Kevin Street, with the park-lights on, and two men in the front seat with a camera, watching who went in and out. Like the time Joe Cahill, the Chief of Staff of the Belfast Brigade, was in town, when he had to get out of Belfast after that press conference back in August.

Now Alita Hughes was glad to see no black Cortina parked outside the Priory tonight.

Into the room I went with John Martyn, the clerk from Mac-millan's. Behind us, two young women, barely in their twenties, rose up, Martina Kelly, from Galway, and Bernadette Cullen, who came from the small seaside resort village south of Dublin called Greystones. After them trailed a fellow who would never see forty again, much less twenty, Barney O'Toole, a dustman for the Dublin Corporation. Then came Maureen Hughes, Alita's sister, Myles Cunningham, her cousin from Wexford, and Brendan McAndrews, her cousin from Belfast. Last up came Peadar Kenny, from the Trinity College Sinn Féin Club, and, dressed in a green fatigue-jacket, which I now recalled from the rally in O'Connell Street, the ginger-haired 18-year-old with the goatee—Mick O'Corrigan.

"I'll leave yez, then," said Paddy Clarke, shutting the door behind him as he descended the stair. "Call down if yez want anything."

While the others looked about their new, stuffy, poorly-ventilated meeting room, Alita Hughes seated herself at the head of the long folding table Paddy and his son had carried up from the function room at the rear of the ground floor. Alita said, "What do you want for nothing? How would it be to rent a room, with our treasury?"

"Paddy Clarke's more than compensated by us," said Barney O'Toole, holding up a pint and a burning cigarette, both in the same hand.

Alita frowned. No one else had brought up a drink. It was only her respect for her elders that kept her from forbidding Barney. "That's the trouble with this organization," she commented, however.

"Now, Alita," said Barney, "can't a man wet his throat?"

"More time is spent lubricating the talking machine," was Alita's dry reply.

"Ah, start the meeting, then."

"When did we ever start a meeting on time?" Everyone was seated now, and Alita asked her sister for the ledger.

Maureen Hughes was a couple of years older than Alita, but nothing like her. Whether in uniform or civilian clothes, as tonight, Alita always looked proper. She kept her straight golden-brown hair clipped short to her ears so it would look neat under her beret. She was not unattractive, with her hazel eyes, high cheekbones, and trim build, and when she smiled, she had a beautiful set of teeth, but she knew people considered her manner too mannish. Maureen, beside her, was fat and frowsy. For the life of her, Alita couldn't understand why Maureen had to wear her hair so long, but could never seem to keep it out of her eyes. To get the ledger out of the shoulder-bag in her lap, Maureen had to push her chair back from the table. "I have it," she said.

"This meeting of the Cumann is called to order," said Chairman Alita. "Have we a quorum?"

"Yes," said John Martyn, the Treasurer.

Maureen was the Secretary, but Alita said she would fill in the names tonight.

"We have two new members present," John reminded her.

"What are their names?"

John Martyn, next to me, gave a nudge. "Nick Petrovich," I said.

"Spell that?"

I did, and when I looked around the table, saw curious faces. The two girls, Martina and Bernadette, sat together down the bottom, Martina next to Brendan McAndrews, who had his back to the windows and sat facing Alita. The two girls were both easy on the eyes, but Bernadette was a real beauty: a brunette, long, straight hair, resting on her shoulders, a creamy complexion, full, cherry-red lips, and bedroom brown eyes.

Bernadette and Martina were inseparable. They worked together in the Aer Lingus office at the bottom of Grafton Street and they shared a flat in Waterloo Road. Big-bosomed and red-armed Martina, the Galway farmer's daughter, who showed freckles rounding the shoulder of her sleeveless white blouse, was trying to get out of the office and into the stewardesses, and she had the looks and the charm, but she was also doing a line with Brendan McAndrews—when he was in town. It was through Brendan that the girls became members. Bernadette was unattached at the moment, and she looked me over well: the name, the accent, the dark looks. Because of the Aer Lingus office, the girls were used to Americans.

"You'd think this was the United Nations," said Barney O'Toole, "with its quorums and quotas." Born and bred in the Liberties, the ancient walled city, all of Dublin beyond, and the rest of the world, too, often looked cock-eyed to Barney. "Enough to put you off your pint."

None of these glances across the table escaped Brendan McAndrews, but he was biding his time.

Alita pointed her biro at the second newcomer. "And yourself?"

"Mick O'Corrigan. From County Tipp, ma'am. And I hope you won't hold it against me." John Martyn raised one eyebrow. Brendan McAndrews looked at O'Corrigan through half-closed lids. But Mick was incapable of taking anything seriously, and he would have liked nothing better than to rattle their stodgy Dublin applecart. "I'm not long for this kip anyhow. I'm for the IRA, I am."

"Maureen," said Alita, with a sigh, "read to us the minutes of the last meeting, please?"

Maureen rummaged through her bag. "I had them written down," she said. "On that piece of paper." She looked at her sister. "I meant all week to put them in the book."

"Have you got them or not?"

"Well, you rushed me out of the house so, tonight."

"Treasurer's report," said Alita brusquely, and she passed the ledger to Maureen. "We'll just have to have two reports from the Secretary next week, won't we?"

John Martyn said, "We're doing rather poorly on this end, as well. Thirty-seven quid and seven bob in the account tonight."

"That's disgusting." Alita looked murder across the table at her cousin Brendan. But he was heavy-lidded and impassive. "And the worst thing is that we have new members here tonight—what kind of an example are we setting for them? All right, I'll get to the point. In the coming week, we have two main jobs. Number one—selling An Phoblacht. I want Rathmines, Ranelagh, Rathgar and Harold's Cross covered. Now who's going to take Thursday night?"

Martina and Bernadette volunteered.

"Where?"

Martina shrugged. "Rathmines?"

"No, that has a couple of big pubs. Save that for Saturday night."

Myles Cunningham and Bernie O'Toole raised their hands.

"Martina, you and Bernadette can do Harold's Cross on Thursday, there's not much in it anyways. Now I want the money handed in, at this meeting next week."

"Why not Kevin Street?" said O'Toole. "I don't like carrying it about for a week."

"Because, Barney, then you'll be sure to be at the meeting next week, won't you?" To change the subject, Alita looked at Martyn. "John—I'd like you to take the two new lads out selling—when and if they go out for the first time."

I perked up my ears at this, and looking across at Mick, saw him wink at me.

"Now, as to Number Two—organizing a fund-raiser—Cumann Hughes, in Tallaght, last week held a céilí and collected over a thousand quid. That's a thousand much-needed by the dependent families. Now, they're a New Town cumann, and you know how they are—I won't have us doing less. Maureen, are you getting this all down?"

"I'm trying, I'm trying."

"I don't want to go too fast for you. Now, we're new, that's true—but even so, we really have no excuse for having fobbed it off this long already. Now I'd like to know just what the difficulty is."

No one spoke up.

"Myles, form a committee, and have a report on progress at the next meeting. And while I'm at it, there's one thing I should say. Recruiting. All over the country, Sinn Fein membership is up—higher than it has been in years. With the crisis on, we can't take them in fast enough. Volunteers everywhere—all except here. Dublin—the South Side, I mean—is absolute dead last in the country in the membership drive. Why, here we are with?—ten, eleven people?—and that's counting two new men who haven't yet been accepted as full members. Nine people to cover all the ground from Ballsbridge to Rathgar—one cumann in the entire South Side, outside of Sandymount, which has the Cumann Saunders. Rathmines, Ranelagh and Rathgar ought each to have a cumann of their own—they're big enough. But who's to organize it? Put that down, Maureen, as Job Number Three." Alita drummed her fingers on the table. "I want to show Kevin Street, by Christmas, that this cumann is moving. And that's not so long away. Have I forgotten anything now, Myles?"

Myles Cunningham seemed to be the mildest of the three cousins. Perhaps it was his straight, cornstalk-colored hair, worn shoulder-length, or his square, trim beard that made him look like one of the Apostles on a wallet-sized prayer-card. "The Sinn Féin fund-raiser?" said Myles.

"Oh, yes. It's being held at the Old Shieling. The date is set for a fortnight from Saturday. It's to be a city-wide event. There'll be a great show—the Barleycorn, down from Belfast— and the ticket includes dinner. Roast stuffed chicken, Myles? Anyway, they do it up right at the Old Shieling. They're good Republicans there. Tickets are four pounds per person. We'll have tickets for you to sell next week. Anything else, Myles?"

"Yes. The Ard Fheis."

"November fifteenth. At the Mansion House. Very important again this year. You might remember that it was the Ard Fheis last year when the split was voted. So everyone from this cumann must be there—and let's hope the new men have their voting rights by then."

"That's all, I believe," said Myles.

"And now, to the new members." Alita straightened herself in her chair, to face me. "You've heard me say we have a drive on for membership. So your interest in joining is welcome. But you musn't think that everyone who signs up at the table in O'Connell Street becomes a member. Lots of them sign at a rally—and are never heard from again. Others turn up but find they're in the wrong local, if you know what I mean. They're not the kind of people we need. Do you know why this cumann is named after Billy Reid? Sorry, what was your name again?"

"Petrovich. Nick Petrovich."

"Well, Mr Petrovich, Billy Reid was a soldier of the IRA who gave his life for the Cause, in Belfast. He was killed just this June. Shot down in cold blood in broad daylight by the British Army. And when he was dead, as the song says, he was kicked in the head, by the hair they dragged him around. The killers who took his life are our enemies. They would kill us, just as they killed him—without compunction—if they could. Now, I want you to think about this—you have to choose us—and we have to choose you. Your first month, you'll be on probation. Someone who's already a full member must agree to be your sponsor during that time. He's responsible for teaching you what you need to know about the organization and what's expected of you on your part. At your fourth meeting, you can bring yourself up for a vote on full membership. Now—take your time—and tell us why one of us should sponsor you for the next month."

"Well," I said, taking a deep breath. "I guess it's a long story." Feeling myself nervous, I cleared my throat. "I've been interested in Irish affairs for a long time. I wish I could tell you I've been in this organization and that, but I haven't. What I've done is to study up the situation and try to learn as much as I could, and now, I've decided to take one more step and, I suppose, you might say, rather than stand by and be a spectator, to do something about it."

"What passport do you carry?" It was Brendan McAndrews, who, until now, had said not a word the entire meeting.

"U.S. Passport," I said, turning to face him.

Brendan wore his dark hair cropped close, like one of the skinheads from Maurice Woolf's, or, in fact, like the Taig street-gang kid from the Falls Road in Belfast that he was. His round shoulders and thick arms, under his denim jacket, lent power to his short stature, and added a certain menace to the somnolent lids of his dark eyes, which didn't blink, but stared at me. McAndrews was 19 years old, and I was 24, but it wasn't age that separated us: we were from different worlds.

John Martyn asked, "What brought you to Ireland, Nick?"

"Well, I'm married to a girl named Sheila Blake, from County Mayo."

"Bring your passport with you to the next meeting," said Brendan McAndrews, and he turned his chair to stare at himself in the mirroring glass of the windows.

Having never heard a true Belfast accent before, I mistook him for someone Scottish, so he sounded to me just as foreign as I was. He certainly didn't sound anything like the Blake family's County Mayo English.

"What passport does your wife carry?" said John.

"Irish. I don't think she'd ever give that up. I guess we always knew we'd be coming back here to settle."

"And is that what you've done?" said Alita.

"Yes. In fact, I have a job here in Dublin."

"And you live in Rathmines Road?"

"With my wife and daughter Aisling. It's a double-bedsitter. A little small, but it's what we can afford."

"You're not one of them draft-dodgers, are you?" said Brendan McAndrews, enjoying himself in the window.

"No," I said, sharply. I was annoyed that he wasn't facing me to say that, and I resented it.

"Because I can understand your wife, or anyone who's Irish, wanting to come home again—but why did you leave your country?"

I fumbled with the question in my mind. I very well knew the answer, I'd repeated it to myself a hundred times. But how would it sound to him? I started slowly, thinking it out as I spoke. "I'm sure you're all familiar with what's going on in the United States at the moment, and for the last several years. I'm sure you all know there's a Movement against the Vietnam War inside America. Well, many Americans are protesting that war, and some are even leaving the country because of it, as you know–."

"No, I don't know that," said Brendan. "I always thought America was the place everybody's trying to get into, not out of. And there's one thing I don't like—and that's a man that won't fight for his country."

"I've fought for my country. I've bled for my country. In Constitution Avenue in Washington, D.C. And I never refused military service to my country, either. They refused me. I spent two years in the U.S. Army ROTC at Boston College, and I was prepared to serve as a 2nd Lieutenant, even if it meant being sent to Nam, which it did, in '68, when I graduated, but they refused me admission to the Officers Corps."

"Why?" said Brendan. "What's wrong with you?"

"Nothing! They made a mistake, that's all. They said I had high blood pressure, which I didn't have then, and I don't have now. I have my draft card with my 1-Y deferment in my wallet right now, if you want to see that."

"That won't be necessary," said Alita.

"I don't mind," I said. "I have nothing to hide."

"Have you ever been in any political organizations?" she said.

"Well, I'm a registered Democrat back home, but I never went to a meeting."

"Never been in the Communist Party, have you?" said Brendan.

"No!" I answered, and I almost added 'What is this, the Un-American Activities Committee?'

"What organizations have you been in?" said Alita.

"The Mobilization Against the War, in '69. The Kent State and Jackson State Strike Committee at the University of Rhode Island, 1970. And this year, the People's Action Committee, in Milltown, Massachusetts."

"Is it joining you're fond of?" said Brendan. "Is it a career of yours—a habit—a hobby?"

"I'll tell you what it is." I was now pretty angry and put off. "I fought as best I could against an unjust war being carried out by my country, not by the people, but by an imperialist military-industrial complex, a war against a country that was small and helpless, but brave enough to fight back, to resist. And because I did what I did, I was photographed by the FBI, and they used that to get me fired from my job. So my wife and I, and she's a native-born citizen here, Irish-born and bred—we came to this country, her country, seeking a better life. And what do I find here? A small country fighting for self-determination, for a scrap of a decent life for people like my wife, who are forced to emigrate because of no jobs, no housing, no factories, no life—a small country fighting against that same military-industrial complex that's world-wide—except, this time, it wears the uniform of the British Empire. Now, you're either a part of the problem, or a part of the solution. Wherever you are. And me? I'm a part of the solution. And if this movement can't use me—then you lose, not me."

Brendan wheeled now in his chair to face me. "Me, I'm fighting for a united 32-county Socialist Worker's Republic, under the banner of Connolly Socialism, and I'm willing to die for it. You understand, then. There are people all over the world interested in the Irish Republican Movement. I don't doubt it. All sorts of people. All we want to know is—which sort are you? Now, is there anyone in this country you know—outside of your wife's family—or does anyone know you?"

"Toss Ribbons," I said. "Kilcross, County Mayo, National School teacher. Frank Delaney, the TD in the Dail for North Mayo. Or you can try Father John Latchford of St Patrick's, Kilcross, County Mayo. Check with them, if you like."

"We will."

I didn't know what I expected that night, or what I hoped for. Or, for that matter, the moment I walked up to the sign-up table in O'Connell Street. And after Sheila expressing her misgivings, and tears, I almost half-hoped they wouldn't accept me, and all this would go away. But now, downstairs, in the pub, afterwards, I said to Bernadette Cullen at the bar, "Thanks for sticking your hand up to be my sponsor."

"You earned it," she said. "After that speech you gave, I couldn't resist it."

"I just hope you're not sticking your neck out, too."

Barney O'Toole came up to us. "Are we having a bit of a song tonight, Bernie?"

"Capital suggestion," said Paddy Clarke. He came out from behind the bar to open the function room. "No sense keeping it open and make the ESB rich and a pauper out of myself. But if there's singing, that'll bring the crowd in tonight."

Alita, Myles and Brendan, the cousins, came down the stair and Brendan asked Martina to wait for him. He went with the other two for a conference, into the snug by the front door. Mick O'Corrigan came up to me and said, "Let me shake the hand of the man."

"He gave me a rough time of it there for a minute, I guess."

"Ah, but you gave it right back to him. Thanks to you, I had the easy time of it myself."

John Martyn entered the circle and I said, "Let me get you a pint, John?"

"No, no," said John. "Tonight, you're our guest."

I took him aside for a moment. "I don't mind telling you, John, I want to be a full member of this Cumann—even more now."

"That's the lad, that's the lad."

Somebody stuck a pint in my hand and Paddy Clarke went back behind the bar, saying to Bernadette and Martina, "I've set up the microphone for yez. Now see if you can get Myles to give us a tune with that lovely voice of his."

Peadar Kenny went in to the stage and set up a single chair for himself, sat down and pulled a tin whistle from his coat pocket. He played a small intro, and Martina and Bernadette began to sing, and everybody joined in as they trooped, up one step, into the function room.

> *I'll sing you a song of a terrible wrong,*
> *When the flags they flew at half-mast,*
> *And a man he lay dead, he was riddled with lead,*
> *and he died on the streets of Belfast.*

It was one of those songs doing the rounds. Nobody knew really when or where it started or who actually made up the words or the tune. It just seemed that one day everybody was singing it, as if they'd known it all their lives. Then the chorus swelled out as the patrons of Paddy Clarke's drifted up the step into the back room.

> *All the radio said was another shot dead,*
> *And he died with a gun in his hand,*
> *But they didn't say why Billy Reid had to die,*
> *For he died to free Ireland.*

The singing brought the conference out of the snug and somebody called out for Myles Cunningham. "Old Wexford Town, Myles!" "Sean South, Myles!"

"One at a time, one at a time," said Myles as he went up onto the stage and adjusted the mike-stand, while Bernadette opened the piano beside the stage.

Brendan McAndrews, with a pint in his hand, leaned up against the door-jamb and called out, "Henry Joy, Myles!"

Mick O'Corrigan said he'd walk me home, he didn't mind, as he had a basement flat in Mespil Road, and that was going my way, and I could keep him company. If that sounded confused, then Mick was, a little. The drinking age being 18, not 21, as I'd learned in Mayo, he might not be used to going easy on the hard stuff quite as yet, whereas myself, I was still getting round to whether or not I even liked Guinness, and so, had sipped slowly.

Aungier Street turned into Camden Street, and then Richmond Street, and they were all one in the dark; traffic was light, few people were on the footpath, yet we managed to cause a man with an umbrella to take a wide berth around us. I had to pull Mick back onto the footpath. "Are you going to make it home, Mick?"

"Are they following us?"

"Who?"

"Who. Who. What are you, an owl?"

"Nobody's following us."

"'Twas the same for Mick Collins. But he gave them the slip, he did, pedaling about Dublin on his old push-bike, and they never could catch him." Mick began to sing softly.

> *Oh, who is the man with blood on his hands,*
> *Such a cold-blooded ambush there never was planned—.*

He almost toppled into the street again. When I righted him, he looked blasphemy at me, and continued, only louder:

> *Oh, shame on the traitor who gave the command,*
> *For to murder the brave Michael Collins!*

"Come on over here, now," he said, as he collapsed onto a park bench in the deep black shade of night under a tree on the far bank of the canal running under the Portobello Bridge. "You go that way, up Rathmines Road, and I go this way, to Mespil Road. And here we'll stay, till I get my head straight." I sat down next to him on the bench, concerned now that I should be walking *him* home, as he pulled a rolled-up plastic bag from the breast pocket of his fatigue-jacket. "Now Guinness is good for you—but this is better."

"I haven't see any of that shit since I left the States."

"Is that what you call it—shit? Ha, ha."

"And to tell you the truth, I haven't missed it."

"Well, don't miss this." Mick rolled a joint in his lap.

I threw my arms spread out on the back of the bench, leaned my head back, stuck my feet out onto the footpath, and relaxed, in anticipation. The stress of the meeting was still in me and I was looking to get past it.

"What other names have you for it?"

"Oh. Reefer. Mary Jane. Uh, weed. Some people call it dope. Mostly we just call it by where it comes from—you know, Hawaiian, Colombian, Panama Red, Acapulco Gold—where's this from?"

"This is no class of marijuana at all. Probably Spain. Maybe the Islands. What you want that's good round here is—hashish." Mick held up his joint. "Now that is what I call a high-flying bird."

I took a hit after him. "I didn't know you could get it round here," I said, letting it out with a rush.

"Like I said, kid—stick with me, you'll learn something."

Another toke and I had a buzz going. "Whew," I said, passing it back, "after this long while, it'll put me to sleep."

"Makes me hungry," said Mick, "and other things, as well, ha, ha." He regarded the number in his hand. "The trouble with this stuff is—if Intelligence gets a whiff, you can forget the 'RA. If there's one thing they hate more than the dirty Commies, it's the dirty dopers." He dragged a long slow hit out of the joint as shook his head like a dog, as if to clear it. "Ha, ha," he coughed, and he laughed till there were tears in his eyes. Blearily, he passed the number back to me.

"What was so funny?" I murmured, as I sipped at the hot little dwindling fish-mouth on the joint. I could hear the night-wind riffing the leaves above my head.

"I was just thinking," Mick sighed, and he chuckled, and after what seemed a long time, exhaled. "I was just thinking." He looked at me. "What was I thinking?"

"What are you, stoned?" I drew in the final short bursts to kill it, whew, whew, whew, held it, let it out, picked at my tongue, offered it back to Mick.

"No," he said, waving it away. "Gets you sleepy. I want to think."

"Listen. Hear the leaves?"

"Yeah."

They were sweeping along the footpath, the fallen autumn leaves of the night, curling around our feet.

"I was thinking," said Mick, "I've got to do something spectacular. Something that'll get their attention. The way we have the troops on the run, if I don't do something quick, this war will be over—and I'll have missed it. I don't know what it is yet. But all I need is my chance, and when it comes my way, I'll know it. And then I'll have me ticket."

At work, on my second Friday at the factory, it was finally payday. Thank God for that. Out of the thousand dollars I'd brought with me from the States (oh, the things I was going to do with that thousand bucks!) I had about forty quid left in our joint account at the Bank of Ireland branch in Rathmines, When Sheila went window-shopping, she went window-shopping. Of course, I'd spent it, too, staying in a B&B by the week, which is how I ended up in Palmerston Road, and then, inevitably, it seemed, in Mrs. McCroomb's grasp. Now things had progressed to breaking point, and it was clear that, not only had I found this job in the nick of time, also, I'd better hold onto it. For the fact was, I'd been living rent-free in Mayo, and that was the only reason, really, that I still had forty quid left.

But the job did have its compensations, aside from the pay-packet. At least, it did to my way of thinking. For one, my muscles ached warmly and sweetly when it was time for bed at night, and I slept like a bear. And from knowing less than nothing about being a Dispatcher in Ireland, after just a fortnight, I could honestly say I was enjoying the learning curve—it wasn't one of Dr Robinson's courses on the New England Transcendentalists—but could he have handled a utility knife and twine-dispenser like I could, now?

As it was nearly lunchtime, I twirled, spun and laced the twine, looping it through my slip-knot, pulling on it, tying it tightly around a bundle of five brown-paper-covered bunk-bed mattresses. Tuck your flap and cut off the triangular tail, so it's squared off. The utility-knife slicing. Snap goes the twine with a squeak, as the loose end fish-tails in the air. Then I flung the knife and it landed squarely on the shelf. Two points!

On the Dispatch floor, repetitions added up, and with increasing manual dexterity, my mind was left free to deal with information overload. I took my black marking pen and wrote out my label on my bundle: that's J.C. Penney's, Cork City. Throw it on the pile. Schedule it for the morning, for Wee Willie to drop it in Pearse Street, where they would they run it out of the warehouse on the big rig down to the country. Along with—I grabbed my clipboard and crossed off a column of destinations: Woolworth's, of Limerick City, Clery's in Galway, Wellworth's in Londonderry—that's a British-owned factory for you: *London*derry—British Home Stores, Belfast City Centre, branches in Lisburn, Newry, Strabane and Derry; Casey's of County Wicklow, Ryan's in Kilkenny, small shops dotted all over the map, with the names of the proprietors, towns and counties, a regular road-atlas, two Mitchelstowns, one Palmerstown, a Wicklow, Arklow, Wexford and Waterford, Macroom, Clonakilty, Kanturk and Letterkenny, a Newtown Butler and a Newtown Stewart, New Ross, and Newcastle (but nary a coal to carry) a Castleblayney, Ballycastle, Ballymoney, Ballyshannon. Ballyghadereen—even the International Store in Ballina, County Mayo. I looked up from my clipboard of touring. Done!

I threw the clipboard on the shelf after the knife and started for the open door of Sugarman's cubicle, where he was hanging his head, worrying his brow over a stack of papers. "Those doodlers in P-Street," he said. "Expecting me to inventory the place. Like it was the press in your pantry. You wouldn't mind, only a tribe of trained monkeys'd make a better factory staff than this lot we have here." Sugarman leaned back. "I tell you, Nick, it's near to impossible to find decent help these days. Now I made the mistake, this morning, of sending the Larkin lads back there to clean out the Disaster Area. Fridays, it's the usual delivery on the lorry from Woolf's in Cork, raw foam. I need room, space, back there, to stock it. Might as well have sent those two to excavate the Sahara with a spoon! What is it I'm running here, a baby-sitting service?—an asylum for lunatic children? Bleeding hell—if your granny stood still for half a mo, they'd steal the knickers off her! There is more inventory disappearing from this kip than—than–than I can shake a spoon at! It's a disaster!"

I knew better than to ask Noel Sugarman, in the apoplectic state he was in, for my pay-packet. I met Higginbotham in the aisle between the edger-benches.

"Are you lunching with us today?" He meant it kindly—he meant with himself and Sugarman.

"No," I laughed. "I'm on a diet. No food. One quarter of a fag at morning tea. One quarter at lunch, and the last bit at afternoon tea."

"Suit yourself."

I nodded toward the office. "Just between us, Mr Higginbotham—he hired me in a fit of enthusiasm, and then forgot I existed. I was the one who got us behind a day this week, going after my insurance cards on a Monday."

Higgy rolled his eyes. "Say no more. How long have you been here now?"

"A fortnight, today—and looking forward to it, since the company's kept back a week. But I like it. I'm learning the map of Ireland."

"Not to worry, lad. I'll see to your pay-packet. I'll have it sent up to you."

I liked Higgy. Imperturbable, he just supervised his department quietly, fiddling with a needle and thread, or pinning a button to a cushion, or any little odd job to keep his hands busy. His hands were quite pious. He patted his samples tenderly on the slightly protruding stomach of his clean white smock. But Simon Higginbotham never missed a pin dropping. Malachi might think Higgy missed him pinching Clare's bottom as she leaned over her table with her denim skirt in the air, but Higgy could have told him how many millimeters of arse he got. Higgy looked out for his staff. And he was good with them. If your machine jammed, he came over and quietly fixed it for you, without a fuss, without a reprimand, without raising his voice. In fact, he would say nothing at all. But when he was done he would raise one pale, owlish eyebrow, slightly. Ah, the contrariness of all things touched by human hands. If not for Simon Higginbotham, the factory in Usher's Island Quay might produce nothing at all.

"Higgy got a good arse-lickin' just now, didn't he, lads?" said Malachi, looking at me as I approached, searching for a place to sit down for lunch. "Was that with the university-educated tongue you were tellin' us about, Dizzy?"

'Dizzy' was the nickname Malachi had planted on me. I made the mistake of mentioning to Susan Drummond that I'd been to college, and when Malachi heard about it, he said, "It's no wonder then that he's come slumming with the likes of us. All that learning's made him dizzy."

I decided on purpose to sit down shoulder to shoulder with Malachi, our backs against the wall. He didn't like anyone getting close to him. "Malachi, you're looking more like an Irish setter every day, with your tongue flapping about in the wind."

"If I had your tongue, I'd bite it in half and spit it out, for fear of poisoning myself."

"That'll be the day when my tongue is in your mouth, Malachi. I mean, I like you, but——."

With that one, Tony Daugherty punched Con Lenihan in the shoulder, and the others laughed and jiggled in their seats. The slagging match was on.

"Go on, Malachi," said Connie. "Top that one, can you?"

Malachi turned a droll bridegroom adoration on me, which was accentuated by that earring he wore. "Just because you have hair round your mouth, don't go thinkin' I'll be marryin' you."

"That's disgusting," blurted out Susan Drummond, as, shamefaced, she blushed.

"Somebody give us a fag," said Malachi. "I've tired myself abusin' the poor witless Yank. Here, Dizzy, have a fag and cheer up, it's payday."

I took an unfiltered Woodbine from Tony's packet of ten that Malachi held out to me, to signal that all was taken in good humor, while Malachi in his victorious mood, mockingly magnanimous, said to Susan, "Wha? Wha? What's troubling you, love."

"Oh, nothing," she said, her eyes smarting through the smoke from the fag she'd lit nervously. "It's just the level of the talk these days. I think I deserve a little more respect than that.

I've lived all my life on the edge of the gutter, I don't need to be dragged into it."

She thrust a cup of tea at me, and from that, I knew she was browned off at me, too. Even Malachi, for once, was subdued.

Seeing her opportunity, Susan went on. "And how many times have I warned yez, if Higgy catches you smoking back here—."

"Aren't you smokin' yourself?" said Pascal Larkin, with a look of amazement.

"I know, and don't remind me." Susan stubbed out her fag-end on the tea-kettle board at her elbow.

"Anyway, when's the last time Higgy bothered us about it?" said Malachi, always on the lookout to get in the last word. "Don't you think he fookin' well knows?"

"Malachi Morgan," said Susan. "I've had just about enough from you. It's you has me all out of sorts—never knowin' what's going to happen next. If you want to smoke, you can go in the jacks. And while you're there, you can diddle yourself."

"Aw, shut up, you old sowse."

"I don't have to take that from the likes of you for the pittance in slave-wages I'm getting."

"Here," said Malachi. "We'll have your favorite, the foreigner, put in a word for you with his pal, Higginbotham, and maybe you'll get a rise, now that he's in thick with the management."

"Malachi, I'm not in with them."

"Sure you're not, and tell us there's no difference between you and us."

"There isn't."

"How much are you getting in your pay-packet today?"

They all looked at me with interest, Tony, Pascal, even sleepy Con. "Seventeen and ten a week. And it's not much when you think my rent alone is six and ten a week."

"Do you know what Susan's getting?" said Malachi. "Ask her."

"Eleven quid a week," said Susan. "Me old one scarpered a solid twenty year ago, and haven't I worked to support the house and his children, and mine, ever since, and that's it, not a ha'penny more, and lucky to be getting it, too—I've often worked for less, and wages hasn't always been this good."

"So," said Malachi, "there you are—there's them, and then there's us."

"As far as I can see," I said, "we're all in the same boat."

"We'll see," said Malachi. "We'll see."

The general comments were, "It's a sin, all right." "Ought to be a law against it, wages like this." "Fat chance of that. Only laws passed in Kildare Street is the ones that make the rich richer." "It's a poor world to be born poor in." "What kind of talk is this?" "Drink your tea and shut up." "If you want a good argument, just bring up the price of butter." "Never mind the price of butter, what about my pint?" "You're not old enough to drink water."

"Listen to them." Malachi nudged me. "Try and get this lot to agree on a single thing. A shower of fookin' solicitors."

"You're the one to talk," Pascal said to Malachi, "wid yer magazines in the bollocky-house."

Malachi threw a pillow at his head, and Pascal took off with Malachi chasing after him, up into the Disaster Area. Shouts and cries came out of the shadows and Eddie Larkin was off to help his brother. Malachi had them both by the neck at the rear entrance when a klaxon on a lorry out in Island Street blasted off and a rich round of Cork cursing came through the door when your man found it locked.

"Go 'way, yez eedjits!" Pascal Larkin shouted through the windowless tin wall. "Can't yez see we're on our lunch hour?"

Malachi came back with a hammerlock on Pascal's arm, with Eddie kicking at his heels. "The Corkmen," the Larkins complained, "must they always be arriving exactly just noon of a Friday?"

"Yeah, when we're supposed to be on our break."

Malachi explained. "It's a four-hour drive up from Cork—and your man is in a flummox to be off-loaded and away again, so's not to be late home for his mam giving him the bit of cheese."

"Well, he can go to bloody hell and wait," said Connie, from a reclining position. "Same as going to Cork, anyways."

"Yeah," said Tony, "you wouldn't say so if you were in the Oliver Bond like me—me and la cucarachas." And on they went. "I wouldn't mind livin' downhill from Guinness'–don't you get a whiff now and again when the wind is right?" "The only inhabitants of the Oliver Bond well-off enough to get drunk is the rats." "Yeah—they're plannin' a snooker tournament in my tea-tray, rollin' their little balls of rat-dung, cuein' up their tails, like."

Mr Higginbotham was standing out of the Office, motioning to Malachi Morgan. "Pay-packets," said Malachi, jumping up.

"That's old Needlenose for ya." "We're not to be trusted, yeah." "Put cash in our hands when we've got a free half-hour, and we'd do a bunk on ya for the afternoon." "So—no pay-packets till luncheon is over!"

Malachi came sauntering back, flipping through the names in his hand. "Susan Drummond. Here's your pittance in slave-wages. I see you're not refusn' it. Tony Daugherty, free tickets to you to the bird-watchin' in the Phoenix Park. Eddie, here's yours, if you can manage to count it. Good thing for you it doesn't go above the number six. Clare—new pair of stockings, love? Pascal Larkin—a few bob for your piggy-bank and your copybooks for school. Connie—here's them new pair of Wellingtons you been longin' for." Malachi stuffed his own small brown envelope with the silver clasp and hole-protector on the top flap into his back pocket, and sat down for one last fag . "Jaysus—I'm knackered. The responsibility is staggerin'."

"Where's mine?" I said.

"Ah, you know that shower o' shite in Pearse Street." He shrugged. "Higginbotham says to say, 'Sorry, better luck next week.'"

"What!" they all said. "No way to run a business!" "I'll bet 'twas Needlenose himself forgot to put your hours in." "I wouldn't be surprised." "Yeah—fine way to land home, and have to tell the little woman—sorry, dear, no milk for the babby this week."

"Well, I'm going to see about–," I started.

But Malachi held me back by the arm. "Now, what do you want to go starting a row for, Dizzy? Complainin' isn't going to get you anywhere. Who are you going to complain to?–Needle-nose? He'll tell you it wasn't his fault, nothing to be done, it's those blasted yokes of a bookkeeping department down in Pearse Street—for he won't want to admit it was anything he done, or didn't."

"Well, it isn't right, Malachi," said Connie, sitting up.

Malachi sighed. "Look, lads—is this any way for us to treat a poor wayfaring stranger? Who came into our midst with the best of intentions to help us bear our lots and make things easier for us? To clean up the Disaster Area that used to be the Dis-patch Floor? Eddie, pass us your hat."

"No, don't do that," I said, as I saw Eddie dig down for his pay-packet.

"Now, cough it up, all of yez," said Malachi. "Share and share alike, isn't that what you was preachin' yourself, just now, Dizzy? All in the same boat, aren't we?"

"I won't take it."

"You're not takin' it—we're givin' it. You there, Pascal Larkin, you too, you snivellin' rodent."

Pascal looked first amazed, and then dismayed, and was about to protest, when Tony punched him in the ribs. "Ow!–that hurt."

"Don't say a word," said Malachi, to me. "We'd do it for the bleedin' Corkman out the back, and he'd steal the button-boots off your Ma, and her, still warm in the grave."

They passed the hat to Tony, and all said, with one voice, "Sure, you'd do the same for us, if the shoe was on the other foot."

I looked down in my hand and counted up at a glance an amount that came to a full seventeen quid. Then Clare came up to me, and, with a little upside down smile and bent eyebrows indicating how much it meant to her to be able to do this for me, as little as it was, as small a thing, placed the remaining ten shillings from out of her purse into my hand. I looked round at them. Tony. Con. Pascal and Eddie. Clare and Susan. Even Malachi. Although Susan had her back turned, and I respected her feelings. They were decent people. Good people. Salt of the earth. "I'm touched," I said.

"We know," said Malachi, placing a finger up to tap his temple with a twisted grin and a wink.

I shifted from foot to foot in my uncomfortable gratitude, but I didn't want to put them all on the spot any longer, so I just said, simply, as humbled as I felt, "Thank you. I won't forget this. And you'll get it all back, I promise." I looked around. "I don't know what to say."

"Say nothin' then, and let's get back to work. Here comes Higgy."

At closing time that afternoon, before leaving, I stopped to say, "Mr Higginbotham–."

"Call me Simon, lad."

"Simon—I would like to ask, before I don't see you again for the weekend—just what exactly happened to my pay envelope, do you think?"

"Why? I gave it to Malachi Morgan—to give out with all the rest. Didn't you get it?"

"No, I didn't. But they all took up a collection, and–."

"Oh—they took up a collection, did they?" Merriment was coming into Higgy's eyes, and he laughed, heartily, with lips pressed together, as if trying to hold it back. "My boy, you've been snookered."

I could feel the fuming embarrassment rising in my cheeks. At that moment, I could see Malachi posing at the back of the lorry with my pay packet dangling in the air wiggling from his fingers, and a wicked grin on his face. "Wait'll I get him!"

Seeing this, Malachi took flight and I didn't catch up to him till we were out on the footpath and he and the other boys were all the way up to the corner of Watling Street, where I jumped on his back and got him around the neck in a headlock and gave him a severe noogie on the skull, like I used to do to my little brother Jack back home when we were kids.

"All right, all right," he cried, breaking away, "I deserved that, but mind the liberties you're takin' with me! I've my dignity to preserve when I'm out in public." He stood up to 'straithen' his clothing.

"How'm I going to pay them all back now? They've all gone home their separate ways." I looked around at Tony and Con, who were standing there, laughing. "How in the hell did you all manage to pull this off?"

"It wasn't us, it was him!"

"We only fell in with the master plan."

We were across Watling Street from Timoney's on the corner, and Malachi said, "Come on along with us now—we need a fourth to team up with us for a frame of snooker."

"I'm told I've already been snookered," I said with chagrin.

"Ah, 'twas all in good fun," said Malachi. "Come on, and you can buy the first round!"

As we tumbled through the door, the four of us, I still wanted to know that Susan and Clare, for instance, had been taken care of.

"Not to worry," said Malachi. "I just gave it back to them out of your pay packet when you went back down to the Dispatch floor and you're weren't lookin', that's all. Plus a small commission for meself. I'm jokin,' I'm jokin.' I'll have a pint, thanks."

When our pints had settled, we picked them up and went down the back, where the lone snooker table stood, shoddy and torn green baize covering the surface, hung over with a pallid pool of light from a green-shaded lamp overhead. "Mm, this tastes good," I said as I sipped.

"Coming straight downhill from Guinness' Brewery up in Thomas Street, by gravity, into the tap here in Timoney's," said Malachi. "You won't get a fresher pint in all of Dublin, or in all the world, I daresay, for that matter."

I was standing there soaking in the atmosphere of this Dublin working-class pub, and it reminded me, for all I could think of, of the rare times, back home in Milltown, when my black friend from the Peace Action Consortium, Tmolura, used to take me into the Horseshoe Lounge on Park Street, in his neighborhood, where he was known as the basketball star from Central Catholic, and the pool champion of the hood.

Meanwhile, Malachi was saying, "I'll take the foreigner, but you'll have to spot us."

"Think I never shot pool before?" I said.

"This is a gentleman's game," said Tony, leaning on his cue-stick, the image of Rod Stewart at the microphone. "This is snooker."

"I shoot straight pool," I said. "Eight-ball. But I'll take Connie here—you and me, Con, the Culchies against the Jackeens. Malachi, we can't play on the same side, I have to get even with you."

"Want to settle a score, do you? Are you puttin' your money where your mouth is?"

I pondered, and put my pint down on the bumper—but Con Lenihan said, "No drinks on the table," pointing to a sign on the wall. "Can't you read?"

From this, I was thinking Con took his snooker seriously, and maybe I had a chance. "I'll bet you one single quid, Malachi." I was thinking of the rent I'd have to pay this week. "Yours against mine."

"That's a mental midget's wager."

"Ah, but that's all you're getting, take it or leave it. Are you on, or not?"

"Yer on."

"What's all the colored balls for, Tony?" I asked, novice that I was.

"This table's not regulation," he said, as he sorted red, yellow, green and brown balls. He filled the triangular rack, with red balls. "It's only five foot by ten, when it ought to be six by twelve. Not enough room in here." Fifteen red balls went into the rack, with the black ball behind it, and the pink a millimeter in front of the of the red-ball triangle. "God bless you," Tony recited as he placed three balls, green, brown and yellow, in proper order, G-B-Y, along the 'baulk-line.' "This is a game you'd want to practice all day," said Tony, "to be any good at it."

"Toss for the break-off," said Malachi, but his ten-bob piece came down on the edge, up against the rail. "We win," he said, looking at Con.

Connie just smiled. "Go on."

Malachi set up his 'striker-ball' between the brown and yellow balls on the baulk-line, but behind them. When he shot, hard, almost jumping off the floor, he aimed for the middle of the triangle's near side, and the red balls broke like a single hand-clap! colors scattering across the green baize, whirring. With no less than 15 red balls, a brown, blue, pink, green, and black ball, as well as a yellow, I quickly saw that the rules were too complicated for a first-timer like me to understand straight off. After all that explosion of balls, nothing dropped.

"Right," said Tony. "You've lost. Go ahead, Con."

But Connie shook his head and made a slight motion with the stick planted between his feet, as he throttled the cue-stick by the throat. "You go, Dizzy."

Malachi said, "Are you feeling lucky, Con?"

"Let's see what the Yank can do."

"Do you call your pockets?" I said.

"We all know where you're going," said Malachi, "*if* you do."

"First shoot the red. Then a color, then a red, and so on. First colored ball is the yellow," said Tony, "then the green, then the brown, blue, pink, and last, the black."

"How do you win?"

"You just shoot," Malachi told me. "We'll keep track of the points. If we start explainin,' we'll be here all night. Learn as you go."

I took a last sip of Guinness, and put the pint down on the wall-ledge. I now felt fortified, as I chalked my stick, and said, I don't know why, "Make way for a pool-shooter from the Horse-shoe Lounge." I leaned one hand on the rail to study my shot. "I haven't held a stick in my hands in months, I want you to know."

"Not this sort of stick exactly, anyways," said Malachi, archly. "Making excuses already, are you, ye wanker?"

Now I knew I had to sink my first shot. I had a red ball on the lip at the nearest corner after Malachi's scatter on the break-off, with a yellow to shoot through to get to it, with the cue-ball lie he left me; the yellow lay right behind the hanging red along the rail, and I didn't know if, in any case, I could pot the red without hitting the yellow, too; and, on the other hand, a fairly unencumbered shot to sink a red ball at the opposite corner pocket; but I decided to go for the two. "Can I bank it off the rail?"

"You have a clear shot," said Malachi, objecting, hopping around the table.

"That's too easy," I said.

"I see your game. Then when you've missed, 'twasn't an easy shot, was it?"

"Shoot, man!" said Connie.

I shot, but softly, not hard or fast. My cue-ball rolled steadily but slowly, kissed the rail, and nudged the yellow fairly solidly, which turned over along the cushion, nuzzling the rail cozily for a few inches, till it struck the red ball in front of it gently into the corner pocket, where it had been hanging, and then the yellow proceeded to turn over once more, and, after hesitating, dropped in while I coaxed it with bodily gyrations.

"Brilliant!" said Tony.

"Sheer beginner's luck," I said. I then sank a red and a green, thinking of Tmolura, who'd told me, always leave yourself a shot, which was why I'd gone for the two-fer. But I proceeded to blow my shot on the brown.

Tony stepped up and potted the one brown, then a red, and the blue ball, but then missed on the next red.

"Right, Tony," said Malachi. "We're ahead on points, 10 to 7."

Connie's turn. Smoothly, the man from down the country ran the table and then stood back with his feet planted and his hands gripping the throat of his cue-stick as if to say, 'could *you* build a haycock that pretty?'

That was the first frame for us. I complained that I had to get home to the missus, which was true, so we shortened the game to 5 frames. Con Lenihan turned out to be money in the bank. "Pay up, Malachi," said I, with a laugh, as I added a welcome quid to my pay packet. "Now we're even!"

The Fleet Street Bar was a pub where some of the reporters and editors of the Irish Times and the Irish Press did their drinking. I met Bernadette Cullen there one night after work because it was handy to where she worked at Aer Lingus. Naturally, Martina Kelly came with her, but I left it to others stacked at the bar to try looking down Martina's blouse undetected. I was in deep enough water myself with Bernadette, whose beauty was intoxicating to the point where I had to keep twirling the wedding ring on my finger to keep my balance.

"What was it John Martyn was telling me the other night about a split at the Ard Fheis last year?"

It was my tactic to get Bernadette involved in arcane political matters to keep her talking to me. "A split?" she said. "More like *the* split. Capital letters and everything. It really goes back to '69—between us and the Stickies."

"Why do you call them that?" I would say or do anything to keep those brown eyes looking into mine.

"Because they've come with Easter Lilies made of gummed paper, like a stamp. You lick it and stick it on your lapel. You'll see, when the time comes, next spring. They're great sellers at Easter Week. People in the pubs buy them and stick them on their lapels to show they're supporters of the Republican

Movement. Only ours are the old, traditional kind, plain paper, and we have to give out a pin with each one to pin them on. So they're the Stickies, and we're the Provos."

"So, if I understand this, the Stickies are the Official IRA, right?"

"And the Official Sinn Féin Or Gardiner Street, as they're referred to, because that's where their headquarters are. And we're Kevin Street. Silly, isn't it—Stickies and Provies? Only it isn't, really. There's a new Cumann, in the North Side, like ours, named after Charlie Hughes, a Provos officer who was gunned down this summer in a gun-battle with the Stickies in Belfast. And over at Trinity, where Peadar Kenny is? When the Split came, they had to split the old Republican Club in Trinity, too, and Peadar was one of the few to come over to our side, and now he's having the devil of a time organizing at Trinity because of the harassment the Stickies are giving him—tearing down his announcements, flatting the tires on his bike, disrupting his meetings—they've even rifled his room and stolen papers."

"Why such, um, animosity?"

"Because they're Marxists, and we're not. We're Connolly Socialists."

"So how did the Split come about, originally?"

"Well, it was at first all one Republican Movement, in the Sixties. But nothing was happening. Meanwhile, the Marxists infiltrated and took it over from the inside—got all their own votes on the Sinn Fein Executive, and the Chief of Staff of the IRA. Then Civil Rights came along in the North, and nobody knew what to do—get behind it, or wait for it to fail, or what. And what did the mighty Marxists do in the meantime but ship all the weapons to their brethren, the Free Wales Army. So, when the pogroms came in '69, the people in Divis Street were left defenceless against the B-men and the RUC and the

Loyalists. Brendan is really the one to explain all this—he was there—it's only for him that I know what I know."

"Go on. I'm listening."

"Well, the majority of the Movement never, never went with the Marxist drift. And they were angry after August, '69. Because the 'Ra wasn't ready to defend the people, but there were volunteers—and no guns to give them. And the old-line leadership up north, men like Joe Cahill, who'd been young in the 'Fifties Border Campaign, blamed Gardiner Street—so they split off inside the army to start up their own military campaign against the Brits—and we're talking about the majority of the army splitting off from the leadership, which was left a rump. Then Sinn Féin followed the army's lead at the Ard Fheis last year, when two-thirds of the Convention walked out."

"Man, have I got a lot to learn."

"Well, I hope I've helped," said Bernadette, smiling, in all innocence–or maybe not—perhaps she was enjoying casting the spell on me.

Thank God John Martyn came up at that point.

"John, I've just been receiving an education from Bernadette."

"She would be the one to do it," said John. "Barman! Oh, Barman!"

The next Friday when I opened the back door into Island Street, Meehawl McGuinn, the driver from Cork City, had his lorry backed up and was sitting on the tailgate with his lorry-helper, Fergus. Malachi and the Larkins were coming out to assist.

"We're not lifting a thing unless youz help," said Malachi to Meehawl.

"We load," said Meehawl. "You unload."

Meehawl directed this to Malachi, but, having dropped the Cork brogue for a moment to speak in plain English, so that I would understand, he looked at me. "Noel Sugarman tells me you're in charge of this lot."

"Come on, Malachi, let's just get it done and over with," I said.

I went back inside to survey the job. I really had no idea. The original bins built out of two-by-fours to stack the foam-pieces by sizes were buried. The entire Disaster Area was piled high to the rafters. Inside, it was chaos in the dark—outside, because for once the sun was out, it was blinding midday. I lifted my palm over my eyes to squint at the tailgate—where a full-on Middle East summit meeting was going on, Dubliners and Corkmen, the best of friends.

"Have you got it all sorted out?" said Malachi to me.

"Look the only thing to do is to pile the raw foam on the pavement out here first, and then clear away space inside. At least that way, McGuinn can be on his way."

"Right you are," said Malachi. "Pascal, you assist the gaffer here and me and Eddie'll take care of inside."

"No, Malachi, I'll go inside."

Malachi jumped down. "I wouldn't do that if I was you."

"I'm responsible for seeing this thing gets done right, Malachi, not you."

"You mightn't like what you find in there."

"Yeah? Like what?"

"Spiders. All kinds of creeping and crawling things. Cockaroaches as big as your thumb. Rats as big as cats."

"Malachi, cut the malarkey, willya?"

He pulled me inside while Pascal and Eddie had gotten busy pulling foam-pads out of the lorry and stacking them against the tin wall.

"Listen, Malachi, you may think I'm stupid, but don't you think I know what's going on around here?"

"What?"

"Pilfering pillows. Looting cushions. Stealing, in other words."

"Ah, Jaysus, you don't have to put it that way, do you?"

"What would you call it?"

"What do they call it over the sea there? Profit-sharing?"

"Ah, it's your own ass. I don't care—."

"That's a very sensible attitude to take."

"But if I know what's going on, don't you think Sugarman does?"

"He might think he knows—why? What have you told him?"

"Nothing. What do you take me for—a snitch? But I know he suspects—and maybe he's on to you. How would you know, one way or the other?"

"I wouldn't, I suppose. But what do you think he means to do?"

"How do I know? I'm not a mind-reader. But don't you think it's time to quit while you're ahead?"

"Do you know—if I had my way—I'd burn this fookin' kip down, as a public nuisance—and all the fookin' foam in it."

"Right. And Malachi Morgan'd be out of a job."

"Sure, there's better jobs than this."

"So why do you stay?"

"You're workin' in it yourself!"

"That's what I mean. We're all in the same boat. So, you help me and I'll help you."

"Well, I'm happy we got all that sorted."

"But you've got to help yourself first, Malachi."

"That's what I've been doin,' boss, right along—helpin' meself."

John Martyn was the Sinn Féiner assigned to train me and Mick O'Corrigan on selling and collecting in the pubs and whatever else we needed to ensure we'd qualify as full members when the time came. I found that whenever you went out peddling An Phoblacht, the Movement's weekly newspaper, people could ask some awkward questions. It might help if I sounded like I knew what I was talking about. Unlike Mick, I couldn't pass myself off, laughingly, as a school-leaver from Tipperary.

One night, after our rounds, we were sitting in Owen Roe's, off the Portobello bridge, resting our lagging spirits, as it were. "Dr Roy Johnston, and Professor Anthony Coughlan, who's at UCD, they were the ones who infiltrated the Movement and filled it with their hair-splitting Marxist rhetoric."

I took John as a university man myself, but in that I was wrong. He'd been to the Christian Brothers School in Synge Street, barely two blocks from where we were sitting. With his monkish love of books and his round black glasses I'd have thought surely he was for higher education, and he was, only as he put it, he came from the wrong side of the income tracks. Again I had to revise my estimation of the quality of Irish secondary schools as compared to their American counterparts, and this did not favor my own country. The Irish were just better at it. The man in the street was a cosmopolitan—farmers, like my own brother-in-law, Patrick Blake, were educated, not merely babysat.

"But, John, if we're the majority, and they're the minority, how is it they're the Officials, and we're only Provisional?"

"That's a label the media stuck on us. What difference? We know what we're about, and so do the people. When we win, they'll call us the Government."

When John stepped away to visit the loo, Mick cautioned me not to ask too many questions. "It's not done, Nicky. You don't want to seem to be nosy. And you don't really want to know, do you? Knowledge is easy to pump in, but it's pumping it out again that comes hard. You'd want to forget some of them things you know when they start in on you with the rubber hoses."

"Mick, you're crazy. This is a completely open thing. Why, there's thousands in O'Connell Street at these rallies with the speakers from the North. And John Martyn doesn't tell us anything we can't find out from the newspapers or in a book."

"Exactly," said Mick, and he let that sink in.

I tried it his way, and the less I talked, the more John did. Mick himself said little at our sessions, and when he did speak up, it was always something scurrilous. John took me under his wing, finding me an apt pupil, but he thought Mick was immature. Mick simply looked him in the eye and said he wasn't a politician. And John understood him perfectly. John could be drawn to a point only. His was the voice of official wisdom— or should I say, Provisional. He spoke for the Movement as he would have spoken for Macmillan's Bookshop. "We have one simple rule in the Republicans. Live by it and you can't go wrong. And that rule is—from each according to his abilities, to each according to his deserts."

That night Mick wanted to walk me all the way home to Upper Rathmines Road. He said he wanted to meet the missus. "Does she know where you and me were the other night?"

"No, and don't you tell her."

"And I'll bet that little girl of yours must be the darling."

"That she is. Daddy's little girl."

"Ah, but I noticed that Bernadette Cullen hasn't taken the twinkle out of your eye, either."

"And she won't. I may have gotten married, but I didn't go blind."

"Ha, ha. Spoken like a true philosopher. But I saw how you were lookin' at her the last meeting. It's as well for your immortal soul that you are married. And as well for me. After all, I might fancy a bit of Bernie meself. Did you ever think of that?"

Mick's surprise visit turned out to be a welcome treat for Sheila. She'd already found friends for herself in the house—two girls at the back of the hall on our ground floor, in a bed-sitter there, two sisters from a family of twelve, 11 girls and one boy, from Kinegad, County Westmeath. Eileen worked in the kitchen at the rectory for Mary Immaculate in Rathmines, and Angela clerked in the Ministry of Labour in Mespil Road, prac-tically next door to where Mick lived. Then there was Josephine, a nurse, upstairs, with a son, Desmond, who was Aisling's age, so that our girl could have a playmate to roam with out in the back garden. And Shane and Monica were a couple who lived downstairs, beneath us, and had their own entry under the front stair, and a baby still in cloth diapers—awful things, to be always washing, said Sheila—but still, from Monica she found out where the washeteria was in Rathmines.

Now Sheila was a fund of curiosity about these Sinn Féiners, and Mick was her first chance to have a go at them. Mick delighted her. She liked him immediately. With Sheila, you always knew if she liked someone or not, and it didn't take long to find out. For if she didn't like you right away, she never would.

"Tell us now, Mick from Tipperary, did you ever know a friend of ours from back in the States, Nuala Mulroy?"

"Ah, no," said Mick. "Why? Should I have?"

"You might have. Nuala's from County Tipp."

"As a matter of fact, I did know a Mulroy, her name was Brigid. And her sister was Moira. And her other sister was Aoife. And then was Orla and Oona and Enya. Tallulah, too."

"Oh, go on with ye now, and don't be a goose."

Later, she told me that he somehow reminded her of her little brother Matt. The three of us ended up staying up most of the night, only for the chat, while the babby slept peacefully unawares in her bed. Mick was the kind Sheila could get on with easily. You could depend on everything he said to be either a joke or a lie.

"Tell us now—where were you two the other night?"

"What night?" said Mick, with a look that foretold a sudden loss of memory.

"Nick was telling me he met you the first night he went to that meeting. But he wasn't home till quite late. Later than the pubs closing."

"Did you not know the pubs in Dublin closes between three and four in the afternoon every day? They call it the Holy Hour. I don't know if it's the same custom down in Mayo."

"Don't go changing the subject, Mick."

"I dasn't."

"These meetings don't go lasting that long, do they?"

"To tell you the truth—."

"Oh, here it comes now—where's my Wellies?"

"We were sittin' under a tree by the Grand Canal, feedin' the ducks."

"And what do ducks eat?"

"Fried potatoes."

Sheila laughed. "You're an old slouched caubeen, you are."

"As true as God—it was a bloody drunken debauch we were at in Stephen's Green, bodies in the bushes, orgies in the flowerbeds, disgusting French sexual practices going on, and I only wish I could remember the details, as I can see your dirty, dirty mind has been busy picturin' all the ructions and goin's-on as I speak!"

"Just tell me one thing, Mick," said Sheila, in the end, with a nod towards me. "Does he know what he's getting into?"

"Aw, missus," said Mick. "Do any of us?"

Noel Sugarman was in his cubicle one evening at five when, ready to leave, I went to his door to say goodnight.

A bleak discovery dawned on his face as he looked up. "Do you realize—bleedin' hell—I have ten bunk beds missing, Nick."

"Bunk beds?"

"Ten of them." Sugarman pinched his long nose in thought. "Due for destinations all over the country—and never arrived."

"There must be some mistake, Noel."

"No mistake."

"But each one of those beds is eight or nine stone apiece—I know—I've wrapped plenty of them." It was true—the frames and bedsprings were made of red-painted steel.

"They didn't just grow legs and decide to take a stroll for themselves, did they? And they're not flying out the roof. Did you ever find anything out of the way, that time you cleaned up the Disaster Area for me, back there?"

"No bunk-beds, I can tell you that."

"Anything else?"

"A few old water-logged cushions—nothing anyone would want to steal—nothing of value."

"But those beds. They're an item that could command not only a price, but a buyer."

"Well, they're not walking out the half-door, and they're not going out on Willie's lorry, because I load the lorry."

"This started before you got here," said Sugarman, musing. "Takes a while for stores down the country to report back—and then it shows up in the figures." He pinched his nose again. "Must have been at night, must have been at night."

"Noel? Since this started before I got here, as you've pointed out—I'd really rather stay uninvolved. I mean—I do have to get along with everyone here, to get my work done. Know what I mean?"

"Quite right." Sugarman stood up. "Leave it to me, lad. I shall take care of it. You see, there is simply no way I can write off the loss of that many beds. And let me tell you this—just between ourselves—P-Street is prepared to go to court to recover the damages. Now all I have to do is to find out those responsible."

Mick O'Corrigan and I still did not have our voting rights by the time of the Sinn Fein Ard Fheis for 1971, but we were in attendance as observing members.

Mick was excited when he told me to expect various wild men and women from the North to be there, and they were. Michael Farrell and Eamonn McCann were there from the PD, People's Democracy. "A lot of pinkos and fairies running around waving red banners with the hammer and sickle on them in front of Stormont," said Mick. But to me, they seemed to echo the typical student-Left activists from back home in the States. Bernadette Devlin was there. I had seen her, from a distance, speaking on the Common when she came to Boston in '69, and later on the television news, but now I had the chance to observe her in person under the studio lights and TV cameras in the Mansion House in Dublin. Frank McManus was there, the MP from Fermanagh-Tyrone who was one of the founders of the Northern Resistance Movement that fall. Gerry Fitt and John Hume, from the SDLP, Joe Cahill, from the Provisional IRA, still on the run, but now living openly in Dublin, and frequently to be seen at the Kevin Street Headquarters; they were

there, as well as the National Sinn Féin Executive, with the Ó
Brádaigh brothers, Tomás Mac Giolla and Dáithí Ó Conaill.

Between the tall windows, on folding seats, like a school
auditorium, the big hall was filled to capacity. People were
saying it was the biggest and, by far, most enthusiastic Sinn
Féin Convention since the 1920s.

Mick and I sat with the Cumann Billy Reid and the
other Dublin cumainn, Martin Forsyth, Charlie Hughes, Tom
McGoldrick, Jim Saunders, Tony Henderson, Dorothy Maguire
and Terence McDermott, on the right, at the front, near the
stage. The cumainn from the rest of the country were ranged
behind us, all the way to the back of the packed hall. There
was a continual coming and going, reading of reports, passing
of resolutions, discussion of platform, speeches on programme,
addresses to the assembly. There was cheering and applause
when Ruairí Ó Brádaigh read out a message from the Army
Council of the IRA.

They called 1971 an historic year. They said that the
struggle, this year, had entered its decisive phase. They called
on the Sinn Féin, as the political wing of the Republican Movement, to ensure that it was in position to act decisively once the
Army had won the military victory. They condemned the Lynch
Government for collaborationist treachery for imprisoning IRA
Volunteers from the North in Mountjoy Jail in Dublin.

Other speakers reported on the progress of the war.
Since the year began, over a thousand operations carried out
by the IRA, 700 of them bomb explosions, 300 alone in the
three months since Internment began, recently 60 operations
mounted successfully in a single day. Casualties: 43 British soldiers, 11 RUC men, 5 UDR killed, and an unknown number
wounded; for the IRA, 9 killed, no figure on injuries. Internment had not damaged the Provisional IRA in any way.

A final speaker gave the demands of the Republican Movement on the British Government for the coming year: cessation of the British Army's campaign in Ireland, abolition of the Stormont government in Ulster, release of all Irish political prisoners, and free elections towards a new government for all 32 counties of Ireland.

I turned to Mick. "No withdrawal of British troops? No abolition of the Border?"

"Well, they're taking it in stages—first we'll beat the Brits back into the sea, and then we'll let you politicians have your turn to talk it all away."

A great cheering went up in the Mansion House. It was being announced from the stage that news had arrived this moment that nine IRA soldiers had just escaped from the maximum-security Crumlin Road Jail in Belfast, two of them picked up quickly, the other seven—clean away.

Chapter 5

Christmas in Dublin

Dressed in the universally popular surplus Army fatigue jacket, the new man first appeared at Paddy Clarke's one night in early December. He also wore a shined pair of high-top British Army boots, which smelled of neat's-foot and looked soft as a glove, causing Mick O'Corrigan to ask if he liked them. "I telling you, comrade, they are very comfortable—and I do a good deal of walking."

He spoke in that lilting accent from the Islands, which you couldn't quite put your finger on—was it Jamaica? the Bahamas, or what?

When Alita Hughes said she appreciated his interest in the Movement, he replied, "And I thanking allyuh, comrades, for inviting me to one of your meetings. I have a great respect for the principles of the Irish Republican Movement."

He fondled one end of his Fu Manchu with a couple of fingers while he balanced his elbow on a crossed knee. He certainly looked East Indian: jet-black eyes; and the long, flowing black locks nuzzling the nape of his neck had the sheen of a water-bird.

When Alita asked for his name, he replied, "My name is C.K. Pradesh." She wrote it down and everyone assumed the C.K. stood for something unpronounceable, as he added, "That is the name on my passport, but my comrades call me Krishna." He smiled. "I am Trini, from Port o' Spain, so I carry the British passport."

All this talk of comrades led Alita to ask him who his comrades were.

"I have recently come here from London. I have been a student at the London School of Economics, and a member of the Third World People's Liberation Front led by Tariq Ali—I'm sure you know the name—and a member of the London branch of the Anti-Internment League. At present, I am unfortunately persona non grata to the British Home Office. I have been forced to interrupt my studies, and—." He shrugged, and smiled, and gestured with open palms.

Nobody had seen Alita's cousin from Belfast, Brendan McAndrews, since the night he grilled me, so the new man was spared, but Alita did explain the membership drive and the conditions of probationary membership.

For his part, C.K. Pradesh was attentive, but non-committal. He obviously knew he had to pass inspection, but he also seemed definitely to be judging us, as if he were undecided, but he expected us to make up his mind for him. For the rest of the meeting, he withdrew, saying nothing, adding nothing, but listening, and observing, in the background.

The talk at the meeting was all of Martin Meehan and his spectacular escape from Crumlin Road. Meehan was the C.O. of the Ardoyne battalion in Belfast, and one of the most wanted names on the British Forces' lists. His capture had led British Army officers to boast to reporters that Internment was working. They locked him up tight in their showcase prison.

Just a fortnight previously General Farrar-Hockley, the British Commander of Land Forces, had come on television in the North to announce in a headmaster's tone barely concealing his glee that the IRA were crushed. Then came the escape of nine Provos from Crumlin Road. And shortly thereafter, at the end of November, the Blitz.

The Blitz, as the newspapers and radio-TV were calling it, was a well-planned, daringly-executed operation over two days that successfully mounted thirty bomb-blasts in the heart of Belfast—the 'RA's reply to the announcement that they were crushed. Millions of pounds of damages resulted, and, best of all, not a single civilian casualty or injured bystander. And now, Martin Meehan, most-wanted man in Ireland—flown the coop—and took two comrades with him. An Phoblacht was easily sold out that week—even the United Irishman, the organ of the Stickies, sold out. People were queueing in the pubs, as soon as you stuck your head in the door, hoping to get the inside dope on what they'd read in the Herald, the Press and the Times. The mighty, proud, invincible British Army, in all their fourteen thousands, out-foxed and made fools of by a mere handful of our darlin' lads. The Provos had done it again. That was the mood among the cheerful holiday shoppers in the pubs.

Alita Hughes closed the business of the meeting that night. "We need more money. We didn't do as well with our Sing-along Night as we might have, did we? We need more publicity, more activity, more of everything. It's coming up to Christmas, and there's still 650 men behind the wire for their holidays."

Mick O'Corrigan and I had just been voted full membership that evening. The other members, offering their congratulations, seemed pleased, although John Martyn was reserved, and Alita was her dour self. When it came time for someone to sponsor the 'Comrade,' remembering what Bernadette had done for me, and knowing it would mean I was no longer the 'foreigner' in the Cumann, I raised my hand.

Then I was pleased to find out that Krishna was living in Rathmines, not far from my place. I invited him to walk home with Mick and me, but Mick wanted to take another route, for, he said, "security reasons." I thought sometimes Mick was allowing his fantasies to run away with him.

"My father was a civil servant in Trinidad," Krishna was explaining as we crossed the Grand Canal. "I was expelled from the University. My father did not sympathise. It was my mother who helped me to get to England. And to continue my studies—I telling you, my mother has helped me."

"Why were you expelled from school, Krishna?"

"Well, it wasn't for drugs, you know?"

"No—I didn't mean—I asked because—well, when I left university, I was really pissed off with the whole thing."

"Man—you have a really bad accent."

"Me?"

"Yes, you. I know—if I really goin' Trini talk maybe yuh cyah understand a single ting I say—but I can talk standard English, when I want to, comrade. Can you?"

"Listen, comrade, we speak the best English in the world in Boston."

"Nah, dat's here in Dublin. Dey told me."

"Yeah, and you'll fit right in with dis, dat, dese and dose. In the North Side, anyway."

Krishna laughed heartily. "So—you were saying?"

"About what?"

"About leaving university. Pay attention, comrade."

"During the invasion of Cambodia by Nixon. After Kent State and Jackson State, you know?"

"I know—of course."

"Yeah. Two hundred and fifty schools all over the country out on strike. We took over the Student Union for two weeks."

"We have more in common than you thought," Krishna observed. "I telling you—that was last year—spring semester, of '70. Precisely the time when the riots struck the University of the West Indies."

"Where is that, Krishna?"

"St Augustine. About eight miles outside Port o' Spain."

"So what's the story in Trinidad?"

"'Wuz de scene?' we say. You asking I?" Krishna shook his head and his tone was mixed with irony and awe. "You Americans. Your country is so big—like a big poker table, and you can't see just right over de edge—dere's little old poker-chip Trinidad n' Tobago. The story is: government in a state of siege. Emergency powers, just as here in Ireland—in Ulster, in England, too. Martial law declared de last six years—and not yet lifted. Repression of the Left. Assassinations, imprisonments, exiles. I am one of them. I cannot go back."

On we walked, up Lower Rathmines Road; approaching in the December darkness, across the road, the Town Hall and its tower; beside us, on this footpath, the Rathmines Library—a Carnegie-endowed Library, curiously enough, endowed by the same wealthy steel magnate as the library in my own hometown back in the States. A capitalist exploiter who made his money off the backs of coal miners like my Dad. "What happened to you in London?" I asked my new 'comrade.'

"I liked it in St Augustine. I was in de Medical Faculty. I was studying to be a doctor. But—dose of us who survived—when de word came t'rough, de government let us know—we had tree choices—exile, prison or death. We all got together again in London. I suppose dat was inevitable. You know, for a time, we were tolerated in London—but not ever welcome, I telling you. The British, dey like to afford asylum to dissidents from all over—as long as it's all over de Eastern Bloc. Dey got no dissidents in de former Crown Colonies, you know? It was only a matter of time till de crunch came." Krishna glanced up at the darkened Palladian-style windows of the Library, now closed after hours. "Perhaps here—dere are quite a few people of colour in Dublin, I telling you, in de Faculty of Medicine, comrade."

Internment hung, a shadow in the air over Dublin, that Christmas season. In spite of the rallies in O'Connell Street, the proclamations, communiques, bulletins, interviews and decrees, North and South; in spite of the demonstrations and protests, in spite of marching in the face of a marching ban in Ulster, in spite of the mounting resistance all over the North, and the whole country, through the entire autumn, to steadily higher, more intense levels; the coming of the holiest day of the year seemed to bring only depression, doubt, bouts of back-ward-looking, seizures of soul-searching.

In O'Connell Street, colored lights in the shop-windows, holiday wreaths on the merchants' doors, looked conspic-uous— and incongruous— beside scrawled whitewash slogans and torn bits of pasted rally announcements. It had been a long year, 1971, a year of 'alarums and excursions.' Even six months is a long time for a civilian population to stand with lines drawn against a professional Army. The spirit sagged, just a trifle. People were hoping for a break. No one looked forward to celebrating what they could only concede was the worst Christmas in—well, since '69, anyway. Year's end was coming, time for adding up what 1971 had brought. People woke in their beds in the morning almost certain in their minds they would hear bad news today, perhaps having occurred while they slept. They were reaching out now to the season, too, to rescue them with its customs and traditions, to bring them home to hearth and family, to bring them back to other Christmases when times were better, when The Troubles weren't 'all there was.' And just as they were going on a shopping spree and wrapping up a fit of spending, along came the latest jolt, the newest shock, the media-spotlight of the day. While across the border, no farther than a twist of the knob on the radio or telly, in Belfast, 90 miles from Dublin, 14,000 British soldiers patrolled, raided, searched, arrested, seized, questioned, stopped, detained, interrogated, jailed and interned, all in the name of keeping the peace. The Big Lie stuck in the throat, too noxious to choke down.

It was during this season that our cumann made a decision to take advantage of the added crowds flooding into O'Connell Street for Christmas shopping to mount a three-day week-end hunger strike as a demonstration of our support for all those campaigning to end Internment and bring the boys home for Christmas.

We therefore spent the weekend on blankets spread out on the cold concrete underneath the columns of the GPO, one of the most historical and symbolic locations in the whole island, with our banners and picket signs. We were allowed to drink water and take tea three or four times a day, but nothing else.

We slept all night in the outdoor air in our clothes wrapped in blankets.

For someone like me who had grown up in America, never having missed a meal in my life, it was a sobering and eye-opening experience. In the beginning I was sure I didn't know how I was going to be able to do it, but as the hours wore on, looking around at the faces of John Martyn, only a few steps away from Macmillan's bookshop where he worked; of Bernadette and Martina, beautiful young creatures used to catering to the whims of travelers with credit cards, nevertheless willing to sacrifice their comfort; of young Mick O'Corrigan with his romantic ideal of fighting for his country; of 45-year-old Barney O'Toole, who worked in a labouring position for the Dublin Corporation, and who would sorely miss his pint; of idealistic young Peadar Kenny of the Trinity College Republican Club; of Myles Cunningham, whose singing voice would lead us through *James Connolly* and *Sean South* and *Kevin Barry*; and yes, Comrade Krishna, who had already suffered more disruption to his life than perhaps any of us except Alita Hughes. Our Chairman, Alita, had family members in Belfast facing death daily, or else incarcerated behind barbed wire without charges, trial or hope of release: mistreated, abused and subject to torture under interrogation. When this same Alita Hughes, our Chairman, handed to me a cup of steaming tea, I was never more grateful for anything anyone had ever given me in my entire life; and at the same time, never more ashamed of myself, for the callous, unseeing complacency with which I'd always taken the privileges of my lily-white American life for granted.

From Friday lunch-time at work until Monday morning when I returned from the GPO to Maurice Woolf's at 8 am, no food had passed my lips, but in that short, all-too-brief time, I became stronger than I had ever been, because we had done this together: and together, we were stronger than any one of us alone.

Three weeks before Christmas, during a crowded night of loud drinking and desperate holiday merriment, an explosion ripped through the premises of McGurk's Bar, in Georges Street, in Belfast. When the smoke cleared, there were 15 dead and 17 injured. The newspapers, radio and television called it a sectarian bombing of a Catholic bar by Protestant extremists. The journal of our Republican Movement, An Phoblacht, which we sold in the pubs, called it a cowardly act against a Nationalist pub by Empire Loyalists, and said that the forensic evidence, which showed that plastic explosives had been employed, would leave no doubt whatsoever that the source of such explosives could only be the one organization on the ground in Belfast which possessed such capabilities: the official representatives of State-funded, State-sponsored, State-run terrorism, the British Army.

While I was there selling papers, a man with a pint in his hand, in Madigan's, in Rathmines, said to me, "If that's what we're comin' to, then dead is dead, and neither the Reverend Paisley nor the Reverend Wolfe Tone is goin' to bring you back."

Leinster Square was the eyesore of Rathmines. Opposite the Town Hall, between the Library and the Allied Irish Bank, it was a seedy, vulgarized version of Dublin's grand squares.

The front of No. 33 Leinster Square was nearly overgrown by bushes. No. 33 had no railings of its own, and no gate, like all the others houses had, just a crumbling walk up to the front steps. Absentee landlord-ism. Jane Quill lived in the double-bedsitter at the front of the first floor with her flatmate, Mary McKenna.

The first time Comrade Krishna brought me up, I thought he was living with Jane and Mary in their flat. He entered without knocking.

It had been the sitting-room of the old townhouse. It had a big fireplace with a wide hearth, room for a big circular hook-rug on the wooden floor, space for three armchairs and a rocker, and even a pantry, off to the side, with the regulation sink, cooker and electric-kettle, but also, cabinets, and, a shock to me—a refrigerator. In this flat, Krishna could seat himself in the ample window-seat, with his knee cocked up, and watch Leinster Square, instead of the back of the laneway wall out the rear entry of his own gloomy flat, down below in the basement.

"My father came from a district about 60 miles north of Delhi." When he got on a roll, Krishna could quite forget to show off his Trini talk, and he lapsed into standard, university English. "My father had been jailed by the British authorities for two years beginning in 1940. At the time, he was a District Commissioner when Mahatma Gandhi began his wartime campaign of civil disobedience nationwide to try to coerce the British, bogged down by the war in Asia, into granting India independence. My father abstained from his duties as an elected official of the local Council, refusing to attend meetings, and had to be jailed. When Nehru came to power, after Independence, he found himself on the wrong side of the political fence, and, taking his family, with me, born in '47, the year of Independence, fled to Port o' Spain. I was therefore that son who grew up listening to tales of the old struggle against the colonialist regime. Still, when it came my turn to rebel, my father didn't agree with the new rebellion. It was against his new country, you see, comrade, and he was civil servant to the new state. To be a rebel was for *him*—I was the son, my role was to *obey*—he wanted me to become a doctor. What a true bourgeois! One will always find that it is conditions which determine people's behavior—not people's behavior which determine conditions."

While he teasingly ordered Jane Quill about, Krishna, of course, addressed her as 'comrade.'

"You know what, comrade?—my feet are tired—here—take off my boots for me."

"I will like hell. What did your last servant die of?"

Mary McKenna came from the same place as Jane, the townland of Abbeyderg, Co. Longford, in the midlands. They'd been besties since they were in St Emers National School together. Mary was a girl who looked as placid as a wheatfield baking in the sun. She rocked in her rocking chair, with one leg tucked up under her, while she knitted. Pink and blue baby's bootineers. She would knit the blue pair and hang them on the mantle, then knit the pink pair. When the pink pair was knitted, she would hang it up, unravel the blue pair, and begin again. She was a girl waiting for a man to come along and fill up her bootineers.

Jane was the perfect compliment to Mary. Talkative, brash and irreverent, Jane would pull her chair up in front of you and quiz you, with her elbows on her knees, her chin in her hands, her eyes wide and amazed. It was Jane who organized the parties and Mary who was courted by the fellas. Where Mary had a fine and friendly ample figure, with skin like the cream on top of a pail of milk, Jane, in her favored shapeless sweatshirts and corduroy jeans, would make you think of a pillow that somebody left only half-stuffed with goose-feathers.

Jane was working as a telephone operator all day, while Mary was in the Mater Hospital, nights, training for a nurse's aide. Back in Abbeyderg, before they left, they'd waited on tables together in a bar, the only pub in the townland. When they came up to Dublin and found other employment, they went out to the bars almost every night, on weekends, where, rather than waiting on the tables, they sat at them, and were waited on instead.

When I was there, daytimes, Mary always seemed to be expecting people to leave the flat so that she could go to bed. She never said anything. She didn't seem to have anything to add. Jane did her talking for her, when she was home, late afternoons.

As a good comrade, Krishna pointed out to Jane the contradictions inherent in this way of life, and that was the only way you knew that he cared about her at all, because he never drank, and he certainly wasn't about to go out on a date with anyone.

"Now, comrade, what possible use could you have for a refrigerator?"

"But it came with the flat!" Jane protested.

"Get rid of it! In dis climate, you don't need it."

"But we don't even use it," Jane pleaded. "Or hardly, anyways."

"Jane—do you know anyone who has a refrigerator?"

"No. But—."

"Are you one of de upper classes?"

"No, silly!"

"Hmph."

Jane looked at Mary. "Should we?"

Mary knitted and said nothing.

"Sell it!" said Krishna. "I telling you, comrade, you've got to learn to be practical. Can you use de money?"

Another time, as she was setting the table, motherly Jane said to him, "Come sit and eat."

The comrade looked up from his meditations in the window-seat. "Do you know what I have a craving for, Jane?"

"What?" she said, looking at her steaming potatoes with despair.

"A little glass of mango juice." Krishna's face lit up. "Run out across de road and get me some fresh mangoes."

"But, Krish, where am I going to get fresh mangoes in Dublin?"

"What a country!" sighed Krishna. "No mango juice."

Ireland was one of his fondest topics. He was full of observations. "Tell me—do you really get any benefit from confessing?"

Jane could find nothing to say to that, nor did Mary, naturally.

"Then why do you people feel so compelled to repeat this empty, unsatisfying ritual? Why, you are no better than the sudras of India who bow down to cattle! You telling I?—what is the difference between a mortal sin and a venial one, eh?" And he turned away disgusted. "I telling you—this country is drugged with the opium of the masses!"

But the comrade could be infallibly kind, as well. He was himself very sensitive, and sensitized. I wanted to know, because I was his sponsor for the cumann.

"In London, the English there, if you can find any, they lump me into their big bag of bigotry under the label *black*—which I am not—nor would I claim to be—nor am I a Paki, wog or jolly little Gunga Din. London is race-conscious, class-conscious, even caste-conscious!"

Ireland he found, happily, much more egalitarian. But also he knew quite well how the Irish tended to view the Third World—from their childhood experience of "a penny for the black babies," or from their inevitable second cousin, "gone for the missions."

The saving grace of the Irish, Krishna thought, was that they had never colonized anyone, never conquered another people, or even set out to—that alone, in and of itself, was one of those conditions that determined their character—just as being conquered and being colonized and being oppressed had. Here in Dublin, for Krishna, it was almost like being back home in the former crown colony of Trinidad and Tobago—or, like his father's experience of colonial India.

Krishna might make fun of Jane Quill for her foibles, which seemed to herself to personify her, and of which she would say, "How can I help it?—I'm made that way." But when he found her in one of her "funks," as he called them, he could be gentle and reassuring. "Jane. What is it? Would you like to tell me?"

"No," she would say, looking away.

The next day he would arrive with some little present for her, always something she needed, pantyhose, or new mittens, or even tea for the kettle. "Krish—you needn't have."

He would shrug. "But I wanted to. I don't want to see you brooding. You're a good person. And someday you'll be a good comrade. Now—will you cheer up, please? And get me some tea."

Soon he was berating her again for ruining her hair with a permanent. "Cut it off! Wear a hat! Get a wig! But don't go round moaning because it won't comb out! I don't know what's wrong wid yuh. Your hair was perfectly fine—."

"No it wasn't. I looked a sight. I had to try something. Oh, Krish—I've no luck at all."

The Comrade's sole vice was tobacco. Even so, it was a point of pride that he didn't waste money on it. He always rolled his own brown papers. He could walk Dublin all day and feel no craving, but when he came back to Jane and Mary's in the evening, he would reach into the breast pocket of his fatigues and pull out his pouch. And when he smoked that single cigarette of the evening, lovingly rolled, he would sit back with his whole body tingling, and a smile would come through a cloud of smoke.

That was when Mary McKenna finally spoke. She shoved her knitting from her lap and made for the loo out in the hall, pausing at his armchair. "I hope you're asphyxiated."

It was true that the Comrade was highly opinionated, but then—he was usually right. He was so self-disciplined that he seemed always to be doing things for some ulterior motive. After the first night or two that I spent with him, he never spoke subjectively of himself again. Instead, he steered everything towards what he called 'concrete analysis,' and 'material objectivity, ' and 'constructive self-criticism.'

I noticed that the evening in Jane's and Mary's would often end with the Comrade going down the steps to his own flat. Finally, I asked to see his room.

Although I was supposed to be inculcating in him some of the principles of the Movement that John Martyn and Bernie Cullen had passed on to me and Mick, instead, I found with Krishna that I was the pupil. When I went to his room, it was not so much lined with books as inundated with them. In the middle of heaps of disarray was the floor pallet where he slept. Evidently, a book fell from his hand when he nodded off and was there when he woke. Every book was on politics, history or social theory, except, of course, his inches-thick medical books. There was a complete set of the Works of Lenin and another of the Works of Mao Tse-Tung. We would sit on the floor and talk late into the night. Once I asked him, "Why do you live like this?"

"I'm not living for creature-comforts."

"But—alone, like this."

"It wouldn't be fair to drag other people down wid me when de crunch comes."

"Then where will you go?"

"When you are a comrade, you have comrades all over de world. You will never go anywhere widout being welcome."

"You know—you should really go down to Gardiner Street —with the 'comrades.'"

"I did."

"Yeah?"

"I looked into de Officials pretty t'oroughly."

"Why did you decide on the Provos then?"

Krishna rolled up a smile like a delighted gnome. He was like a chess-master pleased that, although I had made him wait, his pupil had come up with the right question in the end. "Because the Provos are de real revolutionaries in dis island. De Officials say dat dey are Marxists—dedicated to organizing de masses to develop a true revolutionary movement. But what do dey do? Dey trow away their guns! Dey're not revolutionaries, but armchair philosophers!"

"And yet they call us 'gunmen.'"

"Without the gun, there is no revolution. The Officials talk a lot of Marxist cant, but it's lip service. They talk about the vanguard of the people, but the vanguard cannot be lagging behind the proletariat. And in this case, the people of the North have picked up the gun." Krishna once again was lapsing into his professorial lecturing mode. "Once the gun is in their hands, why should they follow the Officials? They will tell the Officials where to go—and show them the direction with a pistol in the ribs!"

"Are you a Marxist?"

"You telling I?"

One day in December was a perfect replica of summertime, sky clearing, sun shining, temperatures soaring up to the sixties, or, I should say, over 15 Celsius. After work, I stepped off the No. 14B bus on the corner of Rathgar Road and walked up to home.

My little girl was growing up. We no longer counted her age in months. I found her sitting on the top step of No. 56. I sat down with her and asked, "Aisling, what would you like for Christmas this year, love?" I was thinking that just a year ago she was still a little young to comprehend. But now she was already going on three. "Have you written your letter to Santa yet?"

"Daddy, you know."

"Oh, yes. I forgot. I'm sorry, pumpkin. Well, what did you ask for?"

"I can't tell."

"Why?"

"Because."

"Because why?"

"Because it's a wish."

"Oh. And you're not allowed to tell wishes, are you?"

I went inside with my little girl by the hand. Sheila was decorating the little flat for the holiday. She'd got some holly to hang over the door, and she kissed me as I came in. "Are you going to Leinster House tonight?"

The time I was spending at Jane and Mary's flat in Leinster Square hadn't escaped Sheila's notice. She had sarcastically dubbed the place where Krishna and I met to dissect and analyze politics "Leinster House," in reference to the Irish parliament, Dáil Éireann, in Kildare Street. "When am I to meet these pals of yours?"

"Come with me tonight." I'd tried to explain to Sheila that Mary and Jane were very plain and homely, but I knew Sheila had to see for herself. "I'm taking Krishna out selling papers. Bring Aisling and you can visit with Jane and Mary. Or Jane, anyway, Mary works nights. You'll like them. They're from down the country, like you."

"Do you hear that, love? Daddy's taking us out tonight. He's going on, and leave us to sit with strangers."

But to my relief, Sheila got on just fine with Jane. In fact, when we returned, very late, and Aisling was already asleep on Mary's big bed, Sheila began straightaway giving out to Krishna.

"Have you got my husband converted by now, you must have, Comrade."

"Hello, Sheila. Nice to meet you. I heard so much good tings about yuh."

"Oh, I heard all about you, too."

"You telling I?—from Jane, eh?"

"No, from the Special Branch, what did you think?"

Krishna thought that was very humorous, quick, and all, and he laughed heartily. "Nick, your lady would fit right in, back home in Saint James, wid de comrades."

"What have you lot been up to in our absence?" I was yawning as soon as I sat down, and thinking of having to get up for work in the morning.

"Oh, we have everything sorted," said Jane.

"What's sorted?" I glanced over at Aisling sleeping on the bed.

"We have the holiday all arranged," said Sheila. "I'm going to give the child the best gift of all—Christmas in Mayo."

"I wish we could afford it. The train tickets alone are near three quid apiece."

"We thought of that, too. You stay here, and we'll go, just the two of us."

"Without me?"

"I thought you and Krishna didn't believe in such nonsense—empty, unsatisfying rituals, and so on."

"So—we're gonna spend Christmas apart this year?"

"Love—when's the last time I had the chance to spend Christmas at home? Why, when I think of it, it must've been '65. And here it is, 1971. Six years already gone by. You'll be fine.

In case you get lonely or anything, Jane here has promised me to keep a fire going in the grate for ye."

The houses lining the long, straight, well-laid-out Waterloo Road had their dignity, each with its proper front garden, prim black railings, respectable front steps. But one house was a drunken wastrel, with her door always flung open. That door, swinging on its hinges, the lock broken, no doorknob, only a hole in the wood, no door-knocker, only a scar on the wood. Inside the ravished door, the hallway tottered, three stories tall. Only a little light seeped in through the tiny porthole onto the top-floor landing, a little weak light from the tall, drooping pods of the art-nouveau streetlamps of Waterloo Road.

Here in a rambling set of rooms cadged into the top floor lived Martina Kelly and Bernadette Cullen. And here, trooping out of the darkness, trudging up the blind steps, strewn about in standing, sitting or stupefied postures, glass in hand, or head in hand, or heart in hand, came the youth of the generation that was going to make 'certain sure' that this time, *this time,* we shall not fail.

They came for a Christmas Party. They came for a spot to sit and rest. A bit of R&R. A bit o' craic. They came for the booze, they came for the love, for the wet kisses or the liquid fortitude or the stinging whisky or a living touch. They came for the woolly warmth of a comfy old electric-fire, and to forget for a minute the streets of Belfast.

Brendan McAndrews and the 'RA were back in town. You knew why they were there. There was one room, all men in that room, all Ulstermen, that was like a wake being held, a brilliant Irish wake, rip-roaring, dancing, drunken, laughing, shouting.

They had no dead body in there behind that closed door, but they did have a wall-rattling, roof-shaking Irish wake going on for those who were going to die.

Dublin in one room, Belfast in the other. Sinn Fein in one room, and the 'RA in the other. The talkers and the doers. The politicians and the Provos.

While, outside, in the chill December night, Bernie and Martina led three of us, Mick and Krishna and me, tip-toeing out onto the gravel and tarpaper roof outside their pantry window. The girls meant to show us their pride, the boxes of a roof-garden where they grew radishes, lettuce, string-beans and potatoes in the rainy Dublin summers. The garden-boxes were covered lovingly in layers of rain-soaked newspaper, to keep the earth in them dark and humid through the fallowness of winter.

Over the lip of the unfenced roof, we hesitated, mindful of keeping our balance, as we looked down in the dark on dingy courtyards, an old cobbled laneway, and the weed-cluttered back-gardens of the houses in Heytesbury Lane. The boards of the fences in the alley had slouched shoulders, like Dublin bus-riders queued up at the bus-rank, weary of standing so long in the rain.

But such is the folly and faith of youth that Martina and Bernadette, true believers, unhesitatingly grew their garden in the middle of a concrete and limestone Dublin, and on a rooftop, as well.

Inside, in the room that was like a wake, one of the Belfast men stood across the floor in the smoke-filled air to throw out the challenge to his comrades, swaggering up and down waving a Union Jack as he sang lustily,

> *You may talk of your harp, your piano or lute,*
> *But there's none to compare with the Ould Orange Flute!*

He was savagely shouted down, and the flag ripped from his hands, and another Volunteer stood in his place to give the riposte:

Craigavon sent the Specials in to shoot the people down,
He thought the IRA was dead in dear old Belfast town,
But he got a rude awakening from the cannon and grenade
Of the fightin' First Battalion of the Belfast Brigade!

Shouts of Second Battalion! Third Battalion! Andersonstown! The Ardoyne! Up the Rebels! Ballymurphy! The Orangeman squirmed out of the grasp of his kidnappers and shoved aside the opposition to claim the center of the floor for *The Sash Me Father Wore,* but he was toppled from his perch by

In Ireland's fight for freedom, boys, the North has done her part,
And though the day is still to come, we've never yet lost heart . . .
For England knows and England fears our famous Northern Gael,
And that's another reason why they keep our lads in Crumlin Jail!

Never a one to be stopped short, your man came back with *The Protestant Boys,* but cries of "Kill the fuckin' Tartan hoor!" and "Stifle that stupid Orange bastard!" led them to rescue the wake before it collapsed into a chaos of broken bottles and broken heads, with a rousing chorus, standing up, arms linked, feet stamping, hands clapping, shouting it out, shaking the whole house, with *Show Me the Man!*

. . . Let friends all turn against me,
Let foes say what they will,
For my heart is in my country, and
I love old Ireland still!

While in a corner of the sitting room opposite sat Peadar Kenny, holding his tin-whistle as if the instrument carried his tune inside it, and he musn't lose his tune. At his foot Jane Quill and some of the other women at the party knelt before a Christmas tree, short and stubby and stuck into a galvanised pail, roots and all. Bernie and Martina had picked it out of the ground outdoors when they went for a tree up to the Dublin mountains south of the city. They had kept it watered and living in the pail until the holidays would be over and it was time to return their tree to its natural place, planted again. That was in the tradition from Galway that Martina remembered from her childhood, and she taught it to Bernie, and they cherished these things, and repeated them in ritual to keep alive the holiness of innocence in their hearts, as the men of action repeated their own verses to keep alive the spirit of resistance and the burning coals of revenge.

As the women collected themselves and knelt before a manger painstakingly glued together out of ice-pop sticks, with sawdust for straw, and the Holy Family, made out of bits of cork from wine-bottles carved up into legs, heads and torsos, stuck together with straight-pins and dressed in daubs of colored cloth-bits, Peadar Kenny began to play on his tin-whistle. The air that came out of it was the haunting, lonesome air called *The October Winds . . .*

The sound of this plaintive playing, whose high, lonesome, piercing waver cut through everything, noise, ructions and all, brought the lads from Belfast poking their heads through the door of the sitting room.

They saw the assembled women, kneeling, with their heads bowed before the makeshift manger, and they quietened down to see what was up.

Peadar played his song and it was a music to soothe the savage breast. A slow waltz that would make you feel like it was the haunted heart of your own mother singing this lullaby to you from before the beginning of time . . .

The men came out of their room and stood in a circle behind the kneeling women. Someone brought out a rosary and began telling the beads as Peadar ended his song. One of the lads dropped down to his knees. Another one yanked the stolen RUC policeman's cap from off his comrade's head. Soon the whole room was kneeling and reciting in unison,

> *Our Father, who art in Heaven,*
> *Hallowed be Thy name,*
> *Thy will be done, Thy Kingdom come,*
> *On earth, as it is in Heaven.*

And a single voice in the back intoned, at the end of each Lord's Prayer, and the close of each Hail Mary,
    "May the Lord in His mercy be kind to Belfast."

Chapter 6

A Fire in Merrion Square

They came in quiet overcoats, every Friday. There were always two of them. They brought the cold blast of January in through the half-door on their heels.

The first time they came, they stood inside as if the lorry-bay were a waiting room. Sugarman rushed out of his cubicle as they removed their gloves. Handshaking all around.

With a sandwich half in his mouth, Malachi muttered, "Fookin' peelers."

They advanced, a phalanx of three, up the Dispatch floor, and into the pockets of his ankle-length, stained white smock went Sugarman's hands. One of the two plainclothes detectives crooked his finger at Malachi Morgan. "Come with us."

Sugarman went back to his office. Higgy never stirred from his tea-kettle in there. Among the rest, looks went back and forth, and a sort of numbed chewing came over them. Old Susan's eyes went up to heaven. Con Lenihan looked as blank as a donkey. Pascal Larkin piped up, as they disappeared Malachi, "Good enough for him—thinks he's so bleedin' clever—he'll get his now."

"Shut yer bleedin' pie-hole," said Tony Daugherty. "You wouldn't be so pleased with yourself if it was you they took off."

I pinched off the bit of fag I'd smoked for lunch. "Where have they taken him?"

"Up to the copshop, most likely," said Clare.

"Why couldn't they talk to him here?"

"Ah," said Con. "They have better methods than that."

Tony kept his voice low, as Higgy was coming. "What I'd like to know is—who's the tout?"

"Maybe you'll all learn your lesson now," Susan Drummond whispered. "Speaking for myself only, I've had enough of shenanigans."

Upon Malachi's return, Simon Higginbotham spent the afternoon walking softly around him. His young rebel had got his knuckles rapped by Mother Superior.

Outside, at five, as we examined our pay-packets, we surrounded him. "I said nothin,'" said Malachi, "and don't none of youz either."

"Did they lather you, Malachi?"

"Not here, you twits—up to Timoney's." In front of Donleavey's Feed and Grain, Malachi noticed Pascal and Eddie Larkin tagging along. "Where do you think you're goin'?"

"Wid youz."

"Scarper."

Timoney's was packed out. There was a man, the night before, knifed to death over a betting agent's quarrel, and it was full of sightseers. We found a corner at the back of the bar. "They try and trick you, see?" said Malachi. "Asking the same questions over and over again. Waitin' for you to trip yourself up. Just feed them the one rubbish."

"But which rubbish?" said Tony.

"Look—I says to them, them bunk-beds are eight stone if they're a feather. You're daft if you think we carried them out on our backs."

"Why would we," said Con, perfectly logical, "when we had Willie and the lorry?"

"I don't know if it's stupid you are or only thick."

"I hope you didn't go dragging my name into it."

"You're in it up to the skins of yer eyes. And so is Tony here, Wee Willie, Clare and the Larkins."

"We're all involved," I said.

"You're not," said Malachi. "Nor Susan Drummond."

"We're all involved," I repeated, "because it's not going to stop here."

"You had nothin' to do with it," said Malachi, "and besides, it was all done and over with before your time."

"But he's right," said Tony to Malachi. "What happens when they get round to Susan? She'll squeal like a stook pig. She was firm against it from the start, wasn't she?"

"That's right, Malachi," I said. "All they have to do is accuse her and she'll have to defend herself."

"Well," said Tony, "what does the Yank think we should do?"

I looked from one to the other. "I haven't a clue."

The next Friday, the pace picked up. They took two: Tony and Con. Though they managed to weather the trip to the cop-shop, both of them were more than a little shaken. Each of them was told separately, in different rooms, that the other was pointing the finger. The mood in Timoney's that night was edgy.

"It's gettin' serious, Malachi," said Tony, into his jar.

"Do you know what they called me, Malachi?" said Con. "To my face?"

"What? Go on."

"A sod."

"I'm not surprised."

"I wish I was home in Meath," said Con, miserably.

"Go on, son. Pour it in my ear."

"They made fun of my accent," said Con. "The jackeens."

"Connie," said Tony. "Let me tip you. All the coppers in Dublin are from the country."

"They're not."

"They are. They have it fixed that way."

"Well," said Con, morosely. "It's because of him they called me a sod. They know well enough, Malachi, I'm not clever that way—but I'm the sod for letting myself be led on by you."

"Con Lenihan!" Malachi exploded. "You bleated for a fookin' week over bein' fookin' left out, till I took pity on you. I was good enough for you then!"

I stepped between them. "Out of the way!" said Con. "I'll kill him!"

"It's all right," I said to the barman. I held onto Malachi and said, "When are you going to learn? The way you do things, all the world couldn't miss it."

"If he thinks he's going to make his own deal–!"

"Sit down and shut up. Nobody's making any deals."

"We'll be all right if youz'll just shut yer gobs," said Malachi, shaking himself loose.

"It's beyond that now," said Tony. "They were telling me about the charges I'm liable to—and the amount of time to be served attached to them."

"What are you, a bleedin' quail? They're only trying to frighten you, ye rabbit."

"It's easy enough for you to say. Jail is where you belong."

"Ha," said Con. "That's the truth. He could get all his reading done in the jacks over there, couldn't he?"

"You'd know what to do in the jacks, Connie, wouldn't you, you fookin' wanker."

"Shut up! Everybody shut up!"

"And you, Daugherty—that's the thanks I get for showin' you the way to improve the standard of your living."

Tony looked at me. "You wouldn't mind if they paid a livin' wage."

"All right. I've got to think. Charges, you say, Tony?"

"As soon as they complete their investigation."

"Oho," said Malachi. "So it's an investigation now, is it? At first, they told me, ah, we're only lookin' into it."

"Look," I said to Tony, "if it's your first offense, you won't go to jail. If I know anything."

"Malachi's not so lucky then."

I turned to Morgan. Bleakly, he said, "Well—what do we do?"

"When did you start taking my advice?"

One night at home, after Sheila lulla-looing Aisling to sleep, when I was sitting at the kitchenette table reading Tolstoy, the lights went out. "That's great. Have you a shilling, love?"

"No," said Sheila, from the dark. "Haven't you?"

"I have the busfare for the morning."

"Will I go down the hall?" I knew Sheila loaned a cup of sugar to Monica downstairs and babysat for Josephine Bagley upstairs. "I'll get you your shilling," she said.

But when the lights came on, I said, "The hell with it. Let's go to bed."

"What is it?" said Sheila when I turned my back in the narrow bed.

"Work."

"What's wrong?"

"Everything."

She gently rubbed along my shoulder and I realized how tight I felt. "It's only temporary. You'll get a position. The letter's probably in the post this moment, only we don't know it. You can't expect yourself to be satisfied with it—after all, you're a teacher."

"It's not that." I turned over. "There's nothing wrong with a little physical labor."

"What is it then?"

"The police have been in."

"You never told me."

"I know. I was hoping it would go away."

"What's the gardai doing in it?"

"Investigating."

"Investigating what?"

"Thievery. Thievery of steel bunk-beds that weigh eight stone apiece."

"Oh, thank God. I thought it was you. Do they know you're a foreigner?"

"They haven't talked to me."

"Please God, let them keep away."

"My turn's coming."

"Why? Nicky—tell me what's going on."

"The lads, you know? They're stealing the place blind. Pillows, cushions, they take them out under their cardigans. They've even stolen bunk beds, for Christ's sake, on the lorry."

"Well, it's nothing to do with you, is it?"

"No!"

"Stay out of it then."

"Oh, yeah. Just like that. Tell me something, Sheila—I can work there, right? Can't I? I mean, I'm married to you, and you're a citizen."

"They hired you, didn't they? And you have your insurance cards."

I felt better for talking to her. Reassured. Unburdened. "You know something?" I said. "I think I love you, Sheila Blake."

Fridays had become almost numbed by the routine of the plainclothesmen and it was hardly commented on when they took Pascal Larkin and his brother Eddie.

After lunch, Higgy was handing out pay-packets, as usual. He might have been handing out arrest warrants. His staff took them from him grudgingly and went off into corners to poke at them suspiciously. Haplessly, Mr. H. watched them walk away. All week long he'd endured the silent treatment. But what could he do? Sugarman made all the decisions. When Higginbotham arrived in the morning, he might as well hang himself up on the coat-hook alongside his brelly, for all his opinion mattered. And now things had taken a decided turn for the worst.

But they would get still worse. Monday morning we found out how.

"What the hell happened to you?" Malachi wanted to know when Pascal Larkin walked in with a puffed-out left eye with a darkening, three-day-old purpling bruise.

"I tripped on a stool," said Pascal, trying to elude him.

Malachi grabbed him by the collar. "If you said a fookin' word–!"

"I did!" cried Pascal.

"I'll break your tosser's neck!"

"Get your mitts off me brudder!" cried little Eddie Larkin, kicking with his boot. "He's had enough! He got it from Mammy, too, when he got home!" Malachi threw Pascal aside on a pile of cuttings. Tony jumped up and slipped in between Malachi and Eddie. I grabbed Malachi's elbow. Pascal massaged his neck. From the ground, he spoke. "They had no need of me to tell them, Malachi—they already know everyt'ing!"

"Fookin' shower o' shite!" Malachi sputtered. "Why don't they just have done with it? Why drag it on and on?"

"What did they do to you?" I said to Pascal.

"They bet him up, can't you see?" said Eddie.

"Into your places, the lot of you," said Susan Drummond. "Here comes Higginbotham."

Not knowing what else to do, I went to the talkshop in Leinster Square to see if they had any ideas. "Look, Krishna, myself and Susan Drummond are the only adults in it. These kids are too ignorant to know their rights, let alone insist on them with the gardai."

Krishna looked at Jane Quill. "Products of your Irish Catholic educational system, eh?"

"'Tisn't funny," said Jane.

"Well, what's Nick to do about it?"

"I'm sure I don't know—you're the expert on social justice."

"All right, all right. Let me think. First of all, forget about anyone's rights. Once the police were invited in, they can do what they like, and who's to stop them?" Krishna reached for his tobacco pouch. "What about this chap Higginbotham?"

"He's a wimp," I said.

"And Sugarman?"

"He's the cause of all this."

"No melodrama, please. Will he listen to reason? He called the cops in—let him call the cops off. Go see him—first thing. Tell him—either he calls off the investigation—or else."

"Or else what?"

"I haven't figured that out yet."

"Great."

"Use your moral persuasion. Appeal to his conscience."

"He doesn't blink at employing child labor, you want me to appeal to his conscience?"

"That's it! You see, comrade? We have him there—dead to rights."

"I feel sick."

"Why? Jane, you do have laws in this country, don't you?"

"That's just it," I answered for Jane. "If I threaten Sugarman, what's to stop him from turning me in?"

"What have you done?"

"I've been thinking lately—am I legal to work here?–I assumed, being married to Sheila—you know?"

"There's a phone in the hall. Ring up the Ministry and ask them a question."

"And what if they give me the wrong answer?"

"Then you're in trouble."

I buried my forehead in my hand. "Shit"

"Look, comrade. Sugarman's breaking the law, in your case, by employing you. If that's the case—which we don't know for a fact. But—but—he's breaking laws all over the map. You're only trying to earn your living and feed your family."

"Can I ask you something, Comrade? How do you feed your tobacco habit?"

"I have two very sympathetic sisters in the States, one in New Jersey, one in New York—and a mother who loves me in Port o' Spain."

"So you don't need to work."

"Eh—a man's got to do what a man's got to do. I have my application in for the Faculty of Medicine."

"This would never have come up but for this fucking investigation."

"Stop the investigation."

"Mr Sugarman." I rattled the door of his cage. Since this investigating began he'd retreated into his so-called office and wouldn't look any of us in the eye. Now he opened up. "Come in, come in."

I stepped up inside. "What's this, an emissary?" he said weakly.

"You've, uh, noticed."

He waved his hand. "Two camps. You'd think we were enemies. You'd think they'd recall who it was gave them their jobs. Well—fire away."

"I don't think you're gonna like what I have to say."

"Ah. Well, I wouldn't be surprised. In fact, I might say, I'm a bit disappointed in you, Nick Petrovich."

"Really."

"Indeed. I'd say, perhaps—just, perhaps—I mistook you, when you first came on. But—there's still time."

"Time for what?"

"Time for you to come to your senses."

"Me! Mr Sugarman, don't tell me you don't know what those investigators of yours, how they interrogated Pascal Larkin— who's 12 years old."

Sugarman cleared his throat, and shifted in his swivel-seat. "What do you mean?"

"They beat him up, Mr Sugarman."

He spied some papers on his desk that needed straightening. "I know nothing about that. The gardai don't tell me their business. I have no control over them."

"Well, you better get some and stop this investigation."

"I don't think I like your tone. You have no idea what I'm up against. You don't understand the situation at all. I'm getting pressure from Pearse Street. And I'm getting pressure from the police, too. It's up to me, they say, to prefer charges. Yes, it's citizens like you, they tell me, that we have to rely upon, they say, to stand up to these hooligans." Sugarman waved his hands in the air. "I'm sorry for the day I ever left the P-Street warehouse. A promotion, they said. You'll be a manager, run your own show. More like a glorified spindle-jockey. How am I to attract adults into the workplace, without even a decent loo to offer? Not to mention what management considers wages."

"Listen, Noel—you called on the dogs."

"Maybe those boyos should have thought of that when they were lifting my beds."

"Do you condone what the police did?"

"It's out of my hands!"

"I'd like you to pick up that phone, call them, and withdraw your complaint."

"I won't. I won't. I can't. And that's all. Now we're finished here. So, just, get back to your department, and carry on."

On the way home, feeling agitated, I avoided my own place. I jumped off the bus and took a dive into the Leinster Square talkshop. I barged into Jane and Mary's and said to Krishna straightaway, "There's no turning back now." My mood was militant, but it made me no happier: I felt angry, frustrated, humiliated and defiant, all at once. "I only wish I knew what next."

Jane brought us tea with her sympathy. For somebody who claimed she wasn't a comrade, she made an awful good friend.

Krishna curled up in his easy-chair to roll a fag and think. "Now we know who our enemies are," he said, finally. "Who are our friends?"

"What about those Sinn Féin pals of yours?" said Jane.

The Cumann Billy Reid had a full quorum that evening. The members were ebullient, full of chat: sales of An Phoblacht had been brisk, going back all the way to the Ard Fheis in November; the Northern Resistance Movement was forging ahead under a full head of steam; Anti-Internment was still the rallying-cry of the moment, marching, mobilizing and organizing were at the head of the agenda.

Alita Hughes opened the meeting for Wednesday, 26 January, 1972, taking the roll. Alita was in her glory now: having purged her fat sister Maureen, for incompetence, she was keeping the secretary's book herself. Though none of the members missed Maureen much, the point was not lost on them. As Comrade Krishna was quick to observe, just between us.

Alita collected the dues: money, money, money, that's what the Movement needed. She opened the discussion and belabored us with plans for fund-raisers. Cousin Brendan, since Christmas, had disappeared over the border again, and Alita was wearing her martyr's halo: over-burdened, over-worked, on call in the middle of the night, in charge of a million details, nevertheless, Alita Hughes would wage the struggle single-handed, if need be. "Northern Resistance, since Christmas alone, has held three very successful marches—."

"Five thousand on the road from Belfast to Long Kesh last week," John Martyn added.

"And Frank McManus and Bernadette D. in attendance," Alita continued.

"Two MPs," said Myles Cunningham, musing. "That's good." It was whispering round that Cousin Myles was not long for the Cumann. You were not supposed to talk about it, or even know it. He would be leaving soon for the training camps. "What about the SDLP?" Myles asked.

"The people are laughing them off the podium these days unless they join in the call to abolish Stormont," said John.

"The Stickies seem to have gone under for good," Alita added. "Thank God."

"If anyone's interested," said John, examining his cuticles, "the NRM has a march on for Derry, on Sunday."

"Bit of agro there, eh?" said Mick O'Corrigan. Mick was the man for agro.

"I'm working," said Barney O'Toole, the dustman. "God bless the Sunday overtime."

"Well, it is a bit distant, for us, and short notice," said John, "but don't forget now the march scheduled for Newry, Sunday a week."

"Right," said Alita. "That's close enough to home. We're working on the details of transportation and I'll have full information next Wednesday. Let's make every attempt to have the best showing of any cumann in Dublin coming out of our Cumann Billy Reid in Newry—you have those bus-tickets—sell them. Oh—I won't be here next week—I've asked John to do the honours."

"Alita." Comrade Krishna spoke up. "New business."

"It's been a long day. I'd like to get home."

Krishna, sponsored by me, had been granted his full voting rights, a feather for both of us. Nor had he ever been less than forthright about adding his tuppence, so he forged ahead. "Our comrade Nick here has a situation at work."

Alita lifted her shoulder-bag from the floor to the table. "What is it?"

It was my turn to explain, so I briefly sketched out the details.

"Well, I don't see what we can do about it," said Alita, glumly. The family owned a car-wash, off the South Circular Road, and, working on the books, Alita knew only too well how difficult it was to find decent help in Dublin these days.

"Well," I ventured, "seeing as this is a British-owned factory—."

"British-owned!" said Mick O'Corrigan.

"What's the name of it, Nick?" asked Myles.

"Maurice Woolf, Ltd."

"We'll torch it," said Mick avidly.

Alita gave him the quare look. Myles registered a furrowed brow. Alita said, "I'm sure you have a case, Nick, and it does sound deserving of all the support we can give you—but just now, this cumann does have important business which we can't jeopardize."

"I think," said John Martyn, making a church steeple of his fingers, "that our direct involvement—that is, Sinn Fein's name being introduced—might have directly the opposite effect with the police, Nick, than what you could wish for. But, you say there are children involved."

"There are social agencies," Alita insisted, "for this sort of thing, run by the Church and respectable people."

"And what'll the priest do?" Mick scoffed. "Give the kids absolution?"

"Actually," said John Martyn, "I was thinking of the Transport Workers' Union. Nick, why don't I give my friend Michael Hegarty a ring, at Liberty Hall. First thing in the morning. And I'll get back to you."

Downstairs, in Paddy Clarke's afterwards, when Alita was gone, Martina Kelly said, "I don't understand at all, at all, why she has to take such an attitude."

"Alita's 'Our Leader,'" said Bernie, with a grimace.

"Oh, that's good," said Mick, handing out the pints. "I love a good pun. Dead on, Bernie. How'd you like her for a passenger on your dust-brush, Barney?"

"I'm afraid the witch might fly away with it."

"Stop this thing, this minute!" cried Mick, in falsetto. "It's making me randy, and I want to get off!"

"Don't be too hard on Alita," said John Martyn. "She's right, in her own way. You understand, don't you, Nick—Krishna?"

"Sure," I said. "I suppose so."

"Some people have blinders on," Krishna offered. "Straight on, and they can't see left or right."

"Some people," Martina interjected, "can see clouds of dust from over the horizon, but they can't see the dirt in their own back-garden."

"Honestly, John," Bernie complained, "she's so bloody self-righteous."

"But when she's right, she's right," said John. "The main thing *is* over the horizon. We have a tenuous balance with the authorities in Dublin, and no one knows how long that will last. Wouldn't they love to bring back Internment in the 26 Counties right now, but they daren't. But we can't forget, they have done so in the past. And the Offences Against the State Act is not off the books, is it?—any more than Special Powers in the North. Isn't Jack Lynch under pressure from London this moment? We can't go giving them excuses to interfere with us. The lads up Belfast and Derry way are depending upon us. Nick—I'll ring you in the morning, soon as I speak to Hegarty."

I got home that night late, tired and hungry. As I fell in the chair, grateful that at least the lights were on—lately we were stretching it so we didn't run out of shillings till Thursday night—I said to Sheila, "Anything to eat?"

"No."

"Pass me a fag, then."

"There's none left."

I stared at the ash-tray full of butts. "You smoked them all?"

"Well, you were out all night. You could've got some."

"With what? You've got all my money, and I'm left with bus-fare."

"You had money enough for the drink tonight."

"One Guinness I had, 17 new pence the pint. And that was bought for me by my friends."

"Maybe you can get your friends to buy your child something to eat, then."

"Why?" I sat up. "Didn't you feed her tonight?"

"Oh, I fed her, all right. That's all I do is feed her, and play with her, and try to keep her amused while you're out gallivanting."

"I went to my meeting tonight."

"Is this what you brought us up to Dublin for?"

"I'm home every other night of the week."

"To make your dinner and wash your clothes and sit and wait for you?"

"I can't afford to go out anywhere, can I?"

"Till you come walking in the door like a lord, and you want something again? I don't know what's wrong with us, lately," Sheila blurted.

"Lumpy potatoes and burnt pudding," I muttered.

"It's all that's in the house."

"You could at least warm it up before you slide it across the table at me."

"What do you expect on what you bring home—caviar?"

"You may not have to worry about what I bring home much longer."

Across the Liffey from Maurice Woolf, Ltd., the shopfronts of Ellis Quay, in the daylight, when I was used to looking at them, were as bland as so many drawn windowshades.

But behind them, on either side of Blackhall Place, a warren of streets spread out like cob-webbed rooms. Benburb Street, Hendrick Street, Blackhall Street. It was said that these were streets of muggers and thieves, hoodlums and skinhead gangs, and that you did not walk there at night if you valued your life. I certainly never ventured there. But Pascal and Eddie Larkin lived there, and now I was going home with them, home across the hump-backed bridge on the darkening river in the wintry isolation of a January nightfall, when the bleak blackness comes so early.

As we left behind the streaking lights of the quays, where the headlamps of commuters going home after work streamed eastbound, as we walked up Queen Street, it grew colder and darker, and quieter; the hum of traffic receded, and all went silent, as the boys, never at any time with much to say, stopped talking altogether. The street narrowed and houses grew closer above our heads, and I could feel myself contract into my pea-coat as I gave a shiver, withdrawing my shoulders, burrowing my head between upturned collars. Soon all I saw was two pairs of heels in front of me as they rose and fell in resigned monotony. The heels were worn down. Their walk was pinched. We turned into the cold stone cobbles of a street called the Haymarket. A man walking towards us passed on the footpath, taking the wall. The boys knew him. There was no hello, no nod, no good evening or sign of greeting, as there might have been in the small places down the country. They grunted to one another. This was the cold, dark, downtrodden North Side of Dublin, in winter.

Under a low arch rinsed with the stink of dog-piss, a single naked lightbulb hung from a wire twisted around a rusty drain-pipe; and, like a lantern in smog, it shed a dirty illumination on the slouched cap of a dented dustbin-cover and the cracked, frost-heaved concrete slabs of a rain-weathered courtyard sur-rounded by balconies. Mount Pleasant Flats. Boasted of by its tenants as the most notorious slum in Europe. This was where the Larkins lived.

Rubbish littered the stairwells. Under lightbulbs encased in wire cages—why? I thought: to keep the residents from smashing them?—graffitti crawled across the sooty brick walls. *Skinhead Heaven*, read the message. A death's head inscribed *Led-Zep*. Mary loves Tom, Dick, Harry, Sean, Seamus, Fergus, Liam, Ned, Bones . . . a chalk-white swastika. The concrete steps grew heavy and thick, sucking you in as you climbed three flights up, turning round at every half-flight till you ended in a darkened hallway, disoriented. Closed doors. Ears listening, eyes watching.

As you passed down the hall between the gauntlet of doors, you heard the sibilance of the breath, sucked in quickly, as a Dubliner will do, when you bump into him, tossed about on the circular stair at the back of the rattling double-decker bus.

We came to a door with no doorknob. My heart sank. I had the distinct feeling that no visitor ever arrived at this door with good news. Pascal Larkin pushed the door open.

"Who's that?"

A room, as musty as an oven, filled with the odor of a coal fire smoldering under a choked flue. The window that peeked out over a balcony was wide open to let air in. An infant lay in a pram under the window pawing at the atmosphere. A woman leaned against a table while she rocked the pram with her jig-gling foot and held onto the handlebar for support.

"Who's that?"

"Mam—he insisted he had to see you."

"Who are you?" the woman who was Pascal and Eddie's mother said. "No one's been here since the woman from the Legion of Decency."

"I came to see you about your sons, Mrs Larkin."

"Is it him again? Pascal? What is it this time?"

"I want to help him."

"Aw, mister, 'tisn't fair to go foolin' with an old woman like me."

I looked at Pascal and Eddie, who shrugged. I said to their mother, "Can I talk to you?"

"Talk. What can I do but listen?"

For the first time I noticed Pascal's older sister sitting in a chair next to the fire across the table from her mother. Two more boys, one older, one younger, sidled into the room past the door from the balcony. Suddenly they were all there and they were waiting for me to speak and I could find nothing to say to them.

"Well?" said Mrs Larkin. "Are you going to help him like the peelers did last week? They ought to have my doctor bills— to send my boy home half-crippled, and limpin' where they kicked him, shakin' with fear. I never saw that one cry, but he did that night. Bawlin' like a babby, and cringin' in the corner. I gave it to him, all right. He knows better than to bring home trouble down on our heads. Can you help my boy, mister? Try and help my boy. I have no man here, y'see. Try and help him. But if you want to know what I think—there's no help for him this side of heaven."

I put my hands in my pockets and stared upwards at the tall mirror of the glass-walled high-rise, Liberty Hall. "Ever been in in it, men?"

"Are we going to ride the lift?" said nine-year-old Eddie Larkin.

It was the next night, Thursday, and as soon as we were let out at five, we'd raced across the bridge, Pascal, Eddie and I, to catch the first No. 65 into the city centre that we could, to try to make it to this gleaming aluminum and glass tower in Eden Quay before they closed.

And we did rise in hydraulic splendor up to the third floor, but there a security guard told us we were in the wrong building. "You want the Amalgamated. Corner of Marlborough Street. The Seaman's Mission. That's it."

One block away, the room we wanted resided in a humbler mansion, where the Mission's sign twinkled over Eden Quay: *The Flying Angel.* There we found a hall like a school auditorium, with a stage, curtain, and lights hanging from block-chains in big yellowed bowls. The hall was filled with union members on pension, sitting in rows of church-pews.

"Me brudder was bet-up by the peelers," Eddie Larkin informed the old men sitting behind us as we slid into a row near the back, "and we're here to get justice."

Michael Hegarty was a man used to exercising authority, a man used to fighting and winning, who ran his own meeting. The Organising Committee sat with him on the stage, but he wielded the gavel. He noted the newcomers, jotted something on a pad with a pencil, and put us at our ease with a glance. "You wouldn't mind waiting a bit, and we'll get to you."

Behind the Committee, suspended in the middle of dusty mauve curtains at the back of the stage, a larger-than-life por-trait hung: James Connolly, in his Citizen's Army uniform, sepia in a gilded frame, a founding father looking down on the assembly room.

"Now," said Michael Hegarty, with a clap of his gavel, having finished other business, "are you the ones I had the message about today?"

"I believe so, sir," I said, standing.

"Would you mind repeating your story, sir."

"Uh, we work in Maurice Woolf, Ltd., in Usher's Island Quay."

"We know them," said Hegarty. "Main offices in Pearse Street. British-owned. Continue."

"Well, the gardai have been in, plainclothesmen, investigating some missing articles, and the methods they've used, we don't think are right. In fact, I'd go so far as to say, the atmosphere at the moment is like a reign of terror. Every Friday, the past four weeks, plainclothesmen came in at lunch hour and took two of our workers for questioning. I've brought this boy–" I put my hand on his shoulder–"Pascal Larkin—who can testify as to how the police questioned him."

"How old are you, lad?" said Hegarty.

"I'm twelve." Pascal stood up.

"And how old did you tell them you were when they hired you on?"

"Fourdeen. And we told 'em me brudder here was twelve. He's nine."

"You ought to be in school. Both of you. Why aren't you?"

"I couldn't stick it. They don't teach you nothin,' and you can't make any money at it."

A laugh went up from the room.

"What about your parents, son?"

"Me fadder's dead and there's no udder support comin' in the house for me mudder, only the dole, which it isn't enough."

"What did the police do to you?"

"They bet me up." Pascal lifted his chin and stuck his eye out in the light.

"What would you like us to do for you?"

"Just to put a stop to it, if ye can."

"Consider it done. Now—I'd like you to do something for yourself. At the end of this meeting, I'd like a word with you and your brother and your friend."

Friday morning, I jumped down from the bus and ducked into O'Rourke's on the corner. When she saw me come in, the old lady put a single cigarette down on the counter. "Majors," she said. I delved deep into the pea-coat pocket and came up with a single penny. A third before start-up. Another third in the jacks about ten, loan a fag from somebody at lunch, have a third left for the afternoon. It was going to be a regular day.

I passed out the little orange union cards surreptitiously. Michael Hegarty had warned me to take due precautions, "so as management can't nip the job in the bud."

The questions came pouring out at lunch-time, once Higgy had gone.

"What good'll this do?" said Con Lenihan.

"It'll put the weight of the union onto the scales on our side, against the power of the police," I said.

"What's this shop-steward thingy about?" said Tony D.

"I'm just a representative, for you. A go-between. You have any probs with the gaffer, you see me. I take the complaint to Michael Hegarty. He's the head of the Organising Committee, and President of the Dublin City Council, as well. He rings up the Head Office in P-Street, and—."

"Which union is it?" said Susan Drummond.

"Amalgamated Transport Workers' Union of Ireland."

"Sounds grand," said Clare, dubiously.

"What are they going to do for us?" said Malachi.

"Pay him no mind, Nick," said old Susan. "Nothing suits him."

"We want more money." "A toilet that flushes." "Get rid of ould Needlenose!" "We could use a tea-break middle of the morning—another one after lunch, now I think of it." "I'll take sausages 'n' eggs," said Clare, leaning back and throwing her hands up behind her head to nestle in the cushions where she stretched out languidly, "—served before start-up—by Mr Higginbotham, in his white coat—." They laughed. "My manicurist to drop in on every Wednesday—me nails do get torn on them edge-stitchers—let's see, the hairdresser, Friday at four—."

"Petrovich."

We all looked up. There stood Sugarman, a pay-packet, dangling like a dog's tongue from his proffered hand, flanking him, the men in the anonymous overcoats.

In the abrupt hush, I got to my feet.

"You needn't stay the rest of the day," said Sugarman.

"What's this?" I said, taking the pay-packet, taking in the three of them.

"Your dismissal."

A steel bolt hit the wall with a concrete bark.

One of the detectives whirled, and Pascal Larkin eyed him from where he sat on the floor, his hands clasped, choir-boy fashion, in his lap.

"You can't do this, Sugarman," I said.

"You're not to tell me what I can do! Now get out of here!"

"What are these, Noel? Your enforcers?"

The other cop stirred in his shoes. "That's enough of that." He took me by the elbow.

"You'll be sorry for this, you bastard," I snarled at Sugarman.

"Move along, you."

"Get your hands off me!" I put my back to the lorry-bay, to face them and walk backwards. "I'm going. Just don't touch me."

One of the detectives asked Sugarman, "What did you say was the name of this one?"

"I need my coat."

Clare rushed to fetch it and brought it to me, though she was frightened, looking nervously at the plainclothesmen.

"I'm going—peacefully. You don't need to use force. You're not dealing with a kid now. I've got witnesses." I stepped back, brushing myself off with sullied hands. "Sugarman—you haven't seen the last of me."

I whirled and stalked off between the stitching tables, flinging my coat over my shoulder.

From behind his bodyguards, Sugarman, on tiptoe, was shouting, "Don't bother to come back! Your last pay'll be mailed to ye!"

Outside, Wee Willie Bermingham was dismounting from the cab of his lorry just as I came through the half-door. He was startled. I looked at him, flushed. He saw the coat balled up in my fist with the pay-packet. "What happened?"

"Sacked. Willie—fill out that orange card—don't let them take you in for questioning—I'll be back, but right now, I've gotta get outta here. I can't afford to get arrested. Mind yourself, and say nothing."

How I got through that night is a mystery. I absolutely dreaded telling Sheila. If she were to give up on me, how could I blame her? If she were to throw me out, how could I blame her?

Yet where could I go, but straight home to Rathmines Road? I had no place else to go, and no money to get there. The pay-packet in my pocket? Useless. A full third of it would be gone by 6 pm. Parceling it out to last the week—all that was predicated on having a job to plug away at, week after week. This time next week, getting my final check in the mail—what then?

Yet how could I blame myself? It was Noel Sugarman who'd done this to me, when all I had done was to try to do the right thing by those poor benighted kids who worked in that dosshouse of his.

But—would I have blamed myself as much for failing to stand up for the rights of those kids if I had just put my head down, ignored the situation, and thought about saving myself instead of them? If I had stopped to think—you know, I'm taking a risk here, I've got a family to support, I better not. The answer was—I don't know. How could I know, when I never did stop to think?

And so I came back to it's your own stupid fault, you asshole—how could you have been so stupid?

So, as I rattled homeward on a No. 14B, my head went round and round and kept coming back again, full stop: *sacked!*

True to form, the estate agent, Jeremy Flynn, was there at the door to No. 1A, 56 Upper Rathmines Road, by 6 pm, with his hand out for the rent.

As I closed the door, I turned to face the facts. I'd been putting it off—as long as I could—now the rent was paid, and we had exactly one more week—maybe two—for the three of us in our little bedsitter. "Sheila—I need to tell you something—you better sit down."

I was pushing out the chair for her at the little table in the kitchenette with my foot. I was already seated. She turned, with oven mitts on, with steak-and-kidney pies in two tins she'd just pulled from the oven in her hands. She put them down on top of the cooker. She could tell from my demeanor, not wanting to look her in the eye, that this was bad. She sat down. "What is it, Nick?"

I looked at her glumly. "Sacked."

"What?"

"Fired."

"Why? What happened? What did you do?"

"I didn't do anything." Not true—oh, this was coming out all wrong. I had to drag the whole story out of myself. Thank God little Aisling was busy playing with her imaginary friend and her dolls over at her bed, which doubled as her play area. Her imaginary friend came from England. Why England, I don't know. Perhaps she heard us talking of it so much that it seemed to her a faraway, idyllic place. How I wished just then that I could escape into imagination myself.

"How is it," said Sheila, "that I had no clue any of this was going on? Oh, aye—you wouldn't have wanted to worry us."

I stood accused, and I had no defence.

"Is this what we're to expect from now on? That when you get fired—you just leave on a jet-plane for another country?"

That was decidedly below the belt of Sheila. She was referring to my firing from my job back home in Milltown, when leaving on a jet plane for another country was precisely what I did.

We had to eat our dinner together that night. We had to conspire together to make it pleasant enough for the child. But for both of us, those delicious Fray-Bentos steak-and-kidney pies, from the tin with the little screw-key, tasted like cardboard.

And when the child had been put to sleep with her rag-dolls and her teddy, we had to sleep together, because in a double-bedsitter, there is no-place else. Sheila wasn't about to sleep with Aisling because then the child would have known—lately, we'd been training her to sleep in her own bed, instead of between us in our bed—Sheila was still afraid of rolling over and smothering her. So we slept together.

At some point, I said, "Say something."

"What is there to say? Hip hoorah?"

The next day, Saturday, I fled—to Leinster Square. I couldn't stick it in the woe-is-me miasma of our flat—I had to get to Krishna and the girls to get the fight back into me. Krishna would know what to do. Krishna would see it from my working-class solidarity viewpoint. He was always full of ideas—or, at least, could get me to screw my thinking-apparatus back on. And the bonus was that Jane and Mary would flock to Sheila's side so that she had a shoulder to weep on.

"We organize," said Krishna. "Organize to fight back on them."

We went down to the Oliver Bond to see Susan Drummond and urge her to keep the lads together behind me, as she was the eldest, and most responsible, the den-mother of her unruly cubs. We then crossed the river to the Mount Pleasant Flats to see Pascal Larkin and his mother. We laid out our plans. We then hurried on to the city centre to see Hegarty at the Amalgamated, and we stopped in at Kevin Street, too, where, by luck, we found John Martyn. Although we knew he would reiterate his Sinn Féin-can't-get-involved-line, still, we needed him to know, and the rest of the Cumann, too. After all, John had helped already by putting me on to Michael Hegarty.

The next morning was Sunday, the last Sunday in January, and I did something I hadn't done since the morning Sheila and I were married: I asked her to go to Sunday Mass with me. Of course, we'd been to Mass every Sunday down in Mayo, all three of us, but that was different. That was at the behest of Sheila's da, and under the watchful gaze of censorious neighbors, who, the Blakes felt, or knew, would be quick to comment should we not. Since coming up to Dublin, out of sight, out of mind: we'd reverted back to living by our own lights, as we would have, say, in Boston. Now, however, I needed the help of God, or the Mother of God, or the Irish Saints, even Lucifer himself, anyone who could help me glue back together the fractured unity of my little family.

So there I was on my knees under the high dome of Mary Immaculate in Rathmines, trying to pray, and I realized I could make it through an Our Father, more or less, but I'd forgotten half of the Hail Mary, and my Apostle's Creed—that eluded me completely. Bless me Father, for I have sinned. That single phrase kept recurring, spinning off the walls of my brainpan. Sheila knelt stiffly, her gaze locked straight ahead. Aisling fidgeted, and her mother was annoyed. I sat back and picked up my little girl and held her and her teddy close.

We walked home slowly. Winter lay bare along Rathmines Road. I looked up as we passed the Library on the opposite kerb—locked doors, broken promises—Leinster Square—the talkshop of the unemployed masses—at the curving away of Rathgar Road, the Bank of Ireland branch, where our account was still open only because our last five pounds were still in it. Finally, I sighed, and said, "I'll find another job. You'll see."

"I can't wait to find out if you will or you won't," said Sheila. "The girls and I have our minds made up. I'll just have to find the job myself. We all agreed that you can't live your life depending on a man, because they'll always let you down."

"What am I to do then, Sheila? Stay home and babysit?"

"Someone has to. What do you think I've been doing? You should be happy, Nick, that I've friends here who'd give us the loan of a quid or two, if it came to that. In the meantime, I can't let it, so—."

Church-goers were hurrying home, huddled in overcoats; chimney-pots were puffing smoke-balls. When we got back to our flat, out of sheer perverseness, I turned the electric-fire up high. At least that was already paid for. I flopped down on the wall-to-wall carpet to warm myself. Aisling brought a cardboard box in her hands. She had her dolls and teddy sitting up in it. "Will you play with me, Daddy?"

"What shall we play?"

"Well, probly—," *probably* was the word of the month my little angel was learning— "probly, we should play house."

"Okay—let's play house."

"All right—now, Teddy will be the Daddy, and Dolly will be the Mammy—here, you take Teddy—."

"Did you hear the news?" It was Krishna, bursting in without knocking. "Six dead in Derry!"

"What?" I looked up from the floor with Teddy in my hands.

"The troops! They're shooting people in the streets!"

"Oh, no!" Sheila came over from the kitchenette. I was scrambling to my feet. "How do you know?" I said.

"It's all over Rathmines. Look out your window, man."

I rushed to the glass. People were coming out of front doors, up and down Rathmines Road, standing on steps in their cardigans and jumpers—a little knot was already gathered in the doorway of Campbell's shop. Krishna was saying, "Has anyone got a telly?"

"Down the back," said Sheila. "In Eileen and Angela's."

Angela was already in her open door, her face white as flour. "Oh, God, it's awful."

"What happened? Who did it?" We crowded into the tiny, angular, windowless room. A portable Japanese-made television was balanced on a night-table. "How did it happen?" Images were scurrying across the screen, black-and-white video clips of a grey Derry, a man in a doorway waving a white hankie—.

"Look—it's a priest!" A man crawling on his belly across a foot-path to grab someone by the collar who was lying prone in the gutter—. "Ssh! Listen! We're trying to find out!" Lamp-posts, armored cars, cameras swiveling swiftly, erratically, tipping the view-finder crazily, shaking the picture into blurs. Josephine, the nurse, and her son, Simon, were in the room, and Shane and Monica, from downstairs in the basement, came in right behind them. An announcer came on the screen, he was sitting at a desk, reading from a paper. "At last report—ten dead—several wounded—at the hospital—."

"Ten! I thought you said six."

"It's a bloody massacre."

"—a battalion of paratroopers—."

"The fuckin' Paras."

From the edges of the Bogside the shock waves emanated into the tiny triangular bedsitter at the back of the hall of the ground floor of 56 Upper Rathmines Road in Dublin. From the forecourt of Derry's Rossville Street Flats a deathly silence, like the echo falling in the wake of a rifle's report, came over the room belonging to Angela and Eileen, two sisters from Kinnegad, in Westmeath, while the women crowding into this room held hands up to open mouths, and the men pressed their hands into doubled fists. I turned to Krishna with my baby girl in my arms, and when I spoke, it came out in a hoarse whisper, like someone stunned at a deadly road accident. "Just last week, John Martyn was saying anyone who liked might go up to Derry for the big Civil Rights March this Sunday, remember? Could've been any of us."

Eleven dead. Twelve confirmed. Through the afternoon the toll mounted.

We sat, we stood, we muttered half-finished thoughts—we watched, but we could hardly believe it—we heard, but we didn't want to. Report after report grew into an incessant refrain of statistical death until we were numb. We stood, we sat, we spoke out, fell silent, got up, walked out, came back, paced—anything to get out of that irrevocable room. "Oh, God, what's going to happen now?" We honestly expected civil war that day. We thought the Irish Army would be announced as pouring over the border any minute. "The bloody Paras—scum of the British Army—thugs in uniform—and the poor Bogsiders, killed for no other reason than walkin' out in the daylight of their own town."

And somebody said, "Being Irish is reason enough."

The phone rang out in the hall and Shane from downstairs answered it. I was told it was for me. Half-distracted, I went to see who it could possibly be. "Mick! Right. Yes. Come on over. There's a telly here."

When I went back, the television spoke, RTE: "—an unconfirmed report from an official spokesman of the British Army indicates that the soldiers fired in self-defence, in response to gunmen—."

"The liars!"

"Don't believe it!"

"What did you expect them to say?"

"Yeah. Gettin' their lies all lined up in good marchin' order."

The screen comes alive with a tearful, fearful, angry old woman's face, as tight as the kerchief knotted under her chin. She's crouching behind the shoulder of a priest. You spot the white collar, the black overcoat. It's quick, and there's no sound. A mini-scene when a soldier holds a rifle pointed at the priest and the old woman. The padre holds out his hands, palms down, palms up, to show he's clean. But his hands are streaked dark with black-and-white blood. The soldier grins nervously, self-consciously, waves them on with his pointing SLR. They flee around a brick corner. The soldier kneels to the wall, in shooting position. The rifle-stock pumps in his outstretched left hand three times. You never see the finger that squeezes the trigger.

"Well, something's got to be done."

"Why?–do you think Jack Lynch'll disturb his round of Sunday golf for a few poor sods up in Derry?"

"He was quick enough sending the Army up to the border in '69, wasn't he?"

"And just as quick pullin' them back again."

"The Irish Army! Good for nuthin' but sunnin' themselves in Cyprus."

"What have we a Ministry of Defence for, then, if it's not to defend us?"

"I wish I knew. It's plenty of taxes I'm payin' to keep them in brass hats. I don't know—I only know somethin's got to be done."

"Well, if you're waitin' for Jack Lynch, you can wait till another thirteen's dead." It was Mick O'Corrigan, who had just come in behind us.

"Thirteen? Christ. Thirteen."

In the streets of Dublin frustration collected around the GPO. It grew into anger, moved up through College Green, and focused itself outside Leinster House in Kildare Street. The Gardai were all called in from off-duty and made their appearance in rings around the government houses. Somebody said they were up in Merrion Square, too, guarding the British Embassy. Irish Gardai, is it, guarding them? They must be expecting trouble.

The curious went up to see for themselves. Placards appeared. The Gardai were reinforced. All night on Sunday the crowd gathered outside the Embassy. They looked sullen at the police. The cops looked back at them, uncomfortable. The thought, the discordant thought, of Irish police protecting British property, and a symbol of the age-old British imperial presence, at that, was on the mind of every single person there, in uniform or out. How could you help but think it, on this day, of all days, if you were Irish.

The word spread throughout Dublin. A wake was to be held, this night, for the thirteen dead. In dignity. In silence. A protest of all-night candles. We'll show them how we mourn our dead. The phone out in the hall at No. 56 Upper Rathmines Road was ringing off the hook all evening. Every person who'd been around the telly, looking on in Eileen and Angela's flat, wanted to go. Not one declined. Somebody rushed over to Campbell's to get candles before they'd all be gone. The wake was to be held at the British Embassy in Merrion Square. Who called it nobody knew but the word was going round with every ring of the phone. We'd take our grief and lay it at the door of those responsible for the slaughter.

When we went out we found the buses were jam-packed and not stopping at the bus-rank to take on more. We were going to have to walk there. A tributary stream joined us on the other footpath coming from Rathgar Road. Soon it was apparent we'd get there walking before the buses could reach the Portobello Bridge. I was carrying Aisling seated on my shoulders. Sheila was beside me. Krishna and Mick and the rest formed a cohort around us.

It seemed the entire city was there that night, but, of course, how many people could Merrion Square actually hold? Somebody estimated 50,000, and it did not seem unreasonable when you looked out across the sea of bobbing candles in the chill winter darkness. Our little party from Rathmines was unable to get anywhere close to the front door of the Embassy. But nobody turned away. Nobody went home. We stood in the street packed shoulder to shoulder. The silence of the vast crowd actually sounded like a murmur of the sea falling on the pebbled beach of Sandymount Strand. And every few seconds you would feel a wave rippling restlessly through the crowd, a wave of wrath.

By morning the newspapers were calling it 'Bloody Sunday.'

Dublin came to a standstill. Rumours swept the buses in and out of the city centre. People arrived at work only to find committees organized to down tools. There's to be a nationwide general strike. Everyone's being called out. When's the funerals going to begin?

Thousands never went to work at all. They stayed home behind locked doors, afraid. The situation seemed so palpably unsettled. The government was urging restraint. Wives and mothers ventured out early to rush the shops. Early Monday morning masses in the churches were crowded. The work-stoppers did not leave their benches till it was time for the pubs to open. Did you hear?—the Taoiseach has called a national day of mourning—to be held on Wednesday. Doesn't he know there's a national work-stoppage on? Who called it? Nobody called it. *We* called it. Things are gettin' out of hand. I kept the kids from school, I did. They're fastened to the telly. Did you see the Gardai in the street? They looked nervous to me. Have they called out the Army? They have. In the pubs, patrons opened newspapers spread out over the bar counters. Ah, don't mind the Irish Times—here's the Herald. What does it say in the Press? Look at this. It says—.

By late afternoon on Monday, word filtered out that the BOAC offices at the foot of Grafton Street had been smashed. The crowd in the streets paraded by the flames twinkling in the broken glass littering the footpath. The pubs emptied as the winter twilight settled early over the city. By half-five it was pitch black out. That's what they'd been waiting for, the cover of darkness. The boil was not yet lanced. The hand trembled with the drink added to the anticipation added to the universal outrage. The GPO was surrounded. The Dáil was encircled. The British Embassy was besieged.

All day Monday at our house, the rhythms of a regular day were discarded. The little one-room flats that normally husbanded their privacies turned inside out and dumped in the first floor hallway their frailties and anxieties.

The women of the house gathered again around the television in Eileen and Angela's flat. Josephine the nurse had no choice but to be at work at a time like this, but the two sisters were staying home from their jobs at the Ministry in Mespil Road: on screen they'd seen the Irish Army vehicles parked in the driveway of Leinster House. Monica joined them with her infant and they had Sheila and Aisling and Josephine's Desmond, too. The angular little room grew close with cigarette smoke and the water-vapor from the baby's bottle standing cooling on the cooker. Desmond had to be watched constantly as he would crawl under the bed and slip your shoelaces untied, or dash down the hall defying you to catch him, or stand wearily against the wall, banging his head on it to get some attention. "Sit down in the chair now—can't you sit still?"

"I'm bored." "Well, watch the telly with us." "I don't like it." Aisling shrank into the corner. She kept her eyes on the boy, as if he were about to explode. Angela and Eileen took turns trying to amuse him by reading to him but he wouldn't tolerate it very long. "Why can't I go out?" They went upstairs to fetch his toys for him but he threw them on the floor in spite. "God, he's terrible spoiled," said Eileen. "Give him to me for a week, I'd soon sort him." Desmond pretended to be playing with Monica's baby, and when they turned their backs, he tweaked the poor boy's ears. The baby yelped. "Here, you," said Angela. "Here's two bob. Go in to Campbell's and get yourself a sweet." When the boy was out of earshot, she muttered, "Maybe you'll get hit by a bus." "Angela!" said Sheila. But Eileen replied, "I'm with Angela. It'd be a blessing to his mother!"

They turned back disconsolately to the telly. The voice droned on. Thirteen killed. Sixteen admitted to hospital with gunshot wounds. All of them men and boys.

But the women in Rathmines Road were thinking of the mothers, wives, sisters, sweethearts. There seemed a special province of suffering set aside for Irish women. Spared, themselves, the blunt impact of the bullets of that fatal Sunday, they were yet condemned to go on living with their dead buried in their hearts.

I brought Krishna and Mick back to the flat for a quick bite early in the evening. "Can you get us some grub, love?"

Sheila looked worn out and disgruntled. "I was hoping you'd take us to Wimpy's tonight for a hamburger."

"Come on, babe—we're in a hurry."

"Why?"

"Nevermind."

Sheila looked from me to Krishna. *"Wuz de scene*, Comrade?"

I looked at her hopelessly while Krishna replied cheerfully, "Merrion Square."

Sheila grabbed Aisling's coat and hat. "If the whole of Dublin is going to protest tonight, I'm not stopping behind."

"But what about the kid?" I said testily.

Krishna said, "There might be trouble."

"Well—we'll only watch, then."

I barred the open door with my arm.

"Get out of my road," said Sheila. "It's not even your country!"

"Woo-hoo," cried Krishna. "You telling I, Comrade!"

Mick gave me a wink. "No messin' about with a Mayo woman."

The bus was halted. We peered out. Across the mouth of Great Georges Street, a procession was passing.

We paused on the step of the bus. Where the procession poured down the hill past Dublin Castle and into College Green, placards bobbed. On the corner, others shuffled slowly forward, an eddy melting into the main river.

Then in Dame Street we witnessed something like a solemn swelling of the sea. From D'Olier Street, Westmoreland Street and Pearse Street, tributary streams merged into the bottleneck of Grafton Street. There they inched past the burnt-out hulk of the BOAC offices. Though it was not raining, water flooded the pavements, and the procession walked on flattened firehoses. "Jaysus, you fellas got late to that one, didn't you?" said Mick O'Corrigan. A firefighter chuckled. "Oh, the traffic, you know?"

Gradually, we rounded the corner into Nassau Street. Some of the more impatient scaled the black iron fence of Trinity and could be seen racing ahead through the college grounds. They climbed back out at the corner of Kildare Street. "That was a mighty quick education you got there!" says Mick.

On Monday night, in Kildare Street, you looked about and you could see mothers with their children, fathers with their families, barristers rubbing elbows with men on the dole, magistrates mingling with the accused, managers shoulder to shoulder with the workers they supervised. Maybe it was the deepening shadows the government buildings cast over the street, or maybe it was the sibilant hum of the streetlights glowing through the darkness in ghostly blue haloes, but you were moved by the spectacle of whole neighborhoods of Drumcondra and entire streets of Ballyfermot moving silently together. Our little party from Rathmines, plus one from Mespil Road, was by no means unique. And the muffled tramp of thousands of feet rose like a drifting mist from the pavements.

In Stephen's Green, guests of the Shelbourne Hotel came out onto floodlit steps to stand in their nightgowns with their winter coats draped over their shoulders. The night-clerk stood on the running board of a Rolls at the kerb, his arms crossed on the roof, his chin balanced on his forearm. The windows of the Baggot Street Hospital were thrown open and nurses stood looking down beside their patients.

Then we were entering Merrion Square, and through the bare winter trees, distant streetlights flickered. They were like pin-wheels in the muslin of the night. A calligraphy of black branches traced itself on a canvas of billowing clouds, the boat-bottoms of which reflected the cold luminescence of the city at night. I gazed around, mesmerized by the scene, and wishing to memorize it. Looking up, large raindrops began to fall, one by one, at intervals. They crowned the shoulders of the crowd and blessed the foreheads of upturned faces, the holy water of the heavens bestowed upon our mission. The rooftops were closing in. From Clare Street, a second procession was funneling into the rectangular amphitheatre of the square. Between the buildings on either flank and the railings of the green in the middle, two streams flooded forward, closing nearer and nearer on Merrion Square East.

The British Embassy was a narrow-faced building, prim and sedate, pinched into a row of proper Georgian facades, all joined hip to hip. It had only a single door, as if modesty became its matronly demeanor. Tall windows on the first floor, graced with balconies, like the black lace on the veiled hat of a sea-captain's widow. She drew herself up straight, the Palladian pretensions of her neighbors toned down to a classical severity, no hint of rouge on her cheeks, only a respectable, powdered grey wig. But her eyes were blind and blank. No light came from within, and all the drapes were drawn. She had stood there in formation since the 18th century and always successfully before closed her eyes to the gallows where Robert Emmet hanged, to the wagons full of corpses in the Famine, to the sixteen executed rebels of the Easter Rising. She was well-used to not seeing what she wished not to see. That Monday, with the searing images of the day before on the telly still fresh and vivid in our minds, before the single door, formidable squads of the Dublin Gardai formed up in a baton-wielding phalanx, and we wondered, did they intend to stand up for the old bitch?

We edged forward with our backs up against the railings facing the Embassy. It was the only place we could find to squeeze through the jam. I led the way, with Sheila clutching the back of my pea-coat to keep in touch with me. She was holding Aisling up, at first, so that the child could see, but then, increasingly, as she realized with a sinking feeling, so that she could breathe. I looked back to make sure Krishna was following close behind her. I couldn't see the Comrade, nor Mick, for that matter, but I thought it might be because huge floodlights on the roofs of Garda vans were playing an intense white light over the crowd. In the wash of the blind-spot this caused, I could just detect police reinforcements massing in the mouth of Fitzwilliam Street, like a swarm of crows.

Then I saw the coffins. A queue of black caskets bobbing on the shoulders of men whose faces were submerged. Hands sticking up with outstretched fingers passed them forward. The crowd pressed in, craning to see. Thirteen black coffins, one after the other, they came on, up and down, up and down, like narrow-prowed black boats, bobbing on a sea of upthrust hands. A white cross painted on the black lids, which would appear when the thing tilted. A white-washed number 13 repeated again and again. The crowd swayed as the momentum of the caskets surged. Thousands pressed forward to see, and they all seemed to be behind me, so that I was beginning to get alarmed for Sheila and the child's safety.

The lines of Gardai at the Embassy door shoved and heaved and finally opened a path to allow two men to wrest the first casket from the shoulders of the mob. They carried it up two short stone steps and dropped it on the doorsill of the Embassy with a hollow wooden knock. The spectators surged inwards. The police linked arms and attempted to hold them back. A second coffin was laid to rest at the feet of the British government, then a third and a fourth. Then there was shouting and the path to the door was choked off. With a shiver like fever, mass claustrophobia broke out into a full-scale riot in Merrion Square East.

Aisling began to wail. I tried to look at Sheila, but I could not even turn my shoulders to face her. With a massive twist, I turned my back on the Embassy, but then I was up against the railings like toothpaste being squeezed out of a tube. Tears were streaming down my little girl's face, and her mouth was wide open, but I could not hear her screaming, there was so much noise. I caught a glimpse of people going over the top and I knew I had to get the kid out of there. I grabbed the iron spikes on top of the railings and tried to lift myself. No go. I had to get a footing somewhere but the soles of my shoes could find no purchase on the slick, rain-pearled black iron. Then my foot was in the small of someone's back. I pushed off, felt the yielding body, and vaulted upwards. With a desperate heave, I found myself up, my chest impaled for a heartbeat on the spikes in my hands until I flipped my body like a fish and fell over on my back on the other side.

I scrambled to my feet. I was aware of peripheral shadows fleeing from the inside of the fence. Someone was holding Sheila up on tiptoe on the bottom rung of the railings as she passed Aisling across the spikes to me. There was nothing to do but stand her up on the ground next to me, where she stayed, shaking, sobbing and crying, her hands covering her ears and her eyes shut tight. Sheila's face on the other side of the fence was a plaster-cast of fear. It was the sudden, panicky fear of being trampled, the awful, visceral fear of being crushed. I planted my feet spread apart on the lower rung of the railings, put my head between two spikes and my arms through the gaps on either side, and lifted her under her arm-pits. Christ—she was heavy, in that impossibly awkward stance. The iron ground into my chin, the spikes scraped my cheeks. Sheila skinned her knees up the bars on the other side. With a groan, I felt her coming, as I strained lifting, and she first pulled herself up, and then pushed herself over, just as the red, rotating lights began cutting through billows of CS gas.

For three days and three nights, for three members of the Cumann Billy Reid, Dublin was transformed into a personal battleground. To the day-time belonged the planning, plotting, scheming, waiting for the cover of darkness. The night was our ally. Our adversary was the Dublin Gardai. Our refuge was at the bottom of No. 33 Leinster Square.

Krishna's book-strewn kip was not exactly mid-way between my flat and Mick's in Mespil Road but at least it was in-between. "I lost contact with you and Sheila completely, last night," said the Comrade.

"What a mess. Did you two get home okay? I had to leave, because we had the kid."

"I was glad to see you get over that fence, all right," said Mick.

"I know! Somebody gave me a boost up!"

"That was me!" he said, "—you dosser."

"Who's a dosser?"

"You are, you fookin' unemployed bollocks. Soon enough, I reckon, you'll be on the dole, and added to the rolls I'm called upon to support."

"I was sacked, you asshole, so I won't be eligible."

"Comrades, comrades," said Krishna, "let's attend to the task at hand!"

Strip off the mask of your every-day self. The one who always wanted to please, to be a good-boy, to be accepted, one of the herd, a conformist, nobody special. Strip off that mask and underneath you'll find the uncivilised, unsocialised savage, with all his nursed grievances, and primal urges, and un-mixed motives: revenge, hatred, love. Thus, Comrade Krishna:

"The contradictions inherent in the neo-colonialist puppet regime under so-called normal circumstances lie dormant and inactive. But inevitably developments proceed and incidents do occur wherein the true nature of these contradictions are rendered unavoidable, or suddenly stark and clear, and then we move to confrontation. It's the duty of the organizer, or the individual cadre, during the period of confrontation, to develop the confrontation along the path towards the collective goal."

All that being true and well-stated, I suspected that underneath the cogitated analysis lay the raw feelings of revenge dating all the way back to his father's exile at the hands of the Nehru regime: exactly the part of Comrade Krishna that he'd never analyzed, and never would.

As for me, I had a score to settle, and I had no fancy Marxist dialectic to dress it up with. The commonplace civilities of my past life fell away, disowned, as compromises, as the empty gestures, made in bad faith, that they are, and always were, and always will be. They take my job away. They deny me my rights and try to strip me of my manhood. They gas my wife and kid. Now it's my turn. "The spikes on top of the black railings in Merrion Square? They don't give you any room for sitting on the fence, do they?"

The one who remained opaque, and all surface, no depth, to me, was Mick O'Corrigan. Was he just, as he would've said himself, a raw yout'—dropping the th? I hadn't yet figured out what made a 19-year-old kid up from Co. Tipp, far away from the streets of Belfast or Derry, far from the provocations of living cheek-to-jowl with the British Army, so avid for the Republican cause. Or, so dead-set on self-immolation. "We're the riot squad. To hell with the Sinn Féin. To hell with the Cumann."

"Sometimes the leadership must be led by the people," Krishna agreed, "and this is clearly one of those times."

"Right," said Mick. "It's us three, we're a unit. We stick together, and we fight together." Gleefully, he rubbed his hands palm to palm. "Time for a bit of agro!"

That night, Tuesday night, we were ready, and resolute. Thousands of marchers invaded Merrion Square. Too many to count. Maybe not as many as the night before—but then, the women and children were left home on Tuesday.

The Gardai, too, were ready, and after the previous night, spoiling for a fight. Across the intersections, at both wings of Merrion Square East, hundreds of riot-clad Gardai in helmets, long truncheons and shields, formed up in human barricades. Loud-hailers called on the moving masses of demonstrators to disperse. There was no reply but the steady wordless onset of the tramp of hundreds of rhythmic boots on the pavements, approaching inexorably the ranks of police from two directions, the two claws of an encircling mob. The lines of police stiffened to resist. No choreography tonight, no symbolic theatre, orchestrated to appeal to and assuage the deep underground pool of grief and hatred. Tonight was pure anger, unalloyed madness. The loud-hailers whinnied with a futile keening. Somebody in the front rank of the marching mass on the south side of the green ran out ahead a little and, skipping like a javelin artist, launched a broken paving stone through the high and arching, flood-lit mist.

At the beginning, though they were hopelessly outnumbered, the police refused to give an inch.

On Monday night, they might have been merely doing their reluctant duty, of two minds about it, but being attacked by rabble, by the end of the night, they had taken a personal stake in the matter. Now that they'd had a chance to sleep on it, even if only for three or four hours, on Tuesday night their pride was invoked, their appetites were whetted, they wanted to break heads. So they withstood the opening barrage of flung objects, waited for orders, and braced for the clash.

The two sides collapsed into one another in a milling embrace and the parliament of insults broke out. "We're going to burn the fooker, and youz'd better get out of our way!" "You're not playin' in the sandbox now, ye bleedin' shite!" "Go home and beat yer wife, maybe she can't hit ye back!" Threats, vows and oaths accomplished nothing, and the gardai cured that with a whistle and a baton charge.

Despite our resolve, Mick O'Corrigan's self-styled Riot Squad got separated at the very first opening bars of the jig. I went down in the first charge and got up again with my face shining with glee. The nervous part was over, we got the first bump out of the way, and now I could cut loose. A confused thrashing on flying feet was going on all around me while I stood there like a statue. I turned to face where I thought the lines of peelers were still standing but they were already past me and I began to walk backwards slowly with a sense of beatific calm.

A knot of coppers were chasing fleeing rioters along the black railings of a house on the corner across the street. They caught one and began to bludgeon him with their sticks, three onto one. A fourth could get no opening, and twisted round to look for another target. He spotted me in the street and he leapt from the kerb, charging straight at me, giving a terrific wind-up for a knockout blow. At the last moment, I dodged my head, the baton went whistling past, I stuck out my foot, and the peeler went sprawling on his face.

I hopped up on the footpath and ran straight into a pair of arms. It was Comrade Krishna.

"Come on, let's get outta here, man." He began pushing and shoving me up Fitzwilliam Street.

I said, "Didja see that bastard go down?" "Yeah, yeah—move!" "No!–I wanna go back." "All right—but first, let's get some ammo."

Over my head I raised a paving stone, and staggering, I hurled it down with all my might onto an exposed kerb beside the excavated base of a fireplug, shattering it.

Under rusty-piped scaffolding, the streetfighters clambered up a Croagh Patrick of bricks on their knees. They were adding a wing onto the National Library in Kildare Street, and the demonstrators were stealing away with the government's building materials to throw at the government's police.

With our pockets sagging, Krishna and I filtered through stooping shadows with other shadows hurrying all around us. We crept along Leinster Street past the Trinity walls and then through Clare Street and infiltrated Merrion Square from the north side.

Inside the railings of the green, the red and blue lights of the police splintered through the trees like the revolving blades of a kaleidoscopic windmill. In Mount Street, fire engines stood coiled in snaking hoses. Light darted brilliantly off chrome and glazed the visors of the gardai's riot helmets. It was the fault of those high-intensity floodlights on the roofs of the garda vans— they were intended to light the scene, but they afforded our side a fringe of deep shadow to hide in. As we crept up, we could see, in the first floor windows of the Embassy, glass gleamed in shards, and the drapes hung down, charred rags. The Embassy door still stood locked and paralyzed in the doorway and the beleaguered peelers peered out of their cage of light, hunting the darkness beyond it for their hidden attackers. They were lit up for us, while we were protected by the night.

The gas was your only hazard. But even the CS gas could put you out of action only momentarily. You retreated and recovered and went right back again. When the Gardai charged, you faded away into the lanes and side-streets. They could not venture too far from the Embassy lest the mob streak in behind them and finish the job. They were trapped in their defensive posture. Even the gas was blown back in their faces every time the breeze shifted. The Gardai could muster only so many men, and for these, there could be no rest, while the rioters came on in waves, each one fresher and more daring than the last. There were too many vulnerable points in too many directions for the attackers to come at them, too many vehicles to protect, there were the firefighters to be defended, and the costly engines, without which they could not hope to save the Embassy when it did go up. It was going to be a long night.

Somewhere in the confusion of the ebb-and-flow fighting, Comrade Krishna and I bumped into O'Corrigan again. "Where the hell've you been?"

"Mount Street," said Mick. "The Embassy's on fire from the rear. There's a bit of a laneway—." Mick grabbed me. "I saw you go down. I couldn't get to you."

"It's okay, I got up again."

"What about the lane?" said Krishna.

"I'll show you," said Mick. "Come on with me."

Reunited, our Riot Squad set out on a long detour around Stephen's Green and Fitzwilliam Square. Mick lived nearby in Mespil Road, so he knew all the back lanes and shortcuts.

Powers Court, for instance, was a lane leading out of Mount Street Crescent and down between the backs of the buildings to the rear door of the Embassy. It was engulfed in darkness broken only by a single bare bulb wired to a drainpipe. Past the dissipating pool of light, the lane curved a little and you saw smoke, curlicues of flame, the silhouettes of firemen in their black slickers with the yellow hems, the sheen of water in the gutters, heaps of hoses.

In the dark, I stumbled against a rubbish bin, but the Gardai never heard the clangor because they were caught in an enclosed space trying to ward off a surge of rioters attacking the firefighters down a lane leading in from Mount Street. I held my breath, as if that would keep me from making a noise, and looked at the other two. Mick signaled, and the three of us crept forward again, keeping close to the shadow-walls of Powers Court. Mick spotted a fireman's short-handled axe which had fallen on the cobblestones in the melee. He cupped his hand and hissed over his shoulder, "Hit them while I get in there." He stole up with small steps, stealthily, and we jumped out and launched our missiles.

Mick was chopping with short, two-handed strokes at the canvas-covered hide of a firehose.

"Look out!" I called.

A cop squared off with his baton raised over Mick's head. Mick looked up, and the cop caught the gleam of the axe-blade. He hesitated. He must have feared that if he came down on Mick's head, the fooker might not like it and might swing that axe at his knees.

Reinforcements wheeled about from the main fray, and one garda shouted at Mick, "Drop it!"

Krishna was dragging Mick backwards into the shadows and managed to wrest the axe out of his hand. It clattered to the cobblestones and lay there gleaming like a chipped tooth.

Four of the gardai stepped over it and advanced cautiously into the well of darkness in Powers Court. We retreated backwards up the lane, step by step, shouting imprecations like a numberless tribe. I picked up the rubbish bin-lid and sent it bouncing loudly over the cobblestones at our adversaries. The three of us turned and ran quickly as we could through the pool of light from the bare bulb on the drainpipe. Over our shoulders, we could see the police start picking up their flat feet to sprint after us. Now they knew there were only three of us.

In the Crescent, Mick shouted, "Split up!"

"Rendezvous tomorrow!" yelled Krishna, "At my place!"

I peeked out from behind the lane I found myself hiding in. I was thinking: home—by the Burlington Road, Appian Way, Ranelagh—stay off the main streets.

But I was facing the critical crossing, the open air of the Grand Canal and the lights all around the Baggot Street Bridge. Once across the Canal, I thought I would disappear in the shadows again.

I sauntered across the bridge with my hands in my pockets and turned calmly down the footpath along the concrete post-and-cable fence that ran knee-high along the grassy canal-bank of the Mespil Road. I had the feeling that Mick must be safe home by now, behind closed doors, as he lived just a short distance ahead at the rear of the row-houses on the left coming up. I was just turning to cross over to Burlington Road, thinking I had made it, when a spotlight over my shoulder froze me.

A dark car on the bridge with the interior light on and four hatless men shoulder to shoulder in the front and back. I heard the car-door open and slam shut again. Then the sweep of their spotlight back and forth blinded me again.

I turned and walked straight along the canal bank. I wouldn't wait for them, but I wouldn't appear to run away either. I needed a second to think.

Slowly the car nosed around the balustrade of the bridge, and slowly in first gear, it crept past me, blinding me with the spotlight again, so that I had to squint and throw my hand up over my eyes as they were rolling to a halt up ahead. Three men in a sudden hurry tumbled out. Blue suits, silver buttons, no hats or helmets, no badges. When I saw the batons in their hands, I knew they were not going to ask me any questions.

I jumped over the low cable-fence and slipped down the banking. Two of the peelers jumped after me. The third danced along the footpath, beating his baton on the chain-link black cables suspended between each concrete post. The fourth waited ahead of me, peering over the balustrade of the Baggot Street Bridge. They had me hemmed in.

I scrambled. The slope of the banking was steep and slippery, and already my feet were water-logged. Behind me, the mud of the water-margin sucked at the shoes of my pursuers, bogging them down in clumsiness, but still, I was running out of room. I looked up and the cop on the bridge had come around onto the footpath and was flinging his foot up over the cable.

In the shadow cast by the bridge, a dark mass loomed. The canal-lock. Massive timbers soaked in pitch and gleaming with tar-black splinters. At the wings of the lock, white-washed buttresses sloped into the earth, sunk into the double-bankings of the canal. The cop coming over the cable slipped, and slid on his backside, down the dewy slope, right under my feet. His grasping fingers closed on the sucking whoosh at my heels. On my knees, I clambered up the buttress of the canal-lock.

I grabbed at the metal stanchions. I pulled, and propelled my body forward. I tripped on a protruding bolt and my foot slipped down into the space between the groaning timbers. Looking down, I could hear the wash of the canal-water:

slap, slap. Everything was moving in slow motion. Glancing streetlights hitting sliding facets of little waves, cut into quarter-moons.

I yanked, and my wet foot came, but the muddy shoe stayed. I grabbed at the second stanchion of the lock, and a splinter of the ancient, water-logged black wood scored my sock-soaked foot. I flung myself with a leap onto the grass of the far bank.

I ran along Wilton Terrace and into the dark end of Wilton Place with one shoe on. My only hope was that the keystone cops behind me wouldn't be able to get out of each other's way.

But running as fast as I could with only one shoe, I came out in Lad Lane, and they weren't following. I sprinted across the road and under an arch. I was in a courtyard, and a second arch led out of it into the next street. I slowed and stumbled over the cobblestones in the driveway under the arch. I went close to the wall and looked out from under the overhang. Nothing. A deserted section of street. Where were they? Could they have doubled back to their motor, to pursue me in their cruiser? I wouldn't put it past them. Could they have been called away on their car radio? I just didn't know.

Across the road, a green with the usual black railings. Then I heard the steps on the cobblestones coming distantly behind me. I didn't have to look. I knew who it was. One last chance. I'd try for the green. Maybe there's a back way out.

When I darted into the street, I heard the screeching wheels come careening around the corner from Cumberland Road. I stopped myself, skipped off to the right. Back up on the footpath, and I began my one-footed run again. But when I looked up, my heart sank. There at the far end of the street was the whole floodlit television studio of Merrion Square, the posse of police vans, the full-throated clamor of the riot around the Embassy still going on late into the night.

I'd made a circle, back into Fitzwilliam Street, straight back into the net.

Behind me, I heard gearshifts grinding, and the angry whirr of acceleration. I stopped, not knowing which way to turn, stumbling up against the railings in front of a house, brushing my pea-coat collar on the spikes.

I was tired, out of breath. I staggered up the walk to the house. My unshod foot hurt, it felt like it was bleeding. Maddeningly, I was thinking, thank God the splinter didn't penetrate my foot, I wouldn't have gotten this far. I turned to face them. Three of them were climbing out of the Garda car, right in front of this house. I went backwards up a pair of short steps and leaned with a sigh against the closed door. They came around the fenders of their little Ford with satisfied smirks, arranging the hems of their coats, fashioning their batons. I leaned heavily against the door and my knees were turning to water when the door gave way and I fell on my butt in a carpeted hallway.

A priest in a soutane stepped over me and out onto the front step. "May I help you gentlemen?"

"We want that man, Father. Step out of the way, please."

"This man is here to see me."

I sat up and drew my face back into the shadow of the half-open door.

"It's a bit late for confessions, Father."

"The Lord works his own hours, Sergeant."

"Now, Father—."

"You will not enter a holy house to do this dirty work!" roared the priest. He advanced down the step and glared at them, from their suddenly heated faces to their muddy shoes, up and down. "You men ought to be ashamed of yourselves."

One of the cops hesitated, unsure of himself, the second withdrew a step, like a chastised schoolboy, but the Sergeant was adamant. "I'll not forget this."

"Are you threatening me?" the priest bellowed. "What's your name?" The priest looked down on the other two. "Where are your badges? By what authority do you come here seeking to mete out instantaneous justice, without benefit of judge or jury?"

"We only meant to arrest him, Father," said the embarrassed one meekly.

"On what grounds?"

The Sergeant said quickly, "Incitin' to riot. And disturbin' the peace. Is that enough for ye, or shall I add assaultin' the police in their lawful line o' duty?"

"And how do you know this is your man?"

"If he isn't, why did he run from us?"

"Because he knew, Sergeant, you were going to beat him with your sticks and leave him for dead. No. You had no intentions of arresting him." The priest raised his arm and pointed up Fitzwilliam Street. "Or what do you think the disturbances of this night are all about? You ought to be burning down that Embassy yourselves, if you were any sort of Irishmen! Now get out of my sight, all of you!"

And he slammed the door in their faces.

"They'll be back," said Father Vincent, rubbing his forehead. "With a warrant. Which they can get on suspicion. To search this place. This house belongs to the Columbans, and I'm in enough trouble with my superiors as it is."

It was three in the morning and all over the city ambulances were rushing riot casualties to the hospital. But the priest who rang up from the Columbans' residence in Fitzwilliam Street had been too distraught and insistent to be denied. "He's an elderly priest recuperating from brain surgery, and, of all nights, he's chosen tonight to take a sudden turn for the worst. I know, I know. But his last request is to be taken home to his sister's house to die, and how can I deny him? I'd never be able to forgive myself! Indeed, indeed. But you know, the Lord works his own hours, now, so He does."

And so, in the end, an ambulance pulled up outside No. 56 Upper Rathmines Road and the attendant who went round to open the big sloping rear door held it respectfully open while the first priest, Father Vincent, stepped out. The driver and he then wheeled the second priest, the dying one, whose head and face, except for one eye, were swathed in bandages, on a wheeled gurney up the steps. Once inside the hallway, Father Vincent thanked them profusely, adding "I know you must rush off now, I can take it from here, lads, bless you, bless you."

Sheila had her first shock when she answered the gentle knocking half-asleep and saw the priest standing there—but quickly, so that she wouldn't faint or suffer apoplexy, I stepped out from behind Father Vincent and, lifting the bandages over both eyes, said, "It's just me. None the worse for wear, except for one missing shoe. Would you put on the kettle, love, and invite the good man in?"

The sun never rose on the third day in Dublin, but stayed away to let the rain wash away the fury and flames of the night before, and the cold February drizzle was like an act of contrition after a fit of blasphemy.

I never got out of bed till the afternoon, and I supposed, neither did Mick O'Corrigan, who wandered into our flat about two. We all went down to Angela and Eileen's flat to watch telly. "Well, this is it," said Mick to nobody in particular. "Jack Lynch's national day of mourning."

"Feels like it, doesn't it," said Monica's Shane.

Mick, after a while, whispered to me, "I need a drink. There's a telly down in Madigan's, you know."

I gave Aisling a hug, and Sheila a peck on the cheek. She looked at me mournfully, but, by this time, she had given up on trying to change my mind about anything.

The mood in that little bedsitter I had been through before. The women crouched forward in chairs. The subdued commentary. The communal emotions on the verge of head-shaking disbelief, without the release of tears, which were all used up since three days ago.

It was JFK's funeral cortege on television all over again. Only multiplied by many more coffins than one. Three days. Three days after the events that shocked the world. A ritual you had to go through before the nation could move on.

But it didn't suit Mick O'Corrigan. He couldn't stick it in the midst of mourning women. As we stood at the bar in Madigan's, after ordering pints, he said, "We haven't burnt the fooker down yet, Nick."

"It's got to go tonight," I said. "It can't go on like this."

"And to hell with all this rubbish about 'no confrontation with Dublin.' What the hell were the fookers handing us last night—a holiday in Barcelona?"

I asked him how he made out getting home last night and I finally got a laugh out of him with the story of how I managed to finagle an ambulance ride home.

We had another round, and a bulletin on the telly announced that Sinn Féin

intended to mount a rally, to be held at the GPO at seven.

Then the afternoon in Madigan's drowned itself in the sorrows of the television funerals. The tricolour-draped coffins moved solemnly across the grey screen of Derry and, like a slap in the face, there were the British Army standing grimly by, armed to the teeth, by their Saracens in the road, as the cortege wound its way through Free Derry Corner. At the cemetery, the Honour Guard of the IRA, in olive-drab and green berets and ski-masks, stood over the caskets suspended on ropes over holes in the ground with their arms extended heavenward in a gothic arch: the crack of defiant pistols.

"Come on, Mick. It's time we got over to Comrade Krishna's."

Mick barged into the Comrade's flat and opened the discussion with, "It's got to go tonight. Even Christ went on the third day."

"It isn't all that impossible," said Krishna. "If only you go about it with your heads screwed on. Organization. Discipline. Not mob rule. The Movement's going to have to come out of the closet on this one."

"The people will be out there again tonight," I said, "with or without us."

"It takes two to make a revolution," said Krishna. "The people and the cadre."

"Well—where's the IRA been?" said Mick.

"Not where I've been. Not in the streets."

"We saw them on the tube just now, in Derry. They're not afraid to come out under the noses of the British Army up there, but they won't show their faces in Dublin?"

"Who's the Movement anyway, if we aren't."

"Tell that to the bureaucrats in Kevin Street."

"She'll go tonight," Krishna said calmly.

"How do you know?"

"I've just got a feeling. Besides—John Martyn came by here and told me we're all expected at the GPO at seven for a mass meeting. So—something's up. Anyway—where have you two been all day?"

The thousands that gathered in O'Connell Street that evening arrived with a sense of the reckoning at hand. The placards and banners were there and the families from the North with the women and children were back again. Sinn Féin's flatbed lorry stood parked in the middle of the road with the motor running, and Ruairí Ó Brádaigh, at the microphone behind the towers of portable speakers, kept the instruction short. "Please obey your marshals!" Cheers went up for the green-jacketed men in black berets, dark glasses and black armbands who formed up in precise ranks on the outer margins of the crowd: The IRA was with us, and the Dublin Gardai, drawn up outside the lines of green jackets, were prepared to accord all of us a respectful escort. Among the attendance of fifty thousand, O'Corrigan's Riot Squad was absorbed, like a cell of an amoeba. We were satisfied that we had done our job of softening the thing up so that these others could come along and execute the coup de grâce. Even Mick fell in when the flatbed lorry began to move, and Ruairí Ó Brádaigh made a request. "Please maintain good order—we are going to march to Merrion Square."

Looking about us, we could see the faces of our comrades from Cumann Billy Reid: Alita, Myles, Barney, Martina and Bernadette, Peadar Kenny. We were swimming in the sea, a school of fish with our schoolmarm, our headmaster, and our sideline coaches. It was a relief, to be honest, after the night before. "This is more like it," said Mick.

At Grafton Street, a few people, non-Movement members, no doubt, tried to dash on up ahead through the shopping-mall street, but the marshals formed a wall. In Nassau Street, the packed-close marchers got the idea it would be just as easy for some of them to go up Kildare Street. A bulge appeared in the side of the stream, and the marshals rushed in, nervous, one of whom was our own John Martyn. Behind them, the burly Gardai added a bit much of pushing and shoving. The crowd reacted testily: glancing to the right, up Kildare Street, you could see the Irish Army vehicles in the road outside the Mansion House and the rear gates of Leinster House. Just for the craic, Mick O'Corrigan began chanting "lynch Lynch, lynch Lynch, lynch Lynch," making hand-gestures of hanging himself by the neck—the crowd took it up, stamping their feet and clapping in time–"lynch Lynch, lynch Lynch, lynch Lynch!" On the flatbed, O' Bradaigh became very excited, waving directions and shouting orders through the speakers to his marshals. A shoving match ensued, but the Sinn Féin lorry moved out again, space opened into Leinster Street, and the marshals managed to move the milling crowd into the vacuum of the right road again.

The marchers found their release finally in Merrion Square North. They spilled over into the west side of the Square, rounded the south-west corner of the black-railed green, and began a mad dash down the north and south sides pell-mell for the Embassy. Every man and woman there wanted a seat in the first row.

A truce was in force in Merrion Square East. The Gardai were there in numbers, but it was plain they'd surrendered to the inevitable. Either that, or, as we in the Cumann suspected, they'd sat down to parley and struck a deal with us. The anti-British crowd present tonight in the denouement after the funerals of the afternoon were not the only ones with a grievance against Jack

Lynch, the Taoiseach: short of calling the Irish Army out to shoot the people down, nothing was going to save that building on this night. So—a deal must have been consummated. The police offered no objections as their nominal traffic barricades were knocked down and trampled. As the mob flooded in between the railings of the green and the Embassy, they did nothing but interpose a little sheer bulk before the offending door.

The chant went up. "Brits Out! Brits Out! Brits OUT!" They clapped their hands. They stamped their feet. The floodlights on top of the Garda vans took it all in. The Embassy began the third night a battered shell. On the ground floor, the windows, boarded up now, stared at us like bandaged eyes. The stains of petrol bombs wept down the limestone face like tears of rust. She had the shabby look of an old hag lamenting her vanished prime, her breath turned foul.

An olive-drab-jacket with a ski mask over his face began scaling a drainpipe under the first-floor balconies. The Gardai turned their heads to watch with everyone else. The crowd cheered him up, up, up, inch by inch. With his head beneath the floor of the balcony, hanging on with one hand, he reached inside his jacket and pulled out, one by one, three bottles. He reached up and placed each one in a row on the balcony floor. Then he let go with his legs, while he held onto the railings above his head, and swung his whole body out over the open air. The crowd went "Oooh!" *Up* swung his leg, he caught the heel, he pulled himself up by main strength, as they wildly cheered him. Standing there feeling the ebullience of the crowd, Krishna nudged me. "Do you recognize those boots?" "British Army boots?" I said. "Same as mine. Soft as velvet. The best." Two more men went up the drainpipe and the masked man on the balcony helped his comrades up over the railings. "They're up! They're up!" The three men kicked in the glass of the windows of the first floor. One reached inside the jagged bits and pulled out the tails of the drapes. He soaked them in petrol. The others lit the wicks on six more milk-bottles they had and threw them deep into the room. Then they lit the drapes. They bloomed into bright flames burning straight up like fluttering ribbons. The three men climbed over the rail and slid down the drain-pipe. As each one neared the ground, he jumped off into the willing arms of the welcoming crowd.

With the first floor burning, a shout went up. "Make way for the IRA!" The mob parted and three men in ski-masks came forward. "Step aside!" the crowd shouted at the policemen. They politely opened a path up to the stout front door, which was only street-level, a single short doorstep. The men in the ski-masks placed a small bundle in the corner of the door-jamb on the side of the door-hinges. They cuddled it in, turned, and came away quickly, warning in loud voices, "Get back—get back!" The mob swept back like a wave. The charge went off in a burst of sul-phurous smoke. The masked men were already melted into the crowd. When the smoke cleared, you could see the cops taking their hands from their ears, and the door was caved in.

A roar of triumph went up from the crowd. They surged forward again, the police rushed in to fill the gap. The voices were angry now. "Let us in, or you're goin' to get it!" Up on the second floor, at the top of the building, flames flashed from inside the windows. The peelers gave way, and in a second, the inside of the Embassy was swarming with people carrying cans of petrol. The police protested that it was dangerous and attempted to keep the numbers down, but nobody was listening. In a few minutes, the building emptied out again and all three floors were on fire.

I turned to my comrades in the street. Their faces were shining with reflected flames. I smiled to hear an Irish voice behind me reciting, "Burn, baby, burn!"

Between the railings of the green and the burning British Embassy, a profound hush fell over Merrion Square. Everyone stared, in awe of the majesty of this cleansing, purifying fire. The Embassy was fast becoming a cauldron, a roaring furnace, a chimney channeling the fire upward. Through the second-floor windows at the top, we could see the hungry flames licking at the tall ceiling. There was a muffled crash, and the second floor caved in, collapsing in a spectacular whirling pinwheel-shower of sparks.

Then the flames grew ravenous and with an explosion of glass, they burst through the top-floor windows, in a final fury. The three windows across the top of the Embassy became fountains of flame. The flames rose up in three golden spires. They snarled at the dark sky above, three speaking tongues, sending from their burning throats sputtering sparks spinning, tumbling, dying off into the air.

Then from somewhere in the rear a solitary voice began singing.

> *When boyhood's flower was in my blood, I dreamt of ancient free men . . .*

The crowd took up the refrain and gave the song back to the singer.

> *Of Greece and Rome who bravely stood three hundred men and free men . . .*

In a solemn, deep, basso-profundo thrum that seemed to surge upward through your legs from the pavement, from the earth below, a groundswell from the buried depths of the inner core, in a moment I knew, then and there, in my bones, I would never forget as long as I lived, the sound of fifty thousand voices singing grew gradually into one great communal stream as we all sang together the rising, rousing chorus,

> *A Nation once again,*
> *A Nation once again,*
> *And Ireland, long a province be, a Nation once again!* . . .

Chapter 7

North to Newry

The next morning, passersby looked on the burnt-out hulk of the British Embassy and already the ashes were cold. The nine o'clock news on Telefís Éireann, that very night, gave an instant replay to the flames; but somehow, for most of the city, seeing it on the telly, and copping on to the subtleties of approbation in the tone of Charles Mitchel's authoritative voice: almost instantly, a spasmodic, wild, releasing eruption of pent-up rage—passed into history. For seeing it on the telly made it official. For a horrible moment, Dublin looked too much like Belfast, quench the thought.

From London, the British government demanded reparations, while the Lynch government in Dublin issued their apologies. The Sunday papers printed their editorials at the end of the week, but, sooner than you thought, the housewives returned to Moore Street, the classes opened at UCD, the streets were clogged with nothing more than busses and bicycles.

Euphoric emotions lasted a little while longer for Mick O'Corrigan's Riot Squad. No Cumann meeting could ever match the Wednesday night we'd just been through. The talk-shop in Leinster Square opened a continuous coming-and-going, celebratory rehash, right through the weekend. Jane Quill kept the kettle simmering and Bernadette and Martina brought Waterloo Road by with the hard stuff and Mick came by with a little black-market herb to light up the night. He and I had to duck out the laneway in back to blow away the smoke, for we knew that Krishna would not approve. To share in the craic, Bernie and Martina had to make separate forays to the offo, ostensibly for liquid refreshments, in order to partake. The Comrade wasn't the only one who disapproved: Alita Hughes and her Belfast cousin Brendan would have taken conniptions.

Under the circumstances, I was fairly oblivious to what was going on with Sheila and our daughter. I was expecting my last paycheck in the mail that Friday, or Saturday, but my wife had meanwhile, unbeknownst to me, acted in my absence to secure a pay packet coming in without me. At Leinster Square, Mary was gone in the evening for her shift at the Mater, while Jane was home from her job at the Ministry after five, so Sheila had arranged for rotating shifts of babysitters to watch Aisling while she went to work. On the theory that she'd get a job quicker than I would, she was not taking any chances. Besides, Jane and Mary bought their scones where they knew a vacancy was going, in Duggan's Bakery, next door to H. Williams Super-market, almost opposite Leinster Square, right here in Rath-mines. Sheila could walk to work—although she would have to be getting up at four in the morning. By Thursday the deal was sealed, and by Friday she was already starting.

"And what am I to do?" I asked Sheila. "Stay home all day and mind the child?"

Said Sheila, "I would love to think I could depend on you, Nick, to do just that. But seein' as how this week has gone—Mary's home during the day, Jane's home after five, I'll be off at holy hour, somehow between the lot of us we'll have to manage, won't we? Oh—must we talk about this right now?"

I had not planned on becoming a house-husband. I had not planned on not fulfilling my role as the provider. But I had not planned on burning down the British Embassy, nor losing my job, and a lot of other things, either.

By Friday, it was clear that Comrade Krishna was the only one of us who had managed to maintain an even balance.

"We haven't won a thing yet," was his declaration. He refused all drink and sat rolling fags, which he then smoked at rationed intervals. He got into a debate with Mick, who was a fan of Kung-fu at the cinema: a Krishna-dissertation on the Japanese martial arts ensued, but then the river of talk somehow diverged into an endless discussion of O'Corrigan's 'yout' in Clonmel. Fueled by the high, bags of Taytos and the drink, Mick fell asleep mid-sentence and when he woke, Krishna asked him why the Irish had to get drunk to fight. For answer, Mick grabbed me and Martina and Bernie and the four of us nipped out, starting in Owen Roe's by the Portobello Bridge, and closing out O'Donoghue's in Upper Leeson Street, making a statement which spoke plainer than words.

In the end, I came to a Monday morning when I had no job to get up out of bed for and go off on the bus for. It began to sink in. The first thing I could think of to do was to ring up Michael Hegarty at the Amalgamated Transport Worker's Union of Ireland. It made me feel better, fortified, just to recite the name to myself. I had allies, I had backup. Things were going to work out. I went out to the phone in the hall with a lilt in my step. "Sorry I haven't been in touch," said Hegarty into my ear, "but, needless to say, nothing's been done on your case in the week we've just had, but I'm going to get right on it."

The next time he called, however, he had bad news. "It seems we're out of luck. Maurice Woolf has a by-law that would stand up in court wherein they reserve the right to terminate any employee within ninety days of their first day of employment, I'm just off the phone with our legal man. Yes, three months. They say it's their standard probationary period before an employee becomes permanent. Yes, ninety working days. No, you were one day short. That's why they did it on the Friday, you see—Monday next would've been too late. And, then, of course, we all know what happened on the Sunday, don't we? I know, I understand, Nick. I wish there were."

Sheila came home from Duggan's at three in the afternoon wiping flour from the back of her neck. "I'd bought cakes for Aisling there, and often passed it, but I never once thought I'd be working in it. But now there's nothing for it. We're broke and have to pay the rent and feed the meter and put some food in the house." She was taking down the white kerchief she had to wear to keep her long, fine hair out of the big rotary mixers. "Hello, pumpkin!" she said to Aisling, trying to put some cheer into it.

"Mammy, mammy!" Aisling ran over and threw her arms around one of Sheila's legs.

"What did you do all day? Did you miss me, love?"

"Mammy—are you going to stay home now?"

While the child clung tight, hugging her leg, sliding down to ride her foot, Sheila tousled her hair to shake out the flour and crumbs and limped wearily over to me. "Eleven pound, ten bob a week. Won't feed the pigeons in the Phoenix Park."

Seven o'clock was Aisling's bedtime and Sheila said she was going to try hitting blanket street by 8, "if I can sleep." So after our dinner of smashed potatoes, buttered and salted, and drowned in HP sauce, which we could look forward to, pretty much, till further notice, as long as the HP sauce lasted, the spuds being about what we could afford, and pepper far beyond our budget for the time being, I dramatically did the dishes, and then proposed to read stories to the child to induce sleep. Meanwhile, Sheila, unaccustomed to the switch in roles, looked disconsolately out the window on the hastening winter darkness.

I sat Aisling in the crook of my arm, our backs propped up by the wall, and began *Well Done, Noddy!* by Enid Blyton. Noddy was a very clever little English boy with rosy cheeks who wore a blue night-cap crowned with a bell and drove a yellow jalopy through an English village where grandmothers were teddy bears and monkeys hung out clothes to dry in back-gardens. His grey-whiskered friend, Big-Ears, rode with him, and they were chased through all sorts of adventures by Mr Plod, a British bobby, fat as a blue balloon. I paused at the title-page as I closed the book. Published in London. I shook my head. Materially-speaking, as Krishna might have said, it was evident that the clutch of British cultural Imperialism on the country's economy reached, grasping, all the way down to books with which to acculturate Irish toddlers of pre-school age. I took Aisling by the hand down the hall and waited outside while she used the loo. "Did you do your duties?" I said, using my mother's phrase, when she came out.

"I couldn't do anything," she said.

"Did you wash your hands?"

"I needn't, because I didn't do anything," my daughter, who was nothing if not correct, wished to inform me.

When both my girls were asleep, I sat in the window-seat and watched the February rain streak the roadway with glints and gleams from streetlamps. I lit my last fag for the night. I wanted to think, to try to sort things out. Tonight I was feeling quite mortified, and, at the same time, strangely elated. In the past year and a half, I'd graduated from graduate school and been fired from two jobs. I'd left behind everything I'd ever known or been accustomed to and started over again, a new life in a new country. I was setting a course record of some kind, and I wished I knew what kind it was and where it was headed. I was afraid it was a dubious trail of repeated failure. All I had to do was to look over my shoulder to see my innocently sleeping wife and daughter, who never asked to get dragged through all this because of me. Yet, the instant that thought crossed my mind, I resisted it. How could I possibly be a failure? I'd succeeded at everything I'd ever really wanted—including getting Sheila to marry me—not to mention graduating with honors and two advanced degrees—including the incredibly life-changing experience of becoming a father. If I were a failure, why didn't I feel despondent, discouraged, depressed? Why did I feel so free and unburdened?

The mystery entered my thoughts through the fractioning globular raindrops that clung to the window-glass, the street-light from outside refracting and pin-wheeling in starbursts from the interior of these suspended pearls.

The world is so beautiful and so strange. Life is so inde-cipherable. Our minds can only reflect on the valley of the moment from the peaks of our past experiences.

And, as always, it seemed, it was reflections in glass which triggered reflections in me.

Instantly, I passed from the parking lot through the back door into the Stardust Lounge where I took my seat at the bar with the long mirror, where, I realized now, of a sudden, and much, much too late, that I'd forgotten entirely that my own face floated among the fronds and glades of sinuous light-pods and the flowing locks of the lady of the red guitar; that I myself was part and parcel of the mysterious reflections, inextricably linked and interwoven with them; and that I could never escape the consequences of my own perceptions. And once again, by that very subtle process of thought, by this new-forged path of connections between the synapses of the deep-diving ocean of the mind, I felt the hand on my shoulder: the hand of the muse.

I went to the sink and dragged out from underneath my pens and the extra copybooks I'd bought in Hiney's in Crossmoliney, months ago, in Mayo. I knew now where I wanted to be. In that barricaded room of mine in the farmhouse in Kilcross, confronting the clean white page while lines floated into my head from the clarity of the sky. I set a candle burning—my latest scheme to save shillings from the greedy mouth of the electric-meter—and to shut the overhead lights out so Sheila and the child could sleep—I opened my last remaining blank copybook and began to write. *A house is burning in Merrion Square . . .* I was sitting in our kitchenette in Rathmines Road, with the double-leaves of the table turned down, making it more compact so that it would fit in this tiny kitchen alcove of ours. But, then, I was no longer sitting in our kitchenette. I was somewhere else.

In the days ahead I seemed to devise dozens of ways to evade any hint of hunting for a job for myself. I told myself I was probably blacklisted anyway by the employers of Dublin after what happened at Maurice Woolf. I told myself I already knew, since I didn't have the H. Dip., that it was a futile waste to send out more resumes to National Schools, or even to independent Catholic schools. What would I tell them?—that I was a good Jesuit-trained Catholic boy from BC?—or a member of the Provos' Sinn Féin who found it hard to believe in God anymore? I told myself that after the riots at the British Embassy, I couldn't afford to have the police get interested in my working status, that I'd better hope that, in all the public emergency, they'd forgotten that Noel Sugarman had given them my name. I told myself I'd be better off spending time on firing letters off, in tiny handwriting, on aeropost tissue paper, to Ray Deeds in New York enclosing new poems, exciting updates on the Irish scene, and so on, hoping to get reassured that I wasn't forgotten in my poet-persona back home—if I could scrape up the pence for the postage.

In fact, my days were full of activity, I wasn't the type to be easily bored, I wanted to finish Tolstoy's *War and Peace,* as it seemed to be the perfect companion to my current situation, I was too busy minding the child, cooking and cleaning up, too busy with Sinn Féin, and, of course, unwilling to miss any sessions of the talkshop in Leinster Square. In short, I never lacked something I had to get to, right away. I collected on the babby-sitting favors Josephine Bagley owed Sheila and got her to mind Aisling in the afternoons when she was on night shift at the hospital and home in the afternoon. Aisling was content to be left outdoors in the back garden to play with Desmond and I knew Josephine was there to mind them—and Desmond was perfectly well-behaved when he was not confined to a small triangular smoke-filled room—so I was off the clock. Mornings, I could enlist Shane's Monica, in the flat underneath us, as she had her infant, who kept her in. Then there was always Jane and Mary in Leinster Square, Angela and Eileen down the back, and

Bernie and Martina in Waterloo Road. They all adored Aisling and she got on with all of them as long as they'd read Noddy books to her out loud and walk her to the shop for a sweet and did not scold her for writing with crayons on her dollies. I also managed to spend quite a bit of Daddy-daughter time with her myself, much more than when I was working, and I decided I rather liked being a house-husband.

The Dubliners had a word for it. "Ah, the life of the dosser!" Tony Daugherty said to me, the Friday night I dropped into Timoney's for a gab-fab with the lads from Maurice Woolf, Ltd.

I was hoping for a round or two of donated pints, in exchange for only one round at my expense, and the boys didn't let me down. We had a game of snooker, the usual five frames, and talked about the great old times. Malachi Morgan had got the sack, but he was the only one, and with him and myself gone, things had settled down for Higgy and Noel Sugarman. "Old Needlenose is running the Dispatch himself, Nick," said Con Lenihan. Pascal and Eddie Larkin were still in it and I asked my friends to say hello to them for me, and to ould Susan. "I'll be by to see her one of these times," I said. "It's the Oliver Bond she lives in, is it not?" Tony Daugherty said he'd be leaving Woolf's soon. "Tisn't the old kip it used to be. Pot that one, if you can."

I couldn't, and Tony was right—it didn't seem the same anymore without Malachi there, and having to ask in someone hanging on the end of the bar to make up our four. I even asked after Clare, and the lads said they'd be sure to give her a pinch on the arse from me.

For money, I decided I would have to exercise my good old American ingenuity. I dropped in one afternoon to Mick O'Corrigan's in the Mespil Road, as I knew Mick to be a dedicated odd-jobber himself. Of course, he had no visible means of support, that we, both Krishna and I, knew. I suspected what anyone would suspect, which was that he was dealing the stuff, but I was loath to share that with our socialist morality-barometer, Krishna. I liked Mick, and besides, he was in the Cumann, and befriended me, before Krishna was even there. It was a matter of loyalty.

Mick had a little flat in a tiny house raised on blocks, round the back behind the big row-houses fronting Mespil Road alongside the Grand Canal. You had to enter his house from the back-garden, which doubled as a car-park. His sub-divided little house looked quite like a house-boat. It leaned, as if it were about to float away down the canal. Mick had enough in the way of block and tackle and fishing gear strewn about his room to make you believe he'd somehow been involved in the 'angling' back in Clonmel, pun intended. But the little I knew about County Tipp did not include its lakes and rivers, or even where it was. I didn't ask. I didn't want to know, really. As Mick would've said, the less you know, the less you can tell.

I sat down and said, after making sure he put the kettle on, "Do you know that one summer, when I was in college, myself and another chap earned upwards of 500 dollars per week—painting houses?"

"Five hundred? Jaysus—a dollar must be worth next to nuthin.'"

"I'll never forget him. Russell Sage was his name. Did me a favor, he did."

"And not a penny to the taxman, I'll wager."

"Not to mention the birds you could chat up in the pubs, introducing yourself with a little printed card."

"Christ," said Mick, "anyone could get a card printed up—but what you need—I have right here."

He reached into a wooden milk-crate with a pair of hedge-clippers and a lot of oil-cans and pulled out a white muslin peaked cap, suitably dotted with pastel green and blue paint-drips. "And here's me scraper and me brushes and me buckets—and the drop-cloth, mustn't forget that. We could use a ladder or two. I have the planks for a right scaffold."

One afternoon in Rialto, Mick and I sheltered against the chill in a chipper for a couple of hours of downpour. Across the street, men with a van had been doing up the front of the Head-line Bar, till it began to come down, whereupon they set down their brushes, put lids on their buckets, shrouded the equip-ment with tarps, and went inside to warm up, dry out, and, no doubt, discuss the situation over a couple of pints. Having waited for a discreet two hours, and no sign of either the rain stopping or the owners re-emerging, we crossed the road and sauntered off with a stepladder apiece across our shoulders.

An elderly woman beneath an umbrella paused on the footpath to watch us at our work. Mick politely made way for her and gave her a kindly "G'day" with a tip of his painter's cap.

It was catch as catch-can, interrupted by the baby-sitting schedule, but our new little sideline served Mick and me quite well, extemporaneously, for a couple of quid here and there, which were never wanting for a pint to be spent on or a steak-and-kidney pie in a tin with a screw-key for openers.

"So—you are a Trotskyist," said Krishna, as, having just finished skimming through my poem on the burning of the Embassy, he passed the blue copybook back to me.

"What do you mean?" I asked. He made it sound like a dirty word.

We were sitting at the white-clothed table in the window of Bewley's in Grafton Street, where the Comrade occasionally held two o'clock office hours in the afternoons. We were both coffee-drinkers, a Trini, and an American, and Bewley's was the coffee-aficionado's refuge in Dublin. They had one shop in Westmoreland Street and one in Grafton Street. Krishna preferred Grafton Street as it was on the first floor and you could sit in the window with a bird's eye view of the pedestrian mall below. Security was his rationale, but I was sure he equally enjoyed bird-watching the pretty young things with shopping bags going in and out of the expensive shops.

In Bewley's, you could taste the flavors of java, espresso, Turkish, Brazilian and Colombian, in an exotic Lincoln-green-and-brass, Victorian-styled emporium of potted palms and black wrought-iron frames on the tall bay-windows, which let the afternoon sun come streaming in with tropical splendor. It suited Krishna's mood sometimes to just sit there and watch the dust-motes circle through the bars of sunlight, if there was any.

It was convenient for him, too. One of his contacts worked in a walk-up across the street, that side being bathed in shadow at this hour. Mohammad Moneim was the Charge d'Affaire of the Office of Arab Affairs. This Office substituted for the lack of representation in Ireland of the Arab countries, all of which kept their Embassies located in London instead. Mohammad Moneim had been in Dublin for seven years and dearly loved it, but he still kept the office hours he would have were he living in Beirut. At two, he would close up shop, cross the street to Bewley's for lunch, then home by taxi to Balls-bridge for his nap until four, then back to the Office to work until eight.

Soon after he landed from London, Krishna met Moneim in Bewley's. They were at adjacent tables and happened to strike up a conversation, Moneim perhaps intrigued by Krishna's positively Asian-subcontinent looks and complexion; but then he found he enjoyed the young Trinidadian's company for the same reason I did, or so Krishna claimed: to cross words with Krishna permitted one to sharpen the sword of his own wit.

"What do you mean I'm a Trotskyist?" I said.

At the next table a white-haired widow in a hat with a spidery black veil, obviously a denizen of one of the South Side's posh Georgian squares, sipped her coffee as if it were a delicious transgression. Accenting the appellation with scorn, Krishna said, "Trotsky, too, was a writer."

The widow raised an eyebrow at the offensively muddy military boot which Krishna had insolently fixed on the rung of an empty chair at our table.

"You believe in revolution as a romantic inspiration. An excuse for getting emotional on paper."

"You were in Merrion Square. Did it seem so blasé to you?"

"I wouldn't be human if I were unaffected. But, comrade, the secret for the revolutionary, especially the trained, objective cadre, is to channel that emotion. Your feelings, my feelings, they don't matter—what are we, compared to the revolution?"

Oh, my, the things you overhear sometimes in Bewley's, the widow-lady might have said, and the aquatic creatures who swim about in there.

"Emotion is wasted, unless it is used, and it can only be used if it is put to the service of the revolution."

The widow cleared her throat and settled her hat on her head and Kirshna threw his leg rudely across the seat of the chair. He sometimes could not pass up the opportunity of shocking the bourgeoisie.

I had my reply on the tip of my tongue. "Didn't Mao himself write poetry?"

"You telling I? You cite Mao without even having read him! He had a great deal to say about that very subject. Have you read The Yenan Forum on Art and The Revolution?"

"No."

"Then please don't talk about it until you have. I have it in my room. I'll lend it to you."

"Good. I want to read it."

"You ought to."

"I will."

"And Lenin's Imperialism: The Highest Stage of Capitalism, and Das Kapital, and—."

"I suppose Lenin and Marx and Engels weren't writers?"

"Now you are grasping."

"If I'm a Trotskyist, you're a Stalinist."

"I am a realist. Remember this: from practice comes theory. Not the other way round."

Our coffees came. I said, "What are you doing, comrade?"

"Brown sugar." Krishna looked up from a spoonful. "I, too, have my weaknesses. Ah, Mohammad. Sit down, sit down, my friend. Meet an interesting young man who fancies himself the new Rumi."

The Rathmines Library was a relic of the Art Nouveau architectural style of the 1890s: an imposing, imperial front, with massively-tall oaken double-doors, equipped with brass handles rather than door-knobs. Inside, you were cloistered in a revisited neo-Renaissance enclosure, apart from the workaday world. A marble staircase descended from the inner doors with the sweep of Browning's Last Duchess trailing her sibilant gown to her death at the hands of the Duke. The bustle of the street outside, the tumult of Lower Rathmines Road, was severed, and seductively, you were ushered into a world of contemplation.

I loved the place. The irony was not lost on me, that my first love, among libraries, was the Carnegie-endowed brownstone on Beach Street in Revere, beloved of my earliest years, repository of the first books I treasured; and this Library, here in the enclave of Rathmines, a monument to its separateness and individuality, as distinct from Dublin's City Centre, this Library, too, was bestowed by Carnegie. Thus had I come full circle to my home-away-from-home.

The reading room was at the top of the stair to the left. To the right was the Children's Room. I read the signs as I brought Aisling by the hand up the stairs. Under my arms were the books I had just retrieved out of Krishna's room, right next door in Leinster Square.

How I loved spending the afternoon like this, locked up in sweet study. In the library, with everything in life ahead of me, with so much material for thought behind me. All the best the world had to offer was stored in this house, all that I ever wanted to give to the little girl at my side. I was thrilled to think that, now that I didn't have to spend my days in drudgery in a benighted, covered laneway on the Dublin quays, functioning as a wage-slave, my labor devoted to creating profits for people and entities who exploited the working class in their destitution—I was thrilled to think that now I could spend whole afternoons in perfect, tranquil liberty to share the true wealth of the world with my beloved daughter, who, I was sure, shared my own personality and outlook to an absolutely perfect degree. At last—no longer a wage-slave, but instead, an independent, intellectual-worker—I was working not with my hands, but with my mind..

But, I knew, the world never did measure up to its own libraries—and better men than me have tried to right it—so—let me see if I can find out what they learned.

The reading room was packed out with the young ladies of St Louis High School, the local girls' secondary school, in their school uniforms with the navy-blue knee-socks and blue-and-grey tartan skirts and neat navy jumpers adorned with rounded white shirt-collars poking up. I looked around to see if there was a seat. It was quiet and orderly, though the students squirmed with their assignments of books and papers, and a group of girls giggled and whispered at a table-corner. One of them politely offered me her seat. The girl who gave up her seat pushed a friend half-off another chair and took Aisling on her knee. "What a lovely little girl! Is she yours? What's your name, love? Do you know how to play paddy-cakes, Aisling?"

Lenin was like a drink of pure, clear water. Every sentence. Every phrase. And the wit, so sharp, acerbic, so pleasingly unexpected. He was, after all, no heavy-handed theorist, but a childishly playful intelligence who delighted in debunking the hypocrisies of the established order. Scorn dripped from the page. The mind that spoke up here seized the platitudes of the system, chewed them up, spit them out again with all their folly and deceit peeled away, like a man biting into an orange and spitting out the indigestible rind.

I recalled my grad-student days back home, when I was a teaching assistant instructing American schoolgirls on English composition, especially an occasion when Mark Rudd and the Weathermen visited the campus in Kingston, Rhode Island. I watched from the very back of the auditorium, and kept aloof, especially because one of my students was with me, and I didn't want, in front of her, to appear approving of the Weathermen, who advocated violence in the name of the Anti-War Movement. We tended to label the homegrown Marxists in the Anti-War Movement back then as irrelevant, obsolete, dishonest—especially accusing them of dilettantism, as sons of the privileged, scions of the wealthy, supercilious student-bodies from Yale and Cornell, merely masquerading as 'working-class.'

Somehow all my life growing up in America, Marxism had been surrounded with taboos, and yet had been strangely alluring, like forbidden fruit.

Now it was America, and my own former life that seemed foreign to me.

And the subtle, self-imposed censorship of my upbringing there, which now seemed riddled with lies, invidious falsehoods, pernicious distortion.

Only now was I breaking free at last. And there was so much to do, so much I needed to know.

On the way out I asked at the librarians desk, "I wonder might I take out a library card?"

"Certainly. Do you live here in Dublin?"

"Right here in Rathmines."

Going down the steps, with Aisling by the hand, books under my other arm, I thought of the library card in my pocket, with my name signed on it, Nicholas Petrovich, and that library card, to me, was the equivalent of an Irish passport: it signified to me that I belonged here.

The meeting of the Cumann Billy Reid was crowded that week. Some people, in the room upstairs at Paddy Clarke's, Mick, Krishna and I had never seen before. We knew that the burning of the British Embassy was still vivid enough, the wound of Bloody Sunday still bleeding enough, to attract the curious and motivate fence-sitters. When we were out in the pubs that week selling An Phoblacht, people were paying with pound-notes and refusing their change. Morale was high: the people were with us.

A well-dressed woman named Mary who had charge of accommodations for men on the run from up north was soliciting phone numbers and addresses to add to her network. She was responsible for all of Dublin. It was important at times to keep people changing the place where they slept every night. She'd had a lot of experience in these matters, going all the way back to the Belfast pogroms in '69, when they'd had to put up whole families. She was very well-spoken, a tidy woman, who had worn white gloves to the meeting, which she kept folded on top of her purse on the conference table. I volunteered my double-bedsitter, as small as it was—but then, everyone was eager to offer help. Even the new people were conscious of accomplishing important things, of being a part of a network, because of Mary's visit. The Irish Republican Movement was on the move. The next order of business was to prepare for the march on Newry on the weekend.

The movers and shakers of the Northern Irish Civil Rights Association in the north had organized this march as far back as Christmas, but Bloody Sunday had intervened. In the succession of planned protests of Internment, now, in spite of a couple of postponements, more people than ever were flocking to the NICRA banner. Stormont still had a ban on marches, and the British Army would be there to enforce it. Nothing could have been calculated better to set afire the reactions of nationalist-minded people all over the country, north and south, than this. All those who'd witnessed on television that deadly day in Derry were not now inclined to stay home. All Ireland, it seemed, defiant, and determined, was going north of the border.

Sunday was turning out a clear, sunny-bright spring day. The Cumann members met at the Northern Aid Office in Eden

Quay because it was next door to Busaras, where the numbers of buses now necessary to transport all those eager to cross the Border would be collecting. Myself and Mick were there, along with Martina and Bernadette, our little core of Cumann veterans, along with the newcomers, with whom we had not yet formed personal connections that could compare—and then there were the dozens, literally, of strangers we'd all sold bus tickets to in the pubs, on demand. But two of our own were conspicuous in their absence—Myles Cunningham—and comrade Krishna. Everyone knew why Myles was not going, but Krishna played down his reasons, keeping them to our own little close-knit circle. "I'm banned from British territory," he told me. "This thing will be just too wide-open. When I cross that border, it will have to be for a good reason. Let's leave this one to the Civil Rights types."

Newry was a small town set between the hills of a green and pleasant valley on the borders of Down and Armagh, just inside the Occupied Six Counties, on the estuary of Lough Carlingford. It was the centre of the Operations Area of the South Down and South Armagh Provisionals.

I had been north of the border before, under different circumstances, months ago, with my brother-in-law, Patrick Blake. But this was the first time for Mick O'Corrigan.. At the thought of viewing the Brits face to face, he was like a stoked furnace held in by an iron door. Still, we didn't really notice from the bus-window when or where we actually crossed the border. The passage was so free and uneventful we might have been a load of children going on their school picnic.

When we halted on a hill outside of Newry, buses from all over Ireland were already there. Rumour had the size of the crowd to be at least fifty thousand. There seemed to be literally hundreds of marshals wearing the blue NICRA arm-bands, visible under the black arm-bands for the victims of the Bloody Sunday massacre. While we were assembling, marshals walked up and down giving instructions and reminding everyone that this was to be a non-violent demonstration. Peace and orderliness were the tactics of the day. "Stay together, hold to the line of march, no stragglers, no deviations from the planned route, no going in separate groups or gangs, and if they want another Derry, let them start it."

The world was a green bowl of banners, signs, pennants and placards, sunny faces, hillside pastures, distant blue mountains, cerulean, cloudless sky, empty buses, anticipation that brought you almost breathlessly up on your toes. The grey houses of the town were tiny below us in the cradle of the valley.

When we started, the going was easy and downhill, and our feet were inclined to gallop away with us but soon we were into streets of crisscross row-houses and corner shops. Then there was a halt, and then a stall, and word went back and forth. Roadblocks. Diversions, up ahead. The centre of Newry was cordoned off, ringed with troops. The Brits were not going to allow us to march our planned route. For a time, indecision reigned, but then the impasse dissolved, because the NICRA marshals and organizers set off on a diversion of their own, on a spontaneous, unplanned, unscouted route. We climbed uphill, to the west side of Newry, uphill between juttings of rocky road-cuts, winding toward a bald hilltop, in a huge circuit around the town. At the crest of the bald hill, we halted again, caught in the hairpin curve of a little-used paved road curling beneath a railway trestle. The bald hill was high, and the town was below us, and behind us. Then we saw the IRA.

High up on top of the trestle, the silhouettes of dark figures, carrying what were said to be Armalites, or could have been Kalashnikovs, appeared briefly, cut-out against the sun.

And just as quickly disappeared again. A show of force. *Just so you, and the Tom Tits, know we're here.*

Down through the hairpin of the road. Descending down into the bowels of the town. Haggling and negotiating with the British Army officers. After hours of blocking the way, delaying, temporizing and impeding, when the Occupiers were finally convinced the marchers would not just simply fade off, they finally agreed to allow us to pass.

Our banners entered a small square ringed by tall houses, closed on one end by barbed-wire entanglements; Land Rovers. Saracens and Centurions, ranks of soldiers in riot gear, with bayonets fixed on the muzzles of their shoulder-slung SLRs, bright blades sticking up above their shoulders; batons held with two hands, invariably across the loins, in front of themselves, with their feet spread; riot shields standing on the ground, leaning against their hips. Not a word was spoken on either side as the Civil Rights marchers passed in review in front of the British Army, in deadly silence.

We might never know whether it was the presence of the IRA with a show of force on the hilltops surrounding the town which prevented another massacre that day, for certainly, our march, with so many Sinn Féin adherents from south of the border augmenting the numbers of NICRA, was provoking the Brits.

Chapter 8

Road to Rosslea

By the road to Rosslea lay an empty field, a field with four corners, tilted under a dripping sky, climbing a hillside, to crest on
a ridge surmounted by a ragged fence of jagged stone slabs: a
charcoal underlining to a watercolor heaven. *What have I now?*
said the fine old woman, in the song by Tommy Makem. *I have
four green fields, one of them's in bondage . . .*

Up the near side of the field ran the road to Rosslea, a
dirt road, rutted with spring mud, known officially as an unapproved road, meaning it was considered an unauthorized border
crossing. This road had a large crater at the base of the hillside,
hard by the actual border, blasted into it by the British Army,
using explosives to blow a hole in the road big enough to render
it impassable to wheeled vehicles. The road thus cratered separated the open field on its left from a dogleg of forest that
came draggling over the ridge to settle out in a boggy bottom
on the right side of the road-margin. At the top of the rising
road, where it disappeared over the apex of the ridge, in a hovel
of dark, sodden trees, still wintry and bare but for a few spring

buds daring the weather, there was an observation post of four British soldiers; flanked on their right, our left, by the stone fence; protected by thick woods on their other flank. The Army in their riot gear stood openly watching.

On the far side of the field, to our left, a hedgerow, widened and interspersed with tall, singular ash-trees, formed a windbreak. Beginning at the terminus of the stone fence, it descended the hillside to an enlarged ditch that ran all the way back to the road along the bottom, lower edge of the sloping field. In the ditch, a trickle of brook wound over rounded rocks beneath banks of long grass. Through the brook-water ran a wavering line. This line was invisible. You could not detect it traced on the grass. It was washed away in the running trills of the brook. But it was this line, the 'border,' that one of the soldiers in the observation post was examining, back and forth, thoughtfully, through a pair of binoculars.

A week ago a stubbed causeway carried the road to Rosslea across the little brook as it tumbled through a pipe. The pipe gathered the leakage in the lee of the forest and funnelled it under the road. Now it lay with its galvanised ribs exposed and twisted, and the bog, wounded in the side, bled into an upturned bowl of stagnant brown water, a hundred-foot-long crater, where the drizzle from the sky pinged, a hundred blinking eyes.

This was once a simple road that local farmers and others used to travel to Rosslea. This was once a forgotten, neglected outcropping of the Northern State Forest, where only picnickers would bother to occupy the ridge. This was once a pasture where cattle browsed in a sheltered amphitheatre. Now no cattle fed in the field, the birds were fled to the branches of the ash trees, to be nearer to the sky, and their escape. They had abandoned the rectangular field, enclosed by the brook, the windbreak, the stone fence on the ridge, and the cratered road, to the burrowing worms. No flies lazily followed cows. It left the scene eerily silent. Only the rain still came to the field by the road to Rosslea, as if the rest of nature knew that nothing good was about to happen.

Putting up posters was a night-job for the Cumann Billy Reid. Just a precaution. Less chance for the Garda Síochána to harass you. Not that they were stopping anyone. Or, not yet. Still, the coppers were not forgetting the British Embassy. *Either turn us loose or let us join the rabble, but don't put us out there with our hands tied behind our backs.* So the Cumann hit the streets in pairs, late. Pasted the Action Day posters up on the boardings all over the South Side from Ranelagh to Harold's Cross. One carried the brush and bucket, the other followed along with the posters rolled up under the arm. Bring a bicycle with a large satchel to carry them all. Pick out an empty space—or if the spot was covered over already with notices for jazz at Slattery's, slide lectures on Taiwanese cottage industries at Trinity, Irish lessons to be had at UCD, phone 371-648, ask for Liam—slap ours on top. Quick with the brush, one, two, peel off a poster, up on tip-toe—the higher the poster, the harder to rip down again—from the top down, smooth out with the hands, roll of paper between your knees, then, quick, duck out of the spot of the street-lamp, and round the corner. Trade bucket for posters, and off to hunt up the next boarding, blank wall, bridge abut-ment, unadorned arse-end of a post-box. Next night, half of your hard work ripped in strips, defaced or covered over, and you were out till three in the A.M. again.

Funny how volunteers for this necessary but routine and boring task were shy in forthcoming. Alita Hughes had to pair them off and give them their streets. "Our assignments," I said, drily, downstairs afterwards in Paddy Clarke's with a half-pint in my hand, a full pint being 17 new p and a half only 11. "What are you filthy conspirators up to now?" said Martina over Mick's bony shoulder. "Slaggin' Alita," Krishna replied. "Our Leader couldn't organize a henhouse to lay eggs," said Mick. "Cackle, cackle," said Bernie. "You boys are just browned off because a woman is giving out to ye." "She's not a woman," said Mick. "She's a Nazi in drag."

Mick stepped back to appraise his workmanship after plastering over the identical spot for the third night in a row. The poster said,

ACTION DAY
SUNDAY, 19TH MAR.
BREAK THE MARCHING BAN !
<u>FILL IN THE CRATERS</u> !
Contingents from all over the 26 Co's.
Will assemble at Clones, Castleblayney,
& Monaghan and MARCH INTO THE NORTH.
On completion of the road-filling A PUBLIC
MEETING to be held in each Area

<u>INSIDE OCCUPIED TERRITORY</u> !

SHOW THE BRITISH WHO OWNS IRELAND !
Organised by the Republican Movement

"There better be some action at the end of all this," said Mick O'Corrigan.

"Shut up and pass the bucket," I said.

"Take it. I'm glued to meself."

Alita had miscalculated putting Mick with me, or with Martina Kelly, for that matter, but she wanted me and Comrade Krishna separated, as she probably suspected him, and me, wrongly, of plotting to take the whole Cumann over to the Stickies.

"Was I tellin' you last night I was out posterin' with Martina Kelly? Quit early so we could stop into Owen Roe's."

"Get anywhere?"

"Only out the door again. But it wasn't for want of tryin'."

"Isn't she still doin' a line with Brendan McAndrews?"

"Yeah. These skinheads from the Grovesnor Road get all the graft. I tell you, a decent bloke from Clonmel can't get a how-do-ye-do these days. But I found out—he's gone away out of it again—and while the cat's away, the mouses do play."

"Come on, let's get these done."

"Not to worry," said Mick. "I'll be there when there's some real work to do." He looked at his gooey-white fingers. "Jaysus, wouldn't I love to get glued to Martina Kelly."

Mick O'Corrigan lost his wish when we boarded the bus at the Northern Aid office in Eden Quay on Sunday morning. Martina Kelly sat in the front—with Brendan McAndrews' arm flung over her shoulder. Alita Hughes sat in front of them, just behind the driver. Her fat sister Maureen sat glumly imprisoned in the window-seat beside her while Alita chaperoned the aisle. "Good morning," said Mick to them all, very decently, before he led us in a hasty file down to the back of the bus.

"What's the 'RA doin' here?" I said under my breath.

"Maybe Brendan McAndrews knows something we don't," said Mick.

"It's protection for us," said Krishna. "The artillery."

"You talk like you're worried or something," said Mick, who worried about nothing.

"In London, we never went up against the pigs without helmets and ax-handles of our own."

The comrade looked disapproving at his bareheaded friends.

Mick pinched the sleeve of his heavily-padded fatigue jacket, as well as my thick pea-coat. "You're not in London now. We'll show you how the Irish go to war."

Bernadette Cullen was coming down the aisle carrying her guitar, with Peadar Kenny and his tin-whistle behind her. "'Lo," said Bernie, when she saw Jane Quill. "This is a surprise. What are you doing here?"

"Since when is a Sunday stroll against the law?"

"The more the merrier." Bernie sat down with her, pleased. "And for weeks, we've been trying to get you to a meeting."

"Wouldn't catch me dead. Don't I hear it anyways from himself?"

"Why didn't Mary come with you then?"

"She's to babbysit Sheila and Aisling."

"Why, what's with Sheila?"

"She's a grass widow these days, with Nick never home and out late nights."

"For a good cause," I said.

"Brendan's here," Bernie whispered.

"I wouldn't if I was him," said Jane. "He's probably wanted in ten o' them six counties."

At the front of the bus, long-lost Myles Cunningham was now boarding, and Alita, with all the cousins now present, stood up . "Your attention, please."

The middle of the bus was jammed with supporters, well-wishers, fellow-travelers, sight-seers, three or four to a pair of seats, none of them members of any Cumann—Barney O'Toole alone brought half his street from the Liberties. Eden Quay was thronged with perhaps twenty buses, all packed like ours. Publicity, and a fervent, if un-indoctrinated nationalism, and the promise contained in the words 'Action Day,' and Brian Faulkner—the latest Stormont Prime Minister—with his tough talk of bans on marching and prohibitions on protests, brought them out. There was a bandwagon air about Eden Quay that Sunday, we were as excited as schoolkids on a day-trip.

Alita drew herself up. "Well, how many of you have brought your tools with you?" There was a rattle of spades and picks, an admiring flexing of Wellingtons in the aisle, and groaning from the back of the bus.

"That's Dublin for ye," said Mick. "Pack o' grave-robbers."

"Those of you who have your shovels," Alita continued, "can join in with the road-filling brigade—."

But Mick shouted out, "That's if you're not too knackered from bashin' Brits with 'em!"

When the laughter died down, Alita said sternly, "The rest of us will get our instructions when we get there." The bus lurched into motion and Alita grabbed a seat-back to steady herself. "That's all for now."

"Thanks be to God," Mick muttered, as the caravan of busses began to roll, and then, slapping his thigh with his open palm to give a drumbeat to the tune, he threw his head back and began singing.

> *When I was young, I used t' be*
> *As fine a young man as ever you'd see,*
> *And the Prince o' Wales he says t' me,*
> *Come and join the British Army!*

Laughing, the whole bus took up the song.

Toora loora loora loo,
They're lookin' for monkeys up in the zoo,
an' sure, if I had a face like you,
I'd join the British Army!

We laughed and cheered and hooted and banged on the bus and opened the windows in the rain to holler at the people, startled in the streets, all along the North Side of Dublin.

Sergeant Healy went away
An' his wife, she got in the family way
and the only thing that she could say
Was blame the British Army!
Toora loora loora loo,
I've made me mind up what to do,
Now I'll work me ticket home to you,
An' fook the British Army!

The Soldier's Song came next, the rallying cry of the Tan War, and since then, the National Anthem of the 26 Counties, sung at the end of every concert, barn-dance, and céilí. And it fit the mood of the bus that day with its rousing chorus.

Soldiers are we,
Whose lives are pledged to Ireland,
Some have come from a land beyond the wave,
Sworn to be free, no more our ancient sireland
Shall shelter the despot or the slave;
Tonight we man the Bearna Baoil
In Erin's cause come woe or weal,
'Mid cannon's roar and rifle's peal,
We'll chant a soldier's song.

Whenever Peadar Kenny was about with his tin whistle or his flute, a certain song had to be sung. It was a favorite song of Dublin, *Kevin Barry,* and on this bus, we were carrying the Dublin contingent, or part of it, anyway. "Quick, now, Peadar," somebody said, "before we've left the city altogether behind us."

> *In Mountjoy jail one Monday morning*
> *High upon the gallows tree*
> *Kevin Barry gave his young life*
> *For the cause of liberty*
>
> *Just a lad of eighteen summers*
> *Still there's no one can deny*
> *As he walked to death that morning*
> *He proudly held his head on high*
>
> *Just before he faced the hangman*
> *In his dreary prison cell*
> *The Black and Tans they tortured Barry*
> *Just because he would not tell*
>
> *The names of all his brave companions,*
> *And other things they wished to know*
> *"Turn informer and we'll free you"*
> *Kevin Barry answered "No"*

And the 'No!' was a veritable shout from the voices thronging the seats.

"We have one in Clonmel," cried Mick O'Corrigan, clapping his hands, "it goes like this!"

> *Some say the divil is dead,*
> *the divil is dead, the divil is dead,*

Some say the divil is dead,
An' buried in Killarney!
More say he rose again,
More say he rose again,
More say he rose again
An' joined the British Army!

We hung our heads out the windows and waved farewell to the outskirts of Dublin City, and the column of cars and buses stretched out before and behind us, and we set out to think of a song to while away the miles. Bernadette said, "There's one we can do, but we've to divide ourselves into two sides. Everyone this side of the aisle is Irish, and you, over there, you're the English!" "What!" "Just listen! You English start the song like this,"

Are you ready for a war, for we are the English,
Are you ready for a war, for we are the English soldiers!

"Now you sing it. Go on!" And they did. "Now the Irish on our side sing,

Yes, we're ready for a war, for we are the Irish,
Yes, we're ready for a war, for we are the Irish soldiers!

Mick and Krishna and I were stuck with being the enemy, and the first thing we lost was one eye.

Now we only have one eye, for we are the English,
Now we only have one eye, for we are the English soldiers!

But on the other side of the aisle, the Irish lost both their eyes, and so the battle was joined, back and forth, from verse to verse, as we kicked the song to and fro like a football, and as the English lost one arm to the fray, the Irish lost two, and when the English lost a leg, it was two legs for the Irish, until finally the English had nothing left to lose and they had to sing,

Now we are all dead and gone, for we are the English,
Now we are all dead and gone, for we are the English soldiers!

But the treacherous, though clever, Irish, instead of loyally dying, jumped up in their seats, laughing and taunting,

Now we are alive again, for we are the Irish,
Now we are alive again, for we are the Irish soldiers!

From the front of the bus, Brendan McAndrews called for a Belfast anthem, and we all sang to the American tune of *The Battle Hymn of the Republic,*

Craigavon sent the Specials in to shoot the people down,
He thought the IRA was dead in dear old Belfast town,
But he got a rude awakening with the cannon and grenade,
From the fightin' First Battalion of the Belfast Brigade!

The steel-piped bus-seats rang to the chorus, *Glory, glory to old Ireland . . .* and then we rapidly ran through *The Men Behind the Wire,* a huge hit ever since Christmastime when Barleycorn, the Belfast group, came out with it, and it was banned by RTE from the airwaves of the 26 Counties; and at last we came to a rousing Civil Rights number, just to keep the wheels rolling,

To Derry we went on October the Fifth,
To march for our rights, but oh, what a myth!

They bate us with batons, they bate us with fists,
And they doused us all over with water!

And that was followed with,

We're on our way to vict'ry,
We shall not be moved,
We're on our way to vict'ry,
We shall not be moved,
Just like a tree that's standing by the waterside,
We shall not be moved!

"That's an American song!" I yelled. "And so's Belfast Brigade—that's the Battle Hymn of the Republic—you stole all our songs!" "You stole 'em first, we're only stealin' 'em back!" Shut up, now! Myles is going to give us James Connolly." Peader led in with a mournful line from his flute, and then Myles' lyrical tenor sang,

A great crowd had gathered, outside of Kilmainham,
Their heads all uncovered, they knelt on the ground,
While inside that grim prison lay a brave Irish soldier,
His life for his country about to lay down . . .

Then came the call, "A song from the Yank! Let's hear it now!" "Don't know any songs," I laughed. "Only the ones I learned from yourselves." "And are these the lads then that bate the Brits back out of North America?" "All right, all right, I think I know one."

In 1814 we took a little trip,
Along with General Jackson down the mighty Mississsip—

We took a little bacon and we took a little beans—
("Beans from Boston!" Bernadette shouted)
And we fought the bloody British in the town of New
Orleans!

"Ya-hoo!" someone cried, and the entire bus took up the chorus,

Well, we fired our guns and the British kept a-comin,'
There wasn't nigh as many as there was a while ago,
We fired once more and they began to runnin,'
Down the Mississippi to the Gulf of Mexico!

Well, they ran through the brambles and they ran through
the briars,
And they ran through the bushes where a rabbit couldn't go!
Ran so fast that the hounds couldn't catch 'em,
Down the Mississippi to the Gulf of Mexico!

Indian war-whoops came roaring through the bus as Andy Jackson and the Tennessee Volunteers routed the British. Another voice chimed in: "I've seen them run so myself, from nothin' more than a shower o' women callin' them names!"

"You'll see 'em run again today, so you will!"

We were still singing fight songs when we pulled into Monaghan Town. The caravan made a brief halt before the County Jail, and a man came aboard the bus to consult hurriedly with Alita Hughes. When we looked about and saw where we were, we grew quiet. Why are we stopped? There was a vacated look to the town, a vaguely perturbing emptiness to the streets.

When we resumed our journey, onward to the final rendez-vous in Clones, as we bumped along the country road, with the tall hedgerows of the County Monaghan closing round us, and the buds of March just fashioning a twig of green on the bareness of the trees, we stared out the windows, and looked away again, if our eyes met another's, as we listened to Bernadette singing to her guitar,

> *All the radio said was another shot dead,*
> *And he died with a gun in his hand,*
> *But they didn't say why Billy Reid had to die,*
> *For he died to free Ireland.*

Then we were quiet again as we passed through Clones. Quiet as we passed down the last turn through the trees along the route that would lead us to the field by the unapproved road, the cratered road, the road to Rosslea. Myles' tenor sounded solitary as he took up the lyric, at the last, in Irish, but then all our voices joined, even mine, in the chorus,

> *Óró, sé do bheatha ‹bhaile,*
> *Óró, sé do bheatha 'bhaile,*
> *Óró, sé do bheatha 'bhaile*
> *Anois ar theacht an tsamhraidh.*

And the O-rrr-oh! rolled over me like a chilly wave.

We disembarked, sheltered from the rain in an arbour-like tunnel of trees. Cars and buses tilted on the shoulders of the narrow dirt road. A throng of people clogged the churned-up path between parked vehicles. You could barely open a car door in the press. Everyone moved forward, slowly shuffling. Men, women and children, whole families, entire neighborhoods. *So this is where*

Monaghan Town went to. They stretched ahead, a formidable herd, dressed in their Sunday best, having been to Mass that morning, or wearing their workaday corduroys, with their sleeves rolled up. They came with only their eyes and bare hands, or they came equipped with shovels, spades, pitchforks, hoes, rakes, ice-choppers, saws, hammers and nails, pushing wheel-barrows, trailing children's wagons, shoving prams through the spring mud. They came dressed for the rain or heedless of the weather. There were bare-headed men and men in cloth caps, woolen tams, tweed short-brims, golf-caps, card-dealers' visors, berets, rain-bow-spotted house-painter's caps, old men in long dark over-coats, young men with nothing to hinder them but a cardigan or a vest. There were girls in white vinyl boots and women in house-slippers, girls in baggy sweat-shirts, and women tip-toeing from tuft to tuft to save their Clark shoes. Black umbrellas blossomed through the crowd, and you could not help thinking their stout ferrules made the brellies ready to close into rapiers of attack and defence, yet one woman who picked her way timidly along carried no more protection that a clear plastic parasol with a yellow border, which she held aloft daintily.

Up the road the crowd percolated slowly until it came to a bottleneck where the whin-bushes closed in vise-like. Over this rise, the road opened into a clearing, where the hundred-foot-long crater erased it, with the field empty on the left, and the bog and the fringe of the State Forest straggling on the right.

As we looked for the first time on the afternoon ahead of us, from the vantage of noontime, the ground of our ambitions was tantalizingly unoccupied, and we knew that our numbers, anywhere from a thousand to twelve hundred strong, were sufficient to overwhelm the crater, the field and the bog, if left unopposed. Then we looked up to see the four soldiers standing in the road on the high ground in the wood. A man sent his eyes scanning the stone fence along the left arm of the ridge. "Where the hell are the rest o' the bastards?" We halted, and waited.

Over the rise behind us came three uniformed gardai from Monaghan Town. In their long dark-blue raincoats, the policemen took up a vantage-point with their backs to the whin-bushes. One of them clapped his hands behind himself and looked out into the middle distance. Another noticed that heads were turning and pulled down on the visor of his peaked cap, with a shiver inside his coat-shoulders and an exaggerated glance upwards at the rain. Someone in front of us muttered aloud, "What are *they* doin' here?" Overhearing, the third policeman offered a reply, saying they were there as observers. More heads turned, who looked as if to say *Who asked you?* The policeman then stated, "If a British soldier crosses the Border, we'll arrest him." And he gave a short, embarrassed laugh.

The man who gave out with the original comment then pushed his way away from them and, cursing under his breath, said, "The fuckers'd be at home toastin' their toes on a nice turf fire only they're getting' triple-time to stand out here in the cold drizzle and file their fuckin' reports."

In another part of the crowd, a man was pointing. "Do yez see that crater there?" he cried.

This was a man, you might say, past the prime of life, and so visibly agitated that he could not stand still, and a woman at his side was growing alarmed at the reddening of his face.

"Not a sign-post posted!" he cried, and he spoke with the voice of the North Circular Road, tough, gritty, wizened, with the brick-and mortar accents of Dublin's working-class. "Nor a wall nor a fence—but by that foul hole do yez know there lies the partition of Ireland. And if ever a piece of paper came between a man and his God, it was the day they drew that red line across a map, and cut this poor, long-suffering nation of ours in two! And I ask you, who remembers today the man that did that deed? That red line that was drawn with the blood of Suvla Bay drippin' from the pen! That man who had the life's-blood of a thousand trenches from Ypres to the Somme drippin' from his hands! Is there a man, woman or child coming to this place this day who does not know that the name of that man was Winston Churchill? Let them say what they like–they can believe, if they like, that their dear Winnie was the Second Coming of King Arthur himself!— it's their country—we don't go over there and tell then what to think, what to believe, what to sign their names to!—but we know what he was. And we'll never forget, or let it be forgotten, that it was Winston Chur-chill, in 1921, when poor Mick Collins, may God rest his soul, went out to London—at the head of the victorious IRA, that bet the British military with all their legions of hell fair and square—Winston Churchill it was who threatened to Mick's face to commit genocide on the Irish people if he did not sign his name, then and there, to the partition of this country. Aye, we know what he was—a bleedin' murderer, and didn't he cut us in two! Look at the map of Ireland, if ye don't believe me! Cut the heart right out of us, he did—the butcher!"

Over the knoll came men in hiking-boots, trailing wires and back-packing video-tape cameras. They pushed through the crowd, thrusting microphones toward the disturbance the Dubliner was making, but they were too late. Behind them came reporters, asking questions, photographers, hurrying with their heads down, trying to take the light on the meters in their hands. Local people stopped them by the arm–"I'll tell you what this is all about. It's quite simple, actually. No bloody border's going to stop me picking up the odd pint a bit less dear if I feel like it! Here—write that down." A small group gathered and one said, "Look—people in these parts have been getting along just fine for years—both sides of the line—things were just fine—till they showed up, with their Pol-icy of craterin' our roads." "No, that is not correct, sir," another told a reporter with poised pen, "we've had our own road-fillin's up here, since November, when the Brits started this nonsense. So this has not been engineered from Kevin Street. Quite the contrary—we were the ones who invited all these people up here—and it's about time we had some support from the rest of the country. Or didn't the BBC know that?–weren't you informed?" "It's a simple question of economics—I've to deliver my milk to the Creamery, daily, over beyond, and the customs road is ten miles longer roundabout. Now, I've a family to feed, and the cost of shoes from England for the kids is gettin' no less dear by the day. I tell you, it hurts both sides. They're disruptin' trade!" "As I say, it's the principle of the thing. Go back to your own country, and tell them that they can't cross the street, and see what happens! The 'Border!' The very idea's absurd! Why, I know people, and so do you, with the sittin' room in one country, and the kitchen in another!" "Well, I'm fed up. I've been takin' it too long as it is. And—I'm not takin' it anymore! And them soldiers can get to hell back to bloody England where they belong! Or they'll soon find out what it is to bleed for Ireland's sake!"

The British soldiers standing in the road at the top of the hill made their position quite clear.

They were there to say, You can come this far—and no farther.

They were there to say, This is ours, and that is yours. We have every right to blow up this road, and fifty more like it, because the IRA is using these unapproved, back-country roads, unattended by any customs posts, unguarded by any check-points, to raid havoc on our rear. Stay over there where you belong and no harm will come to you. We can't cross the border without Dublin making an international incident out of it. But step over that line—.

"By Christ! Any fool knows that you don't need a road to cross the Border!"

"That's right. You steal a car this side—dump it down the road—and you walk across! Through the wood, or through the field! Who's to stop you? Pick up another car the other side, and you're on your way. What the hell would the IRA need a road for? What have they to drive across—tanks?"

The road then was not the issue. The road could be filled today and blown again tomorrow. Both sides knew that. The question was, Would the papers next day—and the television news that very night—runs pictures of a horde of ban-defying intruders crossing the Border unopposed? Could the British Army afford to be seen as weak, ineffectual? The issue was the inviolability of a line on a map. The British were come a long way to uphold the legitimacy of that line, and the Irish were come a long way to defy them.

A man with a loud-hailer on the knoll behind us was shouting directions. "Into the wood! Into the wood! Bring timber!"

The observation post in the wood a hundred yards away mobil-ised, and a platoon of soldiers popped up from behind the hill, materialising as if out of the ground.

They advanced down the road toward us at double-time. They were armored in riot-panoply, bulky with flak-jackets, wielding long truncheons the length of rake-handles, as mechanical as olive-drab robots, and their solid phalanx of translucent body-length riot-shields, rattling up and down as they ran, made them look like un-plumed Greeks rushing to a new Thermopylae.

They shouted and hollered, making a din like a troop of chimpanzees trying to frighten off a tribe of baboons, banging their truncheons on the sides of their shields. At their head, an officer strode with long strides, unadorned except for the battle-ribbons haughtily displayed on this chest, bearing himself up undaunted to show his men he feared this rabble not.

And hoping at the same time to impress the Irish with his fearlessness.

But we took it as nothing more than the usual British arrogance, and it pissed us off.

The officer brought a loud-hailer of his own to his lips.

"I order you to disperse! Any persons on this road are in violation of the Executive Order of October, 1968, banning protests, demonstrations and marches—."

"To hell with your ban!" someone shouted.

"——and in violation of the Public Order Act of 5 February—."

"To hell with your Acts! Get out of our country!"

Frustrated, the Britisher shouted into his mouthpiece. "I order you to disperse—at once! You are trespassing on the property of the Northern State Forest—!"

"You're trespassing on our country!" came the angry shout from a dozen throats, and a flock of stones went flying through the air.

The soldiers halted in their tracks, crouched, and raised their shields. A fusillade of rocks descended on their heads with a dented Bang! and a plastic Pop! They hesitated, just at the bank of the muddy pool of water that was the crater in the road, and the moment they hesitated, they lost their forward momentum. A storm of threats and curses broke over their heads.

Another round of rocks went up like dead birds, and plummeted like loaded-lead-weights.

One or two of the soldiers might have taken a backward step, or they were simply ducking, or else they were jolted by a hit. The officer in front hurled commands over his shoulder to 'Stand fast!' But just as he turned his head again to face us, a missile plunked him square in the middle of his medalled chest.

Abuse and invective rose like a cry of joy from the open throats of the Irish.

"Get out of here, ye fuckers!" "You'll not disperse us!" "Run, you maggots!" "So you wanted to be a soldier! Yer mother can't help you now, can she?"

Our side raced around the sides of the big puddle, jumped the brook, and poured into the field over the roadside fence. The soldiers faces when they looked up were like bubbles bursting. The stones were hitting them now, from too many sides. They back-pedaled, holding out their shields at arm's-length. As we pummeled them, they tripped over their own feet. Their forearms were tied up with shield-straps, and their truncheons, tied to their wrists with leather loops, were useless hindrances as long as their tormentors kept out of range of their swing.

They looked behind themselves, with the soldier's fear of being surrounded. Suddenly their only thought was their exposed rear. They crept backward, turning every which way— but—not fast enough.

We had the numbers on our side. The unencumbered Irish were racing uphill inside the fence, inches beyond truncheon-swipe. If we got to the high ground first, we could scale the fence, block the road—Jesus!—we'd cut them off!

The British broke and ran before it was too late. The Irish hooted derisively, jumped into the brown lake, splashing with windmilling arms, clambered up the banking, and pursued the soldiers, now fleeing in full disorder as we ran directly up their backs in the road.

Our boys closest on their heels, however, were those inside the fence, and although they tried to outrace the slower, heavier-burdened troops, they only succeeded in outrunning their own supply of rocks and stones.

They had thus to leave the road to the now-hurrying platoon, and once the Brits were beginning to achieve the crest of the hill, and felt their flanks protected again with the woods on one side, and a small stand of trees, and the stone fence, on the other side, they stopped running, and turned to face us in the road again, and allow their commander, huffing uphill, to catch up with them.

With a livid face and dire cursing, he regrouped them, pushing them bodily into a defensive formation, shields outward. At last they were turned to face the enemy again, with the safety that came with possession of the high ground once more

The Irish coming up the road behind them halted at a safe distance, brought up ammunition as quickly as they could, and bombarded the soldiers between the trees on either side of the road. The men and boys in the field spread out, shouting and waving their arms, sending scouts all the way across the field to the windbreak. They might have taken the stone fence at the top of the hilly field had they thought of it, or had they been certain of what lay behind it. But wiser heads prevailed, and for the moment, they were trying to fall back a bit and get organized.

The boys in the field were the corduroy battalion. They had no officers, no one to give directions. They couldn't hold a meeting or take a vote, so they ended by looking around at one another at a loss what to do next, except the obvious—watch out. How to fashion a cohesion on the spot? They were civilians. All the professionals were on the other side. Perhaps they vastly outnumbered the enemy, for the moment, but—only in unity could their strength equal their numbers—and as for intelligence, who knew how many, and where, the Brits were?

So they looked behind themselves down the hillside of the field. Already the pick-and-shovel brigade was at work on the crater. They had won, but they knew in their bones that it was only the first round. And what had they won? They had won ground and won time—but now, they would have to hold that ground. An idiot could see that the main thing was to keep the Brits off the backs of the diggers down below or the crater in the road could not get filled, because the road-fillers needed time.

But how much time? Nobody knew. We were a citizen army, but an unarmed army, and our foes were paid, trained, armed killers.

And at that point, midday, about half-twelve in the noontime, nobody knew that we'd be there fighting the Brits for another six hours.

Out of the bramble of the State Forest came teams carrying felled trees. The Sinn Féiner with the loud-hailer stood on a mound of freshly-dug earth and directed them. The pick-and-shovel brigade busily scraped and carved and excavated at the edges of the crater, splashed a road-bed of tree-trunks and sturdy branches down in the water, and clambered about, gesticulating like a regiment of worker-ants.

Out in the field the corduroy battalion fanned out to form a defence perimeter. Women and girls appeared with wheel-barrows full of rocks gathered from the brook and around the crater. They pushed the wheel-barrows uphill, shoved prams stocked with stones through the grass, walked backwards pulling wagons. Little ammunition dumps appeared, rock-mounds, what I imagined might be the markers on druid graves, dotting the field. The rock-gatherers shuttled back and forth and the ammo pits mounted up.

In the road the tree-choppers and shovelers erected a stout entanglement, half-way up the rise to the road-crest on the ridge, a barricade of tree-trunks, boulders and branches, intended to keep the Brits from bringing vehicles down the road.

The boys in the firing-line loaded up their pockets, and waited, scanning the stone wall on the ridge at the top of the field. The soldiers were gone. Over the hill and into the wood. Vanished. We waited for the stone fence to move, something out of Macbeth, but it remained rooted to the ridgeline. Medics wearing green armbands moved up. They filtered into the front line with their kits in shoulder-bags. The only sound was a rustle like the wheezing of an oiled weathervane: it was the breeze blowing through the branches of the windbreak.

You looked for your friends. You checked to see was anyone hurt, is everyone all right and present. Take a head count. You slapped one another on the back, there was a lot of loud boasting, and when you saw everyone was all right, still together, it felt good. You were trying to stick close to those you arrived with. They were the ones you knew best. There was some bond there, family friendship, neighborhood, comradeship. You neeeded to know the name of the man next to you in the line, on the right, on the left. You had to be able to trust him, to depend on him, and he had to have the same with you. People did not stray. They stuck to their own. Small groups occupied their own little territories in the firing-line.

We staked out our turf, Mick, Krishna and me. Mick was walking back and forth, his face flushed. "The Riot Squad, ha, ha. That's what we are." After our first contact with the troops, we were all in high good humour. "Good work, lads."

To our number we added young Peadar Kenny. He had not been with us during the Embassy riots, but he was one of our group that went back a ways with the Cumann. We did not invite in any of the newcomers—nor did they seem to want to intrude themselves. They milled about amongst each other, obviously more comfortable that way. We did send back Barney O'Toole, who was full of enthusiasm, but was seen to be puffing his way uphill. "Barney," said Mick, "wouldn't you feel better back with the Iron Brigade down below where you could rest yourself on a spade-handle between exertions?" "Well," said Barney, "if you promise to meet me for a pint afterwards and tell me all about it." "That's the lad, you don't want to be slowin' down the likes of us, and you're too big a target for rubber bullets, anyhow."

"I'm actually surprised by the amount of organization that's here," I said. "The arrival of medics tells you that the locals from the Monaghan vicinity have their act together."

"Didn't you hear your man tellin' the media this's been goin' on since November?" said Mick. He threw his arm round Krishna's shoulder. "Stick close, comrade. We'll watch out for ye."

"Give no ground, take no shit," said Krishna.

Mick punched me in the shoulder. "Did ye see the bastards run!"

"Did anybody see Brendan and Myles anywhere?" I said, looking all around.

"I have a feeling they're here somewhere," said Krishna, "but not where you can see them."

"How come you're breaking your rule about no British territory, Comrade?"

"Today is different. I won't be parading up and down in front of their lines in open view."

Bernadette and Martina were hustling up and down the human chain that was now forming up to regularize the conveyance of ammo up to the dumps. Alita Hughes strode up and down supervising, in full Cumman na Ban regalia. Her sister Maureen and Jane Quill were struggling with a pram: a wheel collapsed, and the load of stones tipped out. Barney O'Toole could now be seen with his neighborly street from the Liberties building up the barricade in the road. John Martyn could be seen among the road-fillers with garden equipment. Wherever Myles and Brendan were, it was well out of sight. The incorrigible O'Corrigan said, "I wonder now—do ye think I could get Martina to go bra-less and loan it to me for a slingshot?"

The man with the loud-hailer and the other leaders of the overall operation were Sinn Féin officers out of the Kevin Street Headquarters. They had to be men and women with a name known to every Republican present, so that when they spoke, they would be listened to. Only the Kevin Street leadership had faces and names that widely traveled. Everyone accepted their status, in the name of unity, discipline and practicality. The road-filling they were attempting would otherwise be impossible. No one could be allowed to be there who acted off his own bat or let things get out of control or jeopardize comrades. And with so many hundreds of non-members out here today, just for the one day, it could be dangerous. The Sinn Féiners had to be the cadre, and lead by example. Seán Ó Brádaigh, the President's brother, and Information Officer of the Republican Movement, was the man with the loud-hailer. His brother Ruairí stood on the knoll behind the crater with Tomas MacGiolla. And there were others who were taking care to keep further back even than that.

Throughout the arc of the forest and the road and the field there was a natural sorting-out taking place. Only those who volunteered were allowed to go into the firing line. No one who wanted to hang back, or work only on the road, or keep busy some other way closer to the border itself, in comparative safety, was told or ordered or forced to go up front. You had to be ready to give and take punishment to go up there. Those of us who went had it well in mind what we were there for: to fight.

But just now there was no fighting. Now there was a lull. The thrill of the opening assault was slipping away. Over in a flash, it seemed now you had caught your breath ten times over. The flush drained out of the faces of the Irish. Through the field and across the road and into the forest, the umbrella of men and boys formed a perimeter of defence, centered on the just-completed tree-trunk road-block. We watched and we waited. "Now," I said, if you were them, what would you be doing—what would you be up to?"

"I know what I'd do," said Mick, "but Christ knows what they'll do."

"Look out!" cried Peadar.

Out of the earth they came, hurdling the stone fence at the top of the ridge, and, screaming, charging downhill. The firing-line stiffened for a head-on clash. Out of the two loaded hands went the rocks and stones. But they were coming fast, dodging and weaving, crouching to make themselves smaller. Without their clumsy shields and phalanx formation, they were more mobile, quicker. Into the pockets went the hands, and got tangled in cloth, threads, bulging rocks. The fingers were grasping frantically and barely closed on a stone before it was flying from the hand. The stones hit nothing but the ground at the opposition's heels. In a second, the long truncheons would be upon us, cracking heads. Rocks spent, the firing line bent.

The soldiers wheeled where they scented the weakest links, the slower ones piling in after the sprinters. The wings of the firing line were sucked in toward the whirlpool in the center. Both sides collapsed into the maelstrom in the middle of the field where the Brits were breaking the line, swinging wildly, hitting nothing but air, but repelling their targets, ducking and head-dodging, back onto the wings rushing to their support. A confusion of curses broke out and bodies were snatched back out of the grasp of the grappling enemy. The Brits broke through and suddenly found themselves on the other side of the line they had broken in two. They closed ranks, back to back, and tried to clear a space around themselves by swinging their truncheons at head-level and, at the same time, at shin-level, too. The melee in the middle broke down as the Irish rescued their comrades from pile-ups all over the ground, pulling out bodies by the arms and legs, hauling then back by the scruff of the neck. Then it appeared the British officers were rushing up, starting to shout at the rank-and-file to disengage. Our boys retreated, step by step, grudgingly, back down the hill. The Brits organized a line and advanced menacingly forward again in pursuit. The Irish got their backs up against the fence along the roadside, at the rim of the crater, only steps from all the open-mouthed shovelers, and stopped. The British officers advanced their men to within ten paces of us, and halted, spreading out their line of forty or fifty men in a threatening posture that challenged us to try them again.

The corduroy battalion, thrown back on the pick-and-shovel brigade, seethed with dismay. Having surrendered our ammo-mounds, we now had to watch while the troops scattered them with their truncheons. The soldiers kicked the rock-piles savagely, leaving no doubt in the minds of their audience what they would do if that were a live victim they had on the ground. "Go on!" shouted the Irish. "Kick 'em! They won't roll far!"

"It's easy when they don't kick back."

"Look at them—the pride of the British Empire!"

"Ah, what did you expect out of a pack of hyenas?"

"You!–yes, you!–what bung-hole did you crawl out of?"

"Who. Him? Found him in the Home, they did, certified mental defective."

"Is that where they get them these days? Well–the British Army's come up in the world since I knew 'em—they used get 'em outta the Borstal!"

"Hey, Tommy!–take that truncheon and stick it up yer arse!"

"I'd rather stick it up yours!"

Both sides laughed at that one.

"Yerragh, I'll bet you would. You look just the type, you do!"

"Come on over here and say that, Paddy!"

"I'm comin,' Tommy. Never you fear, I'm comin.' Look to your rear, Tommy, cause I'm comin.'"

Their officers shouted at the soldiers. "No talking in ranks!"

"Blimey, Jack, wasn't that your Ma I seen, last week, in Little Denmark Street, solicitin' on the corner?"

"Naw—his Ma's in a house in Earl's Court—only takes on the Officers' Club!"

The women knew how to be provoking. "Come on over here, Johnny. Aw. What's the matter? Afraid of a wee girl like me?"

"I wouldn't waste yer time, Siobhan. Yer not his type. He likes 'em with hair on their ballocks."

"Shut up, you stupid bitch!" called out the soldier.

"You there!" the officer shouted at him. "Back in ranks!"

"Look, son, what's yer name? Well–how the hell can I talk to ye if I don't know yer name? All right—I know—the officers won't let ye talk. I know lads your age. Out of a job, no pocket money, fed up—no, wait, wait! Listen to me!"

"Ah, give over, Frank. They won't listen. You're wastin' your breath. They're not worth it, I tell you. Lot of hooligans in uniform."

"Fuckin' scum you are," a soldier replied.

"I'm not a hoor like you. Sellin' yerself for a mess o' porridge. Not a hired killer. Not an assassin for pay! Not a terrorist cloakin' himself in the law!"

"Get back, you filthy Fenians!"

There were several black faces in the British line. Someone on the Irish side called out, "What's this you sent us? Mercenaries, is it? From the Colonies, are they? Ah, the youth of Britain—too lily-white for this work?"

Someone else yelled, "Swear to Jaysus—won't have to blacken their faces on the duck squad of a nice Falls evenin'!"

"Smile, so's we can see yez! What are you—the cook?"

"Naw—he's the scullery-maid, that one."

"Come on," said Mick O'Corrigan to Krishna. "We'll shut up that lot for ye."

"No, man, leave them," said Krishna. "It's not the colour of their skins—it's the colour of their uniforms."

"'Tisn't right," Mick insisted. "It's bigotry."

"You telling I?" said Krishna. "And you've had enough of that? Mick—don't be a hothead—think!— it's bad tactics, that's all. You come with me—I have an idea."

Krishna led us pushing through the crowd back towards the knoll where we could see Seán Ó Brádaigh looking over the field anxiously.

Ó Brádaigh had the loud-hailer in his hand. Krishna motioned towards it and said, "I want to make a speech."

Ó Brádaigh looked at the others behind him, his brother and MacGiolla. They said, "He's with us, Sean."

"What do you want to do?"

"I want to talk to the blacks on the other side."

Ó Brádaigh considered a moment before he asked Krishna, "Is it worth a try?"

"You can either taunt them till they are thrown back on the side that gives them support—or you can split them from their white comrades—let me talk to them."

Ó Brádaigh handed over the loud-hailer.

The four of us, Mick, Krishna, Peadar and I plowed back to the front line. Krishna took up his position out in front, surrounded by us, his bodyguard. He raised the mouthpiece to his lips.

"Brudders!"

He looked at the horn and checked the trigger—I nodded at him to go ahead.

"Brudders!—I want to address yuh—can yew hear me?"

The senior officer on the British line, a lieutenant, looked momentarily perplexed.

"Brudders—can yew hear me?" The breeze lifted his words, and the lieutenant cocked his ear in the rain. "De leaders of de Republican Movement here today have asked me to speak to yuh."

The lieutenant heard that. He shouted, "Don't listen to that man!"

"I don't talk to de white soldiers," Krishna said.

That lilting island accent of his and the loud-hailer and the novelty of the situation all of a sudden had everyone on both sides transfixed.

"I don't talk to de white soldiers. Dey don't need to listen. What I have to say is only for de brudders. You dere! You see me standing here?" He pulled open the collar of his combat jacket, and tore down the buttons of his shirt. "I'm black, like yew!"

The Irish all turned their heads to see, who was that? The lieutenant, worried at a motion he was not in control of, shouted at his troops again. "I order you not to listen to that man!"

"So, brudders—he orders yuh—and yew obey??—yew jump when the man tell yuh, yew lie down when he want to step across yer body! I ask yew—who yew gonna listen to?—dat lackey of de colonialist class, who has kept yuh in servitude for centuries??—or me, your brudder!"

Krishna was striding back and forth, excited. He was getting into it now.

Then the lieutenant made his crucial error. He hurried along his line, trying to reach every black, to whisper in his ear, to pat him on the butt, to tell him he knew he could count on him.

Emboldened, Krishna stepped forward.

"Dese people—." He swept his arm, gesturing at the mob of Irish people standing behind him. "Dey are not your enemies! *Dere* is your enemy! I will not lie to yuh—but he will! What's he whisperin' in yer ear now?—in a minute, he will tell yew to raise your baton and strike me down!—to show de white man next to yuh dat de nigger can be trusted!"

The black soldiers toyed nervously with the truncheons in their hands, and looked back and forth to check one another's reactions. That devil with the loud-hailer, he's clever, all right— there will be trouble over this—.

Krishna edged forward. The whole crowd of Irish made a motion with him. "What's de matter wid yuh niggers? Have you lost yer senses? I know yuh! I know de streets in Putney yew walk on—I know de stinking cous-cous shop where yuh meet in the kitchen so yew can smell home. Eh?—dat's it, man!— take a good look at de white man next to yuh. Because when we come—if yew go down—he gonna stop running to save *yew?*"

The Irish were cheering now. The lieutenant was becoming frantic. The dogs sniffed the quarry. Mick O'Corrigan, his back turned insolently to the troops, was waving his arms, orchestrating the chanting response behind Krishna.

"Get the officers! Get the officers! Get the officers! Get the–!"

Krishna cried, "Yew see me here? I'm a free man! I standing on dis side of de line because I want tew! Nobody making me! I know what yuh thinking—how will I get a job, man? How will I get a wife, wid no money? How will I eat?—who gonna feed me? Yew hoping yew will please de master, and he will reward yuh for it. But yew will never be a white man walking down Shaftesbury Avenue! Yew want to know what is a nigger? A nigger is a black man what puts on dat uniform—and forget who he is! You wanna be a nigger all yer life? Brudders, I appeal to yuh—trow down your weapons, and cross over to us!–yew have friends here!"

The Irish were cheering wildly, chanting vehemently, and lifting Krishna off his feet up onto their shoulders. He shouted into the mouth-piece with the horn pointed at the sky. "We will help yuh to escape!–we will protect yuh from de officers who oppress yuh daily—we will hide yuh, we will feed yuh!–Brudders, yew don't have to die for de Empire!"

The lieutenant looked behind him, up the long hill, to where his superiors were, to where help, advice, counsel lay. *If I tell them to attack*—but his initiative was gone, his white platoon-members were looking at him to save *them*—not just from that ravenous Irish mob, but from their own black comrades! And what of them? The niggers! *That black bastard has outfoxed me!* The lieutenant knew that his line, divided, was a line untenable. He looked longingly up the hill. He wanted desperately to pull out every black on his line and send them packing, up there, out of the way, and leave him only his own kind, lads he could trust to obey his commands because, because—we're all Tommies, in this together! He knew now that whatever he did now he'd be castigated for it by the brass-hats up on the hill. It's their fault! What do they expect a man to do with the rejects and misfits they send him! A hail of rocks came flying through the rain, beating down on his indecision. "Pull out!" he cried, startling himself. The Irish charged. The Army fled, as fast as they could, the blacks faster than all the others, not stopping till they were safe behind the cover and security of the stone fence at the top of the hill.

Out of the misty woods of the Northern State Forest an apparition appeared. As it emerged, it grew arms and legs and a humped back, like a spotted cow.

It was a white-washed wooden gate, torn from a farmer's fence, hastily hammered with timbers for legs, a crude shield that took eighteen or twenty heaving men and boys to lift and move.

Once they got it in the field, they pushed the beast uphill inch by inch. At first we laughed, then started cheering, and finally hailed onward the onslaught of our champion, so that we crowded behind it. The laughable madness of this stratagem was matched only by the absurdity of British troops cowering behind a stone fence from our ragtag battalion. Emboldened, we renewed our stone-and-rock bombardment of the defensive foe, and launched a head-on frontal assault.

Helmets popped over the fieldstones. Shoulders scrunched, elbows cocked. Loud pops. Black rubber-bullets came hurtling bombastically through the air. They thudded and plunked on the slats of the farmer's gate. Shouts of "Watch yourself!" We scattered and ducked. "Them things can snap the thigh-bone on a twelve-stone woman!" We fell where we stood and flattened ourselves prone, hugging the earth. The soldiers were re-loading. Up we popped and let go a thundering rattle of rocks. The barrage skipped and skidded off the flat-top fence, or winged high, or bounced back dead, as our firing-line shot quick, fell face-down again, and waited, trying to gauge our timing, waiting for the next flight of rubber-bullets to go *whoooshing* end-over-end over our heads. In the space of re-loading, the gate-crashers pushed ahead again, and then the warnings shouted out– "Duck!"

The Brits were rising, standing, crouching, raising their hand-held 9mm grenade launchers fitted with the bulbous black housing over the muzzle. They assumed their firing position, weapon crossed over the elbow, or balanced on the fence, tried to pick out a moving target, or else shot fast, without aiming, fearfully from the hip.

The game was all about the timing of your fusillade, for them, for us. All we were trying to do with our gate-shield was to get close enough to pick off one or two of them when they exposed themselves. How long to re-load? Now! Quick! The next shower of stones came rearing up high and looped, like mortar-shells, raining down punishment on the bent backs of the troops. The cries from direct hits came back to us from over the fence. The gate pushed on. Every time we fell down flat again, we fell forward, inching closer. "Careful, now!" On came the rubber-bullets, and spent themselves bouncing over the grass, or thudded with a futile *bump!* on the gate-slats.

The women behind us were now venturing once more halfway up the hill in back of our advancing firing-line, and they hurried about the business of collecting scattered ammunition and stock-piling it. Those of us with empty pockets rushed back during the firing-lulls to re-supply at the head of the chains, where the wheel-barrows spilled out their loads.

Down at the crater, work on the road-filling was resuming with re-doubled energies. It was critical for us to keep the Brits off their backs or that road would never get filled. They had their job and we had ours.

The black rubber-bullets flew through the air, eight inches long, nosecone-pointed and hard as steel. Their spin held them to their flight-path till the nose dipped, and then they faltered, spinning crazily, tumbling finally end-over-end. A boy jumped out from behind the gate. "Here I am! Try and get me, you bastards!"

You could see these projectiles coming. As long as the distance was enough. If you were to get one in the gut at three feet—broken ribs or worse. There were cases of people being killed by them. That's why we pushed and pushed, but only up to our limit. The idea was to keep the troops from interfering sufficiently with the road-filling to prevent it. The idea was not to beat them in a battle, to win the day, the idea was simply to prolong the stand-off as long as possible, or as long as necessary to get the road filled.

So the exchange was rocks for rubber-bullets. The Brits usually missed because they had no time to pin down a moving target, and their missiles had an erratic, unpredictable trajectory. After aiming true and squeezing off soft, the rubber-bullet still went wild, from the force of the kick-back, or it lost its spin and flew harmlessly end-over-end. And while the soldier was taking all this time, he was exposed to the rock-artillery. This riot-tactic of theirs was really meant for urban situations, where space was confined and bunching-up of their opponents prevailed. Out in the open air like this, in such a large meadow, they were much less effective.

Our gate-shield was looming closer. The Brits were using their stone fence for a parapet more effectively, to steady their aim, and as we edged closer, we were easier to hit. They started tempting and teasing us to crawl up nearer and nearer. A few lads were close enough to stand up and spit in a soldier's eye. I freely confess I was not one of them. But Mick O'Corrigan actually crawled up to the stone fence itself, and lay there, lobbing rocks over the top till he ran out. The soldiers never saw him, and then they were getting hit, and Mick got away again clean, to the noisy delight of the corduroy battalion.

The fighting flashed a fury, and sagged a lull, and fell into a round of give-and-take, shoot-and-duck, back-and-forth, swaying, moaning, punishing, wearying.

Frustrated, the Brits stood up all at once and all together, at one point, and took aim, for massed fire, at the gate-fence—it was the closest, biggest, most stationary target they had—they couldn't miss. They fired off their salvo, and wood-splintering splattered the air.

We heard wounded cries from the men and boys hit by the hard-hearted projectiles. Our medics rushed up to the vicinity of the gate and were bandaging heads as they lay down in the field-grass with their injured man.

The casualties had to be cleared out from behind the gate. It took time and took men away from the battle, and forced others into ever-more-risky, ever-more-foolhardy forays, to try to keep the Brits with their heads down and give cover to the injured and the medics as they tried to get away.

But the soldiers also could find no way to exploit a moment's advantage—they too were taking casualties, for rocks also could draw blood, and a quarter of their force was gone, with the lieutenant who had spirited away their black comrades under the pretext of restoring discipline. Now a sergeant was left in charge and, in a defensive posture, their initiative was sapped, and they hung on grimly. It's not what they signed up for, to sit there and take it. Once again, our hands are tied! If only they let us un-sling our rifles, we'd clear out a good few of these fucking Fenians.

But in the backs of their minds, and ours, was the thought that was forbidden to think: could this turn into another Bloody Sunday?

At all costs, the Brits had to prevent that from happening. And we knew it. That's why we attacked so fiercely. We counted on it. It was a far better shield than a broken-down farmer's fence.

Besides, we had another motive, which they lacked: revenge. There wasn't one of us in that field that afternoon who didn't want to get them back for that day in Derry.

And so the fight for the field by the road to Rosslea that day was degenerating into a quagmire of attrition, lacking any scrap of honor or nobility, drowning in grit.

We were taking a time-out at the bottom of the ammo-chain.

"How're you lads getting on?" said Martina, anxiously.

"Oh, grand," I said. "Just grand."

"Smashin,'" said Mick. "Have you any water?"

"Feel like I'm running in sand," said Krishna.

"I'll go fetch the water," said Jane.

Bernadette came up. "Everybody okay?"

We looked around at one another. We were covered in dirt and grass-stains, and the sweat was plastered on us. We were as tense as a clenched fist. "Anybody got a fag?" I said.

Bernie lit one up with a puff and handed it to me, filter up.

"Are they shootin' at you girls down here?" Mick asked.

"No," said Martina. Jane came back with a jogger's water-bottle with a spill-proof drinking cap, and we passed it around.

"How're they doin' with the crater?" asked Peadar Kenny.

"They're getting on," said Peg, one of the new girls in the Cumann. Bernie and Martina were more welcoming than us men were, as Jane Quill well knew.

"We need more time," I said, wiping water from my chin with the back of my hand.

"This could go on like this for hours," said Krishna.

"I haven't hit a soldier yet," said Peadar. "Maybe we could get around to the side of them somehow."

Mick looked at Krishna. "Out-flank 'em—yeah."

"Leave it to Trinity to come up with a plan," said Krishna.

We were looking for any kind of a break instead of this endless rallying. Mick looked up towards the ridge, over to where the road went over the top into the woods, on our right, on the troops' left flank. Then he scanned down the line of the stone fence the other way, and we all followed his gaze with the same thought: the windbreak.

"Give us some ammo, Martina," said Mick, "and a kiss for g'luck!"

"Go 'way, ye gob-shite!" said she, more tender than aggravated.

From the unapproved road, the brook at the bottom of the field trickled all the way to the windbreak, where it ran down gently, through a gully with some teasing white-water over rocks. There was then a sharp drop, and then a gradual levelling as the stream disappeared into a welter of tall standing rushes. There, on the far side of the windbreak, everything was treacherous boggy-bottom where you wouldn't want to get chased. It was a long way across a marsh to the distance where a small river gleamed. And all that was north of the Border: a no-man's land for us, especially in the case of Krishna.

The field where we'd been fighting for all this time was also in the North, for that matter, but solid ground where you could run away.

Therefore, if we were going to use the windbreak for cover, with its hedgerow, closely packed tree-trunks and low-hanging branches, to try to get up closer to the exposed right flank of the troops round the end of the stone wall, if we were discovered, our only way out was back into the open field.

Or, stand up and run for your life through the windbreak. But you would have to reach the brook at the bottom and cross it to get back into the 26 Counties, where the troops couldn't follow to pursue you—theoretically.

It was Mick's show. It was his Riot Squad. We were only the rank-and-file.

He gathered us together back at the road-filling brigade's rear. The idea was to disappear from the view of any Brits with binoculars up on the ridge, to meld in with gangs of people, and thus to disappear. That was the plan. Next we crept through the whin-bushes, low scrub and straggling trees south of the brook till we came up even with the foot of the windbreak. Then one by one we lunged across the narrow gully containing the brook so that we landed flat on the banking of the ditch below the windbreak where we couldn't be seen from the field. Mick was the last to cross.

The first third of the windbreak was hedgerow, and we crawled, hand over hand, holding onto the roots of the hedge. For this part of the climb we were completely hidden on the far side of the hedgerow, where our skidding heels sent loose dirt and pebbles sliding down into the bog on that side. We, too, were blind as to what was out of view on the other side of the hedge. Finally, we had managed to clamber up on our bellies inside the beginnings of the tree-planted section of the windbreak.

Here we were in a leaf-carpeted nave where the rain pitter-pattered distantly, a whisper at the tops of the tall young trees. It would have been lovely to just lie there and rest awhile, perhaps turn over on your back, look up above your head at the far-off inter-twinings of branch and cloud-bubbled sky, and listen to the rain.

Instead, we crawled on our bellies, leap-frogging one another, pausing only to hook an eyeball around a crevice of bark.

Then the ground thickened and the windbreak grew tangled with bushes. We were near to the top and Mick held out a hand to signal stop. He whispered, "When you see me jump up—all let loose at the same time, right?"

Raise your hand soundlessly, lift a leaf-corner with one finger, peek. We were eyes in a blind thicket and every gap in the leafage spelled exposure.

"Now!"

The startled expressions in the soldiers' faces seemed to be caught in a slow-motion whirl of stop-time as I jumped up. A mouth dropped open. Two eyes winced. More heads swiveled. I was pumping rocks out as fast as I could. An arm went up across a forehead in reflex. They dodged, tripped, fell. I jumped out of the bush that clawed at my ankles. "I got him!" I cawed, the voice coming out of my throat a crow's croak. I saw the black toothless muzzles of the rubber-bullet launchers slowly wheel round at us, or tilted skyward, or uselessly firing into the ground as soldiers went sprawling behind the stone fence.

Then I was running, crashing, wind-milling back down the slope, dodging tree-trunks, branches whipping the skin of my cheeks until they pulled tears out of my eyes.

The four of us collapsed, winded, on the banking of the gully on the safe side of the border. Mick O'Corrigan stretched himself out on the long grass. "Christ—we got 'em good!"

"Yeah," said Peader, breathing so hard you could see the heart jumping in his chest. "We could hardly miss 'em!"

"Did you see their faces?" I said. "We must have been within ten feet—that close."

Krishna's black eyes gleamed. "I saw fear, man."

"Oh," I said, "I love it—Jesus!"

Mick sat up. "Well, lads—yez did well for a pack o' trainees."

"Fuck you, ye feckin' fooker," we all chorused.

"I'm going back up there," said Mick.

"Are you out of your head, comrade?" said Krishna.

"I don't know about you," I said, "but I'm stayin' right here."

"It's just what they won't be expectin,'" said Mick, leaning forward.

"The tactical element of surprise," said Krishna, "is the only reason we tricked them—once. Once burnt, twice warned."

A sudden, surprising, rapidly escalating *whuppa-whuppa, whuppa-whuppa* came roaring past our heads, and we looked up to see the blur of a helicopter's belly coming soaring up out of the marsh at tree-top level only to scuttle across the field and rise, disappearing over the ridge of the State Forest.

Krishna's head was shaking back and forth. "The cavalry. Can you fancy that, comrades!"

Mick turned to us with his pockets bulging full of rocks from the stream-bed. "Who's with me?"

"They can't beat us." Krishna was filling his pockets. "They can shoot us, but they can't beat us."

"I'll get you for this, O'Corrigan," I said.

Down on our bellies again. I could hear my heart beating. I was afraid we were really pushing it this time. Out in the field the ammo-dumps were hip-high. The pick-and-shovel brigade now had their bull-dozer over the hump and engaged in smoothing out the crater-filling. The fence-gate in the field was now a battered pulp, but the beleaguered troops were still trapped behind their stone wall. We launched our missiles again, this time not from quite so close-in, but—as soon as we delivered the first salvo, rubber bullets came flying at us from our blind side, on our left. A squad of soldiers came running at us from the downslope behind the stone fence. Krishna yelled, "Reinforcements! Get out!"

The four of us broke cover out of the windbreak into the open field. It was our only option. We never would have made it back down through the windbreak. We needed open space—and had to hope we could run fast. We erupted into the field just as the Brits behind us were hurdling their wall.

Our boys in the field around the gate and going up and down to the ammo-dumps saw what was happening and redirected their aim. But we were also in the path of the rock-flights, so they had to hold their hand. The helicopter suddenly came swooping back down over the field head-high and everyone flattened. The women below were fleeing and heads were turning to look up from the road-filling. It was now a foot-race, and we were climbing up the backs of boys in front of us, when Mick suddenly turned and took the lead solider closest on his heels head-on. Then the two lines crashed and bodies were falling down tangling with arms and legs flying everywhere in a sort of a rugby scrum. It took three of us to drag Mick out of there and stand him up. Squirming, he tried to break loose, but we too had the strength of emergency in our hearts and we dragged him off, walking backwards, afraid now to turn our backs on the Brits, who were picking themselves up off the ground, chasing helmets rolling away.

The battle was three hours old. The rain dribbled down. The Brits carried away their injured, and harried their fresh men forward. Our bulldozers withdrew from the crater hastily back over the knoll, back behind the border. The pick-and-shovel brigade scrambled for safety. The lieutenant from the stone fence arrived at the crater in the road; there is only so much of this you can absorb before you turn blear-eyed and mean.

"That was close," I said.

Mick was incensed. "Why didn't yez stick in the boot?" We were sprawled on the ground behind the knoll, exhausted. "We had 'em. We could've killed 'em."

Peadar was gathering his breath. "What happens if we start killing them?"

Obviously, the thought entered our heads that we knew the 'RA was present, but they were holding their fire.

"If we start shooting, they start shooting. Too many unarmed civilian targets here—it would be a slaughter—women and children."

"If they want another Derry," said Mick, "we'll give it to 'em."

"Can't do it, comrade," said Krishna. "It's not on the programme for today. Sorry!"

"I haven't seen any guns in their hands," I put in.

"Not yet," said Krishna, cynically.

Peadar spotted two men in black, who appeared a hundred yards off, up on the ridge at the curve in the road by the British observation post. Two men dressed all in black. "Come and see this."

We crept up to the top of our shielding knoll and peeked over gingerly. After the latest round, the Brits were in complete control of the sloping field and were perilously close to us, held back only by the presence of the border. One of the men in black raised his arm and pointed, as if straight at us. "B-Specials," muttered Mick.

"It can't be."

"They're outlawed."

"It's them all right."

"They've been disbanded."

"What's that to them?"

"How do you know it's them?"

"Those peaked caps."

"It could be RUC—the green of their uni's is very dark— and they're a long way off."

"No. You'd know them by them old-fashioned stiff collars of theirs."

Mick borrowed opera glasses from a young lady with a shoulder-bag. "And unless I'm dreamin,' they've ripped off their insignia—why would the RUC bother? Here—have a look yourself."

"You're right."

At that point the two B-Specials turned and faded into the gloom of the forest.

"Let's go," said Mick.

We went looking for the Ó Brádaigh brothers, but we found Tomas McGiolla first. "We saw them, too," he said.

"What are they doing here, do you think?"

"Whatever it is they're up to, it's no good. Maybe they were called in to identify certain faces. I don't know. Be careful, lads."

But the day was a bit beyond being careful, now. Things were getting quite reckless. Beer-cases and milk-crates of bottles stuffed in the neck with petrol-soaked rags were being brought up to the hedge atop the knoll. From behind this screen, we launched our petrol bombs.

Our purpose was drive the Brits back off that fence surrounding the cratered road again. The glass jars exploded, splattered and died out. Some throws fell short into the water. Out in the open, there was no danger of petrol-bombs setting the wet grass on fire—but the troops were leery of them. Their uniforms were stuck to the skin with sweat already. The thought of burning petrol sticking to them caught them up and they were leaping out of the way.

Next, nail-bombs pursued them—packets of nails wrapped in corrugated cardboard, tied with string, and inserted with a stick of gelignite with a lit fuse. Get that one thrown out of your hand in a hurry, or else.

The lieutenant could not hold his position. It was too exposed, too much within range of the bombers. He was holding what was probably a VHF wireless set to his ear. Neither could he send his men across the border to batter us or chase us down—cheated by the yellow card again, he withdrew, and sent his platoon packing, back up to the high ground.

Upon this maneuver, our pick-and-shovel brigade swarmed over the knoll once more to resume the road-filling operation, our corduroy battalion moved out to occupy the field again, the bulldozers returned into action, and the job we'd come to do carried on.

But if we thought we'd won anything, we'd have to think again.

This time they changed their tactics and came at us from the sky. Rising out of the lowland bog like a gleaming motorized moth, skimming the windbreak at the tree-tops, descending out of the increasingly low overcast, came a single helicopter. It buzzed our crowd, zoomed up, and held there, fluttering. A viral voice floated down upon us, metallic and disembodied.

"You are ordered to disperse!"

Jeers and clenched fists.

"All those who do not disperse—immediately!–will suffer the consequences!"

Stones flew up, but the impervious chopper tilted, and scurried out of range, over the ridge-top of the State Forest.

It's hard to overstate the terrorising effect of flying war-machines. They make you want to dive for cover, when you know there's no place to hide. You feel stripped of your ordinary human powers in the face of technology. It's devilish how it plays with your mind. The menace of the floating mechanical voice issuing threats of who knows what is frightening with a science-fiction horror.

With a guttural squawk, the 'copter resurfaced and came swooping back, tipped onto its nose, blades chopping with the grind of a chainsaw, and it scoured the field, twenty feet from the ground, then, up, up, abruptly over the windbreak. Our people dove for rabbit-holes, and when we dared to raise our heads, the hurricane of the rotary blades blew back the hair over our ears.

We were just getting up and brushing off when a sortie of three choppers consecutively came roaring over the windbreak and soared to hover a hundred feet up, spotting themselves at intervals over the wide field.

Smoketrails came ribboning down in three thin orange streaks, then three blue ones, and then three scarlet. *Poof!* An orange cloud billowed on the ground. A pink mushroom. A blue rose. Dye-gas!

The field erupted with the prankish colours of carnival tents torn from their stakes by a swift, cruel wind. The children's balloon-colors then grew interspersed with an acrid grey, which it seemed they were intended to mask: CS gas.

Dye gas to stain your clothing and identify you to the uniformed gardai and Dublin Castle Special Branch waiting back south of the border, and tear gas to choke you before you could get there.

The canisters exploded when they hit the ground, blossomed brilliantly, and then were twisted into inverted geysers, as the whirring chopper-blades sucked them up and turned them into whirling dervishes of acrimony. The field became a cacophony of day-glo colors tuned to the terrible *taka-taka-taka-taka* of the helicopters.

Then the choppers lifted straight up and sped away, leaving the pasture strewn with shifting banks of gas, drifting slowly in the gaggles of crying, choking people, who, blinded, fled stumbling from the field.

I was one who came tumbling out of a cloud. My legs moved, but they felt very far away, involuntary companions, out of my control. My one overwhelming need was to breathe, and I bent all my will to suck down deep enough to hit bottom and expel just one breath. When I made it, I knew the worst was over. I'd been gassed before, in Washington, and I knew it didn't put you out of action, that you recovered and continued on.

The ones to worry about were the ones who were never gassed before. You panic. You think: I'm going to die. My mind registered: help them—help them. I stumbled about, looking for Mick, Krishna, Peadar—but we were separated in the confusion and stampede. Helping a girl to get up off the ground, I pulled her unwilling over the fence by the crater. "Come on," I kept saying, "you're gonna be all right—keep going."

I had never forgotten the moment in Washington when I was trapped behind a government building in Constitution Avenue by police who chased us down a driveway, only to come up against a ten-foot wall behind a row of parked cars—when, out of nowhere, a hand came down from above the wall and lifted me up to the top so that I could escape.

Helping a frightened girl I didn't know get away was my opportunity to return the favor.

The road behind the border looked like a field hospital. Draped over the bonnets of cars, slumped on the ground, wheezing and coughing, the gas casualties waited for air, fresh, pure, delicious air, to return to their seared lungs. The medics in the green arm-bands were attending them, dispensing lemon-juice, helping them up, to walk them, to get back their legs. The scene was devastating with the air of the sickened and disabled lending defeatism to the atmosphere: our two bulldozers were on loan from a sympathetic building contractor, and could not be lost—now they were stuck butt-end into the road, just over the knoll, barely snatched back out of capture. The Irish were filled with a bitter taste in their mouths. Maybe the chance to re-open the road was slipping from them—but now, the chance to get back at the Army was all that mattered.

Her friends found the girl and I found Mick. "Are you right?" he said.

"Yeah. I got a whiff, but not enough. Where's Peadar—Krishna?"

"Don't know. I want to go back."

We got lemon-soaked hankies from the medics and tied them around our noses like bandits' bandannas. We smeared vaseline into the red rims of our eye-sockets and all over our faces. Mick picked up a knobby stick, and I found an umbrella, ruled, the ferrule a chromed dagger-point. We weren't going to go back out there unarmed. "Ready?" We crawled up to the hedge at the knoll.

Looking out, we saw a moonscape. The field was saturated with gas. The overcast was weeping a foggy mist on the amphitheater of the meadow, sinking it in a blank, bleak greyness: the long afternoon was falling towards five-o'clock. Out of the shifting banks of fog and gas, soldiers emerged, clanking like mechanical frogs, with the goggle-eyes of gas-masks staring blankly.

A dose built up a tolerance. Boys danced in and out of the cloud-banks, crying "Give us more, it's good for us!" Gone were the ammo-chains of women and the tentative sparring at the fence from the beginnings of the fight, hours ago. Gangs roamed the field searching for targets in the drifting gas. Quarry pursued quarry, now the hunter, now the hunted. Fires of petrol-bombs flashed, sputtering, lighting up the fog like gas-lamps. Soldiers materialised out of the gas carrying rifles.

Slowly Mick and I walked out to join the deadly minuet. Our nostrils were plugged with vaseline, it filled our ears and greased our adam's apples and the backs of our necks. Our pockets were loaded with rocks, we carried our jabbing and stabbing weapon, but—where were the Brits? CS canisters came flying at our feet, and we picked them up, still smoking and flung them back. The choppers thrummed overhead, invisible washing-machines whooshing through cloud-banks, *slosh, slosh, slosh.* Their dye-bombs no longer bloomed in gay colours, but sludged into the ragged grey soup. Only when you entered a spout of the stuff did it coagulate, clinging to you in crytsal granules of pink, purple, yellow. And when it covered your skin, it would not come away on your hand, but smeared into the oils of the flesh until you were painted like an aborigine.

A cloud of gas billowed in front of us. New gas. Healthy and vigorous, like bread-dough rising. Through the white screen a solider came leaping, as if clearing a barrier. Behind him, his mate emerged, clothed in ghostly togas of gas. Slowly they advanced, brandishing rifles, step by step, inch by inch, intent on occupying ground. More men emerged. Their line spread out across the field, intending to clear it, now stark and robotic, now vaporous and dream-like, swallowed by drifting gas.

The gang that Mick and I were caught up with retreated grudgingly, yielding a foot of ground only paid for with a barrage of rocks. Still the soldiers came on. Then the cry of treachery rose behind us.

"Snatch-squad!"

Out of the State Forest six Brits came galloping on foot. From the other end of the brook, six more from the windbreak hedge. We broke for the Border. Some of us outraced the snatch-squad and leapt to safety over the brook. But others were not so swift, or lucky. Down went soldiers and rioters in a dire struggle. I had to credit the Irish. They fought ferociously, hand to hand. They were fighting to escape arrest. If taken north of the border, what could they expect? A beating? Jail? A spell in the Kesh? Some of the boys crossed back over the brook to make sure the snatch squads were outnumbered, and knew it. After all, if there were twelve of them, there were hundreds of Irish. They were fighting against Internment—their own. Time was critical. The other Brits in the field were coming rapidly to the aid of the snatch-men. The Irish fought desperately, hellishly, with sticks and boots, fists and bare hands, and they fought through the net without a single man taken, pulling each other, pushing the Brits away, throwing them down, until finally they stood free on the soil of the 26 Counties and could look back and survey the spectacle of their fierce escape, soldiers in flak-jackets writhing in pain on the ground of Occupied Ulster, a hop and a jump away.

Together the pick-and-shovel brigade and the corduroy battalion gathered about the grease-and-mud-stained bulldozers pulled up at the knoll in the road on the southern side of the border. Floating dregs of gas were drifting away as the deepening gloom fell over the field, the forest, and the road to Rosslea.

A man climbed the knoll overlooking the still uncompleted fill-in, with the loud-hailer in his hand, to address the troops with their SLRs and gas-masks. John Kelly was a well-known Republican from the North. He had been interned in the Six Counties during the Border Campaign of the Fifties, and he was on the run again now. The men who gave the orders to British troops in the North, Brian Faulkner, Ian Paisley and the rest of the Stormont regime and the Orange Order, the UVF, the UDR and all the bigots and anti-civil rights forces of the Loyalist diehards, would love to lay hands on John Kelly. But, at this moment, he stood to face them openly, just beyond their reach.

"Today we have seen British democracy. Today we have tasted British freedom. Here they lie—sunk in the mud of a road in Ireland!"

Three young boys stood with John Kelly. One clapped, one raised two fists in the air and jumped up and down, one put two fingers in his mouth and whistled.

"And who did these high ideals to death? There you see them— for underneath all the protestations of law, behind the smoke-screen of propaganda, is the mailed fist of naked force, for all the world to see, honest at last, and as brutal as ever!"

Wildly the crowd hooted and cheered. A banner unfurled, green in the deepening twilight, and bold lettering shook at the soldiers:

SINN FÉIN DUBLIN SOUTH JOIN THE REPUBLICAN MOVEMENT

"For it is only by this brutal, deliberate, calculated use of force that an empire can be shored up! They talk about violence? We condemn the official violence we've seen here today! We condemn the waging of British war on the Irish people on Irish soil!"

The crowd went delirious.

"Let the world know that we aim for peace, but we will never settle for peace at any price! The British government can have peace any time it wants. They know our demands. An end to Stormont. An end to Special Powers. Withdrawal of the British Army. And the final abolition of this illegal Border!"

The crowd at his side, the assembly at his back, Republicans, one and all, who stood with John Kelly, every man, woman and child, that evening by the road to Rosslea, were wild with a thirsty, hungry joy of resolution.

Calm and reasonable, John Kelly's voice rang out: "Let the British Army be warned—withdraw from Ireland—or suffer the consequences!"

Chapter 9

Our Secret Weapon

The Fall of Stormont came only two days after our battle with the British Army by the road to Rosslea.

So you couldn't blame the Cumann Billy Reid if they put the two together in their minds and said to themselves, by God, we've got the troops on the run now.

I went to the Cumann meeting on that Wednesday evening and shared the elation that seemed to course through all the comrades.

The afternoon previous the news had broken over Ireland. Doors opened in the hallway at 56 Upper Rathmines Road. Just as on the Sunday of the Derry Massacre we gathered in Eileen and Angela's flat down the back to watch, in amazement this time, rather than grief, dismay and anger, the bulletins crossing the screen on Telefís Éireann,. Again, the phone was ringing out in the hallway. Krishna and Mick, Bernie and Martina, our network lit up the switchboard at the telephone exchange.

Something which had seemed so permanent and formidable as to be adamantine, even eternal, was suddenly gone.

Poof. A bygone era. For fifty years, and a bit more, since 1921, Ulster had been ruled by the Unionist Party from its parliamentary redoubt on the lawns of Stormont Castle, outside Belfast. Now, with a decree from Whitehall, in London—not even by a vote in the British Parliament, or any kind of referendum by voters—merely with a wave of the hand, and a phone call—Stormont was gone.

Swept away by the dustman's brush.

Sent packing by order of Ted Heath.

The British were washing their hands of their lackeys in Ireland.

Henceforth, said their announcement to the world, it would be Direct Rule from London for that troublesome little province in that obscure corner of their formerly worldwide Empire, a benighted, neglected, downtrodden place which could not even be called a part of the home island, but which was obviously so maddening because it was a part of bloody Ireland.

So up the stairs in Paddy Clarke's we trooped that Wednesday evening to our meeting room with pints in our hands and a bounce in our step, and in truth, at that point, we would have followed Alita Hughes anywhere, even if it were up the Shankill Road on the 12th of July in the teeth of King Billy and all his parading Orangemen.

Chairman Alita dispensed with the usual meeting minutes and so on in rapid fashion in order to get to the next Action on the schedule for the Cumann Billy Reid: a three-day Hunger Strike, like the one we held back at Christmastime, to be undertaken again at the GPO in O'Connell Street.

"We'll be public witnesses—on the occasion of Easter Monday, the 56th anniversary of the Easter Rising—to protest the continuation of Internment—now that Stormont's gone."

Gone was the Party that gave you Internment. Gone was the world's most cartoonish puppet of a so-called Prime Minister, the egregious Brian Faulkner, the architect, chief advocate, and evil genius of Internment.

In the past several years, Ireland had seen elections and reform movements and marches and riots, pogroms, pitched battles and ambushes, Prime Ministers and MPs coming and going; the sudden rise of Civil Rights, Burntollet Bridge, the Battle of the Bogside, the fall of Terence O'Neill and the fall of Chichester-Clark; Jack Lynch and his Merry Men assembling Irish Troops on the Border, only to ineffectually pull them back again; the trial of Captain Kelly and the Fianna Fail ministers, the Split, the dawn raids of Internment, the Blitz and Bloody Sunday, and survived them all.

Only one of them, Bloody Sunday, compared in magnitude, or meaning, to the Fall of Stormont.

No matter what the future might hold, we in the Republican Movement had won the first of the objectives we listed for our Liberation Campaign back at the Ard Fheis in November—the Abolition of Stormont—and it was a great victory for the Struggle.

Fulvio Grimaldi was departing Dublin and he was throwing a farewell bash for the comrades at the North Star Hotel.

Grimaldi was the chap from Milano who became the darling of the newspapers and radio interviewers after Bloody Sunday. 'The Italian photo-journalist,' he was dubbed. But he was known throughout Europe as a leading member of the left-wing Milan outfit, La Bandera Rossa.

Grimaldi was a tall, handsome, sandy-haired man with a dashing touch of Alpine ski-instructor about him. He captured the hearts of Dublin the second Sunday after the Derry Massacre when the Movement put him on the podium of the flatbed lorry at the GPO. His photographs of that day in Derry had flown around the world on the wires of Reuters and UPI, and the lasting impact of the print-images of the incident came from his camera. "I have traveled in many countries," Grimaldi told the people from the railing with the bunting in O'Connell Street. "I have seen many civil wars and revolutions and wars," he told his rapt audience, in fluent, if accented, English "but I have never seen such a cold-blooded, organised, disciplined, planned murder."

Now Stormont was fallen and Grimaldi and his comrades had accomplished all they could for their Irish brethren and it was time for them to be leaving the country.

The North Star Hotel. A long, low-slung white-brick block, straddled by the shadow of the Loop Line railway bridge in Amiens Street. I remembered it from my first day in Dublin, but at that time, I hadn't known that the management were Republican supporters. The Gresham or the Shelbourne wouldn't have hosted a party such as Grimaldi was throwing.

Over the broad doorway to the backstairs ballroom on the ground floor, a long white banner was hung:

VICTORY   TO   THEIRA

Over the back windows behind the stage that was shadowed by the gritty black-iron railway bridge across Talbot Street, another banner read **VICTORY TO THE NVA**. Multi-colored balloons looped over the chandeliers of electric candles. Flags and posters all over the walls: the green, white and orange of Wolfe Tone, the green, white and red of Giuseppe Garibaldi, the red, black and yellow of Yasser Arafat, Huey Newton in his wicker chair, the PLO, with their head-dresses of red checks, Frelimo in bandoliers, Workers of the World, Unite! *Solidarietà sempre.*

I came along with an eye to re-visiting that familiar little slice of Dublin where I'd first landed, now so many months ago. Sheila came along with Aisling because it was a cheap night out that we could afford, a night away from staring at the four walls. Krishna came with Jane Quill on the closest thing he'd ever get to a date. Mick O'Corrigan came on a real date with Bernadette Cullen. She had to share him with Martina Kelly because nobody had seen Brendan McAndrews for a long time now. Even John Martyn brought along a lady-friend: Alita Hughes, who told her sister Maureen, who was tagging along, "if anybody tries to make anything out of it, you tell them I paid for the tickets."

Leaders of the Movement were there that night, too. Ruairí Ó Brádaigh brought his wife and the PD brought their sweethearts and girlfriends from up north. Dáithí Ó Conaill was there with Maria Maguire, the darling of the tabloids. Seán Ó Brádaigh and Joe Cahill and Old Joe Clarke in his wheelchair were together under the one roof with long-time comrades they had Split with, Cathal Goulding and Tony Heffernan, from Gardiner Street. Paddy Kennedy and Ivan Cooper, SDLP MPs from Ulster, Terry Kelleher, the editor of the Hibernian Review, Tim Pat Coogan, the historian of the IRA, who was an editor of the Irish Press. Such was the mood of farewell and reconciliation inspired by Grimaldi's leave-taking. If Tom Wolfe had been there, covering the event for The New Yorker, he would have called it a gathering of the "radical chic of Amiens Street."

"Speech, speech!" they called, clinking glasses for Grimaldi.

He held his arms up in a Nixon-style V-sign. "No, no," he cried. "We want to sing for you, comrades!"

La Bandera Rossa came out on the stage with guitars, mandolins, trumpets, banjos and a tambourine, and began to sing in Italian,

Sono farmuolo Irlandese . . .

which caused the audience to chime in, hilariously, in English, *Oh I am an Irish plough-boy . . .*

Grimaldi clapped his hands, everyone stamped their feet, and when the song was over, Grimaldi made his longest speech of the night. "We have translated many of your songs into every language we know, so that when we go back home, and when we travel through the world, we can explain to our comrades the Irish Revolution—with the original music, too!"

I found Krishna in a corner with Jane and a couple of his contacts, Mohammad Moneim, from the Arab Office in Grafton Street, and Kader Asmal, a professor at Trinity, who was a Palestinian married to an Irish woman, and who was himself the Chairman of the Committee for Human Rights in Ireland. They were chatting with Terry Kelleher and Des Halloran, also from the Hibernian Review.

Krishna introduced me to Kelleher and Professor Asmal. Sheila and Aisling began chatting with the professor's wife, who was from Kildare, and had also brought their daughter along for the party. She was called Fatima, a name with sacred associations to both the Arabs and the Irish.

Kelleher was just saying he'd seen a broadside on the Derry Massacre posted around Dublin by a young Stickie poet called Hayden Dunphy, a poem that he thought deserved wider circulation. Tim Pat Coogan joined in and we all talked about the impact of Yeats' poem in the wake of 1916. Which brought Krishna round to the mention of a poem I had written on the burning of the British Embassy, and Kelleher and Halloran enquired after my credentials and then said they'd love to see what I'd done. So we opened negotiations to get it into either the Hibernian Review or the Irish Press, which ran a literary page in the Saturday edition.

"Now everybody listen!" shouted Grimaldi from the middle of the dance-floor. "Let's everybody sit down in a circle, eh? Like this." Fulvio sat on the floor, crossing his legs under him. "That's it. Join hands. Okay. And we go round the circle and each one must give us a song!"

Mick O'Corrigan said, "Where I come from, there's a little song we made up, to the tune of 'The Wearin' of the Green,' and it goes like this–."

> *Oh, Paddy dear, and did ye hear, the awful things they say?*
> *Princess Margaret and Lord Snowden they have joined the IRA!*
> *Aye, they're drillin' in the mountains, to the sound of fife and drum,*
> *Young Tony's takin' snapshots, while Maggie fires the gun!*

> *While Maggie fires the gun, while Maggie fires the gun,*
> *Young Tony's takin' snapshots, while Maggie fires the gun!*

Some of the Italians on the stage looked baffled trying to follow the words, but they picked up the melody and the tempo and jumped down anyway, banging the tambourine and plucking the banjo.

"Second verse!" shouted Mick.

> *Ah, now Paddy dear, and listen here, there's ructions in the land,*
> *The Queen and DeValera, they're walkin' hand in hand,*
> *And what's the funniest thing, me boys, that you have ever seen?*
> *Prince Philip playin' polo on his ass in Stephen's Green!*

> *On his ass in Stephen's Green, on his ass in Stephen's Green!*
> *Prince Philip playin' polo on his ass in Stephen's Green!*

Then the songs came thick and fast as the ballroom rocked to the rumble of a train passing over the elevated line behind the back windows. John McGuffin, from the PD, got up and sang 'The Men Behind the Wire,' telling the origins of the song in the barbed wire boredom of the Nissen huts of Long Kesh—he'd been one of the lads picked up Internment Day himself, and was in for six weeks. All together, our Cumann sang 'Billy Reid.' A gang from up north got up to sing a song I knew well, and I banged my palms on the floor, in time to the tune, shouting "Woody Guthrie! Woody Guthrie!"

> *This land is your land*
> *this land is my land*
> *From the northern highlands*
> *to the Arran Islands,*
> *From the hills of Kerry*
> *To the streets of De-e-rry—*
> *This land belongs to you and me!*

I held Aisling in my lap and clapped her hands patty-cake for her, in time to the rhythm. Then it came to my turn and I asked them if they knew a song called "Joe Hill," and everybody did, to my surprise, so I asked them to join in and help me along, and we all sang,
> *I dreamed I saw Joe Hill last night,*
> *Alive as you and me . . .*

Internment was continuing, Grimaldi had gone home to Italy, Sheila was working at Duggan's Bakery, I was babby-sitting at home and moonlighting with Mick when the odd-job of painting came up. Mary was home sleeping daytimes in Leinster Square, Jane doing the reverse, Krishna stuck in his room downstairs. Everything as usual, topsy-turvy, upside-down, people all over the map, coming up to Easter, on Sunday, the 2nd of April. One night at No.56, I said to Sheila, "Did I remember to mention we're doing a fast this weekend?"

"No. On Easter Sunday?"

"Easter Monday, too. Isn't that your Independence Day, kind like the Fourth of July? We're going three days without food again, at the GPO, like last time."

"What are you protesting this time?"

"Internment—North and South."

"Well—it's Easter Weekend—I'm taking three days off."

"Yeah? And?"

"I think I'll go home to Mayo."

I shrugged. "Of course, of course."

"It's Easter, and I can take the weekend return. Save us a bit."

"Did I say anything?"

"Mammy and Daddy will be glad to see their granddaughter."

"Honey, go. Say hello to everybody for me. And wish 'em all a Happy Easter."

"Besides—who knows when we'd get the chance again. I'm lucky Mrs Duggan is giving me the time off in such a busy weekend for the bakery. But then—she's a mother, you know?"

Sheila was picking pennies out of her hand-bag, counting them up.

In a circle, we knelt, squatted and reclined under the portico of the GPO. Cross-legged on blankets, leaning, backs against our tuckle-bags, shawls draped over our shoulders, some using the pillars for their support, Cumann Billy Reid followed the Debate of the Acolytes.

"We are the party of physical force," insisted Mick O'Corrigan.

"But that's the just the point," I said. "History is why we're here."

"Don't talk in riddles. What does that mean?"

"Look—we're trying to stage a demonstration—why here? Why not in front of the Allied Irish Bank across the street?–or the Television Club?–or just any-old-where. Why this precise spot? Because this is holy ground."

"This is not Croagh Patrick. It's not Lourdes."

"In the sense that this is the very spot where the Easter Rising martyrs sacrificed themselves to save the nation."

"All you fookin' philosophers are the same. All we're trying to do here is have a good, simple, regular old-fashioned go at the Brits."

"No we're not. This time we're supposed to win," somebody put in.

"And haven't we won before?" said another. "Do you think Connolly and Pearse dyin' on the spot where you're loungin' yer arse at the moment wasn't a victory for the Irish people?"

"Then why are we still here, so many years later?"

"And they were men of action—they weren't sittin' here cross-legged like some hindu mojo-man—they weren't talkin' here—except the only language the Brits understood. Or understand, still."

"Let the comrade have his say," Krishna refereed. "Criticism is not unhealthy—as long as it is constructive—in fact, self-criticism is the duty of the Movement, continually."

I said, "I'm not saying it's religious mumbo-jumbo, or like unto the opiate of the masses—but there is a mystique attached to the noble failure."

Mick said, " You're making a big mistake, you know?—confusing everything up—it's all so simple—you can't pick everything apart, and look for hidden meanings, at the same time you're doing it—you just have to do it."

"How did we get onto this?" Martina Kelly complained.

"What else is there to do?" said somebody. "Sit here and starve?"

"That's gallows humour—right? Right?"

"That's what we came here for," said the always-serious John Martyn.

"Aye," said Mick. "And you call that action? What we had that day up on the border—that was action."

"Not everything we do is so direct, Mick. But if you think that Terence MacSwiney or Thomas Ashe didn't act against the enemy, you're wrong. Starving themselves to death was a deed, and a strong one, an almost invincible action—just as much as Michael Collins ever accomplished with a gun."

"Don't lecture me about MacSwiney or Ashe or Collins —I'm a student of history meself, lest you forget."

"We can't forget—none of us can forget—we're here because we remember—you see that lot passing us by, looking down on us? They're the ones who are trying to forget—and they can't, either. If anything, we won't let them, and that's why we're here—to make sure they don't."

"History," I intoned.

"I still don't see how you can make out the Famine coming into it at all."

John Martyn spoke up. "The Irish have a secret weapon. We've employed it in all our wars of national liberation—down from the monks in their round towers in the times when they were under attack by the Danes. It's not a bomb. It's not a rocket. It doesn't come from our superior technology, which we haven't any, nor from our wealth of natural resources, because we have none of those, either—or, none to call our own, that are not sold out to the Canadians—it comes from the fact that we've gone through this long history of suffering, deprivation, and national calamity, including the Famine, chief of all—until we've turned it into our defence, and our pride—the weapon the British enemy used, to try to stamp us out altogether, genocidally, turned back against the very perpetrators themselves."

Someone laughed rather bitterly. "Isn't that Irish logic for you."

"We've taken the anonymous, mass slaughter of un-named and un-heralded millions, dying unbeknownst by the roadside—and focused it, like a prism focusing light on a blade of dry grass till it bursts on fire—from the hapless death of millions in chaos, down to the deliberate self-destruction of a single human being—that's our secret weapon."

Bernadette Cullen shuddered. "And when you think of it, it works, too. The world paid more bloody attention to Terence MacSwiney dying on hunger strike than it did to all the poor suffering creatures of the Famine."

"Yeah, yeah," said others, "didn't the newspapers follow it day to day like a soap opera."

"Who was the last Republican to die on Hunger Strike?"

Nobody seemed to know, but a separate argument developed on that question behind one of the pillars, until someone concluded, "It's shocking we don't even know ourselves."

Martina Kelly, who grew up in the West, leaned forward. 'Does anyone ever remember feeling guilty about the Famine?" She gave an involuntary twinge. "I remember, when I was a little kid–"

"And a gorgeous wee thing you were," said Mick, delighted at the thought.

"Shut yer gob, you feckin'—male chauvinist!" said Martina indignantly.

"Time out!" said Krishna. "Martina—continue."

"When I was a child, studying in school, and we were made to learn about the sadness of the Famine—I remember thinking, why did God let me live, and not them? Jesus—the horrible things we put into the minds of children."

"But we have to," said John Martyn. "The Famine was the Holocaust of Ireland. We should never forget."

"And it confers a great guilt on all of us," Alita Highes put in. "Because if ever a people had a reason to rise and revolt—but they didn't, and fell into their mass graves without a protest, the length and breadth of the land."

"That's not entirely true," said John Martyn. "I've read where there was plenty of resistance. Why, the country was full of edible bread-grain, even at the worst time, in the middle of the Famine—the Brits had to reinforce their troops here to guard the grain-wagons going up from the midlands to the ports, for export to Britain—it was being sold in England as a cash crop by the absentee landlords—plenty of those trains never made it."

"True, true," said someone from behind a pillar. "But it was a sporadic rising. Disorganised, split up, spontaneous—that too went down as lessons to be learned for the future."

Mick O'Corrigan looked disgusted. "Well, if we resisted at the time, even if it was sporadic—and just another noble failure—then why feel guilty about it? After all, we're alive, aren't we—and we didn't even ask for life, did we? We can't help that they died, and it's none of our fault."

John Martyn said," "Well, the version you get of it is like everything else, from Strongbow to Parnell—depends on which side of the Irish Sea you're standing—but, to save their own conscience, the British started the rumour, which became the myth, which some will repeat down to this day as a fact—that the Irish were responsible for their own demise—that they gave up, and went to the roadside to die in their rags—that they begged for the Big House to save them, but they wouldn't work to save themselves—that begging with a bowl, they were still too stiff and proud to go into the Workhouse where they would've survived—it was put about that God killed them, for their wickedness—or how else would a Paisleyite, even today, explain to you such a devastating act of Nature as the potato blight?—see what I mean?—the Irish were cursed, and good riddance to all their race—and that's the way the Oppressor got the Victim to cooperate in his own destruction."

"Sometimes I think God did forget about us."

"Aye. And in His place, he sent us the Catholic Church."

Mick O'Corrigan said, "I'm sick to death of all this guilt ballocks. You ought to lock up all the intellectuals in a confessional and throw away the key—the priests have them so bloody guilt-ridden."

"Is that what we are?" I laughed. "Intellectuals?"

"Right. Bloody hammering it to death."

"God forbid that you should get your convictions shaken, Mick."

"You'll never, I know what I'm about."

"We're not saying you have to agree. Just be able to discuss it reasonably. What I'm saying is we're using a moral weapon because we're engaged in a moral confrontation."

"Indeed. Let us not be immoral."

"Don't be such a cynic about everything."

"Mick's simply being a realist," said Krishna.

"Another country heard from," said Mick. "Well, what's the realist say?"

Krishna considered a moment. "The moral weapon is a correct one to use against the British, because if they have a weakness, it is their haughty moralistic puritanism, comrade. After all, their argument in the North is that it isn't right to break the law. Now, to be a realist, we must admit that the Struggle is a Struggle of the mind as well as the body—that the mind is one with the body—therefore, starving the body to win a psychological victory in a psychological sector of the war is correct tactics."

"All right, all right. Don't get your knickers in a twist."

Saturday, the first day of our Easter Fast, was shopping day in O'Connell Street. Shoppers flooded the city centre with a sigh of release at the coming of the holiday. The morning was foggy at first and then turned wet as we huddled close to the pillars of disputation and warmed ourselves with argument, but the afternoon cleared, and, unlike Christmastime, when it was so much chillier, in the warmer weather of the opening weekend of April, instruments appeared, out of pockets, cases and blankets, guitars, fiddles and, to my astonished eyes, an accordian.

Danny White played the fiddle. Roy Blaney on banjo. Our own Peadar Kenny, tin whistle. Jimmy Kane on the box, squeezing off reels and jigs. I moved over to watch Jimmy's fingering on the keyboard. It was not a full-size squeezebox, only 12 bass-buttons and an octave and a half on the keys, a child's beginner model, bright red, but Jimmy knew his way around it. "Do you play yourself?" he said, noticing my interest.

"I do, a little," I lied. I'd been trying to forget the ten years of lessons for some time now. "But I haven't played at all in the last six years, or so."

"No excuses," said Jimmy as he pulled off the shoulder-straps and handed me the box.

I explained that I grew up on Italian tarantellas and Serbian polkas, back in the States, and my Irish repertoire was limited. "Do you guys know the Washerwoman?"

"What key?" they said.

"Key of C?"

"Go on."

"I don't have a C-whistle," said Peadar.

"Okay," I said, "slowly, please."

They let me do that for about the first two A-parts, and then started to quicken the tempo. I struggled to keep up but they pushed me on, and after three A's and B's, I was done.

"Give us that back," said Jimmy with a grin.

"I didn't pass the audition?"

"You said yourself you were out of practice."

Everyone laughed and someone said, "Good man, yourself," and clapped me on the back, and I basked for a bit in the era of good feelings.

Then, in keeping with our earlier discussion of the Famine and so on, I asked them if they knew 'Fields of Athenry,' and they played that for me, with Peadar leading the lyrics till everyone joined in on the chorus, and we made the pillars of the GPO echo with ringing music that afternoon, as we cycled through all our Republican favorites.

> *Take it down from the mast, Irish traitors,*
> *It's the flag we Republicans claim,*
> *It can never belong to Free-Staters,*
> *For you've brought on it nothing but shame!*

By the time Saturday evening came, we were getting quite hungry, and after watching all day the parade of shoppers intent on the pleasures of spending their hard-earned cash on some of the things that man lives for, such as company in the house, the relations you see only once a year, roast goose, curried pheasant and stuffed chicken, all the good things of Easter to eat, the topic turned, naturally, to food.

"Herring roes." "Kidney soup." "Marinated kippers, my mam used to make." "Roast leg of lamb, lamb livers, lamb brain, lamb tongue." "Boiled cabbage—ugh!–if I never see another pot of that–." "Boiled crubeens!" "What in God's name is that?" "Oh, that's a delicacy—boiled pig's trotters—the nicest part of the animal, so it is." "Coddie and colcannon." "Mashed turnips." "Cucumber and leeks, Visitor's Trifle, treacle bread, oatcakes and boxty, barmbrack and whisky-cake, toffee custard and strawberry flan!" "And, oh, the Guinness, that's good for ye." "Stop! You're killing me!"

The darkness of Saturday night settled down, and the fog, and the shoppers evaporated from O'Connell Street, leaving the young ones, out for the night in the clubs and the dance-halls, clinging close to one another in the shadows of the doorways, when the pubs called time. One after another the comrades on fast turned over on top of the blankets spread on the cold pavements and pulled more covers up to their chins to go to sleep. Two in the morning. Three o'clock and the mist crept over us and we were heedless. Our minders, the watchful uniformed gardai, crept into their police cruisers to doze.

At some point I woke, catching my breath. The darkened roof of the portico loomed high above us. I rubbed my cheek on the coat-collar pulled up around my head. I peeked out over Bernadette's shoulder, next to my chin. Rows of hips and elbows. I sneaked a cigarette out of my coat-pocket, trying to move by centimeters so as not to wake anyone. I lay there smoking.

. . . is this how the slaughter comes to the sheep? Because we fear to wake them? Where is our shepherd? You are the shepherd.

But the pillars of Samson's temple tower over me with an overbearing weight. And the roof of heaven is so vaunted high . . .

I must have dozed off—and when I woke with a start, it then galled me to think of Sheila picking pennies out of her purse. Not that we could afford the fare to Mayo and back for the three of us. But I know that she'll spend the weekend lying, pretending, covering up. For me.

The family will never learn that she's working, and I'm not. Go to sleep, you maudlin fool—it's great running around playing the big revolutionary in the daylight—*but let the night come, and you're afraid of the dark . . .*

Sunday we made music again. It rained in the morning again, but we kept ourselves dry under the portico, and warm with our singing. Danny White played the fiddle. The rain increased and the gardai gave in and put on their raincoats.

After Easter Sunday mass, the street began to fill. The flatbed lorry arrived and the traffic horses went up. Everyone joined in to set up the rally. The rain slowed up and the musicians stepped up the tempo as the audience gathered.

Sunday was the Movement's day. O'Connell Street belonged to the Republicans. To the true heirs of 1916. The speechmakers bestowed their finest rhetoric on the 56th anniversary. There were tributes to Connolly and Pearse. Reminiscences of O'Donovan Rossa. Quotations from Fintan Lalor and Thomas Davis. Reminders of the border, renewals of the vows taken after Bloody Sunday, reviews of the Fall of Stormont, and predictions of the Victory to come. The coin canisters jiggled through the crowd. The assembled throng listened in the waning drizzle, and went home happy to their snug, Easter holiday, family get-together weekend, their duties fulfilled, their guilt assuaged, their allegiances re-dedicated.

We hunger-strikers went back to our blankets for the night.

Easter Monday was Independence Day, and O'Connell Street would belong to the official state apparatus of the 26 Counties, the official cars, the elected officials of the Dáil, the TDs and the Senators, members of the talkshop at Leinster House, the government in office which the other governments of the world recognized, but which we did not.

The flag of this so-called Irish Republic was the same Irish Tricolour of Green, White and Orange which our Movement flew, the banner of the Irish War of Independence of 1918-21, bought and paid for by the sacrifice of the patriots who fought and died in that war, following in the footsteps of the Martyrs of 1916. But we said, 'Take it down from the Mast, Irish traitors," because that's what the government was to us, the bastion and refuge of those Free State opportunists who had sold out their country by accepting the Partition.

Likewise, the armored cars of the so-called Irish Army, which so distinguished itself in Cyprus and on the Golan Heights, so far from the devastated homeland—where the Volunteers of the 'outlawed' IRA gave their lives for Irish freedom.

Today was the day of The Big Parade. The Big Parade of the Big Lie.

Now everybody loves a parade. And the people came out to line O'Connell Street in droves from end to end. The green, white and orange bunting hanging from every cornice in the street the whole weekend long grew brighter as the afternoon sun broke out like a flashbulb. The strolling politicians waving to the crowd. You couldn't blame the people. The people of Dublin, to me, were salt of the earth. Fathers holding up little kids to see. Fingers pointing at the rumble of tank-treads.

They were the same people who, the day before, on Sunday, had turned out to cheer and support the Republican Movement. You couldn't blame them. They were proud of their country. They were proud of their Army. And Jack Lynch and his Fianna Fail, the ruling party, spared none of their money, collected from taxation, to entertain the ordinary citizens on this one day of the year. Divisions of the Ancient Order of Hibernians from New York, Chicago and Boston paraded in the line of march. Units of Irish organizations from London and Sydney followed in their wake. A great day to be Irish. You wouldn't want to miss it. Pipe bands and accordian bands and kilted bands and uniformed bands and floats from the big department stores and the building societies and units of police and fire engines, and, oh, what a grand parade.

Only the people didn't flood over the island in the middle of O'Connell Street to listen to speeches in the rain, as they had the day before, but remained behind the lines of gardai, glued to the footpaths where they were told they belonged, because in the street, the saddled gardai were walking their muscular horses up and down.

"There goes the Fianna Fail," Peadar Kearney remarked as he put away his whistle in his pocket.

We hunger-strikers watched from under the brow of the GPO as the Land-Rovers of the Irish Army rolled by, and our thoughts turned to the Republican prisoners in Free State jails.

Chapter 10

Riot at the Joy

I winced in the semi-dark, my back to the room while Sheila and Aisling slept. To save shillings from the greedy mouth of the electric meter, I had a candle fixed to the kitchenette table. Our one window was slightly lifted and a breeze slipped in underneath it, disturbing the flame and throwing wavering light-shadows dancing over the cooker and the walls. I wrote out the title again:

A House Is Burning in Merrion Square

It was the two-line refrain repeated at the end of each stanza where I had to get the rhythm right:

Remember one Sunday in January
And the dead in the streets of Derry.

I crossed out "one Sunday," and changed it to read,

I sat back. *Leave it there, for now. Look at it again in the morning.*

Books stacked on the table cast a deep shadow on the flickering wall over the cooker to my left. Vol. IV of *The Collected Works of Mao Tse-Tung.* Title page turned up: 'The Yenan Forum on Art and the Revolution.' Krishna. Others in the stack were volumes I chose myself at the Rathmines Library. *The Exile of John Mitchel. The Life of Garibaldi. The Little Green Book: Quotations from P.H. Pearse.* 'Butcher's Dozen,' Thomas Kinsella's poem on Bloody Sunday, cut out of the Irish Times for me by Krishna.

And then there was the mysterious Captain Bayo, who made his mark with the Madrid Republicans of '38, only to disappear in the wake of the fabled Lincoln Brigade, and materialise, years later, in Castro's column, marching into Havana. Marching with rhymed feet. Through the refrain of Revolution. My eye strayed across my name, signed along the bottom of my library card on the table: *Nicolas Petrovich, Cultural Worker.*

When I woke, it was morning in the window.

I had fallen asleep with my head in the crook of my elbow and one arm stretched across the table.

I lifted my head, stretched, yawned, made tea. Sheila had left for work at the bakery without waking Aisling and me. Before the child woke, I changed it back to 'one Sunday' again, for the sake of the rhythm . . . it still wasn't right. I changed it again, then, to read

And I thought I'd finally got the meter and cadence, and the sense, right . . .

Then I flipped the page and began a new poem.

I was now expanding the manuscript I had started in Mayo, adding new chapters carved out of the struggle in the factory, the work of the cumann, the battle by the road to Rosslea, my wanderings through the pages of the thought-leaders of the past. Sometimes I had to scribble as fast as I could because a burning sensation would grip my fingers, as if my nerves were on fire from a flashpoint in my brain, where words were rolling across a smoking white screen, and I had to copy them down quickly before my hair was singed:

> *From far, the voice of the roaring Tatu,*
> *mingled in twilight with birds of dew.*
>
> *Liu Ting Chiao is one hundred centuries old,*
> *made of thirty iron chains, a serpent of bold*
> *design, flying above the chasm of Tatu.*
>
> *But the planks are gone, and the men are few*
> *who dare to swing, hand by fist, on the bare links,*
> *under fire from every crack and clink*
> *of the enemy cliffs: the first to try*
> *is the first to die.*
> *But as his body drops, straight as an arrow,*
> *through the canyon of the narrow*
> *gorge, ten more arise,*
> *and under the disbelieving eyes*
> *of the enemy, dance and swing,*
> *hand over hand on the groaning*
>
> *chain—as if to defy*
> *the obdurate sky.*

The child woke me when she got up. I had fallen asleep again with my head across the scrawled lines.

William Whitelaw had come to power in Ulster by edict of London. The personal appointee of the British Prime Minister, Ted Heath's little boy. Nothing could have been more revealing of where the real power in the North lay than the manner of Brian Faulkner's departure.

Like an errant schoolboy, Faulkner was called to London for "talks" on the 22nd of March. The Headmaster, Heath, gave him a choice: accept Whitehall's takeover of all security powers belonging to Stormont, or he would abolish the parliament of Ulster.

After fifty years of the puppet dancing the puppet-master on a string, to the puppet's tune, the shadow hand of Britain was cutting the strings, taking off the blackout glove, and descending to the stage, a naked fist.

Faulkner ran home to Belfast, his tail between his legs, but he got no comfort there. His erstwhile colleagues, the Unionists, his own party, gave him a choice, too—refuse Heath and resign in protest, or dangle in the wind of London's desertion of him. Faulkner was loath to let go the reins—for a couple of days more, he temporized, but then, he faced up to it, and resigned on the 24th.

The Prime Minister is dead. Long live the Secretary of State. Isn't that how the refrain goes?

It is, when London's calling the tune.

Newly-appointed Secretary of State for Northern Ireland, William Whitelaw, arrived in Belfast with his brief stocked with concessions, gestures and promises. One of his first acts of office was to declare an amnesty for the NRM and NICRA organisers who'd been jailed on the mandatory 6-months count for breaking the ban on demonstrations. Next he announced he was going to release the Internees.

He closed Magilligan, the notorious concentration camp in County Derry. The first batch of prisoners came home. More would follow, Whitelaw promised, in batches, at intervals, dependant, of course, on the proviso that, with Stormont gone, and the British Army in sole charge of security, the war with the IRA could be wound down.

"He's holding our prisoners to ransom," was the verdict of Mick O'Corrigan, one afternoon at the talkshop in Jane and Mary's flat. "He's made effin' hostages out of them."

"You telling I?" said Krishna. "He's damned clever, that Willie, too damned clever."

He was there in the newspapers every day now, on the telly every evening at nine, on the airwaves all week. There was no haven from the kind-smiling English country squire, with the mantle of hair grown white with decades of doing his duty, and the fatherly voice, full of good advice: Uncle Willie.

"You know what he wants from us," said Mick. "Surrender. And he's not getting it. Why should he, when we're kicking the liver out of the Brits."

Nobody could now legitimately say that the truncated province had independence or self-government of any variety. That was the Unionists' reward for fifty years of sucking-up, alternated with fits of pouting, exchanged for bouts of arse-licking, followed by seizures of deliriums grandioso. The Occupied Six Counties were now just a precinct of London, Westminster's ward-of-the-state; and Ted's bully-boy on the corner, the British Army, who were posted there to keep the restive step-child down, strained at the leash. Whereas at Christmastime, there had been 650 internees, there were now, four months later, nearly a thousand, despite the batches released. Both wings of the IRA, Provos and Stickies, vowed to fight on.

The reaction of Dublin was more subtle. The Fianna Fail government of Jack Lynch, which stood idly by when the thirteen were shot down in January, and half-heartedly attempted to save the British Embassy in February, welcomed the Fall of Stormont in March, and in April, stepped up their campaign of border surveillance, to appease Ted Heath. Lynch started hunting down militant Republicans south of the border, to arrest and jail them, to quiet his critics on the right in the Dáil, the Fine Gael. To the surprise of the naive, but not the cynical, the Catholic Church, whose flock in Ulster the Provos defended from deadly pogroms in Free Belfast and Free Derry, issued a call from the bishopric of Maynooth for the 'RA to cease-fire.

North of the border, the SDLP, whose slate of MPs at Westminster had vowed all the way back on the first day of Internment to boycott the Parliament in London till the very last lad was out, sided with the bishops.

"The worms are itching to crawl out of the woodwork," said Mick, "and sit up in their seats and talk like men."

Among the people, the proverbial sea in which the IRA had to swim or else sink, the Nationalist camp was beginning to show cracks: renegades, peace-mongers and dividers. In the ghettoes of Belfast and Derry, where British soldiers stopped you in the streets every hour of every day, and boarded buses with pads and pencils taking names, and watched you with their surveillance cameras and telescopic view-finders from hidden observation posts in lofts or under factory-eaves, *No Surrender* remained the battle-cry. But elsewhere—"anyone well-off enough," said Krishna, "or far away enough from the agro—I telling you, they're always the last to act, and the first to weary."

"What puzzles me," I said, "is the Unionist reaction. Come the Fall, and not a murmur. Where's the backlash? Where's the imminent civil war they've been scaring us with for months?"

"They're still a shower o'shite," said Mick. "Didn't Billy Hull with his LAW join up with the Vanguard and that Nazi, Craig—first time ever—and throw that big protest in Ormeau Park?"

"They might have rallied," I said, "but they didn't riot in the Shankill—they haven't attacked the ghettoes—and they haven't attacked the Brits in Sandy Row, for that matter. It's strange."

"Not so strange," said Krishna. "I telling you—the Army is our lads, you know?–now more than ever."

"And as for the ghettoes," said Mick, "maybe they're just biding their time—if I know our fellow Irishmen, they'll find the trick where to play their Orange card."

"I telling you, comrade, look out for that Willie. After all, fifty years of Stormont is gone—what more do we want?"

Mick got up, rubbing his hands. "No, comrade. The war's not over yet."

"What are you reading?" I asked Mick.

Mick tucked the book under his arm as he got ready to leave. "Brigadier Frank Kitson," he said. "The British Army Manual of Counter-Insurgency Tactics."

On Thursday, I made my rounds. I spent the morning minding Aisling and Desmond while they played outdoors in the back garden. Then I dropped the child off at Duggan's at 3 pm, when Sheila was getting out: something sweet from Duggan's display case, like a milk-cream Viennese strudel or, her favorite, chocolate apricot-jam cake, was our daughter's daily treat, her reward for doing the big-girl job of walking her mother home from work. Then I walked down to the Pearse Street offices of the Hibernian Review to drop off the clear copy of my poem to Terry Kelleher. Then round to Fleet Street to leave a copy with the barman for Des Halloran when he dropped in. By then it was time for Krishna's Office Hours, about four, so I went upstairs in Bewley's in Grafton Street and waited at the white-clothed table in the palm-potted bay-window corner. Krishna came in, greeting me with, "Wuz de scene, man?"

"I was at Kelleher's."

"Is he going to print it?"

"It's in his hands."

"Good. We can use the frontage. Sometimes it's not a bad idea to get your name in print. Sometimes the more people know you, the more protected you are. I telling you, comrade—that way, at least your friends, when they read that little item in the inside page where it says you've been picked up?—they'll go looking for you. When you are anonymous, they hit you and nobody at all objects."

"What's the matter, Krishna."

"Nothing."

"You look nervous. What've you been up to?"

"I've been on the phone to London. From the GPO. Got through to Tariq himself this time. That was good. Caught up on all the news—at the meeting, I can tell the cumann—what the Anti-Internment League's got in the works across the water."

"Good. Is that all? Why do you keep looking around?"

"Now—when you get that poem in print, we send it to Ali. Then, when the crunch comes, and you have to go there, he knows you."

"What are you going on about? You're freaking me out. You're unusually paranoid today."

"If you ever see me in the street, and I walk by, without recognising you, like this—I don't turn my head—don't seem to see you—just keep going, because it means I'm being followed."

"Were you followed today?"

"Not to worry, I didn't bring him here, comrade."

When I hit O'Connell Street later, the Evening Press carried a fresh headline:

JOE McCANN SHOT DEAD IN BELFAST

When the newsboy went down the step to sell a paper, I nicked a copy from the top step of Eason's. I read the account on the No. 14A home to Rathmines.

> A spokesman for the Official IRA maintained that Mr. McCann was unarmed when he was spotted in the Markets area of Belfast by a squad of the Coldstream Guards on foot. The Army has refused comment, but the spokesman for the Marxist-oriented Officials stated, "The squaddies are shown photographs of wanted men every morning—Joe hadn't a chance even to give himself up." McCann, alleged to have been the commander of the Officials' 1ˢᵗ Battalion, Belfast Brigade, was high on the wanted list since Internment was instituted. "Joe was gunned down in retaliation for the Provies' bomb blitz," the spokeman said. "Two days previous in Belfast, the Provisional IRA detonated 40 bombs in what has been taken by observers as a show of strength in

response to Secretary of State William Whitelaw's latest initiatives and calls for a unilateral IRA cease-fire from other quarters of the community."

On Wednesday night, Chairman Hughes was not happy with the cumann members for not selling their quota of papers in the pubs that week.

"You know how it goes, comrade," said Krishna at the conference table. "People are voting against the bomb blitz, by withholding their weekly donation. This week—I telling you, it will be different—Joe McCann was very popular. They'll buy up, to read our reply to the Stickies' accusations. Everybody loves a family spat."

"We are not putting out a gossip column," said Alita.

The table grew unsettled. Everyone remembered how Alita banished her own sister. John Martyn finally spoke. "Unfortunately, I think the bishops' call for a cease-fire on our part has influenced some of the faithful."

"We don't need their sort," said Alita. "Sunshine patriots. Weekend warriors."

"No guerilla army can afford to alienate the support of the people," Krishna stated.

"Do you think we might leave the theorizing aside," said Alita, "as a practical matter, a matter of getting our business done?"

"But this is very practical," I said, feeling like I should come to Krishna's defence.

If Alita Hughes had had a gavel, she would have thrown it at me.

I blustered on. "I'm not so sure the bombing is helping us anymore." I looked around to find fidgeting and staring at the table-top. "People are getting war-weary."

"I will not permit defeatist talk at these meetings," said the Chairman, firmly and finally.

"Comrade, comrade," Krishna counselled. "Nobody is questioning you. We are simply discussing what has become an issue."

"Joe McCann was brutally eliminated this week—and you people sit here and talk as if to aid and comfort the enemy!"

Everyone objected at once. "Alita, we're just talking among ourselves." "Nobody's listening in on us." "Don't be too sure." "You can't stifle discussion." "Self-criticism is the duty of the Cumann."

"May I remind you, one and all, that we are the political wing of the Republican Movement. Military tactics are none of our business."

"You're the one who wanted to know why we didn't sell papers last Friday," said Barney O'Toole, the dustman.

When Barney spoke up, the rest of us heard the voice of The Liberties—Dublin's underclass.

"This is your first meeting in five weeks," Alita shot back at him.

The meeting ended in discomfort. Alita left the pub downstairs so abruptly, we were all sure she was going straight round the corner to Kevin Street "and tell on us."

John Martyn sighed, and said to us, "We've ruffled her feathers, I'm afraid." Then John followed her quickly out the door.

"Rubbish, isn't it?" Mick O'Corrigan said to me at the bar as we ordered pints. "Thanks for starting it," he said to Krishna. "She's been asking for it for months, but nobody had the nerve to speak up."

"She's getting impossible," I said.

Bernadette and Martina tried to make peace. "Can't you boys give Alita a chance? You know what it is, Martina?"

"I do. They can't stand having a woman over them."

"Bernadette, you can stand over me anytime," said Mick, with his trademark twisted grin.

"Oh, dún *do* bhéal. That's all you ever think of."

Krishna and I looked at each other. We stood apart when the Irish started slagging one another. It was the curse of the native race.

"Maybe Alita's hoping for Joe McCann to come back to life," said Mick, "and I'll tell you, that's just what that woman needs, is a good stiff Stickie between the legs."

There was a knock at the door of our flat.

"Are you going to answer that?" Sheila was crying because we'd had a fight. I'd come home hungry, there was nothing to eat in the house, I asked her if she'd brought home any cakes, she said, yes, but we ate them, why don't you go and get those Sinn Féin pals of yours to get you your dinner, and burst out crying. Now she slumped in her chair as I went to the door, while she was saying, "I'm not at home."

"Phone call for you, Nick." Eileen, from the backstairs flat, looked up at me, afraid she was intruding. "It kept ringing so long—." She backed away apologetically.

I mumbled something and went to pick up the receiver dangling from the wall-phone. The line said, "Hello?"

"Uh—yeah—hello?"

"This is Mary. Do you remember me?"

I hesitated: the voice wasn't familiar.

"One night you said—you'd do us a favor—if we needed it."

"Uh—."

"It's just for one night. Now do you know who I am?"

"Yeah."

"Can you help?"

"Yeah. I guess so. I mean—I'll figure out something."

"It's all right then?"

"Right. First door on the corner—."

"We know." The voice went away, but came back. "Thanks ever so much." Click.

I hung up slowly. I put my hands in my pockets and went slowly back to the flat. Eileen was still by the open door. "Is everything all right?" she said.

"What? Yeah." I was shutting the door in her face. "Just fine—thanks."

"Who was it?" said Sheila. Her voice was small and weak. Aisling was in her lap, cuddling her mother, her light-haired curly head laid against Sheila's dark shoulder.

"Someone's coming."

"Who?"

"I don't know who he is." I went to sit in the window and watch.

"What is it then?"

"Someone who needs a kip for the night. Someone who has less even than we do. Someone who hasn't even a place to put his head down for the night." I didn't have to spell it out: Sheila knew exactly what I meant.

"We'll go," she said.

I looked at her from the window. "Where?"

"Down to Angela and Eileen's—or upstairs to Josephine's—haven't I looked after her kid for her, often enough?—I'll tell them we had a fight, that's all."

"My business is in the hall enough already."

"Well," said Sheila wearily, "I suppose your man would like a cup of tea." In a few minutes after the kettle whistled, she said, "The tea is steeped now. We're going. You should collect Aisling in the morning. At Josephine's. I've to let myself out early for work."

It was raining out when the slight, dark figure came up the steps to spend the night at No. 56 Rathmines Road Upper.

Jeremy Flynn, the estate agent, was an affable sort, always full of the chat, always dressed up, rain or shine, in one or another of a wardrobe of checked sports jackets, always with a smile and a handshake for the missus when he came to collect the rent, promptly at five of a Friday. And one of his dodges was to always leave his Triumph TR3 double-parked out in Rathmines Road. That way, he could take the money and run—"Sorry, love, really must go—double-parked, you know."

But Jeremy didn't care to visit that long any more once he found out that Sheila was working and I was not, and that I'd be answering the door. "That's the lad—always the exact change. Some of our tenants think I'm a ruddy bus conductor! Well—till next time. Ta!"

Nowadays the rent of six pound ten bob a week was coming off the top of Sheila's eleven-ten a week from Duggan's instead of my 17 and 10 from Maurice Woolf's. That left exactly five quid in round numbers to parcel out through the week for the support of three people, one of them not yet three years old.

Desperate times called for desperate measures.

Clothing was out of the question. New shoes for the growing kid? Forget it. When Sheila went home for the Easter weekend, it wasn't a holiday excursion—it was a relief expedition.

Shamelessly, Sheila dropped in, while she was home, on a girlhood friend of hers, Mary Grogan. Mary was married to Edmund Grogan III, who had a big house, ensconced in its own wood, which he'd inherited from his parents, and he'd set himself up as a gentleman farmer, which meant he never did any work if he could help it. Still—the Grogans were well off, or, so everyone said.

"Mary had to show me the house, naturally, what with all the years I'd been away, and of course, I oohed and aahed over her four children, so polite and well-mannered and well-dressed, as we poked into all the wardrobes and all the chest-of-drawers and all the old sea-trunks. Edmund Grogan I, the grandfather, had brought them home with him from Cape Horn and Australia, years and years ago." Sheila was telling me the story. "And every one of her kids with Clark shoes! 'Mary,' I said, 'I remember when we were kids, Daddy used take us up to Hiney's twice a year, in Crossmoliney. Even when he was out of work for months, when he was with the foresters, we always had a new pair of Clark shoes to start school in. And I searched and I searched in Jordan's and Filene's and all them big stores in Boston, but you never will find shoes like that in the States. Now, Mary, are you sure you won't need these for Fiona in a year's time?' 'Well, if I do, says Mary, I'll know where to find them, won't I?'"

I realized sadly, as Sheila was talking, that these stratagems of hers were necessary, in her mind, to keep news of our destitution from reaching the ears of her parents and the rest of them.

It was also a godsend that she had found work just down the road in a bakery, Duggan's of Rathmines.

Mr Duggan wasn't about as often as Mrs Duggan as they had two shops at opposite ends of Rathmines and he spent most of the day in a traffic jam trying to get from one to the other. But the missus was as good as two misters. Sheila said, "The missus would use the string we ties the boxes up with twice, if she could get the customers to give it back when they were done with it." Another story: "One Monday morning, at half-four in the morning, Mrs Duggan found rat-turds in the cupcake frosting, and wee zig-zag tracks of their feet over an entire tray of them. 'Must've popped out while we were away for the night,' says she, 'the little biters. Ice 'em over again and put 'em back. I'll not have my profits eaten up by rodents!—at least, not the four-legged variety.' But let Mrs Duggan find fleas in a sack of flour she'd bought and paid for!—and not the Holy Pope Himself could make it right with a dousing of Lourdes holy water! Mrs Duggan'd be on the horn to every minister in and out of office, until she had the operator's ears red with the language. 'Well, that's a fine state of affairs when you can't get a sack of flour in the whole country without fleas makin' their bleedin' beds in it. Of course I want my money back. But what I really want to know is what are you going to bleedin' do about it! Such folk ought to be behind bars!' However, this did not apply to Mrs Duggan herself. She'd go the Queen of France one better. 'Let them eat spider's web!—I have the cleanest roaches in Dublin city!' Everything into the big batter-mixer– dust, crumbs, flakes, the lot. Then she'll stand there, hands on hips—'Don't bite your nails over the mixer, please, dearie?'"

It was thanks to the Duggans and their bakery business that we ate at all those weeks. Between stale baked goods and day-old bread and ten-pound sacks of potatoes our weekly diet consisted of starches and frosting for breakfast, lunch and dinner, daily.

Still I grew thinner and thinner. It was embarrassing beyond bearing to covet the food going into Sheila, who was working, and Aisling, who was growing, so I had to push a pencil on other stratagems. I sat down and budgeted our four-and-a-half quid per week of available food money, once the electric-meter money was deducted first, so that we could have lights till Thursday next: an exercise in self-delusion. So much for tea for Sheila, don't fancy it much myself—so much for milk for the child—at 1.03 Irish punt per gallon at Campbell's or the Five-Star Supermarket! And the brother-in-law, Pat Blake, with a whole dairy farm in Mayo! The tea, 98p for a loose pound, mince meat at 88 new pence per pound, eggs 53 p per dozen, that leaves so much for cigarettes, which neither Sheila nor I could get along without—something had to be done. Here's what we did. Sheila would scrape off the confectioner's sugar from the little round biscuits at work into a paper napkin which she would fold in her apron pocket to take home. At home, she would put two drops of milk in her tea to color it, then open the napkin over the cup. Ah. Lovely. Tea with milk and sugar. I would drink coffee, most times, once a day, which would come about by Krishna standing me one at Bewley's when we met for office hours. For nourishment, I would drink a pint of Guinness once a week on Cumann night when the comrades were going for it, as they knew I was impecunious.

In these circumstances, we actually ended up eating better than ever as necessity became the mother of shoplifting.

If I was going to steal it, it was going to be worth stealing. Tenderloin steak. Kidney lamb chops. Inch-thick pork chops. Fat, juicy Castlebar sausage. Luscious black pudding. Delicious white pudding. No chicken or mince-meat. That I paid for. It was part of my routine. I would arrive at the Five-Star Supermarket, where Rathgar Road branched off of Rathmines Road, or at H. Williams, a little further down on the right, past Madigan's, bundled up in my Navy pea-coat, not unusual in a rainy climate where the temperature rarely went above 21 or so Celsius. Underneath, I wore a shirt, and over it the grey woolen cardigan I got in Mayo, a hand-me-down from Sheila's Uncle Martin, whoever that was, and this cardigan was tucked into the belt-line of my trousers all the way round the waist, and then inched up, to billow out, forming a baggy pocket that wasn't visible under the pea-coat. I'd take a shopping carriage and stroll through the aisles, fussing over a list in my hand, watching the housewives and the supermarket help over the tops of the shelves, sticking a can of peas here, a jar of carrots there into the cardigan at the small of my back, maneuvering myself over to the meat counter.

When the butcher went inside the double-doors, and the housewives looked self-absorbed, I'd pick up a steak or a plastic-wrapped tray of chops, with a packet of mincemeat. The mince-meat went into the shopping basket and the chops into the cardigan. Never a bulge showed under that pea-coat, God bless the US Navy! My absolute favorite was the Fray-Bentos Steak and Kidney pie in a tin. I could slip three of them inside the back of the cardigan with ease, and we could eat supper for three days. I'd time it till the housewives piled up at the cash registers near the front doors and the uniformed help had to hurry to open a new aisle, and then I'd join the queue, smiling, chatting and joking, pay for the mincemeat, and walk out with our supper warming the small of my back.

The cameras in the Five-Star were my great challenge. Shiny, metallic-blue bowl-shaped vessels suspended from the sound-proofing tiles of the lowered ceiling along with the Muzak playing, they had lenses protruding in four directions. The red poster in the automated front doors warned: *Shoplifters will be Prosecuted—Cameras Operative*. They never caught me. Somehow I figured out every inch of that store where there was a blind-spot for the cameras.

But there were days I'd spend the morning planning, scheming, fantasizing, visualising the act, building up my resolve till I made for the Five-Star, with full confidence at fever pitch, only to approach the plate-glass windows on the car-park side of the store, look in and see those cameras and lose my nerve.

Once I *was* caught. It was one of those days, and I found myself having wandered away down Rathmines Road past Duggan's where I encountered a bag of five pounds of spuds on the vegetable pushcart outside the little grocery shop next to the bakery. I checked inside the dim interior, and spotted the white-aproned proprietor with his back turned, and I snatched up the spuds. I never saw the owner's boy watching me do this from the shadows.

The boy tried to get his father's attention, but the oul' fella was deep in the act of weighing up a paper bag of pears for an old pensioner in a beret, friend of his. The boy grew agitated. Then he dashed out onto the footpath to chase me down.

I was walking away toward the Wimpy Bar when a tug came at my sleeve. The boy's scared face looked up at me. He couldn't have been more than 9 years old. "Give them back," he said.

His eyes darted back and forth. He was mortified lest a passerby should catch him at this wicked act. He whispered his demand hoarsely. I thought he was going to cry.

I said, "I have a child at home to feed." My own eyes were wide with a self-righteous glare of affrontage, brutally genuine. Suddenly, I thrust the bag of potatoes into the boy's hands. "Here. Take it. Now my little girl won't eat tonight."

The boy backed away slowly up the footpath, clutching the plastic bag in his hands, as the potatoes slipped and slid inside. He went back to the outdoor pushcart under the shop's awning and placed the bag back on top of the hill of spuds, adjusting and patting the swimming plastic sack till it was snug and secure up against the pushcart wheel where it wouldn't slide off. He looked about himself warily and turned his back on the shop's interior. I knew he wouldn't dare tell his father.

That's the way with the poor. We steal from each other. I imagined the full larders of Blackrock, the actual refrigerators of Ballsbridge. We'd go steal from them—if we had the bus-fare.

I was a visitor in the land of poverty. Growing up in America, I never took a thought for food. It was always there. There was always enough, more than enough, plenty. It was the land of plenty. I never asked where it came from. My parents, aunts and uncles, retelling the days of the Great Depression they lived through, never made a dent on my mind. That was their life, not mine. They were only trying to scare me. I always believed it couldn't happen to me.

But once you descend to stealing to eat, as a regular thing, not as a lark or a prank, but out of necessity, the creeping suspicion crawls into your soul: you've taken the last step. You're down and out. This is rock bottom. You can no longer hold your head up. How in the name of hell did I ever let this happen?

Brendan McAndrews and the 'RA were back in town. Brendan was kipping awhile in the Mountjoy Hotel, free room and board courtesy of Jack Lynch and the Fianna Fail.

The phone rang out in the hall of No. 56. "Hello, John Doyle?"

"Hello yourself," I replied.

"Yours truly here." It was Bernadette.

"What is it, love?"

"Trouble."

"Where?"

"Up in the Joy."

"Oh, shit."

"Bring the comrade."

"Did you get the others?"

"He's here with us. Listen—we've got to go. Meet you there."

"I'll look for you."

I walked down Rathmines Road as quickly as I could, pulling on my pea-coat and cap. Recently, with alarms raised by shifts in the public mood, but more, with steps being taken by the Dublin government to increase repressive measures against our Movement, our little group of friends in the Cumann had spoken, half-jokingly, of using more caution, especially on the phone—no more calling people by their real names in the open. "You don't know who's listening in these days." Mick was the one who came up with 'John Doyle' for me, because that name tickled his fancy. The real John Doyle was the Chief Superintendent of the Dublin police.

Krishna wasn't in his room. I took the stairs two at a time. Only Mary was home. "Where is he?"

"He's out, visiting Ranjan and his wife."

"What's he doing there?"

"He was invited for something to eat, maybe mango juice and fried beetles, I don't know, and he took Jane."

"Have you the number to ring him?"

"No. Why?"

"Nevermind." I was rushing out again when I stopped. "Look—give us a couple of bob, will you?"

"But what's the matter?"

"Mary, I have no time for puzzles." I grabbed the money from her hand as she was pulling it from her purse. "If he comes home, tell him to shift his arse up to the Joy."

From the upper deck bus-window, I could see billowing smoke rising, and red lights swiveling, rimming the rooftops of the city centre. The high hill of Mountjoy Square was beckoning. At the bus-rank in O'Connell Street, when I was letting myself off the still-moving rear-deck, the sigh of fire-engine sirens gave out, fading in and out of focus. As I went hurrying up the crowded footpath, people were looking for taxis to get home in or cafes to get out of the way in.

At the Rotunda, traffic butted into a logjam from three directions. Traffic cops were snarling everything up by directing people to turn back, away from Parnell Square and the hill of Dorset Street; while motorcycle cops were ramming their bikes between back fenders and front bumpers, trying to force a passage through and get moving uphill.

I slowed down and skipped between the cars in Parnell Street, swiveling my hips, slipping sideways, setting off protesting horns. I went up to the top of Parnell Square past the offices of An Phoblacht and behind the back of the Garden of Remembrance and cut up the hill by the Granby Lounge, trying to take a circuitous route up to Dorset Street. There I saw an ambulance careening through the red light while cars peeled off to the kerb in front of it. Drivers were changing their minds and reversing directions to head back down Dorset Street, away from the North Circular Road, where all the sirens were wailing.

I crossed over Dorset and went up by the Protestant church in St Mary's Place. Paradise Place was quiet. Blessington Street hushed and quiet, cut off from the noise. But when I swung into Berkeley Road and rounded the curve below the Carmelite church where five streets met, I thought I was too late.

Twilight was falling against a violet backcloth of turgid clouds massed in the east over Dublin Bay. The last lights of the dying sun behind me fell over my shoulder to gold-plate the monumental cornices of the Mater Hospital. Before its pillared temple facade, lorries of the Irish Army were filing out of Eccles

Street past the small, triangular, black-railed green flanking the Berkeley Road Church, with its gnarled apple trees and ancient headstones. Across the brow of the massive hospital, the sun electrolized the bold-face gold lettering of the Latin masthead: MATER MISERICORDIAE.

Down at the corner of the hospital wall, where the rear of the grounds met the North Circular Road, a full-scale riot swirled. I ran up Berkeley Road past the church toward the agro. Now I could see the violet mask of the sky was embroiled with a widening, inverted funnel of oily black smoke pouring out of the roof of Mountjoy Prison, across the road from the back of the hospital. I slowed as I pulled up even with the Army lorries and almost fell in with the lines of soldiers, marching double-time to the riot alongside them. What the hell's going on? I looked over the heads of the surging street. And spotted Martina Kelly.

Overturned cars were staggered in the intersection of Berkeley Road and the North Circular. Someone was rolling a burning rubbish bin down the incline of the North Circular towards the front gate of the Prison, where the beleaguered Gardai, who had come out of the Garda Station directly beside the end of the prison buildings, were pulling at their collars to loosen their necks, wiping the sweat from their foreheads with their sleeves. Chipped paving stones and bricks and bottles flew through the air down the street at them as the rioters took a running jump and then ran back again. A CIE bus was burning in the intersection. The soldiers of the Irish Army were trying to beat their way in past the makeshift barricade of cars as the numbed gardai tried to beat their way out. A thousand people milled in the street, shouting, screaming, giving out orders, yelling threats, throwing their missiles. I grabbed Martina and yelled into her ear, "What the hell's happening?"

She turned and looked at me with a smeared, streaked face. "I don't know, I don't know. Nobody knows. They're inside—there–and we're outside—they set their beds on fire, and nobody knows what to do—thank God you're here."

"Where is everybody?"

"I don't know. I haven't seen anybody. Alita's here, and John. I came with Bernie and Mick, but now I don't know where they've got to. I think I saw Peadar. Did you bring Krishna?"

"He wasn't home. He's out at some dinner with Indian friends of his. Did you bring Mick?"

"I just said so!"

"I can't hear a thing! This don't look good, Martina—." We were shouting. "Don't look good at all."

"Come here." She grabbed my hand and led me down the North Circular towards the main gate of the prison. We stopped short about fifty yards from the lines of gardai. From the bus shelter under the high back wall of the hospital, we could see over the roofs of the warders' cottages. Under the burning roof of the prison, a row of faces could be seen, inside barred windows. The glass was broken and men had their arms out, waving. Martina shouted in my ear. "They've taken over the A-wing. Nick, Brendan's in there. If the soldiers or the pigs get in, I'm afraid they'll kill him. They won't let them get away with this without an awful beating. What are we going to do?"

"Who's in charge of this fucking riot?"

"I don't know, but I'm afraid for Brendan—I know him, he won't take it sitting down, I know he won't."

"Where's Bernie? Where's Mick?"

"Over there they are."

We spotted them behind the burning bus in a council-of-war with Alita, John, Bernadette and Peadar, and a knot of others I didn't know. When we got there, Mick was shouting at Alita. "What did we come here for if it wasn't to fight the troops?"

"We didn't call this riot," Alita answered hotly. "We didn't want it. They're rioting inside, and that's all. We had no control over that. We're only here to prevent bloodshed and wait for Kevin Street to settle this!"

"Wait for Kevin Street! What are they going to do?—send the Ó Brádaigh boys up here on their ass'n'cart to ask the soldiers to please go away?"

"Mick!" said John Martyn. "It's important to settle this without reprisals to the prisoners—we've got to give the prisoners a chance!"

"Let me go," said Mick. He looked down murderously at John's hand on his arm. "Let me go, John, or I won't be responsible!" He tore away and turned to run off in the gathering gloom of the North Circular Road in the direction of Phibsboro.

Bernie grabbed me. "Go after him!"

I said to Alita, "Is anybody in charge of this thing?"

"It's a riot, comrade. What do you think? Where did all these people come from?—kids—skinheads—the dregs of the North Side!—look at them!—it's a lark they're having—our enemy is the British Army, not the Irish Army—this is all a breach of discipline—Kevin Street's on the line to O'Malley this minute, I tell you!"

I ran off. Bernie called after me, "Bring him back!"

I found Mick in Geraldine Street. In a lane beside a back-garden of a Berkeley Road rowhouse, there were people bending over milk-cases. "What are you doing, Mick?"

"Give us some of those," said O'Corrigan. He pushed a loaded milk-bottle into my hand. "Are you with me or against me?"

"I'm just along to see you don't get lost. Bernie's worried about you. She's acting like she's in love with you, or something, God help her."

"Bernie's in love with herself."

"She's the one who sent me after you."

"Well, she'll have to wait. Right now I'm busy. Come on."

We took a pair of petrol-bombs apiece and headed for the mouth of Goldsmith Street. At the corner, we peeked out on the wreckage of the North Circular Road.

The dying flames of the burnt-out bus flung a hologram of light on the charcoal-grey walls of the prison. Rotating red lights cut a pink swath through a cloud of CS gas drifting off the pavements the way a foul frost of bog-gas drifts from a bog.

"There's your negotiations," said Mick.

Refugees from the broken barricade were crouching along area railings and crawling for shelter down basement stair-wells, coughing and sputtering, while the search-lights on the prison guard-towers swept the street, punching holes in the oily smoke-clouds to light up the Army joining forces with the gardai. "What happened?"

A man in a cutting North-Side voice who was helping one of the injured to get away said, "Baton-charge. They're getting reinforcements in, to the prison gate, up from Dorset Street."

"That's what you get from Jack Lynch when you ask mercy," said Mick. We pulled back into Goldsmith Street to get out of the way of the gas and Mick started to unbutton his trousers. "I can never keep an undershirt."

We tore his tee-shirt in shreds and made masks for our noses. "These are no good without water or something to soak them in," I said.

"Hold it out, I'll piss on it for you," said Mick, with a wicked laugh.

At the bottom of the street, we could see the troop-lorries edging forward in the Berkeley Road. "Now's the time to hit them, before they get organised."

The petrol-bombs were effective street-weapons. A layer of sugar in the bottom of the glass was there so that the fire would stick when it splattered. Sometimes they didn't explode when they hit, but only shattered. But the sight of the ragged flame sailing through the air, with the gleam of glass toppling end over end was fearful enough to seasoned riot police—to the young, untrained and untested recruits of the Irish Army, they were a good deal more terroristic.

Thus, the street-fighters would rather face the troops than the gardai. The gardai knew them and vice versa. The gardai bore them a grudge from the fight at the British Embassy, when they got no help from Lynch or the Army or anybody. The troops were outsiders, called in for this sudden, unscheduled emergency—it was their first time in the streets. In all the period of the Troubles, since '69, they had never been called out against their fellow Irishmen. Their idea of service was a tour on a U.N. Peace-keeping mission overseas. Nobody knew how the agro in their own front garden would react on them. Would the rank-and-file follow orders from officers to assault citizens on the streets of Dublin? Such a thing hadn't been seen since the Civil War of the Twenties. "Somebody upstairs must've got nervous," said one man. "Somebody lost their head," came the reply.

When the petrol bombs hit and splattered, they cleared the intersection in the North Circular Road quickly. The government forces were thrown into disarray. There were two commands, Army and police, and wireless sets only confused the issue. To complicate everything, the fire-engines were trying to get down the road from Phibsboro to fight the fire in the prison. The warders' families were huddling behind locked doors, scared out of their wits, and a special detail of gardai had to be stationed in the gates of Arranmore Ave. and Cowley Place to reassure them. At the hospital wall opposite, the regrouped police maintained ranks, but it was the Army in their gas-masks who were trying to dismantle the barricades to get the fire-engines through. The brave, or foolish, or foolhardy police did without masks. They wore handkerchiefs, scarves and napkins, like the rioters. The Army were exposed in the street, the gardai protected by the wall, armed with their batons, equipped with their riot shields. The Army were encumbered with rifles they had slung on their backs, which they had no orders to shoot, while the police were itching to crack heads. The rioters took aim and showered the hospital wall with petrol bombs, and a small tree became a golden bloom of fire.

From the corner of Goldsmith Street, Mick pointed. Three Army lorries had breached a hole in the barricade before they could get no further, and now they stood with their tailgates drooping, while soldiers jumped down. "The second two in the queue," said Mick, pointing. "Straight down the filling-pipe."

He tore off rag-sections with his teeth to make wicks for each of us. Then he stuck his box of wooden matches between his teeth so he could use both hands. He loosened the rag in the throat of his milk-bottle, and, tipping the neck into his palm, soaked the rag. Then he dabbed the ends of the wicks. The trick was to get our wicks quickly burning brightly enough so the rush of air wouldn't blow them out

When we had our wicks going good, Mick and I dashed out into the street. Surprise was our only chance at getting away with this.

Fuel-tanks under the lorry-beds. Long, straight filling-pipe, extending up at an angle from the under-carriage behind the cab.

I jumped out between the first and second lorries. The cap was pulled down over my eyes, the mask was over my nose, the pea-coat collar was turned up. I had the glass bomb in one hand

and a bunched-up wick of burning rag in the other. The police shouted from the hospital wall. Soldiers in gas-masks came around the bonnet of the first lorry at me. I glanced quickly over my shoulder. Mick had the cap off the filling-pipe of the second lorry. I saw the pipe swallow the fiery bottle and Mick dive.

The soldiers saw it, too, and ducked away. The police at the wall were starting after Mick.

The lorry behind me exploded and blew me down on my knees. I couldn't get to the filling-pipe now, so I touched the burning wick to the rags stuffed in the bottle-neck and sent it rolling down the footpath at the troops and the oncoming gardai. Then I needed to get away. So I rolled under the lorry-bed till I came out the other side.

Mick dragged me to my feet with the wind knocked out of me. We were two crouching, stumbling shadows in the welter of smoke, gas-clouds, criss-crossing torch-beams, red and blue lights revolving, and sweeping searchlights, and our only hope was to disappear into a pool of deep darkness, and quickly.

But when we got back to the corner of Goldsmith Street, and were swallowed in a curtain of darkness, we were still not sure of our pursuers, so Mick was dragging me along, crying, "We've got to get out of here," as I was trying hard to catch my breath again.

Then it was suddenly quiet and we knew they hadn't followed us. Mick pulled the mask down from my nose. "Are you all right?"

"Go, go." My head was hanging, but I pushed Mick. "Let's go."

When we rounded the corner into Sarsfield Street and were headed back down to the Berkeley Road, we felt safer as we went creeping along close to the railings of the tiny front-gardens. People in the houses had their lights on, but with all that was going on, their shades were drawn. But for a single street-lamp, it was pitch dark, but towards the bottom we had to stop.

Soldiers from another lorry were debarking from the tail-gate in Berkeley Road, across from the triangular green between the Mater and the church. The Army wanted no more lorries blown, so they were halted a considerable distance away from the rioters. A sergeant strode up and down. "Form up! Form up! Single-file! Arms at the ready!" They were only steps away from us.

Mick patted my arm. "Just like the lorries," he whispered. "Pick off the last one in the file."

"Carry-arms! Double-time! Fo-o-or-*ward!*"

We caught the last man in the file still fixing the gasmask on his face. Looking up, the soldier saw his mates stepping out. He lifted his left foot to step off the kerb and Mick caught him with a foot sharp on the shin. Down he went in the gutter.

He couldn't cry-out with the gas-mask on. Mick had him on his back and was struggling with him for the rifle he clung to. The others just kept going double-time and nobody looked back. Why would they? They were worried about what was ahead of them, not behind them.

"Let go, damn you!" Mick hissed.

I stood over them. My chest hurt. My temples pulsed. I was scared. This could end badly. I kicked the soldier in the ribs. Still he wouldn't let go of the rifle. I was getting desperate. I reached down and tore the helmet back from his forehead. Terror-stricken eyes welled up at me from the goggle-glass of the gas-mask. I kicked him in the head, one, two, three times. His head rolled over in the gutter, and the rifle went lax in his hands.

Mick stood up with a brand-new-cleaned and oiled, never-been-kissed Belgian FN in his hands. He backed away into the shadows. "It's my ticket!"

Then he turned and melted away into the darkness of Sarsfield Street.

Chapter 11

Lynch Law

It was very, very late that night, or early the next morning, a Saturday, when I got home to No. 56, and was able to close the front hall door behind me.

When I felt my back against the inside of the closed door was the first time I felt safe. I stood there like that in the darkness of the hallway, unable to move.

I had crossed the whole city on foot in the dark convinced that pursuers must be right behind me.

When Mick disappeared into the impenetrable shadow of Sarsfield Street with the purloined assault rifle, I ran off the other way, my only thought to get into a side street hidden from the streetlamps of Berkeley Road as quickly as I could.

My first rational thought beyond sheer panic was to steer wide of the vicinity of the riot.

So I headed west, knowing that once I got south of Dorset Street, I should just keep turning that way and feeling the pavement beneath my feet trending downhill, towards the river.

I was desperate to get away, so it seemed to me I should try to stick close to pitch-dark residential streets—but what about when I got to the Liffey?

Wouldn't I be out in the open, completely exposed, crossing the river?

I thought my best bet, by far, was to get way upriver, in the neighborhood of streets I knew around the Mt Pleasant Flats, from the time I was working Maurice Woolf"s.

I never thought of the fog, but when I came out on the north-side quays by the little humpbacked Watling Street Bridge, I could have fallen on my knees and thanked God: there was the Liffey breathing up a dense shroud of impenetrable vapor off the water.

The fog of Dublin, then, came to my rescue as I slowed down, crossing the small arched bridge with the hand-high stone railing. All I had to do was calm myself and walk normally—not run, in a panic, as if fleeing. This was absolutely the darkest part of the river, far from the city centre, and yet a long way below the lights of Kingsbridge.

All this flight and the fright that went with it was replaying in my head as I stood there in No. 56 with my back against the shuttered and locked front door and my chest heaving.

I would absolutely have to calm down before letting myself into the flat—and hope not to wake my wife and the child.

Again, I was unbelievably lucky to find that Aisling had crept across to join her mother in bed, leaving a bed for me to slide into without waking Sheila.

I lay there for a long, long time with the covers drawn up to my chin, praying that Mick had gotten away, too, not knowing if he had, telling myself uselessly over and over to never, never, never breathe a word of this to anyone, especially the police; uselessly, I say, because each such thought immediately invoked the very confession it warned against, as I fitfully began to doze off and entered dreadful half-dreams of a big policeman with a doughy heel of half-baked bread for a face putting me up against a wall for a good Dublin lathering.

Saturdays Sheila always slept late. It was her time to catch up after a week of getting up for a four a.m. start at work.

Again, I felt relieved, as the first person I would have to prevent myself from telling was her, and when sunrise came to full bloom in the window, somewhere around six-thirty, I finally fell asleep from sheer exhausted nerves.

When at last I did wake up, Sheila was sitting there in the kitchenette in her quilted housecoat, smoking butts she was digging out of the heap of bent, twisted filters in the ashtray. "Where were you last night?"

"Huh?"

"Never mind. I don't want to know."

I crossed my forearm over my eyes and was vaguely aware of Sheila informing me that she was taking Aisling with her to go down street to visit with Jane and Mary, in case I was looking for them later. I thought she was saying this without much enthusiasm, but I was soon in a deep, heaving sleep.

Later, when I did get up, I crossed the road to Campbell's to scan the headlines in the morning papers. The takeover of the A-wing of Mountjoy by prisoners belonging to the Provos was the lead story, with black-and-white pictures of smoke pouring up from the prison roof, and photos of rioters throwing petrol-bombs. Joe Cahill, ex-commander of the Belfast Provos, and Ruairí Ó Brádaigh, too, were locked up in the Bridewell. The heat was on.

I went back to the flat. It was safer indoors, sitting still. Even the phone out in the hall, when it rang, sounded like nerves jangling.

To say that I felt changed, changed utterly, would be understating the fact. I didn't recognize myself. I had never done anything like this before. To commit an act that was so savage, amoral and cruel, and yet so spontaneous, so unpremeditated: it was beyond anything I had ever expected I would do. And nothing petty. Not mere shoplifting. I was convicted in my own eyes. I was horrorstruck to find that I had such instincts in me. I held myself guilty as charged.

And yet it was no random act of violence. No heedless, thoughtless, pointless attack. My actions were in response to the situation. I had a reason, however deeply buried within me. I was striking back at the Empire. Everything I had ever done since I first stepped foot on Irish soil brought me to that point in time. We were in a war, and when I looked into the eyes of that frightened soldier behind his mask, I was never more aware of it than right then and there. And I was damned if I was going to criminalise myself for it. This was a war I was in, a war with myself, yes, but a war nonetheless with forces far beyond me and out of my control and not of my own making. And it must be said, I felt elation, soaring high, too . . . *I had stuck my foot in, and thereby got my own back, for every injustice, every humiliation I'd ever suffered at the hands of the system, from unjustified abuse when my mother was in the throes of losing it, to the FBI wrecking my life spying on me . . . and—I got away with it!*

In the end, I answered the phone out in the hall, about 3 o'clock.

"Hello, John Doyle?"

I recognized the voice. "Yes?"

With barely-suppressed giggles, Mick said, "Mission accomplished!"

"Ah. Good. Safe home, then?"

"Indeed."

"Well, I better ring off, so. And—I shall see you when I see you."

And when I hung up the receiver, a wave of triumph nearly swept me several inches off the floor.

I thought it better to wait to see Mick O'Corrigan in person again till Wednesday night, at our regular meeting.

I could not afford the Sunday papers, but Krishna could, so I read them down at the Leinster Square talkshop. They were full of speculation. The Dublin authorities were reeling from the riots at the Joy. Cahill and Ó Brádaigh were still being held—did the government feel the Friday disturbances were not so uncalculated after all? Already they were claiming that the Mountjoy Prison, A-wing and B-Wing, were damaged beyond immediate repair. Where did they intend moving the IRA prisoners, then?

There was a big jail in Portlaoise, County Laois, and then there was the Curragh, infamous on several counts. This military camp in Kildare had originally been built as the home of the British Army in Ireland, in the centuries before independence. But more importantly, it was hated as an internment camp during the Civil War of the 'Twenties. If they opened it again, the papers warned, the Republicans would claim that Lynch was instituting Internment in the 26 Counties.

"At the bidding of Ted Heath, I might add," said Krishna. "Worse, the Civil Rights organizations might agree."

"And we all know what Internment brought to Ulster last August," I said, "don't we?"

The press was even more bleak about the developing situation in the North.

It had taken them months to accumulate the evidence and discern the trend, but now they were able to plainly state that a "wave of mysterious sectarian assassinations" had been going on in Ulster, alongside, and underneath, so to speak, the war between the IRA and the British Army—beginning back around Christmastime, or perhaps as far back as November.

John Taylor, Unionist minister in the Faulkner administration still recovering in hospital from the deadly attack on him by the Official IRA, is the exception to the rule of random killings. Mr Taylor is a politician, an office-holder, an activist. Most of the fatally done-in victims of assassination in street-corners and pubs have been ordinary people, uninvolved civilians, unaffiliated citizens. Some of the dead are Protestants, but the vast majority have been Catholics. No one in authority has claimed to know who or what precisely is behind this wave of mystery murders, but William Craig, his Vanguard movement, the UVF and UDA, Protestant para-military counterparts to the IRA, all have been making speeches rife with intimations, indeed, plain threats. To date, no arrests have been made, and it remains as if the authorities are not interested in investigation. In the wake of Stormont's abolition, the situation is deteriorating into an atmosphere verging on nightmare and seemingly calculated to instill terror.

"Now, if you were Brigadier Kitson," I asked, "what would your manual recommend you do? Wouldn't you try to terrorise the civilian population?"

"To sap their resistance," said Krishna. "To undermine their spirit."

"To drain off the sea of support where the urban guerilla sinks or swims."

"You telling I?—there's no mystery to these so-called random killings."

Monday, things got worse. Jack Lynch, the Taioseach, was falling off the fence, finally. After months of dancing the tightrope of pressure from London on the one hand and an uneasy accommodation with the Provos in Dublin on the other, Lynch burnt his fingers on the flames of Mountjoy. The Prime Minister of the Fianna Fail announced the setting up of a tribunal, to be called the Special Criminal Courts. Under decree powers invested in him by the Offences Against the State Act, the judges were to be military officers of the Irish Army. Arrests could be made on the suspicion of wrongdoing by an officer of the Gardai. No solicitor allowed to represent the accused in Court. The usual rules of evidence inoperative, and convictions to be obtained on the testimony of the police or the Army.

Other than Krishna, I saw none of the comrades till Wednesday evening at the regular weekly meeting of the Cumann Billy Reid. The telephone in the hall remained silent. I hadn't heard again from Mick. I had to wait to arrive at Paddy Clarke's to see what would happen.

Bernadette Cullen had her head bandaged, the result of a baton charge by the pigs in the riot Friday night. Martina Kelly wore a splint on a broken finger. Alita Hughes and John

Martyn looked unscathed. The members seemed to be arriving by ones for this meeting. They filed up the stairs separately, even the inseparable Bernie and Martina. I sat waiting. No one had much to say. Krishna got there. Looking at him, I was thinking, he hasn't called any office hours for Bewley's since the Joy. One face was absent—Mick. A bad omen. When Alita opened her ledger to jot down our names in attendance, we grew restive in our seats. That never happened before. The air had changed. We sat there thinking—no more holding mass rallies in O'Connell Street unhindered—no longer will we spend a night of a weekend hunger-strike peacefully sleeping on our toggle-bags in the shadow of the GPO with the kindly shepherds of the Garda Síochána watching over us.

Krishna opened discussion, getting straight to the point. "Did we really believe that Lynch was neutral?" A collective sigh of relief. Just to be able to talk about it with somebody. "Did we somehow delude ourselves that he was our friend?"

"We should have known," said Barney O'Toole. "He was always and ever England's little boy."

"But for him to go so far the other way," Bernadette complained, massaging with her fingertips her sore forehead.

Martina Kelly chimed in. "It's no different here now than the other side of the border."

"When was it ever any different, comrade?" said Krishna. "The Offences Against the State Act has been on the books in Ireland for nearly fifty years—almost exactly as long as Special Powers in the Occupied Province—there has been no more repressive legislation in the Western world—outside of South Africa."

"Is that what these Special Courts are?" asked Peadar Kenny, as a point of information. "Are they in the Offences Against the State Act?"

"Who knows?" said Barney morosely.

"John?" I asked.

"This is a separate decree, as far as I know. Meaning it's—" John shrugged—"instituted by whatever powers are given to Lynch by the Act. I think we'd want a solicitor to speak definitively on matters like that?"

Krishna said, "What difference does it make? Nothing's changed."

For once, Alita Hughes agreed with someone. "I don't see what everyone's so down in the mouth about. Special Powers never stopped Civil Rights in the North. Because Faulkner put out a marching ban, did anyone stop marching? The Bloody Sunday victims were on an illegal march. You yourselves went marching in Newry a fortnight after—or have you forgotten?"

Alita sat back waiting for someone to challenge that statement. No one did. "There'll be a demo at the Bridewell Friday night, if they're still in there. To protest Ó Brádaigh and Cahill being held without charges. We'll see who shows up this time— for a scheduled, disciplined protest." The Chairman shuffled her papers and said, "Now to the Order of Business."

Reports were given from the Secretary and Treasurer and the tally of newspapers and donations and dues covered. Evidently, Alita had made her mind up to avoid any discussion of Friday night's incidents, because she quickly brought up New Business: the Referendum on Ireland's entry into the European Common Market alongside Great Britain, to be held in the 26 Counties on May 10th.

John Martyn said, "We've known that this was coming for a long time, along with everyone else, but with all that's happened, I'm quite concerned that we haven't paid sufficient attention to this Referendum—now, with the latest—if I can see down the road, I think Lynch is going to use the Referendum as—," he paused— "a yea or nay vote on our military campaign."

"Look, John," said Barney O'Toole, "the last vote that counted in this country was 1919, the only vote that was ever taken of the people of all of Ireland, and the people of all Ireland voted Sinn Féin and a United Ireland."

"Nevertheless, if he wins this Common Market vote, he'll label it as an endorsement—a mid-election ratification, if you will—of everything he's doing—including repression of the Republican Movement."

"It's political suicide for us to oppose entry," said Peadar Kenny quietly. "We'd lose."

"Why?" everyone wanted to know.

"Because the people want the Common Market. They want to see the country moving forward. They don't want to be left out. They want all the good things that are going to come with it."

"It's going to be our job to disabuse them of some of their notions," said John.

"This is a load of rubbish they've been fed right along by the Fianna Fail," said Alita.

"That's right," said Bernadette. "It's a big propaganda campaign. And the Fianna Fail have all the money in the world to buy the media. So they're throwing money about at the people, and promises. But the people I saw in the North Circular Road Friday night are not about to vote to join England."

"That's true," said Peadar, "because those people don't vote."

"What do you mean?" "What are you trying to say?" "Explain yourself."

"I'll spell it out for you. Lynch owns the media, he wants to turn this vote into a referendum on the war, the media's killing us on the bombing campaign—."

"There's a war on," said Alita. "People get killed."

"The people of this country have no sympathy and no tears for any British soldier, RUC man, or UDA para-military killed by the Provos—nor do I. But you've all read the papers after Donegall Street in March. And now we've had the Abercorn. Anytime one of our bombs goes off and kills innocent civilians, women and kids—."

"We always give warnings," said Alita. "What do you think the Brits did with them?—in Donegall Street?—at the Abercorn? You know as well as I do. Let the British government pull out their troops, and nobody dies, either side!" Alita closed up her ledger. "I'll be going to a city-wide meeting on Saturday to discuss coordinated efforts between all the Dublin cumainn to mount an effective Anti-EEC Campaign. This meeting's adjourned."

Downstairs, Bernie said goodnight, complaining of a headache. "I'll be just as glad to be getting home," said Martina, who wouldn't have stayed behind without Bernie. Krishna, with his medical faculty background, cautioned both of them about side-effects of concussion. He advised Stephen Street was their best bet, they'd have to treat her, no questions asked. One by one everyone left till only Krishna, myself and Peadar were left.

"Conditions change," said Krishna. He was reading from the manual of left-wing activism that ran continually in his mind. "Where's Mick tonight?"

"I don't know," I said. "I don't think you'll be seeing much of Mick anymore."

"What happened?"

I just looked at Krishna. "Conditions change."

"Say no more." Krishna looked into my eyes. "I wish I'd been there Friday night. I'm sorry I wasn't."

"Hey—you would've if you could've. I know that."

"Right. I think I'll get home. Better we leave one by one."

That left me and Peadar hanging on the end of the bar. And he didn't seem to want to leave. He seemed to want to have someone to talk to, and perhaps he felt easier, being a Trinity lad himself, knowing that I'd been to university, like him. He certainly wasn't there for the drink—so I just waited for him to speak. "Krishna sounds quite the paranoid tonight."

"Maybe if I'd been kicked out of England, I'd be paranoid myself."

"Is that true, he was—deported, then?"

"Yes."

"Well, this country needs all the help it can get."

"For that matter I was kicked out of America myself."

"Were you?"

"Well—not really. They couldn't. I'm a citizen born and raised. But you might say I more or less volunteered to leave."

"I must hear that story some time."

"Peadar—what's on your mind? Maybe you'll feel better if you get it off your chest."

Just at that moment, Paddy Clarke came over to our end of the bar. "What'll it be, lads?"

"Two pints, Paddy, please," I said, and then leaned over to Peadar, as Paddy moved off to pull the pints. "I hope you have 34p, because I haven't."

"Not to worry. I can always walk home."

Paddy came back to wipe off the bar counter.

"Seen any strangers about lately?" I asked him.

"I'm keeping my eyes peeled," said he. "I like to have my friends in. You've always been good for business. I remember the nights we had singin' in here—Peadar, when you and your tin whistle needs a function room, you know where to come, don't you? But it's shockin' the things that can happen to your bar license in this town." Paddy went to retrieve the two pints.

Then he placed them on the counter before us, and I wet my stash. "I have a family upstairs," said Paddy, "and this is all we've got. We do the best we can. But when trouble comes, nobody's going to stop it. Keep your pecker up, boys."

When Paddy was gone, Peadar took a long, soothing swallow of his pint and regarded me. "I'm fed up. You know, it's one thing to fight for the Cause—like the day when we went up to the Border to fill that road—nobody went who didn't want to be there, and we knew the risks involved—but when it comes to—."

"Women and kids," I finished it for him.

"Look, Nick. I wasn't conscripted into this. My eyes are wide open. I'm from a Republican family and I was all the way in since the day I was born, and there's no question of a way out. But it's getting so you can't even bring up a discussion of the issues. Fine—let's have discipline—but let's not fight this thing with our eyes closed. After all—it's not the Cause being questioned—just some of the methods."

"So—what would you like to do?"

"I don't know." Peadar peered into his Guinness, and I thought of Alita—*'lubricates the talking machine.'* "I'd like to go one on one with Ted Heath for fifteen, and settle this whole thing." Then he looked up at me, the way he sometimes looked up from under his brow at his audience when he was playing tin whistle. "You know when we lost this thing, comrade? One night when we had 50,000 people behind us in Nassau Street. All we had to do was to turn up Kildare Street and sit them all down in the Dáil Éireann and occupy it. We could've taken over this whole country. But you saw what happened. What did our leaders on the Sinn Féin lorry do? They didn't want that. They steered us all over to the British Embassy instead. After we'd softened it up for them— after we'd left them no choice—they bring in the artillery to give it the kiss-off. The fix was in with Jack

Lynch that night. They were fighting Jack's war of independence with the Brits *for him,* in return for a blind eye on Partition. For what? So that when the Volunteers kicked the British Army into the Irish Sea, Jack Lynch could form a Fianna Fail government in a United Ireland and bring 32 counties into the EEC with a swipe of his pen? But now the wind's blowing the other way. Now it's going on four months later and we haven't kicked the Brits yet, so Jack's got the knife out, ready to insert in our backs. And you know what's going to happen? It's just going to go on and on, with the women and the kids, innocent victims, and the lads, dying, in a dirty little war, until everybody's dead, or in jail."

"You've done some thinking there, Peadar. And if I were you, I wouldn't do too much of it out loud."

The one window in our flat at No. 56 was right next to the top step and the front door and at this time of the year with the evenings lengthening we kept it open to let a breeze in. A couple of nights later a voice came floating through along with the draft of air. "Hello, John Doyle. Come open the door."

I knew that voice and I went to let him in.

"Mick O'Corrigan, it's about time," said Sheila as her favorite Sinn Féiner came strolling through the door. "You've been neglecting me."

"Hello, Mrs Petrovich, and how're ye keepin'? I thought we weren't lettin' the oul' fella in on our secret, though."

"That's right, what he doesn't know won't hurt him."

"And look at this one—she's grown a mile! Come here to your ould Uncle Mick, Aisling!"

The child, looking doubtful, was swept up by Mick into his arms and placed on his lap as he sat down with us. "What're we havin' for our dinner tonight, love?"

"Pie and chips," said Sheila. "Now that himself has discovered steak'n'kidney pie, I think he'll stay a while in this country."

"And I thought it was your attractions were keeping him here."

"That, too. Blow in his ear and he'll follow you anywhere. Followed me all the way to County Mayo, he did."

"Ah, missus, I'm goin' to miss ye, I am. Nick, she's a rare one."

"What's this new cabbage you're growin' on your chin," said Sheila as she noticed Aisling playing with Uncle Mick's face.

"I'm goin' in disguise these days."

"And why would you be missing me?"

"I think I'll steal just one," said Mick, taking a chip from Sheila's plate and feeding it to Aisling.

"You haven't answered my question."

"Top secret, love, top secret."

"Oh, God help us." Sheila stopped a forkful halfway to her mouth.

"Now, listen. You're not to worry. I know how to take care of myself." Mick helped himself again. "I do think the bachelors of this world would starve if it wasn't for married women," he winked at me.

"Even the likes of Mick O'Corrigan must have a mother somewhere," said Sheila.

"Well," said Mick, placing Aisling on her own chair again. "Come on, Nick. I'm borrowing your husband for the evening, love. We're going out to celebrate by gettin' absolutely soddin' fish-eyed drunk."

We started off down Church Avenue towards Ranelagh. "I think I might be just as glad you're leaving after the way you're flirting with my wife."

"Nonsense. She's a good girl. She meant no harm. And mind you take care of her while I'm gone."

"She likes you, you know."

"Sure, I know that."

"You're one of the few she does like."

"I'm one of the few that's likeable."

"When are you leaving?"

"Soon. Soon. I'm not allowed to say. I've been sworn to secrecy." He threw his arm around my shoulder. "Now, look, we're not going to be serious tonight about anything but the craic, do ye understand?"

"But you must tell me—while we're out here in the open air and no one's listening in—how the hell did you get home that night, and what happened to the—you know."

"It's in the right hands. You know that fella in Kevin Street? The one with the cropped head, always disappearin' into the inside door whenever we used go upstairs to pick up papers at the counter? That's your man."

"How did you get off with it that night?"

"I found back lanes you wouldn't know existed. The North Side's full of back gardens. I didn't touch pavement for miles, like. If you ever need to hide out in Dublin, north of the Liffey is your man. I just kept going over one brick wall after another. I'd toss the rifle over and be waiting on the other side to catch it."

"How the hell did you cross the Liffey with it? Stick it down your trouser-leg?"

"Now I didn't say I walked all the way home, did I? Nor do I care much for late-night swimmin' either. So—I had to borrow a milk-van."

"You took it home, then?"

"I did not. I hid it."

"All right," I said. "The less I know, the better. Where did you hide it?"

"You'll never guess. I'll tell you this—I could watch the spot from my front window."

I tried to picture the section of Mespil Road where Mick's little place looked out. "Not the Ministry of Labour! You're mad!"

"I'm not. Listen. I had a piece of fishing line lying about the house—you know, with all my gear. I always meant to drop it into the canal one day and see what came up. Anyway, under the overhang—you know how the first story juts out over the lane?"

"Yeah." I could see in my mind's-eye the high-rise, modernistic building that housed the Ministry, where Jane Quill worked daytimes.

"Down at the back, the concrete slopes down to a drain— well, I tied the rifle-muzzle to the line, dropped it down between the bars in the sewer-grate, and tied the line to the bar of the grate. Nylon, 70-lb.-test, so thin, 'twas invisible. Kicked some leaves over the grate, and—."

"And what if they'd come to clean off the clogged drain?"

"Ah, you know the Ministry of Labour—allergic to work. Wasn't the leaves lyin' there since last autumn, never raked up?"

"And what did you do with the milk-van?"

"Took it back, straightaway. It was never missed. Sure, I was prayin' your man was a heavy sleeper, though. The time I first took it, I couldn't start the motor till I pushed it by hand some ways down the lane, I didn't dare. That was a job, I'll tell ye. But I wasn't going to take any chances with that. Once I got the rifle hid, my only worry was to get caught in a stolen vehicle. But no one took any notice. They had their hands full elsewhere. Luck was with me, as you'll have it. And if a milk-van was seen out in the wee hours, what of it, wouldn't it be? Ah, but she's a grand one, Nick. A brand-new Belgian FN. Pride of the Irish Army. Wrapped her up in a bit of old canvas I had lyin' about, oiled her all over, and when I went to fetch her for your man, she was better than new. Listen—sorry I had to leave you in the street like that, but there was no sense two of us gettin' caught with it."

O'Donoghue's in Leeson Street was packed out. Girls sat in the open snug behind the front door with fellas in their laps and the fellas had another girl in *their* laps with another pint in *her* hand. You couldn't hear yourself think. After a couple of pints, I shouted into Mick's ear. "Mick—take care of yourself—and God bless."

"You won't mind if I don't write?"

"I'll see you when I see you."

"You won't see me for a long time, I'm thinkin.'"

"Just keep your big mouth shut, and do what you're told. Don't go ballistical with the heroics."

"Not to worry, not to worry. Tell me one thing, though—why wouldn't the fool let go of it?"

Attendance was down at cumainn all over Dublin. No big street rallies were being planned for the GPO. The Mountjoy prisoners were being transferred halfway across the midlands to Portlaoise Jail. And worst of all, the Curragh military camp was indeed being readied for Internment in the 26 Counties.

But there was hardly a murmur of protest. A creeping demoralization was setting in. The Movement itself carried on, defiant as always, but it was the sympathisers and supporters, among the bedrock of the nation, the people, who were frightened by noise from Lynch, by the spectre of the Offences Against the State Act. The Movement needed something big. A bomb blitz, this time all military targets, no civilian deaths. Or, better yet, one of the Provos' brilliant prison escapes. Or, God forbid, another atrocity from the Brits like Bloody Sunday.

Within the depleted Cumann Billy Reid, the lines were now irrevocably drawn. Brendan McAndrews was out of the Joy after a three-month stay, but he wasn't in Dublin at the moment.

Myles Cunningham and Mick O'Corrigan were both now long gone into the training camps and beyond. Even Peadar Kenny wasn't attending anymore because he was cramming for exams at Trinity. The bureaucrats—the Irish chauvinists, Krishna called them—"Green Tories is what they are," he said—were still in control; but reduced to two, Alita Hughes and John Martyn, they were isolated. John stuck by Alita out of sheer loyalty, but he wouldn't cut the others, either.

"No doubt," said Krishna, "Alita thinks we all ought to go over to Gardiner Place. She's stuck in time. That was two years ago now, the Split, ancient history."

"Yeah," said Martina Kelly, "time waits for no woman, eh?"

"Anyway," said Bernadette, 'where's Alita when we're getting our heads battered?"

"She's a functionary," Krishna replied. "Every movement has them—has to. I telling you—her real trouble is she has no political sense of her own—so her concept of the Movement is reduced to 'Follow Orders.'"

In the middle between the two camps sat Barney O'Toole. Barney wasn't a waverer, he knew his own mind, but both sides disgusted him with their intransigence. For the life of him Barney couldn't see why they were fighting amongst themselves when the enemy were the only ones who could gain by it. And he wouldn't help them entrench any further by lining himself up with either side.

"Well," said Alita Hughes. "What are we going to do?" No reply. Shifting in chairs. "Kevin Street is setting up a Speaker's Bureau for the Anti-EEC Campaign." No one asked a question. "They'll accept volunteers. John?"

"No, no," he said. "A public speaker I'm not."

No one was going to volunteer now because it was plain who Alita wanted.

It occurred to me, this is ridiculous. Barney won't—no confidence in himself. Why's John so reluctant?—so maybe he doesn't believe in this campaign? Krishna—knows he won't be speaking in front of black brothers. Bernadette's still recovering her composure—Martina won't go anywhere without her. But I could use the frontage in Kevin Street. "I'll do it, Alita."

Political work is dull, routine, repetitive and boring. Slaving over the phrasing of a handout. Nights at the duplicator churning out copies that you know only the dustman will glance at, and that, when he picks it out of the gutter where it was disposed of. Kevin Street wasn't Crumlin Road Jail and you got no headlines when you escaped from a meeting.

The first meeting I attended, there was a rep sent from every cumann in Dublin, with Seán Ó Brádaigh presiding, and the reps began by airing their grievances.

"I thought this was supposed to get off the ground a couple of months ago, Seán?"

"That would've been two months too late," came another.

"We're up against it from the start," said Ó Brádaigh, "and that's true."

If Sinn Féin were the government, Seán Ó Brádaigh would be the Minister of Information, with a posh suite in Kildare Street, leather upholstery, national treasures on the walls, carpets—here he worked out of a corner as big as a closet, and dealt with media characters every day who asked no questions about politics or the Sinn Fein social-and-economic programme, but wanted only the favour of the latest inside dope on gun-smuggling, bank robberies, prison escapes, ambushes, bombings, sectarian assassinations, and Provo-Stickie knee-cappings. "If we had only six more months, we could be prepared for this properly. But we haven't. We've a month—or more like three weeks."

Ó Brádaigh let the grumbling run on awhile. Not many people in the Republican Movement were as close to the inner workings of the Sinn Féin Executive, and even more, to the Provos Chief of Staff, Seán Mac Stíofáin and his Army Council, as Seán Ó Brádaigh was. He knew more than anyone at that table how difficult it had been these last months to run an underground urban guerilla war. But the men of the Army Council, Ó Brádaigh felt sure, were preparing for a political phase now. Men like Mac Stíofáin or Daithi O' Conaill or his own brother Ruairí had spent their lives in and out of English and Irish prisons, and they above all knew that the only reason for fighting the war to begin with was to emerge from underground, in the end, and make a deal on top of the table with their adversaries. That's how wars are settled—you go to Versailles for a Conference. Ó Brádaigh shifted himself.

"We're committed to this campaign. Labour is in with us, and we cannot appear to stay out. They are trying to drag us, heels first, into Europe. On England's coattails. It would make us more than ever a dependency of foreigners. They want to open up this country to the likes of every industrialist on the Continent to pillage and pollute. This is the policy of the Fianna Fail, and it's a bankrupt policy, waiting only to bankrupt the country. It's looking to the outside for salvation. It's saying we can't make a go of it without Mother England. It'll be the death of the small farmer, in the wake of every struggle going back a century to get him out of serfdom and on to ownership of his own land, the soil he toils on, and has always done since time immemorial. It'll be the end of all hope of independence, and you can toll the bell for our own initiatives. Hasn't it been bad enough for eight centuries to have our lives decided in Westminster? Do we now have our minds made up for us in Brussels?"

"Begging your pardon, Seán, with all due respect—but the tenants in Stillorgan want to know only one thing—what'll it do for the price of butter?"

"Good," said O' Bradaigh. "I'm glad to see someone's got their heads screwed on. Now these sheets I'm handing out have all the data, the facts, on the issues. Study up on 'em. Hammer away at 'em. You'll have all the support my office can give you."

They sent me to the Baymount Shopping Centre in Drumcondra for my first speaker's date.

I caught a bus in Dorset Street on the North Side and it carried me all the way out to Griffith Avenue.

There, Dermot Walsh and Henry Macken swung into the car-park of St Dymphna's Catholic Church in an old scuffed-up, creaking lorry with the door-panels inscribed Walsh Bros, Painting & Yard Repair. Dermot and Henry were members of Cumann Cathal Hughes, up in Finglas. I met their Chairman, Frank Walsh, at the meeting in Kevin Street. "Are you the fella we were sent to pick up?"

I climbed up in between them in the cab and they put the loud-hailer in my lap. "How does it work? What do I say into it?"

"Christ," said Henry Macken, laughing, "and we was counting on you, sent out from Kevin Street, one of them experts, like."

At the shopping centre, Dermot Walsh tore down his canvas top and strung up hand-lettered banners on the stripped stanchions, squared off on the lorry-bed like a triple set of croquet wickets.

DUBLIN SAYS NO TO EEC!

read one side of the lorry,

VOTE NO ON MAY 10th !

said the banner on the other side. The curious among the shoppers and housewives at the entrance to the centre gathered around the business of setting up, and ogled the fine print: *Dublin Citizens' Campaign Coordinating Committee.* Henry Macken climbed up on the lorry-bed in his raincoat.

Our first speeches were carbon copies of our leaflets and the talk O' Bradaigh gave to us that night at the organizing meeting. But each night, the first week, we would have a couple of pints in McNulty's in the Drumcondra Road, after the speeches, and we would wonder out loud.

"Do you know," said Dermot one time, "I said up there tonight that if we went into the Common Market, there wouldn't be any bicycle patches for your inner tubes in Ireland—just to get their attention, you know—because they all come from Bulgaria, says I, and Brussels wouldn't let them be imported unless they came from France. And your man in the audience says, 'Why don't we just send all the bicycles to Paris?'"

The first weekend, we tried a stunt up in Finglas, Dermot and Henry's home-ground, where we toured the housing estate in the lorry, using the loud-hailer to make it into a sound-truck, announcing meetings to be held on the hour at various corners and washeterias. We surprised ourselves with how free and inventive we could be from a moving cab–"It's like hit and run," we laughed, "and we don't have to look at their flummoxed faces before we're gone." But the idea that we went straight to the homes of the neighbors in the estate worked well. Kids and grownups alike began to turn up at the appointed corners well ahead of the scheduled time, for a block party. Finally, someone had taken some notice of Finglas.

"If only we had this type of organisation to carry out this type of thing through all the estates, all over."

"Why?" said I. "Don't we?"

"Do you think there's another team doing what we're doing?" said Dermot with astonishment.

"We are the Anti-EEC Campaign," said Henry, in his sober way.

"I thought all you chaps on the North Side had a dozen cumainn going. All with fat treasuries, too, to hear Alita Hughes tell it."

"That was months ago."

Two or three times a week, I would tour the South Side territory of our own cumann with my hand-picked team, comrade Krishna, Bernadette and Martina, and me. As the rump of the Billy Reid, we tried to cover the same territory that we'd postered so effectively for Action Day, back in March: Rathmines to Ranelagh to Ballsbridge. But this time, there were fewer hands to help, less enthusiasm, and more caution needed against the forces of the Fianna Fail, and even the gardai.

We found the whole area had its lampposts circled with the yellow Fianna Fail and Fine Gael announcements shouting *Vote Yes! To Europe.* We tore them down, or defaced them, or covered them up, as well as we could, one by one, but the next night they were back again, and our own replacements ripped down. Those two parties in the Dáil didn't even need these posters, they had money, they had the Catholic bishops, the newspapers, full-page adverts, the radio, the television: money. As the ruling party, Fianna Fail had control of RTE, the national broadcasting system, and even our Republican songs were banned from the airwaves, nor was our economic programme invited to studio discussions or debates of the issues. We were in an unequal fight. The forces arrayed against us didn't want the Sinn Fein message appearing in public at all.

Nights I was out speaking on the North Side and pacing the South Side, and daytimes I was getting four or six hours of sleep. Other than that, I was out on the hunt for food, or bringing Aisling over to Mary McKenna's to be minded while I napped, or running to catch a bus so that I could meet Henry and Dermot a bit ahead of schedule at McNulty's before starting out and maybe cadge a sandwich or a pint or at least a fag or two. I drove my three comrades from our cumann mercilessly, but by example, trying to show how long and hard I could string myself out, challenging them to keep up.

"Meet the new Alita Hughes," Bernadette jested one night.

"Oh, recovered from our headaches, are we?" said I. "The slagging match is back on."

"A couple of meetings in Kevin Street," said Martina, "and we've created Frankenstein."

It was on the written page that I became my own severest critic. There I caught myself out. I took a slashing knife to romantic notions and self-inflicted illusions. Sometimes late at night, arriving home from one of my tours, I'd sit in the kitchenette at No. 56 with my candlelight while the family slept, to re-write the progress of my political education since the night we burned down the British Embassy. I was stimulated, and over-stimulated. I couldn't sleep. Perhaps this was a phase I had fallen into, of the moon, or the muse, of two or three weeks' duration, under the spell of which I was enlarging upon the three-chapter start I'd made in Mayo the previous summer. No professors, no exams, but I was a student again, this time, learning from my peers, from my equals, my contemporaries, in the hour of our time, in the laboratory of our lives. The streets were my university, politics my classroom, the war in the North my crucible, Belfast the eye-piece of my microscope.

It was strange, but all the roiling energy coursing through me from the dramatic headlines of yesterday, today, tomorrow, the present we were living, right now, came out of me, pouring out, in verses depicting people, scenes, epiphanies— of revolutions of the past, from the tumbrils of Paris to the march of Garibaldi to the assault on the steps of the Winter Palace. Things I'd never thought of before. Things I would have thought myself incapable of knowing or understanding a year ago. Like a troubled volcano, I was at once, choked with noxious gases, and wont to erupt, and I would flow over, late at night, early in the dawn, with the subterranean rivers of the mind coagulated into pure nuggets of glistening gneiss, pumice, frozen ash, glittering lava: tear-drop-shaped poems. On my hands and knees I gathered them, arranged them on my table, gloated at their facets, hoarded my treasure, saw existence itself reflected in their hard, knotty, organic form. Like the Lorca I read of in books from the Rathmines Library, I was the lover of the Alhambra, where verses in an Arabic I could not read were inscribed on the walls, so that poetry itself, the eternal flame, was incomprehensible, in all of its thousand times and places: I became the collector of cooled fire.

I have built a wall of books,
Like an archaeologist
Collecting shards and fragments
Fallen down in the dust,

Buried by the desert wind,
Spending my days, far into the night,
Re-constructing my personal Troy.

The following Sunday, Walsh and Macken and I did the steps of the Phibsboro Church. Our routine was now honed down to a crowd-pleaser. Indeed, we were so successful, we were attracting a new kind of audience; an audience that traveled in pairs, who hovered in the back rows, keeping their hands in the pockets of their suit-coats, and went away afterward in a black, unmarked Ford Cortina.

One evening as I was going out, Jeremy Flynn, Mister Congeniality, the landlord's estate agent, was coming in. Jeremy ushered himself straight into the middle of our bedsitter, with Sheila and the child standing right there. He pointed. "I want that Sinn Féin poster out of the window—right now!"

"Go to hell! And get out of my flat–!"

"Go on, threaten me!"

"Just get out of here!"

"I'm telling you now—either that poster goes—or you go!"

The realist in me walked over and tore the poster out of the windowpane. The vindictive worm in him looked at the torn-up pieces on the carpet and felt cheated of his chance to get me.

That night I gave the speech of the campaign. We'd gone south to a shopping centre in Ballsbridge, where the better half lived and the bread-and-butter issues didn't compute. I lowered the loud-hailer to my side and began by saying, "I won't be needing this tonight, because all I want to do is tell you a little story, and I don't need to make a speech out of it. It's about the century we live in. It's a century in which millions have perished in terrible world wars, and so why should anyone bother about a few odd Irishmen dying in a little corner of a small island? Or why should anyone ask what it was all about? Far greater atrocities have happened. On a far grander scale. And the millions who died and are lost to us now—who remembers *them?* All they ever wanted was to live in peace and be left alone—and they died for nothing, too, for the world isn't that much improved, is it? How do you make sense of the hideous official violence that has visited our century? How do you rationalise the tramp up the stairs of those boot-heels, the rap on the door of those leather-gloved knuckles, the effrontery of those uniforms? One day the bombs came crashing through the roof, and that was it. That's life in our century. Try to live a quiet, unhindered, peaceful life—and hope the knock doesn't come on your door.

Hope that it comes and takes our neighbors on the left. Hope that it comes and takes our neighbors on the right. But we really do believe that it can't come for us! Just like those others did—the millions who perished. Right up to the last second, they believed. And then—it was too late. Too late. If only they'd thought, in time—let us try to do something about it—before we're the last house left in the street, and they come for us. But no, no, they did nothing. Because they always believed it can't happen to us."

"Well, it has happened here. And not so far away, at this very moment. After all, Ireland is a small place. Look over that horizon, and you can almost see the fires burning, 90 miles away."

I knew I had them when they stirred guiltily and some heads actually bowed, having seen the fires.

"My friends, if you read the newspapers, as I do, you know that they have been warning us now for quite some weeks that those fires over the horizon could spread into a momentous conflagration, throughout this whole island. Don't let that happen. There is something you *can* do about it. And you don't have to pick up a weapon and add to the misery of a whole century to do it. All you have to do is to vote on May the 10th and give a simp-le *No!* to all that. We should take Jack Lynch at his word when he tells us in his interviews of recent weeks that a Yes vote in next week's Referendum will mean that the people of this island approve of his policies—not just in the matter of the Common Market—but Lynch's part-and-parcel support of the system of official violence in the Occupied Six Counties—and, his policy of repression, here in the so-called Republic of the 26 Counties. In fact, Jack Lynch supports the status quo all over the 32 Counties, and that involves bringing on our country and on our fellow Irish men and women the system of official violence that is the curse and the shame of our century. There is something you can do about it. You can say *No!*"

Afterward, Dermot joked with me. "Did you know that it's a known psychological fact that it's easier to get people to say Yes than it is to get them to say No?"

And Henry said, "Did you see the Branch men scurry to their cars on that one? They'll have their report for tonight, and a juicy one."

But when you give your heart and soul to something you're certain sure must necessarily prevail, you want it to prevail. That final weekend, as I finished up with Dermot and Henry on the steps of the Dun Laoghaire Church, I felt a turning of the tide, and perhaps not just because we were looking straight out at the Irish Sea.

A phone call from Sean O'Bradaigh came that afternoon. There was a television spectacular planned for the Referendum Eve, tonight. "Arranged at the last minute," said Sean. "With the help of our friends in Labour. I've a contact, and I called him this week, and said, 'How would you like to appear with Maria Maguire?'"

"That would do it, Sean," I commented.

"Well—it could be a breakthrough for us, on the telly aspect. Round-table format with an RTE interviewer. Now—can you make that speech of yours for the camera?"

"Not me, Sean. Why me? I heard that speech myself from one of you in O'Connell Street. Why can't one of you give it?"

"Actually, your presence will lend that argument credibility. People expect that sort of thing from us. It'll seem more objective coming from you. And remember, this is television. It's impact we're looking for. I want people to see a foreigner who's settled here and isn't an industrialist—isn't here to fleece us of the Navan mines profits—will you do it, Petrovich?"

"Since you put it that way—how can I say no?"

"Be at the studios in Ballsbridge at 4 o'clock, for the taping. It'll be shown tonight and you can watch yourself."

We walked down the studio steps into a circle of humid light. Maria Maguire's bodyguard-chauffeur remained watching us from the shadows behind the cameras. She made a cool and formal figure. Her composure, when she met you and gave you her hand, could be chilling. You could sense the cameras responding to a cold magnetism. She wasn't as airbrushed as a swimsuit model, but you could see why she sold copies of the London Daily Mirror when it was her face spread large across the front page with explosive captions about Amsterdam, sexual liaisons and gun-running. The media had made her the femme fatale of the Movement. That was perhaps the reason she was so controlled. It's hard to live up to that picture people already have of you. That was her secret. Maria Maguire seduced you with the distance she put between herself and the lens. And she was the reason we won the debate with the needling, nit-picking RTE interviewer, Charles Butler, in the semi-circle of the lights and cameras.

But that night, as our little rump of the Billy Reid gathered in O'Byrne's Pub in Rathmines under the telly, it never came on. I rang up Ó Brádaigh. "What the hell happened, Seán?"

"Well," he said, "'it's fairly obvious, isn't it? Lynch has managed to block it on us. Maria's here with me now. She says you did too good of a job."

I went back to our table. "Christ—maybe we're winning."

Monday was Referendum Day and not being a citizen, I couldn't vote and Sheila was going to work. For the first time in three weeks, I could relax, with nothing left to hurry and get done. And a wonderful omen arrived in the mail. A letter from the USA. With a refund check from the IRS.

"Seventy-five whole dollars!" I danced around the flat with Aisling. "We're rich!—we're rich! Who could've sent it? It could only be Mamanonna, back home, honey!"

I got on the phone to the comrades, Bernie and Martina. "Listen, I know this sounds crazy, but—I just remembered— tomorrow is May the 16th—that's Aisling's birthday! Now, I've been neglecting the two of them for weeks, and Sheila's not great with me at the moment, can't blame her, but—yeah, she'll be three years old, can you believe it! And Sheila's turned 26, just a few days ago, on the 10th! Now listen. Call everybody and have them here tonight at five and we'll make it a big surprise party for their birthdays! Yes, 5 o'clock. She has to get up for work at 4 a.m., you know."

Brendan McAndrews was back in town, and out of jail, and he and the lads were kipping in at Waterloo Road with Martina and Bernadette, or else, they were in telephone contact.

By the time everybody got to us at No. 56, it was close on six p.m., and we knew we were big losers in the Referendum. But at least it had given me the excuse for having forgotten completely about her birthday, the pretense of which I took care to keep up in front of Sheila once she got home from work after holy hour. Actually, knowing our friends in the Movement, they needed very little excuse to party—losing the biggest poll of the year would do nicely.

At exactly six, Sheila was asking me could I see to the supper tonight, did I mind, she was feeling all in, and—at that moment party-goers arrived in numbers on our front doorstep making a hullabaloo. I feigned amazement and rushed to let them in.

Shouting "Surprise! Surprise!" to make a din, led by Brendan and a whole squad of the 'RA, followed close behind by the likes of Krishna, Jane, Bernie and Martina, plus a platoon of strangers we'd never seen before, to be expected whenever a party somewhere in Dublin was heard of, they all somehow fit through the door and began madly singing "Happy Birthday to you," and so on, which rang in Sheila's ears as she looked at the lot of them in sheer dismay, while a scramble was on to provide a chair for the guest of honour to sit in.

Bernie and Jane caught her by the arms as Sheila stumbled and fell into the chair. Then she saw Aisling stuffed into a corner with all those big people with too much drink in them, and Sheila lost it.

She found my face grinning at her from across shoulders, holding up a drink to salute her.

"Surprise, love!"

Grimly, Sheila said, to me, "Tell all these people I want them to clear out!"

Brendan McAndrews came up behind me as the laughter and the noise of celebration came abruptly to a sag, just like the air going out of a balloon. "We'll go," he said.

I stiffened. "Tell everybody to stay right where you are. This is my house. I invited you."

"No, best not," said Brendan. He was firm and final. He crossed in front of Sheila and looked down at her. "We know where we're not wanted."

Bernadette found me in Madigan's down the street standing alone at the bar. She came up beside me softly. She said nothing at first, but only waited for me. I tried to ignore her, making a show of drinking from the pint in front of me, looking straight ahead, but then she put her hand on my arm. And it made me melt inside just to feel a woman's touch. "Leave me alone," I said, miserably.

"She's sitting in the flat, crying her eyes out. Go back to her, Nick."

"No."

"You're going to stand here and get yourself drunk?"

"What do you know about it?"

"Please, Nick."

"You can't help me, Bernie. Go away."

Chapter 12

The Belfast Europa

One day shortly thereafter I was going up the stairs of No. 4A Kevin Street when I met a fellow called Nugent coming down.

I knew him by sight and I knew who he was, and when I had already started up the stair and looked up, he was just turning the corner at the top, head down, preoccupied, and in a hurry. I knew we were going to meet in the middle with nowhere to go.

The stair being very narrow and closed in by two walls, we made way for one another to pass.

But I was surprised when he stopped himself next to me, almost facing me on the stair, as if he'd had a sudden thought and interrupted himself.

My practice around Kevin Street was to wait till I was spoken to before I opened my mouth. Unless I already knew the person I didn't even say hello. I only went there originally to collect papers to sell, and it didn't do to hang about. I couldn't even remember how I'd learned Nugent's name. He certainly had never spoken to me before. But now he said, "You're the Yank, are you not?"

"I am."

"Would you be interested in doing me a favor if it involved taking a trip up to Belfast?"

"I suppose so."

"Good. Are you free this weekend, on Saturday?"

"I'm not doing anything now that the Referendum's over."

"You see, I need someone to carry a message who isn't likely to draw suspicion if they were to be stopped and questioned. You would have to play the American tourist, and forget about any Irish expressions you've picked up." We were still standing on the stair and he was still in a hurry. "You'll be met by our people in Belfast, of course, and taken where you need to go."

"All right."

"Good. Here's the envelope. You'd best put it on your person somewhere secure. Tell your man upstairs that I said you were to be given the train-fare and a bit more for food and drink. When you get to Belfast City Centre, you're to stand waiting at the kerb outside the Belfast Europa Hotel and you'll be picked up. Cheerio, now."

Nugent hurried down the stair. I put the envelope into my ever-present pea-coat pocket and continued on up.

At this time in my life I was ready to get out of Dublin. My four-year marriage to Sheila Blake, our relationship of six years' duration, was at an all-time low. I needed a change of scenery, badly. Besides, you didn't refuse a task the Movement asked you to do, or you would never be asked again.

I crossed the Border without incident. The CIE-British Rail train I took was a local, and it carried passengers a leisurely 90 miles from Westland Row in Dublin to the Victoria Street

Station, in the heart of Belfast's City Centre. I was alone in my compartment, and only a Customs Officer who paid me a visit marked the passage of the border. He was very polite and circumspect and asked few questions, explaining that it was only due to the 'Emergency' that he had to bother me at all. He gave a cursory glance to my Massachusetts driver's licence—a passport wasn't necessary to travel anywhere in the British Isles: the borders between British and Irish Territory were as open as those between the US and Canada. The Customs Officer added that they were taking routine precautions. "One of our trains had to be held up three hours the other day till the Army cleared the track ahead." He bid me a pleasant trip and courteously closed the sliding door behind him as he left.

I settled down to watch the countryside of County Armagh roll by, an ordinary tourist on an ordinary holiday, only it wasn't pretty out the train-window: dull monotonous hills that reminded me of southern New Hampshire, but without the white wooden steeples. In their place were the squat square towers of medieval Irish churches in the town centres, and the occasional soaring stone needle of a Protestant cathedral. Outside the town, grim, isolated livestock farms, on knobby terrain. Instead of the winding, dipping two-lane macadam of the 26 Counties, here there were high-speed British-style motorways running parallel to the railway. A country made for motorists and sheep, I thought.

As we went clackety-clacking towards Belfast, we halted to drop passengers and take on riders in Newry. Through the train-window, I revisited the town centre, shops still boarded up, the centre still surrounded by barbed wire, barricades and checkpoints. It was as if not a leaf had stirred since the day I walked with 70,000 people from the 26 Counties past the silent ranks of the British Army after Bloody Sunday. Like a blur, the

British Rail southbound express roared past as we stood in the station, a foot away on the next track.

We went through Portadown and Lurgan, on the south shore of Lough Neagh. Each of them was sealed off in the centre, like Newry, and I couldn't detect much in them that resembled life in Dublin.

Through the windows on the corridor and compartments opposite, Lough Neagh, on our left as we passed between the towns, seemed a vast, flat marsh. It was the largest lake in Ireland. An inland sea that stretched so far from the eye, no land could be seen on its horizon, unless that moored mist out there was land.

When we came to Lisburn, only six miles from Belfast, I saw a sign of life. This was the operational command centre of the British Army in Ulster, a garrison town, and it crawled with Army vehicles speeding the roads between the dotted blocks of box-like council estates: troop lorries, armoured personnel-carriers, armoured-cars and Land Rovers, Pigs, Ferrets and Saracens. And everywhere, the barracks, lurking within compounds of tall cinder-block walls, were captive inside barbed wire, high poles with blank lights waiting for nightfall to shine; the sheen of the perpetual mist blanketing all the olive-drab vehicles parked rank after rank behind closed, corrugated steel gates, formed a universal mask of grey gloom.

Then in the vantage of the train-window, Belfast sprawled, like a vast dun of smog.

Even from a distance, the Queen City of the North was ugly. Under the dome of dust that hid her from the sun's healing light, she lay like a spreading cobweb, clinging to the earth, collecting in the corners. Dropping through the hinterland of television antennas, suburban villas and semi-detached estates from Lisburn to the city itself, you passed the line of demarcation between the living and the dead. Green lawns evaporated, and a colour like mould on the inside of an orange rind seeped in. Train-wheels racketing, Belfast began materialising in the train-window, one long vista of unbroken redbrick streets smeared on the sooty trails of raindrops glued to the glass.

One after another, narrow streets closed in on the railway line, abutting it like so many alley-ways in a scrap-merchant's yard. Aisle after aisle of row-houses with their peaked gables, hundreds of chimney-pots, slate roofs as dour as the interminable drizzle, red-brick, the colour of a dried scab. And in the squalid back-gardens, the family wash, a yellowing flag going damp in the afternoon gloom. I felt like I was being swallowed, not by a pocket of poverty, but by a baggy trouser-leg of destitution. I had just passed the real border of the North, the line between privilege and privation.

The size of Dublin, Belfast had none of her sister capital's Palladian gentility. Payne's gray was the colour of Dublin, burnt umber, Belfast. Dublin was the godchild of the 18th century Age of Reason, Belfast the stepchild of 19th century industrialism. Brought into existence by the arrogance of steam-powered capitalism, Belfast had grown too quickly, too soon proved truculent, wrong-headed, a daughter over-fond of the docks and strolling sailors, a sweetheart wooed away by the Tennysonian swains of the soldiery, a wife betraying the strait-laced strictures of her Presbyterian lord and husband. Belfast matured as the willful strumpet of the Empire, both a dream and a nightmare.

When the 20th century arrived, it brought world war, conscription, ship-building, expansion, Depression and rebellion. The drive for Irish independence from the British Empire in Dublin brought about the drive for Loyalist secession from Ireland in Belfast. Belfast was fortified by the coming of Lord Edward Carson and a neat little arrangement all round: we'll partition the country and rule the North ourselves with a ger-rymandered majority and give all the jobs to the Protestant workers, give all the council seats to the Protestant politicians, and all the housing to the Protestant families, and we'll make a decent profit, won't we?

Now, in 1972, more than half a million people lived in this vast slum, divided into armed camps. The city was pock-marked with pill-boxes, pimpled with road-blocks, scarred with barbed wire. Ulster north of the Border was a province the size of Connecticut, and her five thousand square miles were occupied by 14,000 British troops: one soldier for every two square miles. A third of the population of Ulster was jammed into Belfast, but two-thirds of the British Army were stationed in it. To them, she was the old whore of a forgotten fancy who lay straddled on her back in the street and showed one the teeth of a death's-head grin.

The soldiers met me when I stepped down from the train in Great Victoria Street Station. Portable guard rails channeled the passengers disembarking on the platform into a long queue. At the spout of the funnel, three soldiers of the Coldstream Guards, operating out of Girdwood Barracks, stood by the rail with slung rifles, looking at the faces in the queue. Another squaddie, supervised by an NCO, took names and addresses with a tiny pad and the stub of a pencil. The soldier with the pad had to keep licking his finger on his tongue in order to turn its pages over. "Name? Address? Aw roight—move along. Name? 'Ow do yoo spell it?"

It was my turn. The NCO tapped the squaddie on the shoulder. He looked up from his pad and found my face and looked surprised. "'Ey?" he said, glancing over his shoulder at his sergeant. Then he turned to me and said, "Yoo two. Over there. Bof of yoo."

Myself and the man behind me just looked at him. One of the other soldiers leaned over the rail and said, "Come on. Don't stand there gawkin.'"

We followed him to a spot he pointed to on the platform. Two more soldiers took up positions beside us. We were separated from the queue now, and being guarded, apparently. Passengers admitted through the checkpoint glanced at us with looks varying from disinterest to bewilderment to suspicion to reassurance. But none of them stopped. I noticed how instead they hurried away, or made a show of minding their own business, even as they stole a furtive look. They were memorizing the faces of the pair pulled out of the queue, taking a snapshot to store in the memory. Will I see that face again in the morning news on my front-page doorstep? Listen, love—they were right behind me in the queue—two of 'em. I looked at the backs of the fortunate departing few as they dipped out of sight down the nearby black-iron staircase under the red-and-yellow sign: Way Out.

I said to one of my guards, "Why have we been pulled out of the line?"

The soldier looked at me oddly. "Just routine, sir. Nuffing to worry about."

The shadow of the 10-story tall rear of the Belfast Europa was falling over Glengall Street as I came down the steps of the railway station after being released. I was confused. The rail station seemed to be swallowed up by the big hotel complex. An overpass went over the train tracks leading into the station and you had to cross a long yard that appeared to be a U-shaped turnaround for the Ulsterbus station before you came out in the street. I was to wait at the front of the Hotel Europa, but where was that?

Glengall Street was a stubbed toe of a street, littered with unfinished construction and an elderly bombed-out building on the corner. I had no idea what this was, but on the side facing Glengall Street I could see the single word OPERA on an undamaged section of facade. The street was a bus-rank, and single-decker diesels, cue-ball white, with a horizontal blue stripe, and the logo, *Ulsterbus,* forward-slanted, to convey *'progress,'* were pulled up in front of the bus station entrance. These busses were all empty. Their crews, drivers and conductors, loitered in a plexiglass enclosure on the footpath. Inside the chain-link fence surrounding the bombed out Victorian building, the bus-office-caravan was empty, too.

Five-o'clock of a Saturday afternoon and the entrance of the Belfast Europa was deserted. I headed for the corner where I saw light erasing shadow. As I passed the diagonal of the chain-link fence facing Great Victoria Street, I saw a message scrawled with white spray-paint on a wooden boarding on the fence:

PREPARE TO MEET THY GOD

and I was reminded that I was now in Ian Paisley country.

Emerging, I could see that I was at the front of the biggest hotel in Belfast, and that the entrance in Glengall Street must have been a side or back entrance. Indeed, when I looked up at plate-glass windows of the first-floor, there were several British Army officers standing there in a cocktail lounge in dress uniforms looking down on the deserted street with drinks in their hands.

They were still building Belfast's finest hostel. Or so it seemed to me. A chain-link fence continued all the way around the front of the new ivory-colored high-rise with the tinted glass on the lounge level and the crown of a royal red logo high atop the 22nd story. As fast as they were building it, the hotel was being bombed out into construction delays and cost overruns. Most of the tinted glass at the top of the wing on the other side of the entrance from the British officers' lounge was gone, supplanted by plywood. Despite all the security forces, the Belfast Europa had already been bombed six times since Internment Day.

Thus I found myself at this hour on a summer-tourist weekend the only person out there in Great Victoria Street. Across the broad thoroughfare, humped in the middle, pot-holed and peeling, empty, there were two ancient pubs on the corner of Amelia Street, Robinson's, Est. 1895, and The Crown Bar, Est. 1849, both closed up and shuttered. In this street, scattered large buildings, windowless like warehouses, were staggered with vacant lots, turned into Car-Parks where no cars were parked. Imagine a city centre in Ireland with no pubs open! Left and right, the centre faded into a film of grey. At the bombed-out Belfast Opera House, a flag-pole slanted over the footpath: a huge royal blue and gold banner announced

Rosencrantz and Guildenstern - Tom Stoppard – Direct from its Triumphant two-year London Engagement !

As I came out of the shadow of the high-rise hotel, an armoured personnel carrier shot out of the Grosvenor Road and sped into Howard Street, a rifle poking from under the slit-cover in the rear doors. I crossed the deserted street to the shut-up bars.

Around the corner of Howard Street, Donegall Place resembled a fortified encampment. A fence of steel slats ran wall to wall across Howard Street, and the Army vehicle was being let through gates which shut again after it. Behind them, the Belfast City Hall stood in its grounds, sand-bagged, and ringed with machine-gun emplacements. Everywhere I looked in the city centre, I saw the theatre of war. Out of the glass-doored lobby of the Opera House came a man. Behind him the lobby was empty and as he looked around he could see the street was empty. He and I were the only two people there.

Suddenly a red mini-car came pummeling down the pot-holed street. Brakes whined and it screeched to a halt at the kerb in front of the Europa where the concrete barricades were. A girl, with black shoulder-length tresses waving, jumped out and stopped to look at me. I ran back across the street as she held the front seat down for me.

I found myself bundled into the back and the red mini was quickly in motion, jerking and jolting, grinding up to speed in a leering U-turn, kissing the far kerb, straightening, shifting into third to zoom past the Opera House, back the way it came again .

The girl in the front turned to peer out the rear window. "That fella's still outside the Opera House, Kevin. No cars coming, though. Step on it, will you?"

"I'm going as fast as I can. The street's in bits."

"Where and to hell were you all that time?" said the girl to me.

I unscrewed my twisted neck and tried to sit up. "The soldiers stopped us off the train."

"Ha!" said Kevin. "Wasn't I telling you?"

"I was afraid of that," said the girl.

"Why?" I said. "Were you here at four o'clock?"

"Certainly we were, and so was the train!"

"Honest to God, I'm really sorry–."

"Oh, stop apologising—did they bate you?" she giggled.

"No, but they gave me a good frisking."

"Kevin, tell him—didn't I go into the station myself, looking for him?—petrified, I was—trying to look innocent and all—and afraid to ask after you."

"We were in the guardhouse on the platform."

I could see Kevin, the driver, looking at me in the rear view mirror. "We couldn't hang about in the city centre," he said, "we had to leave and drive in circles—we were about to give in when you turned up at last."

"Well, thanks be to God you're landed and we can get out of this. Turn up here, Kevin."

Kevin turned up, and said, "Who's this we and us you keep talking about? Was someone with you?"

"No, but two of us were stopped out of the queue off the train and taken aside."

"Ah—that's them—standard operatin' procedure. They pick two people at random, y'see."

"Just my luck. Anyway, I got to put on my best American accent and hope it helped me get by with my tourist story. You shoulda seen them when I was sayin' I was out to go sight-seeing—in Belfast, no less. Thought I was daft or somethin.'"

"You don't sound outa practice to me," said Kevin. "Where ye from?"

"Boston."

"Arragh. Boston. Heard of it."

All this time, the girl was hanging over her seat looking straight at me. I smiled and she grinned and held out her hand, saying, "I'm Maggie."

"Nice to meet you, Maggie. I'm Nick." Having taken her hand, I was reluctant to let her fingers go.

"Ooh. Such a Yank, Kevin. 'Nice to meet you' and all— who does he remind you of?"

She had turned in her seat to face front, so—I could breathe once more. She was that gorgeous, this Maggie, that my breath was taken away. I saw Kevin peering at me again.

"I'd say—Jerry Garcia, of the Grateful Dead."

"Ha, ha! You're not the first to say that," said I.

"It's the gold-rimmed granny-glasses," said Maggie. "And the curly-mop. Is that natural, or is it a perm?"

"It's all me," I said, delighted to be flirting with this sexy creature.

In Castle Street, the landscape was whittled down from the monumental stone of the Royal Academic Institute and the Technical College to a wee road choked with tiny shopfronts of wild colors and every conceivable article for sale, from bargain dresses on wheeled racks on the footpath to copper-bottom pots and aluminium pans in bins on tables, and standing tall beside them, stacks of unsold plastic rubbish bins. Last-minute Saturday shoppers hurried on their rounds, choking the streets with pedestrians. It was already blocked up with double-parked delivery vans and throttled with cars parked, two wheels on the kerb. Looking out, I spotted a record shop in bold Carnaby Street yellow and red and in the window, a giant poster was pasted:

Paul McCartney's Hit Single—banned in Great Britain—
"Leave Ireland to the Irish!"–
NOW – only 79p !

We came to the Falls Taxi Association cab-rank: a levelled city block lined on both sides with black London-style taxis with the green-and-white FTA stickers in the corner of the windscreen, and then we were in no-man's land, a stretch of broken buildings where not even a grass-blade grew. Entire city blocks were reduced to the level of Carthage after the Romans. To the left, only a chimney remained, naked and alone, a red butte in a toppled desert of white dust. On the right, a steam-shovel yawned, abandoned in the rubble as if the task were hopeless. Straight on, three stories of half a building, with the triangle of a once-upon-a-time joined roof-line traced on its hollow rib.

"I remember when you could go up this street," said Kevin Rooney, for that was his name, "and not see the sky for the buildings crowding the footpaths. Now look at it."

I said, "It looks like Berlin after the Russians."

"Produced by J Arthur Rank, ha,ha!" laughed Kevin sourly. His hands left the wheel and wiggled a dance in the air. "Malay slave-boy hammers the gong! Up goes the curtain! The Rank Organisation presents—a film of the end of the world—Belfast!"

"Stop, Kevin," said Maggie. "Isn't it bad enough?"

"Don't, love. You'll ruin your nails. We have to go up the Falls to get to Andy-town and we're sure to hit a checkpoint before we get there—what's the difference? It's another day pissed down the old drain only for the chance at a bit of fun."

"I just want to get home, Kevin."

"What? And deprive our newly-arrived guest of his one-and-only chance-of-a-lifetime personal guided tour from the one-and-only Rooney of Unity Flats—the greatest show on earth!–Belfastus Agonistes!–doom, doom, doom, goes the Angelus—come one, come all!–and see the British Army chasing its tail, like a dog tied to a tin of sardines, while a cast of thousands jeers from the jail cells." Kevin Rooney peered at me in the mirror, and then he looked sideways down at Maggie, huddled in her corner of the front seat, chewing a hangnail.

We were coming up the slight incline at the end of the no-man's land, and there Kevin slowed the mini to a crawl as we passed the Divis Street Flats. On the footpath to the left, a monolithic grey concrete blockhouse with no windows fronted the walks and drives of the Flats, decorated on four sides with grafitti in black spray-paint and white brush strokes and pastel mauve chalk-lines—NO SURRENDER—and JOIN THE IRA—and *Fuck Willie!*–but the one that caught my eye was the black-sprayed scrawl that asked—

Is there life before death?

"Look," said Kevin Rooney, pointing up.

Seventeen stories up, the roof of the main tower block of Divis Street bristled with whip-like antennas, swaying a little in the wind of that altitude; a corrugated iron wall ringed the square rooftop, with openings for binoculars and machine-gun emplacements.

"The Army have their OP up there. They can survey the entire area. Shoot anything that moves."

Belfast, like Dublin, was a low-level city, but a pair of high-rise towers symbolised the graphic poles of the province. One, the Europa, the prestige venue, the safe-house for the visiting computer programmer and the traveling foreign investor to spend the night in; the other, Divis Street, the showpiece of the social welfare state. Divis Street had been constructed with the modernistic eye of the city-planner, with its cubist design, its concrete-form geometry, meant to provide every tenant and every child with his own Mondrian-colored balcony. They bombed the Europa, and they machine-gunned the Flats. "Which is either 'No Discrimination,' or a lack of discrimination," said Kevin Rooney, "depending on how you want to look at it."

Then, as if to fling defiance into the lenses of the surveillance, a parade came marching down the curve of Divis Street, and Kevin had to pull over the red mini.

Two marchers in the front rank pumped clenched fists in the air as they gripped banner-poles between them, lifting their pennant ahead of themselves, thrusting it forward and up:

VICTORY TO THE WORKERS' STATE!

Flags and placards behind these two proclaimed *Down with Imperialism!* and *Smash Internment!* The largest flag of all flew sturdily on a stout mast in the centre of the burly parade, a yellow hammer and sickle, rippling in the breeze of the demonstrators' strides. They were chanting to the tune of tramping feet, "Brits Out! Brits Out! Brits Out!"

I leaned forward and asked Kevin, "Who are they?"

"The NLF," said Kevin, as he poked the mini into gear. "National Liberation Front. Like in Nam."

"Och, there's no amount of madmen about."

The Falls Road climbed gradually uphill in its rocky, lumpy *déshabillé*. Broad swatches of the macadam disappeared, and the red mini crossed oases of gravel to clamber onto pavement again. Streetlights on in the daytime, but all the stoplights punched out, only the bare light flashing behind the cracked green or red glass. No cars parked in the margins of the Lower Falls, except for the burnt-out hulks of abandoned vans, lorries and buses.

The Shankill, bastion of the Loyalists, lay a mere 400 yards away, down every sidestreet, behind every crook in those streets of rowhouses flanking the Falls Road that bore the names of British battles of Empire—Balaclava Street, Odessa Street, Sevastopol Street. As you passed the mouths of these rabbit-warren streets, you could catch a glimpse of the Peace Line—the cinder-block and corrugated iron, accordian-wire wall that separated Belfast from itself. Sometimes only the blank wall of a warehouse showed, or the back wall of a factory, but, always, there was the wire.

In West Belfast, four roads led out from the City Centre, the Crumlin Road, the Shankill Road, the Falls Road and the Grosvenor Road—the northern pair in Tartan territory, the southernmost two in the hands of the Taigs. These four roads led out from the hub of Donegall Place and Royal Avenue like the spokes of a wheel, and in that wheel were the lives of West Belfast slowly being ground to grist.

Kevin halted for a redlight at a corner with a long, low building framed in a chain-link cage. I rolled down my window and said to the knot of boys standing on the corner, "What's this—the library, is it?"

"It's the Brew," they said.

"What?"

"The Brew!" they laughed, coming closer and enunciating, so that it came out "Brroo-oo-ooo."

Kevin Rooney said, "It's Saturday, lads—isn't it closed?"

One of them stuck his cropped skinhead into the car, ogling Maggie, and said, "Aye, but you know this lot. They spend so much of their time here, waiting to collect the dole, they come down here of a Saturday out of sheer habit."

On we went with the green light, and women with children by the hand began to appear on the street. They looked up at the red mini quickly as it passed them and put their heads down again as they rounded the corner for home. It was habit. A reflex of wariness. Who's that now? Do I know that car? Too many people had been shot lately from a passing car that didn't bother to stop.

Down a bit from the wide intersection where the Falls Road met the Springfield Road, a Saracen armoured car came roaring down from the Royal Victoria Hospital at forty miles an hour, without a siren, but expecting, and getting, everybody, man, beast and machine, to dash out of the road. Too many people had been run down by one of these things, and they didn't bother to stop, either. There were no foot patrols to be seen because it was still daylight, but the British Army manifested its presence in the Falls on wheels, emphatically, recklessly, and the very speed at which they took the winding, crowded street seemed intimidating to the one who darted out of the road onto the kerb, and fearful to the one who stood leaning against her doorway with a show of deliberate disregard.

Here the pubs were fenced with the same chain-link caging as The Brew sported—a wire affair consisting of a fence on the footpath bent over to meet the wall or the roof and completely enclose the entrance. The cages made commercial buildings look like they were wearing a squash racket for a mask. But too many pub doorways had been bombed from passing cars by thrown missiles. And the cages would catch them and bounce them back into the street. Maybe a few lives could be saved. Most of the pub doors had a small sign reading Members Only. You had to practice some elementary security measures in the Falls.

Still, life as usual had to go on, even in the middle of the Falls Road in Belfast. In fact, there was no lack of people about, at least while the daylight lasted. Here they felt safer than they might have, say, in the no-man's land down below Divis Street. There was a safety in numbers and knowing your neighbors and blending in. Even the children were allowed to play in the street. You could see them sitting on the kerbs, feet in the gutter, doll in hand, or pelting around the corner, playing pretend games, chasing the BA with a toy gun. Here pedestrians picked their way from green-grocer to chemist to stationer to curtain shop to yarn dealer to shoe salesman to furniture hockshop to electrical supplier to tobacconist-news-agent to publican. Here it wasn't too far to go from your own front door to the provisioner and back again quickly. You needn't be afraid when you knew your way about. You needed no car or taxi, as you did when you had to cross over for the day to the City Centre. Here you bought your kidney pie and your calves' brains from the local butcher and had your hair cut by the local barber and the butcher and the barber both lived in your own street and everybody knew everybody else.

Just below Clonard Street, I checked off a mental note—investigate later—as we passed a door marked Sinn Féin. Above the bay windows of a tailor's next door, there was another door, the newspaper office, with a bumper-sticker: Republican News. The Irish Republican Movement, too, lived in the Falls Road of West Belfast.

At the corner of Clonard Street, McGuinness' Pub stood with its door invitingly open. No caging surrounded the side-wall where the purple sign with the white-lettered Gaelic script livened the footpath with the quirk of a personality amid the stolid brick.

Maggie O'Neill, for that was the sexy creature's name, wore a resigned look as she climbed out of the red mini. It was on the tip of her tongue to remind Kevin that her mum was waiting and would begin to worry, but—she shivered—it was chilly in the drizzle now, drawing towards the long summer evening. And young Maggie O'Neill was as much a stranger to the Falls, where knowing the man standing at your elbow at the bar could have its mortal import, as I was.

Kevin Rooney shook himself as he stepped out, and stretched his long legs. He was a big man, cramped in the mini. Standing now next to the car, he dwarfed it.

Climbing out of the back, I collected an impression of our surroundings with a squint, like a cave-dweller emerging into the outdoors.

"There was a fella shot here last week," said Kevin, pointing.

I gathered that he found it amusing to try to shock me. The sidewall of McGuinness' facing on Clonard Street was surfaced with blue tiles. You could see the graph-paper pattern of the thin seams of mortar. And also, one, two, three large round bullet-holes, about mid-section-high, just right for cutting a man in two.

"He's pulling your leg," said Maggie, as I went for a closer look.

"I'm not," said Kevin. "They shot from over there." He pointed across the Falls Road. "Didn't kill him, though."

Maggie went to huddle herself in the pub door as if she didn't want to be seen with the lunatic.

In the pub, old men were watching Manchester United in a football match with Glasgow Celtic on the BBC in the dark. They didn't bother with us newcomers, except to notice Maggie and curb their cursing. She was the only woman in it at present. We took a table and Kevin produced a packet of Craven A's, offering them around. I took one. Just what I needed. Filters, too. None of your Woodbines.

"Tell us, then," said Kevin, sending Maggie to the bar to fetch us three pints of Smithwick's, and seating himself. "What brings you to our happy city?"

"Well—I hate to say it—curiosity, I suppose."

"A dangerous disease, in these woods. But a common affliction. And what do you think of Belfast?"

"Detroit—1967? I don't know—first impressions are, you know—first impressions."

"Did the buggers give you a bad time at the Station?"

"I'll tell you, Kevin—they were regulation polite."

"Aye. They're told to be, with visitors. So as to create the right impression."

"Not that they weren't petty and annoying."

"Och, well—they have to prove to themselves that they're the British Army, after all."

"Yeah, well I can see why people don't like them."

"You get used of it. You can get used of anything, really."

"It's depressing, isn't it?"

"It is."

"That's my impression. If I had to choose one word."

"Do you know what it's like, really like, living in Belfast? I'll tell you. It's like living a lie. I don't know if you know what that's like, but as for me—I'm a motorcar salesman, by profession—that is, when I can get it—at the moment, I'm in a salvage yard up in the Ardoyne, as there seems to be more in wrecking them than selling them. Well, I know what it is to be only half-believing the sound of your own words—and to know that they're in on the con, as well—but that both of you carry on regardless, because that's the way the game is played."

"Here we go," said Maggie, setting down the three pints. "Off on your horse again, Kevin?"

Rooney ignored her. "Now you take myself—I consider myself a non-combatant—well, the whole fuckin' city is up in arms—and all my life they've been wanting me to take one side or the other. It's like the question of religion. As far as I'm concerned, nobody ever asked what I thought of it at all. I was brought up Catholic, and that was it—born to it—everyone around you simply assumes that you believe what they've taught you to believe. But do you? Perhaps you do, and perhaps you don't. The point is, you don't say so. It just isn't done. But Belfast is a place where one day you're going to wake up and they're going to make you pay for that—that—tacit whatever-it-is.

So—a man goes about believin' in whatever's goin.' At the moment, it's the season for fuckin' the Pope and drivin' the Brits into the sea. Sure, what the hell, I'm for it, aren't we all? I spend my time dodging the bullets, running in between the rain, and skirting the blown-out bars."

"Don't encourage him, Nick, he'll keep us here all night."

"Now, listen, Nick, my friend, and I'll tell you the true story of Belfast. My father was a bricklayer. Of course, being what we were, he could never find work till he went across to England. He used say, 'twas the bricklayers built Belfast and now they couldn't get work because they done such a good job. My Ma wasn't half sorry to see him go—says she to me, one time, he's better off out of it, and so are we. Even so, he ended his life skinnin' his knees as a day-laborer. My Dad was a terrible man with a temper, and more talk in his tongue than caution. Well, us kids lived in the Falls—and I can remember one day my Ma comin' home outta breath—she ran in all the way from the Tartan green-grocer's down at the corner. The Proddies stoned her from the other side of the street. You see, they're brought up that way, they think it's a gag—they hear their parents talkin' against the lazy, shiftless, thriftless Taigs—and you know how cruel kids can be. Well, they'd get out of the house, no supervision—and this was the way to amuse yourself. Believe it or not, kids are the worst bigots of all, because they know no responsibility about nothin'—not even to pick up their socks or tidy their rooms."

"Well, we moved out of the Falls after that, and in our innocence, or in our ignorance, whichever, we thought, at least in the Ardoyne, we'll still be amongst our own. Little did we know. The Ardoyne's not like the Falls at all. You're surrounded by the Tartans, in fact. There's wee pockets of Catholic houses totally isolated in Protestant streets, sort of islands, stranded among the Orangemen. Well, in August of '69, whatever went on between the Shankill and the Falls, it was nothing compared to the Ardoyne. Now, don't misunderstand. I've no love for the British Army myself. But you should have seen the Catholic housewives of the Ardoyne welcome these bastards. Bringing their tea to them in the street. Chatting them up, telling them what a fine job they were doing. And it is a fact that, at that time, the troops were the salvation of the Ardoyne. But the British are a great people for charging off on their white horse, only to beat the beast to death when she falters. And when the mud thickens on the road, they'll do what they're famous for—muddle through. Nevermind that they've bogged down or they don't know any longer which wood they're in. And of course there were those in the Army that never had any love for the Irish to begin with."

"Well, the chips will fall where they will, and it wasn't long before the very same housewives had turned their tea trays upside down, put a handle on 'em, and called 'em the lid o' yer granny's bin. And rattled her every time a soldier put his nose round the corner of the front garden."

"Thanks be to God my mother passed on before the tide turned. She's blessed to have missed the day. Well, what was I to do? There I was, with my Ma gone. God rest her, the sisters married and set out on their own, and a whole house to myself in the Ardoyne—with whole families burnt out of their homes, sitting on couches in the street. Well, I fell in with this wee gurr-l, nineteen years old, husband gone, two kids, livin' in the Unity Flats, if you coud call it that. Out of the frying pan and into the fire! Some smart-aleck in the City Hall. Some civil servant in England, no doubt. Thought he'd reform Belfast by putting up housing for Catholics in the middle of the Shankill—that's the Unity Flats. Well, if they ask you back home—what message has Belfast? You tell them, that there isn't any hope—except for the hand of the Almighty Brickmason Himself to come down and sweep the place clean and for us to start over again."

Kevin Rooney then paused to down the rest of his pint.

"There. I hope your curiosity's quenched. And now I *have* said too much."

Andersonstown was a community on a hill, self-contained and separate, a residential community of families and children, each with their own semi-detached home on a winding street of terraced houses, trim lawns, and young trees. New, clean, quiet. Andersonstown had its own church, its own primary school, a teacher-training college, a tennis and bowling ground, two post offices, even a bacon factory—and the largest Gaelic football ground in Ulster, Roger Casement Park. It was like any suburban middle-class bedroom community in any social-welfare conscious jurisdiction of any County Council in England, Scotland or Wales—except that it was in Ireland.

The Queen's Writ did not run here in Andersonstown. The Royal Ulster Constabulary did not venture into this enclave. The British Army stayed out. Andy-town was a No-Go Area, governed and guarded by the Provisional IRA.

Maggie O'Neill's house was on a hilltop curve in St Agnes' Drive. From the O'Neill's back windows, you could look down, over the rooftops of descending terraces, on the main IRA checkpoint, adjacent to the tennis and bowling ground.

I liked the house. You came upon it up a short, steep incline, on the linch-pin of the curve, and you swung into the driveway. There was a single-stall garage there, under the bedrooms. A flag walk took you up to the front door. The living room was carpeted wall-to-wall and there was a console colour television, a Phillips, made in the Netherlands. I could have been in any split-level, back home in the States. Only in the kitchen would you know you were in Belfast.

That was where Mrs O'Neill spent most of her time, near the telephone, whenever she was along in the house. She kept the old kitchen furniture from the old house in the Falls where she grew up, and she felt comfortable there. Her husband was away on a job in Dungannon. He was a demolitions man, and his work took him to all parts of the troubled province. But he always phoned every day he was away, early in the evening when he knew his wife wouldn't be outside hanging clothes, but right there, finishing up the dinner dishes.

Mrs O'Neill hated to be alone these times. She was alone in the house, her husband absent on his rounds, when they rang in the wee hours to say her son Brian had been taken from his grandmother's house in the Falls in a British Army swoop in October.

Now, with Kevin Rooney and me, she had company in her kitchen again, and she looked up. As she bustled about fixing tea, she was whispering in her own mind her silent prayer of thanks to the picture of the Holy Mother above the sink, for bringing her Maggie home safe to her.

Kevin Rooney recounted our day-trip into the city centre and back again, but it wasn't calculated to reassure Mrs O'Neill. She liked Kevin—it was her suggestion to have him taking Maggie to the Station whenever she had friends to pick up. It was her cousin's daughter that Kevin was living with, and for the sake of her cousin, she never dwelt on the notion that they hadn't married. "The poor girl needs a good man in the house, after what she went through with the first one—and then, living in the Flats like that, in the middle of the Shankill Road. And I suppose the young people today have a right to do things differently. It's not as if the old ways were so wonderful, is it? For if they were, mightn't we have passed on to them a better world, instead of the Troubles? They've to fix things up where we couldn't."

"But then," said Kevin, "where would be all the fun in living? For instance, today, comin' back up the Falls Road. Soldiers stopped us, and your man sticks his head in and says I, 'Are we on the right road to the Springfield Road Barracks?' And, says he, 'Why?' Says I, 'Well, y'see, we've been asked to place a bomb, and–.'"

"You didn't," said Mrs O'Neill.

"He never did, Mum," said Maggie.

"The devil take you. And did the soldiers stop you at all?"

"They did," said Maggie.

"God save us—where was the checkpoint today?"

"Just outside the Falls Park— at the stone wall under the trees, on this end."

"Well, missus, that was grand, the tay, I mean—and the chat, as well—but I'd best be gettin' back to the woman and the kids. Nick, my American friend—if you're here more than a couple of days, call me, and I'll take you down the Shankill in the mini—I live there, and I'm known, so you'd be all right with me—that way, when you're leavin' town, you'll have something to tell them, where you've been, sight-seein'—and they'll show you preference for it."

The telephone rang as Kevin was showing himself out and it was Mr O'Neill. "Good night!" Mrs O'Neill called after Rooney from the wall-phone. Maggie was pulling me by the wrist with her. Her Mum covered the receiver with her hand. "Are you going upstairs, Maggie?"

In her bedroom, Maggie opened the portable record-player on her night-table. "Do you remember this?" she asked me, as she pulled out an album by Ralph McTell. The first track was

Streets of London. Maggie sat on her bed to listen. I knelt, leafing through the albums in the bottom of her night-table. "It's the last thing I listen to," she said, "when I'm going to sleep at night—some nights, anyway—it reminds me of Matt."

I pulled out an album and tilted it to the light. *Songs of Irish Freedom.* Outlet Recordings, 63/67 Smithfield, Belfast, NI, 1969. "Who's Matt?"

"My boyfriend. My fiancé, I should say. Matt Calloway. We're to be married, when we can, hopefully. At the moment, he's inside with my brother Brian—they were best friends—or, they are, I should say."

"He's a lucky man, Matt Calloway."

I was sitting on the floor, and she was looking down at me, and she blushed. "Not so lucky, I think, or he wouldn't be in the Kesh, would he?"

"He's lucky to have you waiting for him when he gets out."

She looked down at the floor as she said, "You shouldn't be saying things like that."

"You shouldn't have grinned at me so wickedly the way you did in Kevin's motor."

Recovered now, she tossed her brilliant black head of hair as she challenged me. "Tell me about your wife, then. Is she the reason you came to Ireland?"

Since we had never met before, either Maggie O'Neill was psychic or she was very perceptive or she had made a devastating guess. Or—she had made note of the wedding ring on my left hand? Women do tend to notice things like that.

I pursed my lips as I thought it over, but I had to admit, "Yes. She had emigrated to the States from the West. So, we met in Boston."

"Right. I didn't think you would have left her behind you in America just to come all the way here."

"What made you think that?"

"Just the way you looked at me when I grinned at you."

"All that you could tell from just one look?"

"Sometimes that's all it takes."

I thought immediately of the night I had first met Sheila at an Irish dance back home. "Yes, that's true."

"What's she like, your wife?"

"Her name is Sheila. She has dark hair, like yours, but she wears it longer, and she hasn't blue eyes, like yours, but hers are a very pretty, devilish hazel colour."

"Why do you say devilish?"

"Because she's mischievous, and delights in tormenting me."

"I think she's a very lucky girl."

"And she's almost as beautiful as you are, Maggie O'Neill."

"Now that remark is to be stricken off the books as strictly against the law." Maggie rose. "Come on, I'll show you to where you're to sleep, in my brother's room."

I got up off the floor after replacing the album, and I said, "Before we go, tell me about that decoration, hanging over your bed."

She stood in the doorway right next to me as we both looked back. "My brother Brian made it and sent it to me from the Kesh."

It was a wood-carving of an old Thompson gun, and it was hanging directly beneath a framed print of The Sacred Heart of Jesus.

Down the hall in her brother Brian's room, the bedroom was exactly the way it was the last night Brian had slept in it, except that his mother had tidied it, stuffed all his rubbish away in the chest-of-drawers, and arranged his tennis shoes on the closet floor. His communion suit and his confirmation gown were hanging under plastic in the closet. His hairbrush and nailbrush and combs were arranged under the mirror on the doily on top of the chest. On the wall over his made-up bed there was a banner: *Welcome Home, Brian.* The corner of the coverlet was turned down under the pillow, to show a triangle of white, and every day, as Mrs O'Neill or Maggie made that bed, the whiteness of the sheet reminded them never to give up hope.

"We'd better get downstairs. We shouldn't be leaving Mum all on her own."

I stopped her by the hand. "Promise me one thing."

She glanced down at my hand holding her by the wrist. "Are all the boys from America as bold as you are?"

"I saw you in the car checking out my ring finger, and I know what you were thinking."

"You do not know what I was thinking." She wrinkled her nose at me, and stuck out her lower lip.

"Promise me one thing."

"If I can."

"All right. Since we're destined never to be together, since the fates have it that way, promise me that on this very night, ten years from now, you'll be thinking of me. Because I can promise you that, on that night, I'll be thinking of you."

"I will—if you can promise me that you'll come downstairs with me, immediately."

As we tripped down the stairs, I whispered, "You know— you should never have brought me up to your bedroom."

"I know, I know," she whispered back. "Give a woman her moment of weakness, would you?"

We arranged ourselves downstairs on suitably distant pieces of furniture. BBC-1 had Monty Python on. Mrs O'Neill clasped her hands together in her lap and shook merrily but silently. As if she were laughing in a library. We watched a troop of Crusaders attacking a castle in the desert with imaginary catapults. The chieftain of a Scots clan came out on the ramparts in a kilt and called down to the knights attacking, "Send me up your headman!" A knight catapulted through the air and landed on the rampart. "Look here, either you've lost your road, or I'm Saladin the First!" The Crusaders rode off on their imaginary horses.

When this show was over, Mrs O'Neill got up to switch the channel. BBC-3 was showing a documentary: 'Idi Amin—the Long Nightmare of Uganda.' She switched back promptly to ITV. It was a movie, in black-and-white. A model-T Ford was in the yard of a factory. Men in 1920s wardrobe, which looked strangely like present-day Belfast, with the cloth workingman's cap and the stovepipe trousers; these two men came running out of the factory office waving guns and jumping onto the running boards. Mrs O'Neill kept the sound turned down low. She didn't want the TV to interfere with any sounds of Andersonstown at night coming through the open window. Still, when the soundtrack under the credits started playing the theme music, I thought I caught the voice of Joan Baez.

Indeed, it *was* her, singing a ballad, and suddenly I realized I was watching the film credits of something called *Sacco and Vanzetti*, an Italian-made, documentary-style dramatic film directed by Giuliano Montaldi, with Irish actors Cyril Cusack and Milo O'Shea in key roles, and excitedly I explained to Maggie and Mrs O'Neill that this was the famous case of injustice in my home state of Massachusetts. "It became an international cause célèbre of the 1920s when, after seven years in prison, the Italian anarchists Sacco and Vanzetti were executed in the electric chair. In fact," I said, "my mother grew up in the town where Sacco worked in a shoe-shop, and where they arrested him. Let's see, yeah, she would have been 12 years old when they were executed. I wonder why I never saw this film on TV back home? Well—what a silly question—they're still claiming in Massachusetts to this day that those two were guilty and that they didn't wrongfully convict and execute two innocent men. You know, Mrs O'Neill, it was an infamous case of prejudice and bigotry against the Italians—which I am on my mother's side."

I sat back and became completely absorbed in this film that I never knew existed, and, while Maggie excused herself and went upstairs to bed, I sat there and watched the whole thing with her mother, and we kept up a running commentary and question and answer session.

When I went upstairs finally to sleep in Maggie's brother's room, although I was dog tired, I stood in the doorway thinking I just could not sleep in Brian O'Neill 's bed, under the banner welcoming him home. It would have been sacrilege. Instead, I found a blanket in the chest-of-drawers and settled in on the floor. But it was hard to go to sleep. I rolled up my pea-coat for a pillow and shifted it a dozen times and still lay there thinking, I'm glad I came to Belfast . . . what an extraordinary day . . . with signposts along every step of the way . . . *prepare to meet thy God* . . . Maggie . . . Kevin Rooney, the story of Belfast . . . if they could ban Paul McCartney in England . . . why would they not ban this film of Sacco and Vanzetti in Massachusetts . . ? by the time those two poor bastards were breathing their last, Mrs O'Neill and I were old friends . . . that Monty Python sure was weird . . .

On Sunday, we all went to Mass at St Agnes' in the Andersonstown Road. The church could be seen from Mrs O'Neill's kitchen window, just across the end of the back gardens along St

Agnes' Drive. We came back to the house afterwards for Sunday dinner, roast chicken and potatoes with a green salad and Mrs O'Neill's home-made custard pie. It was ages since I ate so well. I asked Maggie if she would like to go down the Falls Road with me, but she declined, saying she'd rather stay home and keep her mother company till her Dad got home, as she'd neglected her to go gallivanting on Saturday, all on my account. I said I just had to go out and walk off that Sunday dinner and she cautioned me, "Make sure that if you should get into a taxi, it's got the green sticker of the FTA in the windscreen, Nick, or you might find yourself going up the Shankill."

I waited at a bus shelter a short distance down the Andersonstown Road from the church. My plan was to explore down the Falls Road till I found the Sinn Féin office, in advance of visiting there Monday morning. I boarded the bus when it came along and stood at the back of the lower deck, strap-hanging, the easier to do a bit of sight-seeing out the windows in both directions side to side. We were waved through the IRA checkpoint at the entrance to Andersonstown. It seemed a normal Sunday afternoon bus-ride in light traffic as we passed the roundabout outside the arched entrance to the Milltown Cemetery. How ironic is that, I was thinking, and I'm coming all the way from Milltown, Massachusetts to see this, where I've seen in the papers IRA burials with the Volunteers in ski-masks firing pistol salutes over coffins . . . I was still lost in this reverie when just at that moment the bus got halted at a roadblock.

Up at the front, where the conductor had retreated after taking my fare, British soldiers came on board. Suddenly, my ears perked up, and dipping my head, my eyes darted like a bird's to see what I could see outside. A low grey stone wall, a black tree-trunk, looks like a park, no benches? Headstones—sandbags, a machine-gun emplacement behind the diagonal corner of the stone wall. This was on my left as I faced toward the front of the bus. My line of sight was cut-off by the top of the bus-window frame. That's all I could make out.

Nobody said a word. It was as if the whole bus was holding its breath. It was not crowded on board—why would it be, when it was a day off from work? All the other passengers were seated. The armed men coming single file on board were advancing, weapons first, muzzles pointed down. The seated passengers were intently looking out windows, avoiding making eye contact. Three riot-geared men in helmets shouldered their way down the bus in single-file, peering at each face as if looking for someone. Their manner was rude and calculated to intimidate. Hands on trigger-guards, they menaced their way down the bus aisle, looking left and right, with an air of taking no nonsense from the Falls Road. They must have noticed me down at the back because I was the only one standing. I got the feeling as they approached me, with curiosity rising and alarm pricked, that I was in for a good dose of ill manners and ruffian behavior. I told myself I'd better try to stay calm and not let myself get provoked, and to watch my mouth.

The Brit in the lead came up to me finally, and he looked me up and down. He said something to me in an accent I'd never heard before, which, to me, didn't sound like English at all. I hadn't a clue what he'd said, so I made no reply. Then the next man peered over his shoulder. Him I understood. He said, "What is it, Derek?" And to me, "Stand aside." When I didn't move fast enough for him, he repeated "Stand aside!" as he pushed in front of the other one and got behind me. "Where are you going?" he hissed in my ear.

"I'm just a tourist," I said, "out sight-seeing."

"Cor—we don't get many of them, do we, Derek? American?"

"Yes."

"Identification?"

"Yes."

"That your wallet in your back pocket?" he said, poking my leg with the rifle-muzzle. "Take it out—slowly—and hold it open for me to see."

The one in front of me was a teen-ager, putting on the skinhead act. He might have been trying to get a rise out of me, showing off for his mates, I couldn't tell. Our eyes met as I held my opened wallet up above my shoulder for the other one to have a look at my driver's licence. My nose was next to the chinstrap biting his neck. He was trying to stare me down. Things were getting quite claustrophobic. I could smell the fear under his armpits.

"O-kay, cowboy," said the one behind me with a jeering tone. "Have a seat. We're done with you. What is it they say— have a nice day? Derek, move out, and stop wasting my time. He's not the sort of madman we're looking for. And you, sir. If we meet again, I'll remember you. I have a good memory for faces. So, for your sake, I hope you were telling me the truth."

They filed off the bus, the same way they came, and when they had gone, you could taste the pure sectarian hatred on that bus: it was stuffed into the air like the burnt odor that came down from the overhead bus-wires.

Back at Maggie O'Neill's house, I found that Mr O'Neill had returned home from his travels and we sat down to get acquainted over the late afternoon tea.

In his own home, Mr O'Neill felt most comfortable in the kitchen, and in that respect, he reminded me of my sister-in-law Mary's husband Tom, from Galway, though Mr O'Neill was a much larger man. He looked like he could handle himself in a rugby match. I could see why having him home made his wife and daughter feel more secure. He asked me to call him Ted, his given name being Edward, and Maggie said he'd been her Teddy Bear all her life, and you could tell how close father and daddy's girl were.

So there we were as Ted poured me a welcome shot-glass of Bushmill's and asked curiously about how I'd gotten involved with Sinn Féin. After my encounter with the British Army, I was glad to have someone to talk to, even if I made sure not to mention anything about that episode on the bus, and, as we conversed, and with a second shot, or maybe a third, sipping, I grew more and more loquacious. Ted O'Neill assured me he was not a member of any movements, 'not even the bowel movement,' and we relaxed into anal humour, R-rated for the family, although Maggie exclaimed, "Poppy!"

At some point, I asked him, "What's it like being a demolitions man, Ted?"

"Well, Nick, it's a dir-rr-ty job, but someone's got to do it. At least you know there's plenty of work going all over the province and you're not likely to find yourself unemployed anytime soon. To tell you the truth, I'm most worried about the competition, the Sinn Féiners, like yourself, who happen to own a building business, and are licensed contractors, licensed to buy and handle gelignite and so on, and some of these have turned it into a profit-making opportunity, going so far as to join the local Brigade, so that the things they blow up at night, they turn up first thing in the morning, putting in the bid to take on the demolition contract thereof resulting, y'see?"

"Is that what's going on?"

"As true as God, I say." And he looked round the kitchen table at his wife and daughter and myself, one by one, and I could see there were no secrets in that family.

"Have you heard of the latest?" said Ted. "It's called 'the black stuff' by the 'RA. It was invented by a chap in Dublin, perfected after months of tinkering, himself being the Quartermaster General of the Provies, at the risk of blowing himself up if he got the proportions of the mixture slightly wrong. I could give you the formula, but then I'd have to kill you, Nick." Ted O'Neill laughed heartily at his little joke.

I went to sleep on the floor of Brian O'Neill's bedroom upstairs that night, thinking there was at least one secret in this family. It defied reason that Ted O'Neill would have his son Brian inside and not be doing everything he could to get him home again, and so I suspected that Mr O'Neill himself must be a member of the 'RA, if not before his son's capture, then certainly after. After all, his occupation gave him the perfect cover.

And so I went to sleep with the sobering and yet comforting thought that things in Belfast (where all was not what it seemed to be) were in good hands.

The next day was Monday, and I used more caution traveling on the bus. For one thing, I made sure I was seated, and next to a window. The bus was deserted more or less on Sunday afternoon, but crowded on Monday morning. I spoke to no one, and made sure to avoid making eye contact when the troops came aboard to roust us. When they had debarked again, surreptitiously I tried to glance outside and see if it was my nemesis of the day before. He was not the only one who would never forget a face. But he wasn't there. Nor was the checkpoint in the same place it had been the day before. This time it was at the big intersection of the Falls Road and the Springfield Road.

I found myself growing increasingly nervous as, in heavy traffic, the bus crept slowly towards the Divis Flats tower in the distance. I seemed to be trapped on that bus into introspective reflection. For one thing, I should have taken care of this already by now—what did I think I was doing hanging about in Belfast? How long could I impose upon the hospitality of the O'Neills? Didn't I have my own place to get back to? I didn't belong here. Where did I belong? The answer came back to me—you belong at home with your wife and child.

How did the people of West Belfast cope? How did they deal with the daily tension of these bus trips, or just walking your own streets. Any corner you turned you could bump squarely into a British foot patrol coming the other way. You could be stopped, questioned, detained at any moment. If your face didn't belong on these streets, they would know it immediately. And there was no such thing as standing on your rights—you had no right to anything, under the Special Powers Act, no right to an attorney, no phone call, not even a reason for your arrest. This was military rule and martial law. How would you like it if this was happening in the streets of Boston? How did they like it when it was—in 1775?

You belong at home with your wife and child.

I got off the bus when I could see we were nearing the looming Divis Tower, and I located my landmark, the dingy-looking, but handsomely quaint, Victorian edifice of the Carnegie Branch Library. I had scouted the area the day before to make sure I knew how to get into and out of it, with my assigned task accomplished, on Monday, it being the sole reason I had come to be in Belfast at all. I was still castigating myself for putting it off this long. Why hadn't I had the sense to get it over and done with and leave town straightaway, instead of mooning about as if I thought this was a weekend at Revere Beach?

The Sinn Féin headquarters were located right next door to the Library, across the mouth of Sevastopol Street. As I crossed, looking right, there was the brooding presence of Black Mountain, which appeared at the end of every side street—just as Nephin followed you everywhere you went in Kilcross.

The Sinn Féin offices here were nothing like Kevin Street in Dublin. This was a small brick two-story building with protective steel shutters closed tightly over the windows, no doubt to bounce back any bombs thrown from passing cars. However, the very same narrow staircase up the side of the building took you upstairs—it made sense that the main office wouldn't be on the ground floor, for security reasons.

Up I went and asked to see someone at the counter up at the top. I was ushered into the presence of one Jimmy Lyons and identified myself as a Sinn Féin member from the Cumann Billy Reid in Dublin.

We closed the door and I slid out the belt from my trouser loops. The back of the leather was wide enough for me to have taped the message I was carrying to the inside of the belt. The letter was written on that tissue-thin blue aeropost paper commonly in use for letters to the States and the Pope in Rome, and the tissue was rolled tight so it was slimmer than a pencil.

Fortunately for myself, I had taped it to the inner side of the belt in the front of my trousers, so that it wasn't visible at all when that officious British Army corporal on the bus was looking at the wallet in my back pocket.

I handed over the letter, thanked Jimmy, said I was fine and I'd be leaving now, causing him to look at me curiously as I beat a retreat, as soon as I'd replaced the belt so that my trousers wouldn't fall down.

Leaving, I swung down the top of the narrow staircase, looked up, and—who should I see but Nugent, coming up!

We passed, again, narrowly, turning sideways, and he nodded at me, but that was all.

I continued on and found myself out on the footpath, flabbergasted. If he was coming himself, why did he not simply bring the letter with him?

The answer, of course, I did not want to know.

Nor would I have wanted to carry it inside my head while I stayed in Belfast with the British Army swarming over all.

I now needed a drink. I needed to sit down somewhere and take a mo to have a nice chat with myself and figure this whole thing out.

I walked quickly away, and two blocks west, a shuttered and boarded up pub with a wire-caged entrance came to my rescue, and I was not going to pass up the first place I came upon where I could get a pint.

Instead, I ordered a half-pint, thinking it would not do at all to loosen Alita's talking machine that much, under the circumstances. I took up a position at the corner of the bar next to the barman's flap where he passed in and out, and I put my back to the wall, and stood facing the front door while I nursed my half-pint.

It was about noontime and the sole waitress was coming back and forth ordering drinks for the mostly sparse attendees, but I did not smile or welcome any interactions. I supposed she was used to it, because she did not bother, either. I had blundered into this place, which turned out to be a sports bar, called Davitt's, though, unlike Dublin, you could not have told from the outside, as this was Belfast and everything was security first. So I spent a half-hour there nursing a drink and being nervous and then could not wait to get out of it again, having not relaxed vigilance for a single moment.

Outside, I felt much freer, and now continued west on foot till I came to a bus shelter with a couple of elderly women who fancied chatting me up.

"You're not from the Falls, are ye?"

"Marian, don't be rude, can't you see he's a visitor?"

"Can't be too careful these days, Dolores, can you?"

"Just visiting, ma'am," I said politely.

"Good God, it's a Yank. Are you on medications or something?"

"Marian, they don't need prescriptions for what they're takin' these days," said her friend Dolores, firmly.

As we boarded, Dolores and Marian made sure to sit far away, and I rode in peace, but got off again, shortly, smiling brightly at the ladies.

This time I was outside a place called The Rock, at the corner of Rockmore Street, though you wouldn't have known it but for the tiny inscription above the, as-usual, barricaded entrance.

Funny how you can have a nose for a pub, no matter how disguised.

Inside, I spent a pleasant hour with a couple of local unemployed dossers named Danny Keegan and Geordie Maher, making sure to let them know that I was leaving Belfast soon, preferably today, so that they could see I had some sense, anyway. However, they delighted in having the chance to ply their war-stories on a fresh victim, just as they would have had I been from South Down or County Waterford, assuring me they did not discriminate against Yanks. Again, I was cautioned about the situation with the black taxis, and I assured them I had not any intention of venturing into the Shankill, which to them, simply proved that I was a man of superior intelligence, to which I replied, "Now you're trying to flatter me."

"No, not at all, isn't that right, Danny?"

"You're right, Geordie."

I left them to their devices, as they saluted me with "Here's to yourself," and "Up the Rebels," and, having passed through the Army checkpoint again without incident, made it back safely to Andy-town.

And, as yet, I hadn't figured out a single thing.

The next day was Tuesday, and this day, this day, I was going to leave Belfast.

But I had one more thing to accomplish, without which I truly believed, since I had by this time convinced myself that I was never coming back again, I truly believed that my exploration of the Belfast question would not be complete. And that was a trip down the Shankill.

So I asked Maggie to ring up Kevin Rooney for me and he soon appeared at her door with the red mini.

Because of the Peace Line separating the two adjacent districts, we had to go all the way in the Falls Road to the no-man's land before heading back out west-by-northwest up the Shankill Road again.

Kevin proceeded at an average slow normal rate of speed up the Shankill, stopping at every red light, and the Army checkpoint, too. He was known by sight there, so my cover story of sightseeing was no probs. The Army were polite and courteous, as I had seen them myself to be, when they wanted to be, when I first landed at the railway station—deferential, in fact—not at all the way they conducted themselves in the Falls. It was obvious why. Everywhere you looked it was red-white-and-blue—the Union Jack was either flying on the breeze or painted on the walls. The Army were at home, performing a police function of protecting British people on British soil. Here in the Shankill they were not on enemy territory as they were right next door in the Falls. It made no matter that the UVF pennant was flying from every lamppost. It made no matter that UDA men, larger than life, stood painted on gable-ends, armed with Kalashnikovs, their faces in ski-masks—the UDA were not the enemy—the IRA was the enemy. Lie down, croppie, was what the Shankill proclaimed, loud and clear.

And, it occurred to me, the soldiers at the checkpoint, or those who did not really know him, likely assumed Kevin was a Protestant, since he lived in the Shankill.

Yet it was a spectral experience to drive slowly up that long road, with the Black Mountain staring you in the face at the aperture of the telescopic narrowing distance.

It was as if you had turned over a mirror, and on the backside, found another mirror where all the images were identical, but appeared in reverse of themselves. In such an odd 'Alice-in-Perverse-land' way. Walls painted with "God Save the Queen." And larger than life, a portrait of a man with short, trim, curly grey hair and a lace-cravat at his throat: James Buchanan, 15th President of the United States, with the quotation, "My Ulster blood is my most priceless heritage." And, of course, Oliver Cromwell, shown in a portrait inside an oval, like a locket worn around a lover's neck, flanked with the old flag of Ulster, the Red Hand at the center of a red Christian cross on a white field, and flanked also with men-at-arms in chain-mail wielding swords of Sheffield steel, all lovingly portrayed on a gable-wall.

"How do you like the Proddies?" asked Kevin Rooney as we finally exited the Shankill again.

He had said not a word the whole time we went up and back down. He had not needed to. The Shankill needed no commentary to elucidate it. It proclaimed itself to the naked eye. And Kevin Rooney had already declared on Saturday that he had said too much then.

I thanked him, saying sincerely, I'd never forget him. I wished him luck, and I honestly meant that, as he left me off at the Belfast Europa so that I could catch my train back to Dublin.

I had not asked Maggie O'Neill to accompany us this time. I did not wish to say goodbye to her at the train station. Nor should she face another trip into the City Centre because of me. We had said our goodbyes in her bedroom, upstairs in Andersonstown, the night before.

That night, late, a fire had been burning, far away in the darkness. I could hear a dull thudding, once, twice, like a rubber mallet on wood. When I lifted the window to look out, the May night came into the room with the after-taste of rain, and with the sound of gunfire chop-chopping in the distant city.

"I want to show you something, Nick," said Maggie, behind me.

It was a wedding gown, under plastic. She had taken it from her closet and laid it out on her bed. Ivory, with French lace on the bodice, and all around the elastic band of the slim waist. It smelled as if it came from a cedar chest. She held it up to her breast for me to admire. "It was my mother's," she said. "Tell me the truth, now, Nick. Do you think I'll ever get to wear it to Matt Calloway's wedding?"

"Yes, I do. And I hope I'll be there to see it. And, uh, I release you from your promise."

"Too late." She tapped her temple. "You're already up here. And when you're up here, you're in my heart, too. So don't you forget *your* promise. Now give us a hug, and we'll say—till then."

Two people in Belfast had admonished me to tell the truth. One was a British soldier. And the other was Maggie O'Neill.

Chapter 13

Radio Free Derry

With summer came the long, lingering twilight that Ireland was known for, which made the daylight seem endless in that northern latitude, and thus transformed Dublin into a city of everlasting light.

This was a real day. With three acts, as in a well-balanced play: morning, afternoon, evening. The curtain rose cool at half-four in the morning. The sun shot up, leaving the east side of O'Connell Street in steep shadow and the length of Rathmines Road as straight as a light-ray, darting south. Clouds came over the late morning and overcast the noon. Showers spilled over the afternoon, to freshen the streets for the final aria. Evening arrived like a glory reborn. Then the sun descended out of the clouds over Kingsbridge, to turn the brown Liffey of the afternoon into the golden river of approaching night.

But the summer of 1972 would bring other colors to Ireland as well, as it did traditionally every summer in living memory. The 12th of July would bring the red, white and blue of Loyalist Unionism to the Shankill Road of Belfast. August would bring

the orange of King Billy circling again with the parade of the
Apprentice Boys along the walls of Derry. With summer came
the marching season, in 1972 as in days of old. But the summer
of '72 was also the green season of the urban guerilla.

Fifty-two British soldiers alive last summer were dead now.
Billy Reid, the Provo Volunteer, was alive last summer, and he
was dead now. Seamus Cusack and Desmond Beattie, Senator
Jack Barnhill, Joe McCann, Bernard Rice, Willie Best, Patrick
McCrory, all of them would see summer no more.

And those were only the names you remembered or chanced
to hear about on the news or to read about in newspapers and
pamphlets. More often, you recalled, not the people and their
names and faces, but the places where they died. St Matthew's
Church in the Short Strand. Three Loyalist petrol-bombers and
a sniper and one Provo killed. The ESB, the Electricity Board in
Belfast City Centre. A young man killed and a lot of girl typists
injured. Two killed by a bomb in a Loyalist pub in the Shankill
Road and fifteen killed in a Nationalist pub in the New Lodge
Road. Then there were the thirteen dead of Derry and Bloody
Sunday, the Army chaplain and six women cleaners killed at
Aldershot military camp in England in the Stickies' reprisal for
Bloody Sunday, the four Provos blown up by their own bomb
in East Belfast, the dead RUC officers and civilians of Done-
gall Street, the dead diners of the Abercorn Restaurant. Who
remembered their names now?

In the summer of '72, Ted Heath and Jack Lynch were
alive and well. Ian Paisley and William Craig were alive and
militant. Falls folk-hero, Provo Billy McKee, defender of
St Matthew's Church, was suffering the effects of his hunger
strike under armed guard in the Royal Victoria Hospital in the
Falls Road, but he was still alive. Ruairí Ó Brádaigh, Dáithí Ó
Conaill, Seamus Twomey, Seán Mac Stíofáin, Martin Meehan,

Martin McGuiness, Sean Keenan, all were alive. Gerry Fitt and Bernadette Devlin and Eamonn McCann and Tommy Herron and Brian Faulkner and Willie Whitelaw were all alive. Gusty Spence and Gerry Adams and Ivor Bell were all in jail, but they were alive. General Farrar-Hockley was replaced with General Freeland who was replaced with General Ford and the British Army was alive. Stormont was dead and gone, but Willie Whitelaw stood alive and fast in its place.

The dead were replaced with the living. Ireland was groaning in rivers of blood that chilled the winter and soaked the summer, but Ireland was alive and kicking, and struggling, as the drums of war danced on into the summer. And Lt. Col. Derek Wilford, commander of the Parachute Regiment on Bloody Sunday, had his OBE.

I had returned to Dublin, but not to 56 Upper Rathmines Road. Instead, I stopped awhile in Leinster Square. Where they were waiting for me.

"How's Belfast?" said Krishna. Mary McKenna was sitting in his lap, her arms around his neck. "Still there, is it?" she said.

"I left it at the Provos' check-point at the entrance to Andersonstown." I flopped in the only available place, Jane and Mary's sheepskin-covered couch by the fireplace.

"You look tired," said Jane Quill. "Have you been home yet?"

"Like Brendan McAndrews said, 'we don't go where we're not welcome.'"

"Aisling's been missing her da," said Jane.

"I miss her, too, Jane. Don't you think I do? I wouldn't be human, would I? But Sheila knows the cure for that. How far away is the telephone on the wall?"

"You're a dirty rotten male chauvinist pig," said Jane, "if you want to know my opinion."

Nobody wanted to listen to a row at this point, so Krishna hastened to interject, "What else happened up there?–anything good?"

"Not much. I stopped into the Sinn Féin office in the Falls—met Jimmy Lyons. You heard that story? And Paddy from Andytown says to say hello."

Mary was playing with the curls on the back of Krishna's neck. "Get off me, you dirty cow!" he said.

Resentfully she shifted herself, over to the couch, saying, "Listen to the official organ of the Republican Movement!"

"Run into any agro?" Krishna continued.

"I stayed away from it," I replied. "In and out."

"And how goes the war?"

"Politics by another name."

"You telling I?"

"There's no difference between the Shankill Road and the Falls Road—I can tell you that. Politicians made this mess—in the service of their own interests—it's nothing but payment for the votes that got them in office."

"It is a political problem—therefore, there exists a political solution."

"So when do we end the war and start the politics?"

"Mary, fetch me some tea, love?" Krishna sat up to the edge of his seat. "We want to talk. We want the solution. We want peace, too. But what power will talk to us—if we do not hold a gun to his head?"

It's said in Ireland that in the summertime you will always get one month of fine weather. Nobody could quarrel with the month of June we had that year.

On a Sunday in late June, once a year, every year, the Irish Republican Movement marches to Bodenstown Churchyard in County Kildare to gather under the apple trees at the graveside of the Father of the Movement, Wolfe Tone, the rebel Protestant from Ulster who founded the United Irishmen in 1791 and was found dead, hanging in his British jail-cell, a martyr to old Ireland, after his capture in the Rising of 1798.

That June, the day we marched to Bodenstown was a risky, parti-coloured day of skidding clouds blanking and peeping the sun: risky for rain. We assembled in the morning in the village of Sallins while we waited for Jack Lynch's Fianna Fail to hold their official government ceremony at the grave-site. Pipe bands in kilts and accordian bands of 8-to-12 year old girls collected in farmers' fields along the road outside the village while their older brothers and sisters and the grownups celebrated in the pubs of Sallins. Na Fianna Éireann in the traditional green uniforms formed up in the village street. Tri-colours and ice-pops, popcorn and hot chips, pretzels and posters, and medallions and medals were being sold by the dozens of vendors who walked up and down hawking their wares. The Movement sold newspapers and commemorative magazines, souvenirs and copies of the Republican Social and Economic Programme, Éire Nua, and a great trade was done among the enormous crowd in their festive and militant mood.

Then in the afternoon it was Sinn Féin's turn to march out to the graveyard, and we set out with flags flying, berets waving and music blaring, clogging the road between the trees so that the official cars of the government had to pull up on the shoulder under the leaves or in the ditch by the stone wall. And in the face of surveillance from Dublin Castle, marching under the rippling green-white-and-orange Irish Tricolour, the Republicans were singing, singing the defiant outlaw ballad of the Irish Civil War,

Take it down from the mast, Irish traitors,
It's the flag we Republicans claim,
It will never belong to Free-Staters,
For you've brought on it nothing but shame.

Won't you leave it to those who are willing
To uphold it in war or in peace,
To the men who intend to do killing
Until England's tyrannies cease.

The Memorial to Wolfe Tone no longer stood in the graveyard at Bodenstown, for the UVF had blown it to dust in '66, as a reprisal for the Republicans blowing up Nelson's Pillar in O'Connell Street; but every year the Movement gathered there nonetheless to renew their vows and restate their faith.

That day, Sean Keenan of Derry was to give the Oration. The silver-haired dean of the Derry Sinn Féin had already spent his time in the Internment camps that year, and the cameras from the Special Branch in Dublin edged forward and clicked once or twice, furtively, before withdrawing. A huge audience packed in shoulder to shoulder under the trees and Keenan arrived, the silver head visible among a phalanx of Derry Provos in dark glasses and black berets, his bodyguard. Jostling, and hoarse threats, and the plainclothes men of the Branch quickly receded behind tree-trunks.

They made a queer spectacle. Other cameras, from our side, were snapping *their* mug-shots, and their vanity was insulted. Like spoiled brats taking their hurley sticks home, when the match hadn't gone their way, they were slinking back to their unmarked black Ford Cortinas wearing their injured sensibilities on their chins. Not a "sorry" out of them, as the people in the audience, there to hear Sean Keenan, made them force their way past stiff shoulders and unbending knees. Hostility buzzed under those trees like invisible bees.

When Sean Keenan got past the obligatory references to history, the bows to the memory of Wolfe Tone, the formulas of the faith, and came to the part he came to say, he seemed to address these stalwarts of the Special Branch of Dublin Castle.

"Our enemies," he said, "accuse us of lacking any politics. They say we are without a plan. They are trying to criminalize us, with their epithets of 'gunmen' and labeling us 'sectarian assassins.' It won't work. The people know who their real enemies are. We are going forward, and we won't stop till our aims are secured!"

His listeners set up a roar that was a cross between applause and ovation, with jeering and catcalls, aimed at the Branch, thrown in, boot-heels stamping on grave-grass for emphasis, blunt toes grinding cemetery gravel.

"Which of us who stood here this time last year," continued Keenan, "would have believed that in just one year we would be talking of that tyrannical monolith, the Stormont regime, as a thing of the past? Just as that machine of repression that once seemed so almighty powerful over our lives was kicked aside, like a stray scrap of paper in the road, under the marching feet of the Risen People, so shall other verities, that seem today so entrenched and formidable, come to pass away. And one day soon, you and I and all our comrades now struggling in the dark tunnels of the Resistance, will emerge, to walk these Irish roads of ours in the broad light of day, unhindered and free!"

Again they interrupted him with wild noise, until Keenan leaned forward into the microphone in his hand.

"And that day is not so far off," he growled, his voice finally gone hoarse. "I promise you, the day of peace is at hand."

Like a cup of hot tea spilled in your lap came the news that made you jump: an offer of a Ceasefire—from the IRA to the British Army.

Four days after Sean Keenan dropped his hint at Bodenstown, the IRA staged a Press Conference in Free Derry. Seán Mac Stíofáin, the Chief of Staff, Martin McGuinness, Derry Commander, Seamus Twomey, Belfast Commander, and Dáithí Ó Conaill, the Movement theoretician, offered Willie Whitelaw an invitation to visit the No-go Area in the Bogside and Creggan to observe, as their guest, how the IRA kept the peace and defended the people.

Willie refused the invite. His second, Merlyn Rees, who happened to be in Derry, fled the city precipitously, lest the Vanguard and the UDA and Paisley accuse him of conferring legitimacy on the 'gunmen' by talking to them.

It was Willie's mistake, and he wasn't long in realising it. Billy McKee and Proinsas MacArt and Gerry Adams were in the Crumlin Road Gaol leading a hunger strike for political status. The Falls was seething with rumours that McKee was dying, right at the moment, with British armed guards in the hospital ward with him. In spite of that, a Provo rescue attempt couldn't be ruled out, and the adoration in which a cross-section of the Falls community held McKee was causing nightly rioting, in preparation for his death and martyrdom. The Army was growing nervous to keep a cap on things. Bombings and gun-battles multiplied and the mystery assassination campaign threw fuel on the fires. The SDLP, whose members abstained from their seats at Westminster, was fit to be tied because of their promise to their constituents not to talk with or bargain with the British authorities while Internment lasted. But now

SDLP MP John Hume went to see Whitelaw, with the twin excuse that Willie was steadily releasing Internees and the IRA wanted a truce. That was all anyone knew, as speculation ripened in the press, on the street, in the studios of RTE, ITV and the BBC.

I hadn't been back to No. 56 since the night of Sheila's aborted birthday party. Now that Krishna had more or less permanently moved into Mary's room upstairs, I was kipping in his room downstairs, since it was paid up till the end of June. I salved my conscience with the thought that I'd pleaded enough with Jane Quill to persuade her to spend most of her free time weeknights up in No. 56 keeping Sheila company, helping out with the kid, and, incidentally, keeping me informed.

Everyone was walking around the two of us on eggshells these days. There were emissaries and peace-feelers back and forth as Bernadette Cullen and Martina Kelly swapped conferences with me for all-night soul-searches with Sheila. I would tell Bernie I couldn't care less, and in the next breath, ask her how your one was getting on without me. Just grand, came Sheila's reply, but Bernie came to me and told me she couldn't sleep nights, and not just because she had to get up at 4 a.m. for work. No wonder, says I, with all her girlfriends stopping by for the chat. Bernie went to Sheila and told her that I was nervous and irritable. A couple of days passed and Sheila admitted she was worrying about me now, too, as well as the kid and the rent and the job and—. Back went Bernadette to me to claim that all Sheila wanted was to be reassured that she wouldn't be rebuffed. "You tell her that I can't live her life for her and it's up to herself." Which Bernie translated to Sheila as, he's falling apart without you, he misses Aisling terribly, and he's desperate.

"Look, Seán, I'm going crazy with nothing to do," I said to Ó Brádaigh one day in Kevin Street.

"Well, I'll see what I can do."

"Does Seamus McGrath need a hand over in Parnell Square?" I asked. McGrath was the editor of An Phoblacht and worked out of Kevin Barry Hall at No. 44. "I have my degree, you know. Two of them, in fact."

Ó Brádaigh scratched behind his ear. "He doesn't have a spot at the moment. But I'll tell you what—could you do a shift at Northern Aid?"

I knew the place, a small office down steps near Liberty Hall in Eden Quay.

"Four hours a day," said O' Bradaigh, "around mid-day, to let the lads slip out for a bite. Just answering the telephone and stuffing envelopes."

"Right. I'll do it."

Dáithí Ó Conaill appeared in the doorway. He was keeping close to Headquarters these days, making himself accessible to the media. Unlike Cahill and the elder Ó Brádaigh, Ó Conaill, so far, had stayed clear of fortnights behind bars. He did it by keeping on the move. If he dropped into Kevin Street, it was to meet his appointment and be gone again. Reporters he would meet in safe houses and safe hotels, safe pubs, too, places he could get to while losing his tail. It was the middle of the after-noon now, and safe enough for him to be in the street or in a car. The Special Branch, like other organisations, preferred doing its dirty work under cover of darkness.

In the narrow space between the counter and the wall, Ó Conaill brushed past us, and Seán and I turned our heads to let him go by. Maria Maguire came out of the back room to join him. She hadn't seen me since the afternoon we taped at the RTE studios, but she acknowledged me with a nod. The two of them were late for their appointment. Back the other way they went and quickly down the stair to the street door.

Breaking my own rule, I leaned over to whisper to Seán. "What's up?"

Ó Brádaigh cast his eyes up to heaven. "Ah—you read the papers, don't you?" Then he said, confidential-like, "Would you ever be available to lend a hand in Derry?"

My ears perked up. "Aye. Sure."

The papers that day bannered headlines shouting out a visit to London by John Hume, from the SDLP, and Paddy Devlin, representing the NRM, who was an Independent, supposed by the British to be in contact with the IRA. These two were sitting down with Ted Heath in Downing Street. The SDLP man, Hume, was talking to the British Prime Minister with Internment still on, and that had to mean something big. Devlin was there to serve as a convenience to the PM, so that he could talk to the Provos 'without talking to them.' Hi-jackings of cars to burn and stoning of British troops with paving stones and bricks and bottles during riots in the Falls were soaring tensions as Billy McKee lay dying in hospital and MacArt and Adams languished in the Crum. Whitelaw was being criticized in the press, Irish and English, for alienating the minority, the Catholics. Editorials pointed out that, one day when the UDA showed up at Stormont, decked out in their para-military uniforms, complete with hoods and masks on, Willie talked to *them*, didn't he?

One afternoon as I rode home on the top deck of a 14A after my shift at Northern Aid, the bus stalled in traffic in Richmond Street. From my stationary perch, I happened to see Maria Maguire, right below my window, walking by herself on the crowded footpath, towards the Portobello Bridge.

Alone—except for the two men in macs walking casually a good way behind her. I ran down to the lower deck, thinking to get in the way of the Branch men, or something, I didn't know what, but the bus was moving again, and I couldn't jump off the rear platform as it accelerated until we were over the bridge and all the way up at the bus shelter in front of Mary Immaculate in Rathmines. I ran back to Portobello, but Maria and the men were gone.

The next day was a Friday and the front pages in Dublin were set on fire with news of a Truce. Billy McKee was saved from death. Gerry Adams was released outright from the Crumlin Road Jail, and MacArt and the others on hunger strike were delivered from a miserable, agonizing death. Not only was Willie Whitelaw going to talk to the 'gunmen,' but the Provos were actually going to go to London, for negotiations with the Prime Minister.

There was ecstasy in Dublin. For the first time since the days of Michael Collins and Arthur Griffith, the IRA was going to negotiate with British statesmen.

According to the terms of the deal, it was to be a bilateral Ceasefire, to begin at midnight, the 26th of June, at which hour both the British Army and the IRA would lay down arms. Both parties were then to enjoy freedom of movement in the streets without hindrance of the other. The IRA was conceded the right to bear arms, and the British agreed to stop searching houses and cars and to cease and desist from the insult of the P-searches, where Army patrols could stop random civilians in the street.

For the prisoners inside, the British Government conceded Special Category. That meant the prisoners were granted the right to wear their own clothing in jail, the right to have visitors, the right to read whatever they wanted, the right to associate freely among themselves, and the right to elect their own prison leadership to conduct their affairs and settle grievances with prison administration. This would prevent another breakdown such as the one which caused the riot at Mountjoy Prison in Dublin. In effect, they were being de-criminalized and granted the status of Prisoners-of-War, with all the rights conferred on POWs by the Geneva Convention.

All that was left now was for the Provos to go to London and negotiate the British withdrawal from Ireland.

"Wait—wait," counseled Comrade Krishna, but nobody wanted to listen.

This was it. All the sacrifices of four years of conflict, all the hard work of the last, terrible year, all those dead and injured, couldn't have been in vain. It was a matter of days now till we saw our long-sought United Ireland—weeks at the most. In the pubs, the talk from the old-timers was all of the days when the Black and Tans withdrew to barracks, going sullenly and full of spit through the silent crowds of onlookers in Dublin and Cork in '21. "Wait—wait," Comrade Krishna advised, but nobody wanted to listen.

For peace was desperately desired on all sides. An end to the warfare, an end to the killing and dying, an end to the jails and the camps, and let the boys come marching home to the kind of peace, with justice, freedom and unity, family and friends, that everybody wanted so desperately.

Krishna came down to me at three in the morning and shook me out of bed on my floor-pallet. "Telephone, comrade."

"Who is it?" I grumbled, knowing full well who it must be at that hour.

Sheila didn't speak at the other end when I said "Hello?" but I could have kissed the sound of her breathing. "Well—you got me up—what do you want?"

"Nick," she said, in a small voice, "don't talk to me like that—please."

I leaned my forehead on the wall. Krishna withdrew discreetly. 'Okay, okay," I whispered, "but why did you call me at this ungodly hour?"

"I had to," said Sheila, "I couldn't sleep."

"Is Jane there with you?"

"Yes, why?"

"Just asking. Don't you have to go to work soon?"

"Nick—are you coming home to us?"

I said nothing.

"Aisling keeps asking after you."

"What is this—blackmail?"

"You know how to be cruel, don't you?"

"Well, that's what it is—emotional blackmail."

"Don't you miss your daughter?"

"It's not me that's keeping my daughter hostage from me."

Sheila was silent. I wasn't giving an inch, and neither was she going to beg and crawl. "Well," she said, but the tears crept into her voice in spite of herself, "–is that all?"

I swallowed a lump in my throat. I felt like I was sweating with a fever. "I'm going back to bed," I said. I waited for the click of the phone at her end, but it didn't come. Finally, she spoke.

"Don't go," she said in a whisper. "I have to talk to you."

"You know where I am. I'm not going anywhere." I hung up before she could.

Now we'll see, I thought. Under the covers on my pallet, I stretched out my toes, placed both hands behind my head, and watched the ceiling in the dark.

When she came in the room she came in so softly you would think she'd walked down Rathmines Road barefoot.

"Oh, my love." I reached up my hand, where the dark form knelt at my side, and felt for her face, inside the mantle of her hair.

"You don't know," she sighed, "this past week—how I thought of killing myself."

"Don't you ever think of hurting yourself. I couldn't bear it. No matter how bad things are, they're never that bad. Come here to me, Sheila."

On the corner next door to No. 4A Kevin Street was the Wexford Inn, a bar where the office help from Headquarters would sometimes stop for a quick pint and a decent roast beef sandwich.

I didn't know why Seán Ó Brádaigh had rung me up or why he wanted me to meet him at the Wexford Inn. I had been back at No. 56 with Sheila and Aisling for a few days only when I took the call out in the hall. Fortunately, Sheila was already home from work, as Sean wanted to see me straightaway, and said he would wait there for me. I told them I'd be home for tea and grabbed the first bus to come by my front door.

"Now I don't want you to be too shocked when this chap walks in the door from Wexford Street," Ó Brádaigh said as we stood at the bar with pints settling. "Remember, this is a public place." And other hints like that. "Just keep your eye on that doorway." He was enjoying himself mightily and grinning away.

Immediately, I thought it can only be the one and only Mick O'Corrigan—but what does Seán know about—?

Then a short shadow crossed over the threshold of light when the door burst open and the shadow made straight for us. But I couldn't make out who it was because the bright sunshine was behind him. Until I put the jaunty step together with the bedspring walk. "Ah, Mayo, God help us!" I exclaimed. "I thought I'd never see you again."

"How're ye keepin,' Nicholas?" said Toss Ribbons, National School teacher of Kilcross, County Mayo, as he grabbed my hand to shake it as if he had a rabbit by the neck. "Is that any way to greet us coming up to Dublin to see you?"

"It's the traditional greeting of the city slickers to the Culchie just up from the country," I said, laughing.

Ó Brádaigh leaned in and said, "I'm glad you're a punctual man, Toss—I didn't know how long I could keep up the charade."

"I couldn't be more flabbergasted," I said to Seán. I turned to regard Toss Ribbons, still amazed to see him, and in the publight, now that the door was closed, I could detect that the wiry little goatee of last summer was now entirely gone, submerged in the full bloom of a pepper-and-salt beard, but the premature grey hair falling over the forehead, only to be brushed back like the forelock on a billy-goat, was the same. "I couldn't be more surprised if you'd fallen from the sky."

"Well, we were never that far away, y'know," said Toss, with the falling-off insistence on 'y'know' at the end of the line that brought the full flower of the Mayo accent back to me instantly. "Why haven't you been back to see us all these months, when Sheila was home for Easter, 'n'such?"

Thinking fast, I nodded at Ó Brádaigh and said, "Your man's been keeping us busy. I'm just back from Belfast, as a matter of fact."

"Well," said Toss, "we've a long ride again, back across the country."

I looked back and forth, from one to the other. "Would somebody mind telling me where, and what for?"

Ó Brádaigh then outlined the situation in the Bogside and the Creggan, up in Derry, as far as the state of his information could make it out, and the job was simple enough. All we had to do was to meet the people up there and go to work. "And now I must get back to the office," he said, shaking hands with the both of us. "Just do whatever you're asked and don't get yourselves in trouble. Sean Keenan runs his own show, and nobody could ask for a better man. And remember who sent you—I might need a favour from him sometime."

When Sean had gone, I said to Toss, "Did you bring a motor with you?"

"Petrol tank topped up," said he.

"Right, then. Back to my place—the missus'll have tea on for us, with baked goods. It's only a minute from here by car."

"I'm afraid not," said Toss. "Oh, not to worry. I've already informed Sheila of the plan. I got her at the bakery yesterday from the Post Office in Kilcross."

"But how did you know about the bakery? And how did you get the number?"

"Nick, my friend, you've no secrets from the Irish Republican Movement,

y'know."

"Apparently not."

"Now come on. We'd best get goin' if we're to get there by nightfall."

Zooming up and zooming down, taking four corners on two wheels, all across the map of Ireland, with Toss Ribbons at the

wheel of the yellow beetle in the summertime, and if ever two
fellas had a lot of catching up to do, we had, and the conversation was as non-stop as the driving.

Beginning with your letter-writing habits, which are
non-existent, what I want to know is, did Pat get another tractor,
certainly he did, and the new pasture's making him more money
than ever, and how is everybody, anyway, they miss you, they
do, you don't expect me to believe that, aye, it's true, there
hasn't been such craic as the day the Yank brought the cows
home, don't remind me, how is it you already know everything
I've been up to, isn't it a small country, and I have my sources,
y'know, well, you're still a secret to me, how did you ever manage
to tear away from that shower of Fianna Fail in-laws of yours,
you're as bad as I am, what did you tell the wife where were
you going, I go where I want to, so I do, and do what I want
to when I get there, you should have no complaints, then, so
what was your story, well, I'm off to do a wee job, that's all, oh,
that sounds bad, now, there's more than one kind of a job, I'm
helping a fella build a wall, in County Monaghan, it's a very long
wall and may take a fortnight, or more, but it's a few bob on the
side while it's summertime and I'm not school-mastering, now
do y'see, you're a rogue, that's what you are, Toss Ribbons, the
same as yourself, according to the little lady, now you've been in
this country a year now and still you don't see, it's the way things
are done, amn't I a son to some, and a father to others, a cousin
to a few, and a stranger to most, a man for all seasons, you're
the staunchest Republican I ever knew that wasn't a Republican,
oh, but I'm not at all, I'm only what I appear to be, a teacher
working for the state, and I have the job and the family and the
whole lot, isn't it a shame now what they did to poor Flipper
Flanagan, of the Garda Síochána, relegating him to duty in the
poor tiny isolated village of Kilcross, County Mayo, the very

arse-end o' the West, after him patrollin' the streets of a big town the likes of Limerick City, you want to watch yourself with him now, the next time you're down in Mayo, he reports everything back up to Dublin, so he does, angling for the promotion, like, and trying to get back in their good graces, why do they call him Flipper? oh, because he has the look of a baby trout surprised to find a hook in his mouth, Flipper Flanagan, that's a good one, which reminds me, I always meant to ask you and you never did explain to me the etymology of the family name of Ribbons, are you sure you have the time, I do as long as you can talk and drive at the same time, well, you see, 'twas back in the days of Daniel O'Connell, before the Famine, and long before the Land League and Michael Davitt of Mayo, and back then, there were outlaw bands, known as the Ribbonmen, which were men evicted from their lands by the profiteering landlord agents belonging to the Ascendancy, absentee landlords many of them were, and the Ribbonmen became notorious for burning down the lord o' the manor's house in reprisal, and murdering the agents, and what-not, and they were hunted down, and one of my ancestors, the great-grandfather, I think it must've been, was on the run and found his way up into the parish of Addergoole, in the wilds of Mayo, the back of beyond, as it 'twere, hiding out from the authorities, and he met a likely young lady and they got married and, of course, that was the time when the parish of Addergoole was just beginnning to keep marriage and birth records, because of the passage of the Bill of 1863 passed in the British Parliament, so there you have it, your man, being a wanted fugitive, but known locally nonetheless as a Ribbonman, a point of pride amongst his own, the Catholics of the parish, gave Ribbons as his name, 'twas his little joke, y'know, and so the name was passed down thereafter to yours truly, and it stuck like egg yolk on a china plate, well, I'm glad to get that finally cleared up, and did you hear the latest from the States, no, what, when was it, Saturday a week, they caught some telephone tappers in the Democratic headquarters in Washington, they didn't, they did, and it's the Republicans spying on the Democrats, you know, I wouldn't put it past that man, you know what we call him, don't you, no, what, Tricky Dick, ha, that's a good one, Tricky Dicky and Silly Willie, sure it's the same both sides of the pond, do you mean I ought to be glad I'm out of it? And how do you suppose I found out all I know about your recent activities, why, Flipper Flanagan, of course, the mouth of the Moy, they call him, all you need do is buy him a pint in Delaney's, when he's off duty, of course, why, they have a nice fat file on you, Nick, up in the Castle, so you'd better mind your step.

And so, great craic was had by all as we made our way across Ireland.

In the border village of Blacklion in County Leitrim, the pub we went into was almost as empty as the street outside. A teenaged barman with the sleeves of his white shirt rolled up stood back from the long bar with the heels of his hands planted on the counter-edge, chatting with a well set-up middle-aged couple. Toss and I parked ourselves a distance down the straight bar.

Your man was distinguished-grey, sipping scotch over ice, while the woman wore the well-preserved look of wealth. They were showing the barman a packet of ostentatiously enlarged colour photos. The woman pointed. "Now that's Hans. He's Swiss-German."

"German-Swiss, dear," her husband corrected her.

"Oh, yes, you're right, darling, of course. You should see the place they live in, Hugh." She was very familiar with the young barman. "A palazzo. That's where we always stay when we're in Geneva."

With courteous difficulty, Hugh the barman detached himself from his guests and slipped down the bar to serve his only other customers, us. I approached the woman when the husband excused himself to the Gents. "Pardon me," I said, smiling my charming smile. "Could that be a Scotch accent I hear?"

"Oh, dear, no, we're from Belfast. Cultra, actually, outside the city."

"Oh, I'm sorry, wow, honestly, I just couldn't help asking. I just love the way people talk over here. Really. I hope you're not offended?"

"Not at all. I'd be quite happy to be considered that British. Are you here long?"

"Less than a week. I landed at Shannon."

"Holidays?"

"You mean—vacation? Yeah."

The husband returned, and insisted I finish my drink with him. "That's the daughter's wedding," he said proudly, showing the photos. "Hollywood Golf Club, you see."

I said, "Oh, she's a beautiful bride. What's her name?"

"Gillian. And this—that's her twin."

"My, oh my. Are they identical?"

"It's the hairstyles, you know. That's Lillian."

"Lillian and Gillian," I sighed. "Well—they're both beautiful. Did Lillian get married, too?"

"Oh, no, no, no," the man laughed. "My boy—think of the expense! Now—this is the entire group, bridesmaids, best man, et cetera, et cetera, on the steps of the City Hall. Registry Office affair, you know."

I spent the next two minutes ooh-ing and ah-ing over the colour enlargements, and another five minutes when the wife made off to the powder room pumping her husband for news of the road ahead.

"Oh, no, no, no. People have entirely the wrong impression. Why—what must they think of us in America? Now, we've just come down from Belfast. Two hours on a perfectly straight motorway. Not a bit of bother. Heading for Galway for our holidays, aren't we, dear?" he said, as the wife was back again. "We just love the coast of Connemara. No, you mustn't think—."

The wife leaned her hand on my shoulder and said earnestly, "It's not what they show you on your television."

The husband said, "Now—have you a rental?"

"Oh, yes," I said promptly. "In fact, that's my driver right over there."

Toss Ribbons was waiting with the motor running on the yellow VW bug outside when I jumped in. "Your driver, eh?" he said. "Pair of feckin' Unionist upper crust."

"Drive on, Jeeves," said I, "they've just come through Belcoo, no stops."

With its bright white railings and its ribs of blue steel, Craigavon Bridge spanned the River Foyle and connected the two halves of Derry, the sole passage between them. It strode across the water with sturdy concrete feet exactly at the point where the river drew its deepest breadth, widening into a magnificent, sweeping curve, a broad blue highway coiled around the outstretched instep of the Derryside.

Derry, like Belfast, was divided into east and west, Protestant and Catholic. Yet the holy ground, sacred to the Protestants of the east bank of the Foyle, lay buried amongst the houses topping the high hill on the west side of the river. Up there were the Walls of Derry, guarding the old city that was defended by the Apprentice Boys in the Siege of 1690, when the city was held by its Protestant defenders against the encircling army of Stuart, the Catholic King of Scotland, who claimed the throne of England by his descent from Mary Queen of Scots. Up there was The Diamond, the four-cornered square that formed the hub of the old city. It was The Diamond the Civil Rights marchers were trying to reach, and The Diamond the RUC were defending, when they drew their batons and charged in the police riot on Craigavon Bridge that began it all on the 5th of October, 1968.

It was a fine, sunny June day and the view was dazzling, with the river a mirror, and the slate roofs of the walled city terracing upward, rank on rank, reflecting a shower of splendor from the sky, when Toss Ribbons pulled the yellow VW into a layover under a set of trees in the Victoria Road, south of the Waterside, the Protestant hillside on the east bank of the Foyle.

"Switch over," he said to me, "just in case. You drive, and play the dumb Yank, and they won't ask you questions."

"Well, hurry up, before somebody spots us." I pushed myself across the stickshift knob while Toss raced round to the passenger side. Off we went, joltingly, as I struggled left-handed with the stick-shift, and the car wobbling back and forth in the Victoria Road.

As we crossed Craigavon Bridge, with the Bogside, still hidden from us on the far side of the old city, three roads splintered off the end of the bridge, and caught in the wrong lane, I was forced away from the Foyle Road along the riverbank and headed into the curving incline of the Carlisle Road. It twisted in the middle and suddenly we were confronted with Bishop's Gate, signs posting the restricted zone, galvanised iron doors standing open in the huge archway of the Walls, and

RUC stopping all cars going under the brow of the Gate. We got closed into the queue of the vehicles, waiting our turn, surveilled by British soldiers patrolling behind the accordian-wire atop the Wall, and an RUC officer watching in the street, the butt of a black Stirling submachinegun planted on his hip, muzzle pointing at the sky.

My window was down in the warm weather and my right elbow planted on the door. An RUC officer asked to see my licence. He looked at the picture and compared it to my face while Toss Ribbons nodded at the officer on his side of the car and a third member of the forest-green-clad police peered into the back seat through the rear window. The RUC man on my window said, "Are you an American citizen?"

"Yes, I am."

"What is the purpose of your visit?"

"Just touring around. Come to see the famous Walls of Derry. I play music, you see, and I know the tune, but I've never actually seen them."

Giving me a look as much as to say 'another talkative Yank full of himself,' the policeman handed the licence back to me and waved us on without having the third officer open the boot.

The four gates in the Derry Walls are called after the four streets leading out from The Diamond: Bishop's Gate, Butcher's Gate, Shipquay Gate and Ferryquay Gate. As we started up the steep hill to The Diamond, a Land-Rover and an armoured personnel carrier came down toward us and swung into the yard of the Bishop's Gate Barracks, but other than that, we found nothing remarkable in these four streets but a succession of small shops squeezed into dowdy Victorian fronts, wooden, and painted ochre, pearl-grey and mauve, and sandwiched between Woolworth's, JC Penney's, and Selfridge's. We parked in The Diamond, thinking that if anyone at the checkpoint had taken any particular notice of the red number plates on the back of the VW, which identified the car as being from the 26 Counties, we'd best do a bit of sight-seeing. In these opening days of the Truce, the shopping district of the old city was a-whirl with shoppers, who mingled with security guards in every shop-doorway, and the Bogside and the Creggan were somewhere on another planet.

At Butcher's Gate, at the bottom of the steep hill, with the bronze monument to the British dough-boys of the First World War up in The Diamond only half-visible behind us, we found a stairway on the inside of the Wall, and climbed up to the top. Our eyes were amazed to find a paved macadam roadway, wide enough to drive a brace of beer-lorries, two-abreast, along the top of the Wall. Toss pointed over the side. There, below Butcher's Gate, lay the Bogside, sunk in the lowland, prone and vulnerable. We were standing atop the perfect sniper's nest.

Up at the corner, where the Wall turned back at a right angle, the British Army had an observation post; covered with canvas and a tin roof, and from which they could sweep the length of the Wall overlooking the Bogside. The outside of the Wall facing the Bogside dropped a sheer twenty feet. At the bottom, the stonework sloped slightly outward, but there was a precipitous grass-covered embankment which fell another forty or fifty feet. The roadway leading out of Butcher's Gate was terraced into the hillside at this point before it wound its way down into the valley of the Bogside.

To anyone standing atop the Derry Walls for the first time, as we were, it became clear instantly why they proved impregnable in the Siege of 1690. For the attacking Stuart Army to have hoped to climb an embankment as cliff-like as this one, and then scale the stout wall at its crest, twenty feet thick, while the Protestant defenders rained down death upon them from above, "would have been madness, or a miracle of all the saints, given the weapons and artillery of those days," observed my friend and fellow history-buff, Toss Ribbons.

But below us, the Bogside was taking no chances, either, in the present-day here-and-now. It was ready to defend itself. Between the winding road out of Butcher's Gate and the valley bottom, the tower-block of the Rossville Street Flats and its lesser companion-buildings intervened, with concrete walks and stairs climbing the hill. But beyond that, we could see Free Derry Corner, and barricades of concrete emplacements embedded at the entrances to the walks and courtyards and car-parks of the Bogside Flats. Barbed wire, over-turned cars, piled furniture, hijacked, burnt-out buses tipped on their sides, wheels out—anything that would help stop a Saracen or dull the blade on a British bulldozer—formed what looked to be a quite formidable barrier at this distance. The Bogside was a fortified encampment.

We fetched the yellow Volkswagen and drove down to Butcher's Gate. Since we were leaving, not entering, the RUC detachment at the checkpoint waved us through. Here their authority ended. Here, the Rossville Flats began and the Provos took over. Toss and I wound down the hillside and leisurely swung round the hairpin curve at the bottom, where the white-washed house-gable-end read in bold black lettering, three feet high,

YOU ARE NOW ENTERING FREE DERRY

The bright clouds we saw crowning the walled city when we were crossing Craigavon Bridge now marched away west-ward beyond the Bogside behind the high hill of the Creggan. Loungers dossed about under the headline of the whitewashed wall, and a young man and a girl counted coins in a cigar-box on a folding card-table. Even the guardians of the No-Go Area, the masked men of the IRA, were doing their watching from the sunny steps of the Bogside Flats— in the last of an Irish twilight, their rifles laid down beside them.

Toss Ribbons and I soon found we weren't the only volunteer political workers landing in the Sinn Féin walkup that week in the Bogside. The Republicans had a house arranged so that all of us could stay together, "out of the way, and all in one place," as Joe Crowley put it. It was an abandoned council flat in the Brandywell, behind the Bogside, in a street called Asylum Road. "Perfect," laughed Toss Ribbons. "Always knew I was mad!"

A one-time fire-bomb target, the house had the roofing gone in places and sagging in spots. But one room in the back, away from the street, was dry, and there ten people took turns boiling potatoes on a gas-ring and eating in shifts at the table. Another room, where the stars at night had only one hole in the roof to peek through, was our dormitory: pallets and sleeping bags lined the walls. The wind went right through the house at night and everyone took to calling it The Whistling Gypsy.

We started work immediately. There were a million things to do, in progress, half-finished, being proposed, up for a vote, abandoned and forgotten, revived and reviled, in flux, out-of-joint, confused and scrambled. All to do with the civil administration of the No-Go Areas of the Bogside and the Creggan Estates, which the Derry people now had carried on for a year in the absence of any recognized or accepted or even feasible governmental, police, fire or social services from the official order.

In that time the Nationalists in Derry had become a community of full-time working people trying their best to make their living, maintain their households, raise their families, and deal with Internment and an urban guerilla military campaign ongoing, in the midst and on the fringes: all at the same time, besides trying to govern themselves. The community needed the help, and they made us visitors welcome. "Would you ever run over to Granny Blackpool's and pick up that load of Green Shield stamps she has?" Joe Crowley would ask the crowd in the office, and somebody, anybody who wasn't tied up on the phone, or tied up typing, or mimeographing, or tied up discussing, arguing or plea-bargaining, would say, "I'll go, Joe." "That's the good lad. I've been promising her for three days, and I'll be lucky to get out of here by midnight again tonight, and she's afraid herself to go into the city, still."

The big project, of course, was the matter of monitoring the Cease-fire. The Bogsiders and Cregganites had been defending themselves for a year, and having suffered through a twelve-month and more of daily tensions and flashpoints, their automatic, hair-trigger reactions tended to linger on in a war-weary nervousness. Above all, nobody wanted some young hothead sparking off resumed hostilities over an insult or an incident. All I had to do to envision the possibility was to think of good old Mick O'Corrigan. How many of his persuasion must there be in a place like this? The Sinn Féiners set up a 24-hour hotline at their office and Toss and I took shifts with the rest answering the incoming. We tried to run down the rumours, establish the facts and defuse situations before they began or before they could escalate into any kind of serious breach of the Truce.

Our days were 12, 14, 16 hours. We drove ourselves till we dropped. Lunch was a pint and a hurried sandwich at the Bogside Inn, when anyone had any money. Supper was potato-soup kept constantly on the simmer at the Whistling Gypsy. At times, the Office resembled a railway station with two trainloads of passengers attempting to take the same train in two directions at once. At times, it resembled the city room of a daily newspaper where every man who had a desk fancied himself the Editor-in-Chief. The community was far from being self-sufficient: essential services, water and lights, rubbish collection, fire protection, all had to be looked after, and the bureaucrats of the Electricity Board, the Derry City Council, the Water Department, were past masters at giving-out with the stall. They could keep the Loyalist community puzzled and put-out, but us, they could simply ignore; we in Free Derry had to make them to respond to our 'community representatives' any way we could, by nudging, insisting, perservering and parrying their malign, willful, and blind malfeasance, when nothing else seemed to work. There were housewives with their family allowances, pensioners with their subsistence cheques, mothers on supplementary benefits, families on the Anti-Internment Rent and Rates Strike to look after. A special eye had to be kept out for the families of the Internees and prisoners on remand. A million things to do, and everything urgent, emergency, stop-gap, even life-and-death.

The Sinn Féiners put out a Newsletter, the Bogside Doodlebug, named after the home-made paint-and-petrol bomb that was Derry's contribution to the fine art of rioting. Not that they had to be inflammatory in its pages—a straight recital of facts was often flaming enough. But news and editorializing went hand-in-hand as the staff tried to instill a perspective, build solidarity. If it was slanted, it needed to be, to counter-act the slant of the BBC, the Derry Journal, the Belfast Telegraph, even the Republican News, since that Movement journal originated in Belfast. And we all took a shift or two at the mike of Radio Free Derry, while we kept the short-wave equipment for our pirate radio station constantly on the move. Derry, in the first week of the Truce, was as volatile, still, as a car-bomb primed to blow, and it wouldn't do to be broadcasting from the same house two nights in a row.

But when you found a spare moment coming your way, you reflected: what's going on here?

The birth-pangs of The Collective, said the Social Theorists. The proof that we can rule ourselves, if only left to ourselves, said the Utopians. A mad, moiling mess of anarchy, said the Doctrinaire Socialists. The Editors-in-Chief all vied for the last word in debate and controversy, but the prize went to the fellow who concocted the formula: we are the experimental society, the Truce is our test-tube, and Derry our laboratory.

Morale was high. We were volunteers with a mission. We were extending a helping hand to a beleaguered city; and the people of Free Derry, Nationalists all, made us welcome wherever we went. Every door was open to us. Nobody went hungry. We met our new friends, new neighbors, new comrades on the barricades of the Bogside, and nobody reminded us that we were outsiders, nobody predicted that we'd be running out on them when we'd had our bit o' craic.

You had to admire the Bogsiders. For their spirit. For their grit. You didn't mind spending yourself for them, and the sleep you took at night might have been brief, but it was as restful as ever you had.

One of the comrades at the Whistling Gypsy was a girl called Deirdre O'Malley. She came from Castlerea, in County Roscommon, next door to Mayo, and so she and Toss Gibbons had "something in ros-common," as he punned. "I was in Castlerea, once."

"It was terrible shocking at the time," said Deirdre. "Nothing ever happens in Castlerea. But it happened that day, all right."

The three of us were sharing fried-egg sandwiches at the lunch table. I looked back and forth between them at the drollery. "There's something in the air in the West," was my comment, upon which the soggy white-bread, which tasted as clammy as a sod of turf from the bog, decided to stick to the roof of my mouth, so that I was suitably chastised for my cheek, and, for once, I was forced to say nothing further.

So it was in that first week of peace in Derry. A provincial connection was enough to form fast friendships.

On the Saturday night, a céilí was to be held at the Bogside Inn, and Deirdre wanted a night out, so the three of us went together, so that Deirdre's dance card wouldn't have any holes in it. Not that she wasn't quite lovely, with her red hair styled like a furze bush, and her dimples and freckles. She was in fact much too young and innocent, according to Toss Ribbons, to be going unchaperoned. "And you're the man for the job, are you?" said I.

"Well, I am a married man," said he.

"I'm an old married man myself," I announced.

"I had no idea you two were so conventional," said Deirdre. "Is that your idea of a Revolution, a pipe on the mantle and a sheepskin to cover your knees with, in the ould rocking chair?"

"A turn around the dance floor," said Toss, "does not a revolution make, it is a mere revolvement."

Deirdre took me by the arm. "Come on. You're not getting out of it."

"I didn't hear them call Ladies' Choice!" Toss protested.

"Aye," said Deirdre, as she dragged me off, "but then, I'm not a lady."

Months of tension were drained out of our dancing feet, and the floorboards vibrated beneath us with the hectic beat.

Eoghan McMurrough and the Bogside Men were on the stage wheeling through the Donkey Reel. The hall was decorated with tricolour streamers and folded bunting, a birthday party for the Truce, now one-week-old. "What are we doing?" I cried above the din as we sped tripping over the floor. "Just follow the others!" Deirdre shouted, laughing. Two lines would form a few paces apart, and the lines would then smash together, and with your partner, facing you opposite, and you were to twirl one another by the forearm, or the wrist, or the hand, I couldn't tell how they were doing it, so practiced were they, one hand crossed on top of the other. I tripped and faltered my way through the fast-paced patterns of the reel till I was dizzy and threw my head back. "Enough!" I steered Deirdre away from the middle of the floor. "Now—there's Toss—he's dying to dance with you. Why don't you give him a whirl off his feet?"

Though the Truce was a week old and the peace intact, the news from Belfast had been nothing but bad. An uncanny series of dramatically brutal assassinations was unnerving the city, according to reports. Six Catholics were dead, and the Loyalists, for the first time, said the newspapers, were attacking their fellow Protestants, for the crime of having Catholic wives or girlfriends. "And what about the UDA?" said someone. "Didn't they take advantage this week to set up permanent barricades—concrete ones, like ours—in the Woodvale, and Portadown, too?" "And why not?–if we can do it, why can't they?" Toss and Deirdre and myself gathered around at the sound of disputation. "We took down three barricades up the Creggan," said Deirdre, who was not one to pass up an argument, "just to point out our willingness, and the Brits reciprocated—didn't they clear out of the Mex Army Post, or have you forgotten?" "That's precisely the point," said a chap called Moses, after the long black beard he wore, "when the UDA evicted Catholics up the Springfield

Road this week, did the Army try to stop them?" "The point," said Deirdre, "is not to keep the No-Go Areas going forever, but to settle the whole thing—when the Brits are out, won't the whole country be an effin' No-Go Area?" "If the Army in Belfast won't protect the people from rampaging Tartan gangs, then we'll have to, won't we? Where's your peace gone then? Up in smoke, that's where!"

With a heavy mind, Father Daly, the parish priest of the Bogside, hiking up the skirts of his soutane, mounted the steps to the stage, as Eoghan McMurrough wound down the music. There was applause, and the popular padre held up his hand to acknowledge the flock as he moved to the microphone. The hall quietened, out of respect. Television viewers throughout the world had seen Fr Daly in clips of Bloody Sunday, exposing himself to the fire of the Paras. The priest with the white hankie, that was him, as he went to the aid of the wounded lying in the street. One of them, a boy 14 years old, died in his arms. In March, Fr Daly had travelled to Washington, to testify in the United States Senate on Internment, with Senator Ted Kennedy presiding. "I congratulate you, the people of the Bogside," the priest now said into the microphone, "for the example of restraint you have given during this first week of this long-awaited Cease-fire. And now, let us bow our heads. Oh, Heavenly Father, we supplicate thee in prayer, that you may look down upon us, and that the suffering and endurance of the people of Derry may win for us the heavenly reward of Peace."

Raised heads watched while the priest descended from the stage and Sean Keenan came forward. Keenan took the hand of Fr Daly, and his silver head bent forward, as the padre wished to confer with him. It was a public gesture. This man in black had done as much as any other to steer the Provos in Derry towards the advantages they might gain from a Truce at the present time.

But the man called Moses muttered his disapproval into his beard. "Look at that—it's as bad as Paisley and Craig."

But in the Bogside, the Provos and the people were as one. The armed volunteer was somebody's son, somebody's neighbour, someone else's father, your husband, my brother-in-law, his uncle, their cousin. And it made as much sense to distinguish the Provos from the people as it did the sand-grains from the beach. Fr Daly could not afford to discount the Provos, and the Provos could not afford to ignore him. And there were ears in the room to hear Moses make his remark.

Then, a whisper swept the hall. Martin McGuiness is here. Hands began to clap and feet to stamp. There were whistles, and then the chant went up, scattered at first, growing in volume. "We want McGuinness, we want McGuiness!"

The O/C of the Derry Brigade, Provisional IRA, Martin McGuinness, was stepping on stage. He shyly removed the ski-cap from the back of his head and approached the microphone. The cheering died down. "Well—I'll just say—that I hope we'll all keep pulling together, as we have in the past week. Some of our people can't be with us tonight. They're in the Kesh still. Others are in the Crum. And more are in the Curragh." He paused for the jeers at Jack Lynch, and the lone yell, "Down with Dublin!" Then Martin McGuinness went on, in a somber voice. "Some of our comrades will never return. But, with this Truce, we're proving one thing, that none of it has been in vain. All of it was worth it, to see you people, on a night like this, in a peaceful Derry, and in a Free Derry. Goodnight!" McGuiness moved swiftly to the exit, calling out "Enjoy yourselves!"

Deirdre pulled me across the floor to Fr Daly and Sean Keenan, and Toss Ribbons followed. "Father, I want you to meet someone who's come three thousand miles to make his confession."

I asked Fr Daly, "Did you enjoy your stay in Washington?"

"I could have wished for a happier occasion. I think we accomplished our mission. Time will tell, time will tell. And you are from Senator Kennedy's part of the world, then?"

"Yes, but you met him before I did, Father."

"Poor man," said Fr Daly. "The things he's seen."

"What did you do that for?" I said to Deirdre, when we were away. "If I want to talk to God, I'll do it in the privacy of my own mind."

"What are you, a Protestant or something?"

"I'm an atheist, how do you like them apples?"

"You're a match for Fr Daly then—he's a politician."

There was a shout from the front door out to the lounge. Toss and Deirdre and I went running with the others.

Outside, armed Volunteers were dragging a man in civilian clothes from a Peugeot in the car-park across the way. People came running ahead of them. "They got him, they got him! It's a nark! He's a tout!"

As we came up, the Volunteers were pushing the man by the coat-collar through an angry collection of vilifiers, trying to hustle him up the stair to Sinn Féin, out of harm's way, before transferring him to a safe place where they could ask him a few questions, as they reassured the mob of vindictive onlookers, who were screaming at him. "Och! He's in for it now. Give it to him, lads! Hey, you!–do you know what we do to your like?"

It was the second week of the Truce, and I was doing an early evening shift at the mike of Radio Free Derry from a house in the Creggan. I bent over the short-wave set with my headphones on waiting for the music to end on the portable turn-table wired to the rear input-jacks. "This is the Voice of the Irish Revolution, coming to you on the airwaves of Radio Free Derry. The time now is half-six. Here is the news."

"In Belfast today the wave of unsolved assassinations continued with the tragic murders of two Protestant brothers in Sandy Row. Pete and Malcolm Orr were discovered shot to death in their home in Albion Street. It is believed that masked vigilantes of the Loyalist para-military organization, the UDA, or persons presently unknown, masquerading as the UDA, were responsible for the double-murder. It was known in the Protestant community that the Orr brothers were associating with Catholic girls. I quote from a report in today's Belfast Telegraph: 'reliable sources believe that the Orr brothers may have been assassinated because of their involvement with Catholic girlfriends. When questioned, the bereaved family stated that the two brothers had received threatening telephone messages, and that they had responded to their callers by refusing to stop seeing their girlfriends. The Press and Media of the Occupied Area have once again today condemned the spectre of sectarian assassination, and the Provisional IRA and the Sinn Féin wish to join in this condemnation, but we point out that it is the responsibility of the authorities to investigate, pursue and prosecute the perpetrators of today's tragic and heinous crime. Paddy Geary, press officer of Sinn Féin in Belfast, said today, 'We have reason to believe these assassinations are part of a concerted effort to terrorise the civil population out of the spirit of resistance to the British occupation which has sustained them for so long now at a high level of commitment—a conspiracy, involving unknown members of the Loyalist para-military with members of secret units of the British Army, presently operating in Belfast, out of uniform, and in disguise, in direct contravention of the Geneva Convention—members of British Army units such as the Special Air Services, the SAS, the MI5, Scotland Yard, Army Intelligence, or other as yet unidentified secret units. The Provisional IRA is conducting its own investigation and will pursue it with all means available to it until these assassinations can be halted.'

"In other news, the Provisional IRA reports from Belfast that General Ford, British Army Commander of Land Forces in Ireland, openly held court today in an Army Saracen at the corner of Ainsworth Avenue, his conferee none other than Tommy Herron, head of the UDA in East Belfast. General Ford, our listeners will remember, was the officer in overall command of the Parachute Regiment when thirteen unarmed civilians were shot to death in this city last January in the incident known as Bloody Sunday. It is believed that General Ford today acceded to demands by Tommy Herron that the British Occupation Forces join together with UDA vigilantes to patrol Loyalist sections of Belfast in an attempt to guard against sectarian assassination. The Provisional IRA condemns this example of open favoritism, which does nothing but foster the spirit of sectarianism. The Crown forces are collaborating with armed Loyalist paramilitaries, while they steadfastly refuse this week the same rights to police their own areas to the Nationalist residents of the Ardoyne and Beachmount."

With the help of the daily papers, I had typed my own copy at the Sinn Fein office, a practice everyone followed who took a turn on Radio Free Derry, and I was vain enough to think that my writing skills had found their perfect utilisation in the service of the Revolution at this post. I was as proud of my radio copy as I was of any poem I'd composed in the little room in Mayo the previous summer or in No. 56 late nights or in the Rathmines Library afternoons that spring. But I was even more vain about my mimicking of the Dublin North

Side accent I'd picked up in Maurice Woolf's, which I thought was pretty perfected, and secretly, I delighted in the thought that the authorities, who were certainly listening in, must be baffled—wouldn't they be surprised to find out that there's an American at the mike of Radio Free Derry?

"That's the news for now. This is the Voice of the Irish Revolution, Radio Free Derry. Now, back to the music—and this is John Lennon, from Liverpool, England—with his Plastic Ono Band—." I gently lowered the tone-arm, and stepped up the volume knob gradually, fading into 'All we are saying, is Give Peace a Chance . . .'

I was alone in the attic. The family was downstairs, but hadn't left the house, so as not to attract undue attention. I wrapped up and went out through the kitchen while they stayed in the living room.

Outside, my lookouts, Toss and Deirdre, were parked in the yellow bug, waiting. I brought out the set in a suitcase and threw it in the boot.

Below, over the roof of the Essex car-parts factory, Derry lay clothed in the evening twilight. The light was coming over the Creggan, over my shoulder, from the West, from Donegal, from Sligo, from Mayo, from the far-off, frothing Atlantic, which whispered in my memory from the last time I'd stood on any of its shores—from America, where I liked to imagine it might be rush hour in Boston, or the middle of the day in Milltown, or New York City, or anywhere, the day just beginning, or over and done with, going home. I paused and lay my arm on the roof of the yellow VW, gazing at the three hills of Derry: the Creggan, where I stood, The Diamond, where the Walls stood, the Waterside, where the great bend of the River Foyle flowed, hidden from my view. Before me, in that long and pleasant light of evening, lay the time and the place—the valley of the Bogside, Ulster, Ireland herself, looking, as always, when you stood back at a vantage, a valley of slumber, a vale of peace, where the mean streets and the troubled countenances sank from view. There—the spires—there—the tower-block of Rossville Street—and there—the Walls of Derry. *The Isle of the Blest.*

"What are you doing, Nick?" said Deirdre, looking up out of the open window.

"I don't know." I smiled down at her. "You know, you can see the clock on the tower of the Guildhall from up here?"

But already, unbeknownst to me, the diminutive clockface on the miniature tower was ticking away the time of peace.

On Friday of the second week, the long-awaited mission of the IRA met in London with the British Government.

Willie. Made promises. To end the sectarian killings. By the UDA? UVF? SAS?–well, to do all in his power, anyway. To protect Catholic families trapped behind Loyalist barricades in Belfast. If I have to post a soldier in the front door of every Catholic, Whitelaw promised.

Seán Mac Stíofáin, Chief-of-Staff of the Provisional IRA. Dáithí Ó Conaill, gun-runner, political mastermind. Seamus Twomey, O/C of the Belfast Brigade. Martin McGuinness, O/C, Derry Brigade. Gerry Adams and Ivor Bell of the Belfast Provos. It was said that without the release of these last two from the Crumlin Road Jail, the IRA would not have agreed to proceed with the London talks. But the British acquiesced.

So. These were the 'gunmen' of the London tabloids. These were the 'terrorists' of official British government *communiqués*. Whitelaw sat down with them in the private house of one of

Whitehall's junior ministers in Chelsea. He served them tea. They drank his tea. He offered the liquor of the junior minister. Dáithí Ó Conaill says to himself—what does he think, we're a lot of Culchies, up to London for a boozer weekend? He spoke up. All six Irishmen refused the liquor. We came to talk. So talk. Willie talked and they listened. They conferred. The 'gunmen' wanted to believe the 'Secretary-of-State' in charge of British rule in Ireland. They went into a separate room.

Ó Conaill led them back, looking pleased. We want to negotiate the end of Internment. We can settle this thing, here and now. Whitelaw promised—a phased end to Internment, dependent upon, he said, a progressive reduction in the level of hostilities against British forces. Agreed. We accept. Can you use your influence in the Catholic community, said Whitelaw, to reduce the level of violence?—can you guarantee that? Certainly we will. But that will mean that you will reciprocate by using your influence to control the renegade elements on your side—in other words, you will use the Crown forces at your disposal to clamp down on the Loyalist paramilitaries, whom you have licenced to arm themselves with 100,000 weapons. Agreed, said Whitelaw.

He stood up, to shake hands all round. Then I may announce that we shall all meet again, in seven days' time? To discuss a British withdrawal from Ireland, of course. Well, then —you may.

I'm not at liberty to say who my source was for this portrayal of that meeting. Obviously, I was not there myself. It may have been any one of several men already mentioned in this story. But I'd rather not say.

Suffice it to say they never met again. At the moment that Whitelaw was making his promises in Chelsea, on the ground in Andersonstown, the Truce was already over.

Perhaps that was why I heard this insider's version. The speaker was under the influence of relieving feelings and re-living the event.

Lenadoon was an estate on the fringe of Andersonstown, to which Protestants had fled in order to escape the barricades of the Provo No-Go Area.

During the Truce, the Andersonstown community reps met with the Northern Ireland Housing Executive, a body set up by Whitelaw when he first came to power in March. The advertised purpose of the Housing Executive was to guarantee fair play in allocation of the hopelessly entangled sectarian housing of Belfast.

The Catholics were saying that 16 houses in Lenadoon, abandoned by their Protestant occupants because of fears of encroachment, were now needed by Catholics ousted from other parts of the city by UDA harassment when the Loyalists set up their No-Go Areas during the Truce. The Housing Executive heard their case, and agreed: they allocated all 16 empty houses to the refugee Catholics.

When the UDA got wind of it, they moved in and occupied 12 of the houses with masked vigilantes, armed, and bearing sawed-off axe-handles. They vowed to the press to prevent the Catholics from moving in.

On Saturday, the Provo Mission was back in Ireland. Ó Conaill and Mac Stíofáin went to Kevin Street in Dublin to stay by the phone; the Northern commanders all sped home by road. The lawful tenants, the Catholics, having met the night before, were already in the courts and walks of Lenadoon, determined, with the help of all the friends, neighbours and support they could muster, to move into the homes awarded to them. A confrontation seemed inevitable, and Seamus Twomey, the Belfast Brigade O/C, phoned ahead from Dublin to order his volunteers into the street. "You don't know what's going on," he insisted to his lieutenant on the Belfast end of the line, but the lieutneant tried to tell him, "Seamus—you've been out of town—." "I'm trying to save the Truce!" Twomey shouted into the receiver, and he slammed the phone and ran out to his waiting car.

The Provos in Andersonstown reluctantly moved out. They knew the people who had lorries out there piled high with furniture expected support from them, not opposition. But they went into the action as stewards, and formed a line between the Catholic tenants and the UDA, using every persuasion they could to keep a cap on the situation.

Until the British Army arrived. They marched in, in riot gear. They announced they were setting up a peace line between the two sides. The Catholic tenants eyed them. Which way would the Brits face their line? They sent a delegation to the British captain. Are you going to help us get into our houses? The Captain looked over his shoulder at the massed ranks of the UDA. "I can't do it. It would cause a riot."

The delegation returned. The Army faced their line toward the Catholics and the Provos. The Catholics began shouting at them. The Provo stewards tried to stop them, but one of the families insisted their lorry of furniture was going through.

The British said no. They brought up a bulldozer. The bulldozer attacked the lorry, and over it went, scattering chairs and beds over the kerb, sending the tenants jumping for safety. The bulldozer pushed and strained and dozed the lorry over on the grass. The rocks started flying. The British charged, and arrested two of the stewards, and eight of the screaming, kicking, lawful tenants, throwing them all in the backs of their Pigs.

In Derry, in the Bogside Inn, Toss and Deirdre and I, on the BBC evening news, saw the bulldozer push over the furniture lorry. Everybody in Ireland who saw the news that evening knew the Truce was over.

Within hours of the breakdown, six people in Belfast were dead, one of them a priest, shot by British soldiers in Ballymurphy. On Monday, the British government flew 1200 more troops into Ulster. Within a week, 14 more British boys in uniform were dead. General Sir Harry Tuzo, latest in the line of British GOCs, Northern Ireland, as the British termed the iniquitous gerrymandered rump of an illegitimate statelet, angrily and vociferously denounced the civil servants in Whitehall for negotiating with 'gunmen.' He proved his fitness for his post by immediately falling into lockstep with all his predecessors, who had always, historically, blamed their failures in Ireland on anyone but themselves.

On the barricades of the Bogside, we were interviewing one another. The fragile pulse of peace wilted hard. We checked reactions. Felt one another out. "Derry's no Belfast," said one. "We've always got on with the Loyalists here." "That's right," his listeners agreed. "No UDA here. The odd bash now and again round the 12th of August, but—truly, we're not sectarian-minded here." "You'll be bloody-well bloody-minded when the Army comes in here to knock down your barricade," said Moses of the long black beard, "with their heavy tanks."

It was midnight, and around us darkness was falling from the peak of the Rossville Street tower-block. Out there, from the OP on the Wall, the Brits were surveying us with infra-red eyes. The Provo Volunteers were crouching in the shadows.

"Did you say tanks?"

"Aye. Tanks. They were seen coming in the Foyle Road, last night, 3 in the a.m."

"You can get yourself into trouble," Deirdre O'Malley warned Moses, "going about rumour-mongering."

"I suppose you seen them yourself," said one.

"The Brits have never used tanks in Ireland," said another.

"It's no rumour," said Moses darkly. "And those lads there—don't you think they'd rather be off and save their pea-shooters than firing them at tanks?"

Sean Keenan, the next evening, came to pay the Sinn Féin volunteers in the office a visit. "I want to thank you for carrying on as you have since the Truce ended. The position here is becoming untenable. I'm afraid I'm going to have to ask you all to leave now."

"We want to stay," said Deirdre.

"This is for your own safety, love," said Sean Keenan. "I cannot guarantee any longer—."

"I was here before the Truce," said Deirdre, "and I'm not leaving."

"I'm going to be very blunt with you, Deirdre—."

"What are the Provies going to do, Sean? Are they going to abandon the Bogside?"

Keenan's face turned as white as his hair. "This is between ourselves—if the Brits bulldoze the barricades, the Volunteers will not resist them."

A chill went through the assembled bodies in the back room. And this time it did not come from the holes in the roof of the Whistling Gypsy. Eyes turned to other eyes, looked down, shoes scuffed the floor. Sean Keenan drew himself up and said firmly, "I would not permit them to stay. I have no doubt whatsoever that the British Army would not hesitate to unleash a full and bloody fury on the helpless civilians if the lads stay. I'm talking about old men and old women, children, and mothers who cannot defend themselves. Who would find themselves the targets of those bastards because the IRA refused to do the sensible thing, the only thing they can do."

"Sean," I said, "are the Brits going to come in?"

"Well, you lads are running the newsletter—the radio— you've seen the reports, like myself. What do you think it means that they've already dozed the Loyalist barricades in Portadown? In fact, haven't they got their propaganda machine in high gear, softening everybody up? Ó Brádaigh and Mac Stíofáin and McGuinness have seen the reports, too. This is a decision. It has been taken with due process of deliberation. And I expect you all to follow orders. Or what do you think tanks in Derry means?"

No one could find anything to say.

"The walls of the Bogside Flats cannot withstand a British Enfield, First World War vintage," Sean Keenan summed up, "let alone Centurion tanks. Hundreds would die."

"Hundreds may die anyway, Sean." Deirdre O'Malley stood up, determined to have the last word before leaving the room. "The Provies may pull out, but the people can't."

Sean Keenan pulled a hand over his ashen countenance. Toss Gibbons approached him. "We all want to stay."

Keenan waved his hand. "I didn't mean right now— tonight. Perhaps not immediately, anyway. We'll see. As long as there's no imminent danger." Keenan patted Toss' shoulder. "Carry on, Ribbons, I'll let you know."

On Friday, 21ˢᵗ July, 1972, the roof fell in on us. People all across Ireland and the UK next door were stunned to hear of an afternoon bomb blitz in the Belfast City Centre by the Provisional

IRA, in which 20 car-bombs went off in the space of an hour or an hour-and-a-half, with the horrific result, on a busy city centre shopping afternoon, that nine civilians were killed and 130 injured. By the time the evening papers came out in Belfast, Dublin and London, they were already calling it 'Bloody Friday.'

In our circles in Derry, among the Sinn Féiners, and amongst the civilian residents of the Bogside and Creggan who were our staunch supporters, the reaction was palpable, immediate, and agonisingly negative. "This is bad." "How could they have miscalculated so?" "Didn't they stop and think that people across the spectrum would be outraged!" "This is nothing but a callous disregard." And these from ourselves, who were supporters of the Provos, who immediately tried to claim that the Brits had ignored warnings given. "That's not gonna shine any spuds with anyone!" "What a disaster." "Would you look at this? Firemen shoveling human remains into plastic bags—on the telly! Who's going to forget that picture?"

"Something's gone awfully wrong," said Deirdre O'Malley.

Saturday came round again, but this time there wouldn't be any dancing at the Bogside Inn. Deirdre came into the room at the Whistling Gypsy to get me. "We're going out tonight—to the theater! How do I look?"

She was wearing boots and had her bell-bottoms tucked into the tops, and a bandanna across the forehead. "You look like a tinker."

"It's at Fr Daly's Derry Bogside, and I don't want to miss it. A play by Sartre." She thought that would excite my interest. "Are you coming?"

"Can I skip it?"

"No. Who knows if we'd get another chance?"

"You won't like Sartre, Deirdre," said Toss.

We left at intermission, the three of us. Deirdre said, "Whatever possessed them to do a show like that at a time like this?"

"Probably they'd rehearsed it for so long," said Toss.

"A week ago it might have been all right," I said.

Deirdre shuddered. "Only out of respect for the priest that I stayed till the first act was over."

Teddy McGrail came running up to us. "Did you hear? They've lifted Moses."

"Lifted him?" sniffed Deirdre. "Gone over is what you mean."

"We were standing under the poster for the Derry Bogside's performance: Jean-Paul Sartre—*Flies*. Deirdre insisted we couldn't go home to the Whistling Gypsy, but had to go up to the office. Outside, she made us locate a spacious block of bare wall. At her instructions, we chalked the message:

INFORMERS WILL BE SHOT

The war was on again now for more than a fortnight. A Wednesday evening. The end of July, more or less. Toss Ribbons was at the wheel of our newly commandeered radio van. At this point it was considered not safe any longer to be broadcasting from someone's attic or cellar, for fear of raids getting women and children involved with questioning and harassment by the authorities. I was in the back lying prone on the boards, with the short-wave set propped against the panel. We could no longer spin records, but we had a cassette-recorder—the sound quality was poor, but the main thing now was information. I was about to start the 9.30 p.m. Bulletin. "Good evening. This is Radio Free Derry, the Voice of the Irish Revolution. Here is the news at half-nine."

"In Belfast today, another British soldier lies dead, shot in Andersonstown by the liberation forces of the Provisional IRA. Two more British servicemen died in an ambush—."

The van jolted, taking my eye away from the copy I was holding up to the light of the rear windows. "Sorry," I said into the mike as I searched for my place. "In an ambush outside Newry. In Warrenpoint, County Down today, an RUC officer was also shot to death. This brings the total British and State security losses in the Occupied Area since the institution of Internment to 138 killed–." The van rose, and fell—and again. I couldn't continue. What's he doing? I thought. As I cut the switch momentarily, I looked over my shoulder.

Toss said, "Somebody's following us."

I hesitated, a fraction too long. The van was speeding up abruptly. *Think.* I flipped the switch. "We apologize for this interruption. Please tune in again tomorrow night at this time. This is the Voice of Radio Free Derry, signing off." I switched off and scrambled to my knees. Shit. 'Technical difficulties'—that was the phrase I simply could not recall in the frenzy of the moment. I was disappointed in myself for giving in to panic. I was jamming myself into the seat next to Toss. "Where are we?" We'd been cruising through the twists and turns of the Creggan Estates. "It's impossible to get out of Creggan without going through the barricades."

"Well, we're not in it now."

I twisted in my seat. Don't panic. Don't—but I felt the flush of automatic fear go hot through me. Toss was accelerating, faster and faster. I saw the Essex car-spring Works through the rear windows—above it, on the left, the houses of the Creggan, glowering like thunder-clouds, already far behind us. Ahead of us, open road. Not a soul or a stick to be seen. High banks closing in the road either side, topped with raggedy hedge. Incredible how quickly the city turned into bare countryside. Ahead of us, open straightaway, two-lane macadam. Behind, an unmarked car, speeding, careening to catch up to us. "Keep going," I said.

"Who's that behind us?" The sweat was popping out on Toss' forehead.

"It's not the Army. Must be RUC. Head for the Border."

"If we knew where it was."

"We do! It's straight ahead west. It can't be more than a couple of miles, Toss! Head for the sunset."

The silent race was gaining on us. No siren. Nothing to alarm the countryside we were now zooming through, up and downhill. We were climbing as we went, and somewhere, not far away, was the Donegal border, and safety. But when I looked through the rear windows again, I said, "Get off this road, Toss, or we can't keep ahead of them."

The van was hurtling downhill between hedgerows. Openings to the fields alongside whipped past before we saw them— muddy with the trampling of cows, the typical steel-rod gate half-unhinged across the track, rutted with tractor-wheels—we were on a secondary road leading to God knows where, the Buncrana Road? or worse to the motorway, coming out of the Foyle Bridge, if we hit that, we're lost, or to the border—but we can't take the chance, on the motorway we're done for. A tall hill loomed up. My heart sank. They'll catch us on the hill! But at the last second, I shouted, "There!–turn in, turn in!"

We made the turn in a cloud of gravel. Behind us, they overshot. Tires squealing, fading. Out the back window I saw them reversing. "Go, go, go!"

A rail-fenced meadow, with cattle grazing, a huddle of three or four. Absolutely flat, on top of a plateau. Far-distant mountain range, glimpsed and gone in a blink. Over the top and we swooped down on a little brook. Worse yet. A wooden bridge, with aluminium rollers across the span, to keep the cattle from crossing. We had to slow up or we'd demolish. Across the bridge finally, and another steep twist up to a stand of trees and a two-story grey farmhouse, quite solidly bourgeois, a trimmed green box-hedge, with purple heather planted along the crew-cut flat-top, very fancy. The road ahead, wind and twist, wind and twist, up and down, over a series of ridges dotted with wee woods and remote farmhouses.

"Ditch the van, Toss! Ditch the van! They're not over the top yet!"

He ran it off into the ditch. Almost ruined the man's nice hedge, but slammed to a stop, windscreen first, into the embankment on the other side of a driveway. The doors flew open on both sides. Toss raced around the front, while I looked round and spotted the unmarked car come careening over the hill. We ran together up the driveway because we could see three out-buildings, the white gable-end of a row of sheds, a stone-barn with a slate roof on the left, and a large tin barn with vertical brown siding in the back of them.

Behind us, two men in tan macs were running up the driveway, reaching inside their coats.

Toss and I turned to face them in front of the stone-barn. It seemed there was nowhere to go, so I waved Toss off with my hand so that he would move away from me, as the men in the tan macs had pulled handguns from inside their coats, while they circled out and approached us from two sides. "I'm unarmed," I said, "and so's he."

"Good," said one, "you're coming with us then."

At that moment the screen door at the back of the grey farmhouse flung open and a boy who looked no more than ten or eleven or so jumped down two concrete steps and heedlessly came running toward us.

"Stop!" Toss cried to him. "Don't come any closer!"

"My da's coming!" cried the boy.

And at that moment, I saw an old man with a walking stick totter down the steps behind the boy. The men in the tan macs were taking this in with eyes darting sideways, while behind us I heard the familiar sound of a tractor approaching. I didn't dare take my eyes off the men holding guns on us but I had no idea what to do or what was going to happen next.

Then the tractor slammed to a halt close behind, coughed and commenced grumbling as whoever was driving put it into neutral and pulled on the brake. I could hear him jump down.

"Here, what's going on? This is private property you're on, you know."

Whoever it was came gingerly forward when he saw the drawn weapons and stood between Toss and me.

The two men in the macs looked at one another. It was clear they, too, didn't know what to do at this point, but they soon fell back on their training and one of them declared, "We have reason to apprehend these two men and you're not to interfere with us in the pursuit of our business with them."

I don't know what possessed me at this point but I spoke up. "You have no jurisdiction on this side of the border."

Toss seconded me. "That's right. This is County Donegal we're in."

"Is that so?" the second man jeered at us.

"It happens to be the case," said the farmer standing between us. "And who are you, may I ask?"

"We are officers of the law," said the first one, "so stand aside."

"Johnny. Run inside and ring up the gardai at the Buncrana copshop. Go on."

After hesitating, looking questioningly at his da, young Johnny did as he was told, and the old man, who must have been the grandfather, made way for him.

The screendoor slammed so that I jumped in my shoes, it sounded so much like the crack of a shot.

The farmer ran both hands over his temples. "You're making me very nervous with those guns. I have my boy to think of. Do you think you could put them away?"

"Or would you rather wait and show them to the gardai?" Toss said, snarkily.

"Oh, I can't wait to see this little drama acted out," I added.

"Oh, oh, oh," said the farmer, "now let's not anyone go losing their heads. Where are you two from, anyhow?"

"The Bogside," said Toss.

"Not exactly," said I. "I'm from the States."

"Well, if we're going to be sticklers," said Toss, "I'm from County Mayo myself. A tax-paying citizen of the Irish Republic."

The detectives looked at one another. You could see that they'd lost the initiative. They were standing on pride at the moment, unwilling to look foolish in front of an audience—at a loss as to how to maintain the dignity of their office and persons. Reluctantly, one of them finally said, "It appears we may have made a mistake about exactly where that unmarked border is out this road. But you two are on notice, aren't you? You're on our radar. We know who you are. We know your MO. We know what you're up to. Now, consider yourselves warned."

They couldn't resist this one final parting threat as they put up their weapons in under-arm holsters again.

Wee Johnny came running back out to his da then, breathlessly announcing, "I rang them up, da. They're coming straightaway."

His father knelt and pulled his blond-headed son close to him. "That's the lad. Fine, son, fine. Good man yourself."

When the two plainclothes officers of the RUC detective branch had climbed back into their motor and gone, the farmer turned to us and said, "I haven't had any telephone in the house, you know, since Johnny's mother passed. I just couldn't seem to bear the thought of the phone ringing in the night with word of a road accident, like the time we lost her. Now Johnny knows that, and he could have blurted it out, and spoiled the whole thing—but, good lad that is he, he thought quick, and made out like as to win the Academy Awards. So you two can thank him for saving your reckless necks for you. Bogside! After all these past years, living so close to it, hoping it wouldn't intrude upon us, now all I can say is I wish the damned border was fifty miles from here, and they'd leave us in peace!"

Chapter 14

Judgement of the Castle

We got out the next night. Toss and Deirdre and me, in the
VW bug. After dark, for a better chance at going unobserved.
Keeping to the motorways, to avoid roadblocks and check-
points, which was easy enough to do if you stayed out of the
town centres. And you could travel fast. The faster the better.
We all knew we were shaving corners now, scraping by, lucky to
be getting out.

And yet we were loath to be leaving. A cloud descended
upon the fleeing beetle with the three Sinn Féiners inside, bottled up claustrophobically with our sense of guilt, our shame
at saving ourselves while we abandoned those who couldn't get
out. The inhabitants of the Bogside and Creggan were not so
lucky as we were. They were stuck in it, for good and for ill.
Theirs was a lifetime sentence while we escaped on parole.

But we were condemned to it. To do anything other than
run away would have caused more problems for the locals, and
the Movement, than any benefit we could have bestowed. In
the changing situation, in the new set of circumstances, the

exigencies faced by the Sinn Féin office, the 'RA, and the people, we could have done no good, and we were no longer wanted. We would have become yet another burden for them, and it was put to us that we ought to do as were were asked, or told, as good Republicans. We reasoned with our consciences that we were running away only to live to fight another day, but it did us no good.

Toss wouldn't go for Donegal, the near way out. Bad memories of the long walk back to the Bogside on foot from the farmer's barnyard and the disabled van, after midnight, to evade detection. We'd had to arrange for the radio equipment to be picked up later. Nor could we be sure whether, at every step, the men in the macs would not be lurking to assail us again, this time to arrest us within their jurisdiction and take us away with their Special Powers Act, no charge, no trial, no reason given. Though we made it back to the Whistling Gyspy in the end, it was with deflation and defeat hurting our hearts.

So now we were headed for Armagh along the dark black high-speed motorway, the A-5, one straight road all the way to Aughnacloy. Toss wouldn't go for Belcoo or Blacklion, either, we'd got in that way, and that was the sure kiss of death.

As we turned the roundabout at the monument in Aughnacloy, we stopped to switch drivers. Lucky we did it there. Once over the dip by the Monaghan Town roadsign, and the hill was that steep, you'd never be able to reverse back up it. The British Army straddled the road at the bottom.

Searchlights. A permanent concrete emplacement. The South Armagh Active Service Units of the Provos kept this border area alive and buzzing with constant multiple operations, and the Brits were taking no chances on a night ambush. A Centurion tank at the abutment on the left. A Saracen parked on the right across the barricade that divided traffic through the emplacement. Soldiers with their weapons unslung. One sprawled with a tripod-mounted machine-gun on top of the concrete abutment on the right. I would have to pass this test as I was behind the wheel. All I had was the old tourist routine. I rolled down my window.

Licence. The soldier examining it under his torch. He wore spectacles and held it up to see, reflected light glazing the glass over his eyes as I looked up. Then he beamed the torch into the back seat and I couldn't see his face. I could only hope Deirdre, back there, was smiling at him. Preferably coquettishly. I waited for questions. But the soldier asked the one I didn't expect. "Why are you traveling so late?"

"Well," I paused—not too long, not too long—"we didn't want to pay for a B&B for another night—I guess we decided too late in the day."

What saved us was the late hour. Deirdre's smile saved us. The fact that we were trying to leave the North and not enter it saved us. Too late at night to ring up the computers for that red number plate, which the RUC must have got when Toss and I went through Bishop's Gate on the first day in Derry. My being a Yank saved us. No international diplomatic incidents for this lot. "They're going for Monaghan, it's the Garda's worry now. Garda See-oh-konnah! What a country! Effin' peelers, wot?"

I didn't speak for the remainder of the trip. Once across the border, Toss took over the wheel again. I packed my pea-coat up against the closed passenger-window and tried to sleep. The other two were keeping their thoughts to themselves as well.

At Deirdre's house in Castlerea, I wouldn't get out of the car. I wouldn't go into the house. I said I wanted to sleep, and they left me there. They wanted me to sleep, too. So far, sleep was eluding us all.

In the morning, Toss came out to me. "Drive me to Dublin, will you?"

"All right, Nick. But go inside first and say goodbye to your one."

We hugged. "I'll miss you, Deirdre."

"Will you write?"

"Of course. Get my address from Toss when you have the chance. You know where he is, in Kilcross, don't you? Deirdre, I have to go. Take care of yourself, love."

Back in the VW, I said. "Drive, Toss, will you? That was not easy."

"I know, I know. The end of something, wasn't it." It was not a question, but a statement.

In the car on the way the radio gave out with the news. "Operation Motorman dawned on Derry today at half-four in the morning. For the first time in a year, the No-Go Areas have been breached by the British Army. There was minor rioting in Derry, in the Bogside especially, leaving two dead and a score injured, including two British soldiers. But the IRA did not offer resistance."

"Minor rioting—two dead!" I said to Toss. "Gawd."

"In Belfast, British Army units bull-dozed the barricades at the Lenadoon Estates, on the edge of Andersonstown. In Claudy, Co. Derry. this morning, a disastrous car-bomb explosion in the village centre has left nine dead, one of them a child of two years—."

Toss switched off the news. "That's too bloody fucking coincidental, that one," he said. "Claudy. You watch tonight—the headlines will all be belating over nine civilians dead—and that poor babby—just so's they could cover their Motorman with a load of incensed distraction."

I sighed deeply, but other than that, I had absolutely no response, nothing to say. Overnight, everything had turned dark, despondent and depressing.

We entered Dublin late in the morning after the traffic from the western roads was somewhat dissipated. From Palmerstown to Chapelizod and down the Coynham Road past the Phoenix Park to Kingsbridge.

"Sheila will still be at work, I believe, Toss, till three o'clock, anyway," I said, as we pulled up at No. 56. "Will you come in?"

"Ah, no, I won't, then. I think I want to get home to Mayo, back to the wife and childers, and it's a long drive, four hours, if I'm lucky, more like six, if not."

"Will you give my address to Deirdre when you get the chance? She wants me to write."

"I will. And now, don't forget us in Kilcross, either, and drop us a line, now and again."

"Toss—how do I thank you–?"

"Not at all, not at all. All for the Cause. Not to worry. I should be thanking you. Remember me to Sheila, tell her I was sorry I couldn't stay and see her. She's a good girl, y'know."

"I know that."

And then Toss Ribbons was gone, and it was time to turn and walk up the steps to home.

I got cleaned up and into a change of clothes and then I was so restless and still upset and all over the map that I just had to go see Sheila right away.

I knew that I wanted to see Comrade Krishna, I knew that I would have to go see Seán Ó Brádaigh in Kevin Street, sooner, rather than later—but before I did anything, I had to see Sheila.

So I went round the back of Duggan's Bakery, in the lane where the screen door attracted all the flies, and I stepped inside. The door banged behind me, and suddenly Sheila turned round and there she was, covered in flour, a hair-net on, by the big mixer, with a big plastic spatula covered in dripping batter, but I couldn't help myself and I went over straightaway and the next moment I had her held tight in a vise-grip with my face buried in her neck and her arms flapping, trying to embrace me without plastering me in batter. "I'm never going to leave you again, " I whispered hoarsely into her ear, eyes shut tight as I drank in the fragrance of her neck, her ear, her flour-dusted hair. "Can you step outside for half-a-mo?"

"I'm popping out for a fag, missus," Sheila shouted over the grind of the machinery, and she pulled me through the door.

"You are a sight for sore eyes," I laughed.

"I'm happy to see you as well," she said, stepping back a little to regard me. "Are you all right, Nick?"

"Did you miss me?"

"I did. But how—?"

"Okay, I've got a million things to tell you, but we can't right now—how's Aisling?"

"She's over with Mary this morning. Here," she said, "you look like you need this." She lit a fag with a match and passed it to me while she slipped the matchbox and a packet of ten Majors back into her apron pocket.

"I thought you were smoking Carrolls? Since when are you on Majors?"

"They're your brand, so I switched. Just to feel you closer to me while you were gone."

"Well, I'm glad I'm back, but I hated to leave the Bogside. Oh, Sheila, I have so much to tell you. Should I go straight over to Aisling, or wait here for you?"

"She's missing her da these days, so you better wait here till I'm off my shift. That way, it won't be so much of a shock to her, seeing both of us together, and not just himself walking through the door, like."

For the next three hours then I sat on the ground with my back against the wall, listless, dozing, wide awake, waiting for the one I loved, the one I couldn't live without, to get off her shift; and then hand in hand we crossed over Rathmines Road to No. 33 Leinster Square to re-unite our little family.

Comrade Krishna wanted to speak with me urgently as soon as he learned I was home, but when he appeared in Mary and Jane's flat from wherever he'd been I put him off, saying I just had to have some time alone with Sheila and Aisling.

"Of course, of course," he said. "It's just that many things have changed in the short time you've been gone."

"I know, I know, Operation Motorman, it was all over the radio in Toss' car on the way back this morning."

"But I'm talking about here in Dublin," he said. "For one thing, you shouldn't be seen walking in the front door here. Do you remember the arrangements we discussed at Bewley's, that time, about how to conduct ourselves when the heat is on?"

"Yes, but can't this wait, Krishna?"

"Of course, of course. I wish it could."

It was so good to be back home and in the arms of someone who loved me, who cared for me alone, and not for what I could do for them on the organising front, or for what my political sympathies were; to be with the one person in the world who could share with me the intense intimacy of having brought a child into the world together, the one person who made me feel, this is where I belong, and no other-where, who could make me feel that, yes, in fact, and in deed, and in the full flower of my entire being, I never want to leave your side again.

For several days then I passed, as in a dream, through a vale of peace and love, and pushed away all the troubles of the world, and languished in quiet evenings at home, frying up a few slices of black pudding for a communal repast, reading a book, holding my child on my lap to play with her or to read to her, looking up to see her mother there, the simple, lost domestic tranquilities, without which the rest of my life was barren and bare, sterile with too much thinking, pestered with agro.

In the mornings Aisling and I would find things to do together, out in the back garden, inside the flat, uncomplicated pastimes born of a pre-school child's world of questioning wonder, in which a blade of grass or a lady-bug on a flower-stalk would reshape the entire universe into the compass-globe of a little girl's eyes; or the pattern of the red-and-black wall-to-wall carpeting would suggest to the imagination a game that could be played in a labyrinth, in pursuit of an elusive part-human, part-animal hybrid-being called, by some, a bull, and by others, a man; and by those who knew, a minotaur. Sometimes we coloured in colouring books, which were available thanks to the bounty of grand-parents and Sheila's trips home to Mayo on the holidays, sometimes it was crayons on the walls, and then the fun of erasing them with water and washcloth, only to compose new cartoons in their place; sometimes we just read books and practiced our alphabet-blocks and how to read words like run and jump and dog and cat and sing and shout. Aisling and I did not need money to be happy together because the Rathmines Library was close enough to our house and Duggan's Bakery for us to walk there, and all the books were free, and besides, the schoolgirls from St Mary's College, in their navy blue blazers and grey-plaid school-uniform skirts and navy knee-socks, all loved Aisling and adopted her as their little sister.

For just a few days I was at peace in this little heaven I made with Sheila and Aisling. I was content to read a book in the library while the St Mary's girls ignored their homework and played happily with Aisling at one of the big tables. They were lovely sweet young innocent things trying out their maternal instincts, and I was thinking, this must be what Sheila was like before she ever met me.

The security arrangements for meeting with Krishna consisted of a scheme of rotating contacts, numbered 1, 2 and 3, with three separate locations and times, one after midnight, the other two in the daytime, to be taken in consecutive order, on three days of the week, and then scrambled the next week. 2,1,3, and then 3,2,1. With check-offs, in case the contact was spotted, but shouldn't be carried through, Krishna to fumble with the tips of his Fu Manchu, myself to push the cap back on my forehead. In case of absence, execute the routine on the next day following, but rotate to the next number. No phone calls, except in case of absolute life-and-death emergency. Krishna was unscrewing the cap of the receiver on the phone in the hall in Leinster Square No. 33 and connecting the wires together backwards, for an hour a day, to scramble any intercept, but you couldn't be sure it worked. And no more contacts through the Arab office, comrade.

I wondered what was going on with my friend Krishna. Why all the melodrama? These spy thriller precautions were straight out of Alfred Hitchcock. Or was he just repeating the procedures picked up from comrades' techniques before his ouster from London? What really happened to him in Trini, in Port o' Spain? I did not know. Was he being super-cautious because he was afraid of being exiled for the third time? Was he running out of countries to run to? Paranoia strikes deep.

I had been too hard on Alita Hughes, and now I realized that. I had condemned her in my own mind for being a wooden replica of a woman, in her Cumann naBan uniform. But Belfast had rocked me, Derry, too, Maggie O'Neill had shaken me to my core, Deirdre O'Malley, too, in her own way. I ought to be checking myself out and curbing my enthusiastic male chauvinist tendencies. As I looked round the conference table at the next meeting of the Cumman Billy Reid, in the attic room of Paddy Clarke's, when I looked at the faces of Martina Kelly and Bernadette Cullen, and yes, Alita, too, I saw Maggie and Deirdre in them, behind them, one with them, even Maria Maguire's face was stamped on them like a hologram. The women of the Movement were the staunchest Republicans we had, they were true and faithful and brave, and they took no nonsense from anyone, and I ought to be ashamed to be in the same room with them.

"Well, here we are," said Chairman Alita, "and it's a long way from here to Tipperary. I look round the faces at this table and I see the faithful few we started with last November, and the rest have all fallen away. That's what happens when the going gets tough. You can't count on the sunshine patriots."

I looked round at John Martyn, Barney O'Toole, Peadar Kenny. Who were the missing faces? Comrade Krishna was lying low, and he was not in attendance, but I knew in my heart he was with us. Brendan McAndrews—who knows where he was? Was he inside in the Curragh, Jack Lynch's new hostelry for wayward Republicans? Was he back in Belfast? I didn't dare bring up the subject. Derry had cured me of my inquisitiveness. Myles Cunningham—and good old Mick O'Corrigan—would we ever see them again?

And Alita was our leader. I knew that now. It was a dirty job that someone had to do, but she was the woman for it.

"Well, we've taken a blow for Bloody Friday," said Alita, "there's no denying it. But we'll have to readjust, we'll have to readjust."

But how? I wasn't so sure anymore. It was hard for me to readjust to the Cumann level of things. It was a temptation to think that I'd moved beyond that, that I was in contact with Kevin Street and the leaders of Sinn Féin. Even Alita looked at me differently, knowing as she did that I'd been sent to Belfast, and sent to Derry, by people in Kevin Street, people above her head. Nothing escaped Alita. She was connected, and she knew everything.

I could see now that Alita Hughes was a younger version of a figurehead of the Movement, a woman regarded almost as a saint, Maire Drumm herself.

How things had changed. It was August now, and we were coming up to the one-year anniversary of Internment—hard to believe—and still the boys were not all back home, and now Internment had been extended to here in Dublin, and I had been in Ireland for almost a year myself.

The following day I was taking Aisling by the hand and we were walking on a pleasant August morning, sunny and 21 plus out, to the Rathmines Library, having stopped for cakes already and to see Mammy at the Bakery, when I noticed, as we approached, crossing the foot of Leinster Square, a scene was going on, kerbside, virtually at the front door of the library

It was a rather large uniformed Dublin garda who was giving a hard time of it to a poor tinker woman and her raggedy children, who had their tumbledown caravan parked on Rathmines Road heading in the wrong direction, directly in front of the library. "Move along now, I say, and be quick about it. Ye're trying my patience now."

"Why don't you leave those poor people alone?" I commented as Aisling and I turned in the library door. "Or try to get them give them some help, instead of rousting them like you are? The travelling people have their rights, you know, and they don't deserve to be treated like that."

"And who are you to be interfering with me in the performance of my duties?" said the policeman, whose beefy cheeks were turning indignantly red as he shook his baton at me.

"I'm a visitor," I said, stretching the truth just a bit, "who's disgusted to see the treatment meted out in the street to Ireland's poor."

And I continued inside with my child, thinking nothing more of this incident at the time.

One reason I did not was the fact that almost the very next thing that happened in the library that day was that, while Aisling and I were settling in to wait for the young ladies from St Mary's to arrive after school, I made straight for the newspaper rack. Now that it was prohibited by Krishna to be hanging out at his flat or Mary and Jane's, as we were wont to do in better days, and not so long ago, at that, the alternative to scooping Krishna's used Irish Times off the floor was, obviously, the library, where I didn't have to pay for the papers.

I grabbed an armful and made myself comfortable at one of the big tables favoured by the girls, just as they began to trickle in, and Aisling contentedly took up with them. For no reason at all I decided to start with last night's Evening Herald. And there at the bottom of page one I found this item:

> *Three men were arrested last night by the Garda Síochána along the border in the vicinity of Drogheda. Activity by Active Service Units of the Provisional IRA along the Northern Ireland side of this section of the border has been recently reported to be heavy and extensive. It is not known at this time whether the three arrested have been connected in any way by the authorities with the bombing of the N.I. Customs Post at Cullaville, outside Crossmaglen, last week, in which two Customs Officers, one RUC, one civilian, and three Provisional IRA Volunteers were killed. Other raiders were believed to be involved in that incident, but the Gardai have refused comment on any possible connection. The three men arrested were Tomas Coote, 23, Warrenpoint, Co. Down, Liam Hargreaves, 21, Ballina, Co. Mayo, and Michael O'Corrigan, 19, Cork City. The three will be charged at the next special session of the Special Criminal Courts in Dublin with membership of an illegal organisation and possession of concealed firearms.*

I sat there stunned. This was not the way I had pictured welcoming Mick O'Corrigan back to Dublin.

The Lynch administration took their first opportunity, Monday morning, to convene a sitting of the Special Criminal Court in the Four Courts. The trial was closed to the public, press and solicitors for the defence. Three officers of the Irish Army were the judges. The Gardai testified that, among other weapons, they found a stolen Belgian FN automatic rifle belonging to the Irish Army in the boot of a suspicious car parked outside a pub in Drogheda. Inside the pub were the three prisoners with a man named Tomlinson. Tomlinson testified that three men had hijacked him in his car, and identified the three prisoners. Under the Offences Against the State Act, they were convicted in twenty minutes and sentenced to eight years apiece. These details were issued via a press release by the office of the Department of Defence.

Mick O'Corrigan did the right thing by the IRA. He followed the code, refused to recognise the Court, refused to recognise the State. Everything according to the principled positions of the Irish Republican Movement. The State was shown once again to ignore principle and rely on naked power. One more Victory in The Struggle, eh?

The item was reported on the front pages of the Dublin papers, as a routine matter, per request of the government, in the side column, in two paragraphs at the bottom. A brief announcement on the RTE radio and television news. A warning to the unruly. The State is secure. The machinery of Justice is well-oiled. God's in his heaven, and we're in the Free State.

Mick O'Corrigan became a casualty of the war against Internment and the British Army's occupation of the North. He might get out in six years or eight, depending on his behaviour and the will of the authorities. Or when the Emergency was over and the State could afford mercy. Or when the war was won and they had a change of government and a 32-county Ireland was established, united and free. Other than that, his Ticket was marked with a new destination: the Curragh Military Camp in Kildare.

The Bridewell was in Chancery Street, behind the Four Courts. A street of shadows cast by the formidable bulk of the bronze-domed buildings of establishment justice in Inn's Quay on the north side of the Liffey. A street hidden from public view, where nobody went quite completely willingly, unless they were getting paid to do so.

The scheduled transfer of the three convicted prisoners for detention at Mountjoy Prison, preparatory to transfer to the Curragh in the morning, was supposed to be routine, and a secret as well. But somebody got word to people who got word to Seán Ó Brádaigh, who got word to me, who got word to Krishna, even though I had to telephone him, and that evening, the wee street was packed out, from the back gate of the Four Courts across to the doors of the jail, with uniformed Gardai, pickets, reporters and photographers, not to mention the RTE cameramen, those blokes not being wont to miss a riot in the offing. This gathering was a tribute to Comrade Krishna's organising abilities, since all he had to work with was the rump of the old Cumman Billy Reid, meaning the two girls from Waterloo Road, Bernie and Martina, and Barney O'Toole and the neighbours from the Liberties he could persuade in half an hour. And it was a tribute to Krishna's connections in the city rooms of the newspapers.

To their credit, all the members of Billy Reid showed up, and that included Alita, John, and Peadar.

But certainly all of us who had known him as our old comrade Mick O'Corrigan could not fail to come out in his support, no matter the circumstances or time constraints.

The inevitable riot was a tame affair as riots went but still a riot like any other. It began with peaceful picketing, the circle of placards going round and round, up on the kerb, down in the gutter, chanting "Let the Freedom Fighters Fight! Let the Freedom Fighters Fight!"

And the Branch detectives, watching with their hands in their pockets, stepping on the kerb, and off the kerb, till one of them decided to take particular offence at a hand-lettered placard with the black-marker message crowding off the card:

INTERNMENT BY ANY OTHER NAME, THAT'S THE SPECIAL COURT'S GAME!

This detective jumped off the kerb, intervened in the circling ring of picketers, and ripped the placard from a young lady's hands.

But that was just a diversion, to create a disturbance and allow the Bridewell warders to erupt from the door of the jail to attack us from the rear. Then the Gardai let loose with the gas and there was havoc in the wee street behind the Four Courts.

Perhaps because of the rioting, nobody, not even the Branch detectives, noticed the burly squad of screws who burst from the jail door to hustle and bundle three prisoners in leg irons and handcuffs into the back of a silver Mercedes parked in Church Street, with a view down Chancery. Nobody but me, that is, from my back, on the ground, and that only because I happened to twist a certain way trying to get up again, and by chance saw Mick. I tried to establish eye contact. I yelled his name.

But it was not to be. He was gone.

We had more time to organize the next riot.

At the meeting of the Cumann the following Wednesday night, we took up the question of what to do about the Curragh Military Camp in Kildare. That was where Lynch was now transferring all his IRA prisoners. To get them out of Dublin, and thereby isolate them from the urban hordes who fueled disastrous riots like the one at the Joy back in April. We Republicans had no intention of letting him get away with it, and Alita and John were strong boosters of Kevin Street's plan for the next big demonstration. This was to involve city-wide all the Dublin cumainn.

I called in my chips from the days of the Anti-Common Market campaign in May and contacted Dermot Walsh and Henry Macken from the Cumann Cathal Hughes. The day for the demo was coming up fast on Saturday, but we managed to get numbers out on the road to Kildare. It wasn't as many as we had for the road-filling operation up on the border, but it was a couple of hundred, at least.

Comrade Krishna was not among them. I would never have questioned any of his decisions, as I had nothing but respect for his substantial political acumen, but somehow, he must have felt he had to explain. "My mother made me promise when I was leaving home that I would enter the medical faculty at London. It was her dream for me, to become a doctor, and she has never stinted in her support for me, but, alas, it was not going to happen in London. Now, here in Dublin, this may be the last chance I get, who's to say? So, right now, I just feel I must lay low for a while, as I'm awaiting the results of my entrance exam."

His face, usually so resolute and in-command, quavered with a kind of a plea, and I hastened to reassure him that nobody was going to hold it against him, but I don't know if he believed that. Guilt feelings have so many ways of disabling even the strongest among us.

I was by now a veteran rioter, and that Saturday, knowing as I did that it was my dear pal Mick who was inside, for whom I was doing this, I had no intention of arriving at the scene of anticipated combat unprepared. So, as we marchers approached on the access road parallel to the main encampment of low huts, where we knew they were holding our prisoners, I made sure to collect as many hefty rocks as I could by the roadside and stuff them into the pockets of my pea-coat.

As usual, Alita and John fulfilled their roles as marshals and attempted to insist on us keeping things orderly and peaceful, or, at least, orderly. But, as usual, we paid no heed to wiser heads, and peeled off the road to charge across an open pasture flanked with tree-lined driveways.

The Irish Army refused the challenge and did not come out to fight us, as the Brits had up on the border. When we pivoted and turned off the road, they stayed uninvolved behind their barbed-wire-topped chain-link fence, and inside the relative safety of their guardhouses with the red-and-white-striped traffic gates at the tops of the driveways.

Thus it wasn't a very satisfactory riot. I expended my supply of ammunition, shouted myself hoarse in the vain hope that our prisoners inside, and Mick, in particular, would be cheered to hear us out there supporting them, and everyone else did, too, but then what? The usual onlookers, the press photogs, TV cameras, and inevitable Special Branch detectives in their unmarked black Cortinas, could have yawned their way through the demo, and they did. It was one of those sunny-and-warm, brilliant Irish summer afternoons, and rioting under the leafy shade of the trees, we didn't even have to work up a sweat, but kept ourselves nice and cool in the breeze that was blowing through the nodding boughs of the windbreaks lining the two driveways.

I knew my friend and comrade Mick O'Corrigan was inside the wire of this camp, and that's what was making me so angry, but I only felt the futility of what we were doing, and it only reinforced the despair I felt at losing all hope of ever seeing him again, for a very long time. The way things were going I certainly wasn't about to show up one day at the gates of the Curragh Camp as some sort of Quaker prison-visitor asking to see him. All we Republicans seemed to be able to accomplish that day was to relieve ourselves of some of the pent-up agro.

I was coming out of the street door of No. 4a Kevin Street, a few nights later, after visiting at a late hour with Seán Ó Brádaigh, upstairs, to sort of brief him about my trip to Derry with Toss Ribbons, and it was by then completely dark out, and I decided for some reason to walk home to Rathmines by some rather circuitous route, to make a wide circle, rather than a straight line, just taking precautions, so, instead of turning at the corner of Wexford Street to head for the South Circular Road, I turned the other way, toward the city centre, heading down Aungier Street, where Paddy Clarke's lay across on the other side of the street.

It was drizzling and dark, with lights darting from the headlamps of the traffic passing, and gleaming streaks of glare from the wet street, and I was just passing into the massive shadow of the pillars of the Mt Carmel Priory opposite the pub, when I saw them, converging on me.

Two men climbing quickly out of a darkened, parked car, over the road opposite, racing across the street, dodging traffic, to block the footpath in front of me. Behind me, two more, already on the footpath on my side of the street, coming on quick, crouching on the balls of their feet, ready to jump this way or that. There was no place for me to go that wouldn't throw me in front of a moving car. I was trapped, and I knew it. They closed in fast, in front and behind, and threw me up roughly against the shadows of the Priory wall.

"Give us your name and address!"

"John Doyle—!"

"Don't give us that!" said the man who was jerking me up against the wall by the lapels of my pea-coat. "We know who you are!"

"What are you asking me for then?"

The plainclothes man shook me. "Have you ever heard of the Offences Against the State Act?"

"That's nothing to do with me. I'm an American citizen."

"Your name and address, I said!"

"Who are you!"

"Detective Sergeant Dooley, Special Branch, Dublin Castle. Satisfy you?"

"How do I know that's who you are?"

"I don't need to show you a thing!"

"Then I don't answer questions!"

"Let me at him, Sergeant!" said one of the others.

"Leave off!" said Sergeant Dooley. He let go of my lapels with a sneer, as if he'd dirtied himself holding me, and then he dusted off my chin with two hands fluttering twice, like brushing me off. He straightened himself with a shudder to his full height while the other three glowered at me over his shoulders. "Your name and address!"

"You know who I am, or you wouldn't be stopping me."

"Yes, and I know you just came out of Kevin Street, too."

"So? There's no law against that!"

"You're going to lecture me on the law? Like you did the garda that time, outside the library? Oho, you didn't think I knew about that, did you? Listen, boyo, I know all about you. Goin' all the way back to Maurice Woolf, Ltd. Oh, we have quite a file on you, all right. Now where's your passport!"

"I don't carry it on me."

"You're wanted for an interview, at the Aliens Department, Dublin Castle, nine o'clock tomorrow morning. Be there, and bring that passport with you. Be there, and don't be late, or we'll come and get you."

They left me standing there and melted away into the night, the same way they materialized out of it.

I was so shaken that I did not even register them getting back into their cars to drive off.

I stood there letting the breath I was holding in my chest cavity, as if I were underwater, expel, with a feeling of all the air going flat in the tire.

I couldn't think of what to do except to turn and start to stumble homeward. I only knew that they wouldn't stop me again or try to interfere with me. They'd done their dirty job of trying to throw a scare into me, delivered their message, and now they were off to do the same to the next poor eedjit, I had no doubt. Never had I hated the police so much or felt so unclean after them putting their filthy paws all over me. No sense in trying evasive movements now, so I trudged home wearily, the same way I'd just come, past the corner of Wexford and Kevin Street, head down, hands in my pockets, and when I was approaching the Portobello Bridge in the rain, it was as if I'd never seen it before, and the whole world had changed from what it was just an hour ago into something else, something strange and unfamiliar and foreboding.

I knew I couldn't go home and face Sheila with this news without talking to Comrade Krishna first. To hell with any precautions.

I banged on the door of Mary and Jane's flat upstairs. One of them let me in and Krishna was sitting in his easy chair by the fire, and he knew it was bad, right away.

"The Branch stopped me coming out of Kevin Street. Put me up against the wall. They say I have to show up at the Castle in the morning and bring my passport. Why do I have to bring my passport, Krishna? Do I have to go?"

He rose slowly and began to pace back and forth in front of the sofa, where I'd collapsed by the fireplace. He sighed deeply. "Yes, you have to go. Looks like the crunch has come, comrade."

"What if I don't go?"

"It might be better if you did. And it would certainly be worse if you don't. Have you thought of Sheila and Aisling?"

"What do they want with my passport?"

"I don't know. But you're going to find out. And then— then, we take it from there. You're still a member of the Movement, and you have to think of that. You're not alone. You'll have back-up. But you must also think of them. The Movement has its needs, too. Why don't we just take it step by step, eh? It's just time now to be realistic, now, and, and— deal with the facts, eh? as they arise, and, uh, see where we are."

Comrade Krishna. The ultimate pragmatist. I knew I wouldn't feel better, feel sane, feel the sand not slipping out from under me, until I'd talked to him. "I'm sorry, Krishna, I had to come straight to you, and blow all our cover like this—."

"Never mind that. They may be coming for me, too, soon enough. Conditions change."

Because the sun rose so early this time of year, it was already mid-morning by nine o'clock, and the sun, if it showed at all, intruded over the back-walls of South Great Georges Street, which bordered on the lower wall of Dublin Castle, where the Aliens Department had their cubicles in a long, low-roofed aluminium shanty.

I trudged over the hump-backed cobblestones of the Yard, feeling low, not with my head held high, as the song about Kevin Barry going up the gallows steps would have it; but more as if all I merited in the eyes of the authorities was this long walk to a shabby fate in a second-class adjunct to the main magnificence.

I said to the receptionist, "I guess they're expecting me."

"Oh, yes, would you have a seat, please, and I'll get your man."

Where had I heard that before? Oh, yes, Macmillan's bookshop. John Martyn. Perhaps I should forget that name. All their names. In case I'm questioned.

A man emerged from a hallway, waving a file folder, a non-descript man in a business suit, about twice my age, wearing bureaucrat-grey on his face with his wire-rimmed spectacles. He could have been a vacuum-cleaner salesman whose hair had gone slightly ashen from sheer repetitive boredom. "Ah, yes. This way, please."

I rose reluctantly. What fastened me to my seat was that I'd been brooding about Sheila. I hadn't yet told her. Well—how could I? She was asleep, obviously, when I got back to No. 56 the night before. And then she was getting up at four in the morning. To go to work to support me. How could I have unloaded on her at that hour?

Down the hall was a vista of cubicles. The Aliens man held open a half door for me. I entered and he said, politely, "Have a seat, please."

I looked down at the ordinary green-vinyl-covered employment-bureau seat he held out for me, and sat down with a sigh as he went round the back of his steel desk to seat himself. The walls of his cubicle, and no doubt, every other one, were made of that dirty white foam material that looks like cork. Sitting there, I felt completely exposed. Anyone on both sides could hear anything I might say. I felt like they'd be peering over the neck-high wall at me soon.

"You know, I've been sitting here brooding over this dossier for the last half-hour," he began. "Nicholas Petrovich. Alias John Doyle." He chuckled. "I like that. Chief Superintendant John Doyle. That's rich."

What an odd fellow. "What's your name?"

"That's not how it works, you see. I ask you the questions. However, I have no objection to telling you. My name is Colm O'Byrne. That's B-Y-R-N-E, in case you're taking notes." He sat back very satisfied with himself, and yet curiously curious. "What particularly nettles me about this case is that I'll have to keep it strictly from Moira. That's my wife, you know. She's very strong opinions on certain things. The sanctity of Irish family life, and so on. I'll have to lie to her. And I'm not good at that. It's a new day, you know. Women's Lib. Have you heard of it?"

I had no idea what was driving him onto this tangent.

"The bastards are testing me, that's what it is." He reached over to the black telephone on his desk and dialed a three-digit number. "Leo? Colm here. Can you answer a question for me?"

"Depends on which one."

He held out the receiver for me so I could hear.

"What are the legalities concerning deportation of a foreigner married to an Irish citizen?"

Deportation! Oh, my God.

"Well, curiously enough, if the alien is a woman, she cannot be deported, her husband being an Irish citizen. But if the reverse is the case—which is it with you?"

"The man is the alien, Leo."

"Worse luck for them both. Another drug case?"

"No. Bloody politics."

"Sounds interesting."

"It's not. Tell us, Leo—how did they ever let that ruling come about?"

"All according to our glorious Constitution of 1937—framed by Dev himself—with a little help from his pals in Maynooth. So much for that much-maligned Irish institution, eh?"

Colm O'Byrne rang off. "Bastards. No loophole there. Looks like old John Doyle is in for it now. But then—they'll have to find him first. Well, that wasn't so very difficult. You made it easy for them. Found you coming out of Kevin Street, where you'd been seen, and photographed, many times before. All in the dossier here. I'm not the type to take a slight easily, you know. I'm smarting still, from the manner the Branch man gave out to me. Supercilious bastard. Just do your part for us, says he—we'll take care of the rest. Damn bloody cheek. Who?—O'Byrne? He's only an old Aliens officer—till they need you—to do the dirty. Well, I told him. Do you mind my enquiring, have you any grounds for this action?"

"Where is all this getting to, Mr O'Byrne?"

"Have you brought that passport with you?"

"Yes."

"May I see it, please?"

I handed it to him across the desk. He flipped through several pages, saying, hmm, hmm, hmm. Then he closed it up, and as I was reaching out my hand to take it back, he quietly slipped my passport into the desk draw at his belly and turned the key, to lock the drawer, extracted the key, and slipped the key in his pocket. All this was done in a trice before my very eyes, as if a magician were practicing his sleight of hand in front of a child. "What are you doing?" I said.

"Regulations, my boy, regulations. Not to worry, you'll get it back."

I felt like I did back in high school in Spicket Falls, when I was sent to sit in front of Mr Lister, the Vice-Principal in charge of Discipline. "When am I gonna get it back?"

"When you're standing across the rope and mounting the Aer Lingus stair for your flight back to the States."

"I'm not going back to the States!"

"That's of no concern to us. You may go anywhere you bloody well like, but you can't stay here."

"Mr O'Byrne. Can I ask you a question? Are you Irish? Do you know what's going on in this country?"

"Yes I do, and yes, I am. May I show you something from this dossier?"

I was completely baffled by this man. What in God's name is he getting at, so fucking politely?

O'Byrne slipped a photograph, an enlarged black-and-white glossy print, across his desk at me, twirling it so it faced me. I leaned over and peered at it. "Is that you?" he asked, pointing with his finger to a figure in the photo.

I recognized myself, bent over, from the pea-coat. "Yes."

It was me, carefully selecting big rocks at the roadside in Kildare, outside the Curragh Camp.

He slipped the enlarged print back into the dossier. "Case closed." Mr O'Byrne sighed heavily. "When I asked your man if he had any grounds, this is what he showed me. And now, you admit to it."

The interview was over, and he was showing me out, but first, he paused to say, "Where is your wife from—do you mind my asking?"

"County Mayo."

"Ah—Mayo, God help us."

"Can I ask you a question? If I'm deported—when can I come back?"

"Never."

"Never?"

"Never."

On the way home to No. 56, of course, I stopped at Leinster Square, and, badly in need of someone to commiserate with me, went in to see Krishna, who, in any case, had been minding Aisling for me the while I went to my appointment in the Castle. "You were right," I said, to start with, "not to go out to the Curragh with us, comrade."

"No use crying over spilt milk, comrade."

"Do you think that garda at the library could have had something to do with this? I'm convinced he was the one who put the finger on me."

"What are you talking about?"

"I made a mistake—and I didn't want to tell you about it. I went shooting off my big mouth." I told Krishna the story, and he looked appalled. "I'll bet he ran to the Branch and insisted they do something about this Yank who insulted him."

"That may very well be the case, but again, comrade, what does it matter? It's done and over with. Don't go blaming yourself. Now we know what they intend it's up to us to develop a strategy for our response. You have to stop blaming yourself. It's not you they're attacking. It's the Movement, through you. They want to get at the Movement, but they can't, because it's so strong, and you are the only vulnerability they can find, you are a weak spot for the Movement."

"I'm gonna fight it, Krishna. I'm not gonna let them just do this to me. I'll go on the run if I have to."

"No, no. no, that's crazy. You can't expect the Movement to support you on that. And where would you be, on the run, without them? And what about Sheila and the child—do you want to bring these hassles down on their heads? Do you think they'd be just left alone—with you out there somewhere?"

"I haven't told her yet, Krishna."

"Why not?"

"There was no chance!"

"Well—we have to tell her—straightaway. *You* have to tell her."

"Can you help me with that, comrade?"

"Yes, yes, yes, of course. I'll go and fetch her when she gets out of work. What time will that be? I'll bring her here—she'll have friends around her—it will soften the blow."

I was sitting with Aisling in my lap on the sofa. Mary was asleep on her bed. Jane was out at work for the day. I was thankful, so thankful, that Aisling was not old enough to fully take in all that was going on. I just cuddled her close to me.

So that's what we did. Krishna brought Sheila back to Mary and Jane's flat. That gave her time to figure out that something bad had happened. Krishna just told her she would have to speak to me to find out what, that he didn't want to be the one to tell her, and that the baby was all right. When she got into the flat, Mary was up, by this time, and she patted the bed beside her, and put her arm around Sheila while I told her that I was being deported.

Later, the three of us walked home together, slowly, up Rathmines Road, and every step we took seemed like the step we would want to memorize and keep preserved in amber for the rest of our lives, and we clung to each other, I put my arm around Sheila's shoulder, she put both arms around my waist and leaned her head on my chest, while Aisling, whom I had by the hand, looked up at us and wisely decided it wasn't the time for her to be chattering away because mammy and daddy were sad.

Seán Ó Brádaigh called the next morning and asked if there was anything he could do, if there was anything we needed. He expressed his support for me on behalf of the Movement. "We're going to get you a solicitor, Nick, the very best. Myles Shevlin. He does all the legal work for the lads inside, on this side of the border. He's a top man. If anyone can do anything for you, it's him. So now, I don't want you going losing hope. How's the missus? Is she bucking up?"

Strangely, Sheila did not blame me. At least, not the way I blamed myself. Maybe she knew me better than I thought she did. Maybe she knew I couldn't help it because I was a hopeless idealist and did not believe that anyone would ever attack me for that, not really. Maybe that was one of the things she loved me for, after all. Or maybe she blamed herself for bringing me to Ireland in the first place. Oh, it was all hopelessly entangled. My biggest fear had been that she would reject me, for having failed her, and the child, for having let her down, in the worst way, that she would turn against me, in anger, and spite, that she would be judgmental, and hurl her epithets at my head, along with the dinner dishes. But no. I did not know her at all. She was a far, far better person than that.

There were other phone calls, too. They started right away. All times of the day and night. The whole building was upset—Eileen and Angela, down the back, Shane and Monica downstairs, Desmond and his mother. I had to tell Sheila and everyone else not to answer the phone—to let me.

I would pick up. And the voice would say, "We know where you are." Click. Or, "Don't let us catch you here after August 24th, or you'll regret it, and so will your one and her baby." Click.

It was chilling. The others in the building, should they chance to answer the ring, got heavy breathing and a click. I got messages that went right through me.

Myles Shevlin was every inch the defendant's legal advocate in his black-plastic-rimmed eyeglasses. His home was in the Phoenix Park and that's where he had his office. I went there full of hopes that I was going to be represented by William Kunstler and that I was the new Chicago Seven, but that was to be quickly dashed.

"There isn't much recourse available to us in this case, I'm afraid."

"But don't you think it's totally unfair that an Irish man's wife cannot be deported, but an Irish woman's husband can? Isn't that discriminatory?"

"Yes, of course, but we're not going to get that reversed. You see, you haven't been arrested, so there is nothing to appeal because there is no case going through the courts. All this is being done to you, Nicholas, quite extra-legally, by which I mean that, if asked, the Special Branch will deny knowing anything about you."

"But they've confiscated my passport!"

"Oh, yes, quite illegally."

"But isn't that illegal?"

"Yes, but if pressed on the question, they will deny they did it."

"But I can't get my passport back from them. They locked it in a drawer."

"But you will get it back when you comply with what they require of you."

"Why can't I get it back now?"

"They will say they have no idea where it is. Why did you surrender it?"

"They asked me for it. I thought the man was gonna look at it and give it back. Instead, he locked it up."

"And you say that you did admit to photographic evidence in their possession showing you with prior intent to commit assault on government officials? Well, in that case—would you prefer that they charge you with that act in the Special Criminal Courts, under the Offences Against the State Act?"

"No. I guess not."

"Because then, being the Republican you are, you would have to stand up and declare that you do not recognise the Court, and so on, down the line. And three Military Officers would sentence you on the testimony of one policeman or the evidence of one photograph. I couldn't be there for you in the courtroom and you might get six months or you might get four years. And your wife might not be able to visit you in Portlaoise very often, that is, if she could find out from them where they had you."

Hearing Myles Shevlin lay it all out like this, I could only reflect sadly that this was exactly what had already happened to Mick O'Corrigan.

"You see, Nicholas—in their minds, they are being eminently fair with you—letting you off the hook easily, so to speak."

"But they told me I can never come back."

Now Myles Shevlin was properly outraged. "Oh, completely illegal, I should say, yes, definitely."

"You mean they can't really ban me for life?"

"Yes, but Nicholas—do you really want to return in defiance of them, having acquired them at that point as your enemies sworn? Think about that, would you, my friend? And Nicholas—if ever you find yourself in the hands of the police, don't talk. Don't open your mouth. Say nothing. Call your solicitor. If I had been there to represent you in your interview with the Aliens Department, perhaps I would have advised you not to turn over that passport, or not to have brought it to the interview with you at all. Certainly not to admit to that photograph." Myles Shevlin looked at me, professionally sympathetic. "I'm sorry. Really, I am." He then looked thoughtful. "There is one point I ought to mention to you, though I hesitate. They have given you that deadline of August 24th, by which time you must be out of the country—because—" and here he paused—

"if you were here within the country for one year and one day, you would then be eligible to apply for Irish citizenship—so they want you to depart before that clause, that option, so to speak, would come into effect."

"Well, Mr Shevlin—would you then advise me to try to stay one extra day—?"

"They would come after you."

"But if I could evade them for just one day—would that be enough time to apply for the citizenship?"

"I cannot honestly put myself in the position of advising you to do this."

"Would I have to give up my American citizenship?"

"That is not my area of expertise."

I left grasping onto this one slim hope.

"Now I find out from Shevlin that everything the Branch did to me is completely illegal!"

"You expected them to play fair, eh?" said Krishna. "Look. There is something I may be able to do for you, after all."

"What?" I recognised a gleam in Krishna's eye. Time was running short. I had only ten days left before the deadline. Sheila and Aisling and I were in Mary and Jane's flat in the evening, Jane was there, too, Mary was out at the hospital, we were all having a strategy session about my case. "Come on, Krishna, what?"

"Well—the Libyan Minister of Education is in Dublin this week, for one week only." He handed over his copy of that day's Irish Times with a want-ad circled in red in the back pages.

"He's looking to interview teachers of English as a Second Language for 2-year contracts to teach ESL in the Libyan schools in Tripoli and Benghazi."

I snatched the paper and scanned the ad. "But this is fantastic!"

"But do you have your transcripts with you, Nick?" said Krishna.

"Yes! Krishna—you're a genius! How did you ever stumble across this!"

"Comrade—you know I'm very tight with Mohammad Moneim of the Office for Inter-Arab Affairs. You remember I brought you to see him and introduced you. Or have you forgotten the days we used to spend afternoons sipping coffee in Bewley's?"

"No, no, of course not!" I looked excitedly at Sheila. "Babe— we're going to Libya! This is the teaching job I've been looking for all this time!"

Sheila and Jane were sitting together on the edge of Mary's bed, and Sheila was grinning sardonically at Jane. "Slow down, love," said she, "you don't know the first thing about Libya, do you?"

"Yes, I do. We had a war with them in 1803—the Tripoli pirates. We were taught all about it in school. From the Halls of Mon-tay-zoo-oo-ma, to the Shores of Trip-oh-lee," I sang.

"Where did you find him?" said Jane to Sheila. "He's eso-teric," Sheila declared, tapping her temple with her forefinger.

"Listen, Jane. It's a far better alternative than the citizenship option we've been throwing around. That one doesn't come complete with a teaching job, does it? And I have to think of some way to avoid being shipped back to the States on a plane, because there's no way I want to be interviewed by the FBI after being deported from somewhere. It was the FBI caused me to leave the country and come here in the first place."

"All right," said Krishna, "everybody settle down. Nick, you haven't got the job yet. We'll have to get you cleaned up. We'll have to be in Mohammad Moneim's office in Grafton Street at ten o'clock in the morning. You're not the only interview he'll be taking, you know. Have you a suit and tie? Good. Your wedding suit. Seems appropriate. Now I suggest we all hit the sack early. It will be a big day tomorrow, and we're running out of time to get everything pulled together. So, out you go. Take your wife and daughter home, and sleep well, comrade."

The next morning on the phone to Krishna, I said, "What do you mean, you're not coming with me!"

"I'm on precautions, you know that. Besides, I have every confidence in you. You're quite capable when you want to be. And considering the importance of this morning to your future—and your family's future—."

"But you're the one who's friends with Mohammad Moneim."

"Nick—consider how it might look to them to have me there to second you, or worse, to speak in your behalf."

"I suppose so, if you put it that way."

Thus I reluctantly boarded the bus in Rathmines by myself. Sometimes I thought Krishna's 'precautions' were thoroughly tongue-in-cheek, that he was indulging in self-mockery with his weird, Asian sub-continent sense of humour. It was as if I'd wandered onto a Monty Python movie set. I couldn't remember if I'd ever heard him laugh. But I would have to put all that aside now, for this was the morning for me to shape up.

In the end, I needn't have been nervous at all. When I got to the Office of Inter-Arab Affairs, Mohammad Moneim welcomed me effusively. He came out from behind his imposing walnut desk and pumped my hand, inviting me to sit on the leather sofa with him while a man-servant set up a small circular tea-table, poured tea, and discreetly withdrew.

Mohammad Moneim quickly put me at my ease with small-talk. "We have two kinds of tea in the Arab world. Green tea and red tea. Some prefer one and some the other. You will see that we make quite a ceremony out of taking tea with our colleagues and friends. Oh, yes. Nothing can be done at the beginning of the work-day before we have our tea ceremony."

Mr Moneim was an Egyptian, and his English, though fluent, was tinged with an accent. Like Colm O'Byrne, the immigration officer at the Castle, and my solicitor, Myles Shevlin, too, he was about twice my age, old enough to be sponsoring me as somewhat of a younger protégé. These people I'd been meeting in recent days, while I was going through personal crisis, and quite a lot of inner turmoil, were all solid citizens, with lives, homes, families, careers. They were taking care of me, solicitous for my well-being, I was being taken under their wing, and groomed, even O'Byrne, in Aliens, with his scruples and concerns, seemed to be in on the game. Mr Moneim even dressed like the other two, like a Westernized businessman.

The door to the office opened, and in came the Libyan Minister of Education. I rose, along with Mr Moneim. To my utter surprise, as he shook my hand, he said to me, "Oh, sit down, please," in a broad American accent that could have come from anywhere north of the Ohio or west of the Mississippi.

Mr Ahmed Omar Jalloud was taller than me, slim, dressed in a black suit, with one button closed, clearly custom-tailored, white shirt, necktie solid red. He smiled avidly, showing perfect teeth. He was tanned, and his hair was black, bright brown eyes; he was clean-shaven. "I can see you're wondering where I got this accent. Six years at USC. School of Education. Phi Kappa Psi, ha, ha, ha. And you're Boston College. Amazing. But I don't believe we ever played you in football, have we? And, I've heard the Boston accent is just atrocious. You're not going to make our poor Libyan students talk that way, are you? At least we can count on you not to inflict a clipped British military jargon on them. Colonel Ghaddafi would not go for that. He's a graduate of Sandhurst, you know, and it would give him bad dreams. "

I'd never been recruited before, until that day. There was no way, when the time came, that I was not going to sign on the dotted line of the two-year contract they presented me with. I would have bought a used Vauxhall from these guys.

"Now," said Mr Ahmed Omar Jalloud, "you'll have to go up to London to get entrance visas for you and your family. All expenses will be paid by us, of course, for transportation to Tripoli via Libyan Arab Airways from Heathrow. Unfortunately, we do not have an Embassy here in Dublin. So—there you are. And now, I must excuse myself, as Mr Moneim and I have another appointment shortly. It's been such a busy week—but isn't Dublin delightful?"

One of the phone calls I didn't expect, out in the hall, came from Seán Ó Brádaigh. "I just got off the phone with Myles Shevlin, Nick, and I can't tell you how outraged I am."

"Seán, I really don't want to talk about it on the phone. I don't mean to cut you short, but I've been getting phone calls, you know what I mean, the threatening kind, and I just have the feeling they're listening in all the time."

"Yes, yes, of course. But it's very important that I see you. Do you think you can come into the office?"

When I was sitting in front of him in Kevin Street, he looked at me with such mortal empathy you would have thought I was Robert Emmet come back to life or something. God bless Seán Ó Brádaigh, I thought, he is a true believer if ever there was one.

"I just really, really feel, Nick, that we must call out the Lynch government on this one. We can't let them get away with it without at least trying to make them face up to the court of public opinion. Now, I understand from Myles that you're under a deadline and that your time with us is running short, but I've consulted with the leaders of the party who are in town, and we're all agreed—now, how would you feel about us mounting a press conference? You would have to be there, of course, and so would your wife, and your child, as she is the Irish citizen who is having her family so wrongfully torn apart. And I do wonder, do the Irish people realize that our women, our mothers, to whom we owe everything in this country, are so wantonly disregarded and heinously discriminated against by these draconian measures being taken by the Special Branch and the Fianna Fail government against the Irish family, the very foundation of our society, the one institution of Irish life which we should be so zealously guarding and protecting? Now we'll have our chaplain, Father Feeney, there, as the Church must be represented, since they have such a vital stake—he will speak—and so will my brother Ruairí —and all of us will be there. What do you say? You'll have to answer questions from the press, and so may your wife, too."

The press conference called by the Sinn Féin was held the next night at half-six at the North Star Hotel in Amiens Street. This was so that the RTE personnel present could rush right back to the studios with everything fresh in mind and get it on that evening's 9 o'clock news with Charles Mitchel. After all, there was bound to be, in the present climate, a good deal of competition for airtime from car-bombings, ambushes, UDA murders, and arrests of suspected members of the IRA. Seán Ó Brádaigh got everything rolling as master of ceremonies, and his opening speech was actually a remarkable, almost word-for-word, reprise of what he'd said to me in his office, in private. The man was born to his post of Information Officer of Sinn Féin. Then his brother Ruairí, the President of the party, spoke, and he gave a detailed rendering of all the evidence the Republican Movement had accumulated through the course of the past year of Internment, North and South, on secret units of the British Army and British Intelligence, MI6, operating inside Ireland, "on both sides of the border, as we can now all plainly see." Next Father Feeney took the mike and he testified that the Irish Government was breaking up an Irish family by expelling the father, that the father was being expelled solely because he'd worked for Ireland's freedom, that they were all, Lynch, Branch, Ministry of Justice and the entire Fianna Fail party, a discredit to their Irish mothers.

Then it was my turn.

The room was packed, front to back. They were kneeling at my feet with pads poised and cameras aimed. I was blinded by flashbulbs going off. I had no doubt whatsoever that the Branch was in the room, probably down at the back, skulking. The news-people were all acting as if they were stunned to find out that there was an American in the Irish Republican Movement. I could see Comrade Krishna leaning up against the wall on the left, dressed in his fatigues, there to support Sheila and me, but trying to be ever so inconspicuous, hunching his shoulders to make himself smaller. I found out pretty quickly that none of these media sharks hungrily circling me, their bait, was the least bit interested in issues of Irish constitutionality or the rights of Irish women or the treatment of mothers or the breakup of Irish families by the government. Their sole focus was on sensationalizing the news of an American caught red-handed as a card-carrying rebel who was due to be deported in the morning by 'de aut'orities.'

"What's Irish freedom to you, as a foreigner?" one shouted.

"You're going straight back to the States, are you?" yelled another.

"Can you give us your views on the use of force by the Irish Republican Movement?"

"One at a time," I had to say.

It was impossible to satisfy them as they scribbled furiously and flashed away. I decided I had to shut them up with a little speech of my own. "I was born and raised in Boston. Boston is the birthplace of the American Revolution." I was warming up to the idea of giving them some good copy. "We were taught at our mother's knee, and in school, too, to oppose British colonialism, and British Imperialism, in whatever form it appears, and wherever, and whenever. I don't believe I've done anything in Ireland, in the time I've been here, that any other American wouldn't have done in my place, born and raised as we are in our traditions of freedom and independence and self-determination for small nations, as President Wilson would have it, as we were taught in school. The British forces ought to get out of Ireland just as we made them get out of Boston!"

The room erupted in hullabaloo, a barrage of questions, while the TV and radio people raced to their vehicles to get their tapes on the air.

There was one question I didn't want to answer. "Since you're not going home, as you stated, then—where are you going?"

Three times that question was asked, and the first two times I simply said, "Well, I don't know yet," or, "I haven't decided."

I wasn't afraid of telling them about going to Libya. What worried me, after my little speech, was admitting that I was going to England.

It was marvelous how quickly that room emptied out when I finally had to say, "No comment," which jumped into my head because I'd seen Red Sox players use that dodge when asked on TV if they hated the Yankees.

Poor Sheila. There she was jiggling three-year-old Aisling, who was getting heavy, up and down in her arms, getting weary having to stand there, and nobody wanted to ask her any questions at all. She was the Irish person in the story and they just ignored her.

The next day dawned as I woke to the calamitous realization that this was to be the last day I would ever spend in Ireland.

Why it did not seem to hit me before that, to sink in, to feel real, I may never know, but there is something to the countdown to a deadline such as I faced, the 23rd of August, 1972, which prevents you from accepting anything as finally final until at last the dread day arrives and you know there is no longer any possible way of avoiding the thunderous finality of that ultimate ending.

Sheila and I had slept together, clinging to one another through the whole night without hardly sleeping at all, but restlessly turning to and fro to face one another or to face away, but almost obsessively unable to, or afraid to, lose contact, or take our arms or hands from each other. Nor did we speak. Words seemed so futile, especially whispered in the dark.

And upon rising, resigned at last, and thinking of some strategy to prolong the day, by taking it slowly, by making it last, by trying to savor the last look, the last word, the last touch, how disappointing to discover that, in fact, no, there were so many things left still to be done that one hardly had a moment left to oneself.

We had to close up the flat at No. 56 and take one last look around at the scene of so much of our family dramatics and yet so much of our love for one another. "I wish I could break open that meter box and get some of my shillings back," I joked feebly, but my humour fell flat.

Aisling had to say goodbye to her little playmate Desmond, we had to receive well-wishes from his mother Josephine, from Angela and Eileen, down the back, from Shane and Monica downstairs. There was a little gathering for farewells outside the door of our flat, with a lot of hugs, followed by standing back and folding arms, and cocking the head to one side with a rueful smile, more like a half-frown. When I looked down at the end of my hand to find myself grasping by the handle the little blue airlines bag with which I'd come to Ireland the year before, almost to the day, it seemed so pathetic to think that all my worldly possessions could fit in that small bag and yet my heart was nowhere near big enough to contain all the real, true riches, the buried treasure of emotions, the past year had bestowed upon me, to the brim of overflowing.

Slowly the three of us walked for the last time down Upper Rathmines Road to the junction where Rathgar Road split off, and passing Madigan's, I remembered the day I was standing there at the bar, devastated, when Bernadette Cullen came in and touched my arm to tell me that Sheila was back at the flat crying her eyes out. And I turned my back on them both. To commiserate with a half-pint alone.

At Jane and Mary's a parade of our friends began filtering in for the rest of the day. John Martyn came in while he was on his lunch hour from Macmillan's in the city centre. He brought Peadar Kenny with him, but they couldn't stay more than half an hour. Barney O'Toole and a delegation from the Liberties came in the afternoon. The 23rd of August was a Wednesday. Tomorrow would be Thursday and the 24th, exactly a year to the day since I'd landed at Shannon. I was not leaving until the 8.40 P.M. boat-train ferry to Holyhead was scheduled to depart Dun Laoghaire on Wednesday evening. So when Martina and Bernadette arrived after 3pm, when they got off their shift at the Aer Lingus office, they joked that I'd cheated them out of the chance to sell me an airlines seat back to Boston. We were all sitting around on the sofa, Krishna's easy chair, and Mary's bed, and the flat was getting crowded when Alita Hughes came in with her sister Maureen. I thanked her for coming and said she needn't have as I knew how she felt and wanted to thank her for all her support and guidance through all the months, but she wanted to apologize for missing the press conference and explain that she hadn't wanted by attending to detract from the focus which should rightly have been on me. "Now I'm going to give you the last instructions, as Chairman of the Cumann, I can give you, which is that you are to return to us as soon as you possibly can and resume your post, and this time, I expect you to obey me, no shadow of a doubt." When to my surprise Alita wanted to hug me, and I was looking over her shoulder at Maureen, who was collapsing into tears, I didn't have the heart to tell them of the sentence given to me by the Aliens man in the Castle. My term of exile was to be lifelong and never-ending. To push away my feelings, I joked, "Hey, all we need is a fiddler and Peadar's whistle and we could have a real American wake for my departure!" Alita and Maureen had to leave, but on their heels, in came Mrs Duggan from the bakery, with cakes for Aisling and commiseration for Sheila, plus a final pay packet, including a generous severance amount on top of it. "Sheila, are you honestly leaving tomorrow?" "Mrs Duggan, I can't stay, really. Aisling and me'll be taking the train home to Mayo." Mrs Duggan found me in the crowded flat and shook her forefinger at me. "If I had had the slightest inkling about you, I'd've swept you out the back door with the rat turds, I would've." It was the first real laugh we'd had all day.

And then, to my utter astonishment, in came Susan Drummond, from Maurice Woolf's, and Tony Daugherty right behind her. "How in the world did you find me?" I asked Susan as I hugged her. "Ah, well," said the matronly ghost from the Oliver Bond Council Flats, "Dublin is still a small town, you know. And besides—you're famous now. We all saw you on the telly last night."

And then it was time for Krishna to take me aside out of the flat and downstairs to his place for a conference.

Once in his room, he handed me a piece of paper. "Now I'm going to give you just a couple of names and phone numbers for when you get up to London, and you'll have to commit them to memory and not write them down. The first one comes from Seán Ó Brádaigh and you'll have to guard that one with absolute security. The name is Tony Boland and the address is Woburn Mansions, No. 26 Torrington Place, basement flat, he lives there with his sister, phone number 01-222-4768. The second one is a dear friend of mine, Dr Sanjay Patel, he's an MD, heart surgeon, he and his wife live in Marble Arch, No.

12 Stanhope Street, 01-330-8325. You're to call Tony Boland as soon as you arrive. He'll put you up. You'll be coming in on the boat-train from Holyhead to Euston Station, and then it's straight down the Tottenham Court Road—."

"Krishna, I won't be in London but a couple of days. I just have to find the Libyan Embassy, pick up our visas and the plane tickets, and I'll be calling Sheila to come over and join me."

"If all goes well, or as planned. This is just in case. Let's hope you won't be at Tony Boland's more than a week, or a couple of nights, if you insist, but I want you to contact Dr Patel, he's in touch with Tariq Ali, and go see him, the doctor I mean, and give him my best regards, will you?"

"Of course, if you want me to."

"Now I'll give you five minutes to get this all down, then I'm taking the paper back, and I'll be sending Sheila in next. You two need some time together—alone."

I sat there in Krishna's shabby bedsitter surrounded by books and newspapers and glumly tried to force numbers into my brain. Then Krishna came back, snatched the paper out of my hand, ran out and shut the door.

The next time it opened, it was Sheila.

She stood there, by the closed door, and didn't approach. I was in a chair, and when I stood up to go over to her, her face began to crumble.

"Don't. Don't, Sheila. Don't cry, love, or I'll never be able to get through this."

"I'm not crying because of us. I'm crying because of my father."

I took her in my arms and held her head close to mine, cheek to cheek, so that I felt the wet tears coming down her face. If it was her father on her lips, these tears were serious. She began to shake. "I called him yesterday, before the press conference. I didn't want him to find out in the newspapers. I asked Toss Ribbons to be sure to buy up all the papers at Delaney's in the morning so he wouldn't see one. I wanted to tell him myself. So when they got him up to the Post Office and he called me back—do you know what he said to me? I didn't want to tell you before the press conference. He said to me I—I should have stopped you before you got yourself in trouble like this—."

"No, no, no, Sheila, how could you have stopped me?"

"He loves you, Nick and he thinks this is all my fault."

"No, no, no, this is not your fault."

"He said to me you didn't know enough about this country, that I should've explained to you how things work over here."

"Sheila, you know better than that. Who knows me better than you do? Nothing in the world could've stopped me—not even myself. It's just the way I am. I never would listen to anybody. Sheila, I never meant to hurt you. Not in a million years did I ever want to hurt you. And now look what I've done. How can you ever forgive me? I can't forgive myself for causing you this pain."

"Nick, what's going to become of us?"

"Nothing's going to become of us." I held her fiercely to me. "I won't let it." I had to let loose a little or I might've crushed her. "Now I'm gonna go over to England there and in a week or so we'll have our visas and our tickets from the Embassy and I'll be on the phone to you down in Mayo and then you and Aisling will come over and join me and the three of us will fly to Tripoli. And we'll be together again, our little family, my salary's going to be 300 dinars a month, we'll be able to rent a whole villa in Tripoli for ourselves, from what they tell me, you'll see, and Sheila, I'm never gonna let anything like this happen again, ever again, and we're never gonna be apart, you and I, you'll see, I promise, Sheila. You've got to believe me, you're all I've got. I can't live without you. I'm never gonna stop loving you. Do you believe me? Will you come with me to Tripoli?"

I held her back at arm's length and I could see that she was trying to bite the tears away from trickling into her lips, and then she wiped them from the corner of her chin, where they were tickling, annoyingly, with the side of her thumb, and laughed a wee bit, a silly, tiny laugh, at herself, at the both of us, as I looked pleadingly up from under my brow over the top of my gold-rimmed glasses, up into her hazel eyes, and I saw the corners of them crinkle with laugh lines, as she mumbled, with a frown, and a trembling lower lip, "Blow in my ear and I'll follow you anywhere."

Dun Laoghaire was a postcard-perfect jewel in the long summer twilight that evening, just south of Dublin, easily reached on the bus in minutes from the city centre, yet pristine as a pearl in its southern exposure to the sea and the sky. And the bus was crowded with holiday-makers heading for Wales, as was the pier when we got there. I thought it just as well. After the instant notoriety I'd acquired the night before, I much preferred to slip out of town anonymously, if I could. And as it happened, the media were through with sensationalizing me to boost circulation, and none of them thought me worthy of any notice now that I was actually departing.

It suited me. I'd asked everyone at Jane and Mary's to not follow us to the ferry, either. Sheila's time alone with me was precious to me at this point, having seen how traumatic this whole thing had been for her. All I wanted now was a quiet leave-taking without histrionics. After all, we'd soon be re-united, wouldn't we? In that mob of summertime travelers going on their holidays, were we really any different?

Thus, nobody really took any notice at all when the two Branch men in their tan macs handed my passport to me, once I had stepped onto the gangplank on the other side of the rope.

For the first time in a year, I stood somewhere not on Irish soil.

The only one I really wanted to be there, to say goodbye to, was Mick O'Corrigan. If only he could have been.

After I got on board, I gravitated toward the stern, keeping an eye on Sheila and Aisling, in her mother's arms, as she stood on the dock below. Sheila was moving Aisling's small hand so that she'd wave to her da. On the bus from the city centre, we'd congratulated each other in whispers, so that the child wouldn't overhear, saying, thank God she's too young to really understand, or for that matter, to really remember, I mean, you know, in the future, as she grows up.

We, however, were not so fortunate. We would have to go through this with our eyes wide open, having our hearts, our minds and our souls imprinted with memories we might never escape.

Then, all of the family members who were not going on holiday with their loved ones on board, but instead, staying behind, were running down the pier to the very tip as the engines of the British Rail ferry, the St Columba, shuddered beneath our feet on the rear deck, and we passengers were thrown from reverse to quarter-speed ahead, and gradually, with a groan of steely, aching engine-might, the St Columba was edging out and away from the dock.

I stood there at the very back rail, and there they were, Sheila and Aisling, bravely waving out of the mass of hankies, hats, white gloves and rolled umbrellas, as we pulled away.

The ship accelerated at a rapid rate and so they were only life-size to me for a few seconds at most.

Then they stepped away from the crowd and stood apart, still waving, as they receded into the distance.

The rest of the people, whose loved ones were simply going on a holiday trip, did not have the strong emotional heart-pull that Sheila had, and so they turned and faded rapidly away to waiting cars, taxis, buses and trains, leaving my wife and daughter standing alone, still waving, though, from moment to moment, less and less, their figures turning smaller and smaller, and looking, to me, more and more forlorn.

I stood there for as long as I could see them, till they were tiny, indistinguishable dots.

Then it occurred to me that, in my self-absorbed concentration, I'd forgotten even to wave back to poor Aisling, so I gave one last wide side-to-side semaphore-wave, hoping they could still see.

Then they were gone.

And I was left alone with the unworthy thought that I had just joined the long queue of Irish emigrants, going back more than a century, more than a couple of centuries, the long line of humanity forced to leave the land they loved, and to leave their loved ones behind them, standing on the shore.

An unworthy thought because, who was I to compare myself to them, to assign myself a place among them, who had gone forth, in sorrow and in pride, forever Irish, no matter where or in what foreign land?

When the St Columba was past the breakwater of Dun Laoghaire harbor, she stopped dead in the water.

The few passengers on the chilly rear deck of the midnight ferry with me exclaimed at this alarming maneuver, and ran inside to make enquiries of the stewards.

I didn't need to. When I looked over the side, I saw the motor-launch churning a wake through the water from a mooring at one end of the breakwater gap, rushing towards our big boat.

Somewhere up the curving hull, at the gangway gate, they were lowering a rope-ladder.

The motor-launch skidded to a halt at the ladder, and black-turtle-necked, knit-capped sailors grabbed the wooden rung at the bottom. Two men in tan macs climbed over the side and down the rope-ladder.

Once I saw that, I reasoned that they must have been afraid I might jump overboard and try to swim back to the pier. They wanted to make sure I was still on board till we got out to deep water before they would feel assured that I was really leaving; that it was not some trick I had up my sleeve; that they could now safely have their pair of Branch men climb down off the ferry and ride back to shore.

Sure enough, once the motor-launch was away again, the St Columba smartly started up and went on her way to Holyhead.

But that made me suspicious. So much for the Irish. But what about the Brits?

I went back to the smokestack house in the dead middle of the big rear deck and put my back to it. I had decided it wasn't safe for me to be standing at the rail. What's to prevent someone from coming up behind me—and overboard I go? Unbidden, a horrendous memory from my previous life back home in the States flew into my head. The death of my childhood friend Jimmy Dillard in Vietnam. Falling off the rear deck of the aircraft carrier *USS Intrepid* and being sliced to pieces underwater by the propeller blades. Coming home to his mother in bits in a closed coffin.

So I would once more put my back up against the wall of the pub and watch that front door.

All too easy to read about myself in the morning papers—deported American, in despair, hurls himself over ferry-rail. Victim not missed till landfall. Verdict: Believed to be suicide. In the sensational case of—.

Nick Petrovich?—or John Doyle?

In the files of Dublin Castle, of Scotland Yard, of Interpol, the FBI, the CIA, and MI6, and yes, the British Army SAS, the only places where it mattered, I was both.

I had seven quid in my pocket, grand total, and I was going to an unknown country, where I'd never been before, a country which I regarded as hostile, to me, and to everything, and everyone, that I loved. The enemy's country. The country which had occupied and oppressed Ireland for eight centuries now.

I was leaving the land in the west, where the last light of day lingered, and proceeding to the land in the east, where darkness was gathering.

The twin church spires of Dun Laoghaire, one Catholic, one Protestant, were dwindling in my eyes now as the St Columba picked up the speed she would need to plough her way through the deep water of the Irish Sea. Nor could I any longer make out the red letters on the forehead of the modernized structure on the hill of the little port town, which I knew spelled out *Royal Marine Hotel.*

The ferry picked up more speed, and the range of the Wicklow mountains rose over the southeast quarter of the now-miniature city of Dublin. Over in the northwest, the double barrels of the red-and-white-striped smokestacks of the Ringsend Electricity

Works poured a flag of black smoke across a cloudbank, which rested like a sandbar across the flowing stream of the sky, and the sunset cut a golden slash of twilight through the archipelago of blue vaporous clouds. Dublin, too, was slipping away from me.

Then gradually, longingly, inevitably, Ireland herself became a mystical cloudland. The Wicklow mountains receded, smaller and flatter, bluish in the distance, till finally they merged into the roseate blushing of the sky. The snub-nosed headlands of the south became a moveable mist creeping over the water. Northward, the coast of Antrim emerged from its lair behind the black-cow carcass of Howth Head. Ireland then reclaimed a full hundred-and-forty degrees of the horizon, as if to reach out, encircle, and draw in again, the fleeing ferry.

At last, over the brow of Howth Head, the sunset burst in a golden showering fanlight, like the one over the door of Mrs Warren's B&B in Lower Gardiner Street, lashing a ladder of light across the waves to my feet, which were nailed to the trembling deck of the St Columba.

I told myself that, as long as this light lasted, I could walk across the water, if need be, over that railway of golden sleepers, back to the country where the northern sun lived, a fiery nucleus, in a golden haze, in a cloud-country of salmon flesh, brass gold, limestone white, grey slate, oyster blue, back to the island of light in the sky that the faithful called *The Isle of the Blest.*

But that was a dream. Or poetry.

In truth, in reality, in the world where other men lived, I was standing with my back to the wall on a ferry taking me to the country of my enemies.

It wasn't, after all, in the end, a time for poetry. It was a time for a dirty little war in a neglected corner of the world overlooked by God and all the other Great Powers.

And that's when it hit me. I suddenly saw my mother-in-law, Jane, that sainted woman, who also loved me, for no other reason than seeing me as a lost child who had wandered into the circle of her skirts, whom she would indeed willingly take in and foster and love and care for, with all her heart, with all her being, and in my vision, I saw her standing in the front door of that little blue-trimmed rain-washed pebble-dash farmhouse in Mayo, making the sign of the cross, blessing herself, as she watched me walking away from her down the boreen.

And the tears came.

They had to come sometime. There is within us an endless reservoir. And life is so sorrowful at times that the only relief we can find is in the gushing forth, which overwhelms us with the sudden perception of the sadness of all things.

And so I stood there with my back to the wall and tears running down my face.

But the ferry ploughed on, plunging and frothing like a driving horse, carving a furrow across the Irish Sea, and nothing could halt the chill that came over me, as the wind dried my tears and I was left with a face stained with fury, fury at myself, fury at my fate.

For our tears are not endless. And when they finally dry up we are left to face the same truth, the same reality, the same set of circumstances, we faced before. What shall we do now? Shall we collapse? Shall we give up? Shall we surrender?

And that was when the words written on the walls of Belfast and Derry came to my rescue: *No Surrender.*

In truth, in reality, better a failed poem . . . than a failed life.

Was mine a failed life? Was Mick O'Corrigan's?

"Nick, what's to become of us?"

I do not know.

In truth, in reality, I do not know.

But there is time yet.

My darling, it is not given to us to be able to foretell the future, nor can we ever fully grasp the past, as it is rapidly overtaken by the all-powerful present, which just as quickly slips through our fingers and becomes, too soon, the past. All we can do is to dwell in the moment, in the succession of moments, and try to see it and hear it and feel it fully. And then we must pass on, just as the ferry passes on across the Irish Sea, to fade into the oncoming night.

The voice of the public-address system broke across the rear deck of the St Columba.

Good evening. Crackle. Welcome to the St Columba, crackle, and thank you, all and each, for traveling British Rail . . . pause . . . We hope you do enjoy your passage across the Irish Sea . . . static . . . Our voyage will take a little more than three hours . . . in a brisk headwind of 12 knots, we should be making landfall in Holyhead at precisely one minute after midnight . . . pause . . . static . . . Your Captain takes great pleasure at this time in inviting you all to join us . . . in the 2nd-class smoke-room bar, on B-Deck . . . for a little game of chance . . . which we like to call Bon Petite . . .

About the Author

Eugene Christy is a novelist, poet and musician currently enjoying retirement in his home in the Berkshires. His maternal grandparents Antonio Scioscia and Giuseppina Fabrizio came from Alta Villa Irpina, near Avellino, in the South of Italy. He has studied under Sean O'Faolain, James Dickey, and Larry McMurtry. Appearing as Gene Christy, he was previously known around the Berkshires as the singer-songwriter and accordian-player who led The Dossers, the Irish-themed pub-band trio featuring Bill Morrison and Rick Marquis. His current project, six years in the making, is called *The Twentieth Century*

Quintet, five novels telling the saga of Antonio LaStoria and his descendants through three generations in America from 1899 to 1972, to be published by Adelaide Books, New York, in 2020 and 2021.